SUPERIOR HERITAGE

Best Wishes!

Tyler R. Tichelaar

SUPERIOR HERITAGE

a novel

Tyler R. Tichelaar

Marquette Fiction
Marquette, Michigan

SUPERIOR HERITAGE

Marquette Fiction
1202 Pine Street
Marquette, MI 49855
www.marquettefiction.com

ISBN: 978-0-9791790-2-0

Library of Congress PCN 9780979179020

Printed in the United States of America

Publication managed by Back Channel Press
www.backchannelpress.com

To Mom and Dad

"Solitary women like me, old men like Cousin Tune: in every day and time there have been many of us, clinging with all the strength of our memories to the old ways--old men and old maids who eye each other on meeting, and in that silent interchange promise to hold fast, by their futile stubbornness, in their own minds--who when they see the life they know not only doomed, but dead and very nearly forgotten, sit down alone to write the elegies."

– Helen Hooven Santmyer, *Farewell to Summer*

PRINCIPAL FAMILIES IN SUPERIOR HERITAGE

Note: some characters are not included so as not to give away the plots

The Whitmans

Margaret Whitman – Family matriarch, maiden name Dalrymple, widow of Will Whitman, mother of Henry, Roy, and Bill Whitman, Ada Lowell, and Eleanor Goldman

Henry Whitman – son of Margaret Whitman, husband of Beth, father of Jim and Ellen

Beth Whitman – Henry Whitman's wife, maiden name McCarey, mother of Jim and Ellen, sister to Monsignor Michael McCarey

Jim Whitman – son of Henry and Beth

Ellen Whitman – daughter of Henry and Beth

Roy Whitman – son of Margaret and Will Whitman

Eleanor Goldman – divorced daughter of Margaret and Will Whitman, mother of Lucy and Maud Goldman

Lucy Goldman – Eleanor's daughter

Maud Goldman – Eleanor's daughter

Ada Lowell – married daughter of Margaret and Will Whitman, who lives in Louisiana with her husband and children

Bill Whitman – son of Margaret and Will Whitman

The Dalrymples

Charles Dalrymple – brother to Margaret Dalrymple Whitman

Harriet Dalrymple – Charles's wife

Joseph Dalrymple – son of Charles and Harriet

Randy and Tim Dalrymple – twins, the children of Joseph

Sarah Rodman – sister to Margaret Whitman and Charles Dalrymple

Joseph Rodman – her husband, a former U.S. Senator

Theodore Dalrymple Blackmore Rodman – son of Sarah Dalrymple Rodman and the late Lysander Blackmore, an illegitimate child adopted by his step-father, Joseph Rodman

The McCareys & Bergmanns

Michael McCarey – a monsignor in the Catholic Church, brother to Beth McCarey Whitman

Thelma Bergmann – cousin to Beth and Michael McCarey

Jessie Hopewell – Thelma's adopted daughter

Lyla Hopewell – Jessie's sister, whom Thelma did not adopt

Other Principal Characters

Scofield Blackmore – half-brother to Theodore Rodman, illegitimate son of the late Lysander Blackmore

Robert O'Neill – famous local novelist

Eliza Graham O'Neill – wife of Robert O'Neill

Bernie O'Neill – Robert and Eliza's son, friend of Jim Whitman

Helen O'Neill – daughter of Robert and Eliza O'Neill

Tom Vandelaare – a young man stationed at K.I. Sawyer Air Force Base

Historical People Mentioned in Superior Heritage

Eve Arden – movie star in *Anatomy of a Murder*

Memo Beyers – a piano teacher in Marquette

Arthur Bourgeois – editor of Chief Kawbawgam's *Ojibwa Narratives*

Monsignor Casanova – a pastor of St. Michael's Catholic Church

Mike Chenoweth – owner of the Lumberjack Tavern in Big Bay

Monsignor Joseph Dunleavy – a pastor of St. Michael's Catholic Church

Mary Dwyer – devoted church lady at St. Peter's Cathedral

Paul Florence – owner of the Delft Theatre

Ben Gazzara – movie star in *Anatomy of a Murder*

Paul Gerard – murder victim

Dominic Jacobetti – longtime Upper Michigan politician

Sadie Johnson – church clerk at First Baptist Church

Ernestine Latour – proprietor of the Bavarian Inn

Ruth Lill – author of Marquette history, and descendant of city founders Amos and Olive Harlow

Maggie – manager of Bookbinders

Lieutenant Peterson – murderer of Mike Chenoweth

Mrs. Peterson – his wife, raped by Mike Chenoweth

Otto Preminger – movie director of *Anatomy of a Murder*

Lee Remick – movie star in *Anatomy of a Murder*

Max Reynolds – grandson of Peter White

George C. Scott – movie star in *Anatomy of a Murder*

Barbara Specker – Marquette resident

Clyde Steele – author of Marquette history

James Stewart – movie star in *Anatomy of a Murder*

John Voelker – Lieutenant Peterson's lawyer; author of *Anatomy of a Murder*

1952

Beth Whitman was attending St. Peter's Cathedral this Sunday morning because her brother, Monsignor McCarey, had been invited by the bishop to say Mass. Beth was accompanied by her children, Jim and Ellen, her cousin, Thelma Bergmann, and Thelma's adopted daughter, Jessie. Beth's husband, Henry, did not join his family because he was one of those Baptists; his marriage to a Catholic had caused such trouble with his parents that he only attended church with his wife and children on holidays. As on every Sunday morning, Jim had grumbled about going to church. He was sixteen and felt he should not have to go anymore, but his mother insisted he go until he was eighteen, and his father supported his mother's decision. Because his parents' marriage had caused family religious strife, Jim had not been baptized or attended church until he was twelve. By then, so his sister thought, Satan had already gotten her brother's soul, and no number of Masses could save him. Being five years younger, Ellen had been baptized at age seven while still highly impressionable; ever since, she had believed and feared every word of catechism she was taught. She had already swallowed several doses of good Catholic guilt, and her artistic temperament found all that guilt dramatically appealing.

Ellen had never been in the cathedral before. She knew it was the church her mother had been raised in, but because the Whitmans lived in North Marquette, they attended nearby St. Michael's. Her mother had often told her how beautiful the cathedral was and that someday they would go there, but Ellen had never dreamt her first visit would include her own uncle saying the Mass. She was always quiet and attentive during church, fearful of doing anything that would increase her years in Purgatory. But today it was hard to be attentive because St. Peter's Cathedral was the most splendid building she had ever seen. She tried hard to concentrate on the homily, but her mind soon wandered into marveling over the pillars and stained glass windows. Paying attention was even more difficult when she noticed her brother's eyes were closed.

Ellen tried to focus on the giant mosaic above the altar where Christ was depicted as ascending toward Heaven. An angel on Christ's right held St. Peter's Basilica in Rome, while an angel on Christ's left held St. Peter's Cathedral in Marquette; both buildings bore the namesake of the first pope of the Catholic Church. Kneeling before Christ was St. Peter himself, while looking on were the other eleven apostles holding various books, crosses, and swords. Below the apostles were several sheep, but Ellen was not sure why. She leaned over and whispered to Jessie, who was twenty-four and a teacher, "What does that Latin mean below the picture?"

"You are Peter, the Rock," said Jessie, while Beth and Thelma frowned at her, "and upon this Rock I will build my Church, and the powers of Hell will not prevail against it, and I will give to you the keys to the Kingdom of Heaven. Alleluia."

Ellen nodded in understanding. Christ was holding keys in his hand and giving them to St. Peter to designate him as head of the church. That must be why the cathedral was named for St. Peter, because it was the seat of the bishop, the head of all the other Catholic churches in Upper Michigan. Ellen loved that the mosaic was so symbolic, elevating it beyond being a pretty picture into a true piece of art. She hoped one day she could create such magnificent art.

Then Ellen realized her uncle's homily was over, and she felt guilty that she had not listened. Now the Eucharistic prayers began. She knelt, listening to the rhythmic Latin and staring at Monsignor McCarey's back as he prayed, but she was also daydreaming of someday painting pictures as beautiful as the cathedral's stained glass windows; she loved the windows, but she thought it unclear which saints were depicted other than St. Patrick because of the snakes in his window. Ellen thought people would like the windows more if they understood the windows told stories. She wanted to paint pictures that told stories; perhaps she would be an illustrator, like N.C. Wyeth, who had wonderfully illustrated so many of her favorite books.

When Communion came, Ellen walked down the aisle with her family. Monsignor presented her with the body and blood of Christ. As she received it into her mouth, she wished it would make her feel different, better; she believed it could if she were good enough and learned to pay attention in church. As she knelt after Communion, she prayed the Eucharist would transform her so she would always be good, or at least quit losing her temper with Jimmy. But she felt God must understand when she lost her temper since her brother would purposely irritate her when he knew she was trying extra hard to be good.

Before Monsignor rose to give the final blessing, the bishop stepped onto the altar to speak. "I'm sure we are all pleased to see Monsignor McCarey, who was raised in this very parish, back among us to celebrate Mass this weekend. You'll all be happy to hear that the Holy Father has invited Monsignor to Rome to teach at the North American College for priests. It is a great honor for him, our parish, and our entire diocese, and I for one am very proud of him."

The church erupted into clapping hands. But Ellen noticed her mother did not clap. Instead, Beth looked over at Thelma and raised her eyes.

"Why didn't Michael tell me?" Beth asked, but Thelma was herself too surprised to answer.

The final blessing was said and the Mass concluded. Monsignor McCarey followed the crucifix down the aisle, then waited outside the front door to greet the parishioners.

"We'll see you later, Thelma," said Beth, heading for a side door.

"Aren't you going to see your brother?" asked Thelma.

"No, I'll talk to him when he comes over for dinner. I'm too upset now."

Ellen and Jim followed their mother down the side aisle. "Beth, that's wonderful about your brother," said a well-wisher. "I wouldn't be surprised if someday he were pope himself," said another. "You must be very proud," said a third.

"Yes," Beth replied. "I am proud of him."

She pushed her way to the door, wishing to escape the crowd. She might be proud, but she was not happy.

"Jim, quit dawdling," she said, although less annoyed with her son's lazy gait than that her husband and the car were nowhere in sight. Ever since she had run into a tree her first time behind the wheel, Beth had refused to drive, but today she wished it were otherwise; Henry never was on time to pick her up. But there was the car now.

"Hurry up, Jimmy," Ellen said, following on her mother's heels.

"How was church?" asked Henry as his family climbed into the car.

"Fine," said Beth, screwing up her lips, unwilling to discuss the topic until she reached home.

"Uncle Michael's moving to Rome," said Ellen, enjoying the drama of the surprise. "The bishop announced it in church."

"Rome!" said Henry.

"He's been invited by the Pope," said Ellen. "He's going to teach new priests."

Henry turned to Beth. "You never mentioned that Michael was – "

"He never told me," Beth said.

Her tone warned Henry to say no more. Ellen now realized just how upset her mother was. Jim closed his eyes and lay his head back on the seat, trying to endure his family until he got home and could escape from them for an hour until dinner. He hated Sundays. Spending the whole day with his parents was almost enough to make him run away from home.

When they reached the house, Ellen went to read in her bedroom while Jim walked up the street to hang out with his friends until dinnertime. Seeing Beth needed time alone, Henry disappeared into his woodshop. He did not come back inside the house until Beth started fixing dinner.

"I imagine Michael must be excited," said Henry, deciding it best to broach the subject before his brother-in-law arrived.

"Yes, it's a great honor for him," she said. "But why didn't he tell me?"

"He probably meant to tell you when he came over. The bishop just beat him to it."

"How can he go? He's the only family I have left except for Thelma."

"You have me and the kids," said Henry.

"That's not what I mean and you know it," said Beth.

"Well, it's not as if we see him that often," Henry said. "Except for that year he was stationed in Ishpeming, he's always been at some distant end of the U.P."

"He was still within a day's drive," said Beth. "Now he'll be in a foreign country."

"Well," Henry rubbed her shoulders as she mashed the potatoes, "it's his choice. He did give his life to God, you know."

"I know," Beth grunted, not willing to be consoled.

"Can I do anything to help you?" Henry asked.

"The roast will be done in a few minutes. You can slice it for me."

"What should I do until then?"

"Tell Ellen to come set the table," said Beth. "Michael will be here any minute."

"I'll set the table," said Henry.

"No, you won't. It's Ellen's job. She can do it."

The back door opened. They heard Henry's brother Roy shout, "Hello!"

"I just came into town for the afternoon," said Roy when he entered the kitchen. "I thought I'd see whether you wanted to go ice fishing."

"I don't understand how you men can go fishing in the middle of winter," Beth said. She also could not understand why Roy did not get a telephone; then he could have called rather than come into town only to learn Henry could not go with him. She did not know what to think of Roy; how could he live as a hermit in the woods in that little cabin without running water, electricity, or a telephone?

"I can't go today," said Henry. "Beth's brother is coming for dinner."

"You can go if you want," said Beth in a tone that warned Henry he better not.

"No," said Henry. "Not when we have company."

"Hi, Uncle Roy," Ellen said. Her uncle's presence made her feel safe enough to emerge from her bedroom. She had always thought her uncle odd, especially now that the bushy beard he sported had started to turn gray. But he was kind, and less intimidating to be around than her uncle the monsignor. "Are you staying for dinner?"

Roy had not expected the offer, but he was lonely today; he did not want to go ice fishing alone. He looked askance at Beth, but she had turned away toward the stove. "No, I can't. I – " he began, but Beth said, "You're welcome to stay, Roy. I'm sure Michael will be happy to see you."

"Thank you," Roy said.

"Uncle Roy, Uncle Michael's moving to Rome," said Ellen.

"He is?"

"Ellen, go set the table," said Beth.

Roy sat down, feeling uncomfortable, while Beth took the roast from the oven and let Henry slice it. Then Michael arrived.

He shook hands with Roy and let Henry take his coat. "It looks as if it's going to snow this afternoon," he said.

"Seems as if it snows every afternoon," said Beth. "Easter's almost here, but you would never know it in Upper Michigan."

Henry scrambled for a topic to discuss. He dared not bring up the subject of Michael moving to Rome; Beth would mention it when she was ready. Michael, who was constantly in demand to console people, had mastered the art of small talk so he began to praise Henry and Beth's home, lightening the awkward moment.

"This is the first time I've been here since you moved in," he said. "It's a beautiful house." He had come into the kitchen by the back door. Now he stood staring into the open dining and living rooms.

"We've been here almost two years now," said Henry. "I'd forgotten you've never been here."

"I apologize," said Michael. "I'm so busy I don't get to see my family like I want to, and remember, we had Christmas at your mother's house."

Henry and Beth had built their current home in the summer of 1950 after a year of living with Henry's recently widowed mother, Margaret. The winter prior to that, they had moved to California, but with the death of Henry's father, they had felt homesick and returned to Marquette and their family. Margaret had been unhappy when Beth married her oldest son, but when she learned Beth had convinced Henry to move home, she had finally softened toward her daughter-in-law. The new house Henry built for his family was only two blocks down the street from Margaret's house; far enough away that Beth did not have to worry about her mother-in-law popping in at any moment, while close enough to Henry's family to keep him satisfied.

On the outside, the house resembled its neighbors in this growing little area of North Marquette, but inside, Henry had displayed his artistic nature. He and Beth had spent their childhood in Victorian homes with numerous tiny cramped rooms, but in California, Henry had discovered space. There he had seen many homes with Mexican or Southwest flavor – homes with arched doorways and rooms that would open into other rooms rather than be separated by doors. The public rooms of his new home – living room, dining room, and kitchen – were built in a straight line so you could see completely from one end of the house to the other. He placed a Dutch half-door between the kitchen and the hall to the bedrooms and another half-door between the dining room and kitchen, but even with the half-doors shut, the other rooms were visible. Beth had insisted on these half-doors so the dog would not track its wet feet on the carpets. The house was "California style" as Henry explained to everyone; even the bedroom windows were large enough to let in the California sun; Henry had not considered how little use windows are in Upper Michigan during long dark winters.

"Let me show you around," Henry told Michael. Roy followed the other men about the house rather than remain with a sister-in-law in no mood to talk with him.

Beth listened to the men's feet shuffling down the hall to the bedrooms; she was annoyed that Henry would let their brothers see her private room. She was even more annoyed by the dirt tracked across her clean floor because Roy had not removed his shoes. She told herself Roy had never been thoughtful, but when she went to get the broom by the back door, she noticed his shoes were next to Henry's. Michael was the guilty tracker of mud. She quickly swept up the dirt before the men returned. As she emptied the dustpan, Jim came through the back door.

"Take off your shoes," she told him.

"Oh, I'm sorry, Beth," said Michael. He was standing in the kitchen doorway, having just returned down the hall.

"It's all right," she said, embarrassed.

"No, it was thoughtless of me." He sat down in a kitchen chair to remove the offending footwear.

"We can eat now," said Beth. She told the men where to sit at the table, then ordered Ellen to help her carry in the food. Jim slumped into a chair, scowling at the disgusting peas and carrots he would be forced to eat and the stringy roast that would stick in his teeth.

Bowls were passed around, and food was dolloped onto plates. Jim lifted his knife to slice his meat when Michael said, "May I say the blessing?"

"Yes, please," said Beth, afraid he would guess they never said a blessing. Roy raised his eyebrows. He was an avowed atheist, but he politely kept his mouth shut. He had kept quiet at his mother's table during many a prayer.

"Amen," said Michael when he finished thanking the Lord.

"Pass the potatoes," Henry said to Roy.

"I don't believe in God," said Jim.

No one said anything. They pretended not to have heard. To keep from grinning, Roy said, "Beth, everything looks delicious."

"God didn't make people," Jim said. "We evolved from apes."

Ellen had never heard this before. How silly to think people evolved from apes. Why did Jimmy say such stupid things?

"Jim, that's enough," said Henry.

"It's true. There's scientific proof to support it up."

"It's not an appropriate subject for the dinner table," said Henry.

"If Uncle Michael can talk about God at the table, I can talk about evolution."

"Not at my table, you can't," said Beth, afraid Michael would think her a bad mother.

"My teacher in school told us about it. Haven't you ever heard of Darwin? He proved we're descended from apes."

"Jim," his father warned.

"It's okay," said Michael. "Everyone has a right to his own beliefs. Jim, can I ask you one question?"

"What?" Jim asked.

"You believe that people evolved from apes? That God didn't create us?"

"Right. I don't even believe in God. You can't prove He exists."

"Can you prove He doesn't?" asked Michael.

"That's not a fair question."

"Still, you have no answer for it, but let me ask you this: if God did not create everything, how did it happen?"

"It's science. The Big Bang theory."

"What caused that big bang?"

"Dust floating around and combusting," Jim smirked.

"What put the dust there?"

Jim did not know; he struggled for an answer. Roy recalled having this same discussion many times with different people. He no longer cared whether God existed or whether the big bang theory could be proven. He simply did not believe in God. Ellen stared at her plate, ashamed of her brother. Now she knew Jimmy would go to Hell. And he would deserve it too, after ruining Sunday dinner.

"You still can't prove God exists!" Jim retorted.

"All right," said Michael. "To each his own. But isn't the idea that there is no God rather frightening? It means we are completely alone in a meaningless world. Do you want to live in a world without hope?"

"Hope in what? That I get to sit on a cloud and sing praises to God for all eternity. If that's what God considers hope, he must be selfish."

Roy frowned. He did not believe in Michael's God, but neither did he disrespect others' beliefs. As a disciple of existentialism, Roy did not live in a world without hope – he believed life had the meaning each individual placed upon it, based upon the individual's experiences.

Beth felt a scratching at her leg.

"Oh, Henry, you forgot to shut the half-door," she said. "Now you've got Bandit in here."

"It's all right," said Henry, trying to calm his wife who was already upset by the conversation.

"No, it's not. He's such a beggar. Don't you give him any scraps."

"He's a fine dog," said Michael, when Bandit settled between him and Beth. "I wish I had such a nice one."

"Why would you want to be a priest if you can't even have a dog?" asked Jim, determined to win the argument by being obnoxious since he could not win by logic.

"Young man," said Henry. "You are excused from the table. You can take your plate with you if you want, but you're not welcome to eat with us anymore."

Jim picked up his plate, tossed his silverware onto it, grabbed his glass of milk, and stomped into the kitchen.

Beth, the dog forgotten, apologized profusely to her brother. "I'm so sorry. Henry will have to go have a talk with that teacher. We should have sent Jim to Catholic school. I can't believe anyone would tell a child something so awful."

"He's not a child anymore," said Michael. "He's almost sixteen and at a rebellious age." He laughed and added, "I was rebellious too at his age, only I rebelled against the evils of the world by entering the seminary."

"Still," said Henry, "we raised him to have better manners."

Silence followed as everyone intently chewed the roast beef.

"I hear, Michael," said Roy to ease the tension, "that you're moving to Rome."

Henry, glancing at Beth, felt this moment the worst to bring up the subject.

"Yes," said Michael. "I go where God leads me."

"It must be exciting for you," said Roy. "I've never been to Italy, but what I saw of Europe during the war was beautiful. Even with so much destroyed, I thought the French countryside and Rhine River Valley among the most beautiful places I've ever seen – even comparable to Lake Superior's beaches and the Huron Mountains."

"Michael, we'll miss you," said Beth.

"I know," said Michael, "but we can always write. I expect many letters from my family."

Roy looked down at his plate, feeling this private family moment did not include him, but Michael touched his forearm and said, "Roy, you must promise to write me. I'll be thirsty for good conversation that isn't only about theology, and I haven't yet given up trying to convert you."

"I'll write," said Roy, "but I can't promise I'll be any less adamant than Jim about my beliefs."

"Fair enough," Michael smiled.

"What exactly will you do in Rome?" asked Henry. Michael explained how he would teach new seminarians at the North American College for priests. Roy listened intently, almost with jealousy. Here was a man who wanted to be his friend – a man who had received great respect in the world's eyes yet managed to forsake materialism. Over the years, Michael had been pastor to numerous parishes, had helped further the goals of the diocese, had learned multiple languages, his French and German being far better than Roy's own, and in addition, he could speak Italian and Latin. He was well versed in history and theology, while Roy knew himself to be only an armchair philosopher. Roy had also forsaken the world's honors, but Michael remained honored because he had not forsaken other people.

The day ended emotionally for everyone. Jim would fume all evening before he got over being bested by his uncle of the cloth. Ellen's respect for priests only increased by her uncle's presence. Beth mourned her brother's departure and would not let Henry comfort her. Michael would remember the day as a pleasant farewell, the afternoon winter sun bathing the room with a warmth reflected in the presence of those he loved. And Roy went home, feeling life was futile; he believed priests were deluded by religion, yet he envied Michael the comfort of that delusion.

All winter, Roy had almost hibernated in his little cabin deep in the woods of the Huron Mountains, reading and rereading books until he had nearly memorized them. Almost daily, he had gone ice fishing or snowshoed through the forest until the late afternoon sunsets proclaimed the end of day. In the forest, he read the seasons in maples, pines, evergreens, oaks, and birches. He knew the different tracks of the squirrels, rabbits, raccoons, and deer. He read the landscape like a storybook of the forest's events. His keen eyes could tell how many inches of snow had fallen simply by marking the trunk of a tree. The clouds never failed to predict for him the next day's weather. He found in Nature a knowledge as great as in any book. He had read that the Druids had known all the secret paths of the forest, and he strove to acquire such knowledge for himself. Roy also read books to understand human nature; he tried to read himself, to obey the great internal sermon, "Know thyself."

Then, with the coming of spring, he emerged from his winter of isolated meditation into active work at the Huron Mountain Club. Yet even there, he was a silent man, often found tucked away in a corner of a crowded room, listening, reading his fellow men's countenances, learning from the inflection of their voices to read their hearts. He flattered himself that he understood human nature; sometimes, he felt superior over others' shallow words and lives.

Roy knew only one man who might understand Nature as well as himself – not the mere nature of trees and squirrels, but the larger meanings. That man was the only one he could not read; whenever he tried to understand that man, he realized his interpretations were simplistic, unfair, even degrading to that man's intelligence. He admired that man, yet detested that the man made him feel so fully his own shortcomings. That man was constantly in Roy's thoughts as spring broke.

On this spring afternoon just days before Easter, Roy returned home from the Huron Mountain Club to find his older brother's car parked before his cabin. He saw Henry standing on his doorstep, laboriously trying to scribble a note on a scrap of paper he pressed against the cabin wall.

Roy whistled to announce his presence.

Henry turned around, smiled, then shoved the note in his pocket.

"What are you doing here?" asked Roy.

"Just stopped by to say hello," said Henry, "and to let you know about Easter. Ma says we'll have dinner at noon."

Roy opened his cabin door without replying. "You could have come in and waited," he said. "I never lock the door. There's nothing to steal except a few dishes, my books, and that old Victrola."

Henry followed his brother inside, noting the cabin's musty smell from the damp winter. He glanced at the wash basin, filled with dishes and dirty water. If he were a bachelor, Henry thought he might also be a bit lazy about his housekeeping, but he could never live like this, in a little shack where even the mice must freeze in winter and bake in summer.

"Have a seat," said Roy. Henry glanced at the bed, the room's only comfortable piece of furniture. The bed quilt was filthy, as if the mice had slept on it. He opted instead for one of the hard dusty chairs.

"Your bookcase looks as if it's overflowing," said Henry. "I could build you a couple more – enough to fill this whole wall if you want."

"No," said Roy. "Some of those books I'll never read again, especially the novels, which are mostly useless with a few exceptions."

"I didn't think you ever parted with your books."

"You can have too much of anything, even books," said Roy. "I don't want my possessions to possess me."

"Your place would look really nice with a whole wall of books," Henry said.

"No," said Roy.

"It wouldn't be any trouble. I could make some shelves in a day or two."

"No," said Roy. "I like it the way it is."

"I don't know how you'll ever find yourself a woman living in a place like this."

Henry regretted the comment the moment he said it. For years he had wondered why his brother was such a hermit; he had tried to avoid asking intrusive questions so as not to aggravate Roy; Henry had enough family cares without worrying about his brother. But the sight of Roy's dilapidated life was more than he could take today.

"Who says I want a woman?" Roy asked.

"What do you mean? Every man does."

"No," said Roy. "That's what's the matter with the world. Everyone assumes men and women have to marry and raise children, instead of having their own lives. This is an awful world to raise kids in, and most love is really just lust in disguise. I'm not going to conform to some mindless social pattern based on sexual urges rather than logic."

"You never will marry with that attitude."

Roy knew it was pointless to explain his feelings to his brother, but he continued anyway. "Two people can never really become one; they're never fully compatible. And to have children is only to be selfish, thinking about the joy children might bring you, but not the troubles and miseries they'll have to face."

"That's silly," said Henry. "If everyone felt that way, humanity would end."

"Would that be such a great loss?" Roy asked. "All people do is make life miserable for the other creatures on this planet."

"That's not true. We do lots of good things, like conservation for instance."

"Conservation is just preserving the world from human exploitation. Think about it. Every time you see a dead animal lying along the road, run down by a car, whose fault is that? What kind of ridiculous, selfish, pomposity makes humans believe we have the right to drive fifty miles an hour, threatening other creatures, as if there is anything so important we have to do, as if our every second is so precious that all other forms of life are expendable. Human extinction would be the best thing that ever happened to this planet."

Henry could see Roy was, as their mother said, 'in one of his moods'. Further discussion would be pointless. Geez, all he had suggested was that he might build his brother a bookshelf.

"Anyway," said Henry, "the reason I came out was to tell you that Ma wants you to come for Easter dinner."

"That's another example of selfishness," said Roy. "I don't want to come for Easter dinner, but just because everyone else celebrates Easter, it's expected that I will. You should know better by now than to think I'll come."

"We always have Easter dinner together."

"I haven't come to Easter dinner for years," said Roy. "I wouldn't even come for Christmas except to make Ma happy. I'll come any other time for dinner, but not for Easter."

"Why ever not?" asked Henry, thinking his brother had become loopy from living alone so long.

"Because I refuse to celebrate the lie of Christianity that has caused so much trouble in the world."

Henry had long ago learned to avoid religious arguments with his brother. Roy was ridiculously atheistic, yet Henry was no match for him when his brother began to quote the Bible, John Milton, Saint Augustine and Saint Thomas Aquinas, the Upanishads, the Koran, and Jean-Paul Sartre to show what was wrong with religion. Henry did not even know who or what most of those things were. He had enough trouble trying to remember all Ten Commandments. But Henry had faith that only God could have created a world so full of infinite splendor and variety. What use were the arguments of all Roy's books next to the beauty of a tree, a sunset, or a newborn baby?

"I don't know what happened to you," said Henry. "We grew up in the same house yet we ended up so different. We all want to see you, and Ma will be hurt if you don't come for Easter."

"We can love each other yet still disagree," said Roy. "Tell Ma I'll come for supper the Sunday after Easter."

"All right," Henry sighed. He felt claustrophobic in this narrow little box of a shack. He got up, muttered, "Goodbye," and went out to his car.

"Goodbye," said Roy. He stared out the window until his brother had driven out of sight. He suddenly felt a lonely urge to go to Easter dinner, but out of principle, he would not give in. When he turned from the window, he went to his coat and dug out the two letters he had picked up that afternoon at the post office; until now he had not dared to look and see whom they were from. He felt hopeful that she had written to him – Chloe, the only woman he had ever loved. But the first letter was from his sister, Ada, in Louisiana. The second letter had no return address, but the postage stamps revealed it was from the man whose approval he craved.

"Mom, can I bring my tablet and pens to Grandma's house?"

"No, it won't hurt you to talk to your aunts and uncles or play with Lucy and Maud."

Ellen sulked but said nothing. Henry came inside from his woodshop. "I'll be ready to go in a minute," he said.

"Daddy, do you want to look at my picture?"

Ellen jumped up from the table where she had been meticulously drawing for the last hour with extraordinary focus for her age. She took the tablet into the kitchen and placed it before her father.

Henry looked at it, not quite knowing what to say.

"It's different than what you usually draw," he said, "but it's very nice."

It was different. Ellen loved to draw the insides of houses, as if they were dollhouses displaying each floor, each room, all the furniture, and the people inside. Henry and Beth thought the pictures reflected their daughter's sense of family security.

But today, Ellen had drawn a giant cathedral, complete with towers and pillars; its surrounding gardens were filled with statues of saints, while nuns walked along the paths.

"Can I bring my tablet to Grandma's house?" Ellen asked her father.

"Ellen, I already told you no," Beth said. "Now go get ready and tell Jim to do the same. Grandma worked hard on Easter dinner so we shouldn't keep her waiting."

Ellen went down the hall to find her brother. Beth looked at Henry, who was still staring at the drawing left on the table.

"Your mother would have a fit if she saw that picture," Beth said.

"I guess so," he replied. A staunch Baptist, Margaret still hoped her Catholic daughter-in-law and grandchildren would someday turn away from idolatry. Henry set down the picture and went into the bathroom to wash his hands and comb his hair.

"Dad," said Jim, stepping into the bathroom doorway, "after dinner, can I leave? Bernie invited me to come over this afternoon."

"I suppose," said Henry, understanding how difficult it was for a sixteen year old boy to be stuck at a family gathering. "As long as you use your best manners at dinner."

"Thanks Dad," said Jim, knowing full well if he had asked his mother, he would have gotten a different answer.

"Let's walk over," said Henry, returning to the kitchen. "It's a nice day."

"Oh, well, I have these pies to bring," said Beth as an excuse. She had grown quite fat in recent years and did not like to be seen in public. If she walked the couple blocks to Margaret's house, the neighbors might think she was trying to reduce her weight. That would be embarrassing.

"I'll carry them," said Henry.

"All right," Beth gave in, then fetched her coat – even though it was a warm day – to hide her fat rolls.

They started down the driveway, then turned down the street toward Henry's mother's house. Jim shuffled his feet along the road, embarrassed that his friends might see him with his parents and little sister. Beth glanced about, equally self-conscious, and constantly eyeing Henry to make sure he did not tilt the pies. Ellen chatted about the houses they passed, why she liked this one, why that one should be painted a different color, what kind of house she would have when she was older. Beth told herself they were now halfway – only one more block to go and she would be safe from being seen.

Henry waved his hand. Beth turned to see Mrs. King, that old snob; Beth smiled politely, hating that the wannabe makeup poster woman with her tiny little waist had seen her. Beth resolved she would not have any pie today. Just because it was Easter did not mean she should break her diet. She always broke her diet, but this time she was determined to keep at it.

They were the last to arrive except for Henry's sister, Eleanor. Beth never understood why Eleanor could never come early to help her own mother. But Margaret was never in the least worried about the meal. It would be ready when it was ready; she had never been much of a housekeeper or a cook, and punctuality was not a word in her vocabulary. Beth immediately delegated to herself the task of seeing everything was finished in a timely manner. Holidays only meant extra work for her because she had to help take care of Henry's family.

And the family was a large one. Over the years, Margaret's home had become the gathering place for every shirttail relation. Ellen knew them all as a group, few of them as individuals, yet she was fond of them, tolerating even their faults as part of the color of family life. Her grandmother, Margaret Whitman, was matriarch of the family. Then came Margaret's brother, Charles Dalrymple and his wife, Harriet. Uncle Charles was quiet, while Aunt Harriet was a shrewish opinionated woman. Their son Joseph was there today with his wife and his twin boys. The twins were only in kindergarten, and usually acted like brats, but Ellen tried to be nice to them because her grandmother had mournfully told her, "They are the only ones to carry on the Dalrymple name." Also present was Ellen's late grandfather's sister, eighty year old Aunt Sylvia. Sylvia's son, Harry Cumming, was present with his wife, Jean, and their two grown sons. Rumor had it that cousin Harry had been quite reckless in his youth, but now he seemed the perfect husband and father. His sons had already graduated from high school, and whenever Jim was around them, he listened to their exploits with girls until he came to idolize them. Then there were Margaret's children: Roy had refused to come, and Ada lived in Louisiana with her husband and children, but three remained to fill the house. Henry was the oldest, and the most responsible of them all. Then there was Aunt Eleanor, whose husband had divorced her, leaving her with two daughters, Ellen's cousins, Lucy and Maud; Great-Aunt Sylvia had moved in with Aunt Eleanor to help her raise the girls. The youngest of Margaret's children was Bill, who at thirty-two, had still not settled down, having a half-dozen girlfriends each year, perhaps more, but the family usually lost count after five or six. Of course, Bill's latest lady-friend was with him today. Also present were Margaret's neighbors, the Rushmores, and Beth's cousin, Thelma Bergmann, who had been adopted as part of the family since Beth was her only relative in town. Thelma was an eccentric spinster, pushing fifty. She was comfortable from a fortune her father had made in the logging industry, and she could play the piano with expertise, but she also suffered from multiple sclerosis. Years before, she had adopted a young girl, Jessie Hopewell, who now at twenty-four, had blossomed into a beautiful young woman. According to Beth, it was a shame "Jessie didn't marry rather than waste her youth taking care of Thelma," yet Beth was also glad her cousin had someone so devoted to her. Surrounded by all these family members, even though some could at times be annoying, Ellen felt safe and loved.

When Lucy and Maud arrived, they immediately attached themselves to Ellen. Maud and Ellen were the same age and in the same class at school. They were best friends and spent much of their free time together playing with their dolls, reading books, and riding their bicycles around Marquette. Today, the girls started to talk about movies, and then which movie star boys they would like to kiss. Lucy had initiated the subject, but Maud, from being around her older sister, had a few ideas of her own. Ellen was surprised by the conversation; she had never yet thought about kissing a boy.

"We can eat," Margaret called to everyone.

"Don't we have to wait for Roy?" asked Harriet.

"No, he won't be coming."

"Did he get an invite somewhere else?" Harriet asked. "Did some woman invite him to her place?"

"I don't think Roy is interested in any woman," Eleanor said.

"At his age, he should have been married years ago," said Harriet.

"Why? Most marriages aren't happy anyway," said Eleanor. "You don't see me trying to find another husband."

"All men aren't like Ronald," Harriet said.

"There's nothing wrong with marriage," said Margaret, "if you find the right person. Will and I were always happy."

"And I found the right one," said Beth, taking Henry's hand.

"Roy just isn't the marrying kind," said Henry. "He's happiest with his nose stuck in a book, and I don't know any woman who would want to live in that cabin of his."

"But who wants to spend their life alone?" asked Lucy, who was experiencing her first schoolgirl crush and dreaming of the husband to come.

Ellen was younger than Lucy, perhaps too young to think about love, but she did not think she wanted to marry either; she liked to be left alone to think, to create pictures and make up stories, without anyone intruding on her. She would rather create beautiful art than spend her time picking up after a husband or raising bratty boys like the Dalrymple twins. Creating art to inspire people seemed more important than being a wife and mother.

"Beth," Thelma asked, "have you heard from Michael since he left?"

"Yes, I just got a letter from him a couple days ago."

"He wrote one to Roy too," said Henry.

"To Roy?" said Harriet. "Why? Roy's not Catholic."

"Beth's brother is a monsignor," Margaret told Bill's new girlfriend, Priscilla, so she would be properly impressed. "The Pope has called him to Rome."

Beth smiled; having a monsignor in the family had softened Margaret, even though Henry had married a Catholic girl.

"I imagine," said Harry Cumming, "that Roy and Monsignor McCarey enjoy each other's company. They're both very intellectual."

"I imagine," said Margaret, "that it's time we eat Sylvia's birthday cake."

Sylvia's eightieth birthday was tomorrow; Margaret had baked a cake so Easter dinner would also be a birthday celebration.

Margaret went to fetch the cake she had baked for her favorite sister-in-law – Harriet being her other sister-in-law.

Sylvia had been estranged from the family for so many years during her unhappy marriage that now she greeted all family gatherings enthusiastically. Clapping her hands at the sight of the cake, she thanked Margaret, then blew out her candles in one breath.

"I never thought I would live to see eighty," she said. "Now if I can just live long enough to see my grandsons married, I'll die content."

Ellen wondered how Aunt Sylvia, after such an unhappy marriage, could wish marriage upon her grandchildren? Ellen's parents were happily married, but they were so boring; in the evenings, they just sat in the living room, listening to the radio and reading the newspaper; when they talked, it was always about Dad's work or someone her mother had met out shopping. Ellen did not want to waste time listening to a husband when she had so many ideas for pictures to draw. She thought she would like to draw a picture of a woman like Aunt Sylvia, who only found happiness after being freed from her marriage.

Birthday cake was passed around. Jim gobbled his down, then took off to his friend's house. Sylvia's grandsons kissed their grandmother goodbye, then went to meet their girlfriends. The rest of the men moved into the living room. Priscilla followed the men; she would have preferred to be with the women, but she did not know any of them well enough to leave Bill's protection; the women knew they would probably never see Priscilla again so they made no effort to include her beyond being polite.

Ellen felt sorry for Priscilla, but that was what happened when you went out with a man; you got stuck with his relatives. Ellen had enough relatives of her own; she loved them, but they could be very dull; she did not need a husband's family to contend with as well. Ellen sat and listened to the women gossiping about who was getting married, what was wrong with the neighbor's children, and best of all, stories about the past – Aunt Eleanor recalled what she had worn at her first dance; Aunt Sylvia remembered the dress she wore on her wedding day – Ellen imagined the poor woman had had no idea what she was getting herself into that day – Grandma said that if she had not married, she would have been an opera singer; Cousin Thelma was asked to play the piano, and Grandma sang, although no one requested her performance. The men talked through the music; Ellen thought them ignorant; they expected women to cook and clean, without appreciating that women had other talents.

On the way home, Ellen asked her mother what she would have done had she not married.

"I don't know," said Beth. "I never thought about it. I always wanted to be a wife and mother."

"Didn't you ever work at all?"

"I worked in the diet kitchen at the hospital until I got married."

"Since you worked at the hospital, did you ever want to be a nurse?"

"No, I had only worked there a short time when I met your father, and then the rest of the time I worked there, I was just waiting to be married."

Ellen wondered how her mother could be so dull. Why did people always get married? Didn't they ever think there might be something else to do? Look at Aunt Sylvia and Aunt Eleanor – they would have been better off if they had never married. Cousin Thelma was a spinster, and she was more interesting than either of them; she loved music and taught the piano. And Grandma – she could have been an opera star, but instead, she had been stuck plucking chickens on a farm. Of course, Ellen knew if Grandma had not married Grandpa, or if her mother had not met her father, she would not be here today, but she wanted more than to wait on a man; she wanted to make a difference in the world, and she thought her art would achieve that goal.

Whenever Roy got a letter from Monsignor McCarey, he did not open it until the next morning. His letters came to the Big Bay Post Office, and he would stop to pick them up in the afternoon after working at the Club, but he knew if he read them before bed, he would not be able to sleep. Instead, he would wake up early, make himself a cup of coffee with sugar – one of the few luxuries his stoicism allowed because he had inherited the Whitman sweet tooth – then tremble as he slowly ripped open the envelope.

After the first paragraph or two, he would sip his coffee. He would read each letter three or four times until he had memorized large chunks of it. The letters were not typical ones, full of gossip and boring comments about the weather just to fill the blank page. Michael's letters always said something. Once Michael's words were in his head, Roy would go fishing or chop his firewood or work at the Club, all the while contemplating his friend's message and composing a reply in his head. Then, after the words had consumed him all day, he would come home to write a response.

Michael had begun the correspondence; despite his orthodox beliefs, Michael thought Roy such an interesting man that he shared with him his deepest thoughts; Roy reciprocated by putting down on paper what he could not have said to anyone else. The two men shared a mutual respect for each other as kindred seekers of truth. Their correspondence was private, but a few glimpses of it may be allowed the reader.

> Dear Roy,
> I had forgotten what a warm country Italy is. The heat of Michigan's Upper Peninsula is rarely over eighty even in summer, but here the country is basked in sunlight, the land seems baked, and the humidity is intense. The Vatican is so full of cement and stone that the heat sores up from it. Sometimes I feel dizzy from the scorching sun. I believe the Lord sent me here – I know you will not believe that, but we can be friends without sharing the same beliefs – still I wish the Lord had sent a younger man. I enjoyed Italy when I first came here to study for the priesthood, but now I feel too old to

be away from my humble U.P. parishes. The young are able to travel about with enthusiasm, but at nearly fifty, a man should not have to leave what is familiar to him. I wrote to Beth and told her I was well, that I felt honored to be here – and that is true, but I am also terribly homesick. What I wouldn't give to hear the unique accents of my fellow Upper Michigan natives over these rich Italian voices. I don't know that too many people other than you would understand . . . .

Dear Michael,

I think you misunderstand me when you say you know I do not believe in God. I do not believe in Christianity or for that matter any organized religion. I do not deny some Force or Being created the universe, but I think that if such happened, it is still meaningless, and that your Supreme Being takes no interest in our lives, so no, I do not believe God or whatever force it is intentionally sent you to Italy. As you know, I have read widely about existentialism; its tenets make far more sense to me than those of Christianity, but perhaps agnosticism is what best describes my beliefs. I feel the greatest wisdom we can admit to is that we cannot know. If man is alone in the universe, then he must act in his own interest. If there is a God above watching our deeds, then all the better, but we should try to do what is best for ourselves rather than depend on a god we can't be sure exists. I find it hard to believe that God has led you to Rome or to anywhere. You would not have gone to Rome if it were not for your own natural inclinations to teach there. You may be homesick, but you also know you are sacrificing yourself for something you believe is more valuable than individual happiness. In other words, priests are not without their advantages to humanity, and you are helping to train future priests, and I am sure you will help them be good ones, in which case they will be much needed, and they will do good – as I know you do. They just cannot claim, as they falsely do, to know the truth.

Dear Roy,

You understand me far better than anyone, despite our theological differences. I believe in Jesus Christ and the Father and the Holy Spirit. That said, I do not know that any of it is true. I choose to believe in it out of Faith. . . . You wrote in your last letter of the meaninglessness of life and how the only meaning is what we make of it. You tell me you have found great meaning in your life. I believe everyone's life is worthy of examination. But please explain to me more what is the meaning you have found. Most people find meaning in a family, but you have apparently chosen not to follow that route. I find meaning by giving of myself to others. But I do not see you active in charity or the consolation of your fellow human beings. I do not wish to cast aspersions upon you, simply to understand you better. I have often thought you lived like a monk, but perhaps you are more like those hermits who lived in the woods alone in ancient times when Christianity was only beginning its hold in Europe. Holy men in those days lived and walked in oneness with God and Nature in a way I do not think our modern world can understand . . . .

Roy had especially enjoyed the images in this last letter. To walk in oneness with God and Nature. Was that not what he had been trying to do all these years? He just did not feel that God, if He existed, wanted to walk with him. What meaning was there in his own life? He pondered the question as he sipped his coffee, but eventually, he looked at his watch and saw it was time for him to leave. He had plenty of work to do at the Club. It was the first of August, the height of the summer season. He would not have much time today to think about what he would write back to Michael. He was looking forward to autumn when he could be alone again with his thoughts.

Hearing from Michael always cheered him, no matter how they might disagree, so Roy whistled with pleasure as he walked to the Club through the beautiful forest. When he came in view of the gate, the keeper hurried out.

"Did you hear the news?"

"What news?" asked Roy, surprised by the man's pale expression.

"About the murder. Mike Chenoweth was shot."

"Shot?" Roy was astonished.

"By one of those hotheaded soldiers at the army encampment."

"Why?" asked Roy, unable to articulate any other word.

"I'm not sure. It's all just rumor at this point, but – " The gatekeeper said more, but Roy was too stunned to hear it. Mike Chenoweth was the proprietor of the Lumberjack Tavern in Big Bay. Roy had known him for years. Mike had always been so friendly that even Roy, who was no great socializer, had willingly spent an occasional evening drinking in the bar and enjoying his company. Mike was known throughout the area for having been in the Marine Corps and as a former Marquette policeman. He was widely respected as one of the best shots in Marquette County. Thanks to Mike's successful proprietorship, the Lumberjack Tavern had become a gathering place for the Big Bay locals.

When the U.S. Army had recently established a firing point near the Big Bay Lighthouse, Mike's personality had caused the soldiers to flock to his tavern. Roy could not fathom why anyone would wish Mike harm, much less want to kill him.

By afternoon, Roy had heard many true details and even more gossip about the murder. The story was repeated a hundred thousand times that day first in Big Bay, then at the Huron Mountain Club, and soon in Marquette, Ishpeming, Negaunee, all Marquette County, and finally, the entire Upper Peninsula. Murders were a rare occurrence in the great North Woods where people felt so safe they did not lock their doors, and they feared assault from a bear more than from a fellow human being. The story stunned everyone; the whispers regarding the murderer's motivation caused a sensation. Soon the story would be told in court, then in the newspapers, and then a bestselling novel and a Hollywood blockbuster film would capitalize upon it. Men would become famous from this murder, but for the moment, the sordid details were hard for anyone to believe.

Wild stories circulated, but the facts were that Mike Chenoweth had been killed by an army lieutenant named Peterson. The lieutenant and his wife lived in the trailer park down the road from the tavern. The night before, the auburn-haired, highly attractive Charlotte Peterson had walked down to the bar with her dog George to pick up a six-pack of beer for her husband. She remained at the bar for most of the evening, playing shuffleboard and having several drinks with Mike.

When she left the bar shortly after midnight, Mike offered to give her a ride home. It was a dark night, and there was always the fear of bears in Big Bay. Charlotte accepted Mike's offer, and she and her dog climbed into Mike's car. He drove her to the trailer park, but when they reached it, the gate was locked. Mike told her he would take her around another road to get her into the trailer park. At this point, he grabbed her arm to keep her from getting out of the car. He then drove her down a lonely road that led nowhere. Mike threw the dog out of the car, then attacked and raped Mrs. Peterson. Then Mike allowed the dog back in the car and drove his victim to the trailer park.

Mrs. Peterson stumbled out of the car, climbed through a hole in the gate, and found her way back to her trailer. She arrived, screaming and crying, and told her husband what had happened. The lieutenant made his wife swear on her rosary that she was telling the truth. Then he lost his mind. He went down to the Lumberjack Tavern and shot Mike Chenoweth dead. Lieutenant Peterson then walked back to the trailer park and turned himself into the caretaker, who was a U.S. Marshal. He handed over his gun and stated, "I just shot Mike Chenoweth."

Many believed Mike would not rape a woman, but others noted he had always had an eye for the girls, and he was a muscular man, easily capable of overpowering Mrs. Peterson. Many wanted to believe the lieutenant had murdered Mike in a fit of jealousy without an actual rape having taken place, but Roy understood how sinister men can be, and how lust can master a person's mind and soul. Roy knew any man could perpetrate such a crime if not in the right frame of mind; he feared even he might behave in such a manner if his self-restraint gave way.

He pitied Mrs. Peterson because Chloe, the woman Roy loved, had also been raped – by her own husband; at the same time, Roy compared himself to Mike because he had also committed adultery with a married woman. Only, Roy had loved Chloe and wanted to protect her against her abusive husband. Roy wondered whether he deserved to be dead, like Mike Chenoweth, because he had committed adultery, even if Chloe had willingly slept with him. Roy did not know whether Chloe's husband, Lex, ever knew they had slept together, but Lex had caught them together once, and had Lex had a gun then, Roy knew he would now be dead; as it was, Lex had nearly beat Roy senseless, and Roy suspected, Lex had often treated Chloe the same.

Roy had tried to drive Chloe from his mind; so many years had passed since he had become infatuated with her, and although he had written to her a few times in the years since the war, he no longer felt a great passion for her. Now this murder had stirred up in him all kinds of repressed and unresolved emotions. He found he rather admired the lieutenant; he wished he had been man enough to kill Lex. Then with Lex gone, he and Chloe might have been together. Instead he had been a coward; he had let her go away with her abusive husband, then spent years trying to accept that he could not be with her because she had to do her duty by her husband and children. He had spent years telling himself how foolish he had been to love her; he would tell himself he was over her and not think about her for weeks. Then the old feeling would swell up in him again, and he knew he had lied to himself that he had gotten over her, and he felt almost unable to endure their separation.

When he returned to his shack, Roy brewed some tea to settle his nerves; he told himself he was just worked up because of the murder, but before the tea cooled enough to drink, he gave in to despair. Collapsing on the bed, he called out Chloe's name and sobbed, "I love you! I love you!" into his pillow. His arms ached to hold her, to taste her lips, her breasts. He indulged in fantasies until he almost believed he was possessing her again, only to hurt more because he lied to himself. He felt he was dying inside because he was separated from her. He told himself elaborate stories of how he would find her and make her be with him. He raged at the God he was unsure even existed; how could he believe in God when he could not be with Chloe, and when it had been in God's own house that he had first seen and begun to burn with lust for her?

Only when his throat ached from sobbing and he could no longer tolerate the snot running from his nose, did Roy sit up and search for his handkerchief. Then he went to the kitchen pump, washed his hands, and drank the now cold tea. He was leaning against the sink, trying to calm himself, when his eye caught Michael's letter laying on the table where he had left it that morning.

"Maybe," he thought. "But – No. He's a priest. He couldn't understand, not when he's never – but maybe. I need to talk to someone. I can't go on like this – but it would almost be like going to confession."

He blew his nose again. Then he went outside to relieve himself, wishing he could overcome his lust. He felt violently ill. He thought for a moment he would vomit or faint. He came inside and washed his hands again. Then he made another cup of tea and tried to talk himself out of writing the letter.

But he hurt so much he had to take up his pen.

> Dear Michael,
>   I never told anyone this, but since you are a priest, I know you will keep it in confidence. Many years ago, I fell in love and what happened as a result I have never known whether I should regret, yet I feel the need to confess it. Perhaps <u>confess</u> is not the right word. I just want to tell someone what happened, and then you may tell me, to the best of your ability, whether I were wrong in what I did.

Aunt Ada's summer visits were always special. Ellen loved her other aunts and uncles, but she saw them all the time. Aunt Ada only came to visit one week out of the year. Other adults were always busy, but when Aunt Ada came, she was on vacation so she could spend all her time enjoying her family. Her children, Judy and Brad, accompanied her; they looked forward to seeing their aunts, uncles, and grandmother as much as Ellen looked forward to seeing her favorite aunt. Ellen's Louisiana cousins would end up at Uncle Henry or Aunt Eleanor's house, while Ellen found herself at Grandma's house, spending the day with Aunt Ada, being taught all the wonderful things only Aunt Ada knew.

Aunt Ada owned a doll shop; she made her own dolls, and their clothes, and even furniture and houses for them. Aunt Ada was a marvel in Ellen's eyes. Grandpa Whitman had built Ellen a dollhouse before he died, but Aunt Ada had taught Ellen how to furnish it properly.

Today the two made mattresses out of sponges, sewed little pillows stuffed with cotton balls, and used thread spools to make end tables. Aunt Ada gave the initial lessons, then Ellen impressed her with her own innovative ways of decorating.

"Ellen, what are you going to be when you grow up?" asked Aunt Ada one happy afternoon.

"I don't know," said Ellen. People asked her that question all the time, but she was afraid to answer it truthfully.

"I think," said Aunt Ada, "that you should be an artist. I wish I'd had your talent when I was your age."

Ellen smiled, but "Maybe" was the most courageous reply she could make to acknowledge her dream.

"Ellen, Ada, would you clean off the table now?" asked Ellen's grandmother. "Bill will be here any minute with Fredrica."

Ellen rolled her eyes when Grandma disappeared back into the kitchen.

"How can anyone marry someone named Fredrica?" she asked her aunt.

"What I don't understand," said Aunt Ada, "is why any girl would want to marry your Uncle Bill."

"Let's just be glad," said Grandma, coming back into the room, and having overheard the exchange, "that Bill is finally settling down."

Fredrica was the girl who had finally manipulated Bill into making a commitment. As he came in the door, he was smooching Fredrica's cheek. Signs of affection disgusted Ellen, and she was further annoyed when Fredrica, glancing at Ellen's miniature furniture, said, "There are more educational things a young lady could do during her summer vacation." Ellen wanted to reply, "There are more educational things you could do than marry Uncle Bill," but she felt it would sound stupid, and she could think of nothing better to say. And if Aunt Ada thought she should be an artist, who cared what Fredrica thought?

"Have you set a date yet?" Aunt Ada asked the newly engaged couple.

"Valentine's Day," said Fredrica. "I think that's romantic; don't you?"

"Oh yes, very," said Margaret.

Uncle Bill and Fredrica kissed again. Then Fredrica began to discuss her wedding plans.

Ellen ate the cake Grandma set before her while trying to block Fredrica's voice from her thoughts. She would be an artist; that was more productive than being Uncle Bill's wife.

By September, everyone in Marquette County was speculating over what would happen with the Big Bay Murder Trial. Would Lieutenant Peterson be charged with murder? Would he get a reduced sentence because his wife had been raped? Would the rape be proven? Then, after ten days of trial and the jury's five hour deliberation, on September 25th, Lieutenant Peterson was declared not guilty by reason of insanity, yet he was now sane and no threat to the public. Lieutenant Peterson was a free man.

Ellen knew nothing about the trial; her parents did not want her to hear the sordid details of a rape and murder, so they hid the newspapers, only reading them and discussing the case after the children were in bed.

Ellen would not have cared about the murder trial even if she knew about it. She was more excited about the new student teacher for her art class at school. The teacher constantly encouraged her, and Ellen believed every compliment about her artistic talents. That autumn, Ellen lived for art class. In her spare time, she drew pictures, trying to do her best so she could bring them to school and have Miss Kendall say in front of all the other students, "Well done, Ellen. You draw so well."

One day Ellen came home from school to find Cousin Thelma visiting her mother.

"Mom, I want to show you the picture I drew in school," said Ellen, fishing her drawing out of her schoolbag. Beth glanced at it, said, "It's very good," then passed it to Thelma.

"Very nice, Ellen," said Thelma, impressed by how well the girl drew intricate churches with statues of the Virgin Mary outside them. "Someday, you'll make a fine nun."

Ellen looked startled. Was it not clear from how well she drew that she wanted to be an artist? She was relieved when her mother said, "Oh, I hope not. I don't want to lose my daughter to the church like I did my brother."

"What do you think you'll be then, Ellen?" asked Thelma.

"I think," Beth answered for her daughter, "that someday Ellen will make a good wife and mother like most girls."

Ellen wanted to shout, "I'm not like most girls!" but she only said, "I'll go put my pictures in my room."

She had been annoyed by Thelma's remark, but she was repulsed by her mother's. She saw little difference between being locked up in a convent and being stuck in the house all day with a bunch of screaming babies.

Just before Christmas, Ellen brought home a painting she had done in school. Miss Kendall had written on the back of it, "Dear Mr. and Mrs. Whitman, Ellen is a very good artist and should be encouraged to pursue her talents."

Ellen beamed with pride when she showed the picture and the comments to her parents. When Jim looked at the picture, he said, "Your trees look like broccoli."

Ellen grabbed the picture and stormed into her room. Her mother was too busy fixing supper to worry over her children's little spats.

Ellen lay on her bed, hurt and angry, until she realized Jimmy had never even tried to draw a tree, so why should she listen to him? She was going to be an artist, and she didn't care what anyone said. She knew there would always be stupid people in the world who would be jealous of her; she would learn to ignore them. Nothing would stop her, certainly not Jimmy.

Dear Michael,

Thank you for the letter. I knew you would understand the anguish I felt and how hard it was for me to write to you of my love for Chloe. It has been fourteen years now, and most days I am fine, but every few months, the pain boils up all over again, just as it did the day I learned she was moving away, and even though I cannot blame her, and I no longer hate Lex, I still feel an anger toward the world and toward myself for what happened . . . .

. . . . I once knew a boy who tore the wings off a butterfly and kept the poor creature in a jar. I hated him for it, and after a couple days, I managed to steal the jar from him and set his prisoner free. I placed the butterfly on a tree where I thought it would be safe, but it climbed from the trunk onto a branch and then stood there at the end of it, looking out at the world, wanting to fly, but knowing it was as much a captive then as when it had been in the jar. I often feel I am a prisoner like that butterfly, except I am a prisoner of my own making; I cannot escape from myself. Sartre says that "Hell is other people" but I think Milton was closer to the truth when he described Satan as having "Hell within him."

I feel I am my own Hell. Hell is within me, in my memories and in the longings I cannot overcome. I am haunted by my memories of how others have wronged me, and even more, how I have let those wrongs lead to my wronging myself . . . .

Your sincere friend, Roy

1956

Since its founding in 1849, Marquette had always been remote, isolated from the rest of the nation, despite its importance as a port to ship iron ore. Most Americans did not know Marquette existed and Michigan's Upper Peninsula was often mistaken as a part of Canada or Wisconsin. The fiercely independent people of Upper Michigan did not care what the rest of the country thought of them. They knew they were a superior people, and they need not be bothered with the rest of the world.

Then Upper Michigan was invaded. The world's largest suspension bridge was being built over the Straits of Mackinac, connecting Michigan's Upper and Lower Peninsulas, two halves of a state as culturally distinct from each other as two separate countries. Simultaneously, Marquette's first television station, WLUC, was established. Newspapers and radio had already brought the outside world into Upper Michigan, but now Marquette's residents could view events from across the globe with more ease than they could see the house across the street during a blizzard, and occasionally, events such as the murder in Big Bay brought the Upper Peninsula into the national spotlight. The modern technological age had come to Marquette.

"Ellen, set the table for me," said Beth, fussing over the stove. "Thelma and Jessie will be here any minute, and I need to keep an eye on the potatoes and corn."

Ellen reluctantly laid aside her book and went into the kitchen, first washing her hands and then collecting the plates out of the cupboard.

"Six?" she asked her mother.

"What?"

"Six? Am I setting the table for six people?" It frustrated Ellen to have to ask twice because her mother was not quick enough to catch her abbreviated language.

"No, for five," said Beth, draining the water from the boiled potatoes. "Your brother has a date tonight."

"Marilyn?" Ellen asked.

"Mmh," Beth murmured, making it clear she did not approve of Marilyn, but that as a mother, she knew you could do nothing with boys.

Ellen envied her brother getting to do whatever he liked. Here it was Friday night, and even though she was fifteen, she was "too young" in her mother's opinion to go out. The last thing Ellen wanted was to spend Friday evening with her relatives.

"Mother, why do you always invite Thelma and Jessie over?" she asked, carrying the dishes to the dining room table.

"What do you mean? They're my family," said Beth, mashing the potatoes.

Ellen's father came inside from his woodshop.

"Hurry and wash up for dinner," Beth told him. "They'll be here any minute."

"What if I don't?" he laughed, grabbing her around her plump waist.

"Then we won't have any supper."

"Then maybe they won't come over so we can be alone."

Beth giggled and allowed Henry to kiss her cheek. But when he tried to steal another kiss, she pushed him away.

"Now, Henry, I need to get the roast out of the oven."

"I'm only hungry for you," he whispered in her ear.

Ellen peeked into the kitchen and saw them hugging in front of the stove. They were a couple of oddballs, but it was sweet how they loved each other.

"Later," Beth said, catching sight of Ellen watching them. She pushed Henry away, then added more milk to the mashed potatoes.

Henry went into the bathroom, then hollered, "They better not stay late!"

"I don't know why they have to come at all," said Ellen.

"They're coming to watch TV," said Beth. "You know that."

Ellen had waited years for her parents to break down and buy a TV. She did not know why they now had to share it with Thelma and Jessie. Ellen knew her father worked hard for every penny he had, so he ought to be able to enjoy his own television set.

"Why can't Thelma buy her own TV?" Ellen asked. "She can afford one."

"I guess she thinks it would be frivolous," said Beth.

"A TV would keep her company since she can hardly play the piano anymore."

Before Beth could reply, Jim came into the kitchen, following a half hour of personal grooming in front of his bedroom mirror. "I'm going now, Mom."

"All right. Have a good time and behave yourself. Be home by midnight."

"Yes, Mother," he said, then kissed her cheek.

Jim opened the back door in time to find Thelma and Jessie on the other side.

"My, you look so handsome," said Thelma. "You needn't get all dressed up for our sakes."

Jim smiled and explained he was going out on a date.

"That's nice," said Thelma.

Jessie shyly nodded "Hello" as Jim slid past her. She was eight years older than him, yet young men always made her nervous. Since Jessie's father had abandoned her as a little girl and her mother had died, resulting in Thelma adopting her, Jessie had had little contact with men. Even at school, she had focused on studying music and avoided boys.

"Hello, Thelma, Jessie," said Beth as they came up the stairs into the kitchen. "Ellen, take their coats."

Ellen did as she was told while trying to think of something to say to her relatives.

"Supper will be ready in five minutes," Beth said. "I'm sorry I'm running behind. I wanted us to be done eating in time to watch the TV show."

Jessie offered to help. Thelma hobbled across the room with her cane until she plopped into a chair.

"How's school going?" Thelma asked Ellen.

"Fine," said Ellen, not volunteering further information.

"How's the piano?"

"Okay," said Ellen, casting her eyes in its direction.

"Have you been practicing much? I expect you to play me a piece later."

Ellen had begun to take piano lessons from Memo Beyers, much to Thelma's disapproval. She did not deny Mrs. Beyers was an excellent teacher, but she was not altogether pleased that Ellen did not take lessons from her. Beth had argued that it was too hard to drive "all the way across town" to Thelma's house for lessons, but Thelma knew it was because her multiple sclerosis made her fingers too brittle for her to play properly. For a short time, Jessie had taken over teaching Thelma's students, but then she had quit giving piano lessons when she found a position as music teacher at one of the elementary schools.

"Here we are," said Beth, setting the roast on the dinner table.

"Hello there," said Henry, appearing in the dining room. "Do you need any help, honey?"

"Hello, Henry," said Thelma and Jessie.

"No," Beth said, "go ahead and sit down. Ellen'll pour the drinks."

Everyone arranged themselves around the table, then waited for Ellen to bring in the glasses and sit down.

"Thelma, did I tell you," said Beth, initiating the conversation as the food was passed around, "that Henry will be going to Florida for three months this winter."

"Florida? Whatever for? Not because of health problems, I hope."

"No," said Henry. "I've been asked by a member of the Huron Mountain Club to go down there and build him a house."

"Really? How'd you manage that?"

"Roy's friendly with the man," said Beth, "who is some sort of big entrepreneur. He asked Roy to come down and build him a house, and Roy agreed, but he told the fellow Henry's a better carpenter than him, so now they're both going to work on the house."

"He's a real nice fellow," said Henry. "Name's Mr. Pryce. He inherited his money, but he's multiplied it several times over since then. He said he'd pay all our traveling and living expenses down there."

"Really?" said Thelma. "That'll be nice. I'd love to see Florida."

"Not me," said Beth. "California was hot enough the year we lived there. I wish we had never gone. We wouldn't have except for Henry's health. I hear Florida's even more humid, and sometimes eighty degrees in the middle of winter."

"I don't blame you," said Jessie. "I hate hot weather."

"Is your brother Bill also going to Florida?" asked Thelma.

"N-no," said Henry.

"I imagine," Beth said, "that his wife won't want him to be gone that long."

"Why not? You're letting Henry go for three months."

"Ellen, honey," Beth tried to change the subject, "pass Thelma the butter."

"No thanks," Thelma said. "The reason I ask about Bill is because I heard he and Fredrica are getting divorced."

Beth laid down her fork and waited for Henry to reply.

"Where did you hear that?" asked Henry.

Ellen wanted to know as well. It was news to her.

"Your Aunt Harriet told me yesterday when I saw her downtown."

"Harriet," muttered Beth.

"Well, we're hoping they'll still work things out," said Henry. "I don't feel it's our place to discuss it."

"I don't see where there's anything to discuss after the way he's acted," said Thelma. "I know he's your brother, Henry, but everyone in town is well aware of what Bill is like. Why Fredrica has stayed with him this long is – "

"Thelma, I bet your coffee's cold," said Beth, thinking Ellen too young to hear such conversation. "Ellen, take Thelma's cup and go get her some fresh coffee."

Ellen wanted to hear the rest, but her mother's eyes warned her to leave the room. She quickly finished chewing her meat, then took Thelma's cup into the kitchen.

"Ellen is too young to – " was all she heard her mother say. Everyone was whispering, and she could not make out the words, but she understood nevertheless; Uncle Bill was running around on his wife. Ellen poured the coffee, then stood, staring out the kitchen window without seeing anything. She didn't understand why her mother tried to protect her – how else was she to learn what men were really like? She needed to let this sink in. It was scandalous – that's what her grandmother must think. Ellen found it hard to understand how Uncle Bill could do such a thing when her father was such a loving husband, and when Uncle Roy had spent his life alone, never having even been in love as far as she knew – she could not imagine any woman loving rough old Uncle Roy. How could three brothers be so different?

"At least there are no children to be hurt," Thelma was saying as Ellen returned with the coffee.

"Henry, when will you be going to Florida?" Jessie asked as Ellen sat back down.

"Probably the first week of January. We hope to finish the job by Easter, but in any case, we'll definitely be home before May 1st."

"Beth, you'll miss Henry terribly," said Thelma.

"Yes, I will."

"I'd miss him too if I had a good man like Henry."

Henry grinned at the compliment.

"Will you be going down through Wisconsin or over the Straits?" asked Jessie.

"I think through Wisconsin. I don't know whether the ferries will be running in January."

"What about the bridge?" asked Thelma. "Maybe it'll be finished by then."

"I doubt it'll be finished in the middle of winter," said Henry. "Last I heard they thought it would take at least another year."

"They've been working on it long enough already, haven't they?" said Thelma.

"It's going to be five miles long," said Ellen, who had just discussed the bridge in school. "It'll be the world's longest suspension bridge."

"It'll be a real wonder when it's done," said Jessie, "that's for sure."

"We should go for a drive to see it," said Ellen.

"I'd like to," said Thelma, "but with my medical problems, I don't think I could sit in the car for a hundred and sixty miles or however far it is."

"It's too bad," said Jessie. "I always thought we'd take a trip to Mackinac Island sometime."

"I don't want to go to Mackinac Island," said Thelma. She had visited the beautiful isle once over twenty years before, only to come away with sour memories.

"Ellen," said Beth, "let's get the dishes done. The TV show will be on soon."

Ellen stood up to gather the dishes.

"Don't we get dessert?" asked Thelma.

"I made cake," said Beth. "How about I cut it up, and we eat it during the show? I want to let my stomach settle for a few minutes."

"Can I help with anything?" Jessie asked.

"Oh no, you and Thelma go make yourselves comfortable in the living room."

"Let me show you the blueprints for that house I'm going to build," said Henry, going into the kitchen to dig through a stack of paper on the cupboard. He returned and sat down on a footstool across from Thelma and Jessie, then proceeded to bore them with the details of house building while Thelma feigned great respect for his skills.

"The show's on!" shouted Henry when it began.

"We're coming," Beth shouted back, quickly wiping the last two dishes while Ellen drained the dishwater. In two minutes, they joined the others in front of the TV.

"My, the picture is so good," said Thelma. "It's like having a little movie theater right in your own home."

"Yes, it is a good picture," Henry said, proud of his television set.

"The screen is small," said Thelma, "but then I'm used to the big screen at the Delft Theatre. Beth, do you remember the first time we went to the Delft to see that movie with Rudolph Valentino? Oh, Jessie, you and Ellen probably don't even know who Rudolph Valentino was, but in his day, he was the heartthrob. He could put that James Dean to shame, even if they did both die tragically young."

Ellen rolled her eyes at her mother. Beth raised her eyebrows in askance of what her daughter meant. Ellen felt all adults were hopeless. How could they watch TV if Thelma were going to talk through the whole program? There was no point in watching anymore.

"My, Lucille Ball's always so well dressed," Jessie said.

"Do you think her hair is really red?" Thelma asked.

"She's a strikingly beautiful woman, even when she's acting silly," said Jessie.

"That black dress Ethel has on reminds me of one of my own," said Thelma. "Oh, Beth, did you know there's a big sale on at Getz's this week. Do you want to go with me?"

"No, I don't have money to buy anything right now."

"Well, it's a sale, so you can probably afford something."

Beth said nothing. Henry would not want her to spend the money.

"I can't believe they let women wear pants on television," said Henry.

"I think they look good on Lucy," said Thelma. "It's about time women wear what they want."

Ellen wanted to yell, "Be quiet!" That would get her sent to her room, but what did it matter; it was too late now to figure out what plot Lucy was hatching to get into Ricky's show.

She gave up trying to listen and thought about Uncle Bill. She had never liked Aunt Fredrica, but still, why did Uncle Bill have to cheat on his wife? And then there were men like Ricky Ricardo, who didn't think their wives should be in show business. Men! She was better off without one.

"Ellen," said Thelma, "remember you promised to play the piano for me."

"Oh," said Ellen, realizing *I Love Lucy* was over.

"Play something from your new piano book," said Beth.

Ellen got up from the couch and dug in the piano bench for her sheet music.

"It's from the new Broadway musical *My Fair Lady*," she explained.

"I've heard of that," said Jessie, "but I don't think I know any of the songs."

"I'll play 'On the Street Where You Live'," said Ellen. She thought it the most romantic song she had ever heard. Everyday when she walked home from school past Andy Travis's house, her heart silently sang that song. Andy was a year older than her, and very cute when he took off his glasses. He was her first crush. She did not smell lilacs when she thought of him, but she thought she might if he kissed her.

Ellen had only played a few bars of the song before Thelma's mouth went off again, "Beth, don't forget to give me that cake recipe before I leave. I want to make it for the church bake sale this weekend." The most romantic song in the world could not overpower Thelma's tongue.

Ellen played through the chatter. When she finished, an awkward moment followed before anyone realized she had stopped. Then Jessie clapped her hands and said, "Very nice, Ellen. I see Mrs. Beyers is teaching you well."

Ellen smiled, then looked to her mother to see whether she could be released from the piano, but Thelma said, "Play us another song."

Ellen turned to "I Could Have Danced All Night". It was a faster song, so her fingers stumbled in several places, but no one noticed while Thelma was yapping. As Ellen finished, the telephone rang.

"Dang it," said Henry. "I wish that thing had never been invented. It only interrupts our lives."

Beth ran to answer it. Everyone was respectfully quiet while Beth spoke. From her tone, they could tell it was bad news.

"I'm sorry, Eleanor. Thanks for telling us. Take care of yourself."

Everyone stared expectantly as Beth hung up the phone.

"What's wrong?" Thelma asked.

"It's Aunt Sylvia. She wasn't feeling well this afternoon so Eleanor took her to the hospital. She just passed away."

There were several moments of deafening silence. Then Henry asked, "What was wrong with her?"

"Congestive heart failure. She'd been wheezing the last couple days. Remember how she was on Sunday at your mother's house?"

"Yes," said Henry.

"When's the funeral?" asked Jessie.

"They don't know yet," said Beth.

Ellen did not know what to say. She tried to look appropriately sad.

A few days later, Sylvia Whitman Cumming was laid to rest in Marquette's Park Cemetery where her family had been buried for a hundred years. Her grave was at the bottom of a sloping hill, gently shaded by a giant oak, beside her late husband.

Ellen had once heard Great-Aunt Sylvia say the happiest years of her life had been those as a widow. Now Ellen felt sorry the poor woman would have to spend eternity beside the man she had tried but failed to love.

"Grandma," Ellen asked, as the mourners left the gravesite after the final prayer, "if Aunt Sylvia was unhappily married, why is she being buried next to Uncle Harry?"

"Where else would she be buried?" asked Margaret. "Wives are always buried with their husbands. See your grandpa's stone over there. There's a space on the stone for my name when the time comes."

Ellen did not want to think of her grandmother dying. She stayed focused on her question. "But Aunt Sylvia didn't love her husband. Wasn't he a mean man?"

"I never met him," said Margaret, "but from what your grandfather told me, he was ornery and hateful. Still, we shouldn't speak ill of the dead. After all those years she spent with him, your Aunt Sylvia must have felt some love for him."

Ellen did not understand. She remembered how Aunt Sylvia had constantly laughed, as if trying to get the most from each moment to make up for years of marital anguish.

"Hello, Jessie," said Margaret, as she and Ellen passed Jessie climbing into her car. "Didn't Thelma want to come?"

"No, she isn't feeling the best today. I could barely get her out of bed and into her wheelchair. I didn't want to leave her, but she insisted I come pay my respects."

"Tell her we hope she feels better soon," said Margaret.

"I will," said Jessie, before shutting her car door.

As they walked away, Margaret said to Ellen, "I don't understand that girl."

"Who? Jessie?" asked Ellen.

"Yes. She's thirty years old, and a pretty girl too, but she doesn't have any gentlemen friends. You would think she'd meet a nice male teacher at school."

Ellen was surprised her grandmother did not understand; Jessie was musically talented and probably only teaching school until she could become a concert pianist. Why would Jessie give up her dream to be trapped like Aunt Sylvia, or even like Grandma, who could have been an opera singer? Ellen was tempted to ask Grandma whether she ever regretted marrying Grandpa, but whenever she tried to ask, she stopped herself; she was afraid to know the answer, either way.

Ellen knew what her decision would be. She liked to imagine kissing Andy Travis, but she knew if she ever did, she would have to break his heart when she explained that being an artist mattered to her more than being a wife and mother. She did not want to hurt him, but she would not let any man trap her.

1957

Family letter extracts from when Henry and Roy built a house in Florida.

January 8, 1957
Dear Beth,

Here we are finally in Florida. Did you get the postcard I sent you from Chicago? I think it snowed all the way there, but once we got to southern Illinois and Indiana and then into Kentucky, we had good weather. Roy and I pretty evenly shared the driving time. It sure is funny to think that just a few days ago, I saw huge snowbanks in Marquette, while down here it's 80 degrees and rainy. These people have no idea what a real snowfall looks like.

Yesterday was the first day we started working. They've just finished clearing the land where the house will be, so all Roy and I have really done so far is buy materials. Mr. Pryce drove over last night to see that we were comfortable here in the trailer park. He's just a regular guy, honey, despite all his millions. He brought us over some soda pop, bread, and lunch meat. He gave us his phone number and told us to call if there's anything we need and he'll stop by the work site whenever he's got a free moment.

I'll write you a longer letter later. Give my love to everyone at home.

Hello, Ellen. Be a good girl for your mother and help her around the house.

Hello, Jim. Keep working and be helpful to your mother, giving her a ride to church or getting her groceries or whatever she needs.

Tell Bandit his daddy misses him. Don't feed him too many snacks while I'm gone. I'll write again soon.

Love, Henry

🍁　🍁　🍁

January 13, 1957

Dear Henry,

I was so glad to hear you and Roy made it down there safely. Now that you've started your job, tell me what Florida is like. I hate hot weather, but lately it's been so cold I almost wish I went down there with you.

Everyone was asking me for days whether we had heard from you until I got your letter. Tell Roy that the one he wrote to your mother came yesterday. Ellen and I went over to her house for Sunday dinner. She said she would be writing to both of you. The kids are fine. Jim is putting in an extra shift at the grocery store today. Ellen is busy reading and painting when she's not going to school. She is like her father – always keeping busy.

Remember that murder a few years ago in Big Bay? Well, John Voelker has written a book about it called *Anatomy of a Murder*. It was just in the papers a day or two after you left. He wrote it under another name, Robert Traver, I think it is, but everyone knows who really wrote it. After all, he was the lieutenant's lawyer. There's talk around town that he's even sold the movie rights to the book. Imagine that. A movie about something that happened right here in our neck of the woods.

We all miss you, me especially. Write as often as you can, but if you're worn out in the evening, don't feel you have to. The kids are being good to me so don't worry. We'll be fine until you get home.

Love, Beth

January 20, 1957

Dear Michael,

I'm sorry I haven't written for so long. Henry and I are in Florida now, building a house for Mr. Pryce, one of the members from the Huron Mountain Club. We imagine we'll be here for about three months so you can write to the return address on the postmark. I wonder what the people at the post office here will think of me sending letters to Vatican City. They always give me a hard time in Big Bay when they see I'm friends with a monsignor in Rome.

It seems funny to be here in Florida in the middle of winter where it's so warm. I'm so used to the snow. I feel more surprised now by the change of climate than I did when I went out West as a young man, or away to Europe. I'll be fifty next year, so I guess I'm getting too old for a change of scenery. You understand – you've told me many times how much you miss the Upper Peninsula. We'll be making some good money working here though, and I know Henry needs it since he has a family to support. I'll just stick mine in the bank I guess. I don't know what else to do with it. I've got about a thousand dollars now. What does a single man even need with that much?

Remember my writing to you about that murder in Big Bay a few years back. I think Beth told me she sent you some clippings about it. John Voelker who was Lt. Peterson's lawyer has written a book about the murder that was just published. I haven't read it yet. I only know because Beth just wrote and told us. I think it's a shame. Why not let poor Mike Chenoweth rest in peace? Whatever wrongs he committed, he doesn't need to have all this fuss brought up again. Beth said there's talk that a movie might be made out of the book. I don't think even John Voelker expected that, but it seems a shame that people will make a fortune off a poor girl being raped and a man murdered.

Well, write when you're not too busy. Give the Pope my best.

Your friend, Roy

February 1, 1957
Dear Henry,

Thank you for the letter. It was good to hear from you. I miss you especially in the evenings. I miss you lying beside me at night, just talking after the kids have gone to sleep. Since you can't be here, if you want to call, I would love to hear your voice, but I know it would be expensive so don't call if you don't want to. We should probably save the money anyway. I did get the money you wired to us. Thank you. Don't worry about anything. The kids and I will be fine until you get back, even if we are really lonesome.

Speaking of money, your mother says that Bill wishes he had come down there to help you; he says he needs the money because in the divorce, Fredrica will take him for everything he's worth. I think he's just lucky they didn't have kids for him to support after the divorce, and I figure she deserves whatever amount he has to pay her for how he acted. Your mother doesn't see it that way, though. He's her baby so she thinks he can do no wrong. He says he's going to write to you to see whether he can come down there, but I've never known him to write a letter in his life, so I don't think you have to worry about it.

I'm becoming worried about Jim. I think he's been running around with his friends too much and staying out late. But he'll be twenty-one soon so what can I do about it? He won't listen to me. Maybe if you were here he'd listen. I'm afraid he's going to get himself into trouble with a girl. This fellow from work he hangs out with is a lot older than him, and I'm sure he's teaching Jim some bad habits. His name is Scofield Blackmore, and when I mentioned him to your mother, she told me he doesn't come from a good family. Maybe you should write to Jim just to set him straight.

Ellen on the other hand is doing fine. She helps me with supper and the housework. She's doing a beautiful painting right now. She went for a walk around Presque Isle and made some sketches of the snow and ice along the rocks. She's been working on the painting for several days, and I can already tell it will be the best she's done yet. I told her maybe we could hang it up in the dining room when it's done.

Write back and don't work too hard, but get done as soon as you can so you can come home to me.

Love your wifey, Beth

February 17, 1957
Dear Henry,

Thank you again for your letter. I'm sorry to hear you've caught a cold. You would think that down in that warm climate you wouldn't have to worry, but I imagine with the rain there you weren't too careful. You better stay in bed and rest if you feel bad because you know how easily you catch pneumonia. I worry a lot about you since I can't be there to look after you.

I had a sociable day. Ellen went to the movie with Lucy and Maud, so Eleanor and your mother both came over to knit with me. Then we had supper together when the girls got back. Of course, I did the cooking, but it was nice to have company since I miss you so much. Thelma invited me to come over Wednesday afternoon while Jessie's busy teaching. I think she must get awful lonely most days since she can barely go out of the house now and has so much trouble walking. I wonder how much longer she's going to last. I'm going to tell her when I see her that she ought to get herself someone to come in during the day to do some housework and sit with her since she shouldn't be alone while Jessie is gone to school. I doubt though that my telling her so will do any good. You know how stubborn and strong-willed Thelma's always been.

I saw Bill the other day and told him you didn't need any more help in Florida, but now I'm afraid he'll be mad at me. I don't know how I got caught in the middle of this. I think Bill's whole problem is that his ego is hurt since Fredrica left him, although your mother says he's already going out with another girl. I didn't ask him how he was when I saw him, because frankly, I don't care what he does after how he treated Fredrica.

Well, it's past my bedtime now, but I wanted to write to you because I missed you so much today. You would think that since your family was here, I would have been fine, but I only seem to miss you even more when other people are around. Sleep well my love and know that I'll be dreaming of you tonight.

Love your wifey, Beth

P.S. Jim is still hanging out with that Blackmore boy. They went out together to the bars the other night. He must be ten years older than Jim. I think it's odd that they're friends when they're so far apart in age. Please write to Jim.

February 28, 1957
Dear Henry,

Thank you for the photograph you sent of the house you're building with you and Roy in front of it. It looks like a monstrous home. It must be nice to be so rich to be able to afford such a place. I showed the picture to your mother who was very impressed with it.

We had a snowstorm this week. There's about three feet of snow in the yard now. Jim has been pretty good about cleaning out the driveway. His hours were cut back at the store for next month so he has plenty of time to help around the house. I'm glad his hours were cut back because he won't see that Scofield Blackmore as much. That boy came over the other night to pick Jim up to go to a movie. He was polite, but I just don't like him. I'm not sure why. There's just something about him that bothers me. I know Jim likes working at the Red Owl, but I think he could find a better job. I hope when you get home, that he can help you with some carpentry jobs so he can quit working there.

I ran into your cousin Harry downtown yesterday. His first grandchild was just born. A healthy little girl named Jennifer Cumming. Harry seems to be doing fine. He said he was sorry though that your Aunt Sylvia had not lived long enough to see her first great-grandchild. He said to say hello to you.

I can't believe it will be March tomorrow. That means it's about halfway until you'll be back home. It seems longer than that already, but now that it's getting closer I can start counting the days. I hope we never have to be separated for this long again.

All my love, Beth

P.S. I'm sending you and Roy some chocolate chip cookies. I hope they will still be good when you get them. Ellen wants me to let you know that she helped bake them. Bandit had a few because he jumped up on the table to grab them, but I'll try not to send you any with dog slobber on them. HaHa.

March 6, 1957
Dear Beth,

Thank you for the cookies. They arrived safely. Henry and I both enjoyed them. We're glad people there are thinking of us. We're both homesick, especially Henry. I don't think much of Florida myself. Mr. Pryce is nice enough though. I don't know what a single man like him needs with such a huge house, but Henry and I are doing a fine job on it. Your husband is a heck of a worker and never lets me or any of the other guys have a rest. It's been hot and rainy here. I'd rather have the snow – it doesn't feel as damp and humid. Tell Ma and everyone at home I said hello. Henry's waiting to mail his letter and said I can stick mine in his so I'll say goodbye for now.

Love, Roy

March 7, 1957
Dear Michael,

Henry went over to one of our co-worker's houses for supper, but I didn't feel much like going. I prefer to be by myself in the evenings, and staying with Henry, I don't have much time for that, so I'm enjoying just being alone and only wishing I was back up in my cabin in Michigan. We should be done here in Florida in another month though.

I know you think it's good that I'm having a change of scenery being down here, but it's all the same to me. I had plenty of changes of scenery when I was younger, and I don't know that they were much benefit to me. I used to have big dreams when I was young, but since I lost Chloe and went to the war, I don't see the point in hoping for change anymore. Most of the time, it only leads to disappointment. I never had anything I wanted in life, and whenever I came close, I found it wasn't what I wanted. I went to college only to find my classmates cared more about grades and getting jobs than learning anything. Even though they wanted to become teachers, it was money and security they sought over knowledge. I went out West to find adventure, only to find my country in a depression, and then homesickness drove me back to Upper Michigan. I found a woman to love, only to be unable to have her. I tried to find peace within, only to find war in the world which led me to the worst horrors man has ever known. Now I'm often lonely, but when I'm with other people, I find myself longing to be alone again. I've forgotten how to act normal around people, if I ever knew at all.

I think the other workers here don't like me. It's hard for me to be friendly when I'm not use to these Southerners' ways, and it doesn't help that I get angry when I see the couple blacks we hired being treated ignorantly by some of the white men. But mostly, I'm just used to the few people I know at the Club and in my family; perhaps I limit myself, but I don't feel any need for other friends. It's hard for me when I'm one of the oldest men working here. Most of the other guys are young and single or newly married; they constantly joke about their women and brag about how someday they'll make big money and have giant houses like the one we're building. Mr. Pryce is a fine fellow, but I sure don't know what a single man needs with six bedrooms, four bathrooms, a sauna, and a pool room. I guess I'm just an oddball who sees life differently from others.

I don't even like Florida that much. It just keeps getting hotter now that spring is coming. Maybe all that's wrong with me is I'm homesick for my cabin in Michigan. There I can hide out and just not worry about the troubles of the world, pretend that I'm above them, I guess. Maybe being a hermit makes me just a coward. I don't know how the hermits in the Middle Ages did it, but they had a God they believed in that they could pray to all day. That is no solution to me. I only have books to read, yet even Emerson and Carlyle don't always sustain me. Your letters help, however, so write back soon.

Yours, Roy

March 20, 1957

Dear Honey,

I hope you like the beautiful slip I'm sending you. You aren't allowed to wear it until I get home to see you in it. It sure is made of beautiful cloth, isn't it? I hope you like the apron and the dress too. I thought you'd like the flowers on the dress. I want you to have beautiful things to show your friends because I couldn't think of a better way to keep you happy and show you how much I love you. But you can't show anyone but me the slip. HAHA.

Well darling, there's only 4 more weeks before I'll be coming home. I've saved up quite a bit of money. After I get home and we get things paid off, I want us to take a nice vacation for just the two of us, and boy, are we sure going to enjoy ourselves. I thought maybe we could go to Escanaba for two days and stay overnight. Then we could take it easy shopping and not hurry. We can buy you a new summer coat while we're there. You know you need one. You and I have never really been out by ourselves like that on a trip, and it would be a good rest for you away from home, no dishes or cooking for two days, wouldn't it, darling? Tell me in your next letter whether you want to. Then you can look forward to it and you won't miss me so much.

Love you, Henry

March 22, 1957

Dear Roy,

You sounded very down in your last letter. I understand what you're saying about feeling awkward and lonely around other people because I'm shy like you. Here I teach the other students everyday, but there are days when I feel isolated and distanced from them. Teaching is a rewarding profession, but it can also be a very lonely one. You devote all your efforts to the progress of your students, and for many teachers, that must be frustrating in itself when they have lazy students who do not even care to learn. I have wonderful students, clever and strong in their faith in God. But after a year or two, they move on and I never see them again. The other instructors are my only real long-term companions, and they are all good, kind men. But I have yet to find one I would choose as my bosom friend. We are simply placed together because of our devotion to God.

But my point, Roy, is that even in this loneliness, I find solace in knowing I am doing the Lord's work by teaching priests who will one day bring comfort and solace to thousands of people and bring many to know God. Perhaps some will even be role models who encourage other young men to enter the priesthood. Teaching is full of rewards, only the biggest rewards are unseen and beyond our knowledge.

But beyond all this, Roy, there is a greater friend who loves and wants to console us. I know you have read the Bible, but have you read the gospels closely? Read them again for my sake. Think upon Christ's words and let your heart be open to them. He will guide you in bringing meaning to your life. He will console you even in your darkest hour. Forgive me if my attempts to convert you are an annoyance, but you know that this is my life work, and I know you respect me for it.

May the peace of Christ come to you, Michael

March 25, 1957
Dear Henry,

Thank you for the beautiful slip. I think I want to wear it right away though, so if you don't get home soon, I'll be showing it off to the mailman. HaHa. Ellen loved the earrings you sent her and Jim liked the pocketknife, though I was reluctant to give it to him. I don't know about that boy. I hate to worry you down there but I'm at a loss myself.

Last Saturday he came home so drunk he was sick. He could barely even walk and he made such a racket coming in at two in the morning that he woke up both me and Ellen, but I told Ellen to stay in her room because I didn't want her to see her brother like that. That Blackmore boy was with him, but he wasn't half as drunk as Jim and was good enough to drive Jim home and make sure he got in the house okay. He even walked Jim to his room and took off his shoes and helped him get into bed. I think Scofield is a good young man after all. He seems a loyal friend to Jim, and I think if everyone in town wasn't so down on him, he'd have a chance to do more with his life than just stocking shelves at the Red Owl.

Anyway, I was so upset not having you here to talk to that I told your mother about Jim when I was over there on Sunday afternoon. Bill was over there too with his newest girlfriend, Anita – I don't think she's Mexican at all. She's a blonde. Anyway, your mother told me again not to let Jim stay around Scofield, and she said she didn't care how nice Scofield was, he wouldn't be anything but trouble and she would write and warn you herself. Bill just laughed though and said when he was Jim's age, he got drunk all the time and that was just part of being young. Still, you and I never drank like that. Yes, we grew up during prohibition, but even so, I know we never would have gotten so drunk we'd have been sick. But Bill said when he was in the army, he and all his friends would always get sick from drinking. I told him it's a wonder we won the war if the soldiers were all like him. Anyway, Henry, I don't know what to do anymore. I'm thankful at least Ellen behaves herself for me. With her, all I have to worry about is her getting paint on my tablecloths.

The snow will be starting to melt soon, honey. It's hard to believe I've spent half the winter away from you. I've missed you, but only mainly because Jim doesn't shovel out the driveway as well as you. HaHa.

You know I love and miss you. Beth

March 25, 1957
Dear Henry,

I'm sorry I haven't written to you as often as a mother should. It seems like the older I get the more I have to do. I've been meaning to write to you and Roy for weeks, but only when Beth was so upset a few days again did I really feel the need.

I don't know what is becoming of the young people today. We never got drunk or danced like animals in my day. You wouldn't believe the book that I caught Lucy reading the other day when I was at Eleanor's house. *Peyton Place* it was called. I picked it up and read a couple pages, and you wouldn't believe how filthy it was. Why, I told Eleanor right then that I wouldn't have my granddaughter reading such trash. I tore that book in half and threw it in the fireplace and told Eleanor that she ought to be more watchful since she's Lucy's mother. Lucy wasn't home or I would have given her a good piece of my mind. But Eleanor says Lucy is an adult now, and she can read what she likes. I can't believe any self-respecting person would read such a book, and to think it was written by a woman too. The hussy should be ashamed of herself.

But that's not why I'm writing. Beth says Jim has been hanging out with that Blackmore boy. You probably don't remember Mr. Blackmore who was vice president at the bank downtown. I have kept this quiet all these years, but I'm going to tell you now so that the Blackmore family can do no more damage to the people I love.

Scofield Blackmore is the bastard child of the banker, Lysander Blackmore. Scofield's mother was Hattie Scofield. I never knew her, but I heard plenty of rumors around town about her. She must not have any shame since she gave her child its father's name when she not only wasn't married to his father, but his father was already married. In fact, a couple years after Scofield was born, Lysander Blackmore committed suicide. It was right after the stock market crashed in 1929. I don't think he killed himself because he lost money but because he was ashamed of his philandering ways.

Now I mentioned that the Blackmores hurt our family once before. Your sister Eleanor knows this, because your Aunt Harriet is such a gossip, but I told Eleanor never to mention it to anyone else. Your cousin, Theodore, is a bastard as well. He is not the son of Senator Rodman. In fact, your Aunt Sarah used to work as a maid for the Blackmores, and Lysander Blackmore took advantage of her, then refused to marry her, so your Aunt Sarah had to go to my aunt and uncle in Chicago where she had the baby. She was lucky enough to marry Senator Rodman soon after to make herself respectable, but you know how odd your cousin Theo turned out to be. It's because of that Blackmore blood in him. You will understand now why I think you should dissuade Jim from chumming around with Scofield Blackmore. We certainly don't need any family skeletons to be brought out of the closet, or worse, more created.

Well, I and all your family here miss you. Please don't show this letter to anyone. Tell Roy I send my love and I'll write to him soon. Give my love to Ada also when you stop to see her on your way home.

Love, Ma

April 1, 1957
Dear Honey,

Only two more weeks. Then we'll stop by Ada's to visit for a couple days before heading home. I hope the time goes by quickly. I sure am awful lonesome without you. You and me were ever pals weren't we, wifey dear? I know you must miss me holding your hand in the evenings. I sure do miss you. We have never been apart a night until now since we were married except that time of the big fire in '38 remember, and I hope we never have to be apart again. I know that I will never do this again. There isn't any amount of money that is worth being away from you for a day.

I'm sorry Jim is being so much trouble to you. He sure should have more respect for his mother than coming home in the middle of the night drunk like that. I thought we raised him better so that he would pick decent friends. You tell him I said that when I get home, if he wants to keep hanging around that Scofield, then he'll have to get his own place because his parents and his sister need their sleep and we're not running a private hotel for him. Ma wrote to me too, and I think she's right that he shouldn't hang out with Scofield. I'm sorry if the boy is nice as you say, but he doesn't come from a very ·good family. I'll tell you all about it when I'm home. I'm sorry, honey, that you have to deal with this without me there.

I'm counting the days until I'll be with you again.

Love, Henry

🍁   🍁   🍁

April 6, 1957
Dear Henry,

I imagine this will be the last letter I will send to you since you'll be leaving there a few days after you get this one. The kids and I are counting the days until you're home again. Be sure to call me when you get to Ada's house so I know you and Roy made it there safely. How is Roy? I bet he's anxious to get back home since spring is coming and he can be back up at the Club.

Jim seems determined to keep hanging out with that Scofield, but I don't know that there's any harm in it. Your mother keeps insisting the boy comes from a bad family, but I think he's polite, and he can't be blamed for his family. Jim even said that Scofield gave him a lecture about drinking and how he should appreciate and listen to his parents. I guess both of Scofield's parents died many years ago so he's basically had to make it on his own, and I think he's done okay for himself considering.

I wish you weren't going to Louisiana to see Ada, not that I begrudge you visiting your sister, but just that I wish you were coming home all the sooner. I'm counting the days.

Love, Beth

🍁   🍁   🍁

April 8, 1957
Dear Michael,

You can send your letters to Big Bay again. Henry and I will be leaving here in a couple days. We're going to Louisiana to visit my sister, Ada, and her family, and then we'll be driving back to the U.P.

I appreciate as always your efforts to bring me spiritual comfort. I know you speak from your heart out of great concern for my soul – if I have one – and my well-being. Christianity is a beautiful religion, and I'm glad you find comfort in it, but I cannot believe in it, though I have tried.

I recently read an article by a priest who was explaining the difference between creationism and evolution and why they did not have to be in conflict. He said that evolution explained "how" things came to be, while religion did not scientifically intend to explain how but simply "why" we existed. That at first sounded like a reasonable statement of difference, but the more I thought about it, the more I have to reject it.

Christianity is intent upon convincing us that Jesus is the Son of God and that God loves us and that he governs the world, taking care of each of us, but none of that answers the real question of "WHY?" It is fine to say that if we believe in God, we will be freed from sin, from evil, but why must we be saved from evil? To be preserved from burning in the fires of hell? Why must we burn in hell, or for that matter go to heaven? Why does any of this exist, life, earth, heaven, hell? The Bible tells us that in the beginning, God created the heavens and the earth – whether he did it over billions of years by evolution, or in six days as the Bible proposes, in neither case are we told <u>WHY</u> God created anything. In fact, not only Christianity, but from what I have read, all the other religions fail to explain it. I am not satisfied to be told that man is not meant to know. How can any of us live in this world and know what to do if we do not know the purpose behind it? How can any reasonable person be expected to believe any of these religions? How can Christianity have any truth when it gives no answer to these questions? It only creates a great myth of right and wrong, of heaven and hell and the fear of sin and the importance of love, as if there is a great spiritual war raging, with obstacles to surmount and triumphs to win, but in this messy battle, the purpose has been forgotten. The Bible and religion tries to steer clear of this dilemma by telling us we cannot understand or know anything, we simply need to have faith. That is simply, in my opinion, a mind trick played by a priestly class to keep the rest of us subservient by making us fear sin.

I am sorry, Michael, to attack your faith, but if your religion is true, my attacks will have no effect on it. I hope you understand I desperately want to know the answers to these things. I do not despise religion – it is a noble effort to give meaning to life – but it is an effort I feel has failed. If your God exists, I think he will forgive me for struggling to try to believe in him and make some sense of it all. It is not I, the student here, who is at fault, but rather God, the teacher, who has no objective to his lesson plans.

But we have been good friends for years now, and even different belief systems will not ruin our friendship.

As always, Roy

April 14, 1957
Dear Beth,

You sure are stingy with your man – I planned on keeping him a few days – or more – but I see you have to have him after only two. Don't blame you – he's too good a man to let run loose.

We sure are glad to have him and Roy here to visit. I wanted to shop for Ellen and Jimmy while Roy and Henry are here, but they'll be leaving before I get to town. But tell the kids I'll send them a package soon. Tell Ellen to send me some photographs of what she's been painting as I'd love to see it.

My kids are in high heaven with their uncles here. Poor things – they have no real relatives here so it's a rare treat for them. They always look forward to when we come up north. It'll only be a few months now before we see you all anyway. You know nothing could keep me away from home for long.

We are all fine. Louis is almost done building our boat so we'll be taking it out into the gulf soon. I wish we could just sail all day long. Sometimes I look out at the ocean and try to pretend it's Lake Superior, but it's no good. Louisiana is beautiful. The magnolia trees are all in bloom right now as are our wondrous Spanish moss trees. Every place is special for something. But I still think blueberry season in Michigan is the best of times.

Love to all of you back home and write soon.

Love Ada and All

Ellen spent Saturday afternoon with her grandmother. They usually went to the movies together on Saturday, but this week Margaret had a bad cold so Ellen had brought over her knitting, and they spent the afternoon visiting and listening to the radio. Two pleasant hours they spent together. Margaret was listing in detail how many dresses she owned – she bought beautiful dresses freely now that Will was not around to keep an eye on the pursestrings, and her children were good to her, always insisting on giving her little monetary gifts. While most young people would tire of an old woman's rambling, Ellen enjoyed her grandmother's enthusiasm for life and its small pleasures. But their pleasant afternoon was soon interrupted by Aunt Harriet bellowing a hello as she burst through the door.

"I think we're going to get a spring blizzard," said Harriet, always knowing how to start a conversation on a cheerful note.

"I hope not. I'm sick of snow," said Margaret.

"Ellen, do you think your father will be home today?" Harriet asked as she sat down.

"He called us last night from Detroit so he should be home this evening. Mother is going to hold supper for a couple hours, hoping he'll make it home in time."

"I hope they're home tonight," said Margaret. "I made up the bed so Roy can spend the night here since I haven't seen him in so long. I'm not going to let him go hide in that cabin of his until I get to visit with him for a couple days."

"Well, I hope they get across the Straits before the snow hits," said Harriet. "Ellen, how can you knit in that dim light?"

"I can see all right," said Ellen.

"You'll go blind," Harriet said, getting up to flip the light switch.

"Ellen's young. Her eyes are still good, unlike ours, Harriet," Margaret replied.

"If she sits in the dark like that, she'll have weak eyes and it'll ruin her looks. She doesn't want to be wearing glasses before she finds herself a husband."

Ellen did not reply.

"The way you knit so fast, Ellen," Harriet said, "you'll have to have lots of children to wear all the sweaters and scarves you make."

"I'm not going to have children," said Ellen, keeping her eyes on her clicking needles.

"Oh, you'll have children. Lots of them, I'm sure. All women wants lots of kids. I know I wish I had more, at least as many as your grandmother. But the Lord decided to bless me only with my Joseph."

"I don't want any children," Ellen repeated.

"Well, what if your husband wants them?"

"I don't want a husband either," said Ellen.

"Not have a husband? What are you going to do then?"

"I'm going to be an artist," Ellen said.

Harriet laughed. She had not heard anything so ridiculous since those crazy politicians thought a bridge could be built across the Mackinac Straits, which still wasn't done.

"Artists end up starving in garrets," she said.

"Maybe," said Ellen, "but at least I'll do what I want rather than have a man telling me what to do. I'll be happier on my own."

"No you won't. You'll be awful lonely. Ask your grandmother. She's been lonely since your grandpa died."

"I was at first," said Margaret, "but I'm used to it now. I rather enjoy living on my own, although of course I'd like to have Will back."

"I don't need a man to make me happy," said Ellen. "I'm not going to waste my life doing dishes, changing diapers, and cooking meals."

"Well, young lady," said Harriet, "it seems you have some la-di-da ideas, but you're not a woman yet. I bet you'll willingly give up all your dreams for the first boy you kiss."

"No, I won't," said Ellen, although her thoughts instantly went to Andy Travis. "I'm not going to waste my life. Women don't have to waste their lives anymore."

"Waste your life?" said Harriet, jolted by the thought. "I raised my child, took care of my husband, and kept house. I barely had a free minute to lay around dreaming up grand thoughts like you young people today. When I was your age, we got up early to milk the cows and do the wash. We didn't have no fancy washing machines then either, and we didn't just go to the grocery store to buy a gallon of milk, and we sure didn't have no TV to lay around in front off."

"It's funny," said Ellen, "that if you work so hard, your house is still a mess!"

"Ellen," Margaret frowned.

"You're an impertinent little miss," Harriet said, her face red with anger. She knew her house was a mess, but she did not like it pointed out to her. "When I was a girl, we didn't talk to our elders like that. You bring shame to your grandmother, speaking like that in her house."

Ellen bit her tongue. Only love for her grandmother kept her from lashing back.

Margaret stared at her two guests, unsure what to say. Finally, she stood up and went into the kitchen. Ellen sat silently for a minute, clicking her knitting needles. Harriet stood up and hollered, "Margaret, I'm going home. I'll see you later."

"All right, goodbye," Margaret called back, politely if not warmly.

Ellen continued to click her needles after Aunt Harriet went out the front door. She defiantly knitted as if daring her grandmother to reprimand her. But when Margaret returned into the dining room, she was chuckling.

"I've wanted to tell Harriet her house was a pigsty for years. Well, I imagine she'll be complaining to me tomorrow. I'll probably never hear the end of what a rude granddaughter I have, but it's worth it just to have seen the look on her face. Still Ellen, try to be nice to her next time."

"I won't apologize," said Ellen. "She's always mean. I think she's too narrow-minded even to consider a woman can be anything other than a house-wife."

"There's nothing wrong with being a housewife," said Margaret. "It's a tremendous job with little thanks, but it has its rewarding moments, especially when you have a good husband and children to love."

"I better go, Grandma," said Ellen, uninterested in further domestic pro-paganda. If she knitted, she did it because she liked to, not because she wanted to make sweaters and hats for screaming little babies. "Mom will want me to help her with supper, and I want to be there when Dad gets home."

"All right," said Margaret. "I'm just going to heat up some leftovers for supper and then read until your Uncle Roy shows up."

Ellen stuffed her knitting in her bag, kissed her grandmother's cheek, then walked home. She found her mother in the living room, reading the newspaper.

"I was just going to start supper," said Beth, glancing at the clock and seeing it was a couple minutes after five. "I imagine your father will be home any time now."

"I came home so I could help you," said Ellen.

"Good," said Beth. "I want to fix a nice meal for your father."

They went out to the kitchen and peeled the potatoes. Beth put a roast in the oven. Ellen made jello. By six-thirty, the roast was almost cooked and still no sign of Henry. But Jim finally showed up, after working an hour of overtime. He complained he was starving, so Beth boiled the potatoes. Ellen mixed up the gravy. Jim went to change his clothes and told them to holler when it was time to eat. Beth left the oven on warm so the roast would not get cold while she mashed the potatoes. Ellen set the table.

"I don't know," said Beth. "It's almost seven now. At this rate, your father will probably be so tired he won't want to eat when he gets home. What do you think?"

"Are we ever going to eat?" Jim shouted from his bedroom.

"In just a minute," Beth replied, letting her son make the decision for her. She pulled the roast from the oven. Ellen poured milk for everyone. The food was dished into bowls and set on the table.

"Do you want me to shut the curtains, Mom?" Ellen asked.

"Oh, I suppose," said Beth. "I thought they'd at least be home before it started to get dark."

"It's not dark yet, only just enough to turn on the lights."

Ellen looked out the window as she spoke. At that instant, her father's truck pulled into the driveway.

"Mom, they're here!" she shouted.

Beth scurried to the kitchen window, but she was too slow. She did not see what her daughter did – that the truck had barely stopped turning its wheels when Henry swung open his door, jumped to the ground and raced inside the house. Ellen was startled, first thinking something was wrong. She saw Uncle Roy still sitting in the cab and thought maybe he was sick or hurt. She heard the back door of the house open and her father run up the steps from the laundry room into the kitchen. She turned toward the door in time to see him fling his arms around her mother and squeeze her tightly. Ellen thought she would have been startled if anyone grabbed her like that, but Beth simply joined in the embrace wholeheartedly. They hugged each other for a long time. Jim stepped into the kitchen from the hall. Ellen looked at Jim, and they both smiled huge goofy grins to see their parents so happy. Finally, the lovers let go of each other; Beth started crying, and Henry told her she was a silly old woman as he handed her his handkerchief.

"Don't you ever go away like that again," she laughed through tears of relief.

"I won't, not ever again," he promised.

Then Henry saw his children over his wife's shoulder. He hugged Ellen; then he and Jim patted each other on the back.

"You're late for supper," said Beth. "We've been waiting forever for you."

"Just let me wash my hands and we can sit down to eat," said Henry, rushing into the bathroom.

"Ellen, help me put the food on the table," said Beth.

Jim was no help. He went to stand in the bathroom door and hear all about Florida while his father washed his hands.

As Ellen carried the mashed potatoes into the dining room, she happened to glance out the window and see Uncle Roy standing awkwardly in the driveway, unsure whether he would be intruding if he came inside.

Then he slowly turned and started walking down the street. Ellen hurried to open the front door, but because they never used it, it took her a minute to get the lock to turn. When she finally yanked the door open, she stepped onto the porch and shouted, "Uncle Roy!"

He stopped at the edge of the yard and hesitated to turn around.

"Welcome home," she said, walking down the steps and across the lawn. She felt she should hug him or shake his hand, but he was never affectionate that way.

"Thanks," he said.

"Aren't you going to come inside and have supper with us?" she asked.

"No-o, your parents will want to catch up. I don't want to be in the way."

"You wouldn't be," Ellen said. "We want to hear about your time in Florida."

"There isn't much to tell," he said, knowing she would not understand the thoughts and changes he had undergone in the past few months. "We just built a house is all."

Ellen thought he sounded lonely. It would be awkward for him to go inside and see her parents so happy together. "I was over at Grandma's house today," said Ellen. "She's hoping you'll stay with her tonight rather than go straight back to your cabin." Ellen thought Uncle Roy should know his mother missed him – at least that was something.

"I better walk over there before it's dark then," he said. "She's probably worried I'm not home yet."

"All right," said Ellen. "I'm glad you're home safely."

"Thanks. Goodbye," he said, then continued down the street.

Back inside, Ellen found her father at the table, her mother hovering over him to make sure he got the best cuts of the roast while he adored her with his eyes. Ellen loved her parents; she loved that they loved each other; then suddenly, she felt a strange fear that she might end up like Uncle Roy. While everyone else had married, Uncle Roy had been the oddball. Ellen had a premonition of a potentially long and lonely future ahead of her. Yet within an hour of her father's homecoming, she had locked herself in her room to work on her painting.

🍁 🍁 🍁

April 20, 1957
Dear Michael,
    I just wanted to let you know I'm back at my cabin and that Henry and I had a safe trip home. We stopped off in Louisiana to see my sister, Ada, and her family. They are all fine. I was sorry to leave them. I see them so seldom. Seeing how much they wanted me to stay

longer only made me long all the more for the U.P. and all my family. No, I don't think I'll be traveling again. Eventually, you get too old to care about seeing grand things.

But Henry and I did make a side trip on the way home. It is shorter to drive up through Wisconsin, but we decided to drive through Lower Michigan and take the ferry over the Mackinac Straits just so we could see the bridge being built. It is a sight! Two giant towering white beams hold up the bridge through which the cars drive. It looks as if you are passing through a great gate to enter the North. I tell you I never saw anything like it before. They say it is the largest suspension bridge in the world, and I can well believe it, for it is five miles long spreading over the Straits. It is a great example of man's ingenuity and how humanity is forging its way in this world, showing itself capable of doing magnificent things rather than allowing the natural world to rule us.

Henry is less enthusiastic about the bridge. He admits it's an engineering marvel, but he's afraid it's going to bring a flood of tourists from Lower Michigan into our beautiful Upper Peninsula. I imagine a few will come, but if we are lucky, they will continue their gross exaggeration of our land as a frozen tundra, and stay downstate. We want to preserve our natural resources from those big city folks as long as possible.

Well, I have tons of work to do to get my cabin back in shape. The frost got in and I badly need to do some repairs. At least the weather is getting warmer and the snow is almost gone in the woods. I need to adjust to being back here and spending so much time alone after having Henry constantly around. I'm kind of lonely actually, but I'll get used to it in a day or two. My repairs will keep me busy. I look forward to hearing from you soon.

Your pal, Roy

1958

"Jim, hurry up!" called Beth. "Ellen's waiting and Lucy and Maud must be wondering whether you forgot to pick them up."

"I don't know why they can't just walk. It's not that far for them," Jim said while Ellen stood, impatient and frowning at her brother as he put on his shoes.

"It's snowing too hard for them to walk," Beth replied, "and your Aunt Eleanor is under the impression that you're a polite young man."

"Come on, Ellen," said Jim.

It was a Saturday in January; the snow was coming down slowly but steadily so that three or four additional inches would be added to the already high snowbanks before the day's end. Jim was to drive his sister and cousins to the Palestra that afternoon to go ice skating. Thankfully, Aunt Eleanor had agreed to pick up the girls and bring them home; Jim was meeting Bernie O'Neill and Scofield Blackmore for supper to discuss some big plans they were hatching.

"Thanks for picking us up," said Maud when she got in the car.

"I'd have driven us," said Lucy, "but you know what a worrywart my mother is."

"No," Maud corrected her sister. "Mother knows how you drive; she thinks you'll kill us on these slippery roads."

Lucy felt insulted but did not reply.

Ellen tried to make peace by complimenting Lucy's pant suit.

"It looks really comfortable to go skating in," she said.

Jim ignored the girls. Once at the Palestra, they had barely stepped inside before he deserted them to find his friends.

"Palestra" is Greek for "a place of recreation for young people". The building had already served as the favorite gathering place to generations of Marquette's youth. Although first built in 1904 in the town of Laurium, in 1921, the Palestra had been moved to Marquette. Since then, it had hosted countless hockey games, ice skating competitions, and dances in its upstairs ballroom. Originally, the Palestra had had a floor of real ice that needed to be scraped, but in 1950, an artificial floor had been laid, making the skating better and the Palestra all the more popular. On this snowy Saturday, a couple hundred people were skating, from senior citizens to children, but teenagers and college students made up the overwhelming majority.

The girls sat down to put on their skates, relieved to be free from Jim's company. Girls tend to fuss, and these girls were no exception. They were cold-blooded Northern girls, but they still complained about the chill as they laced up their skates. They took a few minutes to check out the outfits of the other hundred girls at the Palestra. They ogled the hockey players, the heroes of every Northern girl. Their mothers would not allow them to wear lipstick, so they need not ask each other about their makeup. Finally, they went out onto the ice, slowly gliding along the edge, clinging to each other's company. They stole glances at the boys' figures – although little figure could be seen when everyone wore winter clothes – while they hoped and feared the boys were looking at their figures.

They were busy discussing whom they liked better, Elvis Presley or Fabian, when they caught sight of Carol Ann.

"Oh, look who's here," said Maud.

Lucy and Ellen both glanced toward the door.

"Don't look," said Maud. "She'll think we want her to come skate with us."

"We're the only girls here from her class," said Ellen, "so she probably will."

"Look at her coat," said Lucy. "It's so threadbare."

"Maybe her parents can't afford anything better," said Ellen, fully aware that her own parents squeezed their pennies to give her what they could.

"I don't think her family has anything," said Maud. "Her mother doesn't work and her stepfather spends all his money on liquor."

"How do you know?" asked Ellen.

"Janice told me."

Janice was the class gossip. Ellen would not give two cents for Janice's opinion. Janice had started a rumor that Ellen's father had abandoned his family when he had gone down to Florida last year.

"I think Carol Ann is nice," said Ellen. "It's not her fault if she hasn't been as lucky as us." Ellen felt like adding, "Besides, Lucy and Maud, your father abandoned your mother so who are the two of you to talk," but she loved Aunt Eleanor too well to put down her family.

Carol Ann carefully shuffled across the ice, pretending not to see the girls from her class. For the first minute, she steadied herself along the edge until she gained her balance. Then she made a bold stride forward, and in a few seconds, she was able to coast along the ice like a swan floating with the river current.

"Who's that?" Jim asked when he spotted Carol Ann. He and his friends were standing along the side of the rink.

"I don't know," said Bernie O'Neill, annoyed that Jim had interrupted him when he was saying something important. "So, I sent out applications to the University of California in Los Angeles and California State University."

"When will you hear from them?" asked Scofield.

"Probably by April," said Bernie. "One if not both of them will offer me an assistantship while I earn my Master's degree."

"But we'll be going whether you get accepted or not, right?" said Scofield.

"Oh sure, there's lots of good jobs out there, even if you only have a bachelor's degree."

"What if you don't have a degree?" asked Scofield.

"Well, even if you end up working in a grocery store out there, it won't be worse than here; the weather's better, and the girls sure are better looking."

"And your parents are okay with you going?" asked Scofield.

"I'm twenty-two. I can do whatever I want. They think I should go to Duke University in North Carolina because I have family roots down South, but – "

"I thought your family was from Marquette," said Jim, only half-listening as he watched the attractive girl skate by. Even though she wore a coat, she had it opened enough that he could tell she had giant melon-shaped breasts.

"My mother's from Marquette, but my father lived in South Carolina until he was thirteen."

"Whatever did he move here for?" Scofield asked.

"His mother was born here so during the First World War, he came to stay with his grandma because his mother died and his father was off fighting overseas."

"He's never written a book set in the South," said Scofield; he was a great reader and knew Robert O'Neill's novels better than the author's son.

"So?" Bernie frowned with annoyance. "Anyway, I could easily get into Duke. It's an Ivy league school, but my father's reputation would get me in. I'd just rather go to California."

"California is really nice," said Jim, thinking how warm it had been the one winter of his childhood he had spent there. "Scofield, do you think you'll have enough money saved to go?"

"Sure," said Scofield. "I'm going out to smoke a cigarette. I'll be back in a minute."

"He won't ever go with us," Bernie told Jim once Scofield was out of their hearing. "He's afraid to do anything. Look at him – thirty-two years old, and he doesn't have any parents or family, yet he stays here. It's not even that he's stupid; just that he's afraid to go off on his own. If I had his freedom, I'd have left years ago."

Jim said nothing. Who was Bernie to talk? He could have left Marquette years ago, but he had let his parents convince him to go to college at Northern. And what did Bernie know about Scofield? Jim knew Scofield had a half-brother and half-sister in Marquette with whom he had never spoken because they were his father's legitimate children while he was a bastard. Someday, Scofield hoped to make contact with them. Jim knew that was the only reason why Scofield would be reluctant to leave Marquette, yet he said he wanted to go to California.

"People who are like Scofield," said Bernie, "ought to leave small towns where their families have bad names so they can make new lives for themselves."

"I wonder who that girl is," said Jim, as Carol Ann passed before them again. His eye had barely left her as she circled the rink.

"There's Donna," said Bernie, going off to greet his girlfriend, whom he was trying to convince to marry him and move with him to California.

Jim barely noticed when Bernie left. Carol Ann now had her back to him; he imagined skating behind her, his hands around her waist, his chest pressed up against her back as they couple-skated.

"Where'd Bernie go?" asked Scofield when he returned.

"Off with his woman," said Jim, stepping back to avoid his friend's cigarette breath. "Scofield, do you know who that girl is?"

"Which one?"

Jim pointed out Carol Ann.

"Wait until she comes around again so I can see her face," said Scofield. "So what time do you work on Monday? I've got to meet with the store manager that morning; you know it's going to be either me or Ralph that gets the promotion."

"I think it'll be you," said Jim, annoyed because they had already had this conversation a dozen times in the past week.

"I hope so," said Scofield. "I've been there six months longer than Ralph, and besides, he's going to college, so it's not as if he's going to stick around when he graduates. I think I would be the logical pick, don't you?"

"Huh, uh, yeah, of course," said Jim.

"Are you listening to me?"

"Here she comes. Can you see her face now? Do you know her?" Jim was surprised by the urgency in his own voice.

"Oh, that's Carol Ann Kopel. Sure, I know her. She's been coming into the Red Owl with her mom since she was a kid. My ma used to be friends with her ma."

"Would you introduce us?" asked Jim.

"You like her, hey?" Scofield grinned, revealing cracked, nicotine stained teeth.

"She's got a really nice figure," Jim said. "She's kind of pretty too."

"All right," said Scofield. "Hey, Carol Ann! Come on over here!"

The girl looked in their direction when her name was called. She seemed hesitant to approach, as if she had hoped no one would notice her, but Jim hoped she would come over if only to be polite because she knew Scofield. He felt himself trembling nervously as she skated closer and he saw what a pretty face she had. She slowed down, giving Jim a second to catch his breath, then stopped along the rink's edge.

"Carol Ann," said Scofield, "this is my friend, Jim Whitman."

"Nice to meet you," said Jim. She nodded in return.

"How's your mom?" asked Scofield.

"Fine," said Carol Ann.

"Tell her I said hello."

"I will," she said, but she was looking at Jim, noticing how cute he was.

The DJ announced there would now be a couple skate. "Love is a Many Splendored Thing" drifted over the ice.

"Um, would you?" Jim asked Carol Ann.

She looked him up and down. He wished his gut did not show quite so much.

"Okay," she said.

He was nervous, but he took her hand. As they stepped onto the ice, he was surprised by how much taller he was than her. She could not be much more than five feet tall. She was a petite thing despite her large breasts. Jim told himself he was not exactly fat, just big boned. He knew he was tall and broad in the shoulders. He wondered whether they looked like a funny couple. She barely came to his shoulder. He liked that she was so little; it made him feel manly to tower above her.

"Are you going to college?" she asked.

"No," said Jim. "I work over at the Red Owl with Scofield."

"Oh," she said.

"Do you go to school?"

"I'm a junior at J.D. Pierce."

"That's where my sister goes. I graduated from there."

"I know Ellen. She's in my class. She's nice."

Jim held back a laugh. His sister was a nag. But he was thankful if her being nice would help make Carol Ann like him.

"I hate school," said Carol Ann. "I can't wait to graduate and get outta this town."

"Really? I want to leave too," said Jim. "I want to move to California."

"California? How come?"

"I lived out there for a while when I was a kid. It's beautiful there. There isn't all this snow. It's always warm, and there's lots better jobs."

"I wouldn't mind going out there," said Carol Ann. "Maybe I could get a job in the movies."

"I bet you could," said Jim. "You're real pretty."

Carol Ann giggled. "No, I wouldn't be no star. But I could work at a studio, maybe as a secretary. I type real good and I checked out a book at the library to teach me shorthand. Lots of the girls at school want to go to Northern so they can be secretaries, but I don't see what for. It ain't that hard to type, and California's growing so fast I bet the businesses will take just about anyone."

"I bet," said Jim. "I know there's lots of construction work out there. My dad's a carpenter and I work with him a lot in the summers. Out there, it's so warm there's got to be construction work all year round, so I bet I could find a job easy. I'd rather work construction than bag people's groceries."

The song ended. They skated back to Scofield.

"Thank you," said Jim, but Carol Ann was not listening. She had just spotted trouble.

"There you are!" said a balding man with a cigar in his mouth, rapidly walking toward them.

Carol Ann froze.

"What the hell do you think you're doing taking off with my hard earned money?" the man asked.

"Stan, I don't have any – "

"Don't lie to me, you little tramp. Your mother gave you a five dollar bill this morning. You think I bust my ass all day so you can go spend my hard earned money on your boyfriends? Give it here."

"Hey, Stan," Scofield said, "why don't you let her be? She said she doesn't have any money."

"Shut up, you," Stan shot back. "She's my stepdaughter, so I'll take care of it."

"I don't have any money," Carol Ann repeated. Jim thought she was going to cry. He hoped she would not give the man any money.

"I s'pose you already blew it on makeup and crap?" said Stan. "I know you got it 'cause I gave money to your mother yesterday, and she ain't been out of the house to spend it, but it's gone now."

"I don't have it," Carol Ann repeated.

Stan clasped her shoulder and started to shake her. Scofield grabbed his arm and tried to yank him lose.

"Hold off," said Scofield. "Carol Ann gave me the money to keep it safe."

He reached into his pocket and pulled out a five dollar bill.

"Scofield, I – " Carol Ann said.

"Take it and get out of here," Scofield told Stan.

Stan looked at him, then took the money. To his stepdaughter, he said, "You get your little behind home before dark, you hear me. I won't have no stepdaughter of mine out walking the streets in the dark. It's bad enough you're out with all these boys now. I know you're a little tramp."

"It's not true," Carol Ann sobbed as Stan strode away.

"Don't cry," Scofield told her. "That kind aren't worth it. He's trash. Not you."

"I don't know why my mother ever married him."

"She didn't have much choice," Scofield said. "Your dad abandoned her, and she had a child to raise so she grabbed the first man she could find with a paycheck."

Carol Ann looked at Jim, embarrassed that he now knew the truth about her family.

"What's wrong?" asked Ellen, skating up to the group. She had heard an angry man's voice, so she wanted to make sure her brother was not in trouble. She hated that he hung out with such wild people.

"Nothing's wrong," said Jim.

"Hi, Carol Ann," said Ellen, staring at her classmate's red eyes. She had not realized until now that Carol Ann had been involved in the scene.

"Thanks for the money, Scofield," said Carol Ann, too ashamed to speak to Ellen.

"You're trembling," said Scofield.

"I'm just cold."

"Do you want me to go find your coat?" Ellen asked.

"No, I'll get it," said Carol Ann. "I'm going to leave now."

Ellen felt sorry for her. She could see Carol Ann was trying not to cry. She hoped the girl could get out of the building before she sobbed and further embarrassed herself.

"I'll give you a ride home," said Scofield, putting his hand on Carol Ann's shoulder and escorting her back to where she had left her coat.

Bernie now skated up to Jim and Ellen. "What was all that about?" he asked.

"Scofield is taking Carol Ann home. She was upset about something," said Ellen, trying to word things tactfully.

"Figures," said Bernie. "Scofield has to look after his own kind of people."

"What's that mean?" Ellen asked.

"You know what it means. Scofield's from the wrong side of the tracks, and so's that little tramp."

Ellen bit her tongue. She did not like Bernie O'Neill, but her parents allowed Jim to hang out with him because they thought his father a gentleman.

"People can't be judged by their families," said Ellen, thinking it true of Bernie as much as Carol Ann or Scofield. "Everyone has to make it in this world on his or her own merit."

"True," said Bernie. "Only Scofield will never make it. Jim, I don't think we should let him come to California with us. He'll just hold us back."

Jim's shoulders bristled. He had not yet told his parents he planned to go to California, but now Bernie had mentioned it in front of his sister. He felt Ellen's eyes staring at him. Then after a few seconds, she skated off to rejoin her cousins.

Ellen hardened her heart. At first, she did not tell her parents about her brother's plan. She did not even mention it to her cousins. When Jim came home that evening, he looked askance at her and she shook her head. He sighed with relief and mouthed a "Thank you" his parents did not see. He would have to tell them eventually, but he was not ready yet. First he wanted to make sure Bernie was accepted at a college, and he wanted to talk to Uncle Bill, who had promised to get in touch with Cousin Theo in California. "Theo," Uncle Bill had said, "knows lots of people out there, so he can probably find you and Scofield a job. If you boys get everything settled, then when you tell your folks, they won't be so worried."

Jim believed he was being thoughtful not to tell his parents until everything was definite; he did not consider how much time they would need to adjust to the idea of their son living clear across the country.

The next weekend a dance was held at the Palestra. Lucy and Maud were going. Jim was going. Ellen could not go.

"I better get ready," said Jim, setting down his knife and getting up from the supper table. He disappeared into the bathroom to fix his hair.

"Mom, why can't I go?" Ellen asked. "Maud is going, and since Jim will be there, he can keep an eye on me."

"I ain't babysitting my sister," Jim shouted before shutting the bathroom door.

"No, Ellen," said Beth. "And I can't believe your aunt is letting Maud go. It's different with Lucy, she's an adult now, but you and Maud are too young."

"Mom, I'll be seventeen in a few months."

"You won't be going to any dances before you're eighteen."

Ellen looked at her father for help, but she knew he would side with her mother.

"Mom, didn't you want to go to dances when you were my age?" asked Ellen. She knew her mother had never gone anywhere when she was young; she had heard how strict Grandma McCarey had been; if her mother remembered how sheltered had been her own childhood, Ellen hoped she might relent rather than treat her daughter the same way.

"No, I didn't want to go to dances, and I steered clear of the wrong boys. I didn't want to put myself in a situation that would upset my parents," Beth replied.

"But Jim's allowed to go!"

"Jim's an adult."

"I'm more mature than him. I'd never come home drunk."

"You better not," said Henry. Then Ellen knew she had better be quiet; she might argue with her mother, but never her father. But she still wanted to go.

"I suppose," she said slowly, wondering whether she dared complete her sentence, "that you also think Jim is mature enough to move to California."

Her mother looked at her in confusion.

"That's what he's planning to do," said Ellen. "He's going off to California with Scofield and Bernie; he isn't even planning to tell you – he'll probably just leave you a note you won't find until he's halfway across the country."

"Henry," said Beth, setting down her glass, "did you know about this?"

"No," he replied. "Are you serious, young lady?"

"Yes," said Ellen, now almost wishing she had said nothing. Jim would be sure to take his wrath out on her.

"Ellen, how do you know?" asked Beth.

It was no good. Ellen saw that since she had started it, she might as well tell everything now. "I heard him talking with his friends at the Palestra last weekend."

"We'll get to the bottom of this," said Henry, getting up from the table and going to the bathroom door.

"Jim, come out here!"

"I'll be done in a minute!" Jim shouted.

"Come out here right now!" Henry said.

"Ellen, why didn't you tell us sooner?" asked Beth.

But before Ellen could answer, Jim came back to the table to be confronted by his overprotective parents and tattletale sister.

"Ellen says you're planning to move to California," said Henry.

Jim looked at his sister. She expected him to glare at her, but instead he only looked frightened.

"So, is it true?" Henry asked.

Until then, Jim had not been sure he would go through with it, but now seemed to be the decisive moment.

"Yes, I'm going with Scofield and Bernie."

"Why haven't you told us?"

"I didn't want to worry you until it was definite."

"Is it definite now?"

"Yes."

"How can you go to California?" asked Beth. "You don't know anyone there."

Jim thought of telling her that Uncle Bill had been in touch with Cousin Theo, but he did not want to get Uncle Bill in trouble for keeping secrets from his parents.

"I'll know Bernie and Scofield," he said.

"What are you all going to do out there?"

"Bernie's been accepted at a college; he's going to get his master's degree, and Scofield and I are going to work."

"You must be crazy," said Ellen. "It's so hot out there. Don't you remember?"

"Ellen, go to your room. This is none of your business," said her father.

She looked at her mother to see whether she could stay, but Beth just stared out the window, too upset to speak. Sighing, Ellen went to her room.

Jim was determined now. It was his life and not even his parents could stop him from doing what he wanted, even if love made them want him near.

"Dad," he said, "you know there isn't anything here for me. There's a whole world outside of Marquette. California is full of good jobs and exciting things happening. They can build out there all year round so I'll never be out of work. I don't want to work in a grocery store all my life, and I don't want to be stuck working in a mine. You know yourself that we'd be better off if we had stayed there. I don't know why you and Mom ever decided to move back."

"We came back here," said Henry, sitting back down in his chair, "because your grandfather died, and that made us realize family was more important than money."

"Fine, Dad. I understand you feel that way, but I don't. I have big dreams. I want to – "

"You can dream big and still stay here," said Beth. "We told you we'd help you go to Northern if you want."

"I don't want to go to college," said Jim. "I want to go out into the world, to see things, to make things happen, to – "

Henry remembered years ago Roy had given him the same speech. What made the young seek to leave home? He had never been that way, but maybe he had never been young. He had always been the older brother, the responsible one who had to help support the family. But he had been content to have it that way. He never would have gone to California at all, if not for his health, and once there, he felt his health suffered more by his separation from his loved ones.

"Lots of people dream big," he told his son, "but not everyone makes it. Just remember that if things don't work out, you can always come home."

"They'll work out," said Jim. "I don't have a defeatist attitude. And it's not as if I'll never come home to visit, and you can always come out to visit me."

"I'm too old to travel over those mountains again," said Beth.

"We won't stop you," Henry told his son, "but I hope you'll think long and hard before you make any final decisions."

"I have thought it out," said Jim, looking at his watch. "I've got to get going, or I'll be late." He kissed Beth on the cheek. "Don't worry, Mom. It'll be okay."

She did not reply. Jim stepped back, feeling awkward, and looked at his father. Henry nodded and said, "It's okay. You can go."

Jim went down the back steps, put his shoes on, then went out the door.

Henry and Beth silently listened to him start his car and back it out of the driveway. Henry was glad his son dreamed big, but he knew from experience that big dreams usually fail, that people disappear into the daily grind of the herd. He was less saddened by his son's leaving than the disappointment he feared Jim would soon face.

"I don't want him to go," Beth broke the silence. "He's hardly more than a boy."

"He'll be twenty-two this year," said Henry, reaching for her hand.

"He'll get too caught up in his life out there and never come home. We may never see him again."

"Don't exaggerate, honey. He'll be fine, and he knows if things don't work out, he can come back home. We came home. And look at Roy. Roy wanted something extraordinary when he was young, but he ended up back here."

"God, I don't want him to turn out like Roy," Beth moaned.

"Why not? What's wrong with not washing your hair and sleeping in a shack full of termites?" laughed Henry, although he only got a half-smile out of his wife. "Anyway, Jim's old enough to make his own decisions; if we try to stop him, he'll only resent us later."

"I know."

Ellen remained in her bedroom all evening. She did not care whether Jim went or stayed. Maybe if he went, her parents would be so afraid of losing her too that they would let her do whatever she wanted. Her parents said they let Jim do things because he was older, but Ellen knew if she were five years older, they would have still fought with her about going to the dance. Boys, no matter how immature they were, could do whatever they wanted. She turned on her radio and listened to the music broadcast from the dance at the Palestra. She wondered which girl tonight was lucky enough to dance with Andy Travis.

1959

Jim had wanted to move in May, but it was August 1958 before he finally left. There had been some delays. Bernie's parents insisted that before he leave for school at the University of California, he take one last summer vacation with them down South. Then Scofield decided he would not go to California at all.

"I just got promoted to produce manager," he said. "I can't give up an opportunity like that. The job is a sure thing. California isn't."

Jim could not believe his friend's reasoning, but Bernie said, "I told you Scofield wouldn't go. He's self-destructive. He'll never make anything of himself."

The last week of August, Jim packed his suitcase, and Bernie picked him up in the new chevy his parents had bought him. That same week, Ellen started her senior year of high school.

Her son gone, her daughter in school, her husband at work, Beth found herself alone each day. She was used to being alone – she was a full-time housewife. But now she found the quiet of the empty house made her constantly nervous and pining for her son. Soon, she could not stand to be alone. Margaret started coming over to spend time with her daughter-in-law. Sometimes Eleanor would stop by in the afternoon. A few times, Beth even accompanied Henry to where he was working for part of the day. On days when Beth bravely insisted she would be fine alone, Ellen came home from school to find her mother in tears.

One January morning, Ellen was going out the door to school when the telephone rang. She was already running late, but since her mother was getting dressed, she unwillingly grabbed the phone while trying to put on her coat.

"Hello?"

"Hi, Ellen. It's Aunt Eleanor. Listen, I won't be able to come over today. It's so cold my car won't start this morning. Tell your mother I'm sorry, and I'll call her this afternoon to check on her."

"All right," said Ellen, scarcely listening as she tried to remember where she had put her bookbag.

"Thanks. Goodbye," said her aunt.

"Goodbye."

"Who was that?" asked Beth, coming into the kitchen.

"Just Aunt Eleanor," said Ellen. She then explained that her mother would have no company that day.

"Oh, I'll be all right," Beth said. "Just make sure you come straight home from school so I don't worry."

"Yes, Mother," said Ellen. Everyday she came home directly from school. She could not even spend an hour downtown anymore.

"I guess I'll be okay," Beth repeated, wishing Ellen would offer to stay home from school for the day, but Ellen's mind was set on her algebra test, so she quickly gathered up her books, kissed her mother on the cheek, and hurried out the back door.

Beth walked over to the window to watch her daughter rush down the street. She strained her eyes until Ellen disappeared from sight. Then she sat down and continued to stare out the window. The horrible terror crawled up her spine; she felt herself opening her mouth, trying to breathe. She was terrified when the despair of loneliness began to grip her. She felt she would panic. How would she make it through the whole day by herself? What if something happened while she were alone, like if she had a heart attack, or she fell down and broke a leg or hip, or she might cut herself in the kitchen and bleed to death? Sometimes, she thought of taking a knife and cutting herself to end the constantly recurring fear.

She wanted to cry. If she forced her tears, it would relieve her anxiety and then she might be okay for several hours. She sat shaking, fearful. She hated herself. How had she gotten like this? Even if she made herself cry, she would cry so hard her nose would run and her throat would hurt, and then she would be so weak and exhausted she would not feel like doing any of her housework all day. Maybe Henry would stop by at lunchtime, but if he did, she did not want him to find her eyes red; then he would feel he could not go back to work because he had to stay with her, and they could not afford for him not to work. She was nothing but a burden on her family. No one needed her. Jim was gone, and Ellen was grown now. Henry had his work to keep him occupied – she doubted he would even miss her if she were gone – oh, he said he loved her, but how could he when she was such a mess? He would probably be thankful she was gone; but then, he was so good to her that – how could she feel that way? If

Jim had not moved away – she had never felt this way until then. She missed Jim so much. If he had stayed, she might still be normal; she knew these fears had always lurked inside of her, a silent terror she had barely kept at bay until now – she had felt it first as a little girl when her brothers went away to the First World War, and again when she had been afraid Henry would never marry her, and she would be trapped by living with her parents forever – but each of those times, her fears had never materialized – at least one of her brothers had come home from the war, and Henry had married her – but Jim being gone – she could not change that.

She pulled herself out of the chair. She had to do the dishes. She saw the coffee pot still sitting on the stove. She usually finished the coffee; after Henry left for work and Ellen for school, she would sit and have a cup of coffee to relax her before starting on her housework. But the coffee must be cold by now – it was nearly ten o'clock. She had sat for over an hour feeling sorry for herself. She would make fresh coffee; then she would feel better. She took the coffee pot off the stove and went to dump the grounds down the toilet. Then she brewed a fresh pot. While she waited for it to perk, she sat down, feeling too depressed to do anything more.

When the coffee was finished, she poured herself a cup, then opened the refrigerator to find the cream. There was none. There was no milk either. She could not stand drinking her coffee black. She had forgotten yesterday to tell Henry to pick up milk and cream. It was her own fault. Where was her mind these days? Damn it, what was wrong with her?

In anger, she poured the newly brewed coffee down the drain. Then she regretted it, thinking of the waste. She gripped the edge of the counter, and breathed through her nose, trying to stay calm. She tried to count, to take her mind off her desperate loneliness.

The phone rang.

"Oh, now who wants me?" she muttered, but she was thankful. She so badly wanted to speak to someone, even if it were just a salesman or a wrong number.

It was Thelma.

"Beth, Jessie took the day off from school so we can go see the movie crew filming *Anatomy of a Murder*. Do you want to come with us? We don't want to miss all the excitement, and I thought you might like to get out of the house."

"Oh," said Beth. She wanted to get out of the house, but she was shy. She did not like big crowds. Hundreds of people would be there trying to get a glimpse of the movie stars who had come to town to film the murder story.

"We might see Jimmy Stewart," Thelma cajoled.

"I don't know," said Beth. "I should clean up the house."

"You can do that any day. Come on. Jessie and I'll pick you up in half an hour."

"Okay," said Beth. "I'll be ready by then."

She was surprised by her reply. She hung up the phone, then remembered the coffee she had poured down the sink. She went to dump the grounds down the toilet so no one would suspect she had been so wasteful. She quickly washed up the breakfast dishes, then hurried into the bedroom to put on her best dress. After all, she might meet a movie star today. If Thelma had her way, they would definitely meet one. She knew Thelma and Jessie had gone to Ishpeming the morning the train had brought the movie stars to Upper Michigan. She had thought them nuts because it had only been a few degrees above zero that day. But apparently one movie star sighting was not enough for Thelma. Oh well, she might as well go. It might be fun, and she was thankful not to have to spend the day alone. Once she had her shoes and coat on, she sat by the front window for several agonizing minutes, watching each car pass by and telling herself the next one would be Thelma and Jessie. They turned out to be ten minutes late, which only made Beth worry something had happened to them, or worse, they had forgotten her and she would still have to spend the day alone. She felt exuberant when their car turned the corner and pulled into the driveway. Beth was out the front door and had it locked before Jessie could put the car in park.

"Can you believe there are actually movie stars here in Marquette?" Thelma said as Beth climbed into the car.

"Well, we've had other famous people come to town," Beth said. "Remember when John Philip Sousa came, and Abbott and Costello during the war."

"Do you remember when President Roosevelt came?" asked Thelma.

"F.D.R. never came here," said Jessie. "I'm sure I would remember if he did."

"No, Theodore Roosevelt," said Thelma. "I must have been about ten so I guess, Beth, you'd have been too young to remember. I remember because my father and I specifically made the trip down here and stayed with your parents so we could attend Roosevelt's trial at the county courthouse."

Jessie, less interested in presidents than movie stars, said, "I hope we see Ben Gazzara. I didn't get a good look at him when he came in on the train."

"I would just like to see James Stewart," said Beth.

"Me too," said Thelma, "although I do wish Bill Holden or Gary Cooper were in the movie, or Gene Kelly. I do think Gene Kelly the sexiest man alive."

"Mother!" said Jessie.

"Although that Montgomery Clift," said Thelma, "he's a good looker too. If he were a little older, I'd marry him in a second."

"I don't think you'd have a chance," laughed Beth.

"Any woman would leave her husband for a man as gorgeous as him."

"I wouldn't!" said Beth.

"Even if he weren't gorgeous, I might marry him, just to live in California and rub elbows with all those movie stars and producers."

"When I lived in California," said Beth, "I never met a single movie star."

"You and Henry sure missed your chances then. Didn't you ever once want to do something exciting, Beth?"

"No, I guess not." But secretly Beth thought she would move to California if it meant she could be near Jim, to look after him and make sure he was safe.

As the three women drove down Third Street's hill and through the downtown, they spotted people bustling about in front of the Marquette County Courthouse where the trial scenes were to be filmed. Beth remembered a few years before when the real murder trial had caused a similar fuss. She wondered how Mike Chenoweth's family and even Lieutenant Peterson were feeling about all this attention. She was not sure the past should be dug up or a movie made to profit from a tragedy.

Jessie parked the car on Baraga Avenue, across the street from the county jail. She was lucky to find an empty spot. There were vehicles for camera crews, vehicles for movie stars, the cars of several locals hired as extras for the movie, and curiosity seekers maundering all over the courthouse grounds in hopes they might see a celebrity.

Jessie got out and opened the car trunk to get her mother's wheelchair. Beth held the wheelchair while Jessie helped her mother into it. Then they pushed Thelma across the street to the courthouse grounds. When they came to the side door, Thelma stood and pulled herself up the steps by using the railing and Beth's arm. Jessie carried the wheelchair up. Beth could tell Thelma was exhausted when they reached the top. "I better see someone famous after having to climb those stairs," she gasped. They got her through the door and then back into the wheelchair.

"Go down to the county clerk's office," said Thelma. "My friend who works there promised to get us a seat in the courtroom where they're doing the filming."

Beth was half-convinced they would be tossed out by the police. But she forgot her fears by remembering how, twenty-five years earlier, she and Henry had been married here. She had been so happy that day compared to now. She wondered whether she would ever again be happy as she had been when young. She wondered how Thelma remained so cheerful when she had no real family other than Beth – Jessie was not even her real daughter. Thelma's hands had become so brittle she could not even indulge her passion for playing the piano, yet she could find interest in life by going to see movie stars.

Thelma's friend came out of the office and quietly led them down the hall to the courtroom. Beth tried to tiptoe so they would not disturb the filming even though Thelma's wheelchair screeched. When they reached the court-room door, the guard simply lifted his hat pleasantly and said, "You have good timing. Mr. Preminger just yelled 'CUT!'." They stepped inside and quietly made their way to an empty back row, Thelma wedging her wheelchair up against the edge of the aisle.

"Okay, Miz Remick. Ve'll start with your last line," said a large man with a German accent. Beth recognized Otto Preminger from his picture in the newspaper.

"That's Lee Remick," whispered Thelma, pointing to the girl on the wit-ness stand. "She's the one who gets raped in the movie."

"Oh," Beth nodded, uncomfortable at the mention of such a crime.

Lee Remick began to speak her lines. Then the crowd was jolted by Jimmy Stewart's entrance. Beth knew he was playing the role John Voelker had held in the original court case. She was too stunned to listen to the speeches until 'panties' were mentioned. Then she was glad Ellen had not come – she was too young to hear about such things.

"What do you think?" asked Thelma when the cameras quit rolling to do a third retake of the scene.

"It's very interesting," said Beth.

"Do you think she's as pretty as Lana Turner?" Jessie asked, referring to Lee Remick.

"I think she's prettier," said Thelma. "Lana Turner's too old for the part. Although I can't blame her for quitting because of the wardrobe. No decent woman would wear tight jeans like Lee Remick is going to wear."

"Roll 'em!" Mr. Preminger shouted. Beth was more intent on watching the cameramen than the actors. She thought their jobs must be more difficult. She had never realized how much work there was to making a movie. She had heard the courthouse had even been painted and new lamps bought for this room so it would look proper on black and white film. And if the snow did not melt in time to film the outdoor scenes, it would have to be washed away with hoses. This picture must be costing thousands of dollars a day to make.

"Take fifteen everyone," said Mr. Preminger. "Miz Remick needs her makeup fixed."

Lee Remick stepped down from the witness stand while Jimmy Stewart stepped up to speak to her. Otto Preminger came down the aisle toward the door, but he paused when he saw Beth sitting beside Thelma.

"Ladies," he said, nodding his head, "do you have parts as extras?"

"No," said Thelma, to Beth's alarm. They would be thrown out now for certain. "We just came to gawk at all the talent."

Preminger smiled. "My dear," he said, looking straight at Beth, "you are vonderfully plump. I think you would make a perfect extra. Vould you like to be in my movie?"

Beth was startled. She had always been self-conscious about her weight, especially now that she had gained an extra twenty pounds since Jim moved away.

"No thank you," she said.

"Ah, you are a beautiful voman. It is too bad. I know a scene that vould be perfect for you."

"No, I couldn't, really," said Beth.

"All right, vell enjoy yourselves, ladies," he smiled before passing out the door.

"Beth, what a compliment, to be called beautiful by Otto Preminger."

"Well, he did say she was fat, Mother," said Jessie.

"Yes, but he thought my being plump added to my beauty," Beth smiled. She was deeply pleased. The only other man who had ever said she was beautiful was Henry, oh, and Jimmy when he was a little boy and she the center of his world. Why did he have to grow up?

"Ben Gazzara's in the next scene they're shooting," said Jessie, who had just overheard this from the people seated in front of her. "He's the one I'm waiting to see."

"I wouldn't mind seeing Eve Arden," said Beth.

"She won't be in this scene," said Thelma with as much authority as if she had personally written the script and cast the actors.

Ben Gazzara became the focus of the filming now. Beth admitted he was handsome, but if she had a choice, she would rather have Jimmy Stewart – but now she was being silly like Thelma, letting these movie stars go to her head.

The afternoon wore on. She found herself caught up in the storyline. She wished the actors would get their lines right so they did not have to keep redoing everything. It was frustrating to watch one scene a dozen times when she wanted to see other scenes. Whenever Mr. Preminger shouted, "Cut", she noticed Jimmy Stewart looked exhausted. Thelma chattered on about how most of the actors put in ten hour days which sometimes only resulted in one minute of film. Beth thought it all rather insane, but she could see Mr. Preminger knew what he was doing.

"We'll take another fifteen," Mr. Preminger called around four o'clock.

"I should get home to make supper," Beth told Thelma.

"Oh, well, maybe we could just stop and eat somewhere," Thelma replied.

"Oh no, Henry and Ellen will need me to fix their supper."

"Oh, he's coming this way," said Thelma, ignoring her cousin.

Jimmy Stewart was headed straight toward them. In a bold move, Thelma pushed her wheelchair into the center of the aisle.

"Mr. Stewart, could I please have your autograph?"

"Certainly," he replied. If he realized he was being held hostage by the wheelchair in his path, he did not show the slightest annoyance.

"Make it out to Thelma," said the bearer of that name, after digging in her purse for pen and paper. "I think you're the greatest movie star in Hollywood, Mr. Stewart. You've been my favorite ever since you were in *Mr. Smith Goes to Washington*."

"Thank you. You're very kind," he said, returning the pen with his autograph.

"Oh, and would you sign one for my daughter; her name is Jessie. And for my cousin, Beth."

"Of course," smiled Jimmy, looking straight at Beth. "Are you ladies enjoying yourselves?"

"Oh yes," Beth gushed, overwhelmed by this radiant moment.

"You certainly do have a beautiful town here," he said. "It reminds me of where I'm from in Pennsylvania."

He handed back the autographs, and they thanked him profusely.

"Enjoy yourselves," he replied and passed out the door.

"Wasn't he wonderful?" said Thelma, proud she had dared to accost the famous actor.

"Yes," agreed Beth.

"Let's go now, Mother," said Jessie, tucking the autograph into her purse and then standing up. Beth carefully folded her autograph and also placed it in her purse. She took a last look at the room, at all the stars, at George C. Scott, standing in a corner and rehearsing his lines while Ben Gazzara sipped a glass of water. Then she followed the others out the door.

Hollywood had come to Marquette County. For the rest of her life, Beth would never forget this day.

"How dull for you, Beth," said Thelma, as Jessie pushed her across the street toward the car, "that you have to go home and make supper after such a thrilling afternoon. Are you sure you don't want to go out to eat with me and Jessie?"

"No," said Beth. "I have to feed Henry and Ellen, you know."

"I could take all of you out," said Thelma. "We were thinking of going to the Northland."

"I've never been there," Beth replied, "but it's probably too expensive for us."

"Mother," said Jessie, as she helped Thelma into the car, "we should probably get some groceries first."

"Beth, do you need anything from the store?" asked Thelma.

"Do you need to get a lot of things?" Beth asked, not wanting to wait while they filled an entire cart.

"No, we're just out of bread, cheese, and sugar," said Jessie. "I think that's it."

"Maybe we could get a couple chocolate bars too," said Thelma after she was settled in the car and Jessie had put her wheelchair in the backseat.

"I could pick up some cream," Beth remembered.

The Red Owl was the closest grocery store. Thelma optimistically declared that it was now spring, so as long as the temperature was over twenty degrees, and Jessie and Beth only took a few minutes in the store, she would be fine waiting in the car.

Beth followed Jessie inside the store; then they went their separate ways to get what they needed. Beth scurried over to where the cream was kept, pulled out a container, then rushed back to the counter, certain Jessie's young legs would beat her there. Instead, she found herself in line behind a young woman with a sleeping baby in one arm, and a carton of cigarettes in her hand. As the woman stepped up to the counter, she turned sideways enough for Beth to see her face. Beth usually hoped people would not notice her when she was out in public, but she found she could not help saying, "Hello, Carol Ann. I didn't know you'd had a baby."

She had only met Carol Ann once last year when the girl had come over one afternoon to work with Ellen on a project for school. Ellen had mentioned at the beginning of this school year that Carol Ann had dropped out of school, although no one seemed to know why.

"Hello," Carol Ann replied, not recognizing her.

"I'm Mrs. Whitman, Ellen's mother."

"Oh," said Carol Ann. "Yes, this is my little girl, Celeste."

"How old is she?"

"Nearly two months," said Carol Ann. She repositioned the baby in her arms so Beth could see its face.

"She's adorable," Beth cooed, drinking in the little blue eyes that looked at her in wonder. "Oh, could I hold her? I haven't held a baby in so many years."

Carol Ann hesitated, but then passed her precious bundle into Beth's arms. The touch of the baby blankets sent Beth back twenty years to when Jimmy was an infant. She was curious to ask about the baby's father, but she felt this child could bear no taint however it was conceived. This baby was a beautiful gift from God.

"Hi, honey," said a male voice behind them.

"There you are," said Carol Ann, turning around. "I thought you might be gone on break."

"I just got back," he said.

Beth could resist no longer. She had to look behind her.

"Scofield?" she said with a start.

"Hello, Mrs. Whitman. What do you think of my little girl?"

"Oh, she's beautiful," said Beth, but Celeste began to fidget at that moment, so Carol Ann reclaimed her. As the baby changed hands, Beth noticed what she had missed before, the wedding ring on Carol Ann's finger.

"I'm so happy for both of you," said Beth. "I mean, that you found each other and have this beautiful child. You both deserve to be happy."

The cashier interrupted the conversation. Beth fumbled in her purse for change, picked up her gallon of cream, and said goodbye.

"Tell Jim I said hello," Scofield called after her. "I meant to write and tell him at Christmas that I was getting married, but time got away from me. Is he happy out in California?"

"He seems to be," she replied. From the corner of her eye, she saw Jessie standing by the door, patiently waiting for her. "I'll tell him I saw you."

"It was good seeing you again, Mrs. Whitman," said Scofield, while Carol Ann smiled her goodbye.

Beth left the newlyweds to fuss over their baby. Now she knew why Carol Ann had left school, and why Scofield had not gone to California with Jim and Bernie.

On the drive home, she was silent, but no one noticed because Thelma chattered nonstop about how exciting it was to have a movie made right here in Marquette County, and how excited she was to have seen Jimmy Stewart.

"I do think he's the greatest movie star in Hollywood," Thelma gushed. "Probably the most handsome too." Beth did not remind her of her earlier comments about Montgomery Clift and Gene Kelly.

"We'll have to go back to watch the filming again," said Thelma.

"I'd like that," Beth replied. She had expected to be so lonely today, but now the day seemed full, and her head spun with the news she would tell Henry and Ellen.

No one was home when she arrived. It would still be a half hour before Henry got home from work, and Ellen had left a note on the kitchen table saying she had gone over to one of her classmates' houses until suppertime. Through the window, Beth watched Jessie pull the car out of the driveway; she was glad to see Thelma was still chattering away about movie stars. Poor Thelma. Beth imagined her cousin's life was harder than hers because of her multiple sclerosis, but at least today had been happy for her. She hoped they could all make another trip to see the movie stars.

She sat down at the kitchen table, planning to rest for five minutes before she started supper. She spotted the stack of mail Ellen had left on the table. All bills, except on the bottom of the stack, a letter from Jim.

Quickly, she tore open the envelope.

> Dear Mom, Dad, and Ellen,
>
> Hello. How are you? I hope you're all well. I'm writing because I have something important to tell you. I've met a girl. Her name is .
> . . .

"When has he not met a girl?" thought Beth. "He didn't need to go to California to find girls to charm. There were plenty around here for him."

> Her name is Lisa. I met her at a New Year's Eve party and have been seeing her ever since. I know you aren't surprised because I go out with lots of girls, but you will be surprised when I tell you that I've asked her to marry me . . . .

"Marry him!" Beth watched the words on the paper glaze over before her eyes. "But he's barely grown, he's only – twenty-three! But I was younger than that when his father proposed to me."

. . . and she's accepted. We plan to be married this summer, and we hope you'll come out for the wedding. She's a beautiful girl and I know you'll both love her. She works as a waitress right now, but she's going to secretarial school and will finish this spring. She's a good Midwestern girl. Her parents are from Iowa and they moved here when she was only four.

The rest of Jim's letter was filled with plans about possible dates for the wedding, including that Lisa was anxious to meet his parents, that he hoped his parents would be happy for him, and that Ellen must especially be surprised to learn any girl was crazy enough to marry her big brother.

Beth was shocked for a couple minutes. Then she broke into tears; she felt relieved, even happy.

Here she had gotten up this morning, frightened, terrified really, dreading every minute, but now she felt everything would work out. Thelma had always dreamed of seeing a movie star, a Rudolph Valentino. She had settled for Jimmy Stewart, but it had thrilled her plenty. And then poor Scofield, whom she had never had any hope for, and Carol Ann, that poor girl with that wild family, they had found each other, and created a little miracle. And now, now her son was getting married! He had found himself a good girl – she was already convinced any girl that would take him on must be a good girl – and he would settle down now. She missed him and had hoped he would move back home. Now, with a wife in California, she knew he would never come home – but she could bear that if she knew he had someone out there to look after him. She remembered how much better her life had become once Henry entered it. She did not like the idea of traveling out to California again, but it was for her son's wedding. And in another year or two, why, there might be another little miracle like the one that had blessed Carol Ann and Scofield.

She would celebrate by making something very special for supper. What a lot she had to tell Henry and Ellen. She had had a happy day.

1962

Roy loved solitude. Even his little cabin in the great north woods of the Huron Mountains was at times too near for him to the rest of the world. Only in winter did he feel the serenity of isolation, the great silence that was continually broken in summer by automobiles and tourists coming down his road, curious of where it led, and invading his privacy. In winter, the snow became a barrier to protect him from human activity. Roy had bought a truck with a plow so he could get out of his yard in winter and into Big Bay or Marquette, but usually, he was content to let the winter storms drift over his road, leaving him snow-bound in his cabin, alone with the sparkling ice crystals on his windows. On such dark December afternoons, Roy made himself a cup of coffee, slouched at his table, and bathed in the slanted sunbeams of the winter solstice while he read the little gems written by Conrad Richter and Willa Cather.

But today his concentration was broken by thoughts of Christmas, a day he had reluctantly agreed to spend with his family. He loved his family; he went to visit them every few weeks, but celebrating religious holidays was in defiance of his quest for truth; as Roy grew older, he wondered whether there were any truth, or whether truth mattered. Life was so difficult that if people wanted to find comfort by telling themselves the lies of religion, perhaps that was better than admitting the horror of man alone in an existential world. This year, he had agreed to attend Christmas dinner because Ada would be home, and so would Jim and Lisa with their little girl, Margie, Roy's first great-niece. Having a great niece made him realize just how old he was – he might have been a grandfather now if he could have made different choices.

His meditations were disrupted by a banging, jangling, screeching vehicle, chugging and plowing down his rough, snow-covered road. A bleating horn made him jump from his chair, fling open his cabin door, and feel appalled at the infuriating sight of a giant, grossly modern, gas-guzzling truck with a camper nearly as large as his cabin.

The vehicle came to a standstill, as Roy, now on his doorstep, raised his fist and began to shake it. He tried to peer through the vehicle's windshield, but the driver's face was not visible. Then the truck door opened, and out climbed a grey-haired, balding, middle-aged man, in a spring jacket, despite the temperature being just below freezing.

"Hello, Roy!"

Roy's rage transformed into astonishment that the stranger knew his name.

"How are you?" asked the man, stepping up to Roy and shoving forth his hand.

"Fine," barked Roy. "Who the heck are you?"

"Theo – your cousin."

The name took a moment to sink into Roy's memory. He had not seen Theo since they had been young men, when he had gone to California to visit his relatives – that had been over thirty years ago. He scanned the aging man's face, and after a few seconds, he found his cousin behind the wrinkles.

"Theo, what are you doing here?"

"I've come to visit," said Theo. "When I retired, I decided to see the country, and of course, Upper Michigan was on my itinerary. It's been years since I've seen any family."

"Is Melinda with you?" asked Roy, looking toward the camper for Theo's wife.

"No," said Theo. "I wanted to come on my own."

"Oh," said Roy. "Well, um, did my mother know you were coming?"

"No, I thought I would surprise all of you. I just came from seeing your mother and Henry and his family. Then I thought I'd come up here to see this great cabin everyone is always writing me about. I've never forgotten that day I spent up at the Huron Mountain Club with you. I thought I'd come stay up here with you to get a little peace and quiet."

Roy looked doubtful.

"Don't worry," said Theo. "I won't be a burden to you. I can stay right here in my camper just outside your door. Come and see it."

Roy followed Theo into the camper. He did not know what to say about such an unexpected visit. No one except his brothers ever drove out here to see him – even Eleanor had only come once, and his mother declared she had no inclination to see the place after the awful stories she had heard about it.

"Can you believe this?" asked Theo, showing Roy around the cramped little compartment. "An entire house on wheels. Look at this – there's even a bathroom, and a little stove. What do you say to that, Roy? It's almost as big as your place, but mobile so you can go wherever you want. Have you ever seen anything like it?"

"No, can't say I have."

Roy thought it the ghastly epitome of what was wrong with the modern world, but he did not want to be rude to a cousin he had not seen in thirty years.

"So, how long are you staying?" he asked as they returned outside.

"Oh, I don't know. Through the holidays anyway. Since I'm retired, I can come and go as I please."

"Won't Melinda want you back home?"

"No, she doesn't worry about me," said Theo. Roy had his back to Theo as they stepped into the cabin, so he did not see his cousin's face blanche, but he understood the tone.

"Problems?" asked Roy, cautiously.

"She ran off with another man – a thirty-eight-year old. Some gigolo – after her money, which isn't even hers but mine. She always was a stupid bitch."

Roy's mother had once met Melinda, and although she was too much of a lady to say so, Roy suspected his mother felt the same way about Theo's wife.

"I'm sorry," said Roy. "When did it happen?"

"Oh, three or four months ago. Say, this is a swell place you've got. It's like living in the old pioneer days."

"Thanks. I built it all myself, except that bookshelf there Henry made for me, and Eleanor made me the curtains."

Theo looked around, wondering how anyone could be content in this little hole. It was hardly bigger than his camper, the whole building smaller than the bedroom back in his California house, the bedroom where Melinda and that fellow were romping now.

"How was your trip out?" Roy asked, not knowing what else to say.

"Great. I stopped off at the Grand Canyon, spent a few days fishing in the Mississippi River. Had a great time in St. Louis. Stopped and saw a few shows in Chicago. Drank some beers in Milwaukee. You know, did all the tourist things. I intend to have a ball now that I'm retired and free from my parasite wife. Since I'm up here in the snowbelt, I thought I might even try skiing. Do you ski?"

"No," said Roy. "Not since I was twenty or so. I'd probably break my neck if I tried now, but I go snowshoeing a lot. I s'pose I could take you ice-fishing."

"That sounds fun," said Theo.

Roy wondered whether it would be. He wanted to be pleasant, but he remembered Theo could be rather prissy at times.

"Let me tell you about the fishing I did on the Colorado River," said Theo, sitting down in Roy's favorite chair.

"Do you want some coffee?" Roy suspected his own cup of coffee was cold by now. He would have to make a new pot, and he only had a little coffee left. He would have to make an extra trip into town to get more groceries if Theo were staying more than a couple days.

"So anyway," said Theo, "I met this fellow in Denver, and he told me he'd show me the good fishing holes on the Colorado River, and I figured, what the heck, I'm in no rush to get anywhere, other than I thought I'd come spend Christmas in Michigan with my family, so I – "

Roy listened to Theo's rambling, still trying to believe his California cousin was sitting in his little shack and pretending to prefer it to the society ballrooms of San Francisco and Washington D.C. that he had frequented all his life.

"Look at all the snow around here," said Theo, "and it's only December. How much more will you get before winter's over?"

"We barely have a foot yet," said Roy. "By March it'll be six or seven feet high and blocking the windows."

"You should see the snow up in the Rockies. Absolutely gorgeous. Why I saw this one mountain pass where – "

Theo chattered so much about his recent adventures that Roy could see he was covering up his hurt over the divorce. Roy understood why his cousin had felt the need to get away from California, but Theo had lived the good life, filled with money, rich and powerful friends – movie stars, governors, even a Nobel laureate. He had been honored nationally for his role in helping science progress by his laboratory work. What was he doing in Marquette?

"This looks great, Roy," said Theo, when the modest supper of hot dogs, pork and beans, and bread was placed before him. "I'm so sick of all that damn lobster out in Los Angeles. You've got the life here, Roy. You don't know how lucky you are to be away from all those crowds of crazy people."

"Oh, I think I do," Roy replied.

Theo sighed. "Sometimes I wish I had grown up here, but no, my mother had to marry the senator and move to the big city."

"So how are your parents?" Roy repeated.

"Didn't Mother write to tell you? The senator died six months ago."

Roy groped into his memory until he vaguely recalled his mother mentioning it.

"I'm sorry; that's right," he said. "How is your mother holding up?"

"All right, I guess. She got the house and his money so she can't complain," Theo laughed, "and he can't push her around anymore."

"Oh," said Roy.

"Don't look so shocked," said Theo. "You must know he wasn't my real father. Granted, I never would have had what I did if Mother hadn't married him, but money can't buy love. He wasn't much of a father, or a politician as far as I'm concerned."

"I see," Roy said, unsure what else to say. The way Roy's mother talked, Aunt Sarah and Uncle Joseph seemed like the world's happiest couple and Theo the perfect son.

"Roy, you know what I'd like to do after supper? Play some poker. I haven't played cards in years. I've some good cigars we can smoke while we play."

Roy did not play cards. He had no one to play with. He was too much of a loner to stick around at family parties when his siblings sat down for a game of rummy. But he did not refuse when Theo went to his camper to get his cigars and playing cards.

Theo played uproariously, cracking jokes, inhaling his cigar more than he should, and getting near drunk on the root beer Roy dug out of the snowbank that served as his refrigerator/freezer six months out of the year. Whenever Roy won a hand, Theo patted him on the back until Roy wanted to slug him. He had never seen a grown man try so hard to have a good time. Finally, he told Theo he was tired and had to get to bed.

"All right. What will we do tomorrow, Roy?"

"Actually, I have a couple errands to run up at the Club."

"Oh, great, I'll go with you," said Theo. "I'd love to see the place again. Remember that hike you took me and Henry on up there, and then we all went skinny-dipping in the lake – except you; you were too modest I guess."

"Ye-es, well, we can't go skinny dipping in December," said Roy. He was not sure he wanted anyone at the Club to meet his cousin. Why had Theo not stayed in town with his mother or Henry? His mother would have loved introducing her nephew, the great scientist and son of a U.S. Senator, to all her church ladies.

"Well, thanks for everything, Roy. I'll stay out in the camper. Don't want to crowd you out or anything. Come pound on the door when you're ready to leave in the morning. I'm a pretty heavy sleeper sometimes."

"All right," said Roy, seeing Theo out the door. "It's good to see you. I imagine the rest of the family will want to spend time with you too."

"I told your mother I'd come over with you for Christmas dinner to see all the family. I'd kind of just like to rest here a few days until then."

"Okay," said Roy. Christmas was still three days away – would he have to entertain Theo until then? "Good night. Let me know if you need anything."

"All right. Thanks for having me," said Theo, stepping outside and shutting the door behind him. He paused a minute, shivering in the cold to which he was not acclimated. He had come all this way to get as far from California as possible. He had thought he had escaped the pain until this moment when he found himself alone through the lonely night. He trudged to his camper, noting the light coat of snow on its windows. He would not be able to see out of them in the morning.

He realized Roy thought his divorce was why he had left California. That was fine – Theo did not know how to explain that the divorce was only the end result of several problems. Roy must think him crazy to show up unannounced. He did not know what he expected to find here. Probably no one was left who could tell him what he wanted to know – his mother could, but he dared not ask her now that she was old and sickly. Years ago, she had told him of his father's death, but she had refused to tell him anything except his father's name – Lysander Blackmore. He had not even had the guts to look in the city directory at Aunt Margaret's house to see whether any Blackmores still lived in Marquette. He needed time to decide how he would go about his search – Christmas was in a few days – he would wait until after the holiday to make his next move.

He put on his pajamas and poured himself a drink. He knew he would not sleep for hours. His body was still on California time, and his sleep had been restless ever since the divorce. Even if he learned what he wanted, he doubted he would ever know another peaceful night. Not after the way his life had been destroyed.

When Jim and Lisa came home for Christmas, the entire Whitman clan, along with the Dalrymple, Cumming, Bergmann and Goldman branches, turned out. They came less to see Jim than the newest family addition, little Margie Whitman, already two, yet until this Christmas a stranger to her Upper Michigan roots.

"Just think, Mother," Eleanor said on Christmas morning as the precious little child nestled in Margaret's arms, "that's your first great-grandchild. Hopefully if I can find good husbands for my girls, you'll have more soon."

Lucy and Maud, overhearing their mother's comment, rolled their eyes. Their mother's marriage having been unhappy, their response to matrimony was, "What's the point?" Although their grandparents had been happily married, and Uncle Henry and Aunt Beth clearly adored each other, and they could now witness the prolonged newlywed happiness of Jim and Lisa, Lucy and Maud remained unconvinced of marital bliss. When their mother suggested they find boyfriends, they would argue, "Ellen doesn't go out with anyone, yet her mother doesn't fuss at her to get married." Eleanor would reply, "That's because your Aunt Beth already has a grandchild. I'm still waiting." Yet Eleanor also knew it would be a sad day when her girls left her to start families of their own.

Ellen was too busy trying to please her niece on Christmas morning to worry about marriage. She enjoyed looking at handsome men, but she had vowed not to relinquish her artistic aspirations for the bondage of wifehood. This coming spring, she would graduate from college with a nursing degree. She had chosen nursing because she did not want to be a secretary, and she could not bear to waste her talents by teaching art to children so they could make trivial projects to please their parents. As a nurse, she could witness people's suffering and emotions, which might inspire the art that would continue to consume her spare time.

Aunt Ada, who lived to tat, sew, embroider, quilt and crochet, approved of Ellen's artistic goals. Ada's own children had not inherited their mother's creative genes, so Ada tried to make Ellen into her protégée. Yet even Aunt Ada had told her, "What you need, Ellen, is a rich man to support you so you can paint all day long."

Ellen would have none of it. She firmly believed a great artist was married to her work. She did not want a husband to tell her what to do; nor did she want the burden of looking after children – she was content enough on Christmas morning to have little Margie sit on her lap and open her presents.

Margie tore the paper off one package after another to reveal Teddy Bears, dolls, adorable outfits with ribbons and laces, blocks to build doll houses, and play dishes for tea parties. At two, Margie had enough toys to last until she was twenty.

"How will we ever get all these presents back to California?" asked Lisa.

"It's a good thing we didn't fly," said Jim. "I don't think even the car trunk will hold them all."

"What did you expect when you kept our granddaughter away from us for so long?" laughed Beth, who had not known such a happy Christmas since Jim had moved away.

Margie was not the only one to make a haul. There were boxes of chocolates for Henry, fancy gloves for Eleanor, flannel shirts for Jim, who admitted it got cold even in California, lotion and perfume for Lisa, pretty handkerchiefs for Beth, new pocketbooks for Lucy and Maud, slippers for Ada, oil paints for Ellen, and for Margaret, a thick, luxurious bathrobe.

Margaret looked upon all this bounty, surpassed only by the richness of her still growing family, four generations in one room. She wished Will were still alive to see how their family prospered. She and Will had never had much during all the years they struggled on the farm, through the Great Depression and the wars. Now her children were thriving, thanks to God rather than to anything she had done as their mother. And for the first time in over a decade, all five of her children would be here for Christmas. Ada had come home. Roy had agreed to come for dinner, and Bill would be bringing over his new and second wife, the woman he insisted would make him happy for the rest of his life.

"Well, we better clean up this mess and start dinner," said Beth.

"I still don't know where I'll put everyone," said Margaret. "I can't even keep track of how many are coming."

"Let's see," said Eleanor, trying to count on her fingers, then giving up. "We better write a list so we know how many places to set."

"Even with two sets of china, I doubt we'll have enough dishes," said Margaret.

Ada began to write down names while Eleanor recited them. "There's cousin Harry and Jean, and Thelma and Jessie, and Aunt Harriet and Uncle Charles, and cousin Joseph and Bea, and Roy and Theo, and me, and – "

"I still can't believe Theo just showed up out of the blue," said Henry.

"Have you seen him since he showed up?" asked Eleanor.

"Just that first day. Then he went up to see Roy. We haven't heard from him since except when he called from Big Bay to say he and Roy would come for dinner."

"He always was an odd character," said Jim. "Lisa and I went to visit him and his wife right after we were married. He tried to be friendly, but his wife barely said a word. I don't think she wanted us there, so he didn't know how to act."

"Well, they didn't really know you," said Ellen.

"His wife Melinda was always rather a snob," said Beth. "She sure didn't want anything to do with me and Henry when we lived out there."

Margaret said nothing, but she remembered how she had been ignored by the bride at Theo's wedding. She thought Theo better off without that woman, especially if she were so loose as to fool around with a man young enough to be her son.

"It's too bad Aunt Sarah didn't come to visit with Theo," said Ada. "I know you'd love to see your sister, Ma."

"Yes," said Margaret. "I wonder why she didn't come, especially when I know she's been lonely since her husband died. I'll have to write to her soon."

"Letter writing can wait until we get Christmas dinner cooked," said Beth, pushing herself up from the couch and trudging into the kitchen. No one followed her, not that Beth expected anyone to. Margaret had relinquished Thanksgiving dinner to Eleanor and New Year's Day to Beth, but she still insisted on Christmas. Beth had since noticed that Thanksgiving was a bit of a disaster; Eleanor had never been a good cook. As for Christmas, it hardly mattered whether it were at her or Margaret's house, since she ended up doing most of the work; it had been that way since she married Henry. But why complain after all these years? She started stuffing the turkey, knowing that eventually Eleanor or Margaret would come to help. Instead, Ada appeared, asking what needed to be done. Beth gratefully set her to work.

Someone had turned on the radio. Judy Garland crooning about how soon we would all be together so we should have a merry little Christmas. Beth's heart softened; she told herself she should not mind all this work. It was worth it since all her family were here, and best of all, her son, daughter-in-law and first grandchild were home for the holidays.

Before long, the rest of the company arrived, Thelma and Jessie leading them.

"Henry, go out and help Thelma," said Beth. "The steps will be icy."

Jessie got her mother out of the car and into her wheelchair, pushed her to the front steps, then helped her stand up. Henry grabbed Thelma's arm while Thelma grasped the railing; together Henry and Thelma got Thelma up the steps while Jessie stood behind them to prevent any slips or falls. Once inside, Thelma settled back into her chair, then was wheeled through the screened in porch to the front parlor. She was exhausted, yet feeling festive enough to declare, "Margaret, that's an absolutely gorgeous Christmas tree!"

Next Aunt Harriet and Uncle Charles came from across the street.

"Hello, Aunt Harriet. How are you?" asked Ada, going up to hug her.

Harriet permitted this sign of affection, then handed her coat to Ada. "I'm managing as well as an old woman my age can, especially when I have an even older man to look after," she grumbled. "My God, it's freezing out there."

Uncle Charles meekly removed his coat and sat down beside Henry, pretending not to hear his wife, and hoping no one noticed how she was growing more and more infuriated with him. To his advantage, he was going deaf.

Charles and Harriet's son, Joseph, soon appeared with his wife, Bea, and twin boys, now well into their teenage years, and just as annoying as ever. When the twins were little, Ellen had spent many an unpleasant day babysitting them until finally she had told her mother no amount of money would make her watch them again. Half a dozen years had since passed, yet the Dalrymple twins had scarcely matured.

Then came cousin Harry with his wife, Jean, one of his children, and two little grandchildren, Jennifer and Brian. Brian was exactly Margie's age; they stared at each other in astonishment until Margie could no longer bear the awkwardness and pushed her little third cousin over. The child jumped right up and chased Margie around the legs of the grownups to the screaming delight of both children, the laughter of the adults, and the annoyance of Aunt Harriet.

Then came Bill, with his bride, Annette, a dozen years younger than him, on his arm. She was caked with heavy mascara in an ill-judged attempt to look like Audrey Hepburn; everyone was polite despite her appearance; everyone hoped Annette was finally Bill's true love for the rest of his life, and everyone had said the wedding last month had been a beautiful ceremony; not until next month would the family learn Annette was four months pregnant.

"We're almost ready to eat," said Margaret. "We're just waiting for Roy and Theo to show up."

"Roy's coming?" asked Harry in astonishment.

"Now who is Theo again?" asked Joseph's wife.

"My cousin from California," said Joseph. "The senator's son."

"The senator was not his real father," said Harriet.

"Yes, Aunt Harriet, we all know that," said Eleanor, not wanting Christmas dinner to be a replay of family scandals.

"Here they come," said Bill, looking out the window.

Roy had refused to ride in Theo's monstrous camper. Theo, thankful Roy was putting him up without asking too many questions, had suffered without heat in Roy's car all the way from Big Bay to Marquette. Both were frozen when they reached Margaret's house, but Theo quickly warmed to a crowded room as he tripped over feet and shook hands all around with this enormous family he had never known.

"A few of the adults will have to sit at the children's table," said Ada. "We'll have the little kids, and the twins" – the Dalrymple twins rolled their eyes, hating to be included as children – "Ellen, would you mind terribly as well? And then – "

"Oh, no," said Lisa. "I'll sit at the kiddy table. Then I can feed Margie."

"No, you sit with Jim at the big table," Ellen said. "I'll watch Margie." Ellen hoped Margie would keep her too busy to talk with the twins.

"We'll need one more at the children's table," said Ada looking about for volunteers.

"I'll sit there," said Jessie. "I love little kids."

Everyone scrambled to their seats. Then despite the passing of plates and pouring of coffee, Margaret got everyone to settle down long enough so she could thank the good Lord for providing them with such bounty.

Now the eating began in full fury.

Ellen kept reaching over to the grownup table to get food for the children. Jessie tried to fill the plates of Margie and the two Cumming grandchildren. The Dalrymple twins refused to eat most of what was put before them. Tim Dalrymple complained about how crowded he was; Randy Dalrymple stuck black olives on his brother's plate, only to have Tim, who hated olives, pick them up and shove them in his brother's sweet potatoes. Jessie and Ellen ignored the teenage boys, finding it easier to deal with the two year olds. Ellen fussed plenty over Margie, while Jessie's attention constantly turned back and forth from Jennifer Cumming, age five, to Brian Cumming, age two. Jennifer instantly took to Jessie and talked to her nonstop, while Brian grunted, and kept asking for more of everything so he could poke his fingers in the food and make mashed potato and stuffing castles.

"Look at that girl," said Harriet, watching Jessie with the children. "She looks like she needs to get married and have her own babies."

"I don't think Jessie's the marrying type," said Thelma.

"What's wrong with these girls nowadays not getting married. It's unnatural," said Harriet.

Lucy and Maud waited for Aunt Harriet to ask them the dreaded eternal question of whether either of them had a boyfriend.

"Jessie has a whole classroom of children at school," Thelma told Harriet.

"She needs her own kids to look after, not someone else's."

Jessie heard every word but said nothing. She had been happy to sit with the children, but now she felt like crying. What did that old woman know about her? They only met a couple times a year at these family get-togethers; they were not even related, so why couldn't Harriet Dalrymple mind her own business?

"Love isn't for everyone," said Theo. "I should know."

"What do you mean?" asked Margaret.

"I mean, when your wife runs off with another man, you wish you had never been married in the first place."

No one wanted to hear about Theo's divorce, but he found himself giving out the details, his great desire for privacy conquered by a need for sympathy.

"Theo," Bill said, "one failed marriage hardly counts. It wasn't until my second marriage that I found my true love." He leaned over to peck Annette on the cheek.

"Theo, how long are you staying?" Harry asked.

"I don't know. For a few more weeks anyway."

For days, Roy had longed to ask Theo the same question, but he had felt it would be impolite. Now having his answer, he ground his feet into the heels of his shoes, trying not to show his frustration over his unexpected visitor.

"Margaret, everything is delicious," said Thelma.

"Oh, well, thank Beth and Ada. They let me think I'm in charge, but they did most of the work."

Beth smiled in appreciation, then asked, "Did everyone have enough to eat?"

"I couldn't eat another bite," said Henry.

"Well, you better find room because we have cake, and chocolate and lemon meringue pies."

"Lemon meringue for me," said Roy.

Ada and Beth took dessert orders while Margaret and Eleanor cleared the table.

"I hate pie," Tim Dalrymple said. "I'll have cake."

"Can't you just say, 'May I have a piece of cake, please?' without being so negative?" said Ellen, unable any longer to restrain her annoyance with Tim's whining.

Tim ignored her.

"Everything was so delicious," Thelma repeated as dessert was set before her.

"Who made the lemon pie?" asked Eleanor. "The meringue is so perfect."

"I did," Harriet beamed. Even if her kitchen were a disaster, in all fairness, she could make a decent pie.

"The cake is terrific," said Theo. "Who made that?"

"Beth," Henry said. "It's her specialty."

"No," said Jim, "Ma's real specialty is pineapple brownies; she better make me up a batch before I go back to California."

"If I put off baking them, does that mean you'll stay longer?" Beth teased.

At the children's table, Tim Dalrymple said, "Hey, what's this?"

Ellen looked across the table to see Tim pull a wad of gum out of his cake. "How the hell did that get in there?" he said.

Ellen instantly grabbed it from his hand. "For God's sake, shut up."

The adult table was too busy talking to have heard.

Tim glared and opened his mouth to protest, but Jessie said, "If you say one more word, I'll tell your parents how you swore."

Tim bit his tongue, but he refused to eat another bite of cake.

"Ma wondered where she'd set down that piece of gum," Ellen whispered to Jessie. Beth had taken to chewing gum to help her nerves after Jim moved away. Ellen hoped Jim's visit would help relieve her mother's habit now. Her mother had been so much happier since Jim had decided to come home for Christmas.

"Does anyone want seconds for dessert?" asked Ada.

"I sure don't," Tim pouted.

Ellen glared at him.

"What I need is a walk," said Joseph.

"Me too," agreed Bill, patting the start of his middle-age paunch.

"We should take the children for a walk," Ellen said to Jessie.

"It's too cold for walking," complained Randy Dalrymple.

"You weren't invited," Ellen said, "unless you count as one of the children."

She collected the plates from the children's table, then went to ask Lisa whether she could take Margie for a walk. Jennifer and Brian were also allowed to go along.

"There's an old sleigh in the back shed," said Margaret. "You could pull the children on that."

Lisa decided to join the group, not having spent any time outside since she had arrived in Michigan; her California upbringing made the snow intriguing to her.

"Mind if I come along?" asked Theo, needing a break from so much family time he was unused to.

No one refused him. He waited patiently with his coat on while the women wrapped the children in jackets, scarves, mittens, and hats. Once the walking party was out the door, it became fair game for conversation among the remaining company.

"How sad that Theo got divorced like that," said Thelma, "and after nearly thirty years of marriage. I feel bad for him."

"Well, I'm not surprised," said Harriet. "Ask Margaret. She knows. When she went to Theo's wedding, Melinda acted like such a spoiled thing that I'm surprised she didn't run off with another man years ago. Not that Theo isn't stuck up himself since his mother married a senator and brought him up to think he was better than everyone else; it's about time that whole family was knocked down a few pegs."

No one replied. They were all well experienced at ignoring Aunt Harriet's tongue; each had once dared to confront her and then suffered her wrath.

Outside, Ellen had dug the sleigh out of her grandfather's old workshop. Lisa decided to sit in it, holding Margie in her lap with Jennifer between her legs, and Jennifer's arms wrapped around Brian's waist. Ellen volunteered to pull the sleigh down the street. Theo and Jessie were at the rear of the party although Jessie found herself trying to stay a step or two ahead of Theo so his cigar smoke would not blow in her face.

"I don't know how you people deal with all this snow," said Theo, wishing he had thought to buy himself a pair of boots. The streets were filled with newly fallen snow which seeped over the rim of his shoes and soaked into his socks.

"We're just used to it, I guess," said Jessie. "We all get sick of shoveling it, but it is pretty."

"You couldn't pay me enough to live here," said Theo. "The climate's awful, and there isn't really anything to recommend this town."

"I don't know about that," said Jessie although she often thought she would not remain in Marquette if she were not obligated to care for her foster mother.

"Have you ever thought of moving away?" Theo asked her between cigar puffs.

"Yes. I did go away to college, but then I came home to take care of Mother. I don't know where I would go anyway."

"What my Aunt Harriet said about you," Theo exhaled, "I mean about your getting married – that was uncalled for. I'm sure you could find plenty of young men who would be interested in you. You're a beautiful girl."

Jessie was too proud to admit no young men had ever shown any interest in her; she knew she had warded them off by being too involved in her music and caring for her mother. "I guess I'm just waiting for the right one to come along," she said.

"He will," Theo replied. "You're plenty young enough."

"I'll be forty in a few years."

"That's still young, and you'll probably avoid the trouble of having children – my children don't want anything to do with me, and my ex-wife sure doesn't want me around. Sometimes I think I'd have been better off if I never got involved with anyone."

"I don't know," said Jessie. "I sometimes worry about being old and alone."

Theo secretly worried about the same thing. He dropped his cigar butt in the snowbank. He felt pathetic; what must everyone think of him, to have spoiled Christmas dinner by complaining about his problems.

"You ought to come out to California," he said. "I hear you're a talented musician. I know some people out there who could give you a good job."

"Oh!" said Jessie, thrilled by the thought. "But I can't. I have to care for my mother."

"You can't be expected to give up your life for someone else," said Theo.

"She did for me. I'm not her real daughter – she adopted me when no one else would. After all she's done for me, I can't abandon her."

"My stepfather," said Theo, "gave me a lot of advantages I never asked for. I don't feel any obligation to him, but I guess that's easy to say now that he's dead."

"What happened to your real father?" Jessie asked.

"He and my mother never married. I guess he abandoned her." Theo hesitated as he spoke, afraid to divulge his real reason for coming to Marquette.

"My father abandoned us too," said Jessie, "and my mother died, but I consider myself lucky to have been adopted."

She was grateful, but sometimes she thought if she had not been adopted, she might now be living her own life, rather than having spent the last twenty years caring for Thelma. She knew she was selfish to think that way, but she could not bury the thought, and she wickedly wondered what she would do once Thelma was gone.

"What is California like?" she asked.

"Beautiful. Even as far north as San Francisco, there are green palm trees at Christmas. It's always sunny. The ocean is breathtaking – "

"I've always wanted to see the Pacific," said Jessie. "Does it look like Lake Superior?"

"Somewhat, but you can smell the salt water, and it's a lot warmer. Roy tells me only crazy people would swim in Lake Superior even in summer, but you can swim in the Pacific in the dead of winter. It's wonderful there. You should come visit me sometime."

Jessie wanted to see California, but she could not accept a stranger's invitation.

"One turn around the block is all I can take," said Lisa, loud enough to interrupt Theo and Jessie's conversation. "What do you say, Theo? We Californians just can't take this cold?"

"I'm pretty well frozen," he agreed.

"I want to go inside and play with my doll!" said Jennifer.

"Me too!" cried Margie.

Brian jumped off the sleigh and ran into the driveway, then up the front steps before the grownups could catch him.

"I guess he's decided for all of us," Ellen laughed.

Jessie followed the others inside. She felt she would have preferred to stay outside in the cold, talking to Theo about the warmth of California.

"How was your walk?" Bill asked Theo.

"Jessie," called Beth, "your mother wants you to help her to the bathroom."

"Okay," Jessie replied while trying not to sigh at the intrusion of everyday life into her California dreams.

"I would have helped her," said Beth, "but she insisted she'd wait for you."

"Thelma, when you get back, we'll play some cards," said Eleanor, as Jessie pushed the wheelchair toward the bathroom. "I'm feeling lucky today."

"All right," Thelma called back.

"Theo, rather than coffee," Bill asked, "do you want a little Christmas rum?"

"I can't turn that down," laughed Theo as his eyes followed Jessie and the wheelchair down the hall.

Ten minutes later, the women, Henry, and Theo were earnestly playing cards. The other men sat in the front room, drinking and smoking with loosened belts. The children fiddled with their presents beneath the Christmas tree. The Dalrymple twins found corner chairs to curl up in and hibernate until the doldrums of the family party ended. Jessie listened to Maud, Lucy, and Ellen discuss college, the latest fashions, and their big dreams. Jessie remembered when she had had big dreams. A couple times when she looked up from her cards, she caught Theo staring at her.

1963

Marquette's streets were peaceful that morning. The rush hour traffic had subsided an hour ago, if such a thing as rush hour traffic could be said to exist in the little city. Overnight, several inches of snow had fallen, and while the plows had long since cleared the roads, the morning sun had hid behind the clouds, leaving freshly fallen fluff clinging in layers to tree branches, street lights, building fronts, and automobile roofs.

Theo trudged along the unshovelled sidewalks. He marveled at the city's serenity as he walked down Front Street past the Peter White Public Library and the First Baptist Church. How could the world appear so placid when his heart was racing, his ears still ringing from that awful woman's screams?

Christmas was two weeks past; since then, Theo had spent the days sitting around Roy's cabin or socializing with his relatives. Now all pretense of a holiday visit had passed; if he were to stay longer, the task he had set himself must be executed. He had taken Roy's car that morning to drive downtown. He had parked it on Washington Street, then walked up Front Street and into the residential district so the vehicle would not give away his destination. He had stopped before the house where his mother had once worked as a maid, and where he knew he had been conceived. The house had belonged to his paternal grandparents, then to the father he had never known. Now the city directory confirmed his father's widow resided there.

The confrontation had occurred just minutes before, but already Theo had relived it a dozen times; he was still too much in shock to process its meaning. First, he had stood at the street corner, watching the house, summoning courage; each minute he had told himself he would knock on the front door until half an hour had passed; then he had felt so frozen that he had walked around the block to warm himself up, only to return to the same corner and stare at the house again.

Then the house's front door had opened. A young man had rushed down the front steps and entered a car parked in the driveway. Theo had not seen the man's face, and he had nervously turned away his head when the car passed him. The man had looked too young to be his brother, but then, Theo did not know how old his half-siblings might be, other than that they must have been born before 1929, the year his father had committed suicide apparently due to the stock market crash from what his mother had told him. That had been Theo's senior year of college; he had been beginning his life, and he had told himself his real father was nothing to him. Only when older, when a father himself, had he begun to wonder what his father had been like, and by then, his mother had refused to speak of his father. The only other thing Theo knew was his father's name, Lysander Blackmore, and that he had married and had a family.

Now, as Theo walked back to his car, he again tried to persuade himself that since his father was dead, no good could come from contact with the family. That awful woman's words had confirmed this belief – that some family secrets should remain secrets, that skeletons were better left in the closet.

But Theo had learned this lesson the hard way. After the young man had driven away, Theo had approached the front door. He had half-hoped the young man's departure meant no one else was home; then he could leave, both disappointed and relieved. He had climbed the front steps, stood in the shelter of the front porch, rung the doorbell, and wondered what to say.

"Hello."

A woman had answered the door – a middle-aged woman in a flowered dress, her hair in a bun, glasses perched on her nose.

"Is this the Blackmore residence?" Theo had asked, the words nervously sliding forth, making him think he sounded foolish, despite his years of scientific research, of worldly wisdom, of social prestige.

"Yes," she replied, approving his fine clothes, yet fearing he wanted to sell her a set of encyclopedias.

"Are you a member of the family?" he asked.

"Yes, I'm Matilda."

"Matilda Blackmore?"

"I was – I'm Matilda Robinson now. I'm a widow. How can I help you?"

"I – I'm looking for – I'm trying to find out something about the family."

"Why?" she asked.

"I – my mother – I"

The bewilderment on her face made him blurt out the words.

"I think I'm your brother, or a relative anyway."

Then rather than look surprised, she peered into his eyes.

"Why do you think that?"

"My mother used to work here – she was a maid for the family – she – well, she says my father was Lysander Blackmore. Do you know that name?"

"Matilda, who is it?" a voice called from an interior room.

Matilda did not reply.

"I'm sorry," said Theo. "This must be hard for you. I know the surprise – "

"Lysander Blackmore was my father," she said.

"Matilda!" called the annoyed voice, getting closer.

"I'll be there in a minute, Mother!" Matilda hollered back.

"Well, why can't you answer me when I call you?" snapped the voice.

"I'm sorry," Theo said. "I know it's a shock. I – "

"It's not your fault," said Matilda. "But my father's dead – I don't know what to tell you."

"I just want to know something about him. I – "

"Matilda, who is at the door?"

An old woman, cluttering with a cane, spying through her spectacles, appeared in the doorway. When she saw Theo, a look of horror came over her face. "Who are you?"

He tried to find words, but his voice would not come up from his throat.

"Mother, this is – I'm sorry; what is your name?"

"Theodore," he replied.

"Theodore what?" the old woman snapped. "What do you want?"

Theo looked at Matilda for assistance, but she had stepped back, her eyes dropping to the floor.

"My father was Lysander Blackmore," he felt forced to admit.

The old woman paused, then said with surprising calm, "My husband is dead. Only he could say if your statement is true. You can't prove it."

"Mother, he does look like Nigel," Matilda said. She explained to Theo, "Nigel is my brother."

"What foolishness," the widow said. "My husband is dead and should be left to rest in peace; I won't have any fortune hunters casting aspersions on his name."

"I didn't come for money," Theo said. "I'm plenty rich enough – I only came because – "

"You're not welcome here," the old woman huffed.

"Please, I know this is difficult, but – "

"Matilda, shut the door!"

"Mother, I think we – "

"Shut the door unless you want to sleep on the doorstep tonight."

"Please," Theo said. "I only want – "

But he could see it was no use. Matilda's eyes had asked his forgiveness as the door swung shut in his face.

He had then stood there a moment, too stunned to move. Through the door crack, he had heard the old woman shout: "How many more, Lord? How many more of his bastards will come to torment me?"

The words had made Theo swiftly turn and run down the steps and front walk, where he had slipped on the ice and landed in the snowbank. He had skinned his naked hand; for a moment, he lay and watched his blood soak into the snow. Then sucking his wound, he got to his feet and ambled down the street. He had not stopped until he had turned the corner and the Blackmore house was no longer visible. He felt sobs about to break from his throat.

He had tried to compose himself. With determination, he had kept walking, refusing to make a public spectacle of himself. But the old woman's words kept ringing in his ears. "How many more of his bastards?" He was only a bastard to her. But Matilda had said, "It's not your fault." He told himself if given the chance, he might have liked her – his half-sister. But he was angry to be insulted by that old woman. He had been born before his father had ever married her, so what right did she have to be angry? Had his father even told her about his firstborn child?

And now, as he turned the corner of Front Street onto Washington, Theo realized her words "How many more of his bastards?" meant he had other siblings besides the widow's children, Matilda and Nigel. The old woman knew his father had produced other children outside of wedlock. Theo had seen another Blackmore listed in the city directory. He wondered if –

"Hello, Theo."

He had his eyes to the ground, but he lifted them at the sound of his name. Jessie Hopewell was smiling at him.

"Hello," he said, too jolted from his own thoughts to recollect her name.

"It sure is cold today, isn't it?" she said.

"Yes, it is," he said.

"I walked downtown, thinking I could use the exercise," said Jessie. "My car's at the mechanic's, and I didn't think it would be so chilly a walk."

She did not tell him she had gone for a walk just to get out of the house. Thelma had been ill that night, vomiting all over the bed, and too weak and sore from her disease even to sit up. Jessie had repeatedly cleaned up messes, and having hardly gotten any sleep, she had called in sick to school that day. Later, Mrs. Nabor from across the street had come over to stay with Thelma long enough for Jessie to walk to the bank and cash her paycheck.

Theo stared at her, then fumbled in his pockets for a cigarette.

"Would you like one?" he asked. "It might keep you warm?"

"No. I don't smoke," she said.

He shrugged, then lit and puffed on the cigarette, seeking to release the tension of his encounter with his father's family.

"What are you doing downtown?" Jessie asked.

"Shopping," he lied, not wanting to reveal his secrets.

"Would you like to get a cup of coffee? It might warm us up, and I don't think my Mother would mind. She doesn't like to be alone, but Mrs. Nabor is there, and I left her sleeping, so maybe just for half an hour it would be all right."

Suddenly, Theo burst out, "Are you going to let your mother run your life? Christ, she's not even your real mother, and you're a grown woman!" Then he was embarrassed and irritated with himself. He barely knew Jessie, but he hated to see her mother control her, precisely because he had the same weakness.

"No, I just don't want her to worry," Jessie replied. She felt like a schoolgirl beside him; he seemed so sophisticated.

"Where do we get coffee?" he asked as a form of apology.

When he had snapped at her, she had felt like crying, but now she felt a tingling sensation of pleasure because he had accepted her offer.

"Just down the street," she said, leading him west toward the Post Office. They crossed the street and entered The Coffee Cup. They easily found a seat, the morning rush being over, and it being too early for lunch.

Jessie felt pampered as Theo helped her remove her coat. He felt it the least he could do to compensate for his outburst.

"So, are you enjoying Marquette?" she asked, sliding into her seat. "It must be quite a change for you after California."

"Yes," was all he said.

"Do you mean, 'Yes, it's a change', or 'Yes, you're enjoying it'?"

The waitress came before he could answer. He ordered them coffee and pie without asking Jessie what she wanted. He did not know why he had come here with her or why she had asked him. He had felt sorry for her at Christmas when Aunt Harriet had been ignorant to her, but now he thought he could see why she was not married. She seemed like the clinging type, and she was plain, and so sheltered by her mother that she apparently had nothing interesting to say.

"I think it's terrific you came to see your family," she said. "I'm sure they've been a great support to you; I can't imagine how hard it must be to get divorced."

He felt riled; his divorce was none of her business; nor did it have anything to do with why he had come to Marquette.

"I don't really know my family here that well," he said. "You must know them better than I do."

"No," said Jessie, "they're not really my family. My mother is Beth's cousin – I think Margaret invites us because she pities us being two lonely old maids."

"Still, they wouldn't invite you if they didn't care; that's something," said Theo, lighting another cigarette to help him relax; every few seconds his thoughts flashed back to his recent confrontation with the Blackmores. "I never really knew any family other than my mother; even Roy and Aunt Margaret I only met a couple times before."

"Still, they're your blood relatives. I love my mother, but she's not my real one; she didn't adopt me until I was twelve so it's difficult trying to think of all those people as my family. Not that I don't like them. I guess it's just hard to explain."

She felt muddled, tongue-tied. She wondered whether he thought it obvious why she had never married. She did not know what was wrong with her these days – why she felt so selfish regarding her mother. He must think she had some sort of Freudian psychological complex.

"I understand," Theo replied. He paused as the waitress brought the coffee and pie. In that moment, he decided to tell her – he felt he could trust her because she was adopted, so she might understand, and he had to tell someone, just to get the screams of that awful woman out of his head. "I understand because I was adopted too – by my stepfather. I always had my real mother, but I'm nothing like my stepfather. I always felt uncomfortable pretending to be his son, and since I never knew my father, I've never really felt as if I know who I am."

"I understand," said Jessie. "Sometimes I wonder what my life would have been like if my father hadn't abandoned me and my mother hadn't died."

"That's what I want to know," said Theo. "That's why I came to Marquette. I want to find out about my real father."

"Oh, does he live in Marquette?" she asked. Then she lowered her eyes and nervously cut her pie. She was pleased he was sharing his family troubles with her, yet she did not want to pry.

"No," said Theo. "He died back in '29. He committed suicide."

"Oh." She realized his penetrating eyes were waiting for her reaction, waiting for her to judge him because of a suicide in the family. "I'm sorry."

"Maybe it shouldn't matter since I never knew him," said Theo, "but I'd like to know what he was like and what brought him to killing himself."

"Sometimes," said Jessie – she uncharacteristically touched his hand because she saw the pain in his eyes, then pulled her hand away, fearing she was being too forward, "we miss people more because we didn't know them. I was just a little girl when my father went to Russia. He was supposed to send for us, and I remember for a long time my mother kept believing he would, but we never heard from him again. I only have a few memories of him, but everyday I wonder what happened to him. It was especially hard after my mother died because I had no one left who remembered him. I have a younger sister, but she can't really remember him at all, and she went to the orphanage after my mother died, so we've never been close."

Theo was too intent on telling his own story to listen to hers. "My mother won't talk about my father – she's ashamed of her 'indiscretion' as she calls it. So I came to Marquette to find his family. He has a widow here, and I have a half-brother and a half-sister I never met until today, and – "

"Until today?" Jessie exclaimed.

"Yes, I just came from their house. I went to meet them and they slammed the door in my face. I don't think my half-sister wanted to, but her mother was really angry."

"Oh, Theo, I'm so sorry," said Jessie, wishing she had the courage to touch his hand again. "No wonder you're so miserable. What are your brother and sister's names? I wonder whether I know them."

He told her their names. He told her every word he had exchanged with the Blackmore family. He ended by asking her whether he had been wrong to go to the house, and whether he should make another attempt or give up.

"No, you weren't wrong to go," she said. "At least, you're not wrong to want to know your family. You just surprised them is all – maybe you should have written them a letter first. But the question is do you want to see them again?"

"Maybe, after I get over the shock – they probably need to get over it too. But do you know them?"

"No, not really. I know Matilda, but only because her son took piano lessons from me several years ago. Her husband's name was Robinson – he died a few years ago, and then she moved back in with her mother. That must have been her son, Evan, that you saw get into the car. He couldn't play the piano to save his life. He must be in his twenties now."

Theo felt drained from the morning. He crushed his cigarette into the ashtray.

"Can I give you a ride home?" he asked. "I've probably kept you too long."

"No, that's all right, but I'll accept the ride."

Theo motioned for the waitress to bring the check; he handed her a five dollar bill and said, "Keep the change."

Since they had only had coffee and pie, Jessie knew the tip was generous. She saw how pleased Theo looked when the waitress's face lit up over his generosity.

"Maybe," she said, as he helped her with her coat, "you could write a letter to your sister, or even to her and your brother, though I don't know him. I don't think he lives around here actually. But you could suggest they get in touch with you without their mother being involved."

"That's a good idea," said Theo, but he was still uncertain.

They walked back down Washington Street to where Theo had parked Roy's car. Theo opened the car door for her. Jessie had never had a man help her with her coat or hold open a door; she had spent all her adulthood waiting on her mother.

"The streets look so bare since they took down the Christmas decorations," she said as Theo drove onto Front Street. "Turn here onto Baraga, and then take a left at the cathedral. January always seems like the most depressing month to me. There's nothing to look forward to for so long after Christmas."

"I think it's beautiful, even without the Christmas decorations," said Theo. "California is just dark and dead in winter; here you actually have seasons."

"I thought you said it was green in winter?" said Jessie.

"A little but not much," he admitted.

"I guess I'd like to see it just to compare the two," she said.

When they reached the house, Theo parked the vehicle in the yard.

"Would your mother like some company?" he asked. "It might cheer her up." He had hoped to spend the day with the Blackmores, but now it was not yet noon. He was supposed to be at Bill and Annette's for supper at five, and then he was going with them to see his first hockey game at the Palestra. He dreaded the empty hours until suppertime.

"Um, okay," Jessie said, "unless she's sleeping. She likes company because she doesn't get out much anymore, but since she's been sick, I don't know."

Theo followed Jessie inside. They found Mrs. Nabor in the living room.

"I'm sorry I was so long," Jessie told her.

"That's all right. We had a nice long visit. She just laid down for a nap about half an hour ago."

Jessie introduced Theo to her neighbor, then asked whether her mother felt any better.

"I think so," said Mrs. Nabor. "She wasn't as talkative as usual, but she had enough energy to reprimand me for not visiting more often. She kept going on about how long our families have known each other – she said the first time she remembers seeing my husband was when this was her Aunt and Uncle McCarey's house, and Joe was just a boy and came over to announce that World War I had ended. I don't know how she remembers such things. I sure can't."

"She has a remarkable memory," Jessie agreed.

After Mrs. Nabor left, Theo asked whether he might use the restroom. "I'm afraid I drank too much coffee," he said.

"Sure, I'll just go check on my mother in the meantime," Jessie replied.

Theo found his way to the bathroom. He felt he was imposing by being here when Thelma was ill; he decided he would quickly leave. He could always go to the library and read until suppertime. But when he came out of the bathroom, he found Jessie in the living room with her coat back on.

"Mother's awake, but really weak, and she has a bad fever. I think she better go to the emergency room. Would you mind driving us?"

"Not at all," said Theo, alarmed and relieved simultaneously.

"I'm sorry," Jessie said, "but since my car isn't working, I don't have any other way to get her there. It always scares me when she gets sick because of her multiple sclerosis. I worry about her becoming even more crippled up. I'll go dress her and then maybe you can help me get her down the steps."

"I'll go warm up the car and then come back in," Theo said. As he stepped outside, he remembered again how that nasty woman had called him a bastard, but now that Jessie and Thelma needed his help, his troubles seemed to matter less.

When Theo returned inside, Thelma was in her wheelchair. He held the door as Jessie wheeled her outside; then he helped Jessie get Thelma down the couple steps and into the car. Thelma seemed confused and kept calling him "Henry", but no one bothered to correct her. The emergency room proved to be full of people suffering with pneumonia, the flu, and tonsillitis. For an hour, Jessie tried not to cry as they waited to be admitted. Theo felt protective toward the poor girl who had no one but an old woman who was not even her mother. He knew how she was feeling, afraid her world was about to fall apart – as his had when Melinda left him. All he now had was his own aging mother – and soon she would be gone. He wondered whether he should just go home to her rather than trying to learn something he was not sure he wanted to know.

Finally, Thelma was admitted to the hospital. Jessie went with her to see the doctor. Theo sat in the waiting room for two hours, disgusted with the *Reader's Digest*'s watered down articles on his areas of scientific research. He had devoted himself to science, yet been forced into early retirement, his grants and funding taken from him, his whole life purpose gone. No wonder his wife and children had deserted him when he had overworked himself for so many years, and for what? Had his research made any difference in the world? Science had changed the way people lived, but old complications had been replaced with new ones. Now when it was too late, he realized relationships were what mattered. Why could he not have had a father to teach him that, instead of a power-hungry stepfather and a social climbing mother? But he knew a perfect father was only a dream; if his real father had cared about relationships, he would have married his mother, and his father's widow would not be screaming about how many 'bastards' his father had. From what he knew, his father had not been a good man, so what did he expect or hope to find?

When Jessie returned to the waiting room, Theo lay down his magazine. "They want to keep her overnight for observation," said Jessie. "I'm going to stay with her, so you can leave, but I really appreciate all the help you've been."

"You're welcome," he said. "I'll call you tomorrow to see how she is."

"Sure," said Jessie. "Mother will want to thank you herself when she feels better. I'll let her know how good you've been to us once she's less confused."

"All right," said Theo, wanting to say more, but not sure what.

It was almost five o'clock. He drove to Bill and Annette's house and tried to make conversation with them through dinner. He tried to be friendly, but he could tell they found him dull. Bill explained the rules of hockey to him on the way to the game. Seated in the bleachers, Theo tried to follow the puck around the rink, but the cheering crowd made him tired and his thoughts drifted. The chill rising from the ice reminded him of what a cold morning it had been until he met Jessie, and then he had felt a spark of warmth in his chest, the first such feeling in years.

When the game ended, he drove back to Roy's cabin, glad for the long drive, so he could be alone with his thoughts.

Thelma stayed in the hospital for several days. After she finally went home, she spent most of her time in bed. She complained constantly about her back hurting, and she could do little more than hobble from her bed to the bathroom. The doctor warned Jessie that the disease had now debilitated her mother enough that permanent bed rest would soon be required, and a bedpan would replace trips to the bathroom; this last illness had only hastened the inevitable.

That winter, Jessie frequently missed work to care for her mother. When she went to school, she usually got Mrs. Nabor or Beth to spend the day with Thelma. Occasionally Ellen would come for a few hours between classes or when she had a vacation from college; Jessie felt safe when Ellen was present since she was going to be a nurse; Ellen would check Thelma's blood pressure and monitor her heart, perhaps less for Thelma's health than Jessie's mental well-being. Once a week the good parish ladies of St. Peter's would look in on their invalid sister or a priest would bring her Communion; Thelma would jokingly tell them to go away because she did not need extreme unction yet; then Jessie would smile that her mother still had a sense of humor, but her heart cried because she knew the anointing would be needed soon enough.

That winter was the hardest Jessie had ever known. She longed for relief, yet when she hoped for an end to her mother's suffering, she felt guilty over her own selfishness. She told herself the silent, painful waiting was nothing compared to the empty future to come after her mother was gone.

She found comfort in Theo's friendship; he came a few times every week to inquire about Thelma's health; Thelma was flattered by the attention; Jessie wondered whether he had other intentions behind his visits. Sometimes he came in a morose temper, seeking sympathy, and to debate yet again whether he should contact his father's family. Jessie understood his obsession with the Blackmores, but she also thought he would be wiser to return to California and repair his relationship with his children. She did not understand why anyone who could be in California would stay in Marquette.

A few times, Theo tried to give Jessie a break from her worries by pressing Beth or Mrs. Nabor to stay with Thelma; then he would take Jessie downtown to the latest movie – he liked science fiction, and while she would have preferred to watch a love story with Warren Beatty rather than a green alien take over the earth, she was congenial to whatever he planned. One night, when they emerged from the theatre into a blizzard with subzero windchill, Jessie said,

"Theo, I bet you wish you were in California tonight." He replied, "Then I wouldn't be here with you."

These unlikely friends passed the long winter in this way until Easter week. A few days before the holiday, Thelma said she could not abide another minute in the house. For two days, she had sat up in her wheelchair without coughing, so after a little squabble, Jessie agreed to take her out.

"I want to go shopping downtown," Thelma said. "We both deserve a new dress for Easter, and we can get some candy for Henry, Beth, and Ellen. Maybe we could even send something to Jim and Lisa, at least a stuffed bunny for Margie."

"I don't think it will reach California in time for Easter," Jessie said.

"It doesn't matter – Margie's too little to understand about Easter; she'll enjoy it whenever it gets there. Nothing is better than pleasing a child, and she's the only little one in our family now. I think Beth has some great-nephews and nieces downstate – her brother Jeremy's grandchildren, but we lost touch with them years ago. Jeremy's the one who died in the mine disaster back in – "

Rather than listen to another of Thelma's family sagas about people who had lived and died long before Jessie entered the family, Jessie went to put on her coat. Then she got Thelma's coat on her, found both their purses, put on Thelma's shoes, put on her own shoes, found the car keys, went to warm up the car, then returned inside to fetch Thelma in her wheelchair. A fresh inch of snow was in the driveway. Jessie was sick of snow. Mr. Nabor was good enough to clean the driveway for them with his modern snowblower, but Jessie still had to shovel the steps, which was just too much at times on top of teaching school and caring for her mother. Snow was expected again tonight; she did not want to spend her few days of Easter break shoveling. Carefully, she helped her mother out of the wheelchair, praying no ice was hidden beneath where Thelma set her feet. Once her mother was in the car, she went around to her side, crawled in, started the engine, and asked where they should go shopping.

"How about Getz's?" said Thelma.

Getz's was at the bottom of Front Street.

"Didn't you want to go to Donckers too?" asked Jessie.

"Yes, I want to buy Easter candy. And I need to go to the bank so I can get some crisp new five dollar bills to put in my Easter cards."

Jessie did not see why it mattered whether people were given wrinkled money, but she knew better than to argue the point.

"Why don't we go to J.C. Penney instead of Getz's?" she said.

"Getz's always has a better selection," Thelma replied.

"But Penney's is right next to the bank and close to Donckers."

"True," said Thelma.

"I won't have to move the car twice then," said Jessie, although moving the car was less a problem than getting her mother and the wheelchair in and out of the car, and she knew her mother would wear herself out if they made multiple stops. Sometimes, Jessie felt more worn out from all the work of getting Thelma in and out of the wheelchair multiple times than Thelma did.

Thelma did not argue further. She was fantasizing about a stuffed bunny for Margie, and a hollow milk chocolate bunny for herself.

"Look at that," said Jessie when she found a parking spot right in front of J.C. Penney's.

"Yes, look at that," said Thelma, ogling the Easter candy display in Donckers's window.

Jessie parallel parked on the street, got out of the car, stepped over the spring slush, crossed to the passenger side, opened the back door to get the wheelchair out and open it up, then opened the front door and helped Thelma struggle over the curb and settle into the chair.

"Let's go to the bank first," said Thelma.

Jessie pushed the wheelchair down the street, maneuvering around little puddles and snowbanks.

"I still can't get over this building," said Thelma. "Louis Kaufman gave us a masterpiece when he had this bank built." Since the 1920s, Marquette's First National Bank had been housed in a giant structure of Indiana limestone resembling a Greek Temple; its bronze doors were elaborately carved; the human eye was dazzled by its Corinthian columns and its interior gilded walls and ceiling. "They say it was the most expensive building per square foot in the country at the time it was built. Did you know Louis Kaufman also headed the finance committee to build the Empire State Building?"

"Yes, Mother," said Jessie, used to her mother's constant ramblings. She pushed the chair through the door and into the bank lobby.

"Look at those chandeliers," said Thelma. "Each cost over a thousand dollars; that's still big money now, but think what it was forty years ago."

They went up to the teller's window. In her wheelchair, Thelma could barely reach the counter, but she insisted on making her transactions without Jessie's help.

As the teller processed Thelma's withdrawal and tried to find crisp five dollar bills for her, Thelma chattered, "You're so lucky to work in this beautiful building. I love coming here. I bet Peter White would have been pleased to see his bank housed in this beautiful place. You know, I met Peter White once when I was a little girl – he was a jokester – he told me he knew Paul Bunyan personally. Isn't that funny? Oh, those are beautiful crisp bills for my Easter cards. Thank you. Happy Easter."

The teller smiled politely. She was twenty, and ignorant that Peter White had founded the bank where she worked; as for Paul Bunyan, she had never heard of him.

Jessie spun around the wheelchair while Thelma carefully placed the crisp bills into her purse and chatted to acquaintances she saw in the lobby.

"Hello, Ethel; how are you? Yes, I'm feeling better. No use complaining. Hello, Frances. I love your hat. I feel much better; thank you for asking. Marvin, how have you been? I hope to see you at Mass on Easter Sunday."

Jessie pushed the wheelchair forward, knowing if she stopped, her mother would spend all day visiting.

"Should we go to Penney's now and get the candy last?" Jessie asked as they passed out the bank's door.

"Yes," said Thelma. "Oh, can you smell that? Spring is in the air – you can tell when the snow has that wet smell. Soon the streets will be like babbling brooks as the snow melts and trickles down into the sewers."

Jessie pushed her mother through the door of the Kaufman building that housed J. C. Penney's. She knew a side effect of her mother's multiple sclerosis and the drugs was a general feeling of happiness. She was glad her mother was enjoying this little excursion, as trying as Jessie often found her constant chattering; chances were it would be her mother's last outing.

"Now, I want to get you something new, a pretty dress maybe," said Thelma. "Not just something for school either, but something you can wear to parties."

"Mother, I never go to parties."

"Well, you go out to the movies. Something you can wear out with your gentlemen callers."

Jessie only had one gentleman caller if she could even regard Theo as such. She did not feel as hopeful as her mother about her future.

"What else should we get?" she asked.

"How about some pretty scarves for Beth and Ellen?" said Thelma. "And I noticed the other day that Henry's wallet is in a sorry state."

"Can I help you with anything?" asked the saleslady, accosting them before they could look around.

"Yes, we want to look at your scarves," said Thelma.

Jessie pushed the wheelchair in the direction indicated. The saleslady followed and suggested several different items, but Thelma fussed over each one, until she admitted, "You know, the only time Beth wears a scarf is over her head when she's fishing."

"That's true," said Jessie.

"Thank you anyway," Thelma dismissed the saleslady, whose frustrated look went unnoticed by her customer.

Jessie turned the wheelchair toward the dresses; they were halfway there when Thelma decided she wanted one of the scarves for herself, so they had to return to the other side of the store.

"But then what will you get for Ellen and Beth?" asked Jessie.

"Maybe we'll just get them some candy?" said Thelma.

"I'm not sure that's a good idea. You know Beth is trying to reduce."

"She always says she's trying, but it'll never happen; she has my Aunt Kathy's figure and worse. But we can get Ellen candy. We'll keep her sweet so she can find a husband."

Jessie ignored her mother's joke and tried to think of ideas for Beth's present so they would not have to spend an extra hour looking at everything in the store.

"How about a hat for Beth?" she said.

"Oh, an Easter bonnet's a wonderful idea," said Thelma. "Now if only there were a Fifth Avenue in Marquette so we could have a parade. I love when Judy Garland sings that song. I'd like to see that movie again. Fred Astaire and Ann Miller danced so beautifully together in it."

Jessie was not listening. She could never remember who was in what movie; unlike her mother, she did not read the magazines about the Hollywood stars; their glamorous lives had nothing to do with hers.

Thelma tried on various hats, looking in the mirror and making goofy faces at the ones she disliked until even Jessie finally laughed and said, "Mother, you could charm Khrushchev in that one."

Thelma smiled. "I guess if President Kennedy had sent me over to Russia, we could have avoided that whole missile crisis."

"I believe it," said Jessie, picking up another hat. "I think you should get that one for yourself and then this one for Beth."

"Now that I'm feeling better, I could wear this one when I go to church," said Thelma. "I'll get both of them. Now, we'll find you a dress."

Jessie hated buying clothes with her mother. Thelma would insist she try on each prospective dress until she began to feel claustrophobic from an hour spent in the changing room. Thelma thought the pink dress too pink, the yellow dress made Jessie look pale, the blue one made her look too old, the red one like a floozy, and the brown one like a schoolgirl. Green was finally settled upon because it "looks spring-like and spring is when young men think of love and marriage."

"No man will ever marry me," said Jessie. "I'm an old maid. I'll be thirty-seven this year."

"You never know," Thelma said. "Now let's go find Henry a wallet."

J.C. Penney had plenty of wallets. Thelma required one with a place for coins and photos because "Henry needs room to show off all his grandchildren's pictures. I'm sure Margie will have a brother or sister soon, and it won't be long before Ellen finds herself a husband."

"I don't think Ellen wants a husband," said Jessie.

"She only says that because she's afraid she won't meet the right man, but she has wife and mother written all over her."

Rather than argue, Jessie pushed the wheelchair up to the front counter while Thelma balanced the hat boxes, dresses, wallet, and scarf on her lap.

When everything was paid for and bagged up, Jessie asked whether Thelma would mind waiting by the door while she ran to the restroom.

"That's fine," said Thelma, content to sit by the door and watch the passersby through the window. She knew so many people in Marquette that she was always interested to see who was out and about.

Max Reynolds walked by – Peter White's grandson, if she remembered correctly. Then she saw Harry Cumming go into a store across the street. A nun hurried across the road, dodging traffic; Thelma could not remember her name although she had seen her at Mass a hundred times. There went Mary Dwyer – amazing to see her anywhere except at the cathedral; she was always over there cleaning with wholehearted devotion. And there was Barbara Specker, out shopping with one of her daughters.

Thelma was looking in the opposite direction when the man passed in front of Penney's window. Not until he came through the door did she see him. He looked straight at her, or so she thought. Too astonished to think straight, she blurted out, "Hello, Vincent!" He looked at her strangely. Had she sounded happy to see him? "Hello," he said politely, then brushed past her, and headed for the back of the department store.

He apparently did not recognize her. Had she been mistaken? Maybe it was not him after all. So many times she had thought she had seen him, only to realize it had only been wishful thinking, and then she had felt relieved to have been wrong. She hoped it had not been him. She strained her neck, trying to see him again. He was standing at one of the racks – his side profile visible. It had to be him – the same nose. He removed his hat, holding it in his hand, and revealed his thick red hair. With his free hand, he ran a finger over his eyebrow – she remembered that had been one of his idiosyncrasies, although she had forgotten it these past thirty years.

She hoped he had not recognized her. If he had, wouldn't he have fled – shouldn't he have done so out of shame for the past? Why after all these years did he have to see her when she had become so old, in a wheelchair of all things, her hair half-gray, and her face still so pale from her recent illness? And he looked so fine. His hair was as red as ever; he had scarcely gained a pound. Why should he still be so youthful compared to her? He could easily pass for forty.

He turned his head to speak to the same saleslady who had accosted her and Jessie when they entered the store. When Thelma heard his voice, she was certain he was Vincent – her husband, her husband for one night on Mackinac Island, until he was caught and had to go back to the wife he already had. He was examining the men's coats; she watched him move about the store; he looked at nothing for women, but that did not mean anything; the way he held his hat blocked his ring finger. Thelma wished she did not have so many darn packages to hold; otherwise, she would wheel herself over just to see whether he wore a ring. But would it matter? He might have the same wife, or another one he had bamboozled. She thought she had long ago forgiven him, but now, if she were not in a public place, she thought she would have given him a piece of her mind.

"Okay, let's go to Donckers," said Jessie, appearing and pushing the wheel-chair toward the door, blocking Thelma's view of Vincent. "I'll put the packages in the car on the way."

"All right," Thelma muttered.

As Jessie opened the car door, Thelma craned her neck to see whether he would come out of Penney's. She did not know why it mattered, but she longed for another look at him.

When they entered Donckers, Thelma said, "Just leave me here by the door. You go pick out the candy."

"Don't you want to look?" asked Jessie. "Are you feeling all right?"

"Just a little tired," said Thelma. She only wanted to look out the window, to wait for another sighting.

"I was afraid shopping would be too much for you," said Jessie. "I won't be long."

"Remember to get Margie's stuffed bunny," Thelma called after her, then took up scrutinizing the street with preying eyes. She heard Jessie asking the saleswoman for chocolate eggs and jelly beans, and finally, a fluffy blue bunny. Thelma ached for one last glimpse of Vincent, that handsome conniver; how she hated that bastard, still attractive, barely aged at all – he could probably still charm women half his age. Why had he remained so attractive while she had been stricken with illness? Had she really aged so much he did not recognize her? But it had been thirty years since they had eloped. Or had he completely dropped her from his memory? Had she been only one of so many women he had tried to swindle that he had forgotten her face and name? Scarcely a day passed when she did not think of him.

Then he appeared, stared in the window, admiring the boxes of chocolates on display. Thelma glared at him like a cobra trying to freeze its victim with its eyes, but the comparison did not work properly, for he was the real snake, and he could not see her through the reflection in the glass.

"Oh, I wish he'd go away," said the saleswoman. Thelma looked behind her to see the shopgirl staring at Vincent. "Really, Miss Hopewell," the girl said to Jessie, "that dirty old man comes in her all the time to flirt with me. It's disgusting – he's old enough to be my grandfather."

Jessie smiled sympathetically. Thelma turned back around in time to see Vincent walk down the street.

The saleswoman had called him a dirty old man. Thelma had thought him still handsome and charming. She knew he was a scoundrel, but he had been able to hide it better in his youth. Perhaps he had not aged as well as she had thought. She consoled herself by deciding she had spotted some wrinkles on his cheeks.

Jessie finished her purchases and wheeled her mother out to the car. Thelma did not even crane her neck to look for Vincent again. She just wanted to go home.

"Thank you for taking me shopping," she said once they were in the car.

"I hope you aren't too worn out," said Jessie.

"No, but I'll take a little nap when we get home." She was not tired, but she wanted to be alone with her thoughts.

"I'll wrap up the Easter presents then."

"Oh no, I'll do that later," said Thelma. "Except maybe if you want to wrap Margie's bunny and take it to the post office. Then it might still get to California before Easter."

"Sure Mother, if you don't mind being alone while I'm out."

"Oh no, I feel much better."

She did feel better except for her heart, still broken after thirty years.

Jessie helped her into the house, out of her wheelchair, and into bed, where she covered her in a quilt. Once Jessie shut the door, Thelma lay in shock for several minutes; then the tears came.

The saleswoman at Donckers had said Vincent came in there nearly everyday. Then he must be living in Marquette. He had a lot of nerve to show himself in the town where he had hurt her. She wondered whether he even thought about how he had hurt her? No, he had only married her to get her money; he was used to hurting women – after all, he had left his family to commit bigamy by marrying her.

She remembered how they had eloped to Mackinac Island, then how the next day Henry and Roy had come to rescue her, having found out Vincent was already married. Thelma had insisted Vincent had loved her. Beth had scoffed and told her, "Thelma, he was only after your money, and you'd do well never to think about him again." That had been easy for Beth to say when the only man she had ever kissed she had married. But for one night in her life, Thelma had known what it was to be a wife, to be loved as a woman, to lie in a man's strong arms, to be kissed passionately; even if that night had been a false communion, she could not forget it. It had been her awakening, a teasing taste of nectar she had never drunk again. When Vincent had gone to prison for bigamy, she had written him a letter of forgiveness. He had never replied; only then had she realized he never loved her. She suspected he had become a dirty old man; she wondered how much money he had gotten out of other women. She still did not wish to hurt him, but she felt righteous in her anger.

After a couple hours, Jessie came to check on her. Thelma decided to get up and sit in the living room. She knew she was a burden to her adopted daughter; she suspected her disease had stolen Jessie's youth, but perhaps that had also kept Jessie from being hurt by a man.

"I got Margie's bunny wrapped, but I didn't want to leave for the post office while you were sleeping," said Jessie. "I'll run over there now. I won't be long."

"That's fine," said Thelma. "I'm just going to read my new *Good House-keeping*."

Jessie was not gone five minutes when the doorbell rang. Thelma was startled; she had an awful premonition it might be Vincent. She strained her head toward the window, but her wheelchair did not let her see who was on the front porch.

The bell rang again. She wheeled herself over and opened the door.

It was Margaret and Harriet.

"Hello, Thelma," said Harriet. "We heard you were feeling better, so we thought we'd pay you a visit."

"We can't stay," said Margaret. "Eleanor dropped us off for a moment while she ran to the grocery store. We just wanted to bring you a little Easter cheer since you haven't been feeling well."

Margaret handed Thelma an Easter basket while Harriet said, "Eleanor's been taking us shopping. Isn't that sweet of her? She's a good niece. I wish I had a daughter to do things for me. I tell you, that daughter-in-law of mine – " she shook her head. Thelma wondered what the daughter-in-law would say about her mother-in-law, but she only smiled and said, "You didn't need to bring me anything. Thank you. You're so thoughtful, and such a pretty basket. Come in and sit down."

She set the basket on her lap and wheeled herself back into the living room.

"We'll just stay a minute – Eleanor won't be long," said Margaret, sitting down beside Harriet on the sofa.

"Where's Jessie?" asked Harriet.

"She just ran to the post office, but she should be back in a few minutes."

"It looks like spring is finally coming," said Margaret.

"So," said Harriet, uninterested in the weather, "I guess Jessie's going to marry Theo. Then you'll be part of the whole family, Thelma, rather than just Beth's relative."

"Where did you hear that?" asked Thelma. Margaret was equally surprised.

"I just assumed," said Harriet, "since Roy says they go out together every week."

"Oh, they're just friends," said Thelma.

"A man who constantly treats a girl to a night on the town," said Harriet, "is more than just a friend."

Thelma's tongue fluttered in her mouth, but she was too surprised to deny the rumor. She wanted Jessie to marry and have the normal life she had failed to gain, but how could Jessie marry Theo? That was ridiculous – he was too old for her.

"Well, I'm sure they'll tell us when they're ready," Margaret said to placate everyone, "that is if there's anything to tell."

"It'll be a shame if he doesn't marry her," said Harriet. "The girl must be expecting a proposal after all those dates."

"They haven't been going on dates," said Thelma, but then Margaret, who had been studiously staring out the window, said, "Here's Eleanor. We better go. Have a nice Easter, Thelma."

"You too," Thelma replied. "Thanks so much for the Easter basket."

Her guests went out the door, and before Thelma could gather her thoughts, Jessie returned.

"That was nice of them," Jessie said when she saw the basket Margaret and Harriet had brought. "I better make you some supper now, Mother. Theo will be here in an hour."

"So soon?" Thelma barked.

Jessie looked surprised by her tone.

"Yes, I told you he was taking me out to supper."

"I knew you were going to the movie, but not to supper too," Thelma fibbed.

"I told you on Sunday, Mother," Jessie gently scolded. "You're getting forgetful."

"I haven't been well," Thelma defended herself as Jessie went into the kitchen.

Thelma stared at the wall until she was called to eat. She hated that old busybody Harriet Dalrymple. As if Jessie would ever marry a man old enough to be her father. What advantage would there be in that? Why, when she was Jessie's age – she had to admit that when she had been Jessie's age, she had been terribly bored and seeking any possible escape from life's monotony. That was why she had let Vincent bamboozle her; would boredom cause Jessie to marry Theo?

While Thelma ate, Jessie went upstairs to change her clothes. Then Mrs. Nabor came over to spend the evening with Thelma. When Theo pulled the car into the yard, Jessie went outside. Thelma was relieved Theo did not come into the house; she feared she might say something she would regret; she had started to suspect Harriet was right.

That night while Theo and Jessie were at the movie, Thelma had a stroke. Jessie came home to learn that Mrs. Nabor had gone in the ambulance to the hospital with her mother. Mr. Nabor had been waiting to take Jessie to her mother's side.

Thelma's stroke was severe enough to keep her in the hospital for two weeks. The day she returned home, her speech was blurred, and she could scarcely use her right arm. She climbed into her own bed with the realization she would never leave it again. She decided it was time to prepare for her end.

That afternoon, Theo brought Thelma a "welcome home" bouquet. She said thank you, repressing her usual directness by not asking him why he was trying to butter her up. But when he asked Jessie which night she wanted to go out that week, Thelma said, "Oh, not this week please. I'm nervous about having her gone since I just got out of the hospital."

"I'll let you know once Mother has her strength back," Jessie told Theo.

"I'll stop by in a couple days then," said Theo, feeling disappointed.

The moment Theo was gone, Thelma decided there was no time to waste.

"You're not going to marry Theo, are you?" she blurted out.

Jessie's face paled.

"N-no, I – " she fumbled. "He – that is – he – he hasn't asked me to."

"And when he does ask you?" Thelma demanded.

"I don't know. I don't think he will."

"Jessie, if you truly love him, I'll give you my blessing, but I'm afraid you'll marry him just to escape the dull life you've had with me, and to avoid the loneliness you'll feel when I'm gone."

"Oh, no, Mother," said Jessie, clinging to the doorknob, wanting to disappear from the room. "I don't feel my life has been dull with you, and you won't be gone for a long time yet."

"Nonsense. We both know I won't be around much longer. I just don't want you to be frightened to be alone. You're an attractive girl – you have your whole life ahead of you, and you have – "

"I'm nearly forty," Jessie moaned.

"You're still young," said Thelma, "especially compared to Theo. I don't want you to make a mistake. When I'm gone, I want you to be happy."

"I don't want to think about when you're gone." Jessie began to cry; instead of leaving the room, she sat down on the bed.

Thelma found a tissue and wiped her daughter's eyes.

"I know you love me," she said, "but you have to think about when I'm gone. I'm grateful to you, but also sorry that all these years you've put your life on hold for me."

"I was happy to do it. You took me in when I had nothing. I – "

"I know," said Thelma, "and you've more than repaid me by being the best daughter. But Theo's much older than you. After years of taking care of me, I'm afraid you'll just end up taking care of him. You'll be old before you know it and have no chance left. I don't want that to happen to you. I want you to find some real happiness, not to be afraid to live so you'll feel safe."

Thelma's words frightened Jessie because they were true. At times, she had felt selfish and angry that she must care for her mother. Now she just feared being alone. She did not love Theo, but he was better than no one.

"I made mistakes in my life," Thelma said. She had intended to tell Jessie about Vincent, but now she decided it was best to let that story die with her; she did not want the pain she still felt to add to Jessie's sorrow. "I'm too old now to tell you about my mistakes, but I don't want you to make the same ones. I doubt I've been a very good mother to you, but I've always loved you."

"Oh, Mother, I know. I love you too," Jessie cried.

They were both crying now. Thelma choked on her words as she finished, "I knew what it was to be a little girl and lose a mother. I wanted to ease that pain for you all I could."

"You did, Mother."

"I tried for your sister too, but – "

"Don't feel guilty about that," said Jessie. "You did more for both of us than anyone could expect, more than anyone else tried to do."

"Thank you," said Thelma.

Jessie grabbed the box of tissues, and both laughed as they blew their noses and wiped their eyes.

"It's been a hard winter," said Thelma, "but spring is almost here."

Jessie collected the tissues and threw them in the wastebasket.

"Everything will be okay, Mother. Don't worry about me. You better take a nap now."

Thelma lay down and closed her eyes as Jessie closed her bedroom door. She hoped she had gotten through to the girl.

For the twenty years of her illness, Thelma had tried to enjoy what remained of her life, while preparing herself for when her time came. Now she had to prepare others – she hoped the seeds she had given Jessie would make her strong. She also hoped not to leave Jessie with a mess of a house to clean out.

She had bought her Uncle and Aunt McCarey's house thirty years before when her cousin Beth had married, and since then, she had added her own clutter to the McCareys' possessions. The thought of cleaning out the house had gradually become so overwhelming that boxes of belongings were relegated to the attic with the intention to some day sort them. Now Jessie carried down one box after another of a paper trail of forgotten receipts, bills, and other useless papers that went back nearly eighty years to when the house had first been built.

Thelma convinced Beth to help her sort through the boxes since many of the items belonged to Beth's parents, or even their grandparents. Here was Grandpa Bergmann's German Bible, Grandma Bergmann's cookbook, and forgotten letters in unreadable Italian from their Italian stepgrandfather Montoni's sister, whose name no one would have remembered if it were not signed to the letters. Here was a half-century of *Mining Journal* clippings – wedding, birth, and death announcements. Beth sorted through all these, taking what she wanted to keep or to send to her brother in Rome. Here were even a few of Beth and her brothers' toys, brittle and broken, which, after bringing back fond memories, were duly discarded.

One day, when Jessie was gone to school, and Thelma lay in her bed with mounds of paper littered around her so she could scarcely move, Beth pulled out a large packet from a small trunk that had been her mother's.

"Look at this – it has foreign stamps all over it," Beth said.

"Another unreadable Italian letter?" sighed Thelma, already having tossed away a dozen.

"No, it's addressed to my mother and postmarked from Germany."

"What's the year on it?" asked Thelma.

"1908."

"I wonder," Thelma mused. Beth opened the envelope to pull out a hefty stack of paper.

"It's a letter in English," said Beth, looking at the last page for a name. "It's from your father. I didn't know he ever went to Germany."

"Yes, he went when I was a little girl," said Thelma, reaching for the letter, but Beth was too busy turning over the pages to notice. Thelma laid her hand back in her lap. "I don't really remember when he went, except that it was right after my mother died. I stayed with your parents while he was gone. I didn't even understand where he went. I remember crying one day and asking your mother if my daddy were dead like my mother; she told me he had gone far away, but she promised he would come back."

"Why did he go?" asked Beth.

"You know, I never really thought to ask. Children are too involved in their own lives to ask the important questions."

"Well, let's stop cleaning for now and have lunch," said Beth, setting down the packet.

Beth went downstairs to make sandwiches. Thelma endured a few shouts from across the house about whether she wanted mayonnaise or mustard; she wanted both. Did she want her bread buttered? She did. What did she want to drink? Tea. Then she strained herself, hurting her back to reach across the bed for the packet from her father. She was curious now why her father had made that long, and to her, frightening trip, so many years ago.

> November 2, 1908
> Dear Kathy,
>
> Please tell everyone back home I am fine. I know you and mother must be worrying. I don't know when I'll be back yet, maybe another month or two, but I know you will take good care of Thelma until I return. I am well and content with my journey so far. Tell Mother I am sorry I have not written to her. Please share my letter with her.
>
> I have had many wonderful adventures since I crossed the Atlantic. I left New York and landed in Liverpool, then traveled from there to Amsterdam where I began my land journey through the Netherlands and into Germany, a collection of little kingdoms and duchies spread across Central Europe. I knew father had told me he was from Saxony, but I never fully realized it was a separate kingdom from the rest of the German speaking world. The names and distinctions of all these areas can make your head ache. I have passed through Munster, Westphalia, Hanover, Brandenburg, Brunswick, and Saxony, and those are just the places whose names I can remember. They are beautiful, rich lands of rolling hills, along the Rhine, Moldau, and Elbe Rivers, and castles, cattle, and beer galore enrich the land. There is a beauty here distinct from our own Upper Michigan, yet as rich and breathtaking. I have taken a few photographs, but they will never do justice to the land.

"I wonder what happened to those photographs," thought Thelma, hoping to find them amid the attic's clutter. She read on about her father's journey, his attempts to understand German, the quaint little towns where he had stayed, the history of Saxony – not history then but now history for Thelma – of what people said of King Frederic Augustus III, who at the time of her father's writing was a new king, ten years before he would be forced to abdicate his throne following the First World War; she remembered the war had nearly broken her father's heart when he thought what his brave German people were reduced to. Thelma read of the beautiful Dresden china he had bought and planned to bring home, and she realized that delicate old dish Beth owned had been brought back by her father for her aunt, although neither Thelma nor Beth had known before where Beth's mother had gotten it. Most interesting of all was when Karl had found in Dresden the family of his German immigrant father.

> You will find it hard to believe, but perhaps the best part of my trip was when I found in Dresden, our father's brother, Uncle Rudolph, who is ninety years old and quite feeble, but still in his right mind. He lives with his grandson, Hans and Hans's wife, Wilhelmina. Uncle Rudolph only speaks German, but Hans has been to the university and actually is a schoolteacher of English – not good English, I'm afraid, but well enough to understand me and to translate for his grandfather. Uncle Rudolph has a good memory and says I look just like our Grandfather Bergmann did at the same age. He told me all kinds of stories about our father as a boy, and he showed me the house where they grew up. I wish, Kathy, that you could meet our uncle. You would love him. Even at such an advanced age, he is so much like Father. I have always regretted that Father died before you had a chance to know him; if you could meet our uncle, you would have some idea of what Father was like. I have taken pictures of all our family here so you can know them.
>
> Uncle Rudolph had a hard life, working as a weaver for sixty years. His son, who died last year, had the same trade. They worked hard to put Hans through school, and he is a bright young gentleman. He and Wilhelmina are expecting their first baby in a few months, so Uncle Rudolph is excited at the thought of his great-grandchild. Imagine living so long, and we think Mother a marvel at her age.

"Grandma did live well into her eighties," Thelma recalled. She read about more people her father had met, people who during his short time overseas became incredibly important to him, as if he had found an entire new world, a new life, or perhaps more accurately, reclaimed an old one. "And all these people must now be dead," she thought with amazement, "except perhaps our cousin Hans's child, who would be just a year younger than Beth." Thelma felt an incredible interest in all these people, wondering what they would have been like, all of them relatives she may have known and loved. She wondered what would have happened if her Grandpa Bergmann had never left Germany; he would have married there, rather than met her grandmother in the United States. Perhaps then, Thelma realized, she never would have existed, or perhaps she would have been a German girl, and different in so many ways, but that was a silly way to think. It was like questioning God about why things happened as they did, although she could not help wishing some things had been different, especially for Jessie's sake. She still felt she had been a bad mother to permit Jessie's sacrifice of caring for her.

"Here we are." Beth broke Thelma's train of thought by carrying in a lunch tray. She set the glass of milk on the bedside table and arranged the silverware.

"I was just reading my father's letter," said Thelma.

"Oh, what does it say? Anything interesting?"

"I didn't finish it yet. I'll read you the rest, and you can read the beginning later."

Beth saw several pages on the bedspread which Thelma had already read. She had no desire to spend time reading them when there was so much cleaning and sorting to get through this afternoon. Thelma launched into reading the letter, stumbling over her father's poor penmanship. Beth soon quit paying attention, while reminding herself to mail some of those old newspaper clippings to Michael, along with Grandma's old catechism, which he would be sure to want, even though it would probably cost a fortune to send it to Italy. She did not hear a word as Thelma finished reading the letter out loud.

> Finally, I had a hankering to see the Alps, and then go down to France or Italy along the Mediterranean and take a ship from there back home. I'm writing from Geneva now, and I will start over the mountains tomorrow by train.
>
> On the way here, I passed through the famous Black Forest, which will always be one of the most memorable experiences of my life. I traveled in what we would call a stagecoach in English, and I was fortunate enough to sit by the window. It was early morning, and the other passengers were all asleep. The sun was just beginning to peek through the trees, although the forest is so black from the closeness of the trees that I imagine little light ever penetrates into it. It was beautiful, although stark because it is nearly winter, and the leaves have all fallen. I had imagined it would be deep, vibrant greens, or multicolored as the autumn leaves had been in October while I was in Saxony. Instead, the trees were tall, bare, foreboding. A snowfall the night before had coated the earth and all the branches. The grayness of the morning dawn, the fog floating just above the ground

– I don't know how to describe it – almost as if we were riding upon a cloud, or as if it were the very dawn of time, and I could forget the stagecoach, my modern clothes, the ticking of my pocket watch, and imagine myself back in an ancient Europe once completely covered by trees far more numerous than people. Here our ancestors, perhaps two thousand years ago, before the light of Christ spread across the land, must have knelt and worshipped Odin and Thor, among their sacred oaks. Kathy, you may think me blasphemous to dwell on such things, but you share with me our mother's lively Irish imagination so I hope you will understand what I mean.

I guess what I am trying to say is that I came to Europe seeking consolation for the loss of my dear wife, Aino, but her loss has resurrected in me the pain of other losses, of my best friend, Ben, and especially of our father, which though forty years ago, was the severest blow of my life from which I have never completely recovered. I guess I have been trying to recapture his memory by taking this trip. The puzzle pieces of my life all seemed to come together in that forest when I realized what humanity had come from, and not just humanity, but the history, the origins of my own family – my father and Uncle Rudolph and their father, born back in the eighteenth century, and then their ancestors who lived in the German forests long before the advent of civilization. I now understand myself as a link in the great chain of human generations; I realize the progress men have made, not just from stone tools and wearing animals skins to driving a locomotive and having electric light. Humanity has gone from worshiping trees and foolish gods to a better understanding of science and man's place in the universe. I realized what the theologians must have known all along, that none of this world is an accident, but everything is part of some incredible plan, and this realization has humbled me. I believe God does have a plan, and my ancestors were part of it, our father coming to America was part of it, the loss of my loved ones are part of it, and my dear little girl, Thelma, will add to its fulfillment, and I intend to do all I can for her. Kathy, we have a remarkable family, the human family, and my life is reinvigorated with the realization of it. Perhaps you will think my letter crazy. I do not care. Tell my little girl I love her. Tell everyone I am well and not to worry about me, although I know you all worry.

Love, Karl

"That's a sweet letter," said Beth, catching only the last couple sentences, but wanting to pretend she had heard it all.

"My poor father," said Thelma. "He must have really suffered in those months after my mother died. She passed away the same year he wrote it."

"You better eat your soup," said Beth. "It must be almost cold now."

"I will," said Thelma.

"I have to use the restroom," said Beth. "I'll be back in a minute to clean up."

Thelma was thankful for a moment alone. The soup had grown cold, but she slurped it anyway. She wondered whether her father had been right, and that if there were a plan for everything, then perhaps she had not been such a bad mother. Her father had talked about the progress of the family and his hopes for her – at that time, perhaps he had not realized how odd she was. She had not realized herself that she was odd until she became interested in boys, and discovered none would come near her. She wished her father could have lived to see his granddaughter, even if Jessie were adopted. If God had a plan, then bloodlines did not matter. God could bring about His plans however He chose. She had always felt it was so, but now she knew her father had thought the same way – so many times she had wished he were still alive so she could ask his advice – he had always been so wise and good-natured, even when she knew she was a trial to him with her strange fancies and her constant chattering. She had never doubted he loved her, but this letter confirmed it. It also made her feel her conversation with Jessie had been right, that Jessie was loved, and rather than settle for what came easy, she must seek what mattered, just as her father had gone to Germany to search for something he did not understand, only to find more than he expected. She felt now she had done all, little as it was, that she could in this life; she had to trust Jessie would be fine. She was prepared to see her parents again.

While Thelma had been in the hospital, Theo had worried constantly. Jessie had had little time to spend with him, and so he began to question again what he was doing in Marquette. With the arrival of spring, Roy began to spend all his time in the woods or at the Club, making Theo realize he had worn out his welcome. He also began to miss his children, and without Melinda to interfere anymore, he wondered whether he might be able to reconcile with them. But two things still kept him in Marquette – a hope that if Thelma died, Jessie would marry him and return with him to California – but he could do nothing about that until Thelma died – and still, the haunting desire to make peace with his own infamous origins and the father he had never known.

He decided to look up the Scofield Blackmore listed in the city directory. He did not know whether the man were his relative, nor did he know whether he could bear the same rejection he had received from his father's widow and her children; he had not dared to contact them again. But he did know he could not leave Marquette until he made this last attempt to understand his father, and by extension, himself.

He decided it would be safest to telephone first.

When he dialed the number from the tavern in Big Bay, a woman answered. When he asked for Scofield, she told him her husband was at work, but she could take a message.

"I – um, I – um." Theo knew he sounded like an idiot. "I believe I knew your husband's father. I need to talk to him about something important."

What he said was not exactly true, but it was breaking the ice. He could not tell this woman he thought he was Scofield's brother, but by mentioning Scofield's father, it might prepare the man for their meeting.

"I can give him a message," she replied, "or you can call back. He'll be home after five-thirty."

"Actually, I need to see him in person," Theo said. "Can I stop over tonight?"

She hesitated, then said, "He should be available after supper, say about six-thirty. May I tell him who called?"

"My name's Theo. I'll see you then."

He hung up the phone, afraid to tell her more from fear it would make Scofield Blackmore, whoever he was, slam the door in his face.

Theo looked at his watch. It was four-thirty now. All morning he had intended to call, yet kept putting it off. Then at one o'clock, there had been no answer so he had gone back to the cabin to help Roy plant his garden. Now he was a dirty mess. Two hours of agony had to be gotten through until the meeting, but if he went back to his camper to clean up, and then drove into town, that would eat up most of the time.

As he washed up, shaved, changed his clothes, and combed his hair, he silently rehearsed what he would say.

When Roy saw him getting ready to leave, he joked, "I suppose you're going to see Jessie again? When are you going to ask that girl to marry you?" Roy thought Theo too old for a pretty girl like Jessie, but he would not say so. He just wanted some hint of Theo's intentions so his mother and Aunt Harriet would quit pestering him for information.

Theo, however, ignored his cousin's remarks and finished dressing. He decided to wear a suit so he would be taken seriously, despite Roy telling him he looked "like a dude." Soon he was on the road – well, barely; he was too nervous not to weave down the highway, but he made it to town at breakneck speed, found Scofield's house, realized he was twenty minutes early, thought, "The heck with it," climbed out of his vehicle, tried not to tremble, and walked up to the door of a little box-shaped house. He could tell the owners were not prosperous; they could not be closely related to his Blackmore family.

Theo rang the doorbell and cleared his throat. When a young man opened the door, Theo tried to speak evenly. "Hello, I'm looking for Scofield Blackmore."

"That's me," said the man. "What can I do for you?"

"I'm Theo Rodman. I called earlier," he said, almost apologetically, nearly wishing he had not come, wondering whether he should have given a different last name. "I told your wife I would stop by to talk with you because I knew your father."

A young woman just over twenty peered around her husband's tall shoulder, while a little girl screamed "Mom!" inside the house.

"Yes, he's the man I spoke to. I can tell by his voice," the woman said.

"Go see what's wrong with Celeste," Scofield told his wife without turning his eyes from the stranger at his door. Then he stepped onto the little porch and shut the door behind him.

"What do you want? How did you know my father?"

Theo sized up Scofield. The man was thin but obviously strong. He seemed to shake from nervous anger. Theo feared he had made a bigger mistake coming here than he had by going to his father's house.

"Was your father Lysander Blackmore?" Theo quickly spit out.

"Yes," Scofield scowled, "but I never knew him. He died when I was little, and I was his bastard anyway, so I can't tell you anything about him."

The young man was hostile, but Theo sensed guarded pain behind his anger.

"What's it to you?" Scofield asked as Theo paused to choose his words.

"Actually," Theo said, fumbling in his pocket for a cigarette, "I never knew your father."

He made a peace-offering of a cigarette to his half-brother.

"No thanks," said Scofield.

"It's because I never knew your father," Theo said, "that I wanted to see you. I was hoping to find out something about him."

"Then you've wasted your time," said Scofield, turning to go back inside.

"Wait!" Theo said. "I came because Lysander Blackmore was also my father."

The sentence nearly made Scofield walk into the closed door. As he turned back around, he looked like a brick had hit him in the face.

"What?" he asked. He sat down on the steps, his lean, athletic frame looking like it would nearly collapse.

"I guess," said Theo, daring to sit down beside him, "that we're both his bastards, only I was born before he married his wife."

"That old bitch," Scofield said.

"Yes, I can't say she was too pleasant when I met her," said Theo.

"Where've you been all these years?" Scofield asked. "I've never seen you around town."

"Well, our father," Theo started, thinking how strange the words sounded, "refused to marry my mother. He got her in the family way when they were really young; she was a maid for the Blackmores, so his parents didn't think her good enough to marry him. She says she thinks he loved her, but just wasn't strong enough to oppose his parents. That's what my mother told me anyway. My grandparents didn't want their good name linked with scandal, so they sent my mother to some relatives in Chicago, where I was born. Then she met and married my stepfather and we moved out to California where I grew up."

Theo did not mention his stepfather's social status, his own failure as a husband and father, or his expensive education and impressive career. He could wait to tell all that if they truly came to behave like brothers.

"My mother," said Scofield, "was our father's mistress for several years. She thought he would leave his wife to marry her, but when she got pregnant, he refused. Her last name was Scofield, so when I was born, she gave me both her last name and his to get revenge. I suppose he could have sued her for libel, but he didn't. Then he committed suicide a few years after I was born."

"Yes, in '29," said Theo. "My aunt who lives in Marquette told my mother. She said everyone thought it was because he lost so much money in the stock market crash."

"I don't know," said Scofield. "I guess I always hoped he was ashamed of himself. But I never suspected he had other bastards. My mother told me he was a conniver and a cheat, but I didn't know he was as bad as he seems to me now. I wonder how many more bastards he had. No wonder his wife is such a bitch."

Theo actually now felt some pity for that old woman; she was not angry at Scofield or him, but at their father, still angry more than thirty years after his death; what a miserable life their father must have led her.

Scofield stared at his shoes. Theo put out his cigarette and lit another.

"So," he said, "we're brothers."

"Yeah," said Scofield. "Feels funny. We should have always known each other but never did."

"You've got a wife and kid?" asked Theo.

"Yeah, Carol Ann is my wife, and my little girl is Celeste. How about you?"

"I've got a boy and a girl. They're both grown up with kids of their own. My wife and I are divorced."

"So – " Scofield hesitated, "what do we do now?"

Theo saw the agony in his brother's intelligent eyes. They were the only striking feature in an otherwise plain face.

"I don't know," said Theo. "I guess I just came to Marquette because I wanted to know something about my father. I went to talk to his wife and kids, but they slammed the door in my face."

"Me too," Scofield grumbled.

"Is your mother still alive?"

"No, she died years ago."

"I'm sorry," said Theo. "Mine's seventy-five. She says she's too old now to talk about the past."

"Hmm," said Scofield. "You staying in town long?"

"I've been here since Christmas, but I was too nervous to look you up sooner, especially after the reception the other Blackmores gave me. I wasn't even sure whether you were a relative. My mother's family is here, so I've been staying with them."

"You could stay with us," said Scofield, "only we haven't much space, just one bedroom and another room hardly more than a closet for our little girl. Still, I'm glad you looked me up. I never knew I had a sibling, other than his two legitimate kids who apparently want nothing to do with me."

"Our father probably hurt them as much as us by running around with other women," said Theo.

"Maybe, but at least they're legitimate," said Scofield, who felt less charitable. "When are you going back to California?"

"I don't know," said Theo, putting out his cigarette.

"Well, stop by again some time. Maybe we could have you over for supper."

"I'd like that."

"Do you have a phone number?"

"No. Actually I'm staying up on the Big Bay Road with my cousin; he doesn't have a phone. I could just stop by some evening. I don't want to be any trouble."

"Sure," said Scofield. "Anytime."

Theo paused. He wanted another cigarette, but he did not think he would stay long enough to smoke it.

"If you ever come out to California," he said, "you should look me up."

"Yeah?" said Scofield. "I might do that. I have some friends out there too. I've thought about moving out there since the only job I can find in this town is at the grocery store, and I'm getting sick of that. I'd probably be better off where everyone doesn't know my past."

"It's been the opposite for me," said Theo. "My mother married a rich man and let everyone think I was his son. I had all the advantages, except a real father. My stepfather didn't care one jot for me, but through him I know some powerful people. If you came to California, I could probably find you a decent job."

Theo did not know whether it were right, but he felt he should encourage this young man who was his brother. He pitied Scofield, who seemed the personification of melancholy; he could scarcely imagine how difficult it must be to live in this small town with everyone knowing your family scandals. Theo felt his own life had been a failure, but since it was almost over, he would like to do something for his little brother who was still relatively young.

"Well, I'm glad you came over," said Scofield, not knowing what else to say.

"Let me give you my address," said Theo, pulling his card from his wallet.

"Thanks," said Scofield, impressed to see the Ph.D. after his brother's name.

"I'll stop by in a few days after you're better used to the idea of me," Theo said.

Scofield stood up and shook his hand. Then Theo walked to his car and climbed in. When he looked back at the house, his brother had already gone inside.

He wanted to collapse there in the car, to bury his face in his hands over the silent agony he had endured until the small gain of this hour, but he would not risk Scofield's family seeing him through the window. He pulled the car out of the driveway and drove up and down the streets. He was unsure where to go until he turned up Seventh Street and decided to drive into Park Cemetery.

Somewhere in this graveyard his father lay buried – he did not know where – his father's parents were also buried here. And here rested Grandpa and Grandma Dalrymple, who had died in California, but requested they be laid to rest in the town they considered home. Theo remembered when he had visited Marquette years ago before he started college, his mother had taken him here and shone him the stone of his great-grandfather, engraved as "Arthur Dalrymple, who was born in Pictou, Pictou, Nova Scotia" and followed by the dates. The birth date had been nearly a century and a half ago. Here his mother would also someday rest; she had purchased a burial plot beside her parents' graves. Theo thought it odd she had chosen to be buried here rather than with her husband in San Francisco. Once she was gone, Theo knew it would not be long before he joined her. He felt he had become an old man now, but with old age had come sympathy and understanding for life's struggles; most people just managed the best they knew how – why his father had lived the way he had, that was between him and his Maker. That Theo's wife and children had rejected him he was now equally indifferent to. He felt his life almost pointless, but he would go on for a little while longer, if only because he now had a younger brother who deserved some happiness, whom he felt he should look after. If not for Scofield, he would lie down on this cool earth beside his family graves and just wither away.

Then he remembered Jessie. He thought she still cared about him. He pulled the car out of the cemetery and drove to her house.

When he stepped onto her front porch, he did not know what he would say – he feared the moment she opened the door, he would spoil everything.

"Hello. Come on in," she said, as if it were an ordinary visit. "We just finished supper and I have to give Mother her pills. If you want to wait in the – "

"No," he grasped her wrist and pulled her onto the porch.

"Theo, what's wrong?" she asked, startled by the queer expression on his face.

"Jessie, I have to talk to you. I – "

"What's wrong?" she repeated. "You look upset. You – did you go see your brother – is he your brother? Is that what's wrong?"

"Yes, I saw him. He – oh, just forget about him for a minute. Jessie, you're the one who matters to me, the one I want to be with. Jessie, will you marry me?"

She trembled a moment, then tenderly yet decidedly pulled her hand from his.

"Jessie, please," he begged, but his face crumpled in accepted defeat.

"Theo, I care about you, but I – " How could she explain?

"Why? You know I'll take care of you. I – "

"You've been very good to me," she said. "That's why I don't want to hurt you. I don't want to give you the wrong idea. I'm sorry if I already have."

"Can't you even think about it?"

"I have – lots. But – I can't."

"Why?" he repeated.

"You're hurting now; you're lonely." Her words stung her tongue as she unwillingly said them. "I think you love me only for what I could do for you, because you think I'll make you happy. I don't think you've considered what will make me happy. I'm sorry – I can't give up my freedom for you. I – "

"You'll have freedom with me," Theo said; he could not see what freedom she had now caring for her mother. "I can give you everything you want – money, clothes, high society life, trips, a beautiful home."

"Those are just things, not the same as freedom. I don't want to go from being Thelma Bergmann's daughter to Theo Rodman's wife. I want the freedom to be myself."

He wanted to protest, but he could not think of any further arguments. He knew she was right. All these months he had fantasized about how she might fix his life. He had told himself that if he spent money on her, she would feel she owed him. Until today, he had thought himself entitled to her, but now he realized how he had been self-interested without considering her well-being.

He stared stupidly at her, trying gracefully to accept his defeat. When he could think of no appropriate parting words, he turned and walked down the porch steps.

Jessie thought she should call after him, but she knew if she did, it would only be from guilt over having hurt him. She hoped he would be okay, but she could not sacrifice herself for another's happiness. She would keep the rest of her vigil with her mother, and then, whatever she did, Theo would not be part of it.

He went to the car and did not look back. Between clenched teeth, he told himself, "I'm going to be okay."

He did not cry, nor collapse in agony, nor long for death. He felt hungry. He drove downtown and parked at the bottom of Front Street. He went into the Jet Grill and ordered a cheeseburger. He sat in a booth and wondered how his life had deteriorated. His life had always been pathetic; he had always lied to himself, always hid behind the glamor of society, a marriage of convenience, a prestigious job. None of those things mattered to him now – he did not believe they had ever mattered.

As he ate his cheeseburger, a short, stocky, mustached man slid out of a booth and brought his bill up to the counter. While the waitress rung up the bill, a young boy of seven or eight crawled out of the same booth and wrapped his arms around the man's waist, laying his head on his father's protruding paunch. The dad wrapped his arms around his son, patted the boy's back, and then after pocketing his change from the waitress, gently pushed his son toward the door with an affectionate mussing of the boy's hair. As father and son passed his booth, Theo turned his head, ashamed to have observed them, not wanting to show his envy. All he had sought was – not love from his father, an impossibility – but simply hope that his father might have been affectionate toward him if given the chance. From what Scofield had told him, Theo suspected his father never would have loved him. Love always seemed to escape him, no matter for whom he cared.

He was no longer hungry. He left the cheeseburger half-eaten, dropped a couple dollar bills on the table, and went out to the car.

When he reached Big Bay, he parked the car and went into his camper.

After a few minutes, Roy knocked on the camper door.

"I heard you pull up. I've been waiting for you," said Roy, entering when Theo did not open the door.

"I'm leaving tomorrow," said Theo, from the chair where he was sitting, staring into the dark night. "I know I'm in your way, and now even Jessie doesn't want me around. I guess I'll just go where I'm not a burden to anyone."

Roy did not know what to say to this. He already had a prepared speech he had rehearsed for the last two hours. "Henry came up a little while ago to bring you some news. Your son called my ma's house today."

Theo barely listened.

"I hate to tell you this," said Roy, "but your mother died this morning."

After a moment of silence, Roy added, "Your son wants you to come home. He said to tell you that your family needs you; he and your grandchildren miss you."

In his anguish, Theo had nearly dismissed his children, but now he felt the irony of his son's words. He felt sad that his mother had passed away, but even more, he understood that a son needed a father. However useless a father he had been, he wanted to try harder now.

"I'll go down to the Thunder Bay Inn and call my son," said Theo. He went out to the car without another word.

Theo left early the next morning, determined to drive nonstop to California. He made it in time for his mother's funeral, but he went home to rejoin the living.

In early autumn, the *Mining Journal* ran the following obituary:

Miss Thelma Bergmann, age 60, died this past Tuesday following a lengthy illness. She was born in Calumet, Michigan to Karl and Aino (Nordmaki) Bergmann on August 15, 1903. Miss Bergmann moved to Marquette in 1928. She was a well known piano teacher in the area for many years. She was also a member of St. Peter's Cathedral and active in the Altar Society and Lady Maccabees. Miss Bergmann is survived by a daughter, Jessie Hopewell, and a cousin, Mrs. Henry (Beth) Whitman, both of Marquette. Funeral arrangements are pending with the Tonella Funeral Home.

The day after her foster mother died, Jessie was still in shock. She had long desired and feared the day she would know freedom. Now she just wished she could have her mother back.

She lay in bed late that morning, exhausted with grief. When she finally got up, she burst into tears, not knowing what to do because for years every free minute had been spent caring for her mother. Yesterday, she stayed busy making the funeral arrangements and being consoled by Henry and Beth. This afternoon, she would see the family again, but right now, she had nothing to do except suffer amid the unearthly silence of the house. She cried a little, then got dressed and tried to think what she could do to get through the day. She managed to pour herself a bowl of cereal, but her thoughts were so distracted, the cereal grew soggy before she ate it. She was about to drain and throw the cereal away when someone knocked at the door.

She was surprised to find her sister standing on the porch.

"Hello, Lyla," she said, too shocked to know what more to say. Lyla had gone to the orphanage when Thelma had been unable to find someone to adopt her. For several years, Jessie still saw her sister; Thelma had invited Lyla for holidays and given her gifts, and then when Lyla had left the orphanage, Thelma had supplied her with money to attend a secretarial program at the college, but Lyla had flunked out. After that, Thelma had refused to help her anymore. Since then, the two sisters had rarely seen each other, except to pass on the street or in a grocery store aisle.

"I'm sorry to hear about Miss Bergmann," said Lyla. "I came to see whether I can do anything for you."

"Oh," said Jessie. "Thanks." She was pleased to feel there remained some sisterly feeling between them. "Would you like to come in?"

"How are you holding up?" Lyla asked, stepping into the living room and plopping down on one of Thelma's doily covered chairs. She ogled the fancy furniture, although it had been thirty years since Thelma had redecorated the house. A jar of mints was on the coffee table. Lyla rarely spent money on frivolities like candy, so she took the opportunity to pop a couple mints into her mouth.

"I'm okay," said Jessie, trying to believe she was. "I knew it would eventually happen since she had multiple sclerosis for so long."

"It's too bad," said Lyla, groping for other words. "And what will you do now?"

"I don't know." Jessie thought aloud more than expressed any definite plans. "I thought maybe I'd move downstate. Maybe I could find a job as a music teacher down there. I'd like to be where there are more museums and concerts. Marquette has always felt too small for me."

"Yeah, it's probably for the best then," said Lyla, helping herself to more candy. "You're finally free from her after all those years of being her nursemaid."

"I didn't mind," said Jessie. "She took care of me during plenty of illnesses."

She wanted to talk to someone about all the conflicting emotions she had felt while caring for her foster mother, but she did not think Lyla would understand.

"Well, I suppose it was worth it for you," said Lyla, appraising the furniture and knickknacks. "I mean, you'll get the house and everything now. It's the least you deserve after what she put us through."

"What do you mean?" asked Jessie.

"I mean, she destroyed our family," said Lyla. "She had no right to adopt you or to stick me in an orphanage and force us to be Catholics when we were Finnish Lutherans."

Jessie was unprepared for her sister's words. But she understood her jealousy; she knew she had been more fortunate than Lyla. She had not even considered whether her sister would be part of her future once Thelma was gone. Yet she had always felt guilty that she had been adopted over her sister; she tried to apologize and to justify the past.

"Lyla, Miss Bergmann only tried to help us. Mama didn't even take us to the Lutheran Church after Papa went to Karelia. Our family was already broken up when we met Miss Bergmann."

"Don't try to defend her!" Lyla exploded. "Papa left to find us a better life. He was going to send for us. It's not his fault he was blind enough to believe communism would be better. Lots of Finns went over there. And we couldn't help it that Mama died either. But Miss Bergmann broke up our family by separating us."

"But it wasn't Miss Bergmann's fault," Jessie replied, her head aching. She did not have strength to argue right now. "When Mama died, what else could

Miss Bergmann do? She didn't know where Papa was; he was probably dead by then. Miss Bergmann did the best she could to find you a home. She asked lots of people to adopt you before you were finally sent to the orphanage."

"She could have adopted me herself," said Lyla. "What right did she have to send me there?"

"Lyla, it's not her fault," Jessie repeated. "She always remembered you. She always gave you presents at Christmas and your birthday. She even tried to help you go to college."

"Big deal. That's nothing compared to what she did for you!" Lyla shouted. "Sure it's fine for you. You got all her money; what did I ever get?"

Jessie was astonished. She had felt bad for her sister, but she did not recognize this loudmouthed, threatening woman. No place could exist in her life for this kind of a sister. "You didn't come here for my sake did you, Lyla?" she said. "You just think you can get some money out of me. You don't care about Miss Bergmann or me."

"Not about her I don't," said Lyla. "I deserve something from her for how she broke up our family."

"I'm not giving you any money when you're so rude. I think you better leave now," said Jessie, standing up while trying to hold back her tears.

"I don't want your money!" Lyla hollered. She jumped to her feet, her legs banging against the coffee table and knocking the candy dish on the floor. For a second, Jessie was afraid her sister would vault over the table to take a swing at her.

"I think you better leave," Jessie repeated, her voice flinching as she feared an assault.

"I want – I – oh the hell with you!" shouted Lyla. "I'm glad that old bag is gone. She got what she deserved for how she ruined our family! And she raised you up to be just like her, only thinking of yourself. I'm better off without either one of you!"

Lyla turned and stomped out of the room, slamming the door behind her. Jessie collapsed onto the sofa and started to sob; she felt completely alone in the world; why after years of being dutiful to her mother, did she now have to feel guilt over her sister's situation, when she had been too young to have any control over it? "I'm not going to see Lyla again," she thought. "If things haven't worked out for her, it's her own fault. Mother did what she could for her."

Then she heard the door open again. She quickly turned, frightened that Lyla might be back. Instead, Ellen was in the doorway with a tray of pineapple brownies.

"I knocked," said Ellen, "but I guess you didn't hear me. I thought you must be upstairs."

"It's okay," said Jessie. She found a tissue and wiped her eyes. Then she took the brownies from Ellen. "Did you make these?"

"No, Mom did. She thought you might have people stopping over."

"Thank you," said Jessie, taking the brownies and carrying them into the kitchen. Ellen followed her.

"How are you doing?" asked Ellen, seeing Jessie's red eyes. "We were worried about you spending the night alone. I hope you didn't cry all night."

"That's not why I was crying," said Jessie, moving things around in the refrigerator to find an empty shelf for the brownies. "My sister was just here. She was horrible. She just kept screaming at me."

"Your sister?" said Ellen. "I didn't even know you had one."

"I hardly ever see her," said Jessie, "which is just as well since she apparently hates me."

"Why?" asked Ellen as they sat down at the kitchen table.

"When my mother died, my foster mother adopted me, but she sent my sister Lyla to the orphanage. Lyla has never forgiven either of us."

"Oh," said Ellen. "Didn't anyone want to adopt her?"

"My foster mother didn't think she could handle two girls. She tried to find my sister another home, but Lyla was always kind of whiny and obnoxious so no one wanted her. Even though Lyla went to the orphanage, Mother still sent her presents and would have her over for dinner. I know Mother tried to do right by her, but I suspect Lyla has always been jealous of me."

Ellen thought Lyla probably had good reason to feel hurt when her sister had been adopted and she had not, but as a grown woman, Lyla should not hold a grudge.

"Seeing how mean she was today," said Jessie, "it's no wonder no one wanted to adopt her. She always gave my real mother a lot of trouble."

Ellen felt she should try to cheer up Jessie, but she was unsure what to say. She wished she had not come so early so she could head straight for work, but she still had half an hour until her shift began. Politely, she tried to make conversation.

"What will you do this afternoon? It must be hard for you to be all alone now?"

"It is," said Jessie. "I can't bear to look at the piano when I remember how much Mother loved to play it. And last night, the sight of her empty wheelchair set me to crying. I don't think I want to live in Marquette anymore; there are too many memories here, and I sure don't want to keep bumping into my sister."

"You would really move away?" Ellen asked.

"Yes. I've wanted to for a long time, but I couldn't while Mother was ill. I always wanted to be a pianist, but I took up teaching so I could stay here and take care of her. Now I think I'll move to a city where there are opera houses and concert halls. Maybe I could get a job playing the piano or even teaching music at an art school. There's nothing for me here except to teach music to children who aren't even interested."

Ellen thought of her own dream to be an artist – perhaps if she moved away, she would have a better chance. She had thought she would never want to leave Marquette again after that awful time as a little girl in California when she had been constantly homesick for her old house and her extended family. She was proud to think Jessie was strong enough to leave. She had always thought Jessie's life rather dull, but now she understood Jessie had been trapped. Ellen hoped someday she would also find a way to devote herself to her dream, but right now, she was stuck emptying bedpans, listening to screaming children who were afraid of needles, and dealing with dirty old men who flirted with young nurses.

"I think you should move away," said Ellen. "You deserve to be happy."

"That's what Mother told me," Jessie replied.

"Well, I can't be late for work," said Ellen, standing up. "My parents said they'll stop by later to see how you are."

"I'll be fine," Jessie replied, feeling for the first time that she would be. "Thanks for bringing over the brownies."

"You're welcome." .

Ellen drove to work, wondering how she would survive another long, boring afternoon shift. She envied Jessie. She sometimes thought of just driving away without telling anyone until she was free. Instead, she parked her car and went up to her assigned floor at the hospital.

1964

When Mrs. Senator Joseph Rodman died, her remains were shipped to Marquette, and she was buried beside her parents in Park Cemetery. A memorial service was held at Marquette's First Baptist Church; her sister and brother, their children and grandchildren attended, but her son Theo and his family remained in California.

Six months later, the Whitmans and Dalrymples learned that Theo Rodman had died from a heart attack. His passing occurred at his son's home, where he left the world while holding his daughter-in-law's hand, his eyes on his son's loving face, and his grandchildren's voices audible in the next room. His remains were also shipped to Marquette for burial in Park Cemetery as he requested in his will.

The following Memorial Day, Roy Whitman accompanied his mother to the cemetery to put flowers on the graves of his father and grandparents. They brought enough flowers that they decided to plant a few on other relatives' graves. When they came to Aunt Sarah's stone, they were surprised to find that the stone beside it had not been engraved with the name of Theodore Rodman nor even Theodore Dalrymple, but rather, Theodore Blackmore.

That same spring, Henry and Beth received a wedding announcement:

> With joyful hearts
> you are invited
> to the ceremony uniting
> Miss Jessie Hopewell
> and
> Mr. Eugene Goldsworthy
> on Saturday, the 6th of June
> nineteen hundred and sixty-four
> at two o'clock in the afternoon
> St. Augustine's Church
> Kalamazoo, Michigan

A short note was attached.

> Dear Henry, Beth, and Ellen,
>   I am now teaching music in Kalamazoo. It is not the grand life I dreamt about, but I am content. Shortly after I moved here, I met Eugene at church. He works as a chemist in a laboratory for Upjohn Pharmaceuticals. He is a widower with three children. I adore the children and hope to be as good a mother-substitute to them as my foster-mother was to me. I know you will think Kalamazoo too far to travel for my wedding, but please write, and if you ever come down-state, be sure to visit. I think I've found some happiness at last.
>   Love, Jessie

Ellen was glad Jessie was happy, but she was also disappointed. Jessie had told her she was going to be a pianist; Ellen had imagined her performing in concert halls before crowds of people. Instead, like most women, she had settled for marriage. Ellen told herself again she could not be happy with such a small life, with keeping a house, raising children, and pleasing a husband. She refused to be like her mother, her aunts, or Jessie. She would not give up her dreams for any man.

1967

Tom Vandelaare did not enjoy his first year at K.I. Sawyer Air Force Base. He was twenty-six years old, and he had enlisted in the air force when he was eighteen. The summer before, he had been transferred to K.I. Sawyer in Marquette County, and since then, he had been experiencing the dullest year of his life, especially since he had joined the air force with the express purpose of getting as far away from Upper Michigan as possible. So far he had been stationed in Texas and California, but despite hopes of then being stationed overseas, he had ended up back in Upper Michigan, only sixty miles from where he had grown up in Iron Mountain, on the Wisconsin border. He had always thought Iron Mountain a boring town, but K.I. Sawyer Air Force Base was worse. The closest town was the little village of Gwinn, smaller than the air base and containing nothing but a few seedy bars. Then twenty miles north of the air base was Marquette, the largest city in the Upper Peninsula with a population just over twenty-thousand, but Tom, having seen Houston and Los Angeles, thought it an insignificant backwoods town. Since his primary interest was bars and girls, he settled for a trip to Gwinn rather than driving all the way to the Queen City of the North. He hoped the coming spring would bring another transfer, perhaps to somewhere exotic like Germany or Japan, but he would go anywhere so long as it was far from this frozen tundra.

Tom especially hated the cold. It was early April yet snowbanks towered and the temperature was scarcely above freezing. The weatherman said it was eighty degrees in California today. When stationed on the West Coast, Tom had become accustomed to warmth, so he did not want to readjust to Upper Michigan's climate. Even the most humid California days had not bothered him; he had just taken off his shirt and gone to work. As an airplane mechanic, he often worked outside on the runways or in drafty hangers, which was no problem in California or Texas. But in Michigan, it was always raining, sleeting, or just plain snowing. Even when he wore gloves, the bitter cold would chap and crack his hands.

And as if all this cold were not enough, for the last several days, Tom had been having pains in his right side until this morning he had hardly been able to get out of bed. A visit to an air force doctor confirmed he had a ruptured appendix. Tom soon found himself being rushed by ambulance to St. Luke's Hospital in Marquette.

Despite Tom's feelings toward Marquette and its surrounding area, the local residents were pleased to have K.I. Sawyer Air Force Base in their backyard. The base had been established nearly a decade before to provide protection to the Great Lakes in this era of military competition between the United States and the Soviet Union. While the Cold War was a fearful reality, Marquette residents saw the resulting local air base as a sure way to improve the local economy. Some trepidation had existed that air base personnel from big cities would bring crime to Upper Michigan, but other than an increase in reckless driving from young air base men, no trouble had occurred. A century ago, the iron industry had placed Upper Michigan on the map and inspired thousands of pioneers to migrate to Lake Superior's shores, but now the output of iron ore had rapidly decreased, and the gold, copper, and other mineral deposits were slowly being exhausted. Many feared hard times ahead for the Upper Peninsula, so while some locals might complain about their "wing nut" neighbors at K.I. Sawyer, most appreciated the bolster to the local economy.

Lying in the back of the ambulance, Tom was unable to admire any of the jewels that composed the Queen City of the North's crown. The ambulance sped down County Road 553 into Marquette, past the Cliffs Ridge ski hill, then into the city, first onto Division and Genesee Streets, then onto US 41, which turned into Front Street, then through the old downtown, past the statue of Father Marquette, the First National Bank, the Old Savings Bank, the Presbyterian Church and the Peter White Public Library. The ambulance continued through the residential district, past the old Victorian homes, Graveraet High School, now a middle school since the opening of the new Marquette Senior High School in 1964, and finally, onto College Avenue, to St. Luke's Hospital. Tom would not have appreciated all the city's grand old landmarks had he seen them. He was in such searing, blinding pain that even the medication given to him in the ambulance did not kick in before he reached the hospital. Once at St. Luke's, he was quickly whisked onto a rolling bed, then drugged into unconsciousness and taken into the operating room.

After the surgery, Tom slept for many hours in his hospital bed. When he woke, his first sight of Marquette's beauty was not Lake Superior, Presque Isle Park, or one of the distinctive sandstone buildings, but a young nurse he found leaning over him, clasping his wrist in her hand.

"Hello," she said. "I was just checking your pulse. How are you feeling?"

"Okay, I guess," he said, fighting to keep his eyes open. He felt groggy, but he did not want to be asleep when a pretty girl was touching him. In his confused state with slightly blurred vision, perhaps he overestimated her looks, but he thought she had lovely brown hair – even with the nurse's cap perched on her head – and soft brown eyes, a kind smile, and a special warmth in her voice reserved just for him.

"You seem fine to me, Tom," she said, releasing his wrist and patting his shoulder. "I'm Ellen. I'll be looking after you for the next few days. Are you hungry? It's almost dinnertime."

"Yeah, I am a little hungry."

"The doctor says everything went fine with the operation. He'll be by to see you later. I'll go see about your dinner. Can I get you anything else?"

"No," he said, although "just don't leave" passed through his thoughts. He did not like lying in the hospital, not knowing anyone there, except now he knew Ellen. He hoped he would see her often; then he would not be lonely.

"Okay, I'll see you in a little while," Ellen smiled. Tom struggled to lift himself just enough to catch the view as she left, but the pain from his surgery made him fall back with a groan.

"Are you okay?" she asked, quickly returning.

"Yes," he said, only slightly embarrassed.

"Aren't you comfortable? Do you want me to adjust your pillows for you?"

"No, I'm okay. I just didn't realize it would hurt so much," he said, hoping she would not suspect why he had strained himself. He wished now she would leave him to his misery, but instead, she stuffed a pillow under his side, gently brushing her arm against his chest.

"You probably want to favor that side by not putting too much weight on it," she said. "There you are. Better?"

"Yes," he replied, miserably uncomfortable from the lump now beneath him, but he would not complain.

"I'll go see about your dinner then," she said.

Lying now on his side, Tom decided the lumpy discomfort was well worth it because it had raised him just enough to get a fine view of Ellen leaving the room.

"He's a good looker, isn't he?" Vera said to Ellen in the hallway.

"What?" Ellen asked her coworker.

"That Tom. He's a cutie."

"Oh, I hadn't noticed," said Ellen. But she had noticed. She returned to the nurse's station and tried to concentrate on the medical charts. She had had many male patients, but most of them were old men, and even the young ones were often unattractive – being sick in the hospital did not help matters – but Tom was an exception. She was being silly; she could not date a patient. Tom was only aesthetically appealing to her because she was an artist, and he had a sort of masculine beauty about him. That was all. Nothing was wrong with admiring God's artistry in a good looking man – she would rather like to paint his portrait, to capture with her brush his strong chin, his blue eyes, his sandy blond hair. "Stop it!" she told herself. She had better go check on old Mrs. Blackmore – see what that old biddy was fussing about today. Ellen hoped when she was dying, she would have the dignity to go gracefully without whining about every little thing, but Mrs. Blackmore would keep her too occupied to think about Tom – that was what she needed right now.

Tom hated spending all day in a hospital bed. His commanding officer had come to visit that morning, but after saying a few polite words and being assured Tom would soon be back to work, he said goodbye; visiting Tom had been his excuse to go shopping in Marquette. After Tom's visitor left, Ellen brought Tom his lunch. Someone from the diet kitchen should have brought it – Tom did not notice Ellen went out of her way to deliver it to him, but he was pleased when she sat down while he ate and asked him questions about his home, family, and where he had lived while in the air force.

Tom was one of those young men who think the slightest kind word from a girl means she is interested in him. Ever since a girl in high school had told him he was handsome, he had been a bit cocky; several more girls had thought him handsome, but his distorted sense of humor had often made young women dismiss him as unsuitable husband material.

But Ellen was different. She waited on him. That was her job, but he felt she went the extra mile for him, or at least that her fingers lingered on his arm longer than necessary when taking his blood pressure. Now that he had gotten a better, more focused look at her, he decided her smile was her best feature – she smiled at him a lot, and she listened patiently when he spoke, even when he knew he was rambling, and she asked him personal questions that only encouraged him to ramble more.

By the time Tom finished lunch, Ellen had to go see other patients, and Tom was left to stare out the window, terribly bored, while every five minutes, he strained his ears to hear Ellen's voice in the hallway.

Just before supper, the phone rang beside his bed. It was Tom's brother.

When Ellen brought Tom his supper, he told her, "My brother's coming up to visit me tomorrow."

"That'll be nice for you," said Ellen in her friendly nurse voice. She had nursed enough men to know how to sound as if she cared but did not care enough for them to misconstrue her comments.

"I haven't seen him in months," said Tom. "Me and him, we could hardly be parted when we was kids."

Ellen refrained from grimacing over Tom's poor English by allowing that he was excited about seeing his brother.

"That's nice," she said.

"We used to hunt, fish, do everything together until I joined the air force."

"What does he do?" asked Ellen. "Is he your older or younger brother?"

"He's a couple years older. He works for the Chicago Northwestern Railroad. He's got a wife and they're expecting their first baby."

"Do you have any other siblings?" asked Ellen.

"Yeah, sisters, but they don't live around here. Moved away when they were young – can't blame them – there's not much up here. That's why I joined the air force, to get out of the U.P., but I ended up back here anyway."

No matter how handsome Tom was, Ellen would not hear anyone complain about the U.P. – she did not want to live anywhere else. "It's time to take your temperature," she told Tom and stuck a thermometer in his mouth so they would not argue. She did not care what opportunities were in other areas – great opportunities existed here, maybe not for jobs, but for raising a family, and having fresh air, and being active outdoors, and here a person could have peace and solitude. Money was not everything. Yes, she had thought about moving away in the past, but she had gradually come to realize Upper Michigan was her home, and more beautiful, more necessary for the peace of her artistic soul than living in any exciting big city.

"Do you have any brothers or sisters?" Tom asked when the thermometer was removed.

Ellen paused to read his temperature. "Perfect. You should be going home in a couple days."

"Great," he said.

"I have a brother," she replied. "He lives out in California with his wife and two kids."

"There's nothing like a brother," said Tom.

Ellen thought Tom must have a swell brother from the tone in his voice. She wondered whether Tom would make a good family man – it sounded as if he were close to his family, despite his dislike of Upper Michigan.

"Well, I'm afraid I have to check on my other patients. I'll see you later, Tom."

"Be sure to come by tomorrow and meet my brother," he called after her.

The next morning on her way up to her floor, Ellen met an attractive young man in the elevator who looked familiar, although she could not place him. When he got off on the same floor as she did, she watched him walk down the hall and peer at the room numbers until he entered Tom's room. Then she knew he was Tom's brother.

She waited a few minutes, pretending to scan a report at the nurse's station. She told herself not to move from her desk for a quarter hour. She looked up at the clock nearly every minute until fifteen minutes had passed. Then she waited two more minutes before deciding she would make the excuse that she had to check Tom's blood pressure.

"Here's my nurse," said Tom when she entered. "Ellen, this is my brother, Rodger."

"It's nice to meet you," Ellen said. She went to Tom's side and tried not to show how nervous she was as she wrapped the cloth around his strong forearm and told him to make a fist.

"I hear you've been taking good care of him," Rodger said to Ellen.

"Best nurse in the hospital," Tom said.

"Oh, I don't know about that," she replied, although pleased by the compliment.

"Sit down and talk to us," said Tom after she unwrapped his arm and started to write on her chart.

"No, I can't. I have a busy morning, but it was nice to meet you," she told Rodger. She quickly left the room. She told herself she felt comfortable around Tom, and his brother seemed nice, but she was too shy to stay and –

"She's a real fox," said Rodger.

Ellen overheard the remark as she went out the door. Once around the corner, she paused to listen.

"She's beautiful," Tom sighed.

"You got it bad for her, don't you?" Rodger laughed. "I haven't seen your face light up like that since the day you got accepted into the air force."

Ellen was disappointed not to hear Tom reply. She could not see how he blushed.

"You going to ask her out?" Rodger grilled.

Ellen strained her ears.

"I don't know."

"What do you mean you don't know? You like her, and from how nervous she was, I'd say she likes you."

Ellen was mortified. What a presumptuous thing to say! She had not been nervous at all.

"She's out of my league," Tom said.

Out of his league! Ellen was pleased he thought so, but she could not believe it; she had never been popular with boys. But now she suddenly saw herself on a California beach, playing Annette Funicello to Tom as Frankie Avalon. She could feel the sand between her toes, as Tom rubbed suntan lotion on her shoulders.

"You'll never know unless you ask her," said Rodger.

Her supervisor came around the corner. Ellen quickly moved down the hall, pretending she was just walking past Tom's door to the nurse's station. The rest of the day, she kept telling herself she did not care whether he asked her out, but she was afraid to go near his room from fear he would not. Tomorrow he would be released from the hospital; she was glad – then she would no longer have to think about it.

At supper that evening, Ellen was despondent.

"Ellen, what do you think?" asked her mother.

"About what?" asked Ellen, awaking from a daydream.

"Should we repaint the living room white or leave it green?"

"I don't care."

"Well, if we paint it white like your father wants," said Beth, "I think we'll have to get new furniture to match it."

"We can't afford new furniture right now," Henry replied. "Besides, white matches with anything."

"I don't care what color you paint it," said Ellen. "It's your house, not mine."

"Well, you live here too," Beth replied.

The phone rang, ending the discussion.

"I'll get it," Ellen said, jumping up to grab the phone. "Hello."

"Ellen, can I come over? I need to talk to you."

It was Lucy. She sounded as if she had been crying.

"What's wrong?"

"Can I come over? Or better yet, could we go somewhere?"

"Sure," said Ellen. "We're just finishing supper. I'll be ready in ten minutes."

"Who was that?" asked Beth, when Ellen returned to the table.

"Just Lucy. She's coming to pick me up. We're going for a ride."

Henry and Beth returned to their discussion. Ellen often went for rides with Lucy or Maud during the summer, usually around Presque Isle, with a stop to get an ice cream cone, or they would go out to dinner and a movie. Since today had been abnormally warm, leaving only a few patches of snow on the ground, the evening was perfect for a drive. Ellen's parents did not think to ask any questions, and Ellen did not offer any more information about her cousin. She quickly finished eating, carried her dishes into the kitchen, went into the bathroom to brush her teeth, then walked out to the mailbox to wait. In a minute, Lucy drove around the corner. Ellen noticed her cousin's red eyes as she climbed into the car.

"What's wrong?" she asked.

"It's Phil," Lucy sobbed. She had apparently been doing a lot of sobbing. "Mama drove him off."

Ellen did not know what to say. She did not need to ask why. She had seen this coming. She was silent as Lucy headed the car toward Presque Isle.

"Tell me what happened," she said.

Lucy and Phil had been going out at least once a week for the last couple months. Ellen had vaguely known Phil from high school, but he was a couple years older than her. He was nothing to look at, and she did not think he was very smart. He worked at a gas station and did not seem to be going anywhere with his life. But most of the boys Lucy's age were already married so her dating options were steadily waning.

"Mother drove him off. She's selfish – maybe even jealous. I don't think she ever wants me to marry. She – "

"But what did she do?" asked Ellen.

"It's not what she did. It's the way she is. She doesn't like him. Whenever he comes to pick me up, she'll barely speak to him. She'll pass out cookie trays to everyone in the neighborhood, but when I asked whether he could come over for supper some night, she said we were on a fixed income and couldn't be handing out free meals."

"She didn't say that?" Ellen couldn't believe it; Aunt Eleanor could be fussy, but she was never unkind.

"Yes, she did," said Lucy. "And yesterday when he came over to take me and Maud to the beach, Mother said, right in front of him, that she couldn't understand why I would want to go to the beach when I had such a poor figure."

"Oh, Lucy, how could she?" said Ellen. Lucy was a bit chunky, but no mother should say such a thing to her daughter, especially not in front of a boyfriend. "I hope you went to the beach anyway?"

"No. We just drove to Munising and back, and since we had invited Maud along, we couldn't really talk, but I could see he was thinking about what my mother said. Then just an hour ago, he called me up and said he didn't think I was the right girl for him."

"He broke up with you? Did he say why?"

"No. He tried to be nice, to say he wasn't good enough for me, but I know he was really thinking I'm fat, and that no man would want my mother for a mother-in-law."

Ellen did not answer. She thought Lucy's anger was making her exaggerate. A million reasons might exist for why Phil broke it off with her.

"Well, he might change his mind," said Ellen. "Besides, if he gives up on you so easily, he isn't worth it."

"I know better than to think I'll ever find anyone," Lucy moaned. "Look at how my mother drove off my father. She claims it was his fault, but I doubt it since she's such a nag. She's afraid of being alone, so she wants to make Maud and me stay with her forever."

Ellen gazed at the lake as they entered Presque Isle. She did not know what to say. Her parents had told her Aunt Eleanor's husband had been at fault for their marriage ending – he had left her to follow his career – but Ellen knew her family would take Aunt Eleanor's side. She could not really know the truth behind Aunt Eleanor's divorce so many years ago.

"Lucy, it doesn't have to be that way. You're still young. You'll have plenty more boyfriends."

"No, I won't. I'm nearly thirty now."

"Look at Jessie. She was nearly forty when she got married."

"I don't want to wait that long," cried Lucy.

"It'll be worth the wait if you find the right man."

"You're not helping any," said Lucy. "I don't want anyone but Phil."

"I'm sorry," said Ellen, and she was sorry, although she did not like being told she was not helpful, "but frankly, I don't know what's so great about Phil – especially if he's going to leave you just because you're a few pounds overweight or he doesn't like your mother. He sounds shallow to me."

"You don't know him," said Lucy. "You don't know what he means to me."

Ellen admitted she did not know. She had never been in love with a man unless she could count – but that was just wishful thinking. By now, they had circled all the way around Presque Isle and come to the island store. Ellen thought an ice cream cone might cheer Lucy up, but the way Lucy glared through the windshield, she dared not suggest it. Ice cream would not help Lucy's figure or marital prospects.

Lucy drove Ellen home without another word. She did not even pull into the driveway to drop Ellen off.

"I'll call you tomorrow," said Ellen, "just to see how you are."

Lucy made no reply, just waited for Ellen to close the door.

"I hope you feel better. It'll take time, but you will eventually."

"I'll be fine," said Lucy. "I'll adapt to my usual, pathetic, boring life."

Ellen knew better than to reply. She shut the door and let her cousin drive off.

She decided not to ask her parents about Aunt Eleanor's marriage; they would wonder why she asked, and she did not want to discuss Lucy's broken heart. By tomorrow, the entire family would know Lucy and Phil had broken up. Aunt Eleanor would tell Ellen's mother or at least Ellen's grandmother, who would then tell Ellen's mother. Once Ellen's grandmother knew, it would get leaked to Aunt Harriet, and Aunt Harriet would make sure all of Marquette County heard the story as she decided to twist it. Ellen felt sorry for Lucy – thirty was not much farther around the corner for herself, and she had no better marital prospects than Lucy did. She still wanted to be an artist, but as she got older, she was less sure she wanted it in lieu of a husband.

The next morning when she reached the hospital, Ellen went straight to Tom's room, but his bed was empty. She tried to contain her disappointment when she went to the front desk and asked where he had gone.

"He was released just five minutes before you came in," Vera told her.

"Oh," said Ellen. Then he might still be in the hospital. If she hurried down to the lobby, she might spot him. "No," she told herself, "you're being foolish. You're acting more crazy than Lucy."

She felt the doom begin to descend. Like Lucy and Maud, she would spend all her days living with her parents, and when they died, then what? Maybe she could move in with her cousins; they could be three old maids together; they would get a slew of cats for company. Or she could adopt a child, then get a disease and shrivel up in a wheelchair like Cousin Thelma. No, she would not afflict her pathetic life on a child. She would live alone, and if she got lonely, she would talk to her geraniums. She feared she would always be lonely.

"Ellen, there you are."

She had been pretending to study a chart. She knew it was Tom's voice before she looked up. His face was half-hidden behind a bouquet of flowers.

"These are for taking such good care of me," he said, a hesitant, goofy grin breaking across his face.

"Oh, you didn't have to do that. Thank you," she said. "I thought I'd missed you. I went to your room. I thought you'd wait to leave until I came in. I'm glad you came back. Thank you." She realized she was blabbering. The flowers were a declaration of gratitude, not of love. She had to control herself.

"They're not much," he said, feeling embarrassed.

She smelled the flowers, not trusting herself to speak.

"Listen," he said, "I don't have to be back to work until tomorrow. How's about I take you out for supper tonight?"

Oh! Happiness! She felt so happy she could not speak.

"I can pick you up at five," he said, trying to read her reaction. "That's when you get off, right?"

"Yes," said Ellen.

"Okay, I'll see you then."

"All right," she said.

He said something else – she was too excited to hear it – she admired his figure as he walked down the hall. She was so happy.

They had several dates before Ellen brought Tom home to meet the family. Since she had never gone out with a young man before, she was at first undecided what she wanted from him – of course, she thought he was handsome, but was it reasonable to think of him as her future husband? She was not the kind of girl who could date just for fun; she was too serious for that; everything she did had to have a purpose, and if Tom were the right man, the purpose would be marriage and children. She wondered whether she should date more men just to make sure Tom was the right one – but since she liked Tom, why should she date other men? Was she trying to talk herself out of a commitment with any man. Her girlfriends from school were all married now, and none of their husbands seemed half as good as Tom. And Tom was the first boy who had ever really paid attention to her, so she could not help thinking he was special. Sometimes she thought he was the first man she had allowed to pay attention to her, which meant maybe she was just settling because she was afraid she would grow old before another man came along. Then she told herself she was overanalyzing everything; she should just marry him, quit worrying, and be happy.

When her parents finally asked to meet Tom, Ellen did not invite him for supper. She conceded to his coming inside the house to be introduced before they left for a movie. She did not think a mere ten minute meeting would be too awkward.

It was awkward anyway. Henry shook hands, asked about Tom's job, and pretended to be interested. He offered to show Tom his woodshop, but Ellen said they did not have the time tonight. Ellen had expected a more severe reaction from her mother – a repetition of the anxiety displayed when Jim had moved away and married – after all, if Ellen married, she would move out of the house, possibly move wherever the air force sent Tom. Beth, however, merely apologized to Tom for a messy house, although she had spent all afternoon making it spotless for his visit. Then she pushed a freshly baked brownie on him, and when he declared it was "better than my mom's brownies", Beth was won over. Ellen was surprised by her parents' reaction; they did not even make comments about Tom when she returned home that night. She did not realize how much they wanted her to marry; how much they bemoaned not getting to watch their grandchildren in California growing up. If Ellen married, their grandchildren might be right here in Marquette. After that first meeting, Tom was always a welcomed guest in the Whitman house.

Soon Ellen's grandmother insisted she be introduced to Ellen's young man. At eighty-three, Margaret was the grand old matriarch of the family and stubborn enough that few would deny her requests. Ellen reluctantly agreed to bring Tom over for a half hour one evening before they went out to supper. She then spent three days dreading the introduction.

Aunt Harriet, upon hearing Ellen's young man was to meet Margaret, suggested she would drop by on the proposed evening. After fifty years, Margaret was finally impatient with her sister-in-law's idiosyncrasies. Firmly, she replied, "No, you won't. We don't want to scare off Ellen's young man with too much attention." Harriet stayed home, but since she lived across the street from Margaret, no one could stop her from peeking between the curtains when Ellen and Tom, holding hands, walked over to Margaret's house.

"Grandma," said Ellen, stepping into the living room where Margaret sat with the television blasting, "this is Tom."

Margaret got up, turned off the TV, then asked, "Tom what?"

"Tom Vandelaare," he replied.

"What kind of a name is that?" Margaret asked, easing herself back into her chair. Ellen and Tom found places on the sofa.

"It's Dutch, Grandma," said Ellen, protectively holding Tom's hand.

"My father," Tom said, "came over from Holland when he was young."

"My husband's family," Margaret replied, "came to this country on the *Mayflower*, and my own family is descended from the royal house of Scotland."

Ellen had heard her grandmother's grandiloquent claims many times, but her father had told her that Grandpa Whitman had never once mentioned being descended from any *Mayflower* pilgrims. As for the Scottish royalty connection, everyone in the family had heard Margaret make that claim, but what was the chance it was true? Ellen noticed Tom was not impressed, but neither did he think her grandmother's remarks were nutty. He just looked uncomfortable.

"Where are you from?" Margaret asked.

"I'm in the air force. I live at K.I. Sawyer."

"Tom's a mechanic on the airplanes," Ellen added.

"But where did you grow up?" asked Margaret.

"Iron Mountain."

"Then, you're not a local?"

"Iron Mountain isn't that far, Grandma," said Ellen.

"I know that," said Margaret. "We have relatives there named Cumming. Do you know them?"

"Which Cummings are those?" asked Ellen.

"Your father's cousin, Harry, the one who died last year – his son lives there."

"No, I don't know anyone by that name," said Tom.

"They're not much account anyway," said Margaret. "None of those Cummings were except Harry, and he wasn't much good until he was older."

Tom nodded politely. Ellen pitied poor Cousin Harry. She had always liked him. Grandma should let him rest in peace.

"What was your mother's maiden name?" asked Margaret.

"Varin," said Tom, anticipating her next question. "It's French-Canadian."

"Hmm," said Margaret, her tone failing to betray her opinion of such origins.

"She's from Menominee," he added.

"Hmm." She paused, then asked, "What are your hobbies?"

"I like to go hunting," he said. Ellen cringed. She did not like that he killed poor helpless animals. Despite the popularity of deer hunting in Upper Michigan, no one in her family hunted, not even Uncle Roy, wilderness man.

Margaret shook her head. "People don't need to kill deer anymore. It's different if you live on a farm as I did when I was married; then we had to kill the animals to survive. I can tell you, I've chopped the head off many a chicken. But now, in the age of supermarkets, hunting is just a waste of time and money."

Tom remained respectfully silent.

"What else do you do?" asked Margaret.

Tom took a moment to rack his brain. "I like to fish," he said.

"You do?" said Margaret. "My husband liked to fish. So do Ellen's parents. Ellen, maybe Tom could come along for our next family picnic at Pickerel Lake."

"Sure, Grandma," said Ellen.

"I'd like that," said Tom, wondering why it was all right to kill fish but not deer.

Margaret stared at the couple, unable to think of further questions.

Ellen and Tom stared back.

"Well," said Margaret, "I don't want to keep you young people when you probably have somewhere you want to be off to. It was nice to meet you, Tom."

"You too, Mrs. Whitman," he replied, then let Ellen lead him out the door.

Once Harriet saw Ellen and her young man walk back down the street, she scurried over to Margaret's house.

"Well, what is he like?" she asked.

"He's a very nice young man," said Margaret, who would not have given Harriet the satisfaction of saying otherwise no matter what she thought, but her approval was apparent when she stated, "He comes from a good family – half French and half Dutch; you know, the Dutch are said to be the most intelligent people in the world, and the French have always had good taste. And I'll say something else for him, he's a good looking young man."

Harriet did not think the French had good taste; they ate snails and wrote smutty novels, but she thought it sufficient to say, "If he's French, he must be Catholic."

"Yes," said Margaret, unwilling to grant Harriet a score, "but considering all the divorces these days" – Harriet's grandson, Randy Dalrymple, had just that week begun divorce proceedings with his wife of less than a year, and Margaret attributed the divorce, besides the obvious reason that no sane woman should have married Harriet's grandson, to the girl being a Lutheran rather than a good Baptist – "I think it best Ellen marry a man of her own faith. Catholic marriages tend to last because only the Pope can annul them."

Harriet went home, highly annoyed. Margaret was becoming so self-righteous in her old age, but then again, she always had thought she was better than everyone else. Who was she to allude to Randy's divorce? Two of her own children, Eleanor and Bill, had divorced, and Henry had quit going to church when he married Beth, and Roy did not go to church at all. Sometimes dealing with Margaret was enough to make Harriet wish she had never married into the Dalrymple family.

Tom climbed the hill with the nimbleness of a mountain goat, stopping every few minutes to help Ellen over a rock or log. She could hear a robin chirping. She paused to listen as an excuse to rest a moment. If there were not a cool September breeze this evening, she never would have suggested they climb Sugarloaf Mountain. They had gone out to supper, and now they both felt stuffed. Neither thought they could sit through a movie, so Ellen had suggested a walk might help their digestion.

Tom had been in a rollicking mood all evening, cracking jokes and telling her funny stories about mishaps at the air force base. Ellen tried to tell a few stories about the hospital, but she had never been able to make a story sound funny. Neither could Tom, but because he was telling it, she found it funny. Every week, she waited for Friday night when he would come into town to take her out. The rest of the week, Ellen spent reliving their far too few hours together. By the week's end, Ellen remembered Tom's stories as hilarious, unconscious that she had embellished and improved them.

As they hiked up the mountain, Tom commented on the bushes, trees, flowers and ferns. Ellen marveled at all he knew from growing up in the woods of Dickinson County. She wondered why he had not become a botanist or naturalist – if he left the air force, maybe he could go to college to become one; she kept meaning to suggest it, but she doubted he would be interested in college. Not that there was anything wrong, she told herself, with his being a mechanic.

"This is a bit of a workout," Tom said as he waited for her to catch up with him.

Ellen was nearly out of breath, yet she noticed Tom had not even broken a sweat; she told herself that was because he was in the military and probably had daily physical training. She could tell he was anxious to reach the top, to conquer the mountain, yet she was pleased by how patiently he waited for her.

"Come on," he nudged. "I don't want to go up without you. They say it's lonely at the top."

She smiled, then asked him the name of some pink flowers growing alongside the trail as a further excuse to catch her breath.

He told her the name, but she instantly forgot it when he took her hand. Then he gave her a full, long, kiss on the lips. She was surprised. Sometimes, he was so sweet.

"This looks like the last bit," Tom said as he pulled her up the trail.

At the top, they walked to the edge of the rocky cliff and looked out at the bluish haze of Lake Superior, then over at the City of Marquette nestled among the trees. Ellen thought of telling him that her father had helped to build the obelisk at the top of the mountain, but Tom did not even notice it.

"It's beautiful up here," said Tom. "I used to want to get away from the U.P., but I never saw it from this view."

"It was well worth the climb to get this perspective," said Ellen, laying her head on his shoulder in an attempt not to collapse from exhaustion.

Tom had put it off all evening – in the restaurant he had felt too many people were around – in the car, he had felt it too difficult while he was driving. Now, on the mountain, where they were alone, he had Ellen's full attention. He would have a few minutes to convince her before she could catch her breath and run away from him.

As he drew the ring from his pocket, he remembered he had paid three hundred dollars for it, a tremendous amount to him – all he could really afford, but he feared it had not been enough to ensure she would not turn him down.

Ellen was looking out at the lake, but when he moved his arm to open the box, she turned toward him. At first she did not understand – she thought it was an earring box. She started to say, "Oh Tom, my birthday isn't until – "

Then he opened the box.

He was too nervous to kneel; he thought he would look ridiculous if he did. He took her hand in his and with the other hand, pushed the box toward her, too nervous to place the ring on her finger.

"Tom, I – "

"Please, Ellen. You're the only girl I've ever been this crazy about."

"But – " she tried to think of excuses. "You'll be transferred away, and I don't know whether I can go to all those different places with you."

"Why not?"

"I just can't. This is my home." She remembered how frightened she had been as a little girl in California, yet part of her felt she would follow him anywhere in the world.

"What keeps you here?" he asked.

"My parents. I'm all they have. I want to be here to take care of them when they need me." Why was she saying this, she asked herself. Why was she ruining everything?

He nestled his face in her hair.

"My parents are in the U.P. too. I can get a job here as a mechanic in a garage or at the Marquette airport."

"But Tom, what about your air force career? Don't you want to see the world?" She was afraid he would say, "No, I want to stay here," and she was even more afraid he would change his mind and take back his ring.

"I can see enough of the world from up here," he laughed.

"But think of – "

"You're my world now, Ellen."

It was the most romantic thing he would ever say to her. No matter how frustrated she might occasionally become with him in future years, she would never forget those words.

Now he took the ring from the box. She did not protest. She scarcely believed this moment had finally come.

"Soon?" he asked.

She nodded in agreement.

"This is the last year of my contract with the air force," he said. "I'll resign when it's over, and then we can live here in Marquette."

"All right."

They silently walked down the mountain. The sunset shot bolts of light between the trees until the earth glowed as if it were the first day in Eden. Ellen's heart exulted. She was still frightened, but Tom's hand securely held hers. He was to be her husband. Nothing had ever made her so happy, not even the thought of being an artist. An artist could only imitate life; now she was to have life. Tom was life itself, with strong blood coursing through his veins. Soon his heart would be pressed to hers, and she would bear his children, thus creating life. She realized she was not an artist but a fragment of a great masterpiece. Finally, the great artist had found the proper place for her in His painting.

1968

January and February in Upper Michigan can be difficult months. They are bleak with long winter nights and short cold days. Even the dazzling reflection of the sun's rays off the snow's crystals rarely lasts more than an hour. Once Christmas is past, and the long wait for spring begins, cabin fever sets in. For the Whitmans, Henry's birthday in late February was a much anticipated family celebration that gave a brief break from winter's monotony. Instead of picnic baskets or large holiday meals, the festivities were celebrated with finger sandwiches and sweet pickles, chocolate cake and ice milk, coffee and dinner mints. All the family were present: Henry's wife, daughter, siblings, nieces and nephews, cousins, and this year, Ellen's young man. Since Tom had gone to his parents' house for the holidays, tonight was the first time he would meet Ellen's extended family.

Of all the family, Henry made the least fuss about his birthday. He spent the day in his woodshop, sanding table legs and nailing together pieces of wood. Fifteen minutes before the guests arrived, he went into the house to change his clothes. In the meantime, because Ellen was at work, Beth kept herself busy making egg and ham salad sandwiches, slicing cheese, buttering rolls and baking the birthday cake. She grumbled about how she got no help, just loud enough for Henry to hear as he changed his clothes; when he came out to the kitchen to offer assistance, she grumbled that he was in her way. Then he purposely got in front of her so she could not move, grabbed her waist, and smacked a kiss on her. She threatened to stick him with a pin from her apron and warned that the coffee would not be ready in time if he continued to harass her. Ellen came home from work to find bickering parents – she was pleased to see they loved each other so well – until this year, she had told herself she did not want a relationship like theirs, but now she felt she wanted nothing more.

Ellen disappeared into her room to change her clothes, promising to be out in a minute to set the table, but before she returned, Beth had consented to let Henry do it, even though he had to dig out the good dishes from the hutch cabinet, and not knowing where anything was, he had to keep yelling questions to his wife. Finally, in a fit of frustration, Beth marched into the dining room, demanding to know whether he were blind that he could not see the platter in front of his face.

"Now, do you think you can manage by yourself to put the silverware on the table so I can finish frosting your cake?" she asked.

"I don't know," Henry grinned. "Sometimes I get confused about the difference between knives and forks."

"Don't fold the napkins that way," Beth said a minute later when she carried the salt and pepper shakers to the table. She refolded one napkin to show him the correct process, but then Ellen came to her father's rescue and took over. Henry went to stare out the front window in anticipation of his guests and birthday presents.

"Just like a little kid," muttered Beth, shaking her head, but she was pleased to see he was so excited.

In a few minutes, Bill arrived, complete with Annette, and three little boys in jackets, boots and mittens, their mother coddling them while their father paid no attention to how his wife tried to balance Henry's present in one arm, hold the hand of her youngest son, and make sure the other two boys did not dawdle in the driveway. Roy pulled into the yard right behind his younger brother, having been enlisted to drive his mother, Uncle Charles, and Aunt Harriet to the party. By the time Eleanor, Lucy, and Maud arrived, Beth was ready to serve supper.

"Let's wait five more minutes for Tom," said Ellen.

"We told him we would eat at five-thirty," Beth replied.

"But he doesn't get off work until five, and then he had to go home to change his clothes," Ellen said. "Besides, it's a long drive from the air base and the roads are slippery tonight."

"They were clear when I drove here," said Bill.

"You only came through town," Henry said. "Tom has to drive in on County Road 553, and that can be bad, especially around the ski hill."

"I'm starving," Aunt Harriet complained, but she was ignored when gleeful shouts came from Bill and Annette's sons, little William, Jason, and Alan. Everyone turned to see Lucy and Maud on the floor, Jason and Alan respectively in their laps. The girls tried to interest the boys in their coloring books while William Whitman the Third ran back and forth from one female cousin to the next, demanding her to look at "how good I color in the lines." Whatever

Lucy and Maud's opinion of their little cousin's artwork, Alan decided to play art critic by ripping the coloring book from his oldest brother's hand, and then tearing the colored picture in two. William screamed and swung at Alan, but Maud grabbed his fist in time to prevent its contact with his brother's head; Jason opportunely used this moment of conflict to grab the fallen coloring book and scribble all over it with black crayon.

Annette, exhausted from a long day of childcare, ignored her children's shouts and gossiped with Eleanor. Fortunately, Lucy and Maud were good natured enough to have the rumble under control in a couple minutes.

"Eleanor, those girls of yours need to get some babies of their own pretty soon," Harriet said. Everyone heard her, but no one commented; everyone, including Uncle Charles, wondered why Aunt Harriet had to be invited to family functions.

Ellen wondered why Tom had to embarrass her by being late. She worried the family would think ill of him for not being on time, especially since he had not yet met any of her aunts or uncles. When she looked outside and saw a snow squall starting up, she thought she would cry; he might not make it at all.

"Ellen, shut the curtains," Beth said. "It's almost dark out, and I don't like people driving by and staring in the windows when I have all the dining room lights on."

Ellen was reluctant to shut the curtains because she would not be able to watch for Tom. But just as she pulled the drape cord, his car drove into the yard.

"Here comes Tom," she said, trying to keep her voice even, telling herself not to run to the door, although she arrived there a full minute before him. He gave her a quick kiss and apologized for being late. She took off his coat. Then he came up the backstairs to find himself surrounded by future relatives. He momentarily felt overwhelmed until he spotted his prospective father-in-law, handed him his present, and said, "Happy Birthday."

"Thank you, but you didn't need to get me anything," said Henry.

"I hope you're hungry, Tom," said Beth. "Everyone is starving, but since after Henry, you're the guest of honor, we couldn't start without you."

Beth had been irritated that Tom was late, but now she was ready to gush over the father of her future grandchildren. She herded everyone to the dining table, explaining there were place name cards before all their plates. Uncle Charles did not listen so when he sat down in Margaret's seat, he got his ears chewed by his wife; fortunately, fifty-two years of marriage and deafness in one ear had enhanced his selective hearing. Jason, Alan, and William the Third sulked when told they would have to eat in the kitchen until Lucy and Maud agreed to sit with them. Then the boys were overjoyed, their father indifferent, and their mother fully aware of her good fortune.

Margaret said the blessing. Then the sandwiches were passed around.

"Tom, were the roads bad driving in from the air base?" asked Bill.

"It was a downright blizzard until I got to Cliffs Ridge," said Tom, "but once I came up out of that valley, there was only light snow like you have here in town."

"That always seems to be the worst spot on 553," Bill agreed.

"We're lucky to live in town," said Eleanor. "Because of the lake effect, all the snow is carried over the city and lands in Sands Township or Negaunee and Ishpeming."

"You are lucky," said Tom. "At the air base, we sure aren't."

"Does anyone know what the total snowfall is so far this year?" asked Annette. "Have we broken two hundred inches yet?"

"I don't know," said Henry. "It was in the paper the other day, but I can't remember."

"It hasn't been such a bad winter," Roy said. "Not like other years when I thought I would be buried alive in my cabin."

"No, but there's still too much snow," said Harriet. "I like a little at Christmas, but after New Year's, it should all melt. If I were rich, I'd go to Florida for the winter."

"Me too," said Tom. "I hate U.P. winters."

Ellen felt troubled. Tom had agreed to live here with her, but she did not want him to be unhappy or to resent her because they stayed in Upper Michigan.

"Winter is ugly in Florida," said Henry. "Remember, Roy, when we went down there to build that house – everything was all brown and the trees were bare. It's prettier here because of the snow."

"The snow's not very pretty when I have to shovel it," said Harriet.

Margaret and Eleanor exchanged amused glances. Neither had ever seen Harriet lift a shovel. If Uncle Charles did not shovel, their son Joseph or one of their twin grandsons would come over to do it.

"We do get too much snow," Roy said. "I'd like to live somewhere they only get a few inches, like in England. When I was stationed there, they would only get a little and then it would melt, and they'd get a couple more inches. Just enough snow for it to sparkle, but not enough to make you shovel."

"Yes, I remember reading," said Eleanor, "that because winters were so mild in England, the Pilgrims found it really difficult to deal with their first harsh New England winter."

"I guess," said Margaret, "the Whitmans didn't feel that way about winter when they came to Marquette because they had already experienced New England winters."

"Did the Whitmans come from New England?" asked Harriet.

"Of course, Harriet. I've told you that before," said Margaret. "My husband's ancestors came over on the *Mayflower*."

"Gee, I bet that was exciting – to sail with Columbus and all," said Tom.

Everyone was stunned by Tom's remark, but they all would have overlooked his ignorance; only Harriet said, "Columbus wasn't on the *Mayflower*."

"I thought Columbus brought over the Pilgrims," said Tom.

"No, he did not," said Harriet, furrowing her brow. "What do they teach you young people in school these days?"

"Aunt Harriet is right," said Roy to quell the argument. "Columbus arrived in the Caribbean in 1492. The Pilgrims came over on the *Mayflower* and landed at Plymouth Rock in 1620."

Ellen was humiliated by Tom's ignorance of such common knowledge, and even more, she hated to think Aunt Harriet might know more than him.

"I've always loved history," said Roy, trying to diminish the immensity of Tom's error, "so I've studied it pretty closely and memorized a lot of dates. Since I'm descended from those old New England Puritans, I often wonder just what influence they've had upon my character."

Ellen looked at Tom, afraid he was embarrassed, but he did not seem to realize he had any reason to be embarrassed.

"I'm so ready for spring," Eleanor broke the silence.

"I know. I can't wait to go fishing," said Beth. "Tom likes to fish. This year he'll have to go with us."

"Where do you all go?" Tom asked.

"Down to Pickerel Lake," said Henry.

"Or up to the Huron Mountain Club," said Roy. "They let me have visitors up there once in a while."

"Everything was delicious, Beth," said Annette, setting down her fork.

"Yes, it was," Uncle Charles agreed.

"Thank you," said Beth. "Does anyone want seconds?"

"Oh no," said Eleanor. "I still haven't lost all the weight I gained at Christmas."

"I'll go see whether the kids want anymore," said Annette. "Then I'll help you clean up."

"Make it quick," said Henry. "I'm hungry for my birthday cake."

Annette went into the kitchen, and Ellen got up to help her mother clear the table, abandoning Tom to her relatives.

"So Tom, do you ever get to fly airplanes?" asked Eleanor.

"No, I don't have a pilot's license. I just work on them."

"Would you like to fly them?" Eleanor asked.

"Maybe."

"Anyone who goes up in an airplane must be crazy," said Harriet. "You'd never get me in one."

Tom did not know what to say. Bill said the airplanes he had flown in during the war had been perfectly safe, "except when the enemy was shooting at me."

Ellen returned with the cake. The candles were lit and "Happy Birthday" was sung. Next came the presents. The children were allowed in the dining room for that part of the festivities. Henry happily tore open the first package.

"Henry, don't rip the paper like that," said Beth. "It's so pretty we should save it to use again."

"Mother, the Great Depression is over," Ellen said.

"Ellen Elizabeth Whitman," Harriet snapped. "Don't you speak like that to your mother. You young people have no idea how hard things were back then."

"Yes," Henry smiled. "We didn't even have birthday presents back then."

"Or if we did," Roy joined in to annoy his aunt, "it was only an old piece of twine, or a dead mouse."

"A dead mouse!" asked little Jason in disbelief.

"Really Uncle Roy?" William the Third wanted to know.

"Yes, that was all we'd have for our birthdays because we sure couldn't afford a birthday cake back then. Birthday mouse was a real treat."

"Roy, that's disgusting. Don't tell the boys such things," said Eleanor.

"I'm going to get some more coffee," Annette said, more concerned about her caffeine intake than what her children heard.

"Henry, don't crumple the paper into a ball," said Beth. "Give it here."

"We'll save it so I can wrap your birthday presents in it," Henry laughed.

"Married thirty-four years," Beth shook her head, "and he's still not trained right."

"Don't look at me," said Margaret. "I did my best to raise him."

"Margaret, you did better with Henry than with Bill," Annette called from the kitchen.

Everyone smiled and looked at Bill. He good-naturedly replied, "Annette wouldn't know what to do if she didn't have me."

"Yeah, I would," she said, returning to sit beside him. "I sometimes think I have four boys, especially when he doesn't wipe his feet or leaves the toilet seat up."

"Well, he was my last born," said Margaret. "I was worn out by the time he came along."

"I wouldn't wish my marital happiness on anyone," Annette replied.

Uncle Charles burst into laughter, knowing exactly what Annette meant. Aunt Harriet had to poke him in the rib to make him stop laughing.

"Marriage is good for both of you," Roy told his brother and sister-in-law. "I think it probably makes people more stable."

"Oh, listen to Roy," Eleanor laughed. "He's never been in love or had a girlfriend, yet he's an expert on marriage."

Roy turned to Eleanor. "How do you know whether I've ever been in love?"

Eleanor chuckled. "Come on, Roy. You'd have told me if you had a girl-friend."

Roy did not reply; technically, she was right – he never had had a girl-friend. But he had been in love, perhaps more passionately and sincerely than anyone else in the room. Why did he let Eleanor's words rile him? So many years ago – it was best now just to forget about it.

"Well, thank you all for the presents," said Henry. "This is one of the best birthdays I've ever had."

"Does anyone want anything more to drink?" asked Beth, nervous about the lull in her role as hostess.

"Oh, no, Beth, sit down and relax," said Annette.

"Are we going to play cards?" asked Uncle Charles.

"Sure," said Henry.

"Not yet," said Harriet. "Let's have a minute to let the food settle."

"Bill, the boys look tired," said Annette. "We should probably take them home."

"Beth will let them sleep on one of the beds," Bill said.

"Sure," said Beth. "Jim's old bed is still here. I can clean my junk off it."

"We'll just stay for a couple hands," said Bill.

"Well," said Annette, "I'm worried about the weather."

"Fine," grumbled Bill, standing up. "I'll go warm up the car."

"It's not snowing that hard," said Aunt Harriet, pulling back the curtain to peek outside.

"I know," said Annette, "but by the time I get the kids to bed, it'll be late."

"It's hard having three little boys," said Margaret, although she wished Bill and Annette would stay longer.

While Bill went outside to start the car, Annette gathered up her sons' toys. Lucy and Maud helped the boys put on their coats, hats, mittens, and boots.

"Thanks for everything, Beth. Happy birthday again, Henry," said Annette as she herded her flock out the door.

"Those kids are so adorable," said Lucy.

"I wish Annette would let me babysit them," Maud chirped in.

Ellen also thought her little cousins adorable, but she had no desire to babysit them. She and Tom had not really discussed children. She wondered how many he would want; she wondered whether she would want any, other than maybe a little girl.

The women got up to do the dishes while they muttered about how useless the men were. The men retired to the living room. Uncle Charles took a little nap in the corner of the sofa, while Tom perched on the other end, next to Henry's chair, the safest seat for him since his future father-in-law was the only man present he knew well. Ellen was soon dismissed from the kitchen so she could "entertain her gentleman friend". She perched on the sofa between her wheezing great-uncle and her future husband. Roy turned on the TV, although he had often declared it was just a tool to brainwash Americans into believing what the media and government wanted. But since he had no electricity in his cabin, he did watch television whenever he was at one of his siblings' homes. He was deeply concerned about the war in Vietnam, and the full color news footage stirred his soul in ways he had not experienced since he had fought in Europe.

No one else was interested in the war. Even the sound of gunfire did not wake up Uncle Charles. Henry and Tom decided to talk about fishing. Tom had no idea what was happening in Vietnam; he could not have found the country on a map, although he daily worked on airplanes, including some recently used in the Tet offensive to bomb North Vietnam. Henry knew the conflict was against communism, but since he thought Roy had communist ideas, he would not discuss the subject.

"Oh, turn that thing off. Can't we have one day without the war," Beth huffed when she came into the living room.

"I want to see what's being said since the Tet offensive just ended," Roy replied.

"I'll tell you what happened," said Beth. "People were killed. Thirty thousand I've heard."

"Forty," piped in Aunt Harriet from the dining room. "Forty thousand of those devil communists."

"It's not worth it," said Margaret, "not when we've had a thousand American casualties a month."

"Just turn it off," Beth said. "This is a birthday party."

"That President Johnson is never going to get himself reelected now," said Harriet. "That's what happens when you have a Democrat in the White House. I'm not voting for any president who sends my grandson to war."

Randy Dalrymple was the grandson Harriet referred to. Since he had divorced his wife two months ago, all the family had expected he would become a lost cause. Then when his wife announced she was pregnant with his child, which basic math revealed to have happened after the divorce, Randy decided to join his brother by enlisting in the army. He was currently at training camp, but in the spring, he would be shipped overseas to participate in the ground war. The Whitmans were not fond of the Dalrymple twins – especially not Randy – but even Aunt Harriet deserved sympathy when her grandchildren were involved in the conflict.

"We're ready to play cards now," said Beth, turning off the TV.

Roy did not argue. It was Beth's house. He had seen enough in those few minutes of video to feel his heart ache for the young men experiencing such horror.

Lucy and Maud shuffled the cards. Uncle Charles continued to snooze while everyone else gathered around the dining room table. Tom was the only one who did not know how to play, so he and Ellen shared a hand.

Diamond, Club, Heart. Ace, Jack, Queen, Joker, Three. Card after card circled around the table. King of Spades, Six of Clubs, Four of Diamonds, Ace of Hearts, Two of Clubs, Queen of Hearts. Cards were drawn, laid down, runs were played. Anticipation grew until "RUMMY!" was shouted.

"Now," Ellen coached her boyfriend, "you can either play a spade or an eight."

"Okay," said Tom, laying down a club.

"No!" screeched Aunt Harriet. "You can't play that."

"I'm sorry," said Tom. "I thought I could play black."

"No, you need a spade. You don't follow color, just suit," said Ellen.

Another round around the table.

"Can I play a clover?" Tom asked.

"They're called Clubs," Aunt Harriet said.

"They don't look like Clubs."

Aunt Harriet fumed.

Beth asked whether anyone wanted more pop or coffee.

Ellen pulled a card from Tom's hand and put it down.

Around the table again. Spade. Spade. Spade. Nine of spades. Nine of clubs. Club. Club. Then Heart. Then Joker. Then back to Club.

"I have too many cards in my hand to keep track of them all," said Tom, searching for a Club to play while everyone waited.

Aunt Harriet was annoyed. She was an old woman, and it was almost her bedtime. Ellen wished her great-aunt was the one asleep on the couch rather than Uncle Charles.

"Oh, you're doing fine," said Margaret, patting Tom's arm. He felt more stupid for the encouragement, but he was glad Ellen's grandmother did not give him the hard time he had expected when they first met. He still had to contend with the evil forces of Aunt Harriet, but he sensed family solidarity in that battle.

"Look at that!" Maud exclaimed when Tom's last card won him the hand. "You've been holding out on us. Is that your strategy?"

Tom chuckled, but he could not think of a good comeback.

"Beginner's luck," said Henry. "It's my birthday, so I intend to win."

"You better get at it then," said Beth. "You've got the lowest score of anyone."

The phone rang. It was cousin Joseph. He called to apologize for not coming to the party because his wife was not feeling well.

"She's just sick about this war," said Aunt Harriet. "I don't know what's wrong with the president that he doesn't pull our troops out of there. That silly Tet offensive. I knew it wouldn't do any good."

"Well, I'm sure the president knows better than we do," said Eleanor, who was a staunch Democrat.

"Those Democrats have never known how to run the country," said Aunt Harriet. "Look at Kennedy. He almost got us blown up by Cuba."

"He kept us from being attacked," Eleanor asserted.

"Yes," said Beth, "and don't forget Franklin Roosevelt was a Democrat, and he got us through World War II, and Truman got us through Korea."

"And," said Eleanor, "Wilson got us through World War I."

"Well, I can understand Beth taking that view," said Harriet, laying down the two of spades. "Catholics always vote for Democrats. Kennedy never would have been elected otherwise. But Eleanor, I don't know how a girl like you, who was raised to be a good Republican, can support the Democrats. It must be that liberal ex-husband of yours who put those ideas into your head; teachers are always Democrats."

Eleanor refused to argue but concentrated on the cards in her hand. She knew if she told Aunt Harriet that her ex-husband had been a Republican, she would only have a further argument, and thinking of Ronald only riled her anyway.

Ellen tried to help Tom find the right card, but he lay one down before she could stop him.

"Oh, you should have played the higher one," she said, but it was too late. Lucy and Maud had both played theirs.

By ten o'clock, the game had begun to drag. Beth won the last hand. Then points were tallied and Margaret declared the winner.

"Well, I came in second," said Henry. "That's not too bad for a birthday boy."

"If I'd gotten a trophy for winning," said Margaret, "I'd have given it to you."

"I don't want any pity," laughed Henry, "least of all from my mother."

"Well, we better get going," said Eleanor.

"Is it still snowing out?" asked Margaret.

Lucy, closest to the window, drew back the curtain. "It's a regular blizzard. The snow's swirling all over the place."

"Oh," Ellen clutched Tom's arm. "And you have to drive home in this mess."

"I'll be fine," he said.

"Call me when you get home, promise?" said Ellen.

Henry gathered the playing cards and placed them in their boxes. Beth fetched coats. Roy went to warm up his car. Eleanor gave him the keys to start her car as well. Margaret waited patiently while Harriet woke up Charles. Roy came back inside to collect his passengers. Eleanor, Lucy, and Maud said goodbye and went out into the night.

The snow was falling in thick fluffy flakes. An overwhelming stillness filled the night with the peace only possible when the winter cold keeps all creatures in their shelters. Cold tingled Eleanor and her daughters' noses as they walked to the car. The smell of snow was mixed with car exhaust, which triggered Lucy's memory back to a winter night from her childhood when all the family had been at Grandpa and Grandma's house, back when Grandpa was still alive. The adults had all played cards that night as well. Unlike Uncle Bill and Aunt Annette, Lucy's parents had held no qualms about letting their little girls sleep in the back bedroom while the adults played. Lucy remembered falling asleep in the bedroom, the smell of supper's turnips still permeating the house. She had lain there beside her sister, the bedroom door blocking all but a small gleam of light from the room; she had been half-asleep, half-listening to the adults' chatter in the dining room. And then, her father had come to wrap her in a quilt and carry her out into the cold night to the car. The wind had been piercing and she had whined; then to block the smell of the car's exhaust, she had snuggled her face into her father's wool jacket.

"Goodbye, Eleanor. Goodbye girls!" Margaret called, coming outside. Lucy thought it could have been a call from twenty years ago, but Grandma was now coming out of Aunt Beth and Uncle Henry's house, to climb into Uncle Roy's car, along with Aunt Harriet and Uncle Charles. Lucy was glad that as an adult, she still had so many of the people she had loved in childhood, even if Dad and Grandpa were gone.

She climbed into the backseat, feeling homesick for that night so many years ago. She was glad Maud sat in the front seat so her thoughts would not have to be disturbed by talking with her mother.

"I hope we can make it home," said Eleanor. "It doesn't look as if they've plowed the roads yet."

They pulled out of the driveway and turned onto Summit Street. When they reached Presque Isle Avenue, they saw the plows had just gone by. Less worried about driving now, Eleanor asked, "What do you girls think of that Tom?"

"He's okay," said Maud. "Ellen seems to like him."

"Yes," said Eleanor, "but I'm not sure he's the right one for her."

"Why not?" asked Lucy.

"I don't think they have anything in common."

"They both like to go to the movies," said Maud.

"That's not enough to build a marriage on," said Eleanor. "Not that Tom isn't a nice young man, but I don't think he has the same values or interests as Ellen."

"Like what?" asked Maud.

"You know, books, art, and family. He's from a whole different world than her."

"He's from the U.P.," said Maud.

"No," Eleanor said, "I mean I think Ellen is just settling by marrying Tom. I don't think he's going anywhere. I used to think Ellen would never get married, but now I think she's just had no luck finding anyone, and because Tom is the first man really interested in her, she's settling for him. I don't think they'll be happy."

"I hope they will be," said Maud.

"So do I," said Eleanor. "I'm just afraid she's making a mistake."

Lucy thought it was none of her mother's business whom Ellen married. She was glad her mother could not thwart Ellen's love as she had her own.

"Well," said Eleanor, after a minute, "it won't be long until spring now. I was thinking this year when we do the spring cleaning we might paint the bedrooms."

"All right," said Maud.

"What colors would you girls like for your rooms?"

"I'll stay with pink," said Maud, "but maybe a brighter shade."

"What about you Lucy?"

"It doesn't matter," said Lucy.

"Of course it matters. It's your room. You have to live there, don't you?"

"I don't care. Maybe green."

"Oh, not green. It won't match your bedspread unless you want to buy a new one, but you'll have to pay for it then. I can only afford to buy the paint."

"I don't care then."

"How about an off-white?"

"That's fine," said Lucy. She detested the question. Did her mother assume she would always live in that bedroom and never move out? A minute ago, Lucy had felt happy, but now she was miserable. She recalled again the smell of her father's woolen coat. If he had not gone away, would she have been happier? Might she have found love by now? Had her parents' failed marriage spoiled everything for her?

Roy did not feel much happier as he drove his aunt and uncle the couple blocks to their house. Aunt Harriet grumbled that they should have waited longer for the car to warm up. "This cold makes me sleepy. I just want to go to bed, but of course, I'll have to make sure Charles takes his pills first, and then he'll want the bathroom, and I'll have to wait forever."

Roy pulled into his aunt and uncle's driveway. Uncle Charles got out of the car without a word and waded his way through the crunching snow. He went up the porch and waited patiently for his wife to come unlock the door.

Harriet struggled to get out of the backseat while balancing the container Beth had given her with a couple extra pieces of birthday cake in it. "You would think he'd just carry his own house key," she grumbled to Margaret, while paying no heed to how the snow whirled inside the car. "Men are so much trouble, and they only get worse with age. Sometimes, Margaret, I think you're lucky you became a widow so early."

"Goodnight, Harriet," her sister-in-law replied. "Let us all know when you hear from your grandsons. We all hate the idea of them fighting in the war."

"That's another problem with men," said Harriet. "They're the ones who start these blasted wars."

"Goodnight, Aunt Harriet," said Roy. "It was good to see you again."

"Goodnight," she grunted, slamming the car door.

"What an old biddy," Margaret muttered. Roy chuckled in agreement, then backed the car out of the driveway and across the street into his mother's yard.

"Why don't you stay tonight?" Margaret asked as Roy helped her up the front steps. "The snow's coming down awfully hard. I worry about you driving home in a storm. You can always go back to your place tomorrow."

Roy did not want to stay. He wanted to be alone with his thoughts. He loved his family, but he was so used to solitude that more than a few hours spent with other people would wear upon him, and trivial conversations would ring distractingly in his ears for hours afterwards. Tonight especially, he felt annoyed by Eleanor's remarks about his never being in love. But as he grew older, he was mellowing, and he could see it was important to his mother that he stay tonight so she need not worry about him; he suspected she used the snowfall as an excuse when she was really just lonely. He knew she would be pleased to cook him breakfast in the morning. She would not be around many more years, so he should give her what little pleasure he could.

Once Roy agreed to stay, Margaret fussed over his blankets and pillow case, although he knew she was tired. He settled for the first things they could find, then gave her a kiss goodnight so she would go to bed. He slept in his old upstairs bedroom, across the hall from his mother's room; despite her age, she remained too stubborn to sleep in the downstairs bedroom. Lying in bed, he replayed the party conversation in his head.

"Oh, listen to Roy," Eleanor had laughed. "He's never been in love or had a girlfriend, yet he's an expert on marriage."

The words pierced his heart. His romantic history should not be dismissed as nonexistent; he had just never confided in the family because they would have thought it shameful he had loved a married woman. He could keep his feelings locked away for months or a year at a time, but eventually, they would boil up in him again; a simple word, a certain smell, a certain glow of light, and he would remember again something about Chloe that would make him yearn for her with an uncontrollable clawing, gnawing, tearing ache that consumed his whole system. Until the mood passed, he would feel incapable of anything except chest contorting moans from deep in his soul. Tonight was exemplary of his pain; when he drifted asleep, he dreamt of her, then woke, like Shakespeare's Caliban, and "cried to dream again". Even when he would bolt awake after nightmares of exploding shells and concentration camps, he could dismiss the dreams as part of a past no longer real. But Chloe was always part of his present desire; his nightmarish separation from her was constant. In the early morning hours, he lay strewn across the bed, struggling against his exhaustive grief until his mother knocked on the door to call him to breakfast.

Henry and Beth felt the party had been a success. Once the guests were gone, Beth wanted to wash the remaining dishes, but Henry put a stop to it. "You can do those in the morning," he said. "My birthday isn't over yet. Let's have another piece of cake before we go to bed." Ellen refused a snack but waited up for Tom to call and say he had gotten home safely. Henry pulled out the ice milk from the freezer while Beth sliced up more birthday cake. Henry kissed her cheek as he scooped out the ice milk. Ellen shook her head; just eating cake together was marital bliss for her parents. She wondered what everyone at the party had thought of Tom, but she was afraid to ask her parents whether they thought the family had liked him. Then the phone rang. Tom had made it safely back to the air base in a remarkable thirty minutes, despite the blowing snow. After she hung up the phone, Ellen changed into her nightgown, turned off her light, and crawled into bed. She tried to remember everything Tom had said during the party, and she wondered what everyone had thought of him. He had been late, making them all wait for supper, but that had not been his fault. He had been slow learning to play cards, but that had been less annoying than how ignorant Aunt Harriet had been to him. Did it really matter whether a person knew the difference between Columbus and the Pilgrims? Ellen told herself not to care what others thought. What mattered was whether Tom made her happy; one minute she believed he did; the next she was unsure. If she were unsure, why had she accepted his proposal? But it would be unfair to change her mind now, especially when he was so sweet to her. She remembered how gently he had kissed her goodnight, and how fine he had looked in his air force jacket as he walked to his car. She rolled over onto her stomach, trying to fall asleep as she thought of his handsome face. She dreamt of that day when she would be dressed in white, with a bouquet of lilacs. Beginning that day, she imagined life would always be filled with the scent of lilacs.

On Tom and Ellen's wedding day, the emotions of the bride, groom, and their families can well be imagined. Everyone rejoiced in the couple's happiness. But only Roy felt moved enough to record the event on paper as revealed in his letter to his friend in Rome.

Dear Michael,

I promised our niece, Ellen, that I would describe for you her wedding, so you would feel just as if you had been there yourself. Ironically, just as you vicariously will live her wedding through my words, I vicariously lived that of another young lady – you will understand what I mean in a minute; my heart has been troubled again this last week, and you are the only one who is ever tolerant of my ridiculous fantasies.

A few days before Ellen's wedding, Henry brought me some old copies of the *Mining Journal*. I usually just burn them in my wood-stove, but sometimes I read the articles. This time it seems I was intended to read them because I saw a wedding announcement for Janet Weidner, yes, Chloe and Lex's daughter. She just got married last month. Perhaps it was foolish of me, but I kept the announcement, including the picture of the bride. She is as beautiful as her mother. I will even be so charitable as to say her father was always a handsome bastard and his and Chloe's features have complemented each other in their daughter. Michael, I confess that until I saw she had Lex's features, I had always hoped perhaps she was my child – for years, I have wondered whether despite Chloe's denials, I had been Janet's father, and I wished for Lex's death, not so much to hurt him, as to free Chloe so she could be with me and finally admit to me that her daughter was mine as well.

I obsessed over Janet's wedding announcement for many days. It was in the Marquette paper because Lex's family is from here, and his mother was listed as grandmother of the bride, although the wedding was in Wisconsin. Because Lex's mother still lives here, I realize now he and Chloe have probably made numerous trips to Marquette in the thirty years since they moved away. During all those trips, Chloe has never attempted to contact me – of course, she would be afraid of the risk, but if she loved me, she would have found a way. I know you think our adultery was wrong, but our love was so strong I feel that even God, if he existed, could not say it was wrong for her to be with the man who loves her rather than with a husband who abuses her.

But you are tired of listening to my ravings about Chloe. You want me to tell you about Ellen's wedding. I'm not going to describe

Ellen's gown, the bridesmaids' dresses, the cake, or the decorations. Beth told me she would send you some colored photographs, which will show you better than I can describe how handsome Tom looked, and how beautiful and brimming with happiness was our smiling niece. Monsignor Casanova performed the ceremony – he seems a good man, and when I mentioned I knew you, he told me how pleased he was to marry the niece of his good friend in Rome. He mentioned his visits with you when he went to Rome to attend Vatican Council II. My sister Eleanor's two daughters, Lucy and Maud, were the bridesmaids, and Jim's wife Lisa was matron of honor. Jim was one of the groomsmen, along with one of Tom's friends, and Tom's brother, Rodger, was best man. Jim and Lisa's little boy, Ian, was ring bearer and their daughter, Margie, was the flower girl. Jim and Lisa came from California to spend the entire week with the family. Of course, Henry looked proud enough to burst during the ceremony, and Beth and my mother soaked their handkerchiefs. The cake was triple tiered and big enough to feed twice the hundred guests invited, which I'm told is a small number for a wedding, but for miserly me, it seemed a great extravagance. Even though I tend to be a hermit, I enjoyed myself and even danced with my sisters – Ada came from Louisiana for the wedding. I guess the only sad note – if it saddened anyone – was that my Aunt Harriet was too sick to attend; my poor Uncle Charles stayed home to take care of her, and I can't imagine he found her a pleasant patient.

The wedding was held in the new St. Michael's Church. Except for when I was inside Notre Dame Cathedral in Paris during the war, I had never been in a Catholic Church before. I've often passed St. Peter's Cathedral in Marquette, and also the French Catholic St. John's. Many times I've shaken my head over them, thinking them gaudy wastes of money. I still do not understand why you Catholics build such lavish churches when the money could help the starving, the poor, the suffering. If you had seen the concentration camps, Michael, you would have willingly sold every stone of your Vatican to aid those poor souls. Yet I fear I must be getting old and weak in my atheistic existentialism; I confess that since Sartre's last book leaned toward communism, I have been less impressed by his theories, even if my family has often refused to try and understand me by simply dismissing me as a communist. I admit the time I spent in St. Michael's Church made me feel that if God exists, he might be present there. This new church only has a couple statues, and its cement block walls and yellowish/orange paint is very modern and ugly to my old eyes, but I sensed there an absence of the fear of God

I had known in childhood and that I know you Catholics feel even more strongly. The service was spoken in English – I remember you telling me that is a change from Latin since your Vatican Council. The wedding seemed a celebration of life and God's love for humanity rather than the old religious teaching that man is depraved. I still will not admit God exists, but I think this change suggests that the old binding fears that have controlled men's minds are starting to loosen.

Michael, you know I try to be a philosopher, but I am no theologian. I still don't know what to think; perhaps I have moved from atheism to agnosticism, perhaps I've always just been agnostic. It matters less to me whether God exists than that humanity no longer allows religion to punish it. While I've spent the last twenty or thirty years being pessimistic, now I see the young people protest the war in Vietnam, rather than trying to be heroes, something that never would have happened in our youth. I see my nephews and nieces growing up, marrying, willing to start families rather than dread a future I long thought was doomed – I think perhaps now we are coming into a Brave New World where the young have hope and can overlook the mistakes, the guilt and wrongs of centuries past, to begin again. I do believe now in one thing – the power of the human spirit, because my own spirit has begun to soar again this week.

You must be thinking, "Roy has written another messed-up, long-winded letter." I'm sorry, but I know you will be patient and tolerant of me. Write when you can. Your letters are my great comfort.

Your old friend, Roy

Roy remained deeply thoughtful after writing to Michael. It was a warm summer morning. The heat was swelling in his cabin. His usual cup of coffee – one of the few indulgences he allowed himself – had been put aside when he began to sweat. He could not stay inside because of the humidity. Stripping down to his undershirt, he sallied out into the forest, a thermos of cold water in one hand, Perry Miller's *The New England Mind*, that great tome of Puritan history, in the other. As Roy had grown older, his reading interests had changed from the literary classics of his youth to philosophy in his middle age, and now at sixty, to history. Occasionally, he would theorize about humanity's future, but he most wanted to understand humanity's past as a means to understanding himself. After walking fifteen minutes into the woods, he came to a clearing where a great maple had fallen across the ground, creating a crude log bench. He sat down on it, enjoying the coolness of the shade from the trees above, one of which grew up against the fallen log, creating a chair for his back. The sun glistened across the little meadow clearing, lighting the pink tips of the recently opened lady's slippers.

Roy took out his handkerchief to mop his brow which was drenched with perspiration. Then he poured himself a cup of cool water to perk up his drowsy eyelids. He opened his book, his sweaty fingers turning black from smudging the pages' ink because it was so warm. He wanted to read about the Puritans because his father had told him the Whitmans had come from New York or New England, and their ancestors had been in America since colonial days. Roy had always felt a fondness for those stern old Puritans, nearly fanatical in their obsession with God, with salvation, with creating their city upon a hill, their New Jerusalem. The success of their enterprise had been debated, praised, and maligned for centuries. Roy did not know whether they had been right or wrong; he knew he could not hold their beliefs, yet he admired their determined perseverance, their overwhelming desire to perform God's will without question, their unquestioning faith, now nonexistent in the modern world. Roy thought they had been misled, but he imagined they had found comfort in their strict differentiation between right and wrong.

Roy devoured books with the same strenuous effort another man would run a marathon. He knew no difference between work and play; his entire life had become one great quest for truth. But the stultifying humidity distracted his concentration from the subtleties of Puritan theological controversies. After he finished one chapter, he closed his eyes, lay his head back against the tree, and prayed that if God existed, He would send a cool breeze.

Roy sighed, his eyes still closed. Belief in God had never been simple, as the Puritan dogmas proved, not even in medieval times when everyone believed. He could not remember whether he had ever had unquestioning faith, even as a child, so long ago now. He wondered how others could believe so easily – he doubted that Michael ever questioned, but Michael's upbringing and experiences had been different from his. Michael had never been in love, never known the horrors of war, never had a mother push him to be something he did not want to be – never been forced to break free and choose a hermit-like existence. Roy had thought that living a solitary life in the Huron Mountains would help him forget the horrors of the war, his disappointment in love, the binding, constricting ties of family, work, money, society, religion. But he could never escape from himself – he was tired of being Margaret's son Royal, Henry's brother Roy, a Huron Mountain Club handyman, an army sergeant, or eccentric Uncle Roy; he was tired of his identity, his very existence.

He wondered whether anything could have ever been different for him. What if he had not grown up on a farm? What if his parents had not been poor? What if he had been the oldest rather than second born child, or even been an only child? What if he had never met Chloe? What if he had never gone to church, where he had had the misfortune to see and fall in love with Chloe? What if he had never worked at the Huron Mountain Club, had never met Lex, who had unwittingly given him access to the woman he had loved? What if he had never been born? What difference would it have made to anyone?

A branch broke nearby – the startling sound woke him from his stupor. His eyes snapped open. First he saw a beam of sunlight breaking through the trees, illuminating the clearing. He bent his head down to the earth, where four light brown rabbits were chasing each other in a circle, a halo of sunlight lighting up their furry coats. A branch broke again, only closer. Roy turned his head. A black bear was at his side. Roy thought he must still be half-asleep. The bear nuzzled his hand. Roy did not feel afraid, only regretful that he had no food for the creature. His thermos and cup lay on the ground. It was stifling hot. He poured a cup of water for the bear, who lapped it up, its nose nearly getting trapped in the cup. When the creature finished drinking, it took a couple steps backward, licked the remaining drops from its lips, then slowly ambled away until Roy saw it disappear into the thick summer foliage.

When Roy looked again into the clearing, he saw the four rabbits circle again, then make a beeline into the forest, running between what they thought were trees.

Instead, they had passed between the legs of a great buck. Now Roy felt frightened, for the creature seemed to be watching him, just as he had watched the rabbits and the bear, with an assertion of superior intelligence. The buck was the most magnificent creature Roy had ever seen. A sportsman would immediately have degraded the vision by counting the points on its antlers, but Roy had no such interest; he felt only respect for the awesome creature. It stood as King of the Forest, dominant over everything near it, proclaiming the forest to be its kingdom. Roy could have ridden on its back for miles; it was so gigantic, so powerful, yet untamable. This master of the forest stared until Roy felt the full weakness of his own arms, the frailty of his chest, the feebleness of the sticks he called legs. He was completely inferior to this forest god. Yet Roy knew himself to be powerful compared to those weak little rabbits, and even to the ants who crawled the earth, yet could lift so many times their own weight. The mighty stag observed Roy keenly until Roy felt intensely honored to be so regarded by such a superior creature. No fear of man showed in its eyes, only satisfaction that it had gained some insight by watching a human. Slowly it nodded its head in acknowledgment of Roy, then majestically strode back into the forest.

Roy felt overwhelmed. His heart and mind burned with the belief that "Only God could create such a miracle of life."

Then came the refreshing breeze for which Roy had wished. Relief spread through the forest. With it came to Roy's memory a half-remembered line from a poem he had read in his youth, "For every thing that lives is holy."

He tried to pull himself to his feet, but his frail human legs failed. He fell to his knees and remained there several minutes until the breeze had passed through the meadow.

When he had struggled back onto his feet, he picked up his thermos and book.

"For all their confusion," he thought, "the Puritans believed something I've been foolish to dismiss."

He was almost afraid to acknowledge what had occurred. He told himself all he had seen was a bear, an abnormally large deer, and some bunnies, and he had felt a little breeze. In the Upper Peninsula, wild animals were everywhere and the climate constantly changed.

But as he stumbled home, he realized the unbelievable naturalness of the experience made it magnificent, as if he had seen the everyday world correctly for the first time; all his life such magic, such mystery had surrounded him; he had noticed its beauty, but never acknowledged the miracle of its existence. He had spent his life obsessing over his problems, humanity's problems, but never considered the existence of the animals and insects, trees and flowers, all that lived separate from him, all that the Creator allowed to function apart from a confused, weak old man, who was himself linked to so many miracles.

By the time he reached his cabin, Roy had recovered enough from the initial shock to pen a second letter to Michael.

The next evening Roy went to have supper with Henry and Beth. He knew they felt lonely now that Ellen had married. She had gone to live on the air force base with Tom until his enlistment ended, and then they would find a place to live in Marquette. On his way to Henry and Beth's house, Roy stopped to see his mother. Margaret was in the kitchen, busily baking; she hated to cook, but she had learned to bake continually to satisfy the Whitman sweet tooth.

"Who's the cake for, Ma?" he asked, sitting down at the kitchen table.

"For Henry and Beth. I'm bringing it over for supper."

"I didn't know you were invited," said Roy, pulling out a cigarette.

"Don't you light that!" said Margaret. "Do you want to kill us both with that smoke?"

Roy put away the cigarette while his mother frosted the cake.

"I figured you'd be stopping by to give me a ride over there," said Margaret. "What if I hadn't come?"

"I would have walked," she said. Roy did not doubt she would have. Her legs were old but mighty sturdy.

"But why are you making a cake?" he asked.

"Well, I had to do something for Beth," said Margaret, as if he had asked the world's stupidest question.

"Why? What do you mean?"

"Because her brother died. Really, if you'd come around more, you would know what's going on in your own family."

"Michael?" Roy felt as stunned as if his mother had struck him across the cheek.

"Yes, Monsignor McCarey."

"When? How?" He was so upset he lit his cigarette, ignoring his mother's prohibition against smoking.

"Sometime last night," said Margaret. "I guess it was about eight o'clock in Rome. He was found dead in his room, kneeling against his bed. Must have been praying. They say it was a stroke. The priest who called Beth told her the doctor thought it happened quickly, probably in a minute or two, so he could not have suffered much. I hope when I go it'll be that easy. I didn't know what else to do since he'll be buried in Rome, so I'm making Beth a cake."

Roy had quit listening. Rome was several hours ahead of Marquette; when Roy did the math, he figured Michael must have died at – why at the same time yesterday as when he had been in the forest – could it be that – ?

"All right, let's go," said Margaret. "You carry the cake so I can hold the railing as I go down the stairs."

Roy did as he was told, helping his mother to the car and driving her to Henry and Beth's house. He felt like a zombie, just going through the motions.

"Did you hear the news?" asked Henry when Roy came in the door.

"I told him," said Margaret, taking the cake from Roy. "Beth, I made you a cake. I'll put it in the refrigerator so the frosting won't melt."

"Thank you," said Beth, busily scooping mashed potatoes into a bowl.

"Beth, I'm so sorry," said Roy.

"Thank you," she replied.

"Ma said that Michael went quickly."

"In a minute or two," Henry replied.

"Yes," said Beth. "The doctor didn't think he suffered much."

"I'm so sorry. He wasn't even that old – sixty-eight?"

"All my brothers died young. I don't imagine I'll be around much longer myself."

"Don't talk such foolishness," said Henry.

"Wait until you hit eighty," said Margaret. "Then every day's a gift from God and you try to collect all you can."

Beth said nothing, just carried the potatoes to the table. Everyone sat down. Margaret said the blessing, asking God to "Let the good monsignor feast with thee in Paradise."

"I think," said Beth, as the food was passed around, "that it's somehow symbolic he died on Pentecost."

"Pentecost?" said Roy, surprised to realize it was already so far past Easter.

"Yes, Roy. If you went to church," said Margaret, "you would know that Pentecost was when the Holy Spirit descended on the apostles."

Roy knew about Pentecost. But he could not tell them how astonishing it was that Michael had passed away that day, at the very hour he had been overwhelmed in the forest. He attributed that moment as his friend's last act of kindness.

That next Sunday morning, Roy appeared on his mother's doorstep and said, "I thought maybe I'd drive you to church."

Margaret thought of making a smart-aleck remark about prodigal sons, but she decided not to scare him off.

From that day, Roy went to church with his mother every Sunday. After a few weeks, the congregation ceased to be astonished by his presence. Margaret felt proud; did not the Bible say if you raised a child up in the right path, he would not stray from it when he was older? At age sixty, Roy was certainly older.

Interlude
1968-1975

The world was changing again. Overseas the Vietnam War raged. Throughout the United States, people protested the war. The Civil Rights and Feminist movements paved the way for American freedom to expand. Modern communication and technology brought the world to Marquette more rapidly than the freeways coming north from Chicago or the vehicles passing over the Mackinac Bridge. People changed, ideas changed, yet Marquette still remained isolated enough to hold onto its past.

In these years, people first became conscious that the twentieth century was nearing its end. The nineteenth century was only a memory in the minds of a few elderly people who found themselves living in a modern and alien world of technology they had never dreamed would exist. Old ways of doing things had passed away. People had automatic washers and dryers, televisions, telephones, radios, tape decks. No one drove a buggy or even rode a streetcar – the automobile was everywhere until even Upper Michigan was divided by several major highways. The majority of Marquette's citizens knew little about the past that had created their city. Even the elderly residents could not remember those first pioneers. Many residents had not been born in Marquette, but after being students at the college or stationed at the air force base, they had decided to settle in this ruggedly cold, yet welcoming land.

The buildings changed. The old sandstone quarries had long since closed; new structures were now built of cement or brick. The remaining sandstone buildings were monuments to a forgotten era, and not all were lucky enough to remain. Kaye Hall, the beautiful gem of Northern's campus was demolished, to be replaced in 1975 by a new administrative building, named for local banker Sam Cohodas; despite its five million dollar cost, it was the ugliest building in

Marquette's history and a sad replacement for Kaye Hall. Beside it, the Peter White Science building was also torn down, leaving only a solitary and out of place Longyear Hall to bear witness to the college's original triumvirate of buildings. Northern also built a new library, the Edgar L. Harden Resource Center in 1969 at a cost equivalent to the Cohodas building, but with a better aesthetic result. The old normal school was now Northern Michigan University with an enrollment of nine thousand students. Marquette had become a true college town, and with the decline of the iron ore industry, the university became a major player in Marquette's survival. Northern's growth meant the improvement of its hockey team; consequently, the old Palestra, for decades the favorite haunt of Marquette's youth, was torn down in 1974 to be replaced by the larger Lakeview Arena; the new arena might hold a greater number of hockey fans, but never would it be so well-loved as its predecessor.

Increasing population and modern trends caused the city to grow. Westward spread Marquette's streets, city blocks, parking lots, businesses, and homes. The downtown was nearly deserted as the age of shopping malls arrived. Once the City of Marquette had ended at Lincoln Avenue. Now McDonalds, Shopko, motels and the Marquette Mall sprang up until a bypass was built so vehicles would not have to travel through downtown Marquette at all; new businesses grew along the bypass until US 41 West became the focus of the city's commercial interests. Acres that for the city's first century had lain empty save for a farm or brewery were paved into parking lots, used car dealerships, and fast food restaurants. Old timers, grumbling that Shopko and the Marquette Mall were too far away, vowed they would continue to shop downtown, but automobiles carried most residents to the new shopping areas within ten minutes.

The city had begun as a harbor town, but the iron ore industry's decline had reduced the Lower Harbor to only one ore dock, while another remained in the Upper Harbor at Presque Isle Park, and even these docks had not been built until well into the twentieth century. The lakeshore's purpose was transformed from commerce into recreation, the water becoming filled with swimmers and sailboats, and only a rare ore boat.

Tastes had equally changed. The Victorian mindset no longer reigned. Few could name a Victor Herbert operetta or recall reading a Dickens novel except in school. Even the Big Band era was old fashioned. Frank Sinatra and Judy Garland were replaced by Barry Manilow, Sonny and Cher, Tony Orlando and Dawn, Kenny Rogers, and Olivia Newton John. Elvis was no longer as cool as the Beatles, the Beach Boys, the Rolling Stones, the Eagles. Forget the waltz.

Disco had arrived. Radio was no longer groovy. The first generation raised in front of the TV was growing up, and cable television was on its way.

Into this world John Vandelaare was born. He would think it a long ago era that his Grandpa and Grandma Whitman spoke of when they mentioned streetcars and horse and buggy days. The only person born in the nineteenth century he would ever know would be his great-grandmother, Margaret Dalrymple Whitman, frail and fading with her era, but still the well-loved matriarch of the family. John would grow up taking shopping malls and Pizza Huts for granted. Yet Marquette's impressive old buildings and eternal Lake Superior served as signposts to a past he would slowly discover. The Marquette Mall, with its fountain of sparkling multicolored lights, would delight John's eyes, but it would not trigger his imagination. Instead, raised on Disney films like *Peter Pan*, he would think the Old Savings Bank with its clock tower as grandly impressive as London's Big Ben, and if you had mentioned Central Park or Kensington Gardens, he would have insisted Presque Isle far more beautiful. From his grandparents, John gathered that his family had resided in the city since pioneer times, and he would eventually be as proud of the fact as any English baron of his ancient family castle. Many old Marquette families had vanished from the city's present day records, but John's blood was that of the old pioneers, and it would hold him in good stead against the diseases of modern living. Nature's immutability impressed his young mind just as strongly as it had his ancestors. Still just minutes from the old harbor, the wilderness spread out mile after mile. In Marquette, John could still develop a relationship with Nature which few modern children, reared in the great city amid skyscrapers and concrete slabs, could claim at the century's close.

Patient reader of three Marquette chronicles, John is to be the hero of this story's end. Do not expect from him the great deeds the world applauds. He would not walk on the moon. He would not cure cancer. He would live a relatively unspectacular life, much by his own choice because he wished to be more human than many of the great. He was not born in a palace or mansion. No headlines in the world's newspapers proclaimed his birth. He was born at St. Luke's Hospital in 1970, and a small mention in the *Mining Journal*'s birth announcements was sufficient to acknowledge his existence. Yet he was everything to the family who eagerly awaited his coming.

The day Ellen left the hospital with her firstborn child, she could not wait to show him off. Her first stop was her grandmother's house.

Margaret Whitman's eighty-six year old arms reached out to hold John.

"My!" she said, cuddling her great-grandson, "his eyes are so blue!"

"All babies' eyes are blue, Grandma," said Ellen.

"Not this blue."

"They'll probably change color when he's a little older," said Ellen. "Wouldn't it be nice if they became grey?"

"Why grey?" asked Margaret.

"In books," said Ellen, "heroes always have grey eyes, but I've never actually seen anyone with them."

"No, I think his eyes will stay blue," said Margaret. "Deep Lake Superior blue."

"Is it Lake Superior blue," asked Tom, beaming over his son, "or is it Michigan blueberries blue?"

"He's beautiful. That's all that matters," Ellen said.

"Today, I miss Harriet," Margaret wickedly grinned. "Why did she and Charles have to die before little John here was born? She would have been so jealous – none of her grandchildren or great-grandchildren were such remarkable babies."

A baby's life is not remarkable. Nor can its significance be predicted. Since John remembered nothing of his first years, we pass to one of his earliest memories. He would not remember the conversations recorded here, but subconsciously, they may have stirred his ancestral memories.

Tom and Ellen lived at K.I. Sawyer Air Force Base until Tom's term of enlistment ended. Then they moved into an apartment in Marquette, and he found a mechanic's job in an automotive shop. After a few years, when John was a little boy, with a little brother, Chad, a couple years younger, his parents built a house a few miles south of Marquette; the land there was virtually unchanged wilderness, save for a few rough snowmobile trails. Slowly this wilderness, on the edge of the great Hiawatha Forest, was being developed into subdivisions. But unlike city developments, no bulldozers came to rape this land. Plots were purchased and cleared by individual buyers so that houses remained hidden behind numerous trees.

On Tom and Ellen's new little half-acre of land, a fallen tree lay across what would soon be John's backyard. It was the first tree felled by Tom's chainsaw, and it was one of many that needed to be removed so a house could be built. John's mother had chosen this parcel of land because she loved the trees. While Tom cleared the lot to make room for the house, Ellen walked around the property, tying ribbons around every tree she wished to remain in the yard.

"That's too many," said Tom after Ellen had marked several large oaks she refused to part with. "All those trees will drop acorns and ruin the lawn, and they'll be hard to maneuver around when I mow the grass, and when they die, they might fall and crash into the house."

"I don't care," said Ellen. "I want lots of trees. That's why we chose to live in this area. Besides, trees only increase the property value."

"They also cause more work," said Tom.

"They provide shade," Ellen replied. "Look at how that lot was cleared down the road from us. It looks horrible because there's not a tree left on it. The entire point of living in this neighborhood is to be close to Nature."

Six years of marriage had taught Tom that when Ellen was being stubborn, there was no getting around her. He grumbled some more to make his annoyance clear, but Ellen knew she had won the battle. Usually she gave into Tom, even when he was unreasonable, but she would not live in a naked yard.

Ellen did not realize how much Tom hated trees. He would rather have lived on a Marquette city block, but Ellen insisted that building their own home would be preferable to fixing up an old one. Tom did not like being isolated out in the woods; he hoped all fifty empty lots in the subdivision would quickly be bought and cleared. He wanted his neighbors nearby, not far away. Although his parents now lived in Iron Mountain, his father and grandfather had homesteaded in Dickinson County, making their living by peeling poplar, raising Christmas trees, potato farming, and supplementing their income with odd jobs in Iron Mountain when money was tight. Tom had joined the air force to escape that hard, lonely life, yet now he found himself back in the woods he had hated since childhood.

Ellen left Tom to his grumbling and his chainsaw and wandered about the yard; despite the noise of trees being felled, she felt secure now that she and Tom owned a piece of land where they could make their life. Here the children could have a large yard to play in; they could ride their bicycles down the snowmobile trails; they could build forts in the woods. Here would be a retreat from the busy town only ten minutes away.

In town that morning, Henry and Beth babysat their grandsons, but at noon, they drove out to the new homesite and brought along a picnic lunch. John sat down on a fallen log on the land his father had cleared. John knew nothing yet of history, but today started his boyhood spent in the forest.

Henry and Tom quickly ate the sandwiches Beth had made, and then Tom took Henry to look over the land and show him the morning's work. Henry was nearly seventy now, but he remained as spry as a man three decades younger.

He had officially retired at sixty-five, but he still worked in his woodshop everyday. He insisted he would help Tom build the house, and Ellen and Tom readily accepted the offer, knowing his carpentry skills would guarantee them a sturdy home. With Henry's help, the work would be carried out efficiently and be finished before the snow fell.

"Your dad hasn't been so excited about anything in years," Beth told Ellen while the men sauntered about the yard. "I'm so glad you're letting him help."

Done eating, John slid off the log and onto the forest floor, his two year old brother, Chad, beside him. They played with the twigs and pinecones, poking them into the sand, finding the toys rude yet satisfying for pioneer children.

"Dad's doing us a huge favor," Ellen said as she cleaned up the picnic leftovers. "Besides, I know Tom will need the help if I want a house that will stay standing." Tom thought he was a handyman, but Ellen knew better.

Beth inhaled deeply. "I love the smell of freshly cut wood."

Ellen smiled. "Isn't it the same as the smell of all that sawdust Dad has in his woodshop? I would think you'd be sick of it."

"No, it's not the same," said Beth. "Your father uses wood that's already been treated. Fresh timber has a much stronger smell."

"I'm surprised at you, Mom. You've never struck me as being an outdoors woman, other than to go fishing."

"No, I guess not, but I spent a lot of time in the woods as a girl. Do you remember my cousin, Thelma?"

"Sure."

"Her father, my Uncle Karl, was a big lumber baron. Sometimes when he was working near Marquette, my family would visit him at one of his logging camps. Thelma and I would run around, climbing on the woodpiles and playing hide and seek behind the fallen logs. It probably wasn't a very safe thing to do, but we had fun."

"I thought Thelma was a lot older than you? I didn't know you played with her when you were a girl."

"She was seven years older, but I was the only girl in my family, and she was only child, so I guess we were both glad to have the other to play with. I seem to remember we were rather a wild pair of tomboys at times."

"It's hard to imagine you and Thelma running around as little girls, especially since I can barely remember when she wasn't in a wheelchair."

"In her day Thelma could have outrun any boy. The only thing faster than her legs was her mouth," laughed Beth. "But we always had good times together. That smell of cut trees sure does bring back memories. Back then, we had to work really hard – we didn't have all these modern day gadgets – but there was something special about life then. I suppose everyone feels that way about childhood since it's the most care free time in life, but I do miss those times."

"I think the modern world is better," said Ellen. "Women don't have to wear all those layers of clothes. I'm hot enough today in shortsleeves and jeans."

Beth did not mind a little extra heat if it allowed her to maintain her self-respect. She had never worn pants a day in her life – except when she wore Henry's old trousers to go fishing. Henry did not want to see her in slacks, and she wanted to be attractive to him. Besides, she thought she would look fat in pants.

"I have often wondered," said Ellen, "what it would have been like to be one of the first settlers in Marquette. I wonder whether they felt as proud as Tom and I do to clear our land and build our first house."

"My grandmother would have known," said Beth. "She always told us she came to Marquette the year it was founded."

Ellen wanted to ask her mother more about her own great-grandmother. Her mother rarely mentioned the past, and since all her mother's relatives were gone, Ellen knew little about the McCarey side of the family. But the men returned, dispelling her chance to find out more.

"Well, honey, should we head back into town?" Henry asked.

"I suppose," said Beth, straining to lift her old body up off the log.

"You don't have to take the boys back with you if you don't want," said Ellen. "I can watch them this afternoon."

"Oh no, I don't mind watching them," said Beth, "so long as I don't have to read that darn *I Can Lick Thirty Tigers Today* book. John sure is crazy about that story."

"Thank you," said Ellen. "I appreciate your help."

Henry and Beth drove their grandsons back to town while Ellen and Tom returned to work. Ellen had only momentarily wondered about Marquette's pioneers; someday, John would feel as if he had relived their experiences. But he was yet too young to know how Nature spoke in the wind whistling through the trees, or how this land would cast a spell upon him.

1976

Every Saturday afternoon, around four o'clock, John Vandelaare, his parents, and younger brother Chad, would drive into Marquette, just a few miles from their house in the woods, and spend the evening with Grandpa and Grandma Whitman. At five o'clock, Mom, Dad, and Grandma went to Mass at St. Michael's. Grandpa, because he was raised a Baptist, and because his mother might still be upset if he went to a Catholic church, stayed home to babysit his grandsons. This time spent with Grandpa was the highlight of John's week.

The moment the Vandelaares' car pulled into the Whitmans' driveway, John would head into Grandpa's woodshop at the back of the garage.

Henry was now retired, if working eight to ten hours a day in his woodshop at age seventy-one could be considered retired; everyone he knew still wanted a bench, chair, table, or cabinet from him. He was the busiest retired man conceivable, and he would have wanted it no other way, but he always had time to spend with his grandsons.

Today, as John entered the shop, Henry turned off his scroll saw.

"How are you today?" he asked John.

"Fine, Grandpa. What are you making?"

"A lady wants me to fix that old rocking chair in the corner," he replied. "Did your Mom and Dad go in the house?"

"Yes and Chad too."

"Well, I guess we ought to be going in then, shouldn't we?"

"Uh huh," said John, turning around to go through the garage into the house, but his passage was blocked by a chipmunk running toward him.

"Grandpa, there's a chippie coming!" John said.

"I've been giving him snacks all afternoon," laughed Henry, reaching for a bag of peanuts on his workbench. "I sure don't know where he puts them all."

Henry took three peanuts from the bag, bent down to the ground, said "Don't move" to John, and placed his open palm a few inches above the garage floor.

Without hesitation, the chipmunk jumped into Henry's hand and filled its cheeks with peanuts. It had some difficulty arranging the peanuts in its mouth, but once they were all in, he looked up for another, so Henry gave him a little half-sized one. The chipmunk shoved that one in its mouth as well, then jumped back to the floor and ran out the little hole its grandparents had chewed in the garage door.

"That's about his eighth stash today," Henry said as he and John went into the house by the back door. They found the family in the living room, talking until it was time to leave for church.

"You boys be good for Grandpa while we're gone to church," said Tom.

"We will," said John and Chad.

"We'll be fine," Henry replied.

Once the churchgoers were gone, Henry set the kitchen table for supper – the dining room table only being used for company and special occasions. Then the work was done, and the boys had a full hour to have fun with Grandpa, who was always willing to play whatever game they liked, unlike most grownups who had lost their imaginations.

"Tell us a story, Grandpa!" John said when the boys were seated on the couch with Grandpa in the middle.

"Do you want a story too, Chad?" Henry asked.

Chad nodded yes.

"Okay," said Henry, "what should it be about?"

"Flowers," said Chad.

"And a skunk," said John, thinking that would make it more interesting.

"And a tree," Chad said.

"Anything else?"

"Nope, that'll be good," said John, so Grandpa would not have too hard a time making up the story.

"All right, let me think a minute," said Henry. In thirty seconds, he began.

The Skunk Who Loved Flowers

Once there were two little boys, Billy and Fred, who lived in a house on the forest's edge. One day it was their mother's birthday so the boys decided they would pick her some flowers as a present for her special day.

Early in the morning, the two boys went out walking in the woods. They followed a trail running through the forest with flowers growing along it. In their excitement over the flowers, the boys soon wandered away from the trail without noticing where they were going. When their arms were too full of flowers to carry anymore, they turned to go back home, but by that time, they were so far from the trail that they soon realized they were lost.

Then they were a little scared and worst of all, afraid they would be late for their mother's birthday party.

"If we're late, Mom won't get her birthday flowers," said Fred.

"And we'll miss the birthday cake," said Billy who liked cake very much.

"Maybe if we walk in a straight line," said Fred, "we'll find the trail again."

They did not even know from which direction they had come, but after making their best guess, they headed forward in a straight line, hoping to find the trail.

Not far from where the boys had gotten lost, Smelly the Skunk was busy cleaning his house. Smelly's house was a rotted old tree. It had fallen over years ago in a big thunderstorm. When Smelly had first seen it, because it was hollow and big and cozy inside, he had decided it was the perfect place to live. Since then, he had been busy cleaning out the spiders and ants and making his bed with leaves. Today his mom was coming to see his new house for the first time, and he wanted it to be neat and pretty for her. But no matter how hard he worked, he felt something was missing; he just could not decide what it was. He had been up and working since the sun rose, and now he was tired.

"Maybe I'll just take a little snooze," he thought. "Then when I wake up, I won't be as tired and I can think what else I need to decorate my house. Besides, Mom will be worried that I'm sick if she sees I'm tired. Then she'll try to make me drink nasty things like castor oil." And so Smelly the Skunk lay down on his bed of leaves and went to sleep.

Meanwhile, Billy and Fred were still trying to find their way home. Just after Smelly the Skunk went to sleep, they came across the log that served as his house. By this time, the two boys were both tired from walking. Fred was cranky because he hadn't yet had his breakfast. Billy was cranky because he was scared they would never find their way home.

"I don't want to walk anymore," Billy complained.

"We have to," said Fred, "or else, we'll never find our way home."

"You go find home and then tell Mom and Dad to come back and get me," Billy said. He was a stubborn little boy, and to show just how stubborn he was, he sat right down on Smelly's log and refused to move.

"What if I get lost too? Then we'll never get home," Fred replied. "And besides, if we sit here and do nothing, the flowers we picked will all die because they won't have any water."

This argument did not get Billy off the log. Instead, the thought of all Mom's pretty birthday flowers dying only made him burst into tears. Then Fred felt bad for sounding so mean. He sat down on the log, put his arm around Billy, and tried to comfort him.

Billy was crying so loud that the noise woke up Smelly. He did not understand a word the boys said, but he was mad that they were sitting on his roof, and worse, they were making such an awful crying, whining noise that it was impossible for him to fall back asleep. Smelly was usually scared of humans, but when he was tired, he was crabby, and when he was crabby, he did not feel scared of anything. He was determined to make those boys get off his house and quit making such a racket.

Smelly walked out to his doorway at the end of the log. Then he peeked up over the edge and saw Billy crying, and Fred starting to cry too because he could not get Billy to stop crying. Billy's tears had broken down Fred's courage until both boys became convinced they would never find their way home. But the two boys were not all that Smelly saw; he also saw all the flowers Billy and Fred had picked for their Mom's birthday. Smelly did not know why the boys had picked the flowers, but he did know that his own mother loved flowers, and because she was coming to visit tonight, those flowers would make her think his house was beautiful. Smelly was too lazy to pick his own flowers, and he saw an easy way of getting them away from Billy and Fred.

Smelly marched outside and walked around the log until he was standing right in front of Billy and Fred. Then he hissed and scratched the ground with his foot until the boys noticed him. By the time Billy wiped his tears enough to see Smelly clearly, it was too late to escape. Smelly raised his tail and let out a nauseating spray that made the boys jump to their feet and run and run, screaming all the while. They dropped all their flowers as they disappeared into the woods. Smelly waited until they were out of sight, then collected the flowers and carried them home in his teeth.

Now the boys were just as smelly as Smelly, but as they ran through the woods, they saw their house in the distance, and a few minutes later, they were in their own front yard.

All morning, their mother had been worried about her boys. Now, when she heard their cries, she ran outside. The boys stunk so strongly of skunk smell that even she would not hug them. She was very angry they had gone into the woods without telling her, and she told them they had ruined her birthday. She made the boys take baths and scrub all the skunk smell off themselves. Then she made them go to their rooms, and they were not allowed to have any birthday cake for going into the woods alone and without permission.

Meanwhile, Smelly the Skunk laughed about how he had tricked the boys. He decorated his log with the flowers, and when his mother came over for supper, she praised his beautiful house. She was very pleased when he presented her with a bouquet of flowers. As for Smelly, he was happy because his mother had brought for supper a delicious pie of tree bark and red ants.

The End

"Grandpa, that wasn't a very good story," said Chad.

"Yes it was," said John. He thought it seemed true. He remembered times when he had been punished for something even when he had had good intentions.

"The skunk was bad so he shouldn't have gotten the flowers," said Chad. "It's not fair."

"Life isn't fair," said Henry.

"I liked the story!" said John. "I like when the villains win. It's more real that way. Those boys were crybabies anyhow." He did not like the boys because he was afraid he would have acted just like them.

"I don't know why John had to have a stupid skunk in the story," said Chad.

"Well, it's just a story," said Henry. "What do you boys want to do now?"

"I brought my *Humpty Dumpty* magazine," said John. "Grandpa, will you help me make something out of it?" He ran and picked the magazine off the dining room table, then flipped through it until he found a page with directions for making a hanging mobile.

"Let me see what we need," said Henry, consulting the directions.

The mobile required pieces to be cut out, and string to tie everything together, and a drinking straw from which to spread out and hang the different pieces. Henry dug through Beth's kitchen drawers until he found all the necessary equipment. Then he gave John the scissors and let him cut out the pictures for the mobile. Chad watched for a few minutes, then grew bored and fetched the drawing paper Beth always had in ample supply.

"Grandpa, can I watch cartoons while I draw?" Chad asked.

"Yes," Grandpa said.

Chad turned on the TV and found some cartoons, then lay on the floor with his pencil and paper.

Once John had the mobile pieces cut out, Grandpa found the hole punch and punched each piece. He let John cut the pieces of string, then he threaded them through the mobile pieces, knotting the string so nothing would fall apart.

"Now where will we put it?" asked John.

"I don't know," said Henry. "How about over the doorway?"

John nodded his head. Over the doorway was a good place; that was where Grandma hung papier-mâché bells at Christmas time.

"Now everyone can see how it works," said Chad.

Soon after the mobile was finished, Beth, Tom, and Ellen came home from church. Henry emptied the bag from Burger Chef and distributed the hamburgers while John showed everyone the mobile. Beth chuckled over it. Then Chad gave her the picture he had drawn; it was hardly more than a scribble of flowers, but the family thought it showed the promise of greater artistic achievements.

"John, where are you going to sit?" asked his mom.

"Next to Grandpa," he said.

"Do you promise to behave yourself?"

"Yes, Mom."

"We always behave, don't we, John?" said Henry.

"Yes," said John.

"Come on, Dad," Ellen replied. "John always gets half his sandwich on him, and then you get upset."

"Well, John, no crumbs on the floor today, okay?" said Henry.

"All right, I promise," said John.

Ellen looked doubtful but let them sit beside each other.

"How was church?" asked Henry. Although a stranger in God's house, he was still a fan of the Almighty.

"Fine," said Beth. "Ellen, I forgot to tell you I got a letter from Aunt Ada."

"How is she?"

"Fine. She's coming to visit this summer."

"That'll be nice," said Ellen.

"We'll be at Ives Lake then," said Henry.

"I can't wait to go up to Ives Lake," said Beth. "I'm aching to go fishing there."

"When are you going?" asked Tom.

"Next week," said Henry.

Henry and Beth had spent their last few summers at Ives Lake because Henry had taken a seasonal job there as a caretaker for the Huron Mountain Club. Ives Lake had originally been the vacation home of Marquette's pioneer

Longyear family. The property included a barn, a small caretaker's house where Henry and Beth stayed, a large red house, and farther along the lakeshore, a stone house where the Longyears had lived. Henry's job was to maintain the property, mow the lawns, and keep the houses prepared for any guests, who were usually college students the Club had given permission to study the geology and minerals available in the Huron Mountains. Between doing repairs, Henry and Beth had plenty of time to go fishing or to take long walks in the woods; sometimes, Roy even came over from his own little cabin just outside the Club property. Being a caretaker was the perfect summer job for a retired man and his wife, and visiting Ives Lake became nearly a summer festival for the rest of the family; there were frequent weekend picnics when Henry's brothers, sisters, nephews, and nieces came up to visit; sometimes Tom and Ellen would take a little vacation to Green Bay or Mackinac Island for a few days, leaving John and Chad at the lake with their grandparents. Whenever the snow began to melt, the entire family became impatient for another summer spent at Ives Lake.

"We can invite Ada up there," said Ellen. "I don't think she's ever been to the Huron Mountain Club."

"Are her husband or kids coming to visit with her?" asked Tom.

"No, her husband never comes up, and I imagine her kids are busy working or raising their own kids," said Beth.

John remembered Aunt Ada from her visit two years ago, but he was not interested in hearing about the rest of her family whom he had never met. Having finished his sandwich, he asked, "Grandma, are there any cookies for dessert?"

"I want cookies!" said Chad.

"Shh, let Grandma finish eating first," Ellen said.

"It's all right," said Beth, getting up to open a kitchen drawer. "I was going to bake today, but I didn't have time, so you'll have to settle for store bought ones."

John and Chad did not complain. Grandma's cookie drawer was a hallowed place, never allowed to go empty. In addition to Grandma's usual home-baked cookies were packages of Fig Newtons, Nutter Butters, Windmill cookies, and a Little Debbie treat selection.

John took two Windmill cookies, while Chad declared he wanted "Nutbutters".

"Grandpa," said John, "when we're done eating, will you help us turn our funmeal boxes into houses?"

"Sure," said Grandpa. Already the boys had collected boxes that turned into a castle, a gas station, a grocery store, and a hospital. They even had a floor map so all the buildings could be placed on it to make a town. Tonight, John's hamburger box would turn into a haunted house while Chad's would become a seaside cottage.

"I love Burger Chef!" John said, dreaming of the day he would have all the houses.

"All right, now that you're done eating," said Mom, "why don't you throw away your paper plates and go in the living room and wait for Grandpa."

"Don't throw away the bottom plates if they're clean," said Grandma. They always used paper plates on Saturday nights, and Grandpa put double plates on just in case something leaked through.

When John separated his paper plates, he shouted, "Look!"

Chad made a similar discovery before he could see what his brother was excited about.

Grandpa had placed a dollar bill beneath each boy's plate.

"Dad, you spoil them," Ellen said.

"That's all right," said Henry. "I want to spoil them while I can."

"Boys, what do you say?" Tom asked.

"Thank you, Grandpa!"

"You're welcome."

The boys now went into the living room, soon followed by Grandpa and Tom. Grandpa helped the boys put together their houses while Tom watched *Hee-Haw*. The women let the men watch what they wanted on TV while they washed the glasses. But as soon as the dishes were done, the women came to take over the television.

For most Christians, Sunday is the most religious day of the week, but for the Whitmans, Saturday was the holy day, and it was a double religious experience. Supper was just an intermission between Saturday evening Mass and watching the high priest of musical entertainment, Lawrence Welk. When *The Lawrence Welk Show* came on, no one was allowed to speak a word. Even John and Chad understood they must be quiet or Grandma would be upset. Not that the event itself was solemn; the music was full of gaiety and the performers' costumes were so colorful that twenty years later they would appear hilarious. Church was well and good, but true catharsis occurred when Joe Feeney crooned out an Irish tune, Myron Florin played his accordion, and Bobby and Sissy tap-danced away a week's worth of cares. Grandma agreed with Mr. Welk that everything on the show was "Wonderful, wonderful."

John and Chad were not impressed with Lawrence Welk, but they were content to lie on the floor with their coloring books, little realizing that in after years, they would look back on these Saturday nights as some of their happiest, most secure moments when three generations of the family were allowed for a few short years to enjoy one another's company. Childhood may seem endless, but it fleets away all too soon, and grandparents, whose advanced ages make it seem they will live forever, pass on, gaining immortality only in the memories and genes of their descendants.

Once Lawrence Welk ended, it was time to go home. Ellen gathered up the boys' mobile, drawings, coloring books, and crayons. Henry teased his grandsons with slobbery kisses. Beth thanked Chad profusely for the picture he had given her. Then the Vandelaares were in their car and driving away, and Henry and Beth felt a momentary loneliness before settling down to read the newspaper and discuss what they would need to bring up to Ives Lake next week.

Summer came with all its grand times. That June, John's parents decided to take a trip to Chicago for a week, leaving John and Chad with their grandparents at Ives Lake. The day before the trip, Ellen drove her sons up to the lake. The two anxious boys found the hour long drive nearly unbearable. Ellen helped the boys pass the time by teaching them songs until "Here Comes Peter Cottontail," and "Frosty the Snowman" filled the car, regardless of the season.

Once Ellen and the boys reached Big Bay, they took the road to the Huron Mountain Club. Everyone must pass through the Club's gate, and the gatekeeper had the list of who was allowed inside the exclusive if rustic wilderness paradise. John felt important because the gatekeeper always knew his name when they passed through. As the gate closed behind them, Ellen drove down a secluded road through the overarching forest of maples, oaks, and birches that shaded the road. The car turned down the road toward Ives Lake, then crossed over a little bridge. Through the trees the red barn came into view. To its left was the little green cottage where Henry and Beth spent their summers, and several hundred feet beyond were the red and stone houses. All four buildings were surrounded by fields of grass dotted with tall maples and pines; the grass spread to the forest's edge and down little footpaths in the woods that led to the best fishing holes along the lake.

Once all the boys' belongings were carried inside, Ellen said goodbye to her parents and children, then drove back to Marquette. Now began several glorious days for the boys. Chad was often content to stay inside the cottage, to watch Grandma bake cookies, to color in his coloring books, or to sit on the porch and watch the chipmunks run about. But John's days at Ives Lake were spent as Grandpa's helper; the two were always busy cutting the grass with the riding lawn mower or doing minor repairs to keep the houses ready for visitors. The house visits were more an adventure than work for John. The Red House had an outside basement door cut into the hill that could not be entered unless one went down a flight of steps. Henry never used the front door after John told him the basement door was more exciting because it was like an underground secret passage. Once inside the Red House, if no one were staying there, John was allowed to wander through its countless rooms while Henry did his chores. Eventually, John would go back to find his grandpa. Just when John started to think Grandpa had left and forgotten him, Henry would jump out from his hiding place to scare John. Rather than be frightened, the boy would laugh until he felt his tummy would pop right out of his mouth.

John thought the barn the most fascinating place at Ives Lake. Inside, its roof seemed higher than a cathedral ceiling. He would strain his neck backward to view the rafters where the swallows sat in their nests. Several would fly down, expecting Henry and John to feed them. As Henry spread bread crumbs in the yard, the cottage's screen door would screech open. Beth would step onto the porch to announce lunch was ready. Then she would complain about all the bird poop. Henry always replied that he could not let the poor birds starve. Beth would let out a frustrated sigh and return inside.

John would never forget his grandfather's kindness to the animals. When Grandma complained because the raccoons got into the garbage cans, Grandpa started leaving food behind the barn for them. And no matter how many squirrels and chipmunks raced across the lawn, Grandpa could distinguish between them, and John helped him name them. Like those back in Grandpa's woodshop, these chipmunks trusted Grandpa enough to jump into his hand to fetch a peanut, and John learned to hold his hand steady so he would inspire the same trust in them.

Evening was Henry's only chance to go fishing; then John would dutifully follow his grandfather to the lake. Their favorite fishing spot was on a giant rock that jutted out into the water. Here John caught his first fish, a ten inch trout. But even when neither hooked anything except a floating branch, this was John's favorite time of day. Years after John had forgotten the breed and size of fishes caught, he would remember how Ives Lake had looked when his young eyes had gazed across it. Many a day, John listened to the soft lapping of water against the rock and to the gentle breeze coming across the lake that made the trees rustle. Then John would lay his head against Grandpa's arm in complete contentment.

The first night the boys stayed at the lake, Beth discovered Ellen had forgotten to pack John's pajamas.

"Henry," she fretted, "what will the boy wear to bed?"

Henry thought a moment, then said, "There's my red flannel shirt in the closet. It never really fit me, so let him wear that."

"He can't wear a flannel shirt to bed," said Beth.

"Why not? It's a cold night, even for June."

"Can I, Grandma, please?" John asked.

"Well," Beth hesitated until she was won over by the enthusiasm in John's eyes, "all right, but don't tell your mother; she might not like it."

After changing into the shirt, John went to kiss his grandparents good night.

"Well, John, don't you look smart," said Henry. "That shirt's so long on you, it reminds me of the nightshirts I wore when I was your age."

"Didn't you have pajamas?" asked John.

"Not in the old days. Remember when we went to see *Peter Pan*, and Wendy's brother John wore that long shirt to bed; those are the kinds of nightshirts I used to wear. That was over sixty years ago. Do you remember those, Honey?"

"Oh sure," said Beth. "My brothers wore shirts like that."

"Tomorrow," said Chad, "I'm going to color in my *Peter Pan* coloring book."

"Okay," laughed Grandma, kissing him goodnight.

Grandma tucked the boys into bed. Chad was soon asleep, dreaming of his coloring books. But John could not sleep. His imagination was racing; not only was he wearing Grandpa's flannel shirt, but he was dressed as Grandpa had been when he was a little boy. John lay in bed, pretending to live in the old days when everyone wore nightshirts. That night, the touch of Grandpa's shirt made him feel safe, and all his life, the smell of flannel would comfort him.

And then came the wonderful, long awaited day – Aunt Ada had come all the way from Louisiana to visit her Marquette relatives, and she was going to spend today at Ives Lake. Chad could not remember Aunt Ada from her last visit a couple years ago, but John reminded him, "Aunt Ada is just like a kid. She plays with us, and she always sends us the best presents for our birthdays and at Christmas." Uncle Bill drove his sister up to Ives Lake that morning and promised to come back for her in the evening. When the boys saw the car drive into the yard, they ran outside, their grandparents close behind.

Aunt Ada got out of the car and hugged Henry and Beth, then squatted down to the boys' level and said, "Hello, Chad. Hello, John. I've been so anxious to come see you. I've been staying at your great-grandmother's house, but being around all those grownups was boring me terribly. I'm so glad now to be with children my own age."

A second later, each boy had one of Aunt Ada's hands as they pulled her inside the house to give her the grand tour.

Bill refused Beth's offer to have a cup of coffee, then got back in his car and waved goodbye. Once inside, Beth soon had coffee cake on the table for everyone, and coffee poured for the adults, but Ada's coffee grew cold before the boys finished tugging her about the cottage to show her its every nook and cranny.

"Let Aunt Ada have a little rest," Beth told the boys. "She must be tired after the long drive up here."

"No, it was a beautiful drive, and I've been so looking forward to seeing you all," Ada replied, "but I do need a cup of coffee." Beth tossed out the cold coffee and refilled her cup. Then Henry and Beth asked after Ada's children and grandchildren. John and Chad tried to be patient during this conversation by concentrating on the blueberry coffee cake covered with frosting. But once the coffee cake was gone, they wanted Aunt Ada's full attention.

Henry broke up the little party when he said, "I need to go check on the chicken coop in the back. Do you boys want to come with me?"

The chicken coop had no chickens in it, only old leftover furniture, but Henry went every few days to make sure nothing had troubled it. The night before, there had been some high winds so he would have to make his rounds today to ensure nothing was damaged. Usually the boys would have jumped at the chance to go, but today they looked strangely at their grandfather, afraid to disappoint him. Then Aunt Ada laughed and said, "Would you mind if I went along, Henry?"

"Me too!" said John, jumping up and instantly being mimicked by his brother.

Ada and the boys went out on the porch while Henry fetched his cap.

"My, they took to Ada fast," Beth said to her husband.

"That's only natural," said Henry. "Ada's as much a kid as them."

All the way to the chicken coop, the boys chattered about Ives Lake and everything they had been doing, so that Henry and Ada could scarcely say a word. Most men would have been annoyed by childish chatter when they had not seen their sister in a year, but Henry enjoyed listening to Ada answer the boys' questions.

"Is it hot where you live?" Chad asked her. "Mom says it is."

"Yes, it can be very hot, so hot we don't get any snow."

"No snow!" said John. "Why it wouldn't seem like Christmas without snow."

"No, it doesn't seem like Christmas without snow," Ada replied. "That's the time when I miss the U.P. the most. But it's like summer all year round there, and we have alligators and hurricanes and beautiful flowers and – "

"I like flowers," said Chad.

"We have beautiful magnolias trees," said Ada. "They have giant white flowers on them. You would love them."

"I'd like the alligators better," said John, "as long as I didn't get too close to one."

"Here, boys, now hush a moment," said Henry, not because he minded their chatter but because they had reached the chicken coop. "Ada, look at that hole."

"What's in it?" she asked, looking at the hole that ran under the chicken coop. When Henry did not answer, she looked inquisitively at the boys' faces, but even when she said, "I hope it's not a snake hole," they would not give away the secret.

Henry reached into his pocket and pulled out a paper bag. "Chuckie!" he called. "Shh, now watch."

He opened the bag and pulled out some bread crumbs.

"Oh!" gasped Ada. Chuckie the Woodchuck had stuck out his head. "Oh, Henry, are you sure it's safe?"

"Sure," said Henry, dropping the bread crumbs on the ground. Chuckie looked at his visitors for a moment as if to say "Good morning", then carefully stuffed the bread crumbs into his mouth and disappeared down his hole.

"Well, I never," said Ada.

"That's Chuckie!" Chad screeched in delight.

"Wait a minute," said Henry.

Chuckie reappeared and more bread crumbs were dropped for him. He repeated the process one more time before all the crumbs were gone. The last time, he gave the humans a wag of his tail to say goodbye before finally disappearing.

"Chuckie's funny," John told Aunt Ada, "but I like raccoons better. Grandma doesn't though 'cause they get in the garbage."

"Well, raccoons have to eat too," said Ada.

"I bet you don't see woodchucks like that in Louisiana," said Henry.

"No, this is quite a place here, Henry," said Ada, looking about at the giant maples and enjoying the breeze off the lake.

"We like it," said Henry. "It's a good little summer job for me, and Beth enjoys being close to so many fine fishing holes."

"It's just about the most perfect place I can imagine," said Ada.

"Not for me," said Chad. "I like Never Never Land."

"Oh, from *Peter Pan*?" asked Ada.

"Yes," said John, surprised a grownup would know such a magical place. "Did you see the movie?"

"Better than that," she said. "I read the book."

"Oh!" John wished he had that book.

"Sometimes we play *Peter Pan*," Chad said.

"Do you?" asked Ada. "Well, I'd like to play sometime."

"Okay," said Chad. "You can be Wendy."

"And who will you be?"

"I'll be Peter," said John, "cause I never want to grow up."

"Then who will you be, Chad?"

"Michael," said Chad.

"What about your grandpa?" asked Ada.

"He's Captain Hook," said John. "He'll chase us, so before he catches us, we have to run back down the trail, okay?"

"Well, these old legs aren't much for running, but I'll try," said Ada.

"Actually," said John, "we'll fly. Where's Tinkerbell? We need her to sprinkle pixie dust on us."

"Here she is!" Chad said, reaching into the air to grasp the invisible fairy. He shook his fist, pretending to sprinkle first himself, then the pseudo-Peter and pseudo-Wendy.

"Now," said John, "we must fly away or nasty old Captain Hook will kidnap us like he did to Tiger Lily."

"Hurry!" screamed Chad, tearing off down the trail so fast even his older brother had to run hard to keep up.

"Hurry before Captain Hook gets you!" yelled John.

"You better run! Hahahaha!" roared Henry, enjoying his villain role.

"Hurry, Wendy, hurry!" screamed Michael.

"But where will we hide?" asked Wendy.

"Back in the tree house," said Peter. "Then we'll get the Lost Boys, and they'll help us fight old Captain Hook."

"Not if I catch you first!" shouted the evil old pirate.

He darted past Wendy and Peter and caught up with Michael, grabbing his coat until Chad screamed in delightful terror.

"Now I've got you. When I'm through with you, there won't be any fairies left to believe in!"

"What's all that racket?" asked Beth, alarmed by the boys' screaming. She looked out the open screen door to find her husband with Chad tucked under one arm, while Ada and John ran close behind, flapping their fairy-wing-like-arms.

"We were just playing, Grandma," said John, thinking her too grownup to understand.

"Is Grandma a pirate too?" Chad asked, not wanting the game to be over.

"Your grandsons certainly are imaginative, Beth," Ada said.

"That they are," said Beth. "I hope they didn't wear you out."

"No, I remember how important it was at their age to have a grownup join in my games. Henry always played with me, even though he was practically a grownup since he was ten years older than me."

She smiled at her brother as he held open the screen door for them to go inside.

"It's going to be a warm day," said Beth, who was sweating from having just washed up the breakfast dishes.

"I think it's comfortable," said Ada, accustomed to Louisiana's humidity.

"It'll be in the eighties today for sure," said Henry.

"Well, what will we do this afternoon?" asked Beth.

"I have to run into Big Bay to get a few groceries," said Henry.

"I want to go," said John.

"So do I," said Chad.

"I guess that leaves us here alone, Beth," said Ada.

"No, Aunt Ada has to go too," said John.

"You all go ahead now," Beth said. "I'll finish my housework and fix us some lunch and then maybe we can go fishing this afternoon."

"All right," said Henry. He led his troops out to the truck. The seat in the cab was wide enough for them all to fit. On the way, John and Chad told Aunt Ada how Mom always sang to them in the car. "Do you know any songs, Aunt Ada?" they asked. Aunt Ada sang out "Senor Don Gato Was a Cat" and "Oh My Darling Clementine". Her great-nephews responded with a rather confused version of "I Knew an Old Lady Who Swallowed a Fly."

"It's so beautiful here, Henry," said Ada as they passed out the Club's gate and drove into the town of Big Bay. It was only eleven in the morning, but Grandpa could never resist ice cream; he offered to buy everyone a Mickey Mouse shaped ice cream bar. Chad said he wanted a comic book instead. He could not read yet, but he liked the pictures. Aunt Ada told the boys she would buy them comic books while Grandpa got everyone ice cream. John picked out *Superman* and Chad chose *Donald Duck*.

"Now you boys can't read those until tomorrow," said Ada when they climbed back into the truck, "because you promised to spend the day playing with me."

"John'll probably fish with us," said Henry, "but Chad's a little too young to be interested."

"I don't think we'll be fishing," said Ada as she noticed the sky darkening. By the time they were back at Ives Lake, they just had time to run into the house before a horrendous thunderstorm broke.

"No fishing today," Beth said, greeting them at the door. "Oh well, I could use a day just to relax around the house. John, what do you have all over your shirt?"

"We had Mickey Mouse ice cream!" Chad said.

"Yes, I can see it's all over your face." Beth took a dishcloth to wipe his mouth and cheeks. Then she sent John to change his shirt so she could wash it.

"Henry spoils those boys," Beth told Ada.

"What about you?" Henry replied. "I've never eaten so much chocolate cake in my life as you've made since the boys have been staying with us."

"The one I made last night was because Ada was coming."

"Still, it's the third you've made this week," Henry smiled.

"Aunt Ada, look at my coloring book," Chad said, shoving it before her eyes.

"It's very nice," she replied, admiring one of the pictures. "I like all the red you used." Then she said to Henry and Beth, "He colors so well for his age."

"Both of the boys are so smart," said Beth. "I bet they'll go to college someday."

"I hope so," said Henry.

"Oh, they will. Ellen will see to that," Ada said. "She knows the value of education."

The boys were less interested in college than in Aunt Ada's artistic talents. Now that they were settled inside the house during the rainstorm, she was ready to open up the giant cloth bag she had brought with her. Inside were the slippers she was knitting, and her cross-stitch, and a pad of colored construction paper, and her scissors, and a gluestick, and colorful stickers, and several buttons and beads in a little container, as well as several small pieces of material.

"I thought we'd make a little project," said Aunt Ada while the boys' jaws dropped as she drew out all her art materials. "What would you like to make?"

"A pwincess," said Chad. "Only one that's real so she can marry Pwince Bear," he said.

"Who's Prince Bear?"

Chad raced into the bedroom and returned with his stuffed teddy bear.

"Oh, yes, I see," said Aunt Ada. "Well, he looks rather lonely so I guess he does need a princess. Let me see now."

She soon spied a glass coke bottle on the cupboard.

"Beth would you mind if we used that bottle?"

"No," said Beth.

Aunt Ada fetched the coke bottle, then asked what color the princess's dress should be.

"Pink," said Chad.

Ada took out a sheet of pink construction paper, curved it around the bottle, taped it together, then trimmed it. She cut out more paper to make a white face, and she used yarn for hair, and she glued on sequins for jewelry.

"She's beautiful," Chad crooned.

"Now be careful you don't drop and break her," Aunt Ada said.

"I won't," Chad said, carrying her to the couch so she could sit next to Prince Bear. He pretended the two were being married, and he jabbered away with them to his heart's content.

"Now, John, what should we make you?"

"How about a ship," he replied.

Clearly, Aunt Ada could do anything. No picture of a ship on paper would be sufficient. She set John to cutting out rectangles and triangles to serve as flags. Meanwhile she folded paper, taped pieces together, found popsicle sticks in one of Grandma's drawers to create masts, and cut cloth for sails. Henry was sent to the barn to find a piece of wood to make the ship stand up straight.

"Ada, when are you going to grow up?" Henry laughed, seeing she was more excited than his grandsons by the projects.

"Don't pick on her, Henry," said Beth. "She's a treasure. We all know it."

"There's nothing more adult," Ada said, "than to use your time to please a child. And I admit I'm selfish because I get more pleasure from it than the children do."

"Aunt Ada, do your grandchildren love you as much as we do?" asked Chad.

"I hope so," she said, "but most of my grandchildren are too grown up to play with me anymore."

"Do you like Uncle Bill's boys as much as us?" John asked.

"I love them too, but they're at that age where they think they're too big to spend time with their old aunt, so you boys are much more fun."

Beth now insisted the table be cleared for lunch, and then after everyone ate, the boys and Aunt Ada convinced Grandpa and Grandma to play *Cooties* and *Candy Land* with them.

"I wouldn't mind visiting Candy Land," said Chad, "but I'd rather go to Never Never Land."

"So would I," said Aunt Ada.

"There aren't any lakes in Candy Land for my ship to sail on," said John.

"I wish," said Chad, "your ship was bigger so the pwince and pwincess could ride on it."

"What will you name the princess?" asked Grandma.

"Pwincess Ada," Chad said.

Ada laughed, but then Chad kissed her cheek and she blushed.

During supper, they listened to John's Peter Pan record collection. The cottage was filled with "On the Good Ship Lollipop", "Smoky the Bear," and "In the Little Red Schoolhouse". John jumped up every few minutes to turn over the little 45's.

After supper, Beth and Ada did up the dishes, the boys looked at their comic books, and Henry glanced at the newspaper he had bought at the grocery store.

"Ada, who do you think will win the next presidential election?" Henry asked.

"Gerald Ford I imagine," said Ada.

"There's no way," Henry replied, "that any Republican will be reelected after the Watergate scandal."

"I would think since Ford is from Michigan," said Ada, "you would want him to win."

"Gerald Ford?" Henry scoffed. "Downstate, they think Ford's the greatest president who ever lived, and maybe he is for people down there, but what has he done for the U.P.? Henry Ford did more for us than Gerald Ford."

"Well, I don't know that Carter won't be the better president," said Ada. "In the South, we tend to prefer Democrats, and Carter is from Georgia."

"I'm voting for Carter," Henry said. "Dominic Jacobetti is a Democrat, and any president lucky enough to be in Jacobetti's party gets my vote."

"Who's Jacobetti?" asked Ada.

"Dominic Jacobetti? He's the greatest politician the Upper Peninsula has ever produced. He's head of the State's Appropriations Committee, which means he makes sure the U.P. gets a fair share of the state's money for the first time ever, and best of all, he's fighting for the U.P. to secede from Michigan and become a separate state so we aren't always controlled by people down in Lansing."

"Oh, Henry, it'll never happen," said Beth, "they tried last year for U.P. Statehood and the vote failed nearly two to one."

"People just weren't properly educated about it," said Henry.

"They've been trying for U.P. Statehood more than a hundred years," said Beth. "It's never going to happen. At least not in our lifetimes."

"Would the U.P. be able to sustain itself without the lower peninsula?" asked Ada. "Isn't all the industry down there?"

"Don't argue with him, Ada," said Beth. "You can't budge him on the issue."

"It's hard to argue with someone who's right," said Henry. "They may make automobiles downstate, but where do they get the iron for the steel, except in the U.P.'s mines? The U.P. is the best thing that ever happened to Michigan."

"I agree the U.P. does usually get the bum end of the stick," said Beth. "I just don't think U.P. statehood will ever happen."

"Grandpa," John said. "Uncle Bill is here!"

Chad suddenly felt like crying. It was not even dark out, and it was already time for Aunt Ada to leave.

But Uncle Bill had brought with him his three sons, William, Jason, and Alan.

"Annette was going to one of her women's groups tonight," said Bill, "so I brought the boys along for the ride. I thought they might like to run around in the woods or down by the lake for an hour or so."

"Can we go fishing?" Alan asked his dad.

The grass was still wet, but the rain had stopped, and in the last hour, the warm sun had quickly dried the ground.

"Sure, but be careful," said Bill.

"Can I go too?" asked John. He loved his grandparents and aunt, but he did not often get to play with older boys.

"Only if your cousins promise to keep an eye on you," said Beth.

Jason and William looked at each other. They were twelve and thirteen and did not want to be troubled by a six-year old, but Alan, who was not quite eleven, said, "We promise."

"Grandma, I want to go too," said Chad.

"Then go along," said Beth.

William and Jason exchanged displeased glances. John saw the look and instantly offered, "We can bring our wagon, and then if Chad gets tired you can pull him, and we can put the fishing gear in it."

The cousins agreed to this idea. Alan followed John to the barn to get the wagon while William and Jason collected the fishing equipment, and Chad ran inside to grab his coloring book and crayons. At first he wanted to bring the princess made out of a bottle, but Beth was afraid it might break, so a coloring book had to do. While the boys started on their little excursion, the adults settled on the porch to drink lemonade and enjoy the breeze that had followed the thunderstorm.

A short walk down a wooded trail along Ives Lake soon brought the boys to one of their favorite fishing spots. Chad sat patiently in the wagon while Jason pulled it over rocks and roots in the path. John silently listened to the older boys discuss fishing and baseball, on which they seemed to be great authorities. He felt immensely privileged to be with his cousins; under no circumstances would he have ridden in the wagon like a little kid.

When the boys came to the desired fishing hole, they got out their poles and set to work. The river rolled peacefully along the bank, trickling over and around an occasional rock to form a little eddy. The boys, usually talkative, said little while they fished, other than to complain when a line got a snag. Raised in the great north woods, their fishing poles were like extensions of their arms. They would cast and wait for a bite, watching their line float down the river, then reel it back in. They distanced themselves, William going up the river a couple hundred feet, Jason a hundred or so feet down from him, then Alan at the end, while John stayed with Alan, the most congenial cousin because the closest to his age. Chad sat in the wagon, just a few feet from his brother and Alan. He was determined to color ten pages before he was back home. He always started at the first page of the coloring book and persevered to the end, coloring in order, whether or not he liked the pictures. Every once in a while, he would look up to see John and Alan cast their lines, but he said nothing. He was happy not to be disturbed. He wanted to impress Aunt Ada and Grandma with how fast he could color. Thoroughly involved in his own beautiful art work, he overlooked the more vibrant colors of the summer forest.

Finally, the sun began to set, and William, being the eldest, felt responsible for deciding it was time they head back.

Jason dutifully reeled in his line, but Alan and John groaned; no one had caught a fish. Chad was the most disappointed; he had only colored three pages.

They were all a bit tired now from the long day, and less talkative than they had been on the way to the fishing hole. They walked with a bit of urgency because they knew it would soon be nightfall, and the forest's thick trees would block out the remaining light.

Then, as the beautiful summer evening ended, they stumbled upon a little copse, almost a meadow really, where sunbeams broke through the trees, illuminating a small patch of the forest floor.

Suddenly, Chad cried out, "Ooh, look at the lady's slippers!"

All turned their heads to see the meadow packed with the little pink flowers that looked like fairy slippers hanging from their stems.

"How'd we miss seeing all those before?" asked Alan.

"I saw them," said William, who had not thought flowers worth mentioning.

Chad struggled to get out of the wagon.

"Where are you going?" Jason asked him.

"To pick some for Gwamma and Aunt Ada," was Chad's obvious answer.

"Hey, ain't these flowers the kind that are illegal to pick?" asked Jason.

"Why would flowers be illegal to pick?" asked Alan.

"Because they're rare," said William.

"They don't look rare," said Alan. "There's about a hundred of them here."

"Let's pick them all," said Chad. "We can give some to Gwamma, and Aunt Ada, and some to my mom and some to your mom." He felt overcome by a desire to give all the women pretty flowers until they would all feel as beautiful as Princess Ada.

"It's almost dark," said William.

"It'll only take a minute to pick them," Alan replied. "Besides, maybe the flowers will cheer Mom up."

"Mom's not going to cheer up until Dad quits being a jerk," William muttered; as the oldest, he was burdened with understanding his parents' marriage better than his brothers.

"If we pick them all," said Jason, "won't they die from being exposed? We don't have any water to put them in."

"Aunt Beth will give us vases, or at least plastic bags to wrap them in," said Alan.

While his cousins debated, John joined his brother in gathering flowers. William refused to pick any – he was too old for flower picking, even to make his mother happy. But Alan did not mind pleasing his younger cousins by joining in. Chad's little hands filled too quickly, so he enlisted Jason in carrying his flowers to the wagon for him. Meanwhile, Alan picked ferns to make backgrounds so the bouquets of lady's slippers would look even prettier in vases.

In ten minutes, the meadow was cleared. Heaps of delicate pink air pockets of flowers were gently laid in the wagon. Chad did not object when told he would have to walk home so his feet did not crush the flowers. He thought it nicer to walk beside the wagon and look at the pretty flowers.

The boys started back down the path. John looked back to where the flowers had been. He remembered just minutes before how stunned they had all been by the flowers – how there had been a seemingly endless field of pink rising up from the decaying leaves of last autumn. Now, he only saw the decaying leaves and little broken stems sticking up where once the flowers had been. The evening sun had lowered as well, leaving the field almost dark. Already he was starting to strain his eyes to see ahead of him. He wished they had not picked all the flowers; then he could have come back tomorrow night to see the pink field again.

"I hope the DNR doesn't catch us," said William.

"What's the DNR?" asked Alan.

"The Department of Natural Resources. If they catch us illegally picking all these flowers, they'll probably throw us in jail, or make Dad pay a huge fine, and then he'll probably ground us for a month."

John was frightened by the thought of jail. But he felt it would serve them right if the DNR did catch them. It seemed wrong to have picked all the flowers. They had not left behind a single one. He felt the trees would be lonely and sad without the lady's slippers.

When the boys got back to the house, Ada and Beth marveled at so many delicate flowers. Beth quickly found more empty coke bottles to serve as vases so Ada could go home with a bouquet, and the Whitman boys could bring another home for their mother.

"Thanks for having me, Beth," Ada said, as she picked up her vase and kissed her sister-in-law goodbye.

"Any time, Ada," said Beth.

"We wish you'd come to visit more often," said Henry.

"It was a perfect day," Ada said.

"Boys, what do you say to your aunt?"

"Thank you for the pwincess," said Chad.

"Thank you for the ship," said John, and then he turned to his cousins and added, "Thank you for taking me fishing."

William and Jason said nothing, but Alan mussed his cousin's hair.

"We better get home before dark or Annette will be worried," said Bill.

William thought his mother might prefer if they did not go home, but he would not argue with his father in public. Instead, he carried his and his brothers' fishing poles to the car trunk. A sprinkle of rain started up as everyone piled into the car.

"We're going to have another storm tonight," said Henry as the visitors drove away.

"Well, at least the boys got out of the house this evening," said Beth, "though I don't think they minded being inside since they had Ada to entertain them."

"Did you boys have a good time with Aunt Ada?" Henry asked.

Both nodded enthusiastically.

"Well, you better get to bed now," said Beth. "John go brush your teeth while I help Chad put on his pajamas."

John got ready for bed, then came out into the kitchen to get a drink of water before he went to sleep. When he saw the lady's slippers sitting on the kitchen counter, he wished he could replant them in the woods, but he knew they would not grow now.

As he started to fall asleep, a loud thunderclap made him hide his head under the blankets. He was surprised Chad could sleep through the noise. He felt the thunder was a warning he had done something wrong to pick the flowers. They had been so beautiful in the forest; they were nowhere near as pretty sitting on the counter. He wanted to cry, but he felt if his older cousins knew he cried, they would think him a baby. That he refused to cry did not make him feel any less guilty.

The moment she woke, Margaret remembered it was her birthday; still lying in bed, she marveled to think she was ninety-two years old. She looked over at the clock and saw it was only seven. Lucy would not be up for another half hour. Eleanor and her daughters now insisted on taking turns spending the night with Margaret. They wanted her to come live with them, but she was determined to remain in her own home as long as possible. She loved her family dearly, but when they were here, they just seemed to be in her way. Every morning, she felt she had to lie in bed and be quiet until they got up. Then they would tiptoe downstairs as though they were the ones who might wake her; she had never slept past seven o'clock since the day she was married, but then she had spent all those years on a farm; these modern girls had it far more easy.

When Margaret finally heard Lucy moving around, she went downstairs to make breakfast. Lucy came into the kitchen, already dressed for work. She gobbled down her toast, barely touched the eggs her grandmother made her, quickly swallowed her orange juice, kissed her grandmother goodbye, reminded her that her own mother would be over that afternoon to help her get ready for the birthday party, told her to call her at work if she needed anything, then disappeared out the front door.

Margaret finished her coffee and did up the breakfast dishes, then went back upstairs. Since it was her birthday, she decided that rather than do regular housework, she would find something fun to do, such as cleaning out her dresser. She had several items in it she would never wear again, and she also had several diaries in it – that was her main reason for cleaning. She was ninety-two, and she knew the chance of her seeing ninety-three was slim, so she had a fancy to look back over her life and think about how she had become the old lady she was. She had known a lot of sadness over all these years, losing her parents and her husband, and watching her family struggle through tough times, but she knew she had always worked to make a better life for everyone, and they had all come out right in the end. She was proud she had lived long enough to see them all doing well.

When she pulled out the diaries, she was surprised by how many volumes there were; she had often not written for weeks at a time, but eighty years of even sporadic writing had created a heavy tome of life history.

She opened the oldest diary; she remembered she had received it as a gift from her mother on her twelfth birthday, but she had waited almost a year before finally writing in it. She turned to the first page.

> July 16, 1897
>
> The worst thing imaginable has happened. I thought it would be the best day ever because it was the day they unveiled the Fr. Marquette statue and I was to go to a party at the Hotel Superior, and I had a beautiful new party dress to wear. I went with the neighbors but the party was spoiled because my <u>nasty</u> sister Sarah snuck out of the house to come to the party, and I had to take her home. Then just

as I was going to bring her home, Mr. Whitman had some sort of stroke and died. Old lady Montoni asked me to run to the Whitmans' house and tell his family what had happened. Clarence Whitman is in my class, so I had to tell him his father had died. I felt so bad for him because he is so nice. But even though I know it's selfish, I couldn't help feeling upset that the party had been ruined for me by Mr. Whitman dying like that. I even felt bad for Clarence's older brother Will, even though he was such a snob he wouldn't dance with me at the party. He couldn't help it though when a vixen had her hands all over him. I only wanted to dance with him because he's so handsome, but he's several years older than Clarence, and I bet Clarence will grow up to be even better looking. Still, it is a shame that my first adult party had to end that way, but Mother told me I was being selfish to feel that way and that I'd have many more parties to attend. I must try to be a better Christian girl. May God bless Mr. Whitman and take him to Heaven and take care of his family, and may Sarah learn to quit being such a bad girl and running away and doing other hateful things like wearing my clothes without my permission. I'm glad at least I'm not as bad as her.

Margaret chuckled over the entry. She had never forgotten how when she had wanted to dance with Will, that other girl had stolen him away at the dance – it was so long ago now she could not even remember that other girl's name. She remembered what a shock it had been to see Will's father die. How bizarre that back then she had no idea Mr. Whitman would have been her father-in-law, or even that Will, not Clarence, would have been her husband. And "Old lady Montoni" had been Beth's grandmother. How funny life was that the people you least expected could become important in your life. Margaret even felt bad now for having said Sarah was a "nasty" girl, even though Sarah had often misbehaved. Margaret missed Sarah, and long since, she had forgiven her deceased little sister her faults. After all, Sarah had made a good life for herself, found a husband to love, and given her son everything she could; perhaps when they had had conflict, it was only because Margaret and she were so much alike. More than anyone she had lost, yes probably even more than Will, she wished Sarah were still here with her; she would have been the only one who could have remembered the old days of their childhood, when all the world was fresh and their days were filled with dreams for the future.

Margaret flipped over several more pages, just glancing at them until the following entry caught her eye:

February 3, 1903

Ever since Grandpa Dalrymple died, I've been awful lonely. Sometimes I feel as if he were the only real friend I had. I loved all his stories about Scotland, and I am determined that someday I will go there since he never had the chance to see where his father came from.

But I am not so lonely now. That's because – but I can't write it. No, I have to. I cannot help myself. My heart will break if I don't. I am in love with Will Whitman. He is so handsome and so smart. He is a carpenter and works for my father. We started going out after I went to the Longyear mansion one day to bring Father his lunch – I still can't believe they are tearing down that beautiful house – and I saw Will there. I hardly knew him up until then. He walked me home one day and since then we have been seeing each other. One day he caught me singing as I was out walking, and he smiled and told me I had a beautiful voice, and it always cheered him to hear me sing. I wanted to tell him my secret desire to be an opera singer, but I haven't yet. If I marry him, though, maybe I won't be able to be an opera singer. It will be hard to give up my dream, but I think for Will it would be worth it. He is the only man I have ever met that I would give up my musical calling for. But he will bring me other good things. He is very poor, but he comes from one of the finest families in Marquette, and I know someday he will make a lot of money, and then I will be able to go to Scotland and have all the dresses I've always wanted. But I don't love him because he will give me those things. I love him because he is kind and he listens to me. Sarah just came in the room, so I have to stop writing before she tries to peek.

Margaret shook her head. "What a foolish little chit I was. I don't know what Will ever saw in me." But her heart warmed to think that since he had loved her when she was such a silly girl, he had been an even more wonderful man than she had known then. They might never have been rich, and at her age, she knew she would never see Scotland, but she no longer cared because she had known his love. The only time she had ever not thought him a good husband was when she had selfishly wanted things he could not give her, and she knew he would have given her those things if he could. He had always given her his love, which turned out to be the only thing she had truly needed.

December 25, 1908

Christmas Day. I have just put the boys to bed so I wanted to sit down and write in my diary and say I thank God that we have been so lucky this year. My sister has gone to Chicago and I miss her terribly, and poor Will lost his brother Clarence, but we have weathered those storms and come through all right. Will misses Clarence a lot, and I miss him too because he was always good to me. With the money he left us, Will and I yesterday went to sign papers to buy a farm in Cherry Creek. It will be a good place to raise our boys. I don't want to be a farm wife, but I will try for Will's sake. It is hard though – I feel I'm getting old, and now that I have two children and probably will have more, I feel I will never be anything but a mother and a housewife, but I do love my little Royal and Henry, and Will is so good to me. I know I am not always a good wife to him. I complain and nag a lot, and sometimes I am awful ornery until I get my way. He is so good he always gives in to me, and then I feel guilty. Still, I know he loves me despite it all. I will try to be a better wife to him. That is my New Year's Resolution.

Margaret thought she must have been feeling particularly charitable when she wrote that passage because she and Clarence had never gotten along; she suspected it was largely because Clarence had thought his brother deserved better than her, but Clarence was at rest now so there was no sense dwelling on those old feelings. And she remembered how much she had hated the farm, which she had only agreed to for Will's sake. All those eggs to gather and sell, and the cow to milk, and the orchard to water. But at least she had been some use back then, not an old woman like she was now. She had to laugh that she had written she was getting old when she was twenty-four – she would be happy to be twice twenty-four again, especially if Will were with her. He had deserved a better wife, but she had loved him all she could.

She turned to another volume and opened to the following passage:

July 28, 1926

Even Will I cannot tell this too. He is a man and proud and would probably be ashamed that his wife had gone to beg. But I did not beg so much as threaten, and whether or not it was unchristian, I am glad I did it. I don't know why God allows men like Lysander Blackmore to live on this earth, to oppress the poor, but now I see that despite all the preaching that the Righteous will be rewarded in Heaven, there is some justice for the poor on this earth. Good does come from evil, because by my sister's sin, I have succeeded in saving my family from the poorhouse. Even though they are Satan's servants, the evil ones of this world ultimately fear the Righteous. But I will not tell Will, for he would disapprove. Still, I did what I had to do.

Margaret did not need to read the description that followed of her meeting with Lysander Blackmore. She could never forget that moment of strength she had experienced. To stop the bank from foreclosing on her and Will's farm, she had committed blackmail, threatening to expose Lysander Blackmore's sin by revealing to everyone how he had a bastard child by her sister. Eventually, they had still lost the farm, but she had saved it for a few more years. Until then, she had spent her life living in fear of poverty, but that day she had drawn on her strength; she still felt it had been her grandest moment. She had proven that God hears the cry of the poor by helping those who help themselves.

She skimmed over several more entries, not wanting to read more about the hard years on the farm. The mention of the great blizzard caught her attention.

> January 25, 1938
> The biggest blizzard we ever had struck the other night. At the same time there was a horrible fire downtown. The 10 cent store, the Opera House, the Nightingale and many other buildings burnt to the ground. The streets have still not been plowed in most places. Poor Beth's father wandered out in the storm and we found him passed out in a snowbank. We had to take him to the hospital in the blizzard. Poor Patrick will probably die from the exposure and frostbite. Beth and I have never really gotten along, but I hope for her sake that her father makes it. I have never thought she was the right wife for Henry because she's a Catholic, but he does love her, and I know her sorrow will hurt him. I wouldn't wish the loss of parents on anyone – ever since mine died last year, I have spent many a sad and lonely day.

"I really wasn't very nice to Beth in those years, was I?" thought Margaret. "But things were different then. Catholics and Baptists just didn't get married. How strange that Beth turned out to be the best of all my children's spouses."

Then Margaret thought of Beth's poor father, and how she had lost her own parents, and then her sadness made her turn to that worst day of her life.

> April 25, 1949
> Today my beloved Will was promoted to glory. He was very sick with pneumonia and was in the hospital. The doctors were kind to him, but he had a horrible cough he could not overcome. I will miss him terribly. He was always the best of husbands and the children looked up to him so much. I can't write anymore. I am too upset.

A tear trickled down Margaret's cheek; she felt as if she were reliving the grief of that day all over again. "He's been gone twenty-seven years," she told herself, "but I miss him as much as if it were only twenty-seven minutes. These young people, they don't know what love is anymore. They can't even stay married for a year or two. They don't know what it's like to love a man until he becomes all your world. That was true happiness, everyday happiness. I was so lucky to have Will."

She flipped over many pages after that, not wanting to read the numerous pages where she had written over and over again how much she missed Will, and how she would dream about him, and how she wished he were just there to talk with. She had thought her life nearing its end at that point, but she had struggled on, never even letting her children know how terribly unhappy she had been for years after his death. Even now, a day did not pass without her thinking of him. But she had gone on living, first for her children and grandchildren's sakes, and finally for herself. How Will would have loved to see his great-grandchildren now springing up, to see his family tree blossoming. As she turned to the next entry, she realized even Will's death had been a blessing.

> September 16, 1962
> This Sunday the eldest Baptist members now attending church were honored. There were 9 of us but only 5 were there. Sadie Johnson, as church clerk, pinned corsages on all of us and then we had pictures taken for the Mining Journal. We all were requested to get up on the platform and give a little talk of days gone by. I was afraid I'd be stage struck, but this is what I said. "Many years ago when my parents came to Marquette they joined the Baptist church and I was raised in it. When I was 11 years old I went to a revival meeting & was converted. Shortly after I was baptized in this church. Since then, some of my happiest moments have been spent in sabbath school and church. I had good Christian parents who taught me the right way to live and guided me through the years. I have tried to follow their example and am proud to say that I have good children, all of whom act like Christians even if they don't go to church regularly. I think God loves everyone no matter who we are and we each have different tasks to do. I think this church has helped lots of people, and I am proud to have been a member all these years."
> I didn't quite know what I was saying really, I was so nervous, and I was afraid when I said all my children had been raised to be Christians that someone would laugh because Royal says he doesn't believe in God, but I did my best as a mother, and that's all God can

ask, and I think Royal is a very good son and better than many of the people I know who go to church. And I never would have thought Beth was a good person because she was Catholic, but now I think she is a good Christian for being such a good wife to Henry unlike most of these women who parade around going to fancy charity events just to show off their fine clothes. But I mustn't judge people. My dear Will used to tell me I should be more charitable toward others' faults, and now that I've lost him, I understand better the pain some people go through, and the fear that makes them hide behind their false gods of money and social importance. I must try not to be proud over the difficulties the Lord has given me so I can become stronger in the faith.

There were births of grandchildren and great-grandchildren recorded after that, but while Margaret loved all those moments, she did not pause thoughtfully again until she came to:

February 6, 1970
    I just came back from my sister-in-law, Harriet Dalrymple's funeral. At the luncheon, Eleanor said she felt sorry for Harriet because she had been so miserable all her life. I guess I felt sorry for Harriet too, although I never thought about it that way until last fall after my brother Charles died and left her alone. Harriet told me then that she didn't know how she would go on without him. I knew what she meant and I told her she had to live for her children and grand-children – that's what I did when my dear Will died. But I don't think Harriet was ever as strong as me, even if she were more ornery. Charles has only been gone four months, and now she has gone to join him. I never did understand what he saw in her. She led him a miserable nagging life. But now, I think she was a lot more like me than I ever wanted to admit, and maybe that's why I never liked her much, because I saw myself in her – like how she was probably more jealous of Sarah than I was, and how I was always so proud that my sister married a senator yet I used to laugh at Harriet behind her back for naming her son after the senator. Like me also, I think Harriet wanted a better life than she had – only I had a good hard working husband and Charles was always kind of lazy and didn't even try to make his wife happy by getting her better things, and now her grandsons are just as hopeless. Then again, I don't think Harriet ever learned what I did. When I was a girl, I dreamt of big things such as discovering a distant relative in Scotland who was an Earl or a Baron

and when he died, we would all be rich. When I grew up and married, I knew that dream was foolish, but then I dreamed that if Will worked hard, we would become rich. Will always worked hard, but no matter what we did, we never became rich, and we got no help from his family, even though he had some well to do relatives somewhere out West whom we never heard from. Then I dreamed my children would do well for themselves and their success would make us all happy. None of my children are hurting for money, but neither do they have much to spare. It seems as if I lived my life all those years just waiting for the day when finally I could really start living; when at last we could all be happy. But finally I learned this was just the way life went, and that as long as I had my family, I had more happiness than money could ever bring. Unlike me, Harriet never realized she did not need pretty things. But then, maybe I never knew Harriet at all, and even now, am only imposing my experiences upon her. Maybe instead of always being annoyed with her, I should have tried to listen to her more, to be a better friend to her. Then maybe she might have opened up and I could have truly helped her. I wish she could have been happier. I hope she's at peace now.

Margaret remembered she had written that passage immediately after returning from Harriet's funeral, when the minister's eulogy had softened her heart toward her sister-in-law. She had been lucky; Will had been so good to her. She had not deserved happiness any more than Harriet, but most of her life now seemed as if it had been good, and what had been bad was scarcely worth remembering. She leaned over and dug in the drawer of her bedside table until she found a pen. Then she wrote a new entry in her diary.

July 24, 1976
Every human being is such a muddle of good and bad, neither you or I are exceptions. So why expect perfection in others? Although I have made mistakes we all err. To err is human. To forgive is divine. Do not judge others. Only God can be our judge. Simply be thankful for what you are given. Do not envy others and remember you could well be in their shoes except for the grace of God.

When I die I do not want anyone to weep. I have listened to beautiful music I love; I have had the companionship of those I love; I have roamed the woods I love; I have fished in the streams I love; and looked upon beautiful flowers and trees and green grass, and listened to the birds I love, and heard the tranquil waves of Lake Superior, and I feel God has been good to me. He has given me a family to be proud of and they have given me great happiness in spite of the trials and tribulations which now seem only a bad dream. Dying is but going home. I have been heartbroken with the loss of my dear husband, but that was part of God's plan. We must take the bitter with the sweet. I have had a happy childhood being blessed by fine parents. I have seen my children become fine parents and their children as well. I have lived a long, full and happy life. I hope that because I can say I have been happy after all the bad times I have known that someday my children and grandchildren will read these diaries and see I overcame great difficulties, some brought by the world, but most through my own faults, and they will be encouraged to endure by trusting in the Lord.

Margaret read over her words and felt they were good. Then she heard the front door open and Eleanor calling, "Mom!" She remembered it was her birthday and she still had much to do. She shoved the diaries back into her dresser and with a spry step for a ninety-two-year-old, went to help her daughter make her birthday dinner.

John was coloring. He had a color by number book, and he was following the directions, but he did not like it. He felt Cinderella would look better wearing blue than green, and why was Puss'n'Boots in red on the front cover if the directions wanted him to wear purple? John had a rebellious streak in him – he planned to make Snow White black just to spite the coloring book.

The phone rang. His mother answer it. Then she started sobbing. He sat quietly listening, afraid to go see what was wrong.

When Mom got off the phone, he heard her crying again and he ran to her. "What's wrong?" he asked while hugging her.

"That was Aunt Eleanor. My grandma died," said Ellen. She let John hug her a moment. She needed to remind herself there were others she loved, even if Grandma were gone.

"We need to go up to Ives Lake," she said. "We have to go tell your grandparents. You go finish coloring while I get ready. I'll go wake up Chad from his nap and then we'll leave, okay?"

John was sad Great-Grandma had died. He had liked her because she smiled a lot, even if kissing her wrinkly cheek were kind of gross. He felt sad when they drove to Ives Lake. His mother kept crying softly; usually she sang when they made this trip.

At Ives Lake, they found Henry on the riding lawnmower. He waved but did not stop when he saw them pull into the yard. Ellen waved, hoping he would come over, but when he turned to mow down another row of grass, she went into the cottage with her sons. Beth was taking a blueberry pie out of the oven. The boys asked for some, but she told them it had to cool. Then Ellen told her mother that Grandma had died. Beth sat down, dazed for a moment, then said, "Did you tell your father?"

"No."

Then they heard the lawnmower stop. For a couple terrible moments they waited until Henry came inside. He cheerfully started to ask why Ellen had come until he saw how pale she looked.

"What's wrong?" he asked, his voice slightly frantic.

"Aunt Eleanor asked me to come up. Grandma died this morning." Ellen was sitting in a chair. She thought she should get up to hug her father, but she was hurting too much herself. Henry turned his head away; his body fell back as if struck heavily. Beth got up and put her hand on his shoulder; then he broke down and cried, for the first and only time in his grandsons' presence.

"I thought you'd want to go back to town and be with the family," said Ellen.

"Yes, we better do that," said Beth.

"All right. Let me take a quick shower and change my clothes," said Henry.

"Are you okay?" asked Beth.

"Yes. I just need a few minutes alone."

Henry disappeared into the bathroom.

"I'll bring the pie with us," said Beth. "There'll be lots of people, and no one will feel like cooking."

"Can I help you pack?" Ellen asked.

"No, it'll only take me a minute," said Beth. Ellen followed her into the bedroom although she was not needed. John and Chad sat at the table, staring at each other. John wondered whether when they got to Aunt Eleanor's house, she would have ice cream for the pie.

The day of the funeral, John and Chad stayed at Grandpa and Grandma's house with a babysitter. Chad was too young to understand what death was. John had a vague notion, but he did not yet comprehend its finality. He felt it was a sad day, especially since it rained during the funeral. The babysitter was not interested in playing with the boys. She watched game shows on TV while Chad drew pictures, then tried to show them to her, only to get a grunt of "Uh huh" for praise. John tried to read the *Peter Pan* book Aunt Ada had given him, but he mostly just stared out the window. He wished his parents and grandparents would come home. Then he felt everything would be okay again.

After the funeral, Ellen and Tom spent a couple hours sitting with Henry and Beth, just talking to comfort each other.

"I'm glad Grandma went in her sleep," said Ellen, kissing her dad goodbye. "So am I," said Beth.

"It all works out," said Henry. "Now Bill can move into my parents' house."

"I can't believe," said Ellen, "that Annette didn't even come to the funeral."

"Well, I guess I can understand since she and Bill are getting a divorce."

"Poor Uncle Bill. He'll miss having the boys with him more than he'll miss Annette," said Ellen.

John did not understand this conversation. He only knew he was tired of all this sadness. So tired he fell asleep in the car on the way home.

When they pulled into the yard, Tom woke John up by saying, "It looks like someone has moved into that house next door." The house had been built that spring, but no one had yet met the future occupants.

"Look, there's a little girl in the backyard," said Ellen. "Maybe you boys will finally have a playmate."

John said nothing, but he strained his eyes to look at the girl.

"Come inside and change your clothes; then you can go see whether she wants to play," said Ellen. Tom picked up Chad, who had fallen asleep, and carried him inside.

Ellen followed John into his room. She sat down on the bed, opened up his dresser to find his play clothes for him, then started sobbing.

"Mom, I thought the funeral was over."

"It is, but I'm still sad," said Ellen.

John stood stupidly, not knowing what to say. He was glad when she wiped her eyes and said, "Change your clothes and then go outside." Then she left the room. John hoped the girl next door was not one of those girls who cried all the time.

Five minutes later, John went outside by himself. The girl was still in the backyard, digging in the sand with a shovel. She looked over, then turned and pretended she had not seen him. He stood shyly, thirty feet from her, afraid to approach. He stood there for what seemed an eternity. He realized he was afraid of girls. There were girls he knew from kindergarten last year, but there had never been a girl right in the backyard next door.

Tom came out of the house, whistling, carrying his hoe, and headed for his garden.

"John, aren't you going to go play with that little girl?" he asked.

John said nothing. He was mortified his father should ask such a question.

The little girl did not look up. Maybe she had not heard his father. John hoped she had not.

"You can't be shy about girls," said Tom. "Otherwise someday one will talk you into marrying her, and you won't know how to refuse."

He grabbed John's hand and yanked him over to the neighbor's yard.

"Hey, this here is John. He wants to play with you."

The little girl looked frightened, but she whispered, "Hi."

"I see you're both shy," said Tom. "Good. Then you'll get along well. What's your name?"

"Holly," she practically whispered, while laying down her shovel and nervously pushing her long hair from her eyes.

"John likes to dig holes too. Just don't dig yourself into a hole over her, John."

Tom chuckled at his joke. Then he turned and walked to his garden, whistling "Copacabana".

John and Holly stared at each other. John did not know what to do.

Finally, not sure why, he said, "My great-grandma died."

"I had a pet kitten that died," said Holly.

Tom's whistling grew louder. John felt embarrassed.

"It's okay," said Holly. "My dad's a dork too."

John smiled and sat down in the dirt.

He would soon forget his memories of his great-grandma, although he would hear many stories about her until she became pictured in his mind as the legendary family matriarch. But for now his little six-year old playmate became the center of his world, a richly imaginative world that far outweighed the fascination of the everyday.

1980

When he was ten, "mystery" was John's favorite word. To others his age, the word might conjure up thoughts of Scooby-Doo or the Hardy Boys, but John had heard it in reference to God and the mysteries of the Church. He dreamed of experiencing a miracle, of having a vision. He longed for mystery to fill his life.

John and Chad constantly drew pictures. Chad drew houses. John tried to draw mysterious events – abandoned old churches where a bad priest had been cursed by God, haunted houses where vampires lurked, secretly waiting to prey on evildoers. He created fabulous, unbelievable stories he could only depict in his drawings. His mother saw the pictures and decided he was no longer allowed to watch the old black and white horror films on TV's *Creature Feature* Saturday matinee.

One day, John's best friend Holly told him she had heard if a person stood in complete darkness and stared into a mirror and said "Bloody Murder" one hundred times without blinking, the Devil would be seen. "My cousin Diane told me that, and she knows," Holly said, "because she's thirteen and her father's a minister."

On Friday night, John locked himself in the bathroom and looked into the mirror. Scared yet resolved, he turned off the lights. He blinked his eyes several times to prepare for a long stare. "Bloody murder. Bloody murder. Bloody murder. Bloody murder. Bloody murder." He repeated it over and over and over. He tried to count on his fingers, but he kept losing count around thirty or forty. Finally, he kept counting until he got past fifty. Then he lost his nerve and blinked and had to start over. He tried again and got to forty-two, but then he could not help blinking. He wondered whether he blinked on purpose because he was afraid to see the Devil. He was stupid to do this; if the Devil appeared, what would he do? Was there a way to make the Devil go away? He started to shake, but he also started to say "Bloody murder" and count again. He tried to say it faster to get it over with, but then the words became rhythmically terrifying, and in panic he turned on the light and stared at himself. Then he unlocked the door and went into his room.

Holly would want to know whether he had tried to see the Devil. He had told her he would try. He would just tell her it did not work, or better yet, he would refuse to tell her anything and say she had to try it for herself. She would probably think he had been afraid to do it, but he would like to see her try not to blink. If it mattered so much to her, why had she not tried it herself?

When he went to bed, John wished he was not too old to have a night light in his room. He was afraid he would dream about the Devil. Worse, the Devil might come to him in the night, or God might punish him for trying to see the Devil. While he did not dream of the Devil, a restless night's sleep left him exhausted the next day.

John went to church with his family that Saturday afternoon. He had gone regularly to Mass for the last two years since his First Communion. He loved going to church, to see the priest in long flowing robes, the altar boys carrying candles, the gold covered Book of the Gospels, and the Crucifix. He loved the music that he pretended sounded like choirs of heavenly angels. The Eucharistic prayers were long and boring, but he loved when the priest raised up the sacred host and everyone sang out "Amen". That was the supreme moment of mystery, the great transubstantiation when water and wine became the Body and Blood of Christ. John did not understand it, but he did not expect to; his C.C.D. teacher had told him people were not supposed to understand, just to have faith in the mysteries. That it could not be understood only made it all the more appealing to John.

But today John did not enjoy church. He had sinned and it weighed heavily on his conscience. In a few weeks, he would make his First Confession. When his classmates in C.C.D. had discussed what sins they could confess, most had admitted to stealing gum from the IGA or fighting with their brothers and sisters. John knew he had sinned far more grievously; he had involved himself in sorcery – in trying to call up Satan.

The Mass that Saturday was as soothing as ever, but John felt no comfort in it. He knew it would be an even greater sin if he received Holy Communion when he had such a sin on his conscience. He had wanted to tell his mother he was sick and could not go to church that day, but that would be lying, and lying was another sin. As the Communion song began, he watched the people rise from their kneelers and walk down the aisle to receive the Body and Blood of

Christ. Grandma rose from her kneeler and started down the center aisle. His father got up and followed her, and his mother followed his father out of the pew. John waited for his mother to look back, but she did not notice he had not followed her. He sat staring at the floor as he heard the people behind him lift their kneelers and leave the pew. He kept his head bowed, feeling everyone must be staring at him. Only elderly people did not go to Communion, but they had it brought to them. When his mother came back up the aisle, she would see him sitting in the pew.

Grandma came back first. John rose and lifted the kneeler to let her through. She said nothing to him. She let Ellen raise her own children without comment. John's father brushed past him without a thought. Then came John's mother. She gave him a puzzled look as she sat down beside him. Seeing sadness in his eyes, she decided she would not question him until later.

They went back to Grandpa and Grandma's house for supper. The meal was miserable. Chad told John all about what he and Grandpa had watched on TV. Chad would not start going to church until next month after he made his First Communion. John wished now he had lied and said he was sick; he could have stayed with Chad and Grandpa and watched the movie rather than feeling the misery of guilt. But then, next week, the sin would still be on his soul, so he still could not go to Communion. All through supper, John kept waiting for someone to ask why he had not gone, but everyone chatted as if nothing had happened.

On the way home, John waited for his mother to mention it, but she and Dad gossiped about the neighbors instead. He did not want to tell her what he had done, but it would be three weeks until he made his First Confession. He could not go three weeks without his mother asking why he did not go to Communion. And he felt ashamed that he was more concerned about what his mother would think than that he had actually sinned by trying to see the Devil. Who but an evil person would want to see the Devil? The Devil probably would have made him do something awful, just as Eve had been tricked into eating the apple.

When he got home, John locked himself in his room and tried to read his book of Bible stories as an act of contrition, but he could not concentrate on them. At nine o'clock, his mother came to tell him it was bedtime.

"John, you look really tired," she said. "Do you feel all right?"

"Yes," he said, although at that moment his stomach was fluttering from fear she would ask him, and then he would –

"I meant to ask you before. Why didn't you go to Communion tonight?"

What should he say? He tried to find words. His throat dried up. How could he tell? Could he lie? No, she was his mother. She always knew when he lied.

"I couldn't," he said.

"Why not?" she asked, sitting down on the bed.

"I couldn't because – because I – " He stopped and swallowed to moisten his throat.

"It's okay. You can tell me," she said.

"I did something bad. I – "

"What did you do?"

"I – I tried. I – ." He took a deep breath but still could not speak. "I – Mom, I can't tell you. It's too awful. I couldn't go to Communion because I have to confess it first. I have to wait until my First Confession. I can't go to Communion until then. But what if something happens to me before then, like I get sick and die. I – I'm sorry, but I don't know whether God will forgive me because it's so awful."

"Oh, John," said Ellen, putting her arm around him. What harmless thing could he have done to give him so much distress. "When did you do this awful thing?"

"Last night," he said.

She thought for a moment. He had been home then. She could not imagine any trouble he could have gotten himself into last night that would endanger his immortal soul.

"Are you sure you don't want to tell me?"

"Mhhm," he said, shaking his head.

"All right," she said. "It's enough that you feel so bad about it."

"But will God punish me if I don't confess it right away?"

"No, He knows you haven't been able to make your First Confession yet."

"But I won't be able to go to Communion until then," John said.

"You know," said Ellen, "if you pray really hard and tell God how truly sorry you are for what you did, He'll forgive you."

"Even if I don't go to Confession?" asked John, looking doubtful.

"Yes, Confession is a way to remind us to be good. But if you are sorry, God will forgive you, provided you try hard not to do it again."

"Oh, no, I would never do it again."

"Then say your prayers tonight and ask for forgiveness and everything will be fine," she said, then kissed him goodnight.

John had never gotten ready for bed so quickly. He changed into his pajamas, brushed his teeth, then went into his room, turned off the light, and crawled into bed. He did not wish for a night light this time – he wanted to be completely in the dark, alone with only God to see and hear him. He started out by saying the prayer to his Guardian Angel, although he could not help wondering where the angel had been last night when he had sinned. Next he said the "Our Father" and "Hail Mary".

Then he did not know what to say. He simply tried to tell God he was sorry for what he had done. He told God he hated the Devil with all his heart, unless it was wrong to hate, in which case he just disliked the Devil for being evil. He promised he would never try to talk to the Devil again because he knew it was wrong to do sorcery like looking in mirrors and saying bad words. He told God he loved Him, and he wanted to be good, and he wanted to teach others to love God. He hoped God would forgive him, and not punish him, although he deserved it, because it would hurt his mother, who was a good Christian and who should not suffer for his sins.

Then in his agony, John began to cry, muffling his sobs into his pillow. Finally, when no more words of prayer were left to utter, when he was exhausted and his throat ached, he looked out the window. He had forgotten to close the curtains so the moonlight was able to stream across his bed. He found comfort in the soft glow. He was exhausted, but his pain and guilt disappeared. He could not explain it, but he suddenly recalled once, when he had been much younger, he had woken in the middle of the night after a strange dream. He had experienced a sensation of floating in the air – he had only been three or four years old then. He had not thought of it since. He did not know how to describe it then, but if older, the word he would have used would have been "disembodied". Now at age ten, he felt the sensation again, as if his heart were lifting up, expanding, ready to make him levitate into the air. He believed the feeling must be God's way of comforting him, of forgiving him, of letting him know he was a special child of God who would someday go to Heaven.

John decided not to tell Holly about the mysterious feeling he had experienced. She would not have understood; she did not go to church, even if her uncle were a minister. She would have said he had only imagined he was almost floating. He would have thought so too except it had been so powerful and unexpected a feeling that he could not have imagined it.

The next day, as recompense for his sins, he was sitting in the backyard reading his book of Bible stories when Holly came over. Immediately she noticed his book open to the picture of Jacob giving Joseph his coat of many colors.

"Who's that?" she asked, attracted by the colorful illustration.

"That's Joseph. He was Jacob's favorite son, so his brothers hated him. They sold him into slavery, then told their father a wild animal had killed him."

"Really?" asked Holly.

"Yeah, they sold him as a slave into Egypt," said John, "but he was such a good slave he ended up being friends with the Pharaoh of Egypt. Then when he became rich and powerful, he forgave his brothers and they came to live in Egypt with him."

"They didn't deserve it," said Holly.

"No, but he forgave them because he was kind," said John.

"Are there any other good stories in that book?" asked Holly.

"Lots," said John. He turned back a few pages to the picture of Lot's wife turned into a pillar of salt.

Holly was fascinated. They decided to play Bible Story the rest of the day. They might not have strictly adhered to the biblical narratives, but who was to say that things had not happened that were omitted from the Bible? If Miriam had not really been struck down by God for an evil act, and if Moses had not raised her from the dead, well then, the spirit of their play stories remained orthodox. For Holly, they were just great stories, but John felt they explained the purpose of life.

The next evening, Dad had to work late, and Mom had the night shift at the hospital. John and Chad stayed in town with their grandparents until their father could pick them up after work. John watched *Little House on the Prairie* with his grandparents, and he read his Bible stories during the commercials. He had just finished reading the story of Samson when his father arrived.

As Dad drove them home, it was dark enough that the city streetlights had turned on. John opened his book so he could read about Samuel whenever a streetlight's glow moved across his page. Mom would have said he would ruin his eyes, but Dad never thought of such things. The sporadic streetlights of Fourth Street only allowed John to read a sentence or two at a time; then he had to wait a few seconds before reading the next sentence. As he rode down the hill sloping into Washington Street, John turned the page to a picture of Samuel, sitting up in bed with his hand to his ear. God had called Samuel's name, and Samuel had replied, "Speak, Lord; your servant is listening."

John had never thought any of the biblical characters were like him. But here was a little boy, sitting up in bed at night, surrounded by a bluish glow, suggestive of moonlight streaming into the room – just as it had streamed a couple nights before when John had prayed for God's forgiveness. John had not heard God's voice as had Samuel, but the picture lent confirmation to John's mystical experience; John decided if God ever did speak actual words to him, he knew he would repeat Samuel's words, "Speak, Lord; your servant is listening."

That year, John considered his birthday the highlight of his entire life to date. He received tons of wonderful presents, including those from Aunt Eleanor, Lucy, and Maud, who were always overly generous. But when they gave John a thick copy of Charles Dickens's *Great Expectations*, he was a bit flabbergasted.

"I can't read all that," he said, looking at the small print.

"Why not?" asked Aunt Eleanor.

"The print is so small, and there's so many pages."

"Well, we knew you liked to read," said Maud, "and this book is a classic so we thought you'd like it."

"You could just read one chapter a day," Lucy said. "Then you'll have it done before you know it. That's what I do with some books."

John looked doubtful, but he flipped through the pages, finding some interesting illustrations, particularly one of Miss Havisham with her wedding dress on fire.

"All right," he said. "I'll read the first chapter before I go to bed tonight."

"We have one more present for you," said Ellen, "but you'll have to wait for it until tomorrow."

"Why, what is it?" he asked.

She handed him a little piece of blue paper, the size of a dollar bill, which had written on it, "This coupon good for one pet dog on your birthday."

"Really Mom?" he asked.

"Yes, your father and I think you're old enough now."

"How did you know I wanted a dog?"

"You've done nothing but draw pictures of dogs for the last month!" said Chad.

"When can I get one?" John asked.

"There's an ad in the *Mining Journal* for free puppies at a place in Harvey. We'll go there tomorrow."

John could not sleep that night; he was too excited about the puppy. He wondered what kind it would be and what it would look like. It was a good thing tomorrow was a Saturday because sleep would not come. Finally, to try and fall asleep, he snuck his flashlight out of the drawer by his bed, and then under the covers, read *Great Expectations*. The book was so interesting it only delayed his sleep.

But in the morning, lack of sleep did not stop his excitement. As soon as breakfast was over, his parents drove him and Chad to Harvey to look at the puppies. Only two were left. One was white with reddish brown spots, just like its mother. The other puppy, taking after its father, was black with tan coloring on its face and paws. When John saw the black one, he instantly wanted it.

"You're lucky," said the puppy's owner. "A lady took him yesterday, but her landlord wouldn't let her keep him so she brought him back this morning."

"Then I guess it was meant to be that we have him," said Ellen.

The puppy jumped up to lick John's face as he bent down to pet it.

"His name's Bruno," said the man, "but I imagine you'll want to change that."

"We should name him Twinkie," said Chad.

"How about Buddy?" said Ellen.

"Or Blackie," said Tom.

"No, none of those," said John. "I'll have to think about it."

Because it was Saturday, the family brought the puppy to Grandpa and Grandma's house while they went to church, and Henry babysat it during Mass. After that day, Henry joked to Ellen and his grandsons that they were not allowed to visit unless they brought the puppy with them. Henry and Beth had always had pets, but both felt they were too old now to care for a dog, so the puppy became a welcome addition to the extended family.

At suppertime, the puppy sat on the floor next to Beth's chair. When he could no longer stand to watch her eat her hamburger, he pawed at the air and bit her apron string.

Rather than be one of those intolerable fussy women who are afraid to pet a dog while eating, Beth laughed, patted the puppy's head, and said, "Well, you're quite the little dickens, aren't you?"

"Hey, how about that for a name?" said Ellen.

"What?" asked John.

"Dickens."

"That's a funny name," said Chad.

"No, it's not," said John. "Dickens was a famous writer. He wrote *Great Expectations* that I got for my birthday."

"So what do you think of it for a name?" asked Ellen.

"I think it suits him," said Beth, glad to have helped name the puppy.

"I like it if he does," said John. "Here Dickens. Come here, Dickens." The puppy wagged its tail and trotted over to John. It had a name.

From that moment, John and Dickens were practically inseparable. They went for long walks in the woods, John singing and daydreaming, while Dickens dragged him down the trail, stopped to sniff, then ran down the trail some more. When John started to take piano lessons, Dickens would paw the air and whine, though no one knew whether he were singing or begging John to stop. When the boys went sledding, Dickens would have to ride down the hill with them. Whenever Grandpa or Grandma bought John and Chad candy bars, Dickens would get a bite, sometimes half of each bar, until he had more than either of the boys. At night, he slept on the foot of John's bed, or sometimes in the middle of the bed, not always a comfortable place for John, who curled himself around the dog rather than the other way around. And everyday, Dickens would jump up on the coffee table, until Ellen had to put a rug on it to keep it from being scratched. The coffee table was in front of the window, so seated on top of it, Dickens could watch for the school bus to bring his boys home; his life was on pause when they were away.

One Saturday, Tom and Ellen attended a wedding in Escanaba. John, Chad, and Dickens were dropped off at Grandpa and Grandma's for the day. Henry spent Saturday, as he did every day, in his woodshop. The boys knew Grandma would let them watch cartoons on cable television if they stayed in the house with her, but they preferred to work with Grandpa. Grandpa's shop had a scrap pile of rejected pieces from his past projects – ornate pieces of wood from picture frames or mirrors, heart carved blocks of wood intended for shutters, and every odd, round, square, or irregular shaped piece imaginable. The boys were free to take from this pile, and with hammer and nails, make whatever they chose, and if something were not quite the right size, Grandpa willingly cut it to fit. Henry was always busy making mirror frames, tables, benches, cutting boards, and shelves to take to craft sales and flea markets at the Holiday Inn or the Marquette Mall; the work kept him occupied and provided a supplement to his income, but when his grandsons wanted his help, he willingly put his other projects aside.

Over the years, Henry had made little benches for the boys, a desk for John and a bookshelf for Chad, little wagons and chariots for their stuffed animals to ride in or their *Star Wars* figures to use as transport vehicles across a barren planet. Today they wanted to build wooden houses. They chose the pieces and then Grandpa cut out the doorways and a couple windows for the walls. John's house had four walls that sloped in a curving arch at the top of each wall, giving it a distinctive look. He wanted no roof so he could set things inside the house through the top. Chad's house was large and perfectly square, so Grandpa made a large flat roof that could easily be lifted off when the house would be played with. Once the doors and windows were cut into the future walls of the houses, the boys sanded the pieces, and then Henry helped nail them together. Then he found a couple open cans of paint, one red and one blue, so the boys could decorate the houses.

They were silent as they painted. Henry was surprised when he realized it was already four o'clock.

"What do you boys say to our going to Bonanza for supper?"

"Sure," they said.

"I'll go see what your grandma says. I don't think she'll have started cooking anything yet. Don't get paint all over while I'm gone."

An hour later, the houses were set aside so the paint could dry. The boys went to change their clothes, having dribbled some paint on their jeans. Grandma shook her head and decided she would wash their pants that evening so Ellen would not be mad. In ten minutes, John and Chad emerged in corduroy pants and polo shirts, ready to go out for supper.

Grandpa and Grandma were regulars at Bonanza, which ensured that Chad and John got extra suckers with their little wrangler meals. They all overstuffed their stomachs with steak, chili con carne, salad, french fries, and ice cream.

As they left the restaurant, Beth said, "It's such a nice night; let's go for a ride before we go home."

"How about we go see the prison gardens," said Henry.

They took the bypass to South Marquette, then went out of town along the lake.

Looking to the right, John saw the Carp River, which flowed under the road and into Lake Superior. "Grandpa, what's that stone hut?" he asked about a building beside the river.

"That's one of the old charcoal kilns," said Henry.

"What's it for?"

"They used it like a blast furnace to make pig iron. It must be over a hundred years old now."

John still did not understand its purpose, but he did not ask more questions because they were now driving through the prison's gate. The road wound until a towering sandstone structure came into view.

"That's the prison?" asked Chad, thinking it looked like a haunted castle.

"Yes," said Henry.

He drove the car around the sunken gardens where frog statues sprayed out fountains of water.

"They're pretty," said John, meaning the flowers. No other cars were around so Henry stopped the car and they looked out at the gardens.

"They are pretty," said Beth. "But not as pretty as when they first started them. Henry, do you remember when we were first married, and we used to take my dad for drives here."

"When was that?" asked John.

"Oh, back in the '30s," said Henry.

John took a moment to realize that was about forty-five years ago, thirty-five years before he was even born.

"They started the gardens back in the early '20s," said Beth. "Just about the time my father stopped working here."

"Your father worked here?" John said in surprise.

"Yes, he was a prison guard for many years," Beth replied.

"Since the place first opened, wasn't it?" said Henry.

"I think so," said Beth, "but I'm not sure. That was long before I was born."

"How old is the prison?" John asked.

"I think it was built in the late 1880s," said Henry.

Nearly a hundred years ago! John was impressed that way back then, his great-grandfather had worked here, even before Grandma was born, and Grandma was seventy now. It boggled his mind to think his family had lived in Marquette even before his grandparents were born.

On the way home, Henry drove up Front Street and turned onto Washington. John stared up at the Old Savings Bank, with its clocktower that he thought rivaled Big Ben. The bank building was made of the same reddish stone the prison had been built from, and then as they reached Third Street, he noticed the old City Hall was the same color as well. He imagined they must all have been buildings from the 1800s.

"John, see the Post Office here," said Henry, pointing at the tall white building on the corner beside the old City Hall.

"Yeah," John said.

"I helped to build it," said Henry.

"When was that?" asked John.

"Oh, back in the late '30s."

"I guess you did a good job since it's still standing," Beth told Henry.

"I imagine it'll be standing long after I'm gone," Henry replied.

When they got home, they settled down in front of the television. To Beth's everlasting disappointment, *The Lawrence Welk Show* had finally been canceled. Instead, they watched *Love Boat* and *Fantasy Island* before going to bed. Chad glued himself to the TV, but John sat at the dining room table and drew pictures of buildings. He felt obsessed with the old stone buildings he had seen. He wished Grandpa could make him a playhouse to look like the prison or one of the other old Marquette landmarks. He was proud to think his family had been associated with so many of the old buildings in town.

In the morning, Tom and Ellen came and took the boys and Beth to church. They belonged to St. Michael's Parish, but this morning, they decided to go to St. Peter's Cathedral because the Mass was at a more convenient time. John had only been in St. Peter's once before, and then he had been too young to appreciate it. Now as they walked into the church, he said, "Grandma, this church is built out of the same stone as the prison, isn't it?"

"Yes," said Beth, "it's all Lake Superior Sandstone."

"Is it as old as the prison?"

"Older," said Beth. "The cathedral just celebrated its one hundredth birthday."

"I wish Uncle Michael had been here for it," said Ellen.

"Who's Uncle Michael?" asked John. He only knew Uncle Roy and Uncle Bill, and Uncle Jim out in California, and his dad's brother, Uncle Rodger.

"Michael was my brother who became a priest," said Beth. "He and I grew up in this parish, and he said Mass here a few times."

"Is he dead?" asked Chad.

"Oh, yes, for many years now. He became a monsignor, and ended up being appointed to Rome to teach at the college there. He's buried at the Vatican, but I think he always loved St. Peter's Cathedral best of any church."

John had not known before that Grandma had had brothers; she rarely mentioned her family; now he wished he could have known Uncle Michael; he was impressed that his uncle had been a priest. As he stepped inside the cathedral, he imagined Uncle Michael going to Mass here as a young boy among the giant red marble pillars, the Romanesque roof, the stained glass windows and the mosaic of Christ giving St. Peter the keys to the kingdom of Heaven.

The Mass began. The priest and altar boys walked down the aisle while the congregation sang, "The Church's One Foundation". As he joined in, John thought, "How could Uncle Michael not become a priest when he grew up going to this beautiful church." John had heard people talk about the priesthood as a calling. He wondered whether like the Prophet Samuel, Uncle Michael had heard God call his name.

After Mass, the family picked up Grandpa, and then, with the six of them squished into the car, they drove to the Bavarian Inn.

Bonanza was John's favorite place to eat supper, but the Bavarian Inn was the best place in Marquette for breakfast. Even if there were a wait to be seated, it was well worth it. John would have waited an hour for those pancakes, just a bit thicker than crepes and topped with whipping cream and a choice of apples, peaches, or blueberries. He and Chad never had anything else. Let the grownups settle for eggs and coffee. Pancakes with whipping cream and fruit and hot chocolate with more whipping cream was his idea of a German cultural experience.

The Bavarian Inn itself was very German. Four dining rooms were darkly paneled as if the wood itself had come from the Black Forest, while red trim, Alpine decorations, and pictures of Bavarian villages decorated the rooms. The dining rooms were separated by walls containing shadow boxes made to resemble windows looking out upon German landscapes; the windows had ornate red shutters with hearts carved into them for an Alpine flavor. Arranged along the windowsills of the boxes were several little Hummel figures for added effect.

Presiding over this Bavarian world transplanted to Marquette was Ernestine Latour. She had immigrated to the United States from Germany, and now that her husband, who had helped found the restaurant and its motel, was deceased, she had rented out the restaurant for others to manage, but a day never passed that she was not there, making sure all was well. Her husband had hired Henry to do some carpentry work when the hotel was first built, and since then, the families had been friendly. Many times she had been included in family parties at the Whitmans' house when John was younger, but now he was at an age when her friendliness embarrassed him.

After saying hello to everyone, Mrs. Latour asked, "John, do you remember that time you wanted to play hairdresser and I let you comb my hair?"

John smiled and nodded his head politely. He had not played hairdresser since he was five, and he could not imagine what had possessed him then.

The adults laughed, while Mrs. Latour pulled up a chair, lit a cigarette, and visited with the family. Henry and Beth invited her for a Sunday drive that afternoon. Then she went to ensure her other guests were content while the waitress brought those delicious pancakes.

John poured syrup on his pancakes, never considering the possibility of having too much sugar despite the whipping cream already on top.

"Hello," said Beth and Ellen.

John looked up to see Monsignor Dunleavy from St. Michael's enter the dining room with another priest.

"Giving those homilies works up an appetite," he joked as he greeted his parishioners. Then Monsignor turned to the waitress, one of his other parishioners, and said, "See that boy there. If you want to know anything about the Bible, don't ask me. You ask him. He knows it all. His parents have done a good job teaching him."

The waitress smiled. Ellen said, "I don't know that it was me. John reads his Bible all the time. He knows more about it than I do."

Monsignor Dunleavy replied, "I wish all our C.C.D. students were like him."

John smiled with embarrassed pleasure.

The priests went to their table while the Whitmans and Vandelaares dug into their pancakes and eggs. Henry told Tom how many cutting boards and tables he would have ready for his next craft sale. Ellen and Beth made plans to go shopping on Wednesday, and Beth promised to call Aunt Eleanor to see whether she wanted to join them. Chad asked John whether when they got home, he wanted to work on the fort they were building in the woods. John said he would ask Holly whether she wanted to help, but his thoughts were about what Monsignor Dunleavy had said.

Monsignor had referred to his visit to John's C.C.D. class a couple weeks before. He had come to discuss with them that week's scripture reading about Christ's Transfiguration. One of the girls in the class had read the passage from the gospel. Then Monsignor had begun to explain the story, but he had paused to ask whether anyone in the class could tell him who were Moses and Elijah, who had appeared to Christ and his three disciples.

John had hesitantly raised his hand.

"Moses led the Israelites out of Egypt and God gave him the Ten Commandments. He died at age 120, and he never got to enter the Promised Land because he had struck a rock rather than praying to God for water, but God let him look at the promised land from a mountain. Elijah was a great prophet who demonstrated how Baal was a false God; the King of Israel tried to have him killed, but Elijah hid in the mountains and God had the ravens feed him. Then he chose Elisha to succeed him before he was taken by God into Heaven in a fiery chariot."

Monsignor's face had glowed with pleasure to be given so much information. "Yes, that's excellent," he had said.

Monsignor had then discussed how the Transfiguration was a sign to the disciples that Jesus was the Son of God. When he had finished explaining the lesson, he had asked whether any of the children had any questions.

Again John had put up his arm, this time burning with a question.

"Yes, John."

"When Moses and Elijah appeared to Jesus, do you think Moses was able to because he never really died. I mean, Elijah was carried away in the chariot to Heaven. But the Bible says only God knows where Moses is buried, but if no one else knows, then how do we know he was buried and that God didn't take him up to Heaven as He did with Elijah?"

Monsignor had not been sure what to say to this thoughtful question, but after a few seconds, he had replied, "Well, I guess we can't know. If God wanted us to know, someone would have witnessed Moses ascending to Heaven, just as the apostles witnessed Jesus or Elisha witnessed Elijah go up into Heaven. It's a good question. It might be that Moses didn't die and that's why he could appear with Elijah. I don't know that anyone else ever thought of it that way. But what really matters is that their appearance helped to testify that Jesus was the Son of God."

"Thank you for coming, Monsignor. Children, were you glad Monsignor came?" the C.C.D. teacher had then said. All the children had smiled and said thank you as expected of them, all except John who was deep in thought, and did not notice the hostile stares of his classmates who hated C.C.D.

Now, remembering the question he had asked, John still wished he knew the exact answer, but if Monsignor Dunleavy did not know, John doubted he would ever know himself. He believed all the Bible stories. At times, they were hard to believe, but he understood that was why people must have Faith.

1981

When winter came, Tom's wandering spirit reached its peak. He felt trapped amid towering snowbanks that grew all winter long until he could not see to back his truck out of the driveway. Then more snow would fall, and he had to find more places to snowblow and plow it until the banks were so high the snowblower could not shoot the snow up onto the towering banks, so the snow landed on the sides of the driveway, and the driveway began to narrow in. And while Tom cleaned the yard, the wind would blow snow in his face, and with the temperature at zero, the snow melting off his face, and his nose dripping, Tom was completely miserable.

"I don't know why the hell we live here," he said one Sunday morning when he came inside from snowblowing the yard.

"You better hurry if you're going fishing with your friends," said Ellen.

"I don't know where we'll put another inch of snow, and it's only the beginning of February. We could have three more months of this weather."

"Did you hear me? You said you wanted to take a shower before you go, and it's already eleven-thirty."

"I know. I heard you the first time," Tom snapped.

"Well, then why don't you ever answer me?" asked Ellen.

"I know I want to take a shower. You don't need to tell me."

"I just didn't think you knew what time it was," said Ellen. "Don't be so crabby."

In his bedroom, John raised his head up from his book to listen to his parents bickering.

"I'm just tired," Tom groaned.

"Well, you didn't need to clean the path around the house too."

"How else are we going to get out if there's a fire, and we can't get out the front or garage doors? You're the one who wants to live in this Godforsaken land."

"If you don't want to live here, you can just leave," Ellen replied.

"Don't be like that," he said.

"You started it," she replied. "I told you before I married you, I wasn't going to leave Marquette, and you agreed to it, so don't blame me now."

"I'm going to shower," Tom said.

Tom came down the hallway. Since his bedroom door was open, John lowered his head so he would not see his father's face. Tom ignored his son, went into his room for a change of clothes, then went into the bathroom.

Everyone silently listened to the water running in the bathroom. Chad played in his room, pretending nothing was wrong. John went back to his book. Ellen took her cookies out of the oven. Tom came out of the bathroom and went to the back door. He put on his overalls, boots, and coat.

"If I'd stayed in the air force," he said, "I could retire in another ten years. Instead, I have to work at that damn garage all week and then spend all weekend plowing snow."

"Then go back into the air force," said Ellen.

"Maybe I will and never come back," said Tom.

"Fine with me."

Tom said nothing. He finished tying his boot, then went out the door, slamming it behind him. He found his fishing pole in the garage, then got into his truck and drove to the lake. All the way, he cursed the Upper Peninsula and his own stupidity for marrying a woman who wanted to stay here. He did not consider that his passion for ice fishing would be impossible in the warmer climate for which he longed.

Tom cooled off as he drove into Marquette to the Lower Harbor. With his buddies from work, Rick and Don, he usually spent most of his free time in winter ice-fishing, no matter how cold the northern winds blew or how far the temperature fell. When Tom arrived, he spotted a half dozen other shanties out on the lake, which was frozen for a mile out from shore. Even in the coldest winters, it was rare for much of Lake Superior to freeze, but for ice to form a mile or two along the shore was not uncommon. Shipping on the lake usually ended in December and did not revive until the spring thaws started to crack the ice.

The sun was shining when Tom arrived. His friends, having just pulled up a minute before, were collecting their gear from the back of Rick's truck.

"Looks like a good day to catch 'em," said Rick.

"At least it's not damn cold," said Tom. "I hate it when I freeze out here and don't catch nothing."

"It was thirty degrees on my thermometer at home," said Don, "that's a beautiful day in my book."

Inside the shanty was even warmer, despite the lack of sunlight and an ice floor. The three men seated themselves on stools, took out an awl, and drilled holes in the ice. The warmth they had momentarily felt was soon over. The walk out on the ice had warmed them, but now, sitting quietly over their ice holes and gently moving their lines to attract attention, the stillness allowed the numbing chill to creep into their bones. Outside the shanty's protective walls, they could hear the light breeze gradually develop into little gusts that rattled the hut, making them concentrate on the cold since no distraction came from fish tugging on their lines.

Yet a little cold was small price to pay for the tranquility of fishing – they were not philosophical men, given to much discussion; they would not have said fishing brought peace to their souls, although it did. Their joy centered around bragging rights – the fellow who caught the largest trout, pike, or whitefish was hero of the day. When in this tranquil time, their thoughts took the form of words, it was to reminisce and exaggerate the great catches of winters past.

The afternoon passed slowly. Then the wind picked up and the shanty lightly rocked on its icy floor.

"Damn wind's going to scare the fish," Tom said.

"Doesn't seem to matter. The fish aren't biting anyway," said Rick.

Don restlessly stood up to stretch his legs and peek out the door.

"Sun's gone, and black clouds are comin' in. Looks like a big storm's headin' our way."

"What time is it?" Rick asked.

"Quarter after four," said Don.

"About time ta call it quits then," Rick replied.

"Ahh, we've got time yet," said Tom.

"No, I gotta drive ta Ishpeming, and I don't want ta be caught in no blizzard. 'Sides, I told the wife I'd be home for supper at six," Don said.

"Come on, Tom. Let's head out," said Rick.

"You guys go ahead. I'll be right behind ya. I brought my own truck so don't bother waitin'."

"It's snowin' like heck out here, Tom," Rick warned when he opened the door.

"It's not that bad yet," said Tom, peering outside.

"You better come quick before it gets bad," Don said.

"Yeah, yeah. Don't worry about it," Tom snapped. He hated when his friends nagged him as if they were women. He had not caught a fish in three weeks, so he would not give up easily.

"Well, if ya won't come, we won't wait for ya," said Rick. "Come on, Don, 'fore the wind gets worse."

"Buncha wimps," said Tom once his friends were gone, "especially Don. What a worry wart."

Tom sat silently for half an hour as his last hope of catching a fish died away.

"Well, I s'pose," he then mumbled. After reeling in his line, he covered the fishing hole, and collected his gear.

Not believing his eyes when he stepped out of the shanty, he exclaimed, "Shit!" Instantly, he was blinded by snow furies whipping over the frozen lake, completely eliminating visibility. He strained his eyes to see the shore, but only blinding whiteness could be seen on all sides save for the shanty's walls.

"Well, it'll be okay," he said. "Probably only have to walk for a minute, and then I'll be able to see the shore."

The shanty door had faced out toward the lake rather than the harbor, so after he shut the door, Tom walked around to the back of the hut, then headed inland.

The frigid wind made him shiver. Yearning for his warm truck, he kept his head down, hardly daring to lift his face to squint toward shore because the wind and pelting snowflakes would pierce his eyes. He could barely see his own feet when he looked at the ground.

"It ain't more than a quarter mile to shore – that's about 1,300 feet," Tom thought. "I'll count my footsteps. I probably cover two or three feet with each stride, so by the time I count to five hundred I should be there. Won't take me more than five minutes."

He began to count, but it was hard to concentrate with the wind burning his cheeks. He lost count a couple times, but he still thought he was relatively close to the right number.

"Damn, I should have gone with those guys," he thought at step four hundred.

He figured he must be half or two-thirds of the way now. He wished he had never come out here today. Ellen had not wanted him to – he should have stayed home to watch TV or play games with the kids.

"Six hundred-one, six hundred-two, six hundred-three. Any minute now."

The snowstorm only appeared to get worse, moving in vast swirling squalls that looked like spirits whirling before him.

"Seven hundred. Any second now. Seven hundred-one, seven hundred-two. Damn it! Where's the shore?"

He stopped to peer ahead, looking for land, but he saw nothing but blinding whiteness.

"Seven-hundred ninety-eight. Seven-hundred ninety-nine. Eight hundred. Maybe I'm going diagonal. Well, if I am, I should still reach the shore. Keep walking. You'll get there."

"Eight-hundred one. Eight-hundred two. Where's the shore? Dammit! What was that?"

A loud cracking noise, as if something heavy had broken and fallen into the lake. Tom looked about him, but all was white.

"Must be a car engine starting up. I must be close to shore now even if I can't see it. Nine-hundred twenty-eight. Nine-hundred twenty-nine. What is that sound?"

He looked closely at the ground, fearing the worst. Then he looked ahead. This time – a terrifying sight! A giant stretch of black raging water just a yard before him.

"Damn it!" he nearly screamed. He was walking straight out into the lake! He had heard ice cracking!

"I could end up floating out into the lake!" he said. He hoped the ice he had heard cracking was not below or behind him.

Slowly, he turned around, afraid even to walk from fear it would crack the ice beneath him. Gingerly he took each step, careful not to step down too hard and crack the ice. An inch of snow had already fallen that afternoon, hiding any of the ice's frail spots. Tom had not walked back fifty feet before he heard another crack.

Terrified, he went on anyway. He should reach the shanty before a thousand steps. He started counting again.

"One. Two. Three."

He heard cracking again. His knees felt they would collapse. He could barely distinguish the footsteps he was retracing. The blowing wind would soon cause the snow to drift over them all. He prayed they would not vanish; otherwise, he might turn in the wrong direction again, and then – he felt sick to his stomach – if he plummeted into the lake, he knew the water would pull down and trap him beneath the ice. He wondered whether he would first drown or freeze to death.

"Fifty. Fifty-one. Fifty-two."

CRACK!!!

"Shit!" he cried, almost paralyzed. Tears sprang into his eyes, then froze there.

"Stay calm. Keep going," he panted. "If only I could see where I was heading."

A minute of silence passed as he walked. "Thank God," he thought. He wished he had stayed home. He might never make it back. He might never see Ellen or the boys again. He wished his last words to his wife had not been hateful. He had not even said goodbye to his sons.

He wondered whether you could get hypothermia in a snowstorm. He felt completely numb. His legs stiffened. He could not feel his toes or fingers. He would probably get frostbite. Or was his body shutting down from the overwhelming fear? He must keep going. His legs felt like they weighed five hundred pounds each. With the heavy snow clinging to his boots, his feet only became heavier, and that only meant the ice was more likely to crack beneath their weight.

"Why didn't you leave with Rick and Don?" he scolded himself.

"Nine hundred. Is that really the right number? Doesn't seem like I've walked that far back yet. I must have miscounted. Should I start over? I don't think I've gone more than six or seven hundred steps. No, I'll just keep counting. I should get back to the – oh, thank God, there it is."

The fishing shanty was before him. He practically stumbled toward it. He did not know whether he dared to go on from here. He doubted he would find the shore. He was so cold and tired already.

He went into the shanty to rest and warm himself. He brushed the snow off his coat so it would not melt and leave his clothes wet.

"Maybe it'll let up if I wait a while. The weatherman didn't say nothing about a storm like this today. Hasn't even lasted an hour yet. Must just be a big squall."

He tried to believe his recent experience had not been so bad, that he could go back outside again. He looked at his watch and saw it was five-thirty.

"The guys left about quarter to five. That's nearly an hour ago. It'll be dark any minute. If I don't go now, I'll be out here in the dark. If I do go, I might still be trying to find my way in the dark. But I can't stay here overnight. I'll freeze to death."

He hesitated a couple more minutes, afraid to venture out again, but his fingers were so numb he decided it was better to risk falling into the lake than dying from the cold. Muttering "Dammit", he stepped outside again. He could still see a trace of his footprints so he knew now which way led to the open lake. He started walking in the opposite direction, praying this time he was heading toward shore.

"All right, I'll start countin' again. One, two, three, four, five, six, seven."

He still felt terrified, but not as terrified as before. He had been lucky even to find his way back to the shanty. If only the storm had started sooner, he would have gone home sooner, and then he would not be stuck out here in the dark.

"Ellen's probably worried sick about me," he thought. "I shouldn't have gone out at all. Should have stayed home with her. Poor girl. She didn't want me to go. I know she had plenty of housework to do so I should have stayed home to look after the kids for her. Damn, now I've lost count again. I think I left off around one hundred, or was it two hundred. If I had a dollar for each footstep, then I could buy that bandsaw I want. I don't think I'm gettin' anywhere. Looks like the snow is lettin' up though. I hope so. Drivin' in a blizzard's almost as bad as walkin' in one, except it's not so cold."

"Five hundred. Five hundred-one. Five hundred-two."

"What? Is that it? Can't be already. It is."

He saw the shore in the distance, and then he could see the ore dock, and some of the downtown buildings. Another minute and he would be on dry land, or snow covered land, but land at least.

He nearly ran the last hundred feet to shore, forgetting his fear of cracking ice. He came to the land, sloping down to the lake. As he stepped up the hill, he knew he was safe. He saw his truck. He would have to clean it off before he headed home. He set his fishing gear down in the snow, then dug in his pocket for the truck keys. Brushing snow off the lock, he inserted the key, turned it, opened the door, and reaching around the steering wheel, got the engine running.

"I'll let it warm up while I clean the windows."

He brushed off the truck. Then he brushed off himself. Five minutes later, he was driving through the downtown, amazed at how abandoned Marquette looked. "I guess everyone but me was smart enough to stay inside today."

The snow was blinding, but he made it home by driving thirty miles an hour. Ellen grumbled at him for being late. She and the kids had already eaten so now he was making extra work for her because she would have to reheat his supper. He grinned as she complained. He wanted to tell her he had nearly died. He wanted to say he was sorry, even that he loved her. Instead, he ate his meat and potatoes at the kitchen table while she went into the living room to watch the evening news. He did up his own supper dishes. Ellen was surprised but said nothing. She was not surprised when he fell asleep on the couch while the boys watched *The Wonderful World of Disney*.

All year round children find golden moments, especially imaginative children who live in a land of changing seasons. In winter, John, Chad, and Holly carved out snow tunnels, built castles with their snow blocks, went sledding, and created snowmen they pretended were the great marble statues of Ancient Greece, left by a forgotten colony of Athenians who had migrated to Antarctica. When the windchill dropped below zero, they played inside with stuffed animals and *Star Wars* figures, or they turned their bedrooms into haunted houses, creating extra rooms and passageways with blankets and quilts, then chased each other through secret tunnels, threatening to suck out each other's membranes, whatever membranes were. In summer, they built forts in the woods, and tore up the fresh ferns to mat together for roofing and carpets. They wandered down trails, hoping like Dorothy, in *The Road to Oz*, to stumble upon the right path to lead them to a magical land. They rode their bicycles down trails until they came out in Harvey, swearing not to tell their parents how far they had gone. They ran through the sprinkler, then paraded about the yard in their beach towels, pretending to be Julius Caesar, Cleopatra, and Moses. The summer days spread from eight in the morning until ten at night, with sand castles in the backyard, hide and seek at dusk, and childhood stretching before them as if never-ending, until John believed himself like Peter Pan, never to grow up.

They climbed trees. There were so many fine climbing trees with low branches to swing upon. One terrific tree had fallen and wedged itself between two other trees, so its top still remained ten feet above the forest floor. Its trunk was two feet wide, and it was strong enough that the three children could walk straight up to its top. They named the tree Bernard, a distinguished name for a distinguished tree, their naturally formed tree house. Sometimes Bernard was a place to sit and read a book in silence, sometimes it was a lookout tower, or a castle.

Today, the tree was a ship, the *Poseidon XIII*, and John, Chad, and Holly were movie stars in their neverending series of sequels to the greatest disaster movie of all time. In *The Poseidon Adventure*, nearly all the characters had died, but these imaginative children would not let that stop other tidal waves from flipping boats upside down and trapping casts of outlandish characters inside the boats. Today, Holly was the impossibly sexy movie star, Tina Diarrhea, whose boobs were a full foot longer than Dolly Parton's. John was Egbert, the eccentric millionaire, who made his fortune by selling electric toothbrushes. He was madly in love with Tina Diarrhea, and she intended to marry him, being madly in love with his money. Chad was the penniless painter, Pablo, whose favorite artistic subject was to paint Tina nude, a secret he and Tina had long kept from her millionaire fiancé, along with their long time affair. Then the tidal wave hit, and all three screamed and jumped off the tree, pretending they were crashing through windows. They shook tree branches for dramatic effect, as though chandeliers were swinging and falling to pieces. Everyone else drowned, but fortunately, Egbert freed Tina from being trapped under a table. Pablo meanwhile despaired because the water rushing into the ship had destroyed his artistic masterpieces.

"Who cares about your stupid paintings. We have to find a way out of this boat," said Egbert, going to look for other survivors.

"We need to save my jewels," said Tina, shoving them down her cleavage.

Then she found the captain who led her to the bottom of the ship, which floated above water because the ship had overturned. To reach the bottom of the ship, they must climb up the tree. Egbert/John slipped and ripped his pants on a ladder/tree branch, which caused him to hang upside down, but Tina grabbed him before he plummeted into the boiler room's flames. Then she declared her love for him. She told Pablo because Egbert had saved her and now she had saved him, she could no longer love a mere penniless artist. Pablo, in despair, decided he would throw his weight against the only door between them and the surging waters so Egbert and Tina had time to escape to the bottom of the boat. Thanking Pablo for his sacrifice, the lovers made their escape with the captain (now played by Chad because Pablo had died). They reached the bottom of the ship, but they could not break their way through the metal floor.

In despair at their approaching death, Tina Diarrhea declared, "I hope Dolly Parton plays me in the made-for-TV version of our story. Only her boobs are big enough." "Baby," said Egbert, "you're too beautiful for a TV movie. It'll be a bigger box office smash than *Jaws*." Then they kissed passionately as they prepared to meet death.

Suddenly, a saw blade was heard. They were rescued. The Coast Guard pulled them through the cut floor of the ship and flew them off to Hawaii, the nearest island, where the lovers entered marital bliss.

"Holly! It's suppertime!" her mother screamed, recalling the children to reality.

"I better go," she said. "I had fun."

"Me too," said Chad.

"We should write these stories down," said John.

"Why?" Holly asked.

"Because they're cool," said John. "Maybe someday we could even get Hollywood to make a movie sequel from them."

They were fortunately unaware that a woefully bad TV sequel had already been made of their favorite film.

"No," said Holly. "I don't want to share our game with anyone else. Besides, it would take forever to write it all down, and that would be like doing schoolwork."

"Well, maybe we could write it down as an assignment, like for Reading class."

"Maybe," she said. "Anyway, I better go, or I'll be late for supper."

"Okay. Do you want to sit together on the bus tomorrow?"

"Sure. Bye!"

"Bye!" John and Chad shouted as Holly ran into her own yard. John decided to go inside too. Then he would have time to read more of *Johnny Tremain* before supper. Chad wanted to watch *Super Friends*.

When they came out of the woods into their yard, they saw Uncle Roy's car in the driveway.

"I almost forgot!" said Chad. "Aunt Ada's coming for supper."

"She must have driven Uncle Roy's car over," said John. Aunt Ada had just arrived yesterday for her summer visit and neither of her great-nephews had seen her yet. Except for Grandpa, she was the only adult who took an interest in their imaginative worlds, so the boys' enthusiasm was understandable as they raced toward the house. They had barely burst through the back door when Ellen asked, "John, how did you rip your pants? And you're bleeding. What happened?"

"I just fell is all."

"How?"

"I was climbing Bernard."

"What do you mean?"

"I was climbing Bernard."

"Who's Bernard?"

"Mom," said Chad, "it's the tree on the Blueberry Trail – the one fallen between the other two trees, right where the trail curves."

"And you fell out of it?"

"No, my foot just slipped and I tumbled a little. I was only up three feet."

He looked at Chad, hoping his brother would not tattle that he had slipped and hung upside down, suspended by his ripped pants.

"Oh, you boys," Ellen shook her head. "How many times have I told you not to climb trees?"

"We climb trees all the time," said John.

"I don't want you boys climbing any more; do you hear me? One of these days you might really hurt yourself. Go in the bathroom now and take off your pants. I'll be there in a minute to put some mercurochrome on your scrape."

"Mom!" the boys protested. "We climb Bernard and Frederick all the time!"

"I assume Frederick is another tree?"

"Yeah," John said. "Bernard and Frederick are the biggest trees in the woods."

"What if you fell out of one, John, and I didn't hear you yell? You might break a leg and lie there for who knows how long."

"Oh Ellen," Ada said. "Let them be. Children climb trees, and you can't stop them. I wouldn't have stopped at their age because an adult told me to."

"I can't imagine you climbing trees, Aunt Ada," Chad said.

"Oh sure, my brothers and sisters and I used to climb the apple trees on our farm. It was wonderful. We could see clear across Chocolay Township from there."

"Even Aunt Eleanor climbed trees?" asked John, thinking her too fussy for such an activity.

"Yes, I daresay she could out tree-climb any girl in Marquette County."

"Now you're just setting a bad example for the boys," Ellen told her aunt.

"Tell me boys," Ada said, ignoring her niece, "do you name all the trees?"

"We have to," said Chad. "Otherwise, how could we keep them all straight when we talk about them?"

"Yeah, and each one is different and good for climbing in its own way," said John. "They're as much our friends as real people so they deserve names."

"Ellen, you have smart boys," Ada said. "Let them climb trees. It helps their imaginations."

"Chad, go wash your hands for supper, and John, take off those pants and wash out the cut. I'll be there in a minute to bandage it," Ellen ordered.

The boys disappeared.

"Aunt Ada, will you watch that the spaghetti doesn't boil over while I treat John's knee."

"Of course," said Ada.

Ellen did not remonstrate further with her sons. She knew her aunt was right to think she fussed too much, but her boys were all her world, all that brought her happiness, and she was terrified of losing them. She was relieved when they stayed inside to spend the evening at the kitchen table with their aunt, cutting up construction paper and making cardboard puppets out of toilet paper rolls. There was no end to Aunt Ada's creative ingenuity. The boys thought her the smartest grownup they knew.

"Aunt Ada, I wish you were our art teacher," said Chad. "You always make the best stuff."

"Do you like to write too?" asked John. "I like making things, but I like making up stories best."

"Well, I like to write poems," said Ada. "I write mostly about my childhood here in Michigan. Louisiana's a beautiful place, but in winter, I miss the snow, so I write about the games we played all winter. My brothers and sisters and I used to have the best times when we'd go sledding or snowshoeing."

"I wish I knew you when you were a kid," said Chad. "I bet you were a lot of fun."

"I bet," thought John, "that Aunt Ada would have been as much fun as Holly. Only, I bet Aunt Ada would have helped me write down our stories."

1982

Even childhood's golden days must end. For John, the first blow happened when Holly's parents divorced. Her father moved to Negaunee, and then shortly after Christmas, she moved downstate with her mother. Holly's house went up for sale and stayed vacant throughout the winter. Outside of school, John now only had Chad to play with. By summer, they were sick of each other. John did not find his brother as interesting as Holly. Chad was content to watch cartoons, while John's active imagination refused to settle for passively watching television.

John was very lonely that summer. Loneliness made him delve farther into his imaginary world. He began to wonder about his future; after all, he was twelve now; he wanted to do something great and good with his life such as be a priest or missionary; he was an abnormally religious boy; he frequently locked himself in his room to kneel and say his rosary. Then his mother would knock on the door to bring him his underwear from the wash, and he would get angry to be interrupted while praying, and she would ask him why he was so crabby. He would not tell her, but he felt his frustrated efforts to be good only made him behave worse. He wished he could leave home to better the world somehow; perhaps he would have a vision of the Virgin Mary, who would tell him to go to Africa to help the starving Ethiopians. But he did not feel brave enough to do these things on his own; he wished he had a friend to go with him; he began to wonder whether he were a little crazy to be so religious; he was becoming painfully aware he was different from other boys, but then, many of God's saints had been accused of craziness; look at Joan of Arc.

A few days before school started, a new family bought Holly's house.

"I met the father outside," said Tom, when he came home from work one evening. "He has a boy the same age as John. They'll be moved in tomorrow."

"What's the boy's name?" asked John.

"I don't remember," said Tom; he had enough difficulty remembering his own sons' names and often called them Chon and Jad.

"You boys should go over tomorrow to welcome him," said Ellen.

"Maybe," said John, not willing to admit how desperately he wanted a friend.

The next morning, John looked out the window and saw the new neighbor boy in his yard. John asked Chad to go with him to see whether the boy wanted to play, but Chad was still in his pajamas and plopped on the couch in front of the television. After a minute, John said to his brother, "Well, come out when you're ready."

He put on his shoes, then hesitated. What would he say to this new kid? What would the boy be like? What would he ask him to play?

He went into his room and looked at his games and toys. Finally, he pulled out his case of Hot Wheels and Matchbox cars. He went outside and pretended he was just going to play as if he did not know the boy was in the yard. When he saw the boy, he pretended to be surprised, then said, "Hi, I'm John. Did you just move in?"

"Yeah," said the boy. He was an inch taller than John. Thinner too. He had a rugged, chiseled look to his face. He did not look very friendly, but John was lonely.

"What's your name?"

"Paul."

"Hey," said John, feeling himself start to tremble, "I was just going to play with my cars in the sand. Do you want to play?"

Paul looked at John's car case, then at John, then at a car passing by. "Sure."

"Great," said John, unsure how great it was but feigning enthusiasm.

"What grade are you in?" John asked as they walked into the backyard.

"I'll be in seventh this year," said Paul.

"Me too," said John. "Where did you move here from?"

"Just Negaunee."

"Oh," said John.

"I didn't want to. Do you have a good basketball team at your middle school?"

"I don't know," said John.

"I'm going to try out for basketball," Paul said. "But I really want to play football. I'm on a soccer team right now."

"That's neat," said John to be polite.

They had reached the sand. They sat down and John opened up the box.

"This one's sweet," said Paul, picking up a Ferrari.

"I like the old fashioned ones," said John, pulling out a Model-T and a Rolls Royce circa 1920s.

"Those old grandpa ones?" said Paul. "They can't go very fast."

"Let's make some roads," said John, taking sticks to draw out streets in the sand. Paul helped, then started driving the Ferrari along the road. John pretended his Rolls Royce was chasing the Ferrari.

"See I told you it could go fast."

"Yeah, right," said Paul.

John gave his car a sudden burst of energy and crashed it into the Ferrari. Paul made squealing sounds for the wheels.

John mimicked a fake car voice. "Haha, now I've got you. I'm faster than you."

Paul pulled back and looked annoyed.

"Cars don't talk," said Paul.

John stared at Paul. He saw disdain in the boy's face.

"Maybe it's people talking in the car," said John.

"That's dumb," said Paul. "It's not real. Cars only make engine noises and honk their horns."

"It's more fun if they talk," said John, "so they each have a personality."

"Cars don't have personalities."

John did not reply, but he saw no point in just driving cars along dirt roads. When he and Holly had played cars, she had let the cars talk. Paul was boring.

John played Paul's way, but he was relieved when a few minutes later, Paul's dad came outside and hollered for him to come home.

"I'll see you later," said John.

"Yeah," said Paul, and then ran to his house.

John was devastated. It had been a horrible experience. He had longed for a friend, but he would prefer playing by himself to spending time with Paul. He felt overcome by loneliness, by a longing for Holly. He collected his cars and carried them back into the house. He found Chad still glued to reruns of *The Brady Bunch*.

"Did you meet the new boy?" asked his mother.

"Yeah."

"What's his name?"

"Paul. He couldn't play long because his dad called him to go home."

"Well, I'm glad you found a friend," said Ellen.

"I'm going to go read in my room," John replied.

But John was too depressed to read. He went to his desk drawer, pulled out his *Garfield* journal and wrote:

> I met the new neighbor boy today. His name is Paul and he's my age. He's also boring. I tried to get him to play cars, but I could tell he didn't really want to, and when we did play, he said cars aren't allowed to talk. He has no imagination. I'll never be able to have fun with him as I did with Holly. I don't think it's fair her mom made her move away – just because her mom has family downstate. Her parents are both selfish to get divorced; I don't think they thought about what was best for Holly. First she lost her dad and now all her friends back here. Since we don't live in town, there's no one else around to play with, except Chad, and all he wants to do is watch TV. Holly and I used to have the best times together because she's imaginative like me. We used to play Poseidon Adventure, and restaurant, and stuffed animals, and build forts, and ride our bikes, and a hundred other things. We were never bored. I remember one time we pretended . . .

Poor John. He had lost his best friend, but perhaps it was best it happened that way. Teenage girls are fickle and when Holly got to middle school, she would have felt less compelled by John's imaginary world than the prospect of kissing cute boys and dressing in styles inspired by Michael Jackson and Madonna. John's seriousness and his religious inclinations would never make him part of the popular crowd; doubtless, Holly would have spurned him as immature, and instead of his present loneliness, John would have felt the heartbreak of rejection from the friend he most trusted.

But John was too young to realize what had occurred was probably for the best. He moped through the rest of the day. The next morning, when he saw Paul outside, he did not go out to play with him. He did somewhat hope Paul would come over to see him, but when Paul did not, John felt there could be no friendship between them. When Chad once more glued himself to the television, John went in his room to play, but he found himself no longer interested in his stuffed animals or even his Star Wars figures; he knew Paul would think it unnatural for him to play with anything that was not round and could be tossed through a hoop.

He lay down on his bed and decided to read *Little Women* just to spite Paul, who would have been disgusted by a girl's book. John had long loved

Alcott's masterpiece and its sequels, thinking *Little Men* the best of them; he wished he could have lived at Plumfield with the other boys. Now, he came across the passages describing Jo March writing and performing plays with her sisters. He thought how he, Holly, and Chad had created their own stories. Then in a moment of insight, John realized all those make believe stories had been a form of writing, an oral rough draft for a book. Holly had never wanted to write down their stories, but John thought if he wrote them down, it would be like playing with Holly again.

He opened his desk drawer and pulled out the Smurf tablet his mother had bought him last Christmas. He loved the Smurfs, but he suspected if he brought the tablet to middle school that fall, he would be a laughingstock. Instead, he would use the tablet to write down his stories. For the next three days, he worked diligently for a couple hours each day. He soon realized the story would become a novel the length of an Oz book. The story was based on one Holly, Chad, and he had made up with their stuffed animals, but he changed a few things to make it more interesting. The tale follows as John wrote it, but with the grammar and punctuation corrected.

The Chronicles of Sunshineland
by
John Vandelaare

Prologue

For six hundred years, the ancient kingdom of Sunshineland had known peace, and during the last one hundred years of the reign of the good King Rainier, a golden age had flourished. The only sadness in the kingdom had been the death of Queen Susie the year before. Susie had been killed by King Rainier's best friend, Count Benji, but the count had committed this crime while hypnotized by Sylvester, the evil sorcerer. Sylvester had wanted Queen Susie dead because she was more beautiful even than his own wife, the Lady Aurora, the queen's sister, and he would be married to no one but the most beautiful woman in the land. When the court magician, Michael, discovered that Sylvester had enchanted Count Benji, King Rainier's heart softened toward his friend, so rather than being hung by the neck, Count Benji was simply banished from the land. The evil Sylvester was not so fortunate. He was imprisoned in a tower where he eventually died from sheer misery, leaving the beautiful Aurora a widow. Peace had been restored to the kingdom and the golden age of King Rainier continued. Soon after her mother's death, the king's daughter, Princess Desdemona, married the handsome Prince Gregory, and great celebrations were held throughout the land. Now people looked forward to the birth of the king's grandchildren so the throne would be secure. There seemed no longer any chance that war, famine, or flood would strike the kingdom, and every sign existed that peace and happiness would continue forever until . . . .

Chapter 1
The Abduction

One afternoon the lovely Lady Aurora ran into the throne room screaming her gorgeous head off.

"What is the matter with you, Aurora?" asked King Rainier.

"Oh, your majesty we're going to die. They attacked my carriage. All is lost, woe is me, we shall surely die," she started yelling, then burst into tears.

"Calm down, Aurora. Now start from the beginning and talk slowly so I can understand you," said Rainier.

"Oh, okay," said Aurora, sitting down on a chair before the throne. Then she related to the king, her brother-in-law, the following.

"Well this morning I was bored. You know how bored I've been since Sylvester died, not that I blame you, Rainier; Sylvester was an evil man. I tried to warn him not to do evil, but he – "

"Never mind that," said Rainier, not wanting to remember the tragic death of his late wife. "Tell me what happened to you today."

"I was bored. You don't know how boring it is trying on new clothes, being simply tortured by your hairdresser's combs, while she tries to give you a new hairstyle that ends up looking like a fruit salad.

"I was so bored I wanted some adventure so I ordered my chariot, only those stupid people who take care of it had broken one of its wheels. So I had to take that cheap looking carriage of mine."

Aurora's cheap carriage was only made of brass, with hubcaps made of silver, seats of velvet, and doorknobs made of diamonds.

"Well anyway," Aurora said, "I decided to take a trip into the Deadly Forest and discover what dangers lurked there.

"We had only been in the forest ten minutes when those scaredy-cat coachmen of mine wanted to head back because they were afraid.

"Just as I was trying to tell them no monsters were going to get them, we were attacked by a band of elves who took us captive and carried us away to a magnificent palace where their king lived. And you know what one of those cruel elves did? He stepped on my new blue silk, and got mud all over it, he did."

"I'm sorry, and it's such a lovely blue silk dress," said Rainier, knowing she would want sympathy before she would continue her story.

"You should have seen the elves' palace. It had rubies glittering all over the ceiling, and the windows were made of giant diamonds. Rainier, it makes your castle look like a stable."

Rainier would have been offended, but he was too worried to speak.

"Anyway, they brought us to their rotten, mean elf king who was busy playing croquet.

"Well, what do you think that king did? He asked me to play croquet with him; well I was never so insulted in all my life. The thought of me playing croquet with an elf! But I was a prisoner so I had no choice but to accept, and while we were playing I asked him why his guards had captured me.

"You know what he said, he said, 'I'm holding you for ransom.'

"I then asked him how much he was holding me for.

"He said he was going to let me go in exchange that all the Kings and Queens of our Planet Inna Wola would make him King of the World.

"I asked him what he would do when he was King of the World, but he told me he was tired of my asking questions and that he could see I was a bad croquet player. Then he had the guards lock me up in a three room suite with silk rugs, and gold and diamonds decorating the walls, and there were over a thousand dresses in the latest styles.

"I wanted to try on the dresses, but instead, when the guards left, I started tying the silk rugs together to make a ladder so I could climb out the window. Only when I had the ladder made, I realized there wasn't a window in my new accommodations.

"That was when I had a great plan.

"I took all the dresses I could carry, and put them on the bed. Then I started ripping up the other dresses and I found a needle and used the material to sew pockets on my dress, and then I filled my pockets with all the big pieces of jewelry in the room. Then I sat on the bed waiting for my lunch to be brought up.

"The maid looked as if she thought I were weird because of the outfit I had on, but that didn't matter to me. I reached into my pocket, threw a diamond at her, knocked her out, grabbed all the prettiest dresses, and ran through the castle's halls to try and find a door out. Anyone who tried to stop me got a diamond in the eye! After what seemed an eternity I got out of the castle, ran through the forest, and raced here to tell you."

Chapter 2
War is Declared

"Aurora, are you sure the elves want to take over everything?" asked King Rainier in great alarm when she had finished her story.

"Yes. I'm positive."

"Well, what will we do?" King Rainier despaired.

"How am I supposed to know?" asked Aurora, who was crabby because of all the dresses she had left behind and because she had not had her lunch. "You're the king! You figure it out! I did enough by escaping and coming to warn you!"

Just then a chariot carrying the Ancient Sage, the High Lord Condour, arrived at the Royal Palace. The chariot had barely stopped before Lord Condour had flown up the palace steps and burst into the throne room. Following close behind him were his assistants, Pooky Panda and Charlie Mouse.

"We have just come from the Valley of Stuffed Animals to inform you of a very important matter," declared the old bird sage.

"Who are you? And where is the Valley of Stuffed Animals! I never heard of it before!" said the king, shaking like crazy, from sheer nervousness over all the strange things happening today.

"That's doesn't matter!" replied High Lord Condour. "The important thing is that all we now cherish in Inna Wola is about to be destroyed. At this very second your palace is under attack."

"This is nonsense," said King Rainier. "I have the best army on the planet. We will not be attacked. This whole story has to be some sort of joke."

"Looketh out the window if you don't believe me," replied the wise old bird.

King Rainier looked out the window, and as he did so, an elf climbed inside, bopped the king on the nose, and knocked him cold on the marble floor.

Pooky Panda and Charlie Mouse ran to the king and carried him back to his throne to protect him.

"Who are you!" screamed Aurora, looking cruelly at the elf.

"Don't you remember me, my dear?" asked the ugly elf.

"Yes, you're one of those creatures who princess-napped me."

"That's right!" he said, and then drawing his sword, he forced everyone into a corner. With a snap of his finger, a dozen elves burst through the door and made it clear that everyone in the throne room was a prisoner.

Meanwhile in their bedroom, Princess Desdemona and her new husband Prince Gregory had just returned from their honeymoon to Lava Land to visit the volcanoes. Now, as they were unpacking, Desdemona looked out the window to see a zillion elves bombarding the palace with arrows.

"Ahhhhhhhhhhhhh!" she screamed as an arrow zoomed through the window, past her head, and went out another window.

Prince Gregory began to close all the windows while Princess Desdemona left the room to warn her father, King Rainier. Luckily she had her traveling clothes on, and we shall find out why this was so lucky in our next chapter.

Chapter 3
The Escape

As the princess ran down the hall, a legion of elves stopped her and asked her where the Princess Desdemona's room was. (They did not recognize her because they knew nothing about fashion and her traveling clothes made them think she was a maid).

She told them the princess was still on her honeymoon and would not be back for another week.

The legion turned back down the hall. Now Desdemona realized the entire castle, including her father, had been captured. She rushed back to her bedroom, locked the door once she was inside, then dove under her bed to enter the secret tunnel.

Gregory, thinking his wife was nuts, crawled under the bed after her. He found a trap door that opened into a staircase that led down to a tunnel. He hurried down the tunnel after his wife, only to discover it ended outside on the shore of the Muck River.

At the river dock, there was only an old rowboat, but Princess Desdemona was crawling into it. Prince Gregory jumped in and then asked why she was acting so crazy.

"There's no time to talk!" she said. "Just hurry up and row us to Jungleland. It's our only hope!"

Chapter 4
Encounter with the Slime Creature

Thus, for seven days and nights the Crowned Prince and Princess of Sunshineland traveled down the Muck River. If they had gone by land it probably would have taken but a couple days. Unfortunately the Muck River is more mud than river as you may have guessed, so it took all the strength Gregory had in him to row down the mighty river.

On the seventh day of their journey an unexpected happening occurred. They were passing by Waterland (one of the few places on the planet where you can get clean water that isn't full of muck).

"Stop darling I've just got to get some decent water. I'm near death from lack of it," said Desdemona whose skin was already becoming cracked from not getting any water in her system. (After all, she is a princess so you would expect her to worry about her ivory skin, wouldn't you?)

Gregory stopped the little decaying rowboat, and Desdemona cupped her hands together so she might drink the water.

But as she pulled her hands back out of the water, something dreadful bit her. "Ouch! Help! I'm going to die!" she screamed.

Then out of the waters rose a huge monster, twenty feet tall, and thoroughly covered in gobs of green slime.

The monster looked at Desdemona, wondering what was the matter with her.

"I think you would consider it quite an honor to be bit by the last member of the Gigantis Slimatonis Gruesomitis Monsters, or Bertha for short," said the monster with an air of superiority.

"I beg your pardon, Miss Bertha, but my wife has been known to get hysterical at times," replied Gregory with a tremble of fear in his voice.

"Oh well, it doesn't matter," said the slimy beast, "and by the way, I'm a mister; it's just that my mother always wanted a girl so she named me Bertha. Anyhow, my past is none of your business. Now about dinner, I think – "

"Oh, dinner! I'm so starved; let's hurry to your home so we can eat," said Desdemona joyfully.

"Mmhmm," the monster cleared its throat. "Where did you learn your manners? Don't you know it's not polite to interrupt another in the middle of a sentence."

Desdemona looked terribly embarrassed.

"Now about dinner," repeated the creature, "I think I'll eat you first, and save your husband for dessert."

"Oh, no you won't!" Desdemona screamed with determination.

"You can argue if you want, but it won't do you any good," said the monster with a yawn.

The creature grabbed Desdemona and started to place her head in his mouth, when all of the sudden he instead spit her into the mud.

"Bluck, yuck, oh disgustment city!" Bertha cried.

Now the reason the Monster Bertha said this was because Desdemona's hair was so greasy it was worse putting her hair in his mouth than it would be for you or me to eat liver. (Of course, that doesn't mean that Desdemona was a slob, only that she had been too busy traveling to wash her hair, and obviously she could not wash it in the Muck River.)

"Oh, I suppose you aren't any better tasting," the slime monster said to Gregory.

"No, I s'pose I'm not," replied Gregory, "but since you can't eat us, could you possibly help us?"

Then Gregory told Bertha all about the war in Sunshineland, and when he finished Bertha said it would truly be an honor to help. "We can't have elves take over Inna Wola, and if they come near the Muck River, I'll eat everyone of them. Now, if you'll both sit on my tail, I can catapult you to Jungleland in a minute!"

Desdemona and Gregory hesitated, but they knew it would take several more days to finish rowing to Jungleland so they climbed onto the monster's tail. Then, on the count of twenty-seven (Bertha's favorite number) they found themselves flying toward the shores of Jungleland.

Chapter 5
King Benji of Jungleland

"Ouch, my head hurts! That creature! The nerve of him throwing royalty around!" screamed Desdemona.

"Darling, do try being quiet for once," said Prince Gregory as he helped her up off the ground.

Just then a coach came by carrying none other than King Benjamin I (Benji for short). Yes, this was the famous Count Benji who had murdered Queen Susie by mistake. When he had been banished, he had traveled to the distant Jungleland and after many adventures, to be told in another book, had become its king.

When Desdemona and Gregory hollered and waved, Benji stopped his coach, recognizing the princess though he had not seen her since she was a little girl.

Benji left the coach and walked over to his friends.

Gregory explained to Benji their present situation, but not without unnecessary comments from the princess.

Benji was not one to hold grudges so he soon agreed to come to the aid of his old friend King Rainier. The party then went back to King Benji's jungle palace in a giant palm tree. There they made plans for their return journey to defeat the elves. Then all went to get a good night's sleep before leaving in the morning.

Chapter 6
Back to Sunshineland

The next day, the three of them set out on Benji's royal yacht to Sunshineland. Fortunately, this boat was motor powered, so within two days it made it down the Muck River, without any interruptions from Bertha. Soon they had arrived in Sunshineland.

Only one thing was wrong. They had made no plans about how they would conquer the elves. But when Princess Desdemona asked King Benji about this, he simply replied, "With the Magic Bluetonic Berries."

"Bluetonic Berries!" exclaimed Gregory and Desdemona together.

"Why yes, when you eat one you become ten times your original size. When the elves see that King Rainier has giants on his side, they'll immediately surrender or else we'll threaten to step on them. The only disadvantage is that after eating one berry you stay a giant for a week. With so much weight on the planet, the planet could fall out of its orbit and who knows where we'll end up."

"Who cares, as long as those vile elves are totally humiliated and made to surrender," said Desdemona. "Once we conquer them, I'll become their queen and then I can afford a thousand fancier dresses than what I have now because I'll make them work night and day sewing for me."

"Yes, yes," said Benji, realizing the princess really cared little for anyone but herself.

"Land, ahoy, Kingy!" yelled Pillsby the yacht's captain.

Soon the rescuers were upon the shores of Sunshineland. Just as they were stepping off the yacht, Desdemona screamed, for coming toward them were one hundred elf warriors.

Desdemona and Gregory quickly ran and locked themselves in their cabin on the yacht, but King Benji stayed for he wanted to talk to the warriors, and find out why they were fighting against Sunshineland and King Rainier.

But before he could say a word, the warriors had lifted him over their heads and were carrying him off toward the forest as a prisoner of war.

Desdemona and Gregory sadly looked out the yacht's window. King Benji had been their last hope and now even he was captured. The berries could still help them, but they didn't know where on the yacht King Benji had put them. All seemed lost.

John had not yet decided how the story would end, but he was so proud of the opening chapters he had written that he decided to let Chad and his mother read them.

"That's not the way it happened!" Chad said when he had finished reading. "There wasn't any sea monster at all – and him flinging them on his tail to Jungleland – that's just dumb. And King Benji wasn't captured. He just used the pills and killed all the elves. Why'd you change it?"

"Well, it's going to be a book," said John, "so I need to make the story longer, and if King Benji is captured, that just makes it more exciting."

"No, it doesn't," said Chad, "it just makes it more dumb. And how come you don't have any of my stuffed animals in the story?"

"Well, I didn't see where they fit in. Maybe later they can be in the story."

"It was better the way we played it," said Chad. "Now it's just stupid."

"Holly would like it," John said.

"Holly would think it's stupid too."

John refused to listen to his brother. When his mother read the story, her only comment was, "You need to learn the difference between commas and periods."

"But did you like the story?"

"I don't know. I'm not used to reading fantasy stories."

John grabbed the notebook and stomped off to his room. He flung the notebook into a drawer, then threw himself on his bed. He wondered again what should happen next in the story – should King Benji be rescued first or should Desdemona and Gregory save the country – somehow he could not see them able to do that – and he began to wonder whether King Rainier had escaped or been thrown into prison while Desdemona and Gregory were gone? Or maybe the elf king had forced Lady Aurora to marry him? What if that were to happen? But what did it matter? The more he thought about it, the more he thought Chad was right. It was a stupid story.

John felt cranky with himself for being so stupid. He thought about saying his rosary, praying that God would make him a better writer, but he was too angry to pray. Instead, he picked up *Ozma of Oz* and started to read it again because it was his favorite fantasy novel. He read it to find out what made it so good. He would not finish writing *The Chronicles of Sunshineland* because it was too stupid, but he would try to write another story just to prove he could do better. He was sure his next story would be wonderful because it would teach people something such as how to be good – maybe it would be a fairy tale, or a story about a saint, or a good king – John did not know yet, but he was sure he would think of something. He knew he was destined to be a writer, no matter what anyone said.

1985

The winter of 1984-1985 was one of the worst on record. Snowstorms had caused school to be canceled seven or eight times that year, but by March, John and Chad despaired that there would be no more snowdays. Already, signs of spring were visible. Each morning, the snowbanks appeared to have melted down another inch or two. Whereas a week ago, they had towered over John's head, now they were barely chin high when he stood beside them.

Then one evening, just as all hope of another snowday seemed lost, the weather man announced that a giant storm, currently moving across the Dakotas and Minnesota, was destined to strike Upper Michigan. All that night John waited for the blizzard to come. In the morning, he woke disappointed to a clear, blue sky. Throughout the day, he was distracted from his schoolwork by glancing out the window to watch for snow. Not until the bus ride home did John see the slightest appearance of snowflakes in the air, and then it was only a pathetically light sprinkling.

When the school bus dropped off Chad and him, John felt considerably glum. He tried to cheer himself by thinking that at least he would not have to shovel out the driveway, but that would have been a small price to pay for a snow day. When he and Chad entered the house, they were instantly greeted by Dickens, who was aching to go outside to the bathroom. John found Dickens's leash and put it on him, then walked him outside into the neighboring woods. The snow was still falling lightly; John tried to convince himself it was picking up, but it was not enough to make him hopeful. Dickens looked equally disappointed. He loved to bury his snout in newly fallen snow, sucking in the fresh smell of it, then rolling in it, often the only bath he would get for months. The result was wet snow sticking to his leg fur until snowballs the size of giant marbles clung to his legs, while pebble size snowballs wedged themselves between his paws. John would be forced to yank the snow from Dickens's feet without pulling out too much of his fur. Some days the snow was so packed on

Dickens's legs that John could not yank it off; then he would let Dickens in the house, snowballs attached, and hope the snow would melt before his mother noticed. Fortunately, there was no such problem today; the fresh snow made nothing necessary beyond a quick drying off of Dickens's feet.

As John went inside, the phone rang and Chad ran to answer it. It was their mother; she always called from work about the time the boys got home. John let Chad talk to her while he went to hang up his coat. A minute later, John sat down on the bed to start his homework, only to be interrupted by his brother.

"Mom says the snow is really coming down in town. She's going to come home early because it's so bad."

"Did you tell her there's barely a sprinkle here?" John asked.

"Yeah, but maybe it's headed this way, inland from the lake."

"Good, maybe there won't be school tomorrow."

Chad went to gorge himself on Mom's chocolate chip cookies and watch yet another rerun of *Little House on the Prairie* while John lay on the bed doing his geometry. Although there now seemed a slight possibility that school would be canceled, John felt he better play it safe by doing his homework. He hated geometry, but today's assignment was easy enough that he finished it in half an hour. Then, too excited by the prospective storm to do anything more productive, he wandered aimlessly into the kitchen, found some cookies, and went into the living room where Chad was deeply engrossed in Laura and Almanzo's courtship.

"Don't come in here if you're going to bug me," said Chad.

"I'm not. I'm going to watch the show," said John, dropping cookie crumbs on the lazy boy as he sat down in it. He rocked the chair vigorously while he ate his cookies. For a moment, he tried to interest himself in Laura and Almanzo, but he had seen all the episodes too many times before.

Looking out the window, he said, "It's really coming down out there."

"Uh huh," said Chad.

"The wind's picking up too. Have they run any weather advisories on TV?"

"No."

"I hope there isn't any school tomorrow."

"Be quiet."

"How can you watch this show again? You must have seen it five times. Why don't you do something useful with your life?"

Chad ignored his brother. John realized he was only accusing his brother of laziness because he felt guilt over his own lack of energy. He could find more productive things to do than stare out the window. For days an idea for a short story had been in his head, but he felt unable to concentrate on putting it down on paper. He had forgotten to read his daily Bible chapter when he got home, but he did not get up to do so now. He just stared out the window. Winter storms created a strange energy in him that left him incapable of doing anything except admiring Nature's power.

"I bet it's coming down an inch an hour now," he said. Chad was silent.

The snow was not falling anywhere near that fast, but John exaggerated in hopes it would. The wind had started to pick up, which would soon mean drifting snow covering the roads so the school bus could not get through. John hoped so anyway.

"Mom's home," he said when her car pulled into the driveway. He headed for the back door, leaving Chad free to watch television without distractions.

Usually Mom came home from work with groceries, but she had none tonight.

"I wanted to get home as quickly as possible," she said. "The snow was bad in town, but it was even worse on the highway. I could barely see the car in front of me when I passed the ski hill. I hope your father makes it home safely."

The storm still did not look that bad; it could barely be rated a storm, but John knew it always looked worse when you were driving in it. Winter was always filled with accidents caused by cars spinning on ice. Other cities had murders, but in Upper Michigan, most violent deaths were the result of poor winter road conditions.

Ellen set about making supper while Chad kept watching TV. John's restlessness made him sit down on the kitchen floor to pet Dickens, who soon became bored and wandered into the other room. John kept looking outside, watching the snow slowly pile up. Finally he could see an inch had fallen, but it had snowed now for two hours, so it was hardly coming down fast enough to warrant school cancellations. He felt hopeless again. He tried to convince himself that since it was growing dark outside, he could not accurately tell how much snow was on the ground; it probably was a lot more than he thought.

Ellen asked him to set the table, so he got up from the floor, washed his hands, and helped her. Just then, his father walked in the door.

"I couldn't see where I was going," Tom said. "I almost ended up in the ditch because this stupid car passed me. It kicked back so much snow I couldn't see out my windshield."

"That's what causes accidents," said Ellen. "People don't know how to drive in this weather. They're always in a hurry, never thinking about whose lives they are endangering until it's too late."

"It was probably some guy from the air base," said Tom. "Probably some twenty-year old from Florida who's stationed here for his first winter and doesn't yet know how to drive in the snow."

Now John felt the storm was becoming exciting. A storm bad enough to send cars into the ditch was almost a sure sign school would be canceled. But John was glad his father had made it home safely. A few years ago, John had been in the car with his father during a storm. The car had hit some ice and gone spinning in circles across the highway. They had both felt utter terror at their helplessness, the experience happening so quickly they were too afraid to scream. Then just as suddenly, they found the front of their car wedged into a snowbank. They had been lucky. No one else had been on the road for them to smash into. John's father was a good driver, but no matter how well anyone drives, ice can be hidden under snow, and if a driver hits that ice, little can prevent anyone from losing control of his vehicle and being thrown randomly about the road.

John's excitement now expanded into the many possibilities that could result from the storm. Perhaps they would be snowed in; they would be safe in the house, provided the snow did not pile up so much that the roof caved in. That was unlikely, but at least enough food was in the house for several days, so they would not starve.

After the family finished eating supper, Tom wanted to go outside to clean the driveway, but with the amount of snow coming down, Ellen convinced him he might as well wait and get up early in the morning so he did not have to do it twice. He went to lie down on the couch, covered in a warm quilt, while he watched the evening news to see the weather report.

Meanwhile, John took Dickens out again. It was now dark and with the yard light on, John could see how fiercely the snow was coming down. He looked up into the black sky; the snowflakes whizzed toward his face like miniature bullets, as if he were Han Solo in the Millennium Falcon, and he had just geared his ship into warp speed until it looked as if the stars flew past the spaceship. For a moment, John imagined himself flying through outer space until he felt an unearthly realization of the universe's vast endlessness that made him slightly dizzy; then he looked down at the snow covering his feet to regain consciousness of the world.

He watched Dickens leap over snow nearly too high for a short dog to walk through. But Dickens would not let the snow get the best of him. He stopped to roll in it, burying his snout in the cold water crystals. John watched his silly dog while the wind picked up and whipped against his own face, freezing it bitterly despite his knit hat and pulled up jacket collar. Dickens, ignoring the cold, was in one of his obstinate moods. Always during the worst weather conditions, he would decide to sniff every foot of ground, leave his mark on every tree, and take his time examining three or four places before selecting the perfect spot for his final activity. John shook Dickens's leash to make him hurry, but Dickens was indifferent to his master freezing. They walked along the road where the snowbanks were up to John's shoulders. Dickens insisted he had to go up the snowbank before he would go to the bathroom. After several failed attempts to jump up the bank, Dickens sat down and lifted his head pleadingly toward John, giving out a little whine. John picked up his fussy dog and set him on the snowbank. Dickens then walked inward several feet from the edge of the bank, so John foolishly let go of his leash. Ten feet from the road, Dickens found his spot, but by the time he had finished his business, he was so cold he sat down and held up his paws, refusing to make the trek back to John. After a few attempts to call Dickens back, John gave in and struggled up the bank to collect his dog and carry him back down. He rubbed and blew on Dickens's paws to warm them, then carried him to the edge of the snowbank, set Dickens down, crawled down the bank himself, lifted Dickens up again, and set him down on the road. Content to have been spoiled, Dickens now agreed to walk home.

But they only made it halfway to the house when Dickens sat down and held up his paws. By now, John was furious from the cold and the wind whipping snow in his face; he picked the dog up and swiftly walked to the house, lugging the thirty pound burden with him as his boots trudged down the unplowed road. Dickens, rather than being appeased, wiggled the remaining hundred feet to the house. John ignored the stubborn animal's struggles and buried his face in its fur to shield his skin from the threat of frostbite. Once they entered the garage, John's hands were so cold he could barely move them. But he was not finished yet. He took off his gloves and grabbed the old towel hanging on the stairwell to yank the snowballs off Dickens's feet. The dog was cooperative enough to hold up each individual foot as John wiped it. Then, with a guilty kiss on Dickens's head to show he was not mad, despite the dog's pokiness, John let Dickens in the house, took off his own boots, and stepped inside, quickly shutting the door after him. He removed his jacket on the way to the bathroom where he turned on the hot water and stuck his hands under the faucet to thwart the numbness creeping into his fingers.

Once he felt the blood again circulating in his hands, John went into the living room, just in time for the weather report. As the family now suspected, a major blizzard had struck with a predicted three feet of snow falling in the next forty-eight hours.

"Cripes, those banks along the driveway are already five feet high!" said Tom. "I don't know where we're going to put all that extra snow."

"Shh!" said Ellen. "They're going to read the school cancellations."

"Ishpeming Public Schools are closed tomorrow. Negaunee Public schools are closed tomorrow. Marquette Public Schools are closed tomorrow. Gwinn Public Schools are closed tomorrow."

"Good," said John, smiling.

"Well," said his mom, "I guess I won't be going into work tomorrow if the boys will be home."

"Must be nice," said Tom. "I'll be snowplowing all day."

A few years before, Tom had been laid off from his job as a garage mechanic. He had then found employment with the Marquette Road Commission, driving the snowplow. It was not an easy job since he had to work long hours most winter nights during the seemingly never-ending Upper Michigan blizzards, and more and more, Tom wished he had never left the air force.

At that moment, the power went out. Suddenly the entire house was black. The family sat in silence a few minutes, waiting to see whether the lights would come back on, but when the house remained dark, Ellen felt her way into the kitchen to find candles and flashlights. She gave a flashlight to Tom, so he could go downstairs where some wood was stored for the fireplace. Even if the electricity did come back on, the wind chill made everything so cold that a fire would be a comfort.

Tom opened up the flue in the fireplace, then went down to the basement where he collected some scrap pieces of wood to burn. Meanwhile, John's mom found a stack of old newspapers and magazines to kindle the blaze. In a few minutes, the flames made the wood crackle and the room grew warm. Dickens was afraid of the fire, so John sat at the end of the room, petting him to keep him calm. Then John stretched out on the living room carpet with a book, recalling a picture he had once seen of Abraham Lincoln as a boy, lying on the floor reading before a fire. The shadows cast by the crackling flames made him wonder what it would have been like in those pioneer days not to have electricity. He wondered how his ancestors had weathered such blizzards in Marquette a century before without electricity, canned food, or plows to get them out when they were snowed in. History books were full of great events, but John felt they did not evoke the quiet daily courage of those who had struggled simply to survive and feed their families in those far off times amid an incredible lack of comfort few modern people could bear.

When bedtime came, the family slept in the living room since it was the only warm place in the house. Tom watched the fire, while Ellen found extra blankets. Sleeping bags were soon spread on the living room carpet for John and Chad. Dickens cuddled up between the brothers. As John fell asleep, he listened to the wind blowing in great gusts, screeching through the trees, and howling down the chimney with the voice of a banshee. A couple times, John awoke to the sound of a tree branch that cracked, then broke off to be blown across the front yard and buried beneath several inches of falling, drifting snow.

When he woke in the morning, John lay there trying to orient himself to where he was. The house felt strangely cold until he remembered the electricity had gone out. He sat up, clutching his quilt about him, then looked around. His brother and Dickens were still sleeping on the floor. His mother sat in her chair, straining to read in the dim light coming through the window.

"Where's Dad?" John asked.

"He got called into work early. Didn't you hear the phone ring?"

"No, I guess I was too tired."

"The road commission can't keep up with the snow during storms like this. As soon as they get a street plowed and go onto the next, the one they just plowed needs to be done over again."

John felt sorry for his father, imagining how tiring it was to drive with the snow flying in his eyes, the white-out conditions when you couldn't even see where you were going. But the roads had to be clear – not just for those few crazies who would go out in this weather, but so the police or the ambulances or other emergency vehicles could get through. It must have been terrible just for his father to drive to work in the storm. The snow was accumulating so quickly the roads would be covered again shortly after being plowed. Plenty of cars would end up stuck in the ditch today.

John looked out the window to see snow still swirling around the trees. The front steps were invisible save for the very tops of the railings where portions peeked out beneath a foot of fluffy white. John noticed that his father had plowed out the driveway. Since then a couple inches of snow had fallen and the wind had drifted the snow over the tire tracks.

John's stomach began to growl; he would have liked pancakes for breakfast, but without electricity, he would have to settle for cereal.

The morning hours passed slowly. It was a boring day. The weather was too fierce for the boys to go outside and play. They could not watch TV since the power was out. They spent the morning and most of the afternoon sitting on the couch, wrapped in their quilts, trying to read. They found hardcover books that would stay open on their own so they merely had to sneak a hand out from under a quilt, flip a page, and bury their hands back under the warm blankets. For most of the afternoon, Dickens snuggled on the couch between his human brothers. Ellen kept herself warm by doing what housework she could – sweeping the floor and making lunch from food in the refrigerator before it could spoil, although the house was so cold that was unlikely. They were all a little worried about Tom, but no one mentioned it. Ellen worked as if she had no worries, so as not to scare the boys; they engrossed themselves in their books, while frequently wishing the phone would ring.

"I haven't seen a storm like this in years," said Ellen late in the afternoon.

"I don't think I've ever seen a storm like this," said Chad.

"It's not as bad as the storm of '38," John said.

"Was that the really bad one your grandparents talk about?" Ellen asked; the boys knew more about local history than she did because their grandfather was always telling them stories.

"Yes, it was a huge blizzard, the worst that ever struck Marquette," John replied. "It snowed nonstop for three days, and you had to use snowshoes to get around. In some places, the snowbanks were so high people could step out onto the snow from their second story windows."

"Yes, and the snowdrifts were even worse – twelve feet high," said Chad.

"And all the while, there was a fire downtown," said John. "It burned down an entire block. People were out in the blizzard fighting the fire until the streets were filled with slush from the snow and waterhoses."

"It's funny," said Ellen, "that the blizzard didn't put the fire out."

"No, the wind only made the fire worse," said John.

"Grandpa showed me the photographs he took when the blizzard was over," Chad said. "There were huge icicles on everything because the water froze almost the second it left the firehoses."

"Grandpa said that Grandma's father got lost in a drift and died of frostbite a couple days later," said John.

Ellen was less interested in the grandpa she had never known than she was concerned that Tom would share the same fate.

"That reminds me," she said. "I better go call your grandparents to make sure they're all right. At least the phone hasn't gone out yet."

Ellen's phone call revealed that Grandpa and Grandma Whitman were fine. The power had not gone out in town, only in the city's outskirts where

John and his family lived. After Ellen hung up the phone, Tom called. He had put in nearly twelve hours and was finally going to be relieved and come home, but he would probably have to go back out early the next morning even if the storm did let up. It could be days before the snowplows got to all the back roads in Marquette County – just the main highways and city streets had been more than they could keep up with most of the day.

"I guess we'll have to eat sandwiches for supper," said Ellen. "I can't cook anything until the electricity comes back on." But just at that moment, the TV began to blare out noise, breaking the cold silence that had possessed the house all day. Ellen sighed in relief, no longer having to fret over supper. By the time Tom made it home, John noticed the wind had begun to die down. It was still snowing and blowing, but the wind was mild compared to the past twenty-four hours.

Being cooped up in the house all day made John and Chad anxious to explore the newly created landscape left by the blowing wind and drifting snow. Ellen was hesitant to let them go outside, but after supper, when the visibility had increased until individual snowflakes could be distinguished as they fell, she finally consented. It would not be dark for another hour, so the boys had plenty of time to trudge over the snowbanks and burn off their excess energy.

John and Chad put on their long johns and flannel shirts, then their snow pants and jackets. They wrapped scarves around their necks, pulled hats down over their ears, and slipped on boots and mittens. Before they went out the door, they were already starting to sweat from wearing so many layers, but they would be well protected once outside. John suggested Dickens should join them since he must be equally tired of staying inside. During the day Dickens had only made quick bathroom trips into the driveway, just a few feet from the garage door, but now he could wander free until he complained of cold feet.

Soon the boys and Dickens were outside. They quickly discovered the wind was still strong, so seeking protection, they set Dickens up on the high snowbank, then climbed up themselves. They trudged on top of the snow, at times six feet above the buried grass, until they reached the shelter of the neighboring woods. They found a giant pine tree whose lowest branches, usually eight feet above the ground, were now heavily weighed down with snow, until they curved down three feet to touch the top of the frozen banks. The boys were forced to bend down to enter beneath the tree whose branches were too high for them to reach on summer days. Beneath the tree's bent limbs, they felt sheltered in their own little lodge house. A small depression around the tree formed snow walls to provide further insulation from the bitter chill wind, while leaving room for John, Chad, and Dickens to sit and watch the dying storm. Exhausted from the heavy trudge into the woods, the boys and Dickens were content to listen to the storm's fury. The dazzling whiteness of everything was breathtaking – snow was clustered against the brown and gray tree trunks, turning them into giant white poles, while tree branches had glazed over with frozen ice and snow that perched precariously until the morning sun would come to melt it away.

Neither brother was eloquent enough to express his awe over the beauty of the scene, but neither could fail to notice it. Now free from the stifling, still air inside the house, the boys gratefully opened their mouths and breathed in the fresh coolness, enjoying the pleasure of it biting down their throats. They pulled off their gloves to coil their fingers into fists, then replaced their gloves with their fingers curled together to ward off the numbness a short while longer. They took turns petting Dickens with their fisted gloves, while Dickens huddled against them to stay warm.

Serenity filled the moment, yet in this serenity was an exhilaration surpassing yesterday's anticipation of the storm. As the wind slowly died down with less frequent gusts, the boys felt proud to have survived the storm. Nature's fury had left behind three feet of snow, broken tree branches, enormous snow drifts, hundreds of hours of snow removal work, and downed power lines, but it had also revived the courage of its witnesses; they were survivors like their pioneer ancestors who had fought similar storms a century before when snowblowers and electricity had not been imagined; the pioneers' survivor spirit had resurrected itself, making the Vandelaare boys respectful admirers of Nature's sublime power.

John's spirits had been especially stirred by the wind, now no longer a screeching banshee voice wreaking havoc, but a simple whisper carrying the last twinkling fall of snowflakes that resembled confetti more than ice bullets. John recalled the Bible story of God's appearance to the prophet Elijah. There had been a wind, an earthquake, and a fire, but God had not been in any of them. God had been found in a gentle whisper. Now John felt he understood that passage. The wind had subsided to a whisper, a promise of peace and renewal as the snow cleansed the earth to create a new landscape. John felt a deepened sense of contentment, as if he had learned a secret about Nature's incredible power, yet sheltered beneath the pine tree, he felt he would always be safe in the northern wilderness, no matter how fierce the blizzards might blow.

"We better go in," Chad broke into his brother's thoughts. "Mom'll be worried if we're not in by dark."

"Yeah," John reluctantly agreed, "Dickens looks cold."

The boys and their dog trudged back out of the woods. Where before the storm had caused a blinding greyness, now a tiny pink streak in the Western sky promised a fine day tomorrow.

Ellen had seen her sons heading toward the house, so she had water boiling on the stove for hot chocolate when they came inside. She told them to change their clothes before they thawed out and were wet. Then, with the storm all but forgotten, the family sat down to drink hot chocolate and play Monopoly until bedtime.

But in later years, when John would live in a far away city where fierce Northern winters were unknown, the memory of that storm would come back to him. A strong wind would recall the powerful snowfilled gusts of his childhood, and he would imagine himself once more at home, hearing the wind wailing down the chimney, or sitting beneath a pine tree's branches to watch Nature's sublime fury. Then he would realize how impressionable he had been to his native land's natural rhythms where he had formed a bond with the wind, the trees, the snow, Lake Superior, and the seemingly neverending Hiawatha forest that encompassed his childhood world. Wherever he went, John was branded with the knowledge that he belonged to this place; whatever majestic sights he saw, the serenity of a snowfall surpassed them all.

On Saturdays, John and Chad often went to matinees at the Delft Theatre. The movies were not always spectacular, often children's shows they had outgrown. *Robinson Crusoe, The Journey of Natty Gann, The Watcher in the Woods* were films soon forgotten, but that hardly mattered; the true glamor was being at a movie theatre, especially the fabulous old Delft. This theatre, perhaps more than any place in Marquette, evoked history to them. When the boys saw *Annie*, they were impressed by the glamorous scene when the characters from the 1930s go to the movies at Radio City Music Hall, and the ushers danced down the aisle with flashlights to show them to their seats. The boys could just imagine that in its heyday, the Delft had been a similarly magical movie showplace. For seventy years, the theatre had stood along Washington Street, the most notable building on the block. During its long life, the theatre had shown films and been the sight of public performances. Now, as the theatre fell into neglect, its former grandeur made it all the more enticing. It was the only theatre in town with a round little ticket window inside the front door. From there rose a long hallway that led to double doors where the usher collected your ticket so you could enter a splendid fantasy world. Then you went down a tall flight of stairs until you came to the concession stand where a cluster of people competed for the cashiers' attention to buy popcorn, raisinettes, coca-colas, and sometimes, even ice cream! The concession stand was against the left wall while the right wall had a giant window that looked into the theatre itself so even the concession workers could watch the film when they were not busy serving customers.

The theatre walls were covered with winter scenes of children sledding. Protruding from the ceiling was the magnificent big round metal thing no one could define – it was not a chandelier because it had nothing to do with lighting; it had giant rings, one inside another, like a spaceship hovering over the audience, which only added to the atmosphere when watching *Return of the Jedi*, *The Last Starfighter*, or *2010: A Space Odyssey*.

Most impressive of all, the Delft boasted the largest screen in the Upper Peninsula – they did not make movie theaters with such big screens anymore. Drive-ins were now all but extinct and most old movie theaters had been replaced by multiplex cinemas. John had heard tales of such theaters from friends who had seen them downstate; he had heard that if you did not like a movie, you could sneak into another one, so you could see parts of three or four films on the same night. John thought this silly since you would never get to see a full film. He did not imagine Marquette would ever be big enough for a multiplex cinema. Three theaters, each showing one movie, was enough variety for Marquette.

John and Chad got their snacks: cokes for both, raisinettes for John, junior mints for Chad. Then they went into the theater. They had learned from their mother always to sit in the back row so the teenagers could not kick the backs of their seats. John also felt morally obligated to sit in the back row to discourage immoral behavior; otherwise, teenage boys and their girlfriends would sit there so they could make out during the love scenes.

John and Chad found seats where the floor was not too sticky from spilled pop. Then they ripped open their candy boxes, sipped their cokes, and sucked in the movie atmosphere. Chad looked at his new digital watch; six minutes remained until the movie would start, so he decided to talk.

"I wonder whether they'll ever open up the balcony again," said Chad.

"I don't know," John replied. "I've never seen it open."

A door in the lobby led to the balcony, but the balcony's appearance was a mystery since only employees could now enter there. John and Chad were not even sure whether it were still a balcony or just the projectionist's booth, but

Mom said she had once sat up there, so there must be one. The Delft was full of such mysteries. One could enter the theater on Washington Street and exit it on Main Street, yet if you walked along Third Street from Washington to Main, an alley existed between the front and back door. A huge metal shaft connected the buildings on each side of the alley, which made the shaft appear to be the theatre, but if you came out of the exit door on one side, you came out in the alley, and on the other side, you came out on Main Street. It was all very confusing. John and Chad had often discussed this mystery, but neither could figure it out.

"The first movie we ever saw here," John recalled, "was when Dad took us to see *Pinocchio*."

"I don't remember that," said Chad. "The first movie I remember seeing was *Bambi*. I remember crying when Bambi's mother got shot."

"They didn't have the balcony opened back then either," said John.

"You know, Grandpa and Grandma sat in the old Opera House's balcony the night Grandpa proposed," said Chad; he knew John knew this, but there was something grand about his grandparents sitting in the balcony at the Marquette Opera House that made it worth repeating.

"Yes," said John, "and Grandma's cousin was there as chaperone that night."

"I wish I could have seen the Opera House," said Chad. "It's too bad it burnt down. I've heard it was nicer inside than the Delft. A lot fancier too I imagine."

"Grandpa told me," said John, "that when he was a boy, his father would give him a quarter for washing the kitchen floor, and then he and Uncle Roy would come here and have enough money to buy two tickets and candy."

"They must have come to see silent films," said Chad.

"Yeah, old westerns I guess."

The lights dimmed. The boys' anticipation grew. They heard that comforting sound of static as the movie reel began to turn. The screen lit up with previews of movies to come. The boys forgot the real world for the next two hours.

"I never thought it would happen here!" said Ellen.

"What?" John asked. He was eating breakfast while his mother sat at the table reading the newspaper.

Ellen pointed at one of the paper's headlines.

"The Delft is being remodeled; they're replacing the big screen so they can split it into two smaller theaters. We already have three screens in this town. Marquette isn't big enough to have four movies playing at the same time."

"I can't believe they would do that!" John was as upset as his mom. He and Chad enjoyed going to matinees at the Delft, but now that would change forever. There might still be matinees, but he did not want to go to them if the Delft were completely ruined. He frantically read the *Mining Journal* article about how the theatre represented the city's cultural history. In years past, the Delft had been a theatre in every sense of the word; its large orchestra pit had allowed for concerts and plays in addition to the movies shown; John Philip Sousa had once played there to a crowd that lined Washington Street to gain admittance; walking backstage in the Delft was like stepping into the past of the early twentieth century. All that was about to change now. The paper quoted the Delft's owner, Paul Florence, as saying, "I hate to see it happen, but I have to go with the times . . . It kind of breaks my heart to do it because I believe we have the largest screen in the U.P. – 38 feet."

It broke John's heart as well.

"What is the world coming too!" he said, letting out the full fury of his teenage indignation. "Why can't people ever leave well enough alone?"

"Calm down," said Ellen, surprised by his anger. "I'm sure it'll look nice remodeled. I just can't imagine Marquette able to support four movies at once."

"But it will ruin the theatre," said John. "It's the atmosphere that matters."

"Well, maybe they won't have sticky floors anymore after they remodel," said Ellen, "and I always thought it dangerous to let you boys go downstairs to the bathroom, especially with all those hoodlum college kids smoking cigarettes down there."

John wondered how his mother could not consider this remodeling as a travesty against history. He could do nothing about it, but he remained furious.

Not every Saturday was spent at the movies. Once every few weeks, John worked as his grandpa's assistant at a craft sale or flea market where Henry would sell the tables, cutting boards, benches, and lazy susans he had made in his workshop. John and his grandpa would arrive early in the morning in Henry's large station wagon where everything was packed to overflowing. Usually, the organizers of the sale would provide the tables. First, John and Henry would cover the tables with sheets. Then they would carry out and open up the boxes in the station wagon. Out came lazy susans and cutting boards. Table tops were chosen; then Henry got out his screwdrivers so the legs could be fastened on to display them as actual tables. John and Henry had a system down to be set up in twenty minutes. For several years, they had been doing this, and both felt they were experts in the matter.

Half of Marquette County knew Henry Whitman was whom you went to if you wanted a sturdy bench or nice picture frame at a good price. Yet, this year, John began to notice that his grandfather's work was beginning to slip. John occasionally spotted a little nick in the wood, a board cut slightly crooked, or a spot Grandpa had failed to stain. At first, John pointed out these flaws to his grandfather; Henry would strain his eye for a moment, say he would bring it home to fix, and then the item would go back into the car rather than be sold. But one day, John spotted several nicks, specks of paint that had landed in the wrong place, and crooked cuts. Henry's cataracts were making it hard for him to see, but unwilling to admit his eyesight was poor or his work a tad shoddy, he became annoyed with John. After that, John never mentioned these little flaws, and to prevent the customers from noticing them, he tried to arrange items so the flawed ones were least noticeable. Now that Grandpa was eighty, John wondered whether there would be many more sales for them to attend.

Today, the sale was in the parking lot of St. John the Baptist's Catholic Church. Last year, Henry had made over two hundred dollars there and given John ten for helping out. John suspected the sale had been so successful because God favored a church sale. Once the tables were set up, Henry told John to go size up the competition. It was an active little sale. Church ladies sold crocheted afghans and knitted clothes. Church volunteers sold hot dogs and pop. Several ladies sold plastic canvas crafts, from kleenex boxes to coasters and Christmas decorations. Rummage from attics and basements flooded nearly every table. John was pleased by the sale's size and the number of people it would attract. But he saw no books for sale. He was ready to head back to his grandpa's table when he spotted a curious little display with statues and pamphlets.

Neither lady behind the table wore black, but both had crosses around their necks. John soon realized the women were nuns selling religious items for the church. Little prayer books and biographies of saints were scattered about. The back of the table displayed beautiful tall statues of St. Francis of Assisi and the Virgin Mary, and little founts to hold holy water. John's attention was especially drawn to numerous prayer cards with vibrantly colored pictures of Mary's ascension into Heaven, her appearance at Lourdes, and her sacred heart.

"How much are the cards?" John asked.

"A nickel a piece," said one sister.

John decided he needed one of each of the ten different cards. He dug in his pocket and drew out a dollar, enough to buy the cards and the little plastic glow-in-the-dark statue of St. Joseph.

The nuns treated him as grandly as if he had spent a hundred dollars while they put everything in a bag for him. Then John noticed a little statue, about nine inches tall, of a young man with blond hair. He thought the statue must be of a king or a bishop. The figure wore a red robe and held a round ball with a cross in one hand, while holding up the fingers of its other hand. On its head was a crown with a cross.

"Who is this statue of?" he asked.

"That's the Infant of Prague," he was told.

"I never heard of it," said John.

"Well," said the first nun, "it's the Child Jesus."

"It's quite unique, isn't it?" said the second nun. "Usually, the statue is depicted as a little child, but he looks like a teenager here."

John thought it beautiful, so different from the usual depictions of Jesus.

"Here's your change," said the second nun, handing him back a quarter.

"Thank you," said John.

He walked back to his grandfather's table. Henry asked John what he had bought. When John showed him the beautiful prayer cards, Henry politely admired them. Then John showed him the little statue of St. Joseph holding a square.

"That's right," Henry said. "Joseph was a carpenter like me, wasn't he?"

"The nuns also had some beautiful statues for sale," John said, "of St. Francis of Assisi and the Virgin Mary for five dollars, and there was a pretty one of Jesus as a child, looking like a prince. I'd have bought that one if I'd had the money."

"How much was it?" asked Henry.

"Two dollars," said John.

Henry reached into his wallet and drew out two dollars.

"You better go get it before someone else does," he said.

"No, Grandpa. You don't need to give me any money."

"I'll just deduct it from your wages for helping me today," Henry smiled.

John hesitated a moment. He really wanted the statue; it seemed so grand; he liked that Jesus looked his age, yet so regal, as if in his ordinary carpenter lifestyle, Jesus had inwardly known all the while his greatness.

"Thanks Grandpa," he said, accepting the money. A minute later, he was talking to the nuns again.

"Good, I kind of felt you should have it," said one nun.

"What church do you go to?" asked the other.

"St. Michael's," said John.

"I imagine you'll be wanting to enter the seminary soon," she replied.

"I've been thinking about it," John said. He had never admitted it to anyone, but he had thought about it a lot.

"The Church needs young men like you," said the first nun. She wrapped the statue in tissue paper and a box and handed it to him. "There you are. God bless you."

"Thank you," said John, finding 'God bless you' too awkward for his tongue.

He went back and showed Grandpa his treasure.

"Only two dollars!" Henry said. "It would probably sell for ten in the stores." He was glad to see he had not wasted his money, and even more, that he had pleased his grandson.

"Thank you, Grandpa," said John.

"You're welcome," said Henry.

"The nuns gave me this little paper about the Infant of Prague as well," said John, who then read it to his grandfather.

"Legend states that a man gave the statue of the Child Jesus in bishop's robes to the nuns in Prague. He told them the more they honored it, the more they would be blessed. After that, the convent's financial problems disappeared. Soon the story of the Infant of Prague spread until people everywhere honored him and were blessed."

"Hmm," said Henry. He did not seem overly interested beyond noting the statue was attractive. Still John appreciated that his Baptist-raised grandfather had no problem with buying him a Catholic statue. John decided he would devotedly pray to the Child Jesus to learn whether he were meant to be a priest. The nun's remark about his going to the seminary had put it into his thoughts again.

When afternoon came, the sale began to slow down.

"We'll close up in an hour," said Henry. "That'll give us time to get home and clean up so you can go to Mass."

"All right," said John. It was slow enough that he pulled out a book to read. He did not look up at the customers again until he heard Grandpa say, "Why, hello there."

Henry stood up to shake hands with a fellow old-timer. John shyly looked up; his grandfather knew everyone in Marquette, and Grandpa was constantly introducing him to countless people whose names he soon forgot.

"John, this is Mr. O'Neill," said Henry.

"Pleased to meet you, John." Mr. O'Neill offered his hand over a table full of lazy susans. John stuck a finger in his book, then stood up to shake hands. "Your grandfather and I are old friends, and I knew your Grandma when she was a little girl at Bishop Baraga, although she was several grades behind me."

John smiled, not knowing what to say.

"Your grandfather's a fine carpenter; he's done plenty of work at my house over the years," said Mr. O'Neill. "He built me new kitchen cabinets back in the 1960s, and he fixed up my back porch during World War II, not to mention I don't know how many times he's come to repair the bannister on my staircase."

"I don't imagine I'll have to fix that bannister anymore," Henry smiled.

"No, my days of sliding down it are long over," laughed Mr. O'Neill. "My children are all grown up and my grandchildren live in California so I rarely see them. I imagine even they're too old to slide down it now."

John thought Mr. O'Neill had a playfulness in his eyes that said he might slide down that bannister yet, even if he were on the wrong side of eighty.

"What are you reading there, John?" asked Mr. O'Neill.

John lifted the book cover for Mr. O'Neill to see. It was *Bleak House* in its entire splendid eight hundred pages.

"That's my favorite Dickens novel," said Mr. O'Neill, "even though it's so long; longer than anything I've ever written."

"John, have you read any of Mr. O'Neill's books?" Henry asked.

"I don't think so," said John.

"I'm not surprised," said Mr. O'Neill. "No one reads my books anymore. They're too old-fashioned now, but there was a time when Robert O'Neill made the bestseller lists. I can only hope someday some stuffy old professor or literary critic will rediscover them."

"You – you're Robert O'Neill?" asked John.

"The one and only," said the famous novelist.

"Oh, I've read several of your novels. I'm sorry. I just didn't realize you were that Mr. O'Neill when Grandpa introduced you."

Mr. O'Neill beamed, terribly pleased. "It's good to know there's at least one young person left who enjoys good literature."

"I've always admired your books," said John. "You're one of the people who made me want to grow up to be a writer."

"Really?" said Mr. O'Neill. "People think being a writer means living like Fitzgerald, wild parties and all, but it's more like what Steinbeck said, 'the loneliest job in the world'. It doesn't pay much either. I just happened to be one of the lucky ones, despite my meager talent. But the question is, do you write now, John?"

"I keep a journal," said John. "I write in that almost everyday and I write stories too. I have an idea for a novel, but I haven't started it yet."

"Good. Keep at it then," said Mr. O'Neill. "Even if you never make a penny or publish a word of your writing, it'll bring you great pleasure and comfort. Well," he said turning to Henry, "it was good seeing you. I better head home before Eliza starts worrying about me."

He and Henry shook hands. Mr. O'Neill started to turn away, then stopped. "Say, Henry, I don't have any carpentry work for you to do, but why don't you and John come have lunch with me sometime?"

"Really?" said John, his shyness conquered by enthusiasm. "I'd love to talk with you more about writing."

"Well, I don't know much about it, but I'll try to find some words of advice for you," Robert winked. "I'll give you a call sometime."

"All right," said Henry. Mr. O'Neill walked away as a couple more customers approached the table. Henry went back to selling.

John's heart glowed the rest of the day. He had known Robert O'Neill was from the Marquette area, but he had never imagined he might meet him. Some of Mr. O'Neill's books had been written fifty years ago, so John had just assumed the famous writer was dead. Why had his grandfather never mentioned knowing him? Now he wanted to read all of Mr. O'Neill's novels again. He would go to the library that week and check them out so he could discuss them when he had lunch with the published author.

That night when he got home, John set the Infant of Prague prominently in the center of his dresser. Then he knelt down to thank God for such a fine day and to pray Mr. O'Neill would remember to invite Grandpa and him over for lunch. But when school began in a couple weeks, and no lunch invitation came, John forgot all about Mr. O'Neill.

One Saturday morning in September, John was lying on his bed reading, listening to the rain outside, and enjoying the sight of fog. His mother had gone to work to get paid overtime and his father had gone to breakfast with his friend, Mr. Richmond. Chad was sleeping in late. John had woken not long after dawn, and since then, lain on his bed, wrapped up in the old quilt Aunt Eleanor had made him. He enjoyed the fog because it complemented his melancholy book; he was hopelessly engrossed in a glorious old copy of Sidney Lanier's *The Boy's King Arthur* which he had recently picked up at the Peter White Library's booksale. The old book was complete with thick, crisp pages and lush colored illustrations by N.C. Wyeth that made it feel like a medieval illuminated manuscript. John enjoyed the beauty of the medieval language Lanier had retained from Sir Thomas Malory, although John knew nothing about Malory or that the book was a revision of another book five hundred years older. The book's literary ancestry was uninteresting compared to the magnificent tales compiling the Matter of Britain. And now John had come to King Arthur's death at the hands of his son Mordred, and the sword Excalibur was returned to the lake, and Sir Lancelot and Queen Guinevere became a monk and a nun. In the final illustration, Lancelot sighed over Guinevere's corpse, she having died a holy woman, having redeemed herself for her sins; the picture nearly made John weep. The glory of Camelot had passed away; John felt the loss more strongly than he had ever felt anything in a book before. He wanted to believe, as the legend claimed, that Arthur would return and bring back a golden age.

After reading the last page, John cuddled in his quilt, and stared at the trees peaking through the fog. Fog was so mysterious it always delighted him. He could easily imagine a knight coming out of the forest and riding right through the back lawn of his house. He wished those grand times had never ended. If people would still strive for righteousness as King Arthur had, perhaps good would return to the world, and the threats of nuclear war, the evils of communism, the money-grubbing, the crime, the high divorce rates would disappear. John thought perhaps if he reminded people of King Arthur's story, if he retold the story for a modern audience, they might return to the principles of the great Christian king.

The telephone rang. Reluctantly, John woke from his daydream, unwrapped himself from the quilt, and raced into the kitchen to pick up the receiver.

"I thought maybe you and your brother would like to go to the movie this afternoon," said his mother on the line. "That new Sesame Street movie, *Follow that Bird*, opened yesterday. Your dad could drop you off for the matinee, and then I could pick you up when I get off work."

"I'll have to ask Chad," John replied; he would prefer to stay home and dream of King Arthur. He was too old for Big Bird movies.

"Well, have your dad call me if you decide to go."

"All right," said John. He hung up the phone, then woke up his brother. Chad wanted to go, so when their dad got home, he agreed to drop them at the movie.

Not until they arrived at the Delft did John realize he would be entering the theatre for the first time since it had been remodeled.

At first nothing looked as if it had changed much. The lobby was the same. The stairs down to the concession stand were the same. But then John saw that the open window across from the concession stand had been blocked up, and the concession stand had been moved against the wall where the window had been. On each side of the concession stand were doors, each leading into one of two theaters. The boys got their candy and drinks, then entered the doors into the theater on the right. John instantly noticed that new red carpets covered the aisle, and along them were little runners of lights so people could find their seats. But when he sat down, he became disappointed. The screen was puny compared to the massive thirty-eight foot screen that had once dominated the Delft.

The movie started. John was bored. He glanced at the walls, now covered in red material where once the winter sledding scenes had been. He did not enjoy the movie.

"I like the new theatre," said Chad when the movie was over. "It's a lot nicer. The floors weren't sticky, and it looks classy with the red carpeting."

"The screen isn't too big," said John.

"It's big enough," said Chad. "And now there's more variety of movies in town."

"It's not as nice as it used to be," said John.

"I still have two dollars," said Chad. "Mom won't be here for about ten minutes. Do you want to go into Donckers and buy some candy?"

"I don't care," said John, but he followed his brother. He stood silently at the candy counter while a woman scooped jujubes into a bag for Chad. John looked around and saw the empty back of the store where his mother had told him there had once been booths. He imagined how much fun it must have been in the old days when Donckers had a soda fountain and all the teenagers hung out here. Chad paid for his candy, and then the brothers went outside and sat on a bench. John looked across the street to Amigo's restaurant; he liked the restaurant's Mexican food, but he thought he would have liked it better if the Marquette Opera House still stood there.

"Life nowadays is just like the Arthurian legend," he thought. "All the splendor has vanished; only there's no hope the good old days will return."

1986

When most boys turn sixteen, they want nothing more than to grab the car keys and go for a joyride, but John told his parents he wanted a family party at Presque Isle. His birthday fell on Memorial Day weekend, so it was a perfect opportunity for a picnic, and even when Aunt Eleanor complained it might be too cold out, Ellen talked everyone into coming. Presque Isle Park also celebrated a major birthday that year. One hundred years had passed since the Honorable Peter White had preserved it for the enjoyment of Marquette's future citizens. The pioneer, who once had befriended John's ancestors, would have been pleased to see Presque Isle still considered a near Eden by its visitors.

When the family reached the park, Uncle Bill and Uncle Roy immediately searched for a shaded picnic table not yet desecrated by the incessant seagulls. Then the women spread out the food – sandwiches and chips, baked beans, coca-cola and coffee, Mom's potato salad, and Grandma's pineapple brownies, the last two of which John had insisted upon. Aunt Eleanor had made the birthday cake, and Lucy and Maud had brought special birthday plates and napkins. Everyone set to eating so they could beat the flies to the food. When it was time for cake, John proved himself by blowing out all the candles in one breath.

Before the presents were opened, Ellen surprised everyone by announcing there would be games, and the winners would receive prizes of giant size candy bars.

"First I'll give everyone a piece of paper," she said. "You have to draw a picture of what John looked like as a baby, and then another picture of what John will look like as an old man. John will judge the pictures, and a prize will be awarded for the best one in each category."

Everyone laughed as they began. Tom's efforts produced little more than stick figures. Beth seemed to remember John as a fat baby, while Henry thought he had been skinny. Lucy thought John would be bald in old age, while Maud thought he would be in a wheelchair, but Aunt Eleanor thought he would still be young and wearing a spacesuit. "You never know what science might create in the future," she said. Chad, a dedicated artist, was still working on the baby picture when everyone else had finished both drawings. Ellen and Tom told him to hurry, but everyone else waited patiently.

The winner of the baby picture turned out to be Uncle Bill, who drew John crawling out of his crib with "Troublemaker" written over it. As for the old man picture, John chose Beth's picture of him all wrinkled and shriveled. She told him, "You'll probably take after me." Then an uproar went up from everyone that Beth did not look a day over sixty, until she blushed.

Next came a game of Birthday Bingo, won by Maud and Lucy simultaneously. Ellen only had one candy bar as a prize, but the sisters agreed neither of them needed to eat more than half of it.

The final game was called John Vandelaare Trivia. Ellen had ten questions about John, and people had to write down the correct answers. Some questions were as easy as "How old is John?" or "What color are John's eyes?" while others demanded the test-taker to know John's favorite color was blue, his favorite book was *Bleak House*, and the place he most wanted to visit was London. Tom only got two right, mistakenly thinking his son was seventeen. Only John's grandparents and mother got the book right, while everyone else claimed they had never heard of it. Chad ended up winning, apparently knowing his brother best, being closest in age; his victory softened some of his disappointment in losing the art contest.

"Now can I open my presents?" John asked.

"Yes, now you can open your presents," said Ellen.

Grandpa and Grandma gave him the record album from the Broadway musical of *Les Miserables*. Lucy and Maud gave John a new leather-bound journal with a lock, as well as candy. Cards with money came from Aunt Eleanor, Uncle Roy, and Uncle Bill. Dickens, though not allowed to come, had sent a box of candy with a note that he would share them with John. Chad gave John a pen set with his name on it. Mom and Dad gave him clothing, and then came the present he felt was the best of all.

"Thank you," he said, ripping the paper off the book, then holding it up for everyone to see. It was *Walden* by Henry David Thoreau. The book jacket had a photograph of a trail running through the woods, which reminded John of the Blueberry Trail he and Dickens walked down everyday.

"I've read that," said Uncle Roy. "I have some of Thoreau's other books if you want to read them."

"Maybe after I finish *Walden*," said John. Reading Uncle Roy's grubby old books did not appeal to him. He could get Thoreau's other books at the library.

Roy decided next time he came into town, he would leave the books for John at Henry's house. He had not thought much about his great-nephews over the years, rarely seeing them except at family functions; he had been stunned to learn John was already sixteen, almost an adult, and an avid reader; Roy wondered whether he now had a kindred spirit in the family; he was glad John wanted to read about nature, having grown up like him in Upper Michigan, which despite all the recent foolish technology, had not changed much from the wilderness world of his own childhood.

After the presents were opened, everyone sat for a minute, unsure what to do, not wanting the party to end. Tom commented that he could see some ducks swimming out on the lake. The remark made Henry say, "John, I've got a birthday story for you. Did I ever tell you about the time my dad went out duck hunting and nearly got killed by a bear?"

"No," said John, always interested in a family story.

"This story," Henry said, "really happened to my father when he was a young man. One time my father went out hunting, but after several hours, he saw nothing to shoot at, and he was becoming very disappointed. He badly needed the meat because he was poor and had no money to buy food for his family."

"He wouldn't have been so poor," Bill broke in, "if Eleanor weren't always eating us out of house and home. Cripes, remember how we used to have to kill a pig every day on the farm just to have enough bacon for her breakfast."

"That's enough, Bill," said Eleanor. "With that mouth of yours, it's no wonder you've never been able to keep a woman."

Bill's face grew angry, and everyone suddenly felt uncomfortable. Henry thought it best to continue his tale.

"My pa was so disappointed not to find any game that he was just about to give up and go home when suddenly he came across a mill pond, and in the middle of that pond were a whole bunch of ducks. Well, my father really liked the taste of duck; in fact, he liked it so much, he didn't want to settle for just bringing one duck home with him, and he knew if he fired a shot, he'd just get one duck while the others would all fly away. So he tried to think of how he could get all those ducks. Then he had an idea. He went back home and got himself a rope. When he returned to the pond, he quietly waded in, taking the rope with him. He dove under the water and swam out beneath where the ducks were swimming. Very carefully, he tied the rope around the ducks' legs until he had them all strung up together.

"How could he do that?" Chad asked.

"Very carefully," Henry said. "Then, thinking himself mighty clever, he prepared to swim back to shore and carry all those ducks back with him. But when the ducks felt a tug on their legs, they got scared and started to fly away. Well, they flapped their wings and started up into the air, but my pa was determined not to lose them, so he held onto that rope with all his might. Next thing he knew, he had been lifted clear out of the pond and up into the sky. Before he could realize his danger, he found himself soaring among the clouds; he was afraid to let go of the rope because the clouds were in his way, and he could not see where he was going or where he might fall. When the ducks flew out of the clouds, my pa found that he enjoyed the view of Marquette County so much he did not want to let go. Only, the rope could not hold his weight any longer. Just as he was being carried over the Sands Plains, the rope snapped and he fell out of the sky."

"Did he get hurt?" asked John, not believing a word, but fully enjoying the yarn.

"No, he was lucky, considering what a fall it was. He landed right smack into the hollow of a big old stump and wasn't hurt a bit. Only problem was, he had landed in there upside down, with his arms wedged to his sides, so he didn't know how he was going to get out before all the blood rushed to his head.

"Then he heard this scratching noise. An animal was clawing at the stump. At first it wasn't very loud, so he thought maybe it was just a squirrel or a raccoon, but then it let out a loud, ferocious roar, so he knew it was a bear."

"Did he get away?" asked Chad.

"Well, that bear just kept scratching at the stump, trying to break through the wood so he could have my pa for supper. Pretty soon, it started rocking that stump back and forth to try and knock it over. But all that rocking let my pa jiggle his arm free, until he could stick it out of a hole in the stump. Then he felt around until he could grab onto the back of the bear's coat and give it a good hard pull. The bear tried to turn around to see what was going on, but it was so fat, it couldn't see behind itself. Then it became scared and tried to run away, only to drag my pa in the stump behind it. That bear ran for miles across the Sands Plains until finally, the rough ride broke up the stump, and as it fell apart, my pa let go of the bear's coat, jumped up off the ground and started running in the other direction before the bear could realize it was free.

"You can imagine how glad my pa was still to be alive, but he was also disappointed because he didn't have any bear or duck meat to bring home for supper, and now he was out on the Sands Plains and would have to walk about ten miles home. But fortunately, it was late summer, and everyone knows the blueberries are abundant on the Sand Plains in summer, so my pa started to pick blueberries until he had filled both of his coat pockets and his pants pockets. Of course, he had to walk very carefully to get himself home without squashing all those berries, but he managed well enough. He was really tired when he got home, but my ma, she was pleased to see all the berries, and so that night we all had blueberry pie for supper, and it was the best supper I ever remember having."

Ellen laughed. "You never told me that one before Dad."

"He never told it to you before," laughed Bill, "because not a lick of it is true. I sure don't remember it happening."

"That's cause you weren't born yet," said Henry.

"I don't know that it matters whether it's true," said Roy, "so long as it's a good story. What actually happens isn't always as true as what we want to believe is true, until our beliefs become truth for us."

No one tried to follow this long-winded sentence; they were all used to ignoring Roy's philosophical gibberish.

And still, after the story, no one wanted to go home. It was one of the first truly fine days of spring, and after a long winter of being cooped up in stuffy rooms, everyone wanted to lounge in lawn chairs and enjoy the warm breeze. Yet Roy felt restless; he was so used to being a hermit that he grew uncomfortable if he were around people more than a couple hours. Clearing his throat, he said he was going for a walk; then pausing, he asked John whether he wanted to come along. John was surprised by the invitation, but he agreed to go. Chad asked whether he could tag along. Roy merely said, "Fine." The trio walked up the hill from the picnic tables; in a few minutes, they approached Chief Kawbawgam's grave.

"My pa knew Kawbawgam when he was a boy," said Roy.

"Yes, Grandpa told us that," said John.

They crossed the road and started down one of the trails that cut through the woods. John thought the trail looked like the forest scene on the cover of *Walden*. Chad chattered about the different flowers growing along the trail. Roy began to name all the trees they passed. John was impressed by his uncle's vast knowledge of botany since he could only recognize maples, oaks, birches, and pine trees, and he did not even know the different varieties of conifers. At the same time, he wondered what use it was to know the names of trees. Such knowledge had not seemed to do Uncle Roy much good; he had probably just learned the names because he had been a guide all these years at the Huron Mountain Club. Uncle Roy's solitary life seemed so pointless to John, especially when what little he knew of his uncle had been colored by comments from disapproving relatives and a couple visits to Uncle Roy's dilapidated shack. John could not think ill of a man who had such an overflowing bookshelf, but the last time John had been to the cabin, the couch had smelled so musty, John had refused to sit down, and likewise he had refused to drink Uncle Roy's coffee because the well water was a cloudy brown.

John remembered Thoreau had also lived in a little cabin for a couple years, but he created a famous book to justify it. Uncle Roy had lived in that shack for nearly four decades, with nothing gained. John liked Uncle Roy better than Uncle Bill, but Uncle Bill, like his grandfather, had at least been a carpenter. Grandpa and Uncle Bill could point at buildings all over Marquette and say, "I built that." They knew those buildings would stand for years after they were gone. No such memorial existed for Uncle Roy's life.

The late afternoon sun illuminated the tops of the forest trees. John thought it a beautiful sight; Presque Isle was such a special place that he wished everyone could know of its grandeur just as Thoreau had made the world realize the special magic of Walden Pond. John felt a sudden desire to be alone, to go home and write about Presque Isle. He was more like his Great-Uncle Roy than he realized; even on his birthday, after a couple hours of company, he yearned for solitude, for his books and his pen.

As the three came out of the woods, Chad turned to walk along the road, but Uncle Roy clutched his arm and said, "Stop to look at the view."

They stared out at Lake Superior, serenely blue; a sailboat skimmed over the gentle waves.

"I wish I had a sailboat," said John.

"You don't need one," Roy replied.

"I'd like to be on one," said John, "surrounded by all that water, with a cool breeze blowing."

"You can be on that sailboat anytime you want if you use your imagination," Roy said. "You don't even need to read about it in a book; imagination makes us free to escape to wherever we want to be. Imagination is the salvation of mankind."

John had never heard anyone say such a thing. He did not know how to take it.

"Don't you like books?" Chad asked his uncle.

"For some of us, the time comes when we grow tired of books."

"It won't for me," said John. His mother was right; Uncle Roy was weird.

Roy wondered how he could have thought his great-nephew a kindred spirit. Neither of the boys understood him. No one ever had, except maybe Michael, who had been dead nearly twenty years now. Roy started walking down the road. After a few seconds, his nephews followed.

John had noticed the downcast look on his uncle's face. He noted Roy's faded green work pants and the scarcely matching blue and white flannel shirt. His uncle had long since started to go bald until now he looked as if he had the tonsure of a monk; he was becoming thin and brittle, his eyes retreating into his skull. Soon Roy would look like one of the malnourished living skeletons he had never told anyone he had seen in the German concentration camps.

"Did you have a nice walk?" Beth asked when they returned to the picnic area.

"Yeah," said Chad. "We walked all over the trails in the woods."

"Uncle Roy told us the names of all the trees," said John, trying to sound enthusiastic to cheer his uncle.

"He would know them," said Eleanor. "He's spent his whole life roaming in the woods around the Club."

"Uncle Roy, I don't know how you can live out in the woods like that," said Ellen.

"After all these years, it's home," said Roy. "I'm used to it."

"You really ought to move into town," said Eleanor. "You know Bill wouldn't mind having a roommate."

"Maybe I'd mind him," Roy smiled. After his divorce and his mother's death, Bill had moved into his parents' house. He did not want a roommate, but Eleanor knew now that Bill had retired, he could use someone to help him share expenses.

"Roy, at your age, you shouldn't be alone like that," said Henry. "You don't even have a phone out there."

"If I had a phone," said Roy, "people would be calling me all the time, and that's exactly what I don't want."

"At your age, you should be glad to have people checking on you," said Beth.

"What's all this "at your age"? I'll only be seventy-eight this year, and I intend to outlive all of you," Roy said. His ornery tone made everyone uncomfortable. Usually, only Uncle Bill was ornery, and sometimes Tom.

"We better head home. It's getting late," Eleanor said to her daughters.

The party was soon packed up. As John rode home with his family, he decided this birthday had been his best. It had been a beautiful spring day; Presque Isle had been so green, and Lake Superior so blue; his family had been together, and his mother had made up games to ensure everyone had fun. He had already forgotten the awkward moment with Uncle Roy. In a few more weeks, this birthday would be packed away with his memories, not to be remembered for many years, and then its significance would be based on different criteria than the presents he had received or even where it had been held.

Every Wednesday, Ellen took her mother and Aunt Eleanor shopping. In the summer, John, Chad, and Dickens spent these shopping days with Grandpa, but today, to please their mother, the boys agreed to go shopping and to lunch with the ladies. John hated to shop, but he still had birthday money so he thought he would buy a new book.

The first stop was Shopko. Everyone went their separate ways once they were inside, but John did not know where to go. He was too old for the toy department, and he did not want to go to the record section flooded with headbanging heavy metal enthusiasts. The book section of Shopko was mostly bestselling romance novels, so he decided he would not look for a book until they went to the Marquette Mall and he could visit B. Dalton's.

"Grandma, do you want me to go find anything for you?" he asked.

"Sure," Beth said. "I can never find anything here; I think they move things around every week just to spite old ladies."

John suspected his grandmother just forgot where things were, but helping her gave him something to do. She set her purse in the top of the shopping cart, then leaning on the cart to take her weight off her bad knee, she dug out her shopping list.

"Now where are the snacks," she asked, looking about her.

"They're in the next aisle," said John. He thought of going to fetch them, but he knew his grandmother would want to look at everything. Slowly he followed her toward the next aisle while Grandma paused every couple feet to check out something on the shelves. John knew she was not really interested in cheeze whiz or pez candy dispensers; she only pretended to be interested to give herself short rests.

"Oh, that knee hurts today," she grumbled. John told himself to be patient; they would reach the cookies eventually. After several minutes they did turn the corner and start down the next aisle.

"Okay, Little Debbie, Little Debbie. Do you see them?" Grandma asked.

"They're at the end of the aisle," said John.

"See, they moved them again. They always move things just to confuse me."

A few more minutes, with a stop to look at Planters' peanuts, meaning Grandma needed another little rest, and they reached the Little Debbie section.

"Now, which ones do you like?" Grandma asked.

"I don't care, Grandma. Whatever you and Grandpa will eat."

"Oh, we'll eat anything. I like to have them for when you boys come over. How about these? The chocolate cakes with the white frosting."

John was revolted by all Little Debbie products, especially the white frosted cakes, which tasted like sawdust covered in wax. But Grandma thought he liked them, and he did not have the heart to tell her otherwise. Tactfully, he picked out the most edible items. "I like the Dutch Apple Treats best," he said.

"Okay, one box of those," said Beth, fumbling to pull them off the shelf. John reached over to help her before she knocked an entire row over. "Then we'll get these white cakes too because your grandpa likes those."

John did not object. Grandpa would be afflicted with them, not him.

"Now, I need to buy some birthday cards," said Beth, "so we'll have to go back down that aisle and then in the other direction."

Another ten minute journey commenced. John followed behind his grandmother as she pushed the cart. He sneaked a look at his watch. They had only been in the store fifteen minutes. He was so bored, and his mother had said they would stay at Shopko for an hour.

Once back in the main aisle, Beth maneuvered her cart around the other shoppers and the series of small tables designed to catch people's eyes with the items arranged on them, including bestselling books.

It was the summer of "*...And Ladies of the Club*" and Shopko was determined to sell every copy of Helen Hooven Santmyer's blockbuster novel. The enormous, fourteen hundred thirty-seven page paperback brick had been printed with four different colored covers to choose from: blue, pink, green, or yellow. The cover, depicting women wearing enormous turn of the century hats, declared it was clearly a woman's book, but it was also a historical novel. One woman looked like the old fashioned picture on one of the coke glasses in the cupboard at home. The cover made John feel nostalgic. His grandmother stopped to look at dishtowels on one of the tables; John knew she would not buy any; she had an entire cedar chest full of dishtowels at home, all new, given as gifts, which she refused to use until the old ones were worn out, but she had to feel how soft the towels were as an excuse to give her knee another rest. While John waited, he picked up the yellow copy of *"...And Ladies of the Club"*. The back cover declared the novel was a domestic story of several generations of women who belonged to a literary society in Waynesboro, Ohio.

"Boy, that's a thick book," said Beth. "Do you think you could ever read a book that long, John?"

"Probably," said John. He knew he could easily read it in a week.

"It looks like a romance novel. You wouldn't want to read that would you?"

"It's not a romance; it's a historical novel about a town in Ohio."

"Oh," said Beth. She noticed her grandson did not lift his eyes from the book when he spoke. She knew he must be bored walking around Shopko with her. "Do you want it?" she asked.

"I don't know," he said because it was a woman's book, but he did want to read it.

"I'll buy it for you if you want," said Beth.

"No, Grandma. I have money; I can buy it," John said although he knew his protests would be pointless.

"No, you save your money," she said. "Besides, I can't take mine with me. Put it in the cart and don't say another word."

"Thank you, Grandma."

He placed a yellow copy of the novel in the shopping cart. He liked the copy with the green cover best, but he thought the yellow cover more masculine looking. With the book in the shopping cart, the cashier would think it was for Grandma and not for him. His mom would know it was for him, but she would not object to his reading it, just Grandma buying it, and he knew Grandma would win if there were an argument over that.

John was more patient now as they looked at birthday cards, although he just wanted to take his book and go read in the car while the ladies finished their shopping. Since Grandma's eyes were not what they used to be, he helped her dig through the birthday cards to find one for his cousin Ian in California. He read a dozen of them out loud to her, hoping he was not annoying too many of the other shoppers. He hoped no one he knew from school would see him. But all the shoppers in the aisle thought him a nice young man to help his grandmother.

Ellen and Chad found them half an hour later, still in the card aisle. When Ellen learned her mother was buying John a book, she said, "Mom, you shouldn't do that." Beth only replied, "Chad, I'll buy that record you have so I treat my grandsons equally."

They made another stop at the Marquette Mall, but John saw no books he wanted at B. Dalton's. He decided to save his money until next week since his new book would take a week to read. Then the shopping party went to Ponderosa for lunch.

As they sat at Ponderosa, eating steaks and salads, John looked closely at his mother, grandmother, and great-aunt. They had grown up in the earlier half of the century, when girls did not use the "F" word or talk openly about their boyfriend's anatomical sizes as many of the girls did at his high school. John felt himself too much of a gentleman to go out with such girls. Most of the girls he found attractive ended up repulsing him once they opened their mouths, and those girls would only go out with jocks anyway. John thought if he had lived a hundred years ago, or even fifty, the girls would have been young ladies who appreciated that he was a gentleman. He enjoyed reading books like "...*And Ladies of the Club*" because they promised to let him return to the golden yesterdays.

"Look at that," said Aunt Eleanor, staring toward the salad bar where a plump young woman of not more than twenty-five was helping her little girl of six or seven fill her plate. The mother was dressed in tight pink shorts and a white sleeveless T-Shirt. Her belly protruded out of her shirt, making it clear she was expecting.

"No one dresses nice in summer anymore," said Ellen.

"Those shorts are crawling halfway up her rump," said Aunt Eleanor. "In my day, we would have been ashamed to be seen in public like that."

"Wouldn't your day have been the 1920s, Aunt Eleanor?" asked Chad. "I thought those were wild times, full of flappers, jazz and liquor."

"Not in Marquette," she said. "It's like that new book out by that Clark girl from Marquette, *Twenties that Didn't Roar*. What is her name, Beth?"

"Ruth Lill," said Beth. "Her maiden name was Clark, and her mother was a Harlow."

"No," said Aunt Eleanor, who always had to be particular about things. "Her paternal grandmother was a Harlow. Amos Harlow's daughter I think. Anyway, the twenties sure didn't roar here in Marquette."

Eleanor's cousins, Harry and Serena Cumming, could have told her otherwise, but they were long since gone.

"When we were that girl's age," said Beth, "we never would have gone out in public if we were in the family way."

John thought his grandmother and great-aunt's sense of decorum rather old-fashioned and idiosyncratic, but he admired that they retained their standards despite the world changing around them. In their day, both women had been rebellious, his grandmother marrying outside of the Catholic church, his great-aunt choosing to divorce her husband rather than move away from Marquette; both had shown moral integrity ahead of their time by these deeds, yet their standard for decency had never changed.

In the next few days, John voraciously read '...And Ladies of the Club'. Day by day, hundreds of pages were read, so that by the next week, he had finished the book. When so many books existed to read, even such a massive novel could not be spared more than a week. John was becoming a discerning reader; between reading Jane Austen, Dickens, and the Bronte sisters, he would sandwich in Agatha Christie, J.M. Barrie, Elizabeth Goudge, and Anne Tyler. He learned more about literature that summer than he would in any English class, but of all the books he read, '...And Ladies of the Club' made the greatest impression on him, perhaps because it was most suggestive of his world, colored by a past that seemed more real than the present to him. Helen Hooven Santmyer was an elderly woman who had decided to record the world of her Ohio Town before its daily life had been forgotten. John thought he would like to write a similar tale, recapturing the world of streetcars and silent movies his grandparents had known when Marquette was young.

The morning after John finished reading Santmyer's novel, he sat down at his desk, took out some paper, and started to write a story with characters based on his grandparents. He worked steadily, getting up every morning, quickly eating, then going to his desk to write for a couple hours. He enjoyed whatever he was writing as it flowed from his pen, but a day or two later, he knew it was no good. To make the story more interesting, he set it during World War II and made his grandfather a soldier who wrote love letters home to his wife. But John realized he knew nothing about the war or its battles. After twenty pages, he abandoned the story. He started another, about a little girl who met an interesting lady who moved in across the street. The interesting lady would tell the little girl stories about the olden days. But there seemed no point to the stories. John started again, this time writing about an early settler to a mining town who befriended the Indians, but he knew nothing about Indians or mining, despite being raised in Upper Michigan. He stuffed away all his failed writing attempts until he had a drawer filled with pages of dribble, as he thought of them. As the days passed, he felt the summer was being wasted. He had caught the writer's curse, the nagging feeling that if he did not write everyday, he was lazy, and when he had writer's block, he felt irritable. He worried that he would never write anything worthwhile. He did not suspect yet how his young, elephant-like memory was storing up daily impressions of his everyday world which at the moment he dismissed as worthless, but which would ultimately matter more than all of that summer's scribbled pages.

Then he put his writing away for two weeks. It was time to go to Bible camp.

Bible camp was located at the southernmost point of Marquette County on a small lake surrounded, like all Upper Michigan lakes, by a pine tree forest. The camp was spread across several acres and consisted of nearly a dozen small cabins that roomed ten campers each, a large dining hall, and an assembly hall that served double as chapel on Sundays and lecture hall for weeknight sermons. Mornings at camp were spent in prayer and organized activities; afternoons were free for swimming, sailboating, canoeing and hiking; evenings were for team sports, singing, and prayer service. Here, good Christian men and women, faithful to their pledge to spread God's word, gave up their vacations from grinding jobs to spend time raising the next Christian generation. Here was perfect harmony between young and old, city and country dweller, Catholic and Protestant, a microcosm of the Christian world Christ had intended.

At Bible camp, John was constantly occupied. He and a cabinmate went sailing on the lake to break the record number of times a sailboat could be capsized in an afternoon. The next day he was water-skiing. Tree swings and rope ladders were climbed, silent devotions and prayer meetings held, kitchen duty performed, and practical jokes played. Evening skits and variety shows sent laughter over the lake. Bus rides included singalongs on the way to explore the Laughing Whitefish Waterfall. Ice cream socials followed evening walks around the lake. Water games were succeeded by nighttime campfires. Here was camaraderie as John had never experienced, and he took every opportunity to participate, to win friendship and affection from his fellow campers, whether by cleaning extra toilets or going canoeing. This was the Christian life. Nothing greater could be aspired to – except perhaps to get Gloria to go with him to the Christian dance the last night of camp.

The Christian dance was the social event of the summer camp season. Boys wore suits, and girls relinquished shorts for full length skirts. Hardly anyone failed to spend an hour fixing his or her hair. Most importantly, everyone must have a date. By the middle of the first week, boys were already asking girls to the dance. John decided to ask Gloria. She was pretty – well, honestly, she was hot, although he tried not to think of her that way. For several days, he prayed for courage; then for several more days, he tried to catch Gloria alone, to find a suitable moment. Many times, he came close to asking her, only to lose his nerve. Then one day, he was coming out of the restroom, and she was walking toward the restroom. Feeling it was now or never, John spit out the question, barely hearing his own words.

"Oh," she said in surprise. "Oh, I – well, I know it wasn't easy for you to ask me, but I – "

John felt his face fall.

"The truth is I like you well enough, John, but I – and it's not that I want to go with anyone else, but – I'm sorry, but I can't answer right now. Can I let you know in a couple days?"

"All right," he said, stupidly.

"Okay, I'll talk to you later," and she disappeared into the bathroom.

John was too devastated to tell any of his cabinmates. If he did, they would think him a loser, and besides, Gloria might still say "yes". He did not want to pester her, but he wished he had asked for a timeframe when she would give him an answer. When he got back to his cabin, he was relieved when his friend Mike asked him to go canoeing. He tried to concentrate on paddling and not think about Gloria.

The next day was a camping trip to Lake Superior. Everyone was going to sleep overnight on the beach. Two buses were packed with teenagers, counselors, cooks, and a minister. When John and Mike got on the bus, the only open seat was across the aisle from Gloria and her friend Marcy. As they drove to the lake, everyone started to notice the charred forests. The previous spring a number of wildfires had threatened forests across Upper Michigan. Miles of Marquette County forests had burnt.

"You should have heard the fire engine sirens going off," John told his friends. "We could hear them every night, one after another, as fires popped up all over Sands Township and Gwinn. It was kind of scary. The fires got as near as five miles to our house."

"You live up here?" asked Marcy of Dearborn.

"Yes. I'm from Marquette," said John.

"That's right; I'd forgotten," said Mike, who was from Detroit. "Don't you get bored up here?"

"No, why would I be bored?" asked John.

"There's nothing to do up here."

"We can go to the roller rink, and there's a mall, and lots of restaurants," John replied.

"How many McDonalds are in Marquette?" Mike asked.

"One."

"One?" Mike laughed. "In Detroit, there's one every few blocks."

"We don't need more than one," said John. "Marquette only has twenty-five thousand people."

"Twenty-five thousand!" said Marcy. "Detroit has over a million."

"Do you get any movies up here?" asked Mike.

"Sure," said John.

Mike named some movies John had not seen.

"What was the last movie you saw?" Marcy asked.

John was starting to find these Trolls from below the bridge rather insufferable. Anyone who came from Detroit's polluted crime-ridden streets had no reason to brag. Sarcastically, he replied, "I just saw *E.T.* the week before I came to camp."

"*E.T.*!" said Mike. "That's been out for years. You've got to be kidding."

John pretended to be serious.

"Please tell me you at least have MTV," said Marcy.

"No," said John. "We don't have a TV."

This was too much even for Gloria. "Why not?" she asked.

"It's too expensive to import them over the Mackinac Bridge."

"I could get you a TV off the street from a guy I know in Detroit," said Mike. "I could get you a twenty-seven inch for fifty bucks."

John was afraid to ask how Mike knew this guy.

"You sure are hicks up here," Marcy said.

"We're Yoopers and proud of it," said John.

"What's a Yooper?" asked Marcy.

"Someone from the U.P.," said John.

Marcy and Mike just laughed. They would not understand why they were Trolls, even if he tried to explain. He wished that bill for U.P. Statehood Grandpa always talked about had passed.

The conversation ended when the buses reached shining Lake Superior. The water was only slightly chilly – the temperature that day being in the eighties and the ice having melted three months before. They camped beside a river pushing warm water around a sandbar into the lake. In minutes, the buses were unloaded. Adults arranged themselves in lawn chairs and on beach blankets. Boys ripped off their shirts and ran screaming into the cold water to prove their manliness, while hoping the girls were watching. Eventually the girls were coaxed into the lake since they wanted closer views of the boys' lean torsos. Chicken fights began when the girls got up on the boys' shoulders and tried to push each other down. Those less daring built sandcastles, played frisbee, or rolled down the sand dunes, then went to wash themselves clean in the lake.

John stood in the water, laughing, splashing, and being splashed. Then he saw Mike run across the beach into the lake, his hand firmly clasping Marcy's as she raced beside him. For a moment, he saw utter happiness on their faces; they seemed like a second Adam and Eve, innocent, reveling in each other's company; John had suspected their feelings for each other all along, but today was their first open display of affection. He was happy for them. He wondered whether he could be as happy.

In the evening, a campfire was lit. Besides cold sandwiches and chips, hot dogs were cooked, followed by the great ritual making of the smores.

John found a place to eat on the beach beside Gloria.

Before he could stop himself, he asked, "Have you thought about what I asked you?"

For a moment, she pretended not to hear. When he hopelessly asked again, she said, "John, I can't go to the dance with you. You're from up here, and I'm from downstate. We'd never see each other again because I'm not coming back to camp next year. I don't see the point in our starting anything. I'm sorry."

"It's just a dance," he said. "It doesn't mean we have to date or anything."

"No," she said. "Besides, I think someone else is going to ask me. I'm sorry."

"It's all right," he said. But it was not all right. He ate his hot dog in silence. Then muttering that he was going to get more pop, he got up and did not return. He felt awkward around everyone for the next hour, but no one noticed. He was glad when night came and hid his face. He sat in the back of the group then, away from the campfire's flickering flames, silently eating his smores.

The campfire songs began – church hymns and Amy Grant songs. He noticed Gloria was sitting next to Pete. Pete was a jerk. He was in John's cabin. He boasted that he had sex with his girlfriend back home every Saturday night. He was a poor Christian in John's opinion, but Gloria was laughing as Pete made goofy faces in the firelight. That night, John found little joy singing praises to the Lord.

Finally, bedtime came. Everyone spread out on the beach with their sleeping bags. In the morning, they would be irritated by the sand in their hair, but tonight, sleeping on the beach seemed wonderful in the warm, humid air.

A meteor shower lit the night sky. Many of the campers stayed awake to watch. John pretended to be asleep, but he opened his eyes when his fellow campers began to "Ooh" and "Ah" over falling stars. John knew you were supposed to wish on falling stars, but he had no wishes to make. He heard the wind rustling the trees. Occasionally, a cricket could be heard. The waves lapped on the shore, then rolled out, a silent roar, to wash in again.

Why did his heart have to be broken at Bible Camp? Was his heart really broken? He never would have asked Gloria to the dance except that everyone else asked someone. He told himself he did not really like her all that much. Here they were in the beautiful North, but she obviously did not appreciate it. She had laughed at him for being a Yooper. That was partly why she would not go with him to the dance. Why had she made such a big deal out of it anyway? He had not asked her to be his girlfriend, and what did he care what she did next summer. And how dare she say she thought someone else – probably that jerk Pete – might take her. Why, even at Bible Camp, did girls have to like bad boys? But she was from Detroit, so what had he expected? He hoped she went home to rot in the dirty, stinking, murder capital of the world. He did not care if he did not have a good Christian attitude. But why did he let it bother him? He was only sixteen. He had plenty of time to find a nice Yooper girl.

By the next day, his thoughts had moved on. Last year, a camper from each cabin had been awarded the "Most Christlike Award". John had been extremely proud to win the award. At first he had not felt he deserved it, but his counselor had told him, "Who else in the cabin would I have chosen?"

Now John decided he would be sure to win the award again this year. Pete sure wasn't going to win it. Then Gloria would realize he was the better man. Save now for his silent mockery of the Trolls at camp, he went out of his way to be nice to everyone, to be good. He volunteered when no one else would to clean the toilets. During a volleyball tournament, he missed hitting the ball, causing his cabin to lose the game. When Pete was such a sore loser that he whacked John in the stomach, John saw red for a moment, but he caught his breath, then went up to Pete and said, "I forgive you." Pete scowled and walked off, but everyone else congratulated John for keeping his cool. When one of his cabinmates hurt his leg while water-skiing, John gave up his lower level bunk; his cabinmates said it was kind of him to trade bunks, but John had secretly wanted an upper bunk anyway.

Then, the second to the last night of camp, the preacher reminded everyone that camp was almost over, and that the whole purpose of these two weeks had been to develop a closer relationship with Jesus Christ.

"Soon we will all be returning to the real world with its many temptations," said the preacher. "We won't be in this beautiful place surrounded by fellow Christians who love and support us. We need to return to the world strong in our beliefs. We need to be witnesses to Christ. Some of you may not have been Christians before you came to camp, but during this week, you have come to accept Christ as your savior. Others of you may want to receive Christ as your Lord, but you have not yet found the courage to come forward. Tonight, I ask those of you who feel the need to give your lives to Jesus to stay after the service. If you are too embarrassed, then leave and come back after a couple minutes when everyone else has left. Come tonight and give your lives to His service. Come and know the peace that only the Lord can give. Now let us pray."

John did not hear the prayer. He felt the preacher had spoken directly to him. What was he doing with his life? Did he really know where his life was headed? He had never fully agreed to give his life to Christ. Had he not thought many times he would become a priest, yet what had he done about it? This night would be the start. He wondered whether Gloria had turned him down because God had a greater plan for him. He wondered whether his writing were not very good because being a writer would bring fame and recognition, and he was instead meant to walk humbly with his God.

When the service ended, John stayed behind. In a couple minutes, the only ones remaining besides himself and the preacher were Pete and two mouthy girls who could never aspire to being Virgin Mary's. Why, they were the three least religious people at camp! Had the preacher meant only for people who were not saved to stay behind? John had been saved years ago, besides being baptized a Catholic. The preacher gave John an odd look, as if to say, "What are you doing here?" John did not belong with these people. They were not future priests, ministers, nuns or missionaries. They were guilty sinners. He felt stupid being with them.

But the preacher did not discriminate against anyone. He simply asked each one directly whether he or she were ready to testify to a belief in Jesus Christ as Savior. They all said yes. John thought it easiest to coincide with the others rather than explain himself. The preacher then prayed for God to guide their lives. John felt foolish. He hoped the others would not mention he had been there, but then he realized they would be ashamed to have stayed behind as well. It did not matter why he was there; he silently vowed that now he would dedicate his life to God. When the prayer was over, he walked out the opposite door from the others. He hid himself in the black of night, then merged into a crowd of teenagers lingering along the lake in the last minutes before curfew.

He did not tell anyone else what he had done, but he told himself it had been the most important moment of his life.

The last day of camp, John was anxious to leave, to go into the world and find a way to serve God, but first he had to attend the Christian dance. His cabinmate Luke was "going stag" like him. John felt less awkward when he learned this, but he told himself he no longer cared about girls; he now had higher things on his mind.

The meeting room had become a dance floor, flooded with the music of Leslie Phillips, Amy Grant, Emmaus Road, Harvest, Petra, and Michael W. Smith. Everyone danced to glorify God, just as King David had done centuries before. John danced with a couple girls he was friends with, but he mostly stood on the sidelines, awkwardly watching everyone else, trying not to feel jealous when he saw Pete's arms around Gloria.

At the evening's end, the camp director announced that before the last song would be a presentation. John had forgotten all that day about the awards, but now he listened quietly, clapping when badges were given to the most athletic boy and girl, the neatest cabin, and the best volleyball team. Then he grew anxious. The Most Christlike Awards would be next. He suddenly realized that in his desire to earn the award, he had been the least Christlike, seeking personal recognition rather than to glorify God. Now that he had given his life to God, he would not be so self-centered again. He told himself he did not want the award, that other boys in his cabin were more deserving.

Then the camp director announced, "Finally, this year we have two very special awards. One for the boy and girl who are the most like Christ. We call these the "Servant Heart of Christ" awards. Each recipient will get a plaque with his or her name engraved upon it."

The director held up the two plaques, each a foot tall. These two very special awards had replaced the previous Christlike awards, one for each of the ten cabins. They were more special because more rare. John could not imagine hanging such a large plaque on his bedroom wall.

"The girl awarded the "Servant's Heart" is Christy Brixton," announced the camp director, "and the boy awarded the "Servant's Heart" is John Vande-laare."

John's spine went numb. The room exploded with applause. His cabin-mates pushed him to the front of the assembly. He was too shocked, perhaps too cowardly to resist. Now the camp director was shaking his hand, the crowd chanting, "Speech! Speech!" and everyone clapping. Christy accepted her award, raised it for everyone to see, nodded appreciatively, and returned to her seat. John tried to follow her example but stumbled on a microphone cord and blushed as he made his way back to where he had been standing. Everyone surged around him to see his plaque. He barely had a chance to look at it until after it had passed through a dozen other hands. Then in enormous gold letters, he saw his name engraved beneath a pair of silver hands folded in prayer.

He was mortified. He wanted to say he did not deserve it, but he could not speak with so many people clapping him on the back and saying, "You deserve it, John," and "There isn't a better guy at camp." Once back in his cabin, he quickly buried it in his suitcase.

The next day at home, his mother found the award as she collected his laundry.

"You should hang it on your bedroom wall," Ellen said.

"I don't know," said John.

"Sure you should," she said. Even Chad agreed.

"I'll go find you a screw to hold it up," said Tom.

A couple minutes later, his father had pounded a hole in John's bedroom wall and hung the plaque right above the desk where John wrote his stories. Now John would have to look at it everyday.

"I guess I'll leave it there," John thought. "Since I don't deserve it, it'll teach me to be more humble."

Once every couple weeks, Henry drove up the Big Bay Road to visit Roy. In summer, Bill would come along, and they would stop to dig for worms. Bill had taken to raising worms in what had been his father's woodshop; he sold them to fishermen to supplement his retirement income. Unlike Roy, who lived simply, Bill had never learned to live within his means. With his extra worm money, he bought Michigan Lotto tickets for the Saturday night drawings; that he lost every week could not convince him he never would win.

By contrast, Roy saw most expenditures as wasting money so Henry brought him old copies of the *Mining Journal* which Roy refused to spend money on. Other than an occasional visit to his family, Roy's only way to keep up with Marquette events was to read the newspaper; then he burnt it in his woodstove for extra fuel.

A strong summer downpour had begun that morning while Henry and Bill had been digging worms, so rather than go fishing that afternoon, they just stopped at Roy's cabin for a few minutes to drop off the newspapers.

"I remember days when a little rain wouldn't have stopped us from fishing. It still doesn't stop me," said Bill.

"Wait until you're eighty and it will," Henry replied.

"I can tell you're over eighty by the way you drive," said Bill. "Roy, you should see how he swerves all over the road now."

"If you don't like my driving you can take your own car next time," said Henry; he rarely snapped when criticized, but he was becoming touchy about his driving. His cataracts were so bad the doctor had signed a slip for him stating he could see fine so he wouldn't lose his driver's license; his family were secretly not too pleased with that doctor. Ellen was especially concerned when her mother confided that she had to tell Henry whether the stoplights were red or green.

"We're all getting older," said Roy, trying to keep the peace as he poured more coffee.

"No sugar for me," said Bill, who had recently been diagnosed with diabetes.

Henry plopped four spoonfuls of sugar into his coffee to spite his younger brother.

"So, Roy, when are you going to help me tar my roof?" Bill asked.

"I have some work to do at the Club tomorrow," said Roy, "how about Thursday."

"You want me to help too?" asked Henry.

"No, it's just a two man job," said Bill. He had not asked Henry because he knew Beth would have a fit if Henry were up on the roof at his age. Bill felt there were some advantages to having no wife, even beyond not having to have the same woman every night; he often wondered why he had ever gotten married in the first place; even more, he wondered how he had been dumb enough to do it a second time.

The rain did not let up. Bill hoped his roof was not leaking. Since the brothers could not go down to the lake, they talked about fishing for twenty minutes. Then Henry and Bill made a mad dash to the car. Roy watched them drive away, then set to making his supper. Once his beans and hot dogs were cooked, he poured out the last of the coffee and sat down to read the *Mining Journal* by a kerosene lamp he had lit because of the stormy weather.

As he read the headlines, he reflected that the news became more depressing everyday. More problems with Libya; bombing them had done little good. Tensions continued with the Soviet Union. AIDS was spreading across America. And then there were the obituaries. More and more people he had known in his youth were dying, even people twenty years younger than him were often listed in the paper, people whose parents he remembered as young men and women. Lately, the obituaries had made him start to feel his own mortality. But today, he spotted one that ashamedly lifted his spirits.

Lex Weidner

- Madison, WI. Mr. Lex Weidner, former Marquette resident, died suddenly at his home on Thursday, surrounded by his family. Mr. Weidner was born in Marquette in 1906 and resided in this area until 1938 when he moved to Madison, Wisconsin . . . . He was preceded in death by his parents, Irving and Evelyn Weidner. He is survived by his wife, Chloe, a daughter, Mrs. Richard (Janet) Josephs and three grandchildren, all of Madison, WI. Funeral arrangements . . . .

Roy skimmed the notice to make certain it was Lex. Then he went back and read the details, even about Lex's former professions and the funeral time.

"The damn bastard," he said, his old anger surging up. "I wonder what Chloe will do now."

He had his own idea of what she could do, but he told himself the notion was ridiculous, especially at their ages.

"It must be twenty years since I last let these feelings overpower me," he told himself, surprised by how the old pain suddenly revived. He was relieved to know it was over for Chloe – that the years of her unhappy marriage had finally ended – but she had probably forgotten him by now. And had he not spent the last twenty years trying to forget her? But he never could. Not ever. He had promised her he would not.

"Damn it, Roy," he said to himself. He turned the page and tried to read the funnies, but soon he was staring out the window at the rain. "It isn't right that it should get to me like this," he thought. "Not after all these years."

He had read all those philosophy books. He had been an atheist, an existentialist, and then a Christian again. Religion had soothed his spirit, but it had only restrained, never eliminated those feelings. He had sinned with Chloe, but sinned due to overpowering love, and now that Lex was gone, it would be no sin to be with her.

He would get nowhere thinking about her. How could he honestly believe that she still might feel – but he could not help himself. He had to find out. He did not know why it should still matter at his age, but if she did care –

He would write to her. He could call her, but that might be too awkward. A letter would be better – it would be an easier way to express himself, and she would not have to write back if she did not care. But what if she did reply? Then what? He could not have a wife come live with him in this shack. They would buy a home. He had plenty of money sitting in the bank that he did not know what to do with. Or he could go live with her in Wisconsin – but no, he would not live in that bastard's house, and he would miss his own family if he moved away. She could come here – they could live together, maybe in Snowberry Heights, the new senior citizen high-rise in Marquette. It did not matter; he would let her decide, just so long as he could be with her.

He dug out some paper and found a pencil. How should he begin? He felt overwhelmed by the possibility that their promise to each other might now be fulfilled – this ending was the one he had always hoped for, had waited so long for, and the wait had been worth it. He just needed to let her know he still waited for her. She might have contacted him by now, but she was probably busy with the funeral arrangements, and it would not be proper that she run after him before her husband was buried; besides, it was only right that the man make the first move.

The newspaper said the funeral was tomorrow – if he mailed the letter tomorrow, it would take three or four days to reach her, plus Sunday, so nearly a week would pass after the funeral before she received it; then she would write him back; that would take another three or four days. Once he had her answer, he would go out to see her. Within a month – a sufficient time for her to mourn the husband she had never loved – they would be together. They would not have much time – a few years if they were lucky – but whatever time remained would be enough.

He wrote the letter. He did not focus on their years of separation or all the loneliness he had felt. He only told Chloe what she already knew – that he loved her and he wanted her to be his wife. Then he signed the letter, placed it in an envelope, and addressed it according to the information given in Lex's obituary. He put it in his jacket pocket so he would remember – as if he could forget – to mail it tomorrow. The rest of the evening, he imagined the happiness that would finally be his.

In the morning, Roy walked through the woods to the Club. The sunlight streamed through the trees, causing the remaining raindrops on the leaves to sparkle like little diamonds. He noticed what a dark green the leaves were becoming, a clear sign summer was almost over and autumn approaching. Any day now he would see a touch of red or orange on a maple or oak. He loved each of these trees, having watched them grow for the last sixty years. He knew each tree well, knew each individual distinguishing feature; had he dared confess it, he knew these trees better than the woman he had loved all his life. He would miss them when he left his cabin to be with Chloe, but they were just trees, not a woman. Nature could not hold a man on a cold winter night; it could not run its fingers through his hair. Chloe would be worth leaving the woods. Anything would be worth being with her. He was still stunned by how intense his feelings were after so many years. His chest felt like it would burst if he could not soon speak his love. He stopped to rest against a tree and catch his breath; his love was overpowering.

He looked about, trying to contain his feelings. Yes, the leaves were quite dark this year, even for late August. Not even green really, almost black. Funny, the sun seemed to have gone away suddenly, as if a storm were coming. The love feeling was disappearing now; he felt almost dizzy. His eyelids grew heavy; he tried to push them open; for a second he saw a shot of dazzling blue sky. How odd; the sun never came out that fast. Then a flash of heat coursed through his body, and he knew. He clutched at the tree, but his fingers had lost their strength. Now Chloe would never know he was going to come for her. He would still wait, wait for her until this time it could be forever. What did a few years on earth matter? He could wait again. All was well. His mother's face flashed before him, replacing his beloved's. He remembered the words of his childhood, "Now I lay me down to sleep. I pray the Lord my soul to keep."

He fell to the ground, finally free from his piercing consciousness. From his jacket pocket, the envelope slipped onto the ground. Then a gentle rain began to fall.

That evening, Roy's body was found by two workers from the Club. His clothes were soaking wet. His frame was stiff and numb. The men lifted him into the back of a car; neither noticed the crumpled paper on the ground. Had they seen it, they would have distinguished only a few legible words. The rain had washed away the penciled address. The envelope and paper inside were so wet they would have fallen apart if picked up. Only the silent forest would ever know Roy's great secret.

"That's Mr. Pryce over there," Henry told John. The funeral was over. They were at the cemetery where the casket would soon be lowered into the earth. "Roy and I built a house for his father in Florida about thirty years ago. He's a member of the Huron Mountain Club. They say he's worth about a hundred million dollars."

John was impressed. He hoped his father would not say anything to Mr. Pryce to embarrass him. His grandmother was grumbling behind him. She was hanging onto his mother's arm, her old knees aching in the damp weather.

Once they were all gathered around the casket, the minister began to speak.

"Lord, today, we commit to you our brother, Royal Whitman. Take him Lord to – "

John had a hard time listening. He thought back to the couple visits he had made to his uncle's dirty little cabin, then to that walk with his uncle around Presque Isle just a few months ago. He could not understand how a man who owned so many books – volumes and volumes of literary classics, philosophy, psychology, science, religion, things far beyond John's understanding – had not done something more productive with his life, had not used his knowledge to better the world. Yet here were millionaires, important men at his funeral. John wondered whether he had missed something about Uncle Roy.

When the minister finished speaking, the funeral director herded everyone back to their cars. People turned around, walked a few steps, then paused to chat.

Henry did not move for a moment. John stood silently beside him, not caring that the others had already left.

"I guess I don't know how to feel," said Henry. "I've lost my parents but never a sibling. Your grandma lost all her brothers years ago. I always figured since I was the oldest, I would be the first to go. I didn't think my younger brother would go before me. I'm eighty-one, but I still don't understand life."

"I don't think anyone ever does," said John, feeling the inadequacy of his words, feeling how presumptuous he was to try comforting someone five times his age.

"I'm glad my parents bought these extra plots. My ma liked that she would be buried on top of this hill. She wanted her children to lie beside her, and they all will, except me. I've promised your grandma I'll be buried with her in the Catholic cemetery."

John did not reply, just listened to his grandfather.

"My father wanted to be buried closer to his own parents, but all those spots were filled years ago. My grandparents, they're buried down the hill over there. You see that tall pillar shaped grave? That one's theirs."

"Did you know your grandparents?" John asked.

"Not my father's parents – they died before I was born. I knew my mother's though – they died out in California, but they're buried down there by that tree." He pointed farther across the cemetery.

As John strained his eyes, Henry coughed. It was a cold morning.

"We better go back to the car, Grandpa," John said.

As they turned around, John noticed how frail his grandfather looked. His mother had commented a month ago how fast Grandpa was losing weight, but only now did John notice. Grandpa's overcoat hung from his shoulders as if he were a scarecrow made of sticks. Henry had never been a large man, but now he could not weigh much more than one hundred thirty pounds. John suspected he already outweighed his grandfather. He shivered as a cool breeze spread over the cemetery. Soon it would snow. It was a shame to leave Uncle Roy out here in the cold.

John lay on his bed. He had no homework to do. He was free until suppertime to pore over John Jakes's epic Civil War saga, *North and South*. He had seen the miniseries the year before, along with its sequel, *Love and War*, but he enjoyed the novels far more. Still, he found it hard to believe, as depicted in the books, that people in the 1850s and 1860s had so much sex, especially outside of marriage. John Jakes obviously had wanted to spice things up. John loved historical fiction, but he had already waded his way through the eight volumes of Jakes's American Bicentennial series about the Kent family, finding it unbelievable that someone in one family could be at every major event in American history; the sensationalism of the novels made them enjoyable and hard to put down, but John did find his willing suspension of disbelief put to the test. '*...And Ladies of the Club*' had been a far more realistic historical novel, yet he found himself going back to reread the sex scenes in *North and South*. He had never read anything before like those passages. Of course, even the Victorians had had sex, but was it proper to write about it like this? And all the foul language – did they really use the "F" word during the Civil War? He had never seen it even hinted at in Dickens, but Jakes's characters had no problem using it. Where did a writer draw the line between realism – after all, a soldier would swear when his leg was amputated – and writing with moral responsibility? Could one write believable stories and omit the seedy events of life? Should he even be reading this book? Everyday after school, he read a chapter of the Bible. But even this afternoon, he had only let his eye run over a page of the Bible, not even absorbing the meaning, then set the Holy Book down and picked up *North and South* to indulge vicariously in the titillation felt by Orry Main on his first visit to a whorehouse.

John reread the spicy passage, then set the book aside with extreme guilt. He felt torn. He opened his dresser drawer, pulled out his rosary, and kneeling before the Infant of Prague, read one of the prayer cards he had bought from the nuns at St. John's. He had begun to say this prayer everyday to lessen the years he would be punished in Purgatory for his lust, anger, and selfishness.

Prayer to the Crucified Christ, Our Lord

O my holy and beloved Jesus, behold me, cast upon my knees, weeping fervently for my sins. Behold my soul's fervent desire for Thine love and for Thine mercy. Behold how I pray and beseech Thee that Thou impress upon my heart and conscience sincere repentance for my sins and teach me only to desire the goodness that emanates from our Holy Father. Teach me thy sacred and holy ways, that I may turn from Satan and all his evil works; with great grief of soul I contemplate Thy five wounds, recalling the words of Thy prophet David, "They have pierced my hands and my feet, they have numbered all my bones" (Psalm xxi: 17, 18). Let the remembrance of Thy great love expressed in Thy sacrificial death be a motivation for me to turn from sin and walk humbly in the way of Thy Cross until I feast in Paradise with Thee. Amen.

After finishing the prayer, John prayed the rosary, focusing on the Sorrowful Mysteries of Christ's suffering in the Garden of Gethsemane, His scourging at the pillar, His crowning with thorns, His carrying of the Cross, and His crucifixion. John winced as he tried to imagine the nails being pounded into Christ's hands and feet, the spear piercing His side. John's knees and back hurt from kneeling, but he told himself his pain was nothing compared to hanging from a cross. He wished he could weep and wail over Christ's sufferings, but if he did, his mother would be sure to knock on his bedroom door and ask whether everything were all right.

But as he started the second decade of the rosary, he lost track of how many Hail Mary's he had said, even though the beads were supposed to help him count. He thought about *North and South* and how he should not read sexually explicit novels, although he knew he would keep reading them, and then he thought about what he should read next, and he told himself he had to read everything, and that he had not forgotten his promise at camp to give his life to serving God, but that did not mean he had to be a priest – he did not think he had the patience for it, and he knew someday he would want to be with a woman. He was not compromising his values; God had given him his talent as a writer – that must be what God wanted from him; writing could be a religious calling, even if it were not exactly the same role for which God had called Samuel.

While John's thoughts wandered, and his lips prayed, the phone rang. Then he heard his mother coming down the hall. He quickly shoved his rosary under his pillow. He was not ashamed to pray, but the Bible said to go into your closet and shut the door; do not make a show of your religion.

"John," his mother said through the door, "your grandpa's on the phone. He wants to talk to you."

"All right," said John, getting up off his knees. Why could God not time things so people did not call while you were praying? Was it wrong to interrupt his prayers to answer the phone, or was it more wrong to be rude by not talking to his grandfather?

"Hello," he said when he picked up the phone.

"John, you remember Mr. O'Neill that we met at the flea market last year."

"Yeah."

"He just called me. He said he's sorry he's been so long about it, but he still wants us to come over for lunch sometime. I guess when he saw Roy's obituary in the paper, he remembered his offer. He specifically said I have to bring you."

"Okay," said John, surprised but pleased.

"I told him it would have to be a weekend since you're in school. How about this Saturday?"

"Sure, that's fine," John said.

Henry said he would call Mr. O'Neill back to confirm. John hung up the phone and told his mother the news.

Chad, who had overheard, abandoned the television to come into the kitchen and say, "You mean you get to see the inside of Mr. O'Neill's beautiful house?"

"I don't know where he lives," said John.

"Everyone knows he lives in that big Victorian sandstone house on Ridge Street."

"Oh," said John.

"I wish I could go," said Chad.

John did not reply. He was not going to share this chance with his brother. Chad did not care about literature – he just wanted to see the inside of the house. John went to his room and pulled from the bookshelf the one O'Neill novel he owned. He would reread it so he would have something to talk to Mr. O'Neill about. Somehow, he doubted Mr. O'Neill was a fan of John Jakes.

On Saturday morning, Henry picked up John. All the way to Mr. O'Neill's house, he talked about his carpentry work while John interjected an occasional, "Uh huh." John was too anxious about seeing Mr. O'Neill to say much else. Henry parked the car on Ridge Street; only now did John realize Mr. O'Neill lived in what John had always considered Marquette's grandest home; the neighborhood had larger, more ornate homes, but none seemed to embody such sublime dignity as this sandstone mansion.

"Come in, come in," said Mr. O'Neill, opening the door. He was in a dark blue sweater, and his hair was slightly mussed, but his eyes smiled through his bifocals. "Hurry, it's cold out there."

"Should we take off our shoes?" John asked.

"Yes, otherwise Lyla will get upset. She's our housekeeper; technically, she works for us, but she knows how to make Eliza and me feel as if we work for her."

Grandpa laughed, "I know about women like that." John felt intimidated to think Mr. O'Neill rich enough to have a housekeeper.

"You have a beautiful home," he said to be polite, and because it was true.

"You've only seen the front hall," smiled Mr. O'Neill, hanging up their coats. "I made us soup and sandwiches, but they'll stay warm on the stove. Let me show you around first."

They turned left into a large parlor decorated in what Mr. O'Neill described as modern furnishings compared to the rest of the house. It had been redecorated in the 1970s, complete with spackled, glittered ceiling, giant lamps, and a shag carpet. It was a monstrosity to John's senses. He was disappointed, but he reminded himself he had not come to see a grand house.

"See these mirror frames," said Robert. "Your grandpa made these, and look out here on the porch to the side. Your grandpa practically rebuilt this entire porch back during World War II; there wouldn't be any remnants of the original porch today if your grandpa hadn't come to restore it."

He led them through a smaller sitting room behind the front parlor which was used as a little TV room and contained lazy-boys, a comfy sofa, messy plants, and scattered magazines. Then they went back into the hallway and stopped at the stairs.

"I'm afraid the wife wouldn't appreciate me showing you the bedrooms. But look at this beautiful old bannister, John. Your grandpa put new supports into it more than once because I nearly broke it when I used to slide down it as a boy, and I'm afraid my children took after me."

"Did you grow up in this house?" John asked.

"No, it was my great-aunt's home, but one summer when I was a boy, I had to be caretaker here. That's when I first slid down the banister." He smiled. "How could I resist?"

"Mr. O'Neill," Henry told John, "was originally born in South Carolina."

"Yes," said Mr. O'Neill. "People always wonder how I ended up here, but my mother was from Marquette, and when she died and my dad was off fighting in the First World War, I came up here to stay with my grandma and aunt. Since then, I've never wanted to live anywhere but Marquette. Well, let's go eat."

John and Henry followed their host into the dining room and seated themselves at a long mahogany table while Mr. O'Neill went into the kitchen. John looked at the tall hutch cabinets full of fine china and depression glass. Through the window he could see the grand old Victorian house across the street, almost as much a picture for the room as the old-fashioned Norman Rockwell style paintings on the walls. On the buffet was a good size model train car. Other randomly spread knickknacks spoke of yesteryear.

"I hope my cooking's not too bad," said Robert, reappearing with a tray of food. "The housekeeper has the weekends off. Eliza would have cooked for us, but she promised to help out at the church bazaar this morning. I told her it was too cold for her to go out, but she gets more stubborn as she gets older. Would you like coffee?"

Mr. O'Neill poured coffee for everyone. Then he placed the soup and a platter of sandwiches – egg salad, tuna, and chicken salad – before them.

"John, do you see that hutch cabinet?" Mr. O'Neill said as they began to eat. "Your grandpa built that."

John looked at it admiringly. It was nicer than the one Grandpa had made for Grandma, but Grandma always said a carpenter's wife was bound to have the worst furniture because her husband was too busy to make her anything.

"I've built so many things that I'd forgotten about that cabinet," said Henry.

"I did some carpentry work in my youth," Mr. O'Neill told John, "but nothing so fine as the work your grandfather does."

John smiled. He could hear the slightest touch of a Southern accent when Mr. O'Neill paid a compliment. To John, this old gentleman seemed like the last survivor of a chivalrous, hospitable world.

"Well, I can't write books," Henry replied, "so you surpass me there."

"I imagine," Robert replied, "that people will still be enjoying this house and the furniture you made long after my books are forgotten."

John wondered how a writer could have such a thought. He hoped the books he would someday write would rival those of Dickens, yet he seriously doubted anything he wrote would even be half as good as anything by Mr. O'Neill.

"Where did you get that streetcar?" Henry asked, referring to the model on the buffet that John had mistaken for a train car.

"Oh," Mr. O'Neill replied, "my son Bernie sent it. He lives in San Francisco now. He saw it for sale out there – the tourists like to buy them you know. He claims when he was a kid, I was always telling him about the old streetcars; I don't remember that, but I was always fond of them."

"I miss the old streetcars," said Henry. "I remember when we were boys, my brother Roy and I used to take the streetcar out to Presque Isle to go swimming."

A silent moment followed as Henry remembered the brother he mourned. John concentrated on his soup. Mr. O'Neill got up and stepped into another room. He returned a moment later with a book he handed to Henry.

"Have you read this?" he asked as he returned to his seat.

Henry wiped his hand on his napkin, then picked up the book and held it close to his eyes to read the title. John could see the title from where he sat: *It Seems Like Yesterday* by Clyde Steele.

"The author's only a few years younger than us," Robert said. "He's written this little book about his memories of Marquette and its history."

Henry could not read the print without a magnifying glass, but he looked at the pictures of old buildings he had seen a thousand times although they had long ago vanished from Marquette's landscape.

"The Hotel Superior," said Henry. "Do you remember that?"

"Oh sure," said Robert. "It was a shame when they tore it down. Such a grand building."

"My dad and I were hired to help dismantle it," Henry said. "One of the saddest jobs I ever had to do."

Henry turned over a few more pages, pausing to look at Marquette's vanished churches and forgotten dance halls.

"I can't get over this picture of the horses and buggies going down Washington Street," said Henry. "I remember when I was a boy, my parents used to say how glad they'd be when automobiles went out of fashion."

"My step-grandfather, Mr. Carter," said Robert, "told my dad he was foolish to buy an automobile, but a couple years later, he had his own for terrorizing the neighborhood."

Surprised, John said, "I didn't know there were still horse and buggies when you were boys. I thought after nineteen hundred everyone had cars."

"Oh no," said Robert, "at least until World War I, horses were still the norm. I'd say they were still seen regularly until about the 1930s. If everyone had had automobiles back then, the streetcars wouldn't have lasted so long."

"This is an interesting book," Henry said, laying it down to finish his soup. "I'll have to pick up a copy."

"I wish I had thought to write it," said Robert. "Only people from Marquette will read it, but it'll be read years after today's bestsellers are forgotten."

"You should write a book about Marquette," John told Mr. O'Neill. "I mean, everyone has different memories. Maybe it could be your autobiography and include your memories of Marquette. I bet lots of people would like to read your autobiography."

"It's funny you should say that," Robert replied. "My family has always told me I should write my autobiography. I've tried to get started but just can't seem to piece things together. There's so much to tell after my long life that it's hard to decide what to include and what to leave out."

"I don't imagine I'd have much to say if I wrote mine," Henry replied. "Just that I got married, had a family, and worked all the time. But I imagine yours would be more interesting, what with all your books, and traveling, and the famous people you've met."

"You should write it as a novel with you as one of the characters," John told Mr. O'Neill. "Novels are what you're used to writing, and maybe that way it'll make it easier for you to shape it and think differently about your life and what's important."

"You know," said Robert, setting down his soup spoon, "that's a good idea. Maybe that would give it more shape. I could write a novel about how I moved to Marquette and ended up staying here, just remembering what Marquette was like when I was young. Thanks, John. There's nothing worse than having writer's block, but now that you've given me a different angle, I might just make some progress."

John wanted to tell Mr. O'Neill that he always got stuck in his own writing, and that he could use advice in return. But the front door opened, and the conversation was interrupted by an elderly woman breezing into the room like a college girl. She smiled at Henry and John, then went to Robert who lifted his cheek to meet her kiss. In that moment, John got a good look at her. She was in her mid-eighties, but clearly young in spirit. She was one of the few women left in Marquette who still wore a hat with a brim, a lilac colored hat at that, even if it were almost winter, and it looked grand on her. She reminded John of one of the characters on the front cover of *"...And Ladies of the Club"*. She wore a delicate purple sweater with a silk scarf to match, and although she wore slacks, there was no doubt she was a lady. John felt she was above his and his grandfather's class, and for a moment, he felt nervous, until she said, "Hello, Henry. I hope Robert made you something decent to eat. You must be John?"

"Hello," Henry replied. "Yes, this is my grandson."

She came around the table to give John her hand. "Pleased to meet you. I'm Robert's wife, Eliza."

"It's nice to meet you," he replied, standing up.

"I don't imagine there's any coffee left?" she asked.

"No, I'm afraid not," said her husband.

John felt awful that they had drunk it all. He never would have asked for any if he had known Mrs. O'Neill would want some when she got home.

"Well," Eliza said. "I guess that gives me an excuse to make a nice cup of tea. It's just freezing outside."

She picked up her husband's empty plate and bowl and carried them into the kitchen. John politely collected his and his grandfather's dishes and followed her into the kitchen.

"Thank you, John. Would you like some tea?"

When she saw his puzzled look, she said, "Why, you've never had tea, have you? It's so soothing. I'll make you a cup and then find some dessert for us all."

John thanked her and returned into the dining room. He found his grandpa and Mr. O'Neill talking about fishing. He sat silently until Mrs. O'Neill brought in the tea.

"Here we are," Eliza said, carrying in a tea tray filled with cups and saucers and dessert. "Earl Grey tea is the only kind Princess Diana will drink. As I understand it, the princess refuses to drink anything except what Mrs. O'Neill, wife of the celebrated author, serves to her guests."

"And notice," laughed Robert, "that Mrs. O'Neill insists on serving it with the special tea set we bought in England to commemorate Queen Elizabeth's coronation."

"If a thing's worth doing, it's worth doing well," Eliza replied, pouring the tea and passing out the cups and plates of cheesecake that especially delighted the Whitman sweet tooth John and Henry shared.

John knew his grandpa would drink tea out of a plastic cup without a second thought, but his mother and grandmother would have delighted in the exquisite tea service. Grandma might, out of jealousy, have been inclined to think Mrs. O'Neill snobbish, but in truth, Eliza O'Neill was devoted to making her guests comfortable.

"Let's go into the library," she said. "It's the most elegant room in the house, so we should drink our tea in there."

John was unprepared for the library. He dreamt of having his own book-room someday, but he was stunned to discover a library could be a room of incomparable beauty. The woodwork on the bookshelves was astounding. The shelves themselves rose halfway up the wall, every inch of them stuffed with books. Above the shelves was delicate blue and green Victorian wallpaper which John would one day recognize as a William Morris pattern. Arranged on the wall were large paintings in vibrant colors by the Pre-Raphaelite school, depicting famous literary scenes. Arranged in the center of the room were little escritoires and high backed chairs designed for hours of comfortable reading. At the room's far end were several Boston ferns leading into a little sunroom complete with a fountain that even on a late autumn day brought a sense of springtime to the room.

"Isn't this the prettiest room you ever saw," said Henry, as John found a seat on the sofa beside his grandfather.

"I never had the heart to change it," said Eliza, "and when Robert married me and came to live here, he agreed I had made the right decision."

"Did you live here first?" asked John. "I thought this was his aunt's house."

"It's complicated," said Eliza, "but Robert's great-aunt was my first husband's grandmother. When she died, my husband and I inherited the house. My husband died soon after during World War I so I lived here by myself for many years until Robert and I married. We feel it's like an ancestral home now. His great-aunt decorated this room about a hundred years ago. The rest of the house we've modernized over the years, but we dared not touch this room; Great-Aunt Carolina could be such a fright of a woman that we were afraid if we changed too much, she might haunt us."

"I think it's a perfect room," said John, who felt Heaven would be to sit here on a sunny morning just reading Anthony Trollope's novels and sipping tea.

"I don't think even my woodworking skills could improve it," Henry said. "I remember when I was a boy my Grandma Dalrymple's parlor had curtains like those – you don't see these types of furnishings anymore."

"No, but the Victorian style will come back someday," said Eliza.

"Nothing stays the same," Robert said. "We just have to get used to that I guess, but here at least, we've managed to preserve a piece of the past."

"Speaking of preserving the past," said Eliza, "Mags and I noticed that the steps to St. John's have now been removed."

"I don't even want to drive by there," said Robert. "I can't imagine what an awful empty sight it will be when the church is gone."

"It's a shame tearing that old church down," said Henry. "It's one of the finest buildings in Marquette."

"I've been a parishioner there all my life," said Eliza. "You know, our parish is the oldest Catholic one in Marquette. The French Catholics purchased that land from the Episcopalians in Marquette's first years. I can even remember when I was nine years old and the old St. John's was torn down to build this new grand one, and now the new one is considered too old and not sturdy enough to stand anymore."

"I can't believe they're tearing it down," said John. "It's so distinctive, so Spanish looking, and all those beautiful statues that were on the roof."

"And now it's going to the wrecking ball," said Robert.

"I can't believe it's being allowed," said Eliza. "That church is a Marquette landmark."

"Let's not discuss it," said Robert. "We can't do anything about it at this point."

John shared the O'Neills' frustration. For nearly a year, the paper had run stories about the closing and eventual destruction of St. John the Baptist Catholic Church. The parishioners had made noble efforts to save it, but the bishop had decided the building was no longer structurally sound, and it was not important enough to the diocese for it to be saved. The parishioners felt betrayed. John mourned that there would be no more flea markets to attend there with his grandpa. The church's destruction would be a woeful day in Marquette's history.

Henry looked at his watch, then said, "Well, I suppose."

"Um," said John, not yet ready to leave, "Mr. O'Neill, I brought one of your books with me; only, I left it out in the car. I was hoping you would sign it for me."

"I'd be happy to," said Robert.

John's face lit up. "I'll be right back," he said, disappearing from the room and going out to the car. He felt foolish not to have brought the book in with him, but he had feared it might be rude to ask for an autograph, never imagining Mr. and Mrs. O'Neill would be so charming.

A minute later, he had returned inside and Mr. O'Neill signed his book.

"Henry," said Eliza, "you're so lucky to have your grandson in town."

"I have four grandchildren," said Henry, "but only John and his brother Chad are in Marquette. Jim's children are all in California so I rarely see them."

"We almost never see our grandchildren," Robert said. "Funny our son Bernie and your son Jim see each other out in California, but we never see them. And our daughter Helen is so busy flying around the country chasing her news stories that she's never settled down with a family."

"She's too old to have children now anyway," said Eliza. "But we did see our grandchildren last spring for Robert's birthday, and they're planning to come for Christmas. I'd say we're lucky we get to see them twice this year."

"I feel sorrier for your grandchildren than for you," said John. "I'd hate not to have grown up with my grandparents nearby."

"He's such a good boy," Eliza told Henry. "Watch out or Robert and I might just adopt him as our own grandson."

John glowed as he left the O'Neills' house. As Henry pulled the car away from the curb, Robert and Eliza stood on the front porch to wave goodbye. John liked them so much. He hoped he could be just like them when he was old, in a beautiful room with lovely books and tea to drink, and best of all, someone to love and grow old with. He and Mr. O'Neill had not even talked about literature, but seeing the author in his everyday surroundings made John appreciate Mr. O'Neill more than if they had discussed books. The O'Neills seemed like real people you could talk to about anything, without needing books as an excuse to visit them. John felt not one of Mr. O'Neill's millions of readers was as lucky as he had been this day.

On a gloomy Sunday morning in early December, Henry woke early. Most mornings, he was up before Beth. He usually got dressed, went out to his shop to light a fire in the old barrel stove so it would be warm when he went out to work, then returned inside to cook breakfast. This morning, Beth was awake enough to hear Henry shut the door as he went out to the shop. She looked at the clock and told herself she should get up, but she did not want to leave the warm bed.

She was still half-asleep when she heard the back door bang open and the fire alarm's beeping, screeching, siren. In panic, she jumped out of bed as she had not done in fifty years. She ran down the hall into the kitchen but saw nothing to give her alarm. Then she looked down the stairs into the laundry room; Henry was covered in flames and struggling to turn on the faucet over the wash tub. Her instincts brought youth back to Beth's old legs. She tore into the bathroom, grabbed a towel, soaked it under the bathtub faucet, then ran into the kitchen. By then, Henry had come up the stairs and was shouting for her. She flung the towel around him, heedless of the flames licking at her own clothes. She smothered and soaked his burning shirt. Wisps of smoke and steam shot up as the flame was doused. She held him for a minute, to make sure the flames were extinguished, to assure herself he was still hers.

After a minute, Henry said, "Go turn off the fire alarm."

She pulled the towel away. As she did, pieces of Henry's flannel shirt dropped to the floor, while other pieces appeared melted to his chest and arms. His body was badly burnt and quickly turning black and red.

Beth turned away, unable to bear looking at him. She went into the hallway and smacked the fire alarm until it quit blaring. In silence, her hand clapped to her mouth, she returned to the kitchen where Henry stood, muttering, "Oh God. Oh God."

"I better call the ambulance," she said.

"No."

"I have to. You're really burnt."

"It'll cost too much. Call Ellen. She can take me to the hospital."

Beth was too shocked to argue. Ellen might think more clearly.

Beth dialed the phone, then watched her husband, half-naked, try to sit down at the kitchen table. His skin was black and red, his hair singed, his cheeks ready to blister.

"Does it hurt?" she asked as the phone rang.

"No, but it will," he said. "Oh God."

His wallet fell onto the floor from where his pants pocket had burnt away. His belt held up the rags that had been pants.

"I didn't know what to do," he started to say when Ellen answered the phone.

John was still in bed. His father had just left to go out for coffee. Ellen was combing her hair in the bathroom, but she ran to get the phone. In a few seconds, John heard his mother sobbing.

"Call the ambulance!" she cried. "It can get there before I can."

Knowing something was wrong, John jumped out of bed and threw on his clothes.

"Then call Uncle Bill. He can be there quicker than me. It'll take me ten minutes. I'll call him. Then I'll meet you at the hospital."

John strained his ears until he was dressed. Then he opened his door and went into the dining room as his mother called Uncle Bill. He listened as she explained to his great-uncle how his grandfather had been burnt and needed to be taken to the hospital. When Ellen hung up the phone she found John and Chad dressed and standing beside her.

"Go get in the car. Uncle Bill will take Grandpa to the hospital. We need to make sure Grandma's all right, and that nothing in Grandpa's shop caught on fire."

The boys were too scared to do anything except put on their shoes and silently go out to the car. Ellen hung up the phone and went into the bathroom to finish combing her hair. Then she found her car keys and purse and went out to the car. Within three minutes of Grandma's phone call, they were driving to town.

"Maybe I'm overreacting," said Ellen. "Maybe it's not as bad as I imagine, but I don't know. I can't believe this could happen."

"It's probably not that bad," said John, unwilling to believe the worst.

"Grandma said his whole shirt was just rags, and his arms, chest, and back are burnt. That's a lot."

Ellen had been a nurse long enough to know the seriousness of burns. She also knew Marquette General Hospital was not able to handle critical burn cases.

When they reached her parents' house, Ellen went straight into the shop to make sure nothing was on fire. She turned off the stove and told John to come back out and check on it while she was at the hospital. Then they went inside. Grandma was sitting at the kitchen table, still in shock. The towel she had used to put out the fire hung over one of the kitchen chairs. Charred pieces of clothing were scattered across the kitchen floor.

Beth started to cry when she saw her daughter. "I can't believe it happened. I put it out as fast as I could. Bill came over right after I talked to you."

She was a bit incoherent. Her arm had a second degree burn. Ellen told her she would call her from the hospital, and that the boys would stay with her until then.

Once Ellen left, John asked his grandmother whether she had eaten breakfast.

"No," said Beth. "Did you boys? I'll make you something."

John said they could just eat cereal, but he understood his grandmother wanted to keep herself occupied. He set the table and Chad made toast.

Beth started cooking the eggs, still trying to believe what had happened. In recent years, she had often feared one day she would wake up and find Henry had gone in his sleep, although she had selfishly hoped she would be the first to go so she would not have to be alone without him. Then she grew angry with herself for thinking such thoughts – he was not gone yet, and she would not believe his time had come. Doctors could do almost anything these days – except operate on her old knees. She must not doubt. He would be fine.

Just as they sat down to eat, the telephone rang.

John jumped up to answer it.

"How's Grandma doing?" his mother asked.

"Worried, but okay," said John. "How's Grandpa?"

"He's in good spirits, talking about the next craft show he's going to, but he's burnt really bad. We have to fly him to the Burn Center in Milwaukee. They'll have to do skin grafts on him. I'm going with him. There's an ambulance plane that will be leaving in forty minutes. I'm going to run home to pack my suitcase and meet it at the airport. You boys stay with Grandma for now; I'll call you when I get to Milwaukee. Okay?"

"Okay," said John.

"Let me talk to Grandma for a minute."

John called his grandmother to the telephone and stood listening to her half of the conversation. "I'm fine." Silence. "How is he?" Silence. "Why?" Silence. "All right, I'm sitting down."

Chad did not feel like eating. He started sweeping up the scattered pieces of burnt clothing.

"Grandpa's going to the hospital in Milwaukee," said John, starting to laugh.

"He is not," Chad said. "How can you joke at a time like this?"

"I'm not joking," John replied. He could not keep a straight face; the situation was too ludicrous to believe.

"He has to go to Milwaukee," said Grandma, hanging up the phone.

Then Chad looked at John, wishing his brother had been joking. He laid the broom against the wall, then asked Grandma what their mother had said.

John swept up the rest of the charred clothes, then carried them out to the garbage can.

A long day stretched ahead of them. They finished their breakfast, although their eggs were cold now. After eating, John called his father, who had just come back from coffee at Wahlstrom's Restaurant. When Tom heard what had happened, he agreed his sons should spend the night with Grandma. He came out to the house, checked the barrel stove and garage to make sure everything was safe, then drove John home to collect what he and Chad would need while they stayed with Grandma.

"You don't need to go to school tomorrow," he told his sons. "It's more important you're with Grandma. Will you be okay staying with her?"

"Yes," said John, "we'll be fine." He tried to be brave, but he did not know what he would do except to call the hospital if Grandma had any problems.

Tom stayed until after supper. In the afternoon, Aunt Eleanor and Uncle Bill came over. Bill told Beth that Henry had been in good spirits at the hospital, and the doctors and nurses were being nice to him. He would be in good hands in Milwaukee because he would have specialists to treat him, and since Ellen was a nurse, she would make sure he got the best care.

After all the visitors left, John, Chad, and Beth sat down to watch *60 Minutes*, not knowing what else to do. Then Ellen called from Milwaukee. She told John that Grandpa was resting peacefully, and after they ran some tests tomorrow, they'd be doing skin grafts the next day. He had burnt forty percent of his body; his recovery could take months, but they should only tell Grandma he was doing fine until they knew more details. After John talked to his mother, Chad talked to her, and then Grandma, and then Grandma repeated to the boys what they already knew.

The next day, John drove Grandma to the doctor to get a tetanus shot and have her own burn treated. The doctor and nurse knew Ellen from the hospital, so they expressed their concerns; John thanked them while fighting to keep down his own emotions. At night, John slept in his Uncle Jim's room, while Chad slept in his mother's old room. John spent the night worrying, praying, bargaining with God that he would be good, that he would be a priest, or whatever God wanted, if only Grandpa would live.

After two more nights, Eleanor and her girls took turns staying week-nights with Beth so the boys could get enough sleep for school. John and Chad returned to stay with Grandma the next weekend. They spent that weekend watching TV while Beth slept most of the day in her chair, the newspaper constantly sliding out of her hands. Almost the only thing she ever said now was, "I hope to God he makes it."

John occupied himself by feeding Grandpa's squirrels. The little creatures did not know where their benefactor had gone, but they were scarcely concerned so long as they received their treats. How unfair, John thought, that life should go on, that Nature should not even notice the tragedy in his life. His grandfather had always gone out of his way to take care of the family – his parents, brothers and sisters, wife, children and grandchildren, the men who worked for him, the neighbors, even the least of God's creatures, the squirrels and chipmunks, yet he was repaid with tragedy? Even John's most fervent prayers were ignored; Ellen called to say Grandpa's kidneys were failing from the strain and shock done to his body.

The second weekend, Tom drove the boys over to Grandma's house on Friday night. They bought hamburgers at Hardee's, and Tom stayed for supper. After he left, Grandma and the boys sat down in front of the television waiting for Ellen's nightly eight o'clock telephone update.

Just after seven o'clock, Eleanor, Lucy, and Maud came over.

"They're probably bringing me more soup I don't want," said Beth, although she knew they meant well.

No one went to open the door because relatives always let themselves in. The visitors found their way into the living room.

"Hi, Eleanor, how are you?" said Beth.

"Okay," replied Eleanor, ringing her hands. Lucy crossed the room to sit down in her Uncle Henry's chair. She reached over and took Aunt Beth's hand.

John saw his Grandma's face sink.

"Oh," she gasped. "He died, didn't he?"

Eleanor's face confirmed the bad news.

"Ellen called us," said Maud. "She wanted us to tell you rather than for you to hear it over the phone."

"She's on her way home," Eleanor said, "but she probably won't get here until around midnight."

It was the worst evening of John's life, and he knew it was even worse for his grandmother. He had seldom seen her without her glasses, but now she removed them to wipe away her tears. He watched her eyes become swollen and red, even bloodshot. She told Lucy she did not want to live anymore, but Lucy reminded her that her children and grandchildren needed her. John wanted to hide in the bathroom and cry. Instead, he called to tell his dad that Grandpa had died and Mom was coming home. Soon other relatives and neighbors came over to express their sympathies. Aunt Eleanor played hostess. Lucy and Maud helped lay out food trays, pour drinks, and make snacks for the company. Maud told John to sit with his grandmother and hold her hand. John did as he was told, awkwardly muttering meaningless phrases. "It's okay, Grandma. He's in a better place now. He's with God. It's better that he's not suffering any longer." John wished someone would explain to him how God could let this atrocity happen.

The long evening dragged out until Ellen reached home. Then there were plenty of tears as she hugged her mother and children. Aunt Eleanor insisted she would spend the night with Beth so Ellen could go home and sleep after her long drive home from Milwaukee. The boys rode home with their mother; on the way, Ellen told them about the Milwaukee Burn Center, how nice everyone had been to Grandpa, how good the food had been in the cafeteria, what neat things were in the hospital gift shop where she had bought Mountain Dew and magazines, what Grandpa had looked like hooked up to life-support machines, and how he had hallucinated about building houses and Uncle Bill bringing him the wrong size nails. The boys said not a word. They did not know how to comfort their mother.

When they got home, they went straight to bed. Ellen came to kiss John goodnight. "I'm sorry you lost your grandpa," she told him.

He did not know what to say. How could she even be concerned about him when her father had just died?

The family got through the funeral. Grandpa had not gone to church in fifty years, but the funeral must be religious. Grandma wanted him buried in Holy Cross Cemetery, not in Park Cemetery with his Protestant relatives. To compromise, Ellen asked the priest from St. Michael's to say the funeral service at the Swanson Funeral Home. Then the Baptist minister said a prayer at the Catholic cemetery, and the funeral luncheon was held at the Baptist church.

For days, visitors came to Henry and Beth's house. Everyone stuffed themselves on food from meat and cheese trays, and they wondered what to do with all the funeral flowers. Uncle Jim and Aunt Lisa came for the funeral and stayed with Grandma for a week. Aunt Ada came from Louisiana and returned home with several of her brother's flannel shirts so she could make a quilt in his memory. There were moments when John lost himself in being part of the family gatherings until he nearly forgot his grandfather was not there. Then he would notice Cousin Joseph Dalrymple or Maud or a neighbor sitting in his grandfather's chair, and emptiness would overwhelm him.

Life went on. The visitors quit coming everyday; the out-of-town relatives returned home. Ellen and Beth argued about whether she would continue to live in her own home now that she was alone. Beth won the argument. She insisted she would stay in her house; she would not go live in Snowberry Heights or with her daughter. She wanted things to remain as normal as possible. John felt things could never be normal again.

A few days before Christmas, John went to get his hair cut at Pete's Barbershop on Washington Street. As he left the barbershop, he heard a horrendous noise from the East. He got into the car and drove toward the lake. Within a few seconds, he saw a crowd gathered along the street watching a giant wrecking ball swinging into the walls of St. John the Baptist Catholic Church. He watched aghast as brick and mortar collapsed into what had once been the sanctuary. Fortunately, the stained glass windows had been removed and sold. The antique pipe organ had gone to St. Mary-St. Joseph Church in Iron Mountain, the bells from the tower were sent to St. Francis de Sales Church in Manistique, the rose window donated to John's own parish of St. Michael's. Only the bell tower was left behind, to remain attached to the old parish office that would now be an office building. The ruin was devastating.

"They couldn't even wait until after Christmas to tear it down!" John raged. He had never attended a service there, but it had been a beautiful church, the church the O'Neills attended, the church where he had gone to flea markets with his grandfather. All the way home, sobs burst from his throat as he drove with tear-smeared eyes.

Nothing made sense anymore. He would never again know the innocence of childhood. Never feel the old comforts around him. Grandpa was gone. Life might go on, but now it was a miserable, grey, uncertain life that even God could not control; not when He let His churches be destroyed; not when good, kind men met tragic deaths.

1988-1989

John was embarrassed. It was bad enough to have his dorky little brother along, but his mom and dad were worse. Mom was always fussing over him, and Dad was already crabbing at Chad. John's brother and father could not even carry boxes up to his dorm room at Northern Michigan University without hollering at each other. John was glad he did not meet any of his future neighbors in the hallway. The four Vandelaares lugged suitcases and pillows down the hall while glancing at all the room numbers. At the far end of the building, the bass from someone's stereo speakers was pounding and bouncing off the cement block walls.

"I hope these kids aren't always this loud," Ellen said. "How will you get any studying done?"

"I'll be fine, Mom," John said for the umpteenth time. He knew she was having a hard time seeing her first child leave home, even if he would only be a few miles away. He wished for her sake that everything were going better today; that his family were not arguing and his neighbors were not so noisy. But he also wished she would quit worrying for just five minutes; she was only making him more nervous.

They continued down the hall toward the blasting stereo until they stood before an open door, with John's room number on it, and the stereo visible from the doorway.

"This is it," said John, bravely stepping forward before his family could complain about the noise. His brother and father hesitated. Ellen raised her eyebrows but followed. In the room, a tall, large-chested young man was tilting backward on a chair; his long, jean-clad legs ended in giant tennis shoes that were propped up on a bed; he had a baseball cap turned backwards on his head, and his fingers fiddled with the joystick to a video game, although the TV screen was blank.

"Uh, hi, I'm John, your roommate," John shouted over the harmony of Megadeath.

"Hey, I'm Frank," said his roommate, barely glancing away from the video game. Then, from the corner of his eye, he saw John's parents, so he set down the joystick and stood up. He towered a couple inches above John; John instantly felt intimidated as well as out of place amid video games and heavy metal.

"These are my parents and brother, Chad," John said. "They're helping me move in."

Frank just nodded. The stereo was so loud he could not hear John clearly.

Chad started to remove clothes hangers from a box. Ellen opened the closet door and hung up the clothes. Frank, realizing John's family would be staying for a while, politely stepped over to the stereo and turned down the volume.

"We have to go get some more things from the car," John told Frank.

"No problem. Something's wrong with the way I hooked up the VCR so I'll be here figuring it out."

"Okay," said John, leading his family out of the room.

"He's not too friendly, is he?" said Tom in the hallway.

"Shh, he'll hear you," said Ellen.

"He shouldn't have his feet on the bed," said Chad.

"He could have offered to help us," said Tom.

John was too nervous to say anything, but he did not think he would like Frank.

They returned to find Frank fiddling with a power cord.

"It sucks that there aren't more outlets," he said.

Ellen smiled in sympathy. "Where are you from, Frank?"

"Pelkie."

"Where's that?" asked John.

"Near Baraga. Where're you from?"

"Marquette," said Chad; his tone declared his town's superiority.

"Did your folks come up with you, Frank?" Ellen asked.

"Just my dad. He left before you got here."

"I imagine it will be hard for you at first, being so far from home," said Ellen.

Frank shrugged; his facial expression suggested he was glad to be away from his parents.

"John'll have to bring you over some time for a home cooked meal," said Ellen.

"Sounds good. I hear the cafeteria food sucks," Frank said while putting in a videotape to see whether the VCR worked yet.

Ellen gave up trying to be friendly and started to arrange John's clothes in the dresser. John cooperated by saying as little as possible so his parents would leave all the sooner. He would rather put his clothes where he wanted, but instead of arguing with his mother, he planned to rearrange everything after she left. What annoyed him most was the way she kept commenting about his clothes; he was suddenly ashamed of everything he wore; his mother had insisted he would need nice clothes for college, but Frank's appearance made John feel he would be overdressed.

"Okay, let's inspect the bathroom," said Ellen, once the dresser was full. She was distressed that John could not lock the suitemates' door to the bathroom; any of the other three boys in the suite could walk in while he was in the shower or on the toilet. "At least the floor is relatively clean," she said. "I was worried you'd get athlete's foot. You be sure to scrub out the shower every couple days."

"Yes, Mom."

"And make sure the other boys help you, but don't pick up after them, and don't endanger your health either because they're lazy."

"Yes, Mom."

"Ellen, you about ready to go?" Tom asked, sticking his head into the bathroom while Chad watched Frank play his video game without either speaking.

"I guess so," said Ellen, unprepared to abandon her firstborn.

She came out of the bathroom and said to Frank, "What are you boys going to do for supper? Would you like to go get a hamburger with us?"

"No, thanks. I'll just go to the cafeteria," said Frank. "John can come with me if he likes."

"Do you know where the cafeteria is?" Ellen asked her son.

"Yeah, they showed me at orientation."

He did not remember how to get there, but he would not prolong his parents' visit by admitting it. He figured he would just pretend he knew where he was going by following Frank.

"Let's go then," said Tom, bored and impatient.

"All right," said Ellen. "Call me if you need anything, John."

"All right."

"See you later," said Tom.

"Bye," said Chad.

"Bye."

Ellen wanted to kiss John goodbye, but the look on his face made it clear she had better not.

"Remember, you can call us anytime," she said. "And Grandma only lives a few blocks away so be sure to stop over and see her once in a while."

"Okay. Goodbye," said John, trying to get his family out the door.

"Home will be quiet without you," Ellen said as she stepped into the hall where Tom and Chad waited impatiently. John felt bad. He could see his mother was upset, but he was too embarrassed to step into the hall so she could hug him.

Ellen managed to make it back to the car before the tears came.

"He's only ten minutes away," laughed Tom.

"I know," Ellen said, "but he's my son so I'm going to miss him."

"Do we have to go to Hardee's for supper?" Chad asked. "Can't we go somewhere decent to eat?"

John waited a few seconds after his parents left, then shut the door. He sat down on his bed and watched Frank play his video game for a couple minutes. Neither said anything. Already, John wanted to avoid contact with people by sticking his nose in a book, but he thought he had better try to be friendly. He wondered whether he and Frank would find they had anything in common.

"So, Frank, how come I didn't meet you at orientation?" he asked.

"I was sick, puking up my guts, so I ended up going to a later one," said Frank, madly jolting his joystick. "Damn it! I can never get past that level."

He set down the game controls.

"You wanna go eat now?"

"Sure," said John.

"Just let me take a piss first," said Frank, disappearing into the bathroom.

John waited. When he heard the toilet flush, he opened the room door and stepped into the hall. Frank joined him in a second.

"You got a key, man?" he asked John.

"Yeah."

"I got mine, but bring yours just in case I lose it."

They locked the door and started down the hall.

"Have you met our suitemates?" John asked.

"No, haven't seen any sign of them yet."

Once they were outside, Frank said, "I think the cafe's this way, but if not, we'll just take the scenic tour I guess."

"That's all right," said John, relieved that Frank was as lost as he was. "So what's your major?"

"Business. How about you?"

"English."

"English was my worst subject in school."

"I guess you don't read much then," said John.

"No, it's kind of boring. No offense."

"That's okay. I don't know anything about business."

"You going to join any sports or a fraternity or anything?"

"I don't know," said John, although he knew he would not.

"After supper," said Frank, "I thought I'd go check out the Hyper. You want to come along?"

John nervously asked what the Hyper was. If it were a bar or college hangout, he did not want to go.

"It's the Phys. Ed. building – HPER stands for something like Health and Physical Education and Recreation. But everyone just calls it the Hyper."

"Oh," said John, realizing the word was a string of initials, although there was no "Y" sound in it. "I guess I don't mind going." He had no interest in physical fitness, but he would rather stick with Frank than be alone his first night on campus.

"I want to see what kind of weight machines they have. Do you work out?"

John felt Frank's eyes appraise his thin physique.

"No," he said, feeling inferior to his tall, broad-shouldered roommate.

"You play any sports?"

"I swim a lot," said John, which was partly true.

"Were you on the team in high school?"

"No, I just do it for fun."

"I hear they got a big pool in the Hyper, and a high diving board. I played high school football, but I hurt my knee last fall so I didn't go out for the team here. I was on the wrestling team too. I'm thinking since I can't run no more, I'd like to get into bodybuilding. I got the height and strength for it, but need to work on my tone. I want to learn more about nutrition so I can burn fat and build muscle mass."

"You look really strong," said John.

"Yeah," laughed Frank, "I could bench press you." He gave John a friendly punch on the arm. He was only teasing, but John felt humiliated. Still, John could not help asking, "How much weight can you lift?"

"Two-eighty."

"Wow!" said John. That seemed an impossible number to him, but from the looks of Frank, he did not think his roommate exaggerated.

"So, if you don't play sports, what do you do?" asked Frank.

"I get some exercise. I walk a lot." He did walk Dickens a lot because he enjoyed spending time in the woods. "Otherwise, I mostly read." He figured Frank would think reading bad enough, so he would not mention that he wrote novels. He would break that to Frank later – after all, writing occupied most of his spare time so Frank would know soon enough.

"You ever read any Stephen King? He's the only one whose books I like."

John thought it better to be illiterate than to corrupt the mind with mass-produced, moneymaking bestsellers. "I don't care for Stephen King," he said.

"Really? Then what do you read?"

John decided to confess; Frank would see him read many books while they were roommates.

"I like Charles Dickens."

"You're kidding!" said Frank. "You must be one of the smart kids. Did you have a good GPA in high school?"

"Not that good," John lied.

"What was it?"

Again John decided the truth might as well come out.

"3.7."

Frank whistled. "I had a 2.1. Bet you're surprised I even got into college."

John was more surprised Frank would admit his GPA had been so low. Frank clearly did not know when to keep his mouth shut so he would not look foolish.

"There's the place," said Frank, as they approached the down campus cafeteria.

Soon they were in line with dozens of other confused freshmen and several rude upper classmen who shoved their way through the line in evident despisement of all newcomers. Frank and John were lucky to find a table of their own where they could sit alone and observe everyone else; John spotted a couple kids sitting by themselves, not having yet met their roommates or made friends. John was thankful he was not among them. Frank was a better companion than none at all.

John and Frank's conversation consisted of what classes they had that semester, and critiquing the cafeteria food, which both agreed was better than expected, although within a few weeks they would be sick of it. When they finished eating, they piled up their trays near the garbage cans and stepped back outside. Then they tried to figure out how to reach the Hyper. Frank had no clue where it was; neither did John until Frank said, "Well, I know it's next to the football stadium, wherever that is." Then John used his Marquette native background to lead them down Center Street for several blocks until they reached Presque Isle Avenue. From there, they crossed the street. John pointed out the football stadium behind Hardee's. They took a side road until they came to the stadium and then saw to its left a large brown brick building with writing on the side stating it was the Health and Physical Education and Recreation facility.

"Cool," said Frank. "It's not too far. I can jog over here to get my heart rate pumping before I lift weights."

Once inside, they asked directions from a fellow student, then went down a long hallway and a few shorter ones to the Turf Room, which John thought as big as a football stadium; they checked out the two swimming pools, one for relays, the other with a gigantic diving board that Frank said would hurt his balls if he jumped from it. To one up Frank, John boasted that he would love to dive off it, but secretly he also found it intimidating. Then they went to the weight room.

John followed Frank around as he stopped at each weight machine, looking to see the maximum amount of weight available to lift at each station, and which muscles each machine would help to tone. Next they looked at the free weights, the exercise bikes, and the suggested workout charts on the walls. John pretended to be interested. A couple guys who looked like football players were busy lifting, only stopping every few minutes to flex and admire their biceps. Frank watched them with admiration since they were even bigger than him. John noticed, however, that Frank received several respectful nods from guys his size or smaller. John felt out of place, yet he was pleased when Frank asked whether he wanted to work out with him regularly to get "buff". John agreed, figuring none of the big guys would harass him so long as he was with Frank.

It was almost dark when they left the Hyper. The evening air made John feel relaxed, and he did not mind listening to Frank talk all the way home about bodybuilding.

"Who do you think is the greatest bodybuilder?" Frank asked.

"I don't know," said John, naming the only bodybuilder he knew. "Arnold Schwarzeneggar I guess."

"Yeah, he's incredible. Lou Ferrigno's a lot bigger, but Arnold's got better definition. You know who I really admire though is Mike Mentzer; his pecks are huge, and I think his mustache makes him look more mature and strong. I've thought about growing a mustache to look older. What do you think?"

"I don't know," said John, looking curiously at his roommate's face. "It's getting too dark out for me to see you, so I have a hard time picturing you with a mustache."

"I didn't see many guys at the weight room with mustaches. Those other guys are mostly football players, so they're there to bulk up, not to get toned or define their abs and back muscles. I don't think bulk is as attractive as being really ripped."

"Me either," said John to be agreeable.

"I'm sure glad you know your way back to the dorm," said Frank. "It's good I have a roommate from Marquette to show me around. I wasn't sure I'd like it here since I didn't know anyone, but you can introduce me to people."

John doubted he knew any more people than Frank. He did not have any high school friends who were going to Northern. But he was glad Frank seemed to appreciate him, even if they had nothing in common. They walked up Center Street, then around the Circle Drive, and down the hill to their dorm. When they went in the door, they spotted a coke and a snack machine. John bought a candy bar. Frank said, "I can't eat those since I'm trying to get into condition." But he insisted on buying John a coke for showing him how to get to the Hyper.

Once back in their room, they settled down on their beds to watch *Married With Children*. John had never seen it before; Frank said it was "the funniest show on television." John thought some of the sexual innuendoes were vulgar, but he could not help laughing because Al Bundy reminded him somewhat of his own father. After the show, Frank flipped the channels with the remote control until he found a movie. "Hey, this is *Night of the Comet*; ever seen it? It's about this comet that kills everyone on earth except people in metal buildings; a few others survive but they're mutants and want to eat the people who are still normal. It's awesome."

Frank got involved in the film. John watched for a while, but he was too tired to concentrate. He was also nervous about school. He wondered what his professors would be like, and whether the work would be a lot harder than high school, which had been easy and boring. He was irritated because he was an English major, yet at orientation, he had been told to sign up for classes to fulfill his liberal studies requirements; his first semester, he would not have a single English class; instead, he had chemistry, physical geography, social problems, and history of Western civilization. Only the last class held the slightest interest for him. He started to wonder what he was doing here at all. All he wanted to do was to write and study literature; the university claimed all these classes would make students "well-rounded", but John suspected it was to suck tuition money out of students.

John woke from his daydream when he heard Frank snoring, despite the fascinating, comet-stricken cannibals. John silently regarded his roommate. Stretched across the bed, Frank looked bigger than before. He was not handsome; nor had his conversation made John think him terribly bright. But John liked him. At least he knew someone now, which made him feel safe. And Frank seemed to be outgoing. Maybe the real education of college would be for him to meet people and learn about them, which would help his writing more than extraneous chemistry and geography classes. Maybe the two years of sadness since his grandfather's death were now coming to an end. John had not felt close to anyone in high school, and as much as he loved to read, he had grown tired of always having his nose stuck in a book. Perhaps at college, he might start to live life rather than merely read about it.

He got up to use the bathroom. Then he put a blanket over his snoring roommate, turned off the light and the TV, and crawled into bed.

That autumn, Marquette was shocked by its first murder in many years. In the early morning hours of Wednesday, September 28th, a man's body was found at Presque Isle Park, a short distance from Chief Kawbawgam's grave. Murder in Marquette was stunning enough; that it would happen beside the resting place of one of its patriarchs seemed sacrilegious. In the next few days, gruesome details surfaced. Paul Gerard had already been dead several hours when his body was found; no murder weapon or any substantial clues to the killer's identity were discovered. The murder had obviously been violent; a struggle must have taken place because the killer had stabbed Gerard forty times, presumably to ensure his death.

All of Marquette was outraged, repulsed, and frightened. On the streets, in restaurants, in the privacy of their homes, people speculated about what could have caused anyone in their peaceful city to commit such an atrocious deed. Little old ladies who had never once felt unsafe in their hometown now locked their doors at night. College students did not leave their dorms except in groups. Rumors were rampant, and the criminal investigation proved many of them to be true. Paul Gerard had been openly homosexual and known to have male companions, including hitchhikers he had picked up on the streets. His neighbors reported seeing sketchy characters passing in and out of his little Division Street home at all hours of the night. No one could believe such deviant behavior or such brutal punishment could happen in their town. Marquette was nearly five hundred miles from hideous, crime-ridden Detroit. No. Never. It couldn't be. But it was. What did it mean? What would the future be if this could happen in the Upper Peninsula?

Eleanor Goldman could scarcely enjoy her birthday party a couple nights following the murder. Her daughters had planned a special meal and invited all the relatives. Beth baked a beautiful chocolate cake, and Eleanor managed to blow out all the candles on the first try. But when it grew dark enough to pull the drapes, everyone felt another crime might be committed. After all, the murderer had not yet been caught – worse, he never would be. They were all nervous about venturing out to their cars to drive home. They dared not get in a vehicle without checking whether anyone were hiding in the back seat, waiting to spring out on them. Murder was all they could think about; when they were not discussing it, they were trying to think of other topics to divert their thoughts.

"The murderer must have been from downstate," Lucy said when murder became the birthday party topic of choice. "I'm sure we have nothing to worry about; I bet the murderer has long since left the state; probably gone into hiding in Canada."

"You never know these days," Ellen shook her head. "It could be someone from Marquette."

"The kids at school say it has something to do with drugs," said Chad.

"I didn't hear that," said Ellen.

"If it had to do with drugs, then the murderer probably was from downstate," said Maud. "Those darn people from Detroit are always bringing drugs up here, as if alcoholism isn't already a big enough problem in the U.P."

"Well," said Bill, "those fags are all a bunch of druggies anyway."

"Uncle Bill," said Ellen, "not all gay people are on drugs."

Lucy and Maud rolled their eyes, knowing it was pointless to argue with Uncle Bill.

"I don't see why it's surprising for fags to be on drugs, considering the other stuff they do sure isn't natural," said Bill. "It would serve them fags right if all the ones who don't die from AIDS die from drug overdoses."

Beth felt uncomfortable. She could not believe this conversation. In her day – never – you would never talk about men with those unnatural problems – never – but then, neither would you talk about people on drugs. Even the

Chicago mobsters back then only drank and shot people, but now there was all this cocaine and heroine and shooting up with needles, and films like that *Dirty Dancing* she had seen film clips of on *The Oprah Winfrey Show* – why it had been just like having sex with your clothes on! She felt nauseous just thinking about it. She was glad she would not be around much longer, but she worried about her grandchildren living in such a wicked world.

"I just read," said Eleanor, "something about drug users in *The National Enquirer*. Something about some rock star who overdosed and killed himself. I think he was gay too."

John exchanged amused looks with his brother. He loved Aunt Eleanor dearly, but in a more innocent way, she was just as narrow-minded as Uncle Bill.

"*The National Enquirer!*" said Bill. "That paper's just bullshit."

Beth blushed at such language.

"People are usually murdered by someone they know," said Maud. "If this Gerard fellow was gay, he was probably murdered by a spurned lover or someone like that. It's still awful, but not as scary as a random crime, like a drive-by shooting."

"Marquette's still a safe place," said John, unwilling to believe otherwise. "I'm not going to worry."

"Well, until they catch the killer," Ellen told him, "I don't want you walking around campus at night by yourself. Not even back and forth from the library. You have Frank come pick you up in his car if you're going to be at the library late."

"You're mother's right," said Eleanor. "We can't take our safety for granted anymore. Marquette isn't like when I was young and everyone knew everyone else. Why there's something like twenty-five thousand people living here now and that big sports building they're putting up – the world's largest wooden dome or whatever they claim it is, it's only going to attract more people here."

"I doubt it," said Tom. "No one's going to come all the way up here to see that dome."

"They're only building the dome," said Ellen, "because NMU is going to be an Olympic training center, and they want to impress the governor so he'll give the school more money."

"It just makes me sick to think what that dome and the Olympics will attract to this area," said Eleanor. "All those kids training for Olympic boxing will be coming up from Detroit, nothing but a bunch of undesirables from the ghettos. They'll only bring trouble with them."

"Having them kids boxing is better than their doing drugs," said Tom. "Boxing'll give them a chance to make something of themselves."

"Well," Eleanor said, "people think the dome will attract big entertainers to town like that Madonna. We don't need her type in Marquette, not after the kind of music videos I hear she makes, but there'll be busloads of undesirables coming up from Detroit and Chicago to see her."

"Or else rich people," said Bill. "They'll see how nice the U.P. is, then buy up all the land, and stick up their damn "NO TRESPASSING" signs everywhere."

"It's all about money," said Eleanor. "People just want to bring money into the area. They don't care whether it ruins the town. I'm glad I won't be around many more years to see Marquette destroyed."

John feared he would be around that long – he suspected by the time he was Aunt Eleanor's age, he would not recognize his hometown. He did not like the thought.

"Well, it's getting late. We better go," said Ellen. "We have to drop John back off at the college."

The party broke up, and John's family drove him back to his dorm.

Frank greeted him by laughing, "I see you didn't get murdered yet." John and Frank's suitemates, Derek and Steve, were there, having video game playoffs.

"Hey, John," said Steve, who was sitting out the present round. "A girl in my accounting class invited me to this wild party tomorrow night. You wanna go? The rest of us are."

John felt uncomfortable at big parties, but he did not want to spend Saturday night alone in his dorm room.

"Sure," he said.

Twenty-four hours later, he would think how shocked Aunt Eleanor would be if she went to a college party; so many of the undesirables she feared were apparently already in Marquette.

The boys left for the party an hour after dark. Several blocks south of the university on one of those avenues branching off Fourth Street, stands one of Marquette's innumerable older, but uncared for houses. The eyesore building is undoubtedly owned by a slum lord who charges overpriced rent to struggling students until half a dozen of them must waste their meager assets for a shelter they can scarcely afford and for which upkeep is unknown. The house is the vexation of every neighbor, and because it was rundown when they moved in, the college students feel no need to care for it, so its dilapidation progresses each semester. Such a house was the scene of that Saturday night's great college beer drinking party.

In the growing darkness, Derek and Steve, Frank and John did not notice the house's peeling paint or its blanched and faded siding, and if they had, the sordidness would have only added to its enticement. They did notice a few guys standing under the porch light, beer cans in hand, signaling this place as a party haven. As the four suitemates climbed the porch steps, the half-dozen boyish men, fashionably dressed in jean shorts, sweatshirts and backward baseball caps, beer cans in hand to complete their ensembles, coolly nodded at the newcomers who subtly raised their hands and swaggered through the doors of this underage speakeasy.

A few lamps, collected by the house's residents from St. Vinnie's and their grandmothers' attics, lighted various corners of the two large front rooms where the party animals drifted in and out. The hallways were packed with people holding plastic beer cups inevitably to be sloshed on passersby squeezing their way into the kitchen where bags of chips were laid out amid cases of beer, and a few glasses in which to mix coke and rum. In the bathroom, hidden in the tub, was the glorious keg to which all party animals must pay homage. Then after several visits to the glorious keg, a mandatory final visit must be made on one's knees to the porcelain goddess to offer up libations. Of course, upstairs were beds for more serious evening rituals.

As John and company entered, they were greeted by more cool nods from guys, some appraising looks from blonde sorority girls, and a few shouts of "Hey Frank!" In just a couple months, Frank had become recognized as one of the big freshmen on campus, more because he was big than cool, although to be cool only required being big and the ability to down a half dozen beers without becoming sick. John knew most girls were hot for his roommate; he had first expected that once Frank opened his mouth, his attraction would lessen, but John soon learned he had overestimated many college girls' intelligence.

Once inside the house, Frank tried to tell John about a certain blonde girl in the room, but John could not hear him. Heavy metal was blasting from the stereo speakers, occasionally interchanged with some of the new "rap crap", or so it was called by the white boys present, and save for a couple air force kids, this was the U.P., so they were all white boys. John asked "What?" but Frank did not hear him. Instead, he led John into the kitchen where he grabbed a

Miller can and handed one to John. Steve and Derek had already popped open cans and were guzzling down beer with the aim to get drunk as fast as possible. John knew all about peer pressure, he knew the law said he was a minor, and he knew that surrounded by fifty other beer guzzlers, he could not refuse. He would just sip it slowly. He followed his friends back into the front room, leaned up against a wall, nursed his beer, which he found he rather liked, and wondered what he would do if the cops busted the party.

Frank was hi-fiving football players he had met at the weight room. A couple of them nodded at John, recognizing him from when he worked out with Frank a couple nights a week, although he had seen little improvement in his biceps. Some forward girls came up to talk to Frank. Steve and Derek tried to flirt with the girls by cracking jokes no one could hear over the pounding music. John smiled and pretended to enjoy himself, but he found trying to have a good time rather exhausting when he could not hear himself talk or think.

Frank went to get another beer. He asked whether John needed another, but John said he was good for now. Derek and Steve helped the crowd pull back the furniture so people could dirty dance to "I Want Your Sex". John nervously feigned intense interest in his beer. He lied to himself that he did not feel lonely standing by himself.

Then he saw a guy with a bushy mustache staring at him from across the room. First John thought maybe it was someone from one of his classes, but then he realized the guy was older than him; when the man started walking toward him, John feared because he was a minor, he was going to be tossed out.

"Hey," said the man, "how are ya?"

"Okay," said John, not feeling okay.

"You don't recognize me, do ya? I'm Alan, your cousin."

It took John a minute. Uncle Bill's youngest son.

"Hey," said John. "I didn't know you were going to Northern."

"Yeah, I dropped out a few years ago, but started up again this fall. You a freshman?"

"Yeah," said John. He felt strange talking to Alan. What if Alan told Uncle Bill he had seen him, and Uncle Bill would tell Aunt Eleanor, who would be sure to tattle to his mom that he had been drinking.

"What are you going to school for?" John asked.

"Criminal justice," said Alan.

"Great," thought John, "and here I am, being a criminal underage drinker."

"You must have emptied that beer by now," said Alan. "You don't want that crap anyway. Let me get you some good stuff. Come on."

Alan led him back to the kitchen. John remembered Alan was the closest to him in age of Uncle Bill's sons – Alan was really his mother's cousin, not his, but Alan had always been nice to him when he was little. He was glad to know someone here.

"Here's where I keep the good stuff," said Alan, opening a cupboard and pulling out a bottle of tequila. "I only share it with my special guests."

"Oh," said John, unable to summon the required gratitude for such an honor.

"Say, where you living?" Alan asked, as he handed John a glass. "I got an empty room upstairs if you need a place."

"I'm in the dorms," said John. "My roommate's around here somewhere."

"Oh, is he the tall blond guy you came in with?"

"Yeah," said John, wishing Alan would not pour so much into his glass. He knew tequila was hard liquor so he was afraid of what it might do to him.

"The girls like your roommate," said Alan. "You can bring him to my parties anytime; hunks like him always attract more girls, and since he can't have them all, some are bound to fall for me once they're drunk enough."

John was uncomfortable discussing how to take advantage of girls. He asked, "Is this your house?"

"Yeah. I bought it myself, and the rent from my roommates more than pays the mortgage. I've had it for two years now. Couldn't stand living with my mom anymore, and you just throw your money away when you rent, so I bought this place. I have parties here all the time. Feel free to come whenever you want."

"Thanks," said John, impressed that his cousin owned his own place while still in his early twenties, even if the place were rather a dump.

"Hey, Sheila!" Alan yelled to a girl entering the room. "I want ya ta meet someone. This here's my cousin, John."

Sheila came across the room. John offered her his hand, but she barely touched it. John's Grandma would have said, "Sheila's a hussy", and Frank would have said, "That Sheila chick's a bitch," but Alan clearly liked her.

"Honey," she whined, "when you coming upstairs with me?"

"In a little while. There's too many people here right now."

"You're such a prude," she laughed. "I have to pee."

She disappeared into the bathroom.

Alan whispered in John's ear, nearly spitting, "She's a bitch, but she's sure got great tits. You got a girl?"

"No," John said.

"I can hook you up with one. I know lots of girls, including some fine sorority chicks. Most of them wear too much makeup, but that don't matter in the dark."

Alan leered at John, who noticed for the first time how much his cousin looked like Uncle Bill. Both his older cousins, William and Jason, were married with children, but apparently, Alan was a playboy like his father. John had always liked Alan best of the three brothers, but probably because Alan was closest in age, not for any morals he possessed. Then again, the jury was still out on how successful William and Jason's marriages would be.

"Honey," Sheila shouted from the bathroom. "Come here! My zipper's stuck."

Alan grinned at John, then took the tequila bottle with him into the bathroom, and shut the door.

John wished he could leave. He went back to the living room where Frank was dancing, or rather grinding against a girl, only their pelvises touching. John would have left then except that he had driven Frank here. He found an empty place to lean against the wall and slowly sipped the tequila until he felt light-headed. He knew he should not drink anymore after he emptied his glass, but he was surprisingly pleased by the lightheaded feeling he had.

After a few minutes, Frank came over with his dirty dancing partner.

"Hey, John, what you drinking?"

"Tequila," he shouted, hoping to appear cool before Frank's pretty redhead.

"Where'd you get it?"

"My cousin."

"Who's your cousin?" asked the girl.

"This is Renee," said Frank. "She's in my psychology class."

John thought Frank and Renee would make an interesting Freudian study. "Alan Whitman," he said.

"You didn't tell me you knew Alan," said Frank. "Man, we probably missed two of his parties because you didn't tell me sooner."

"I didn't know he owned this house until tonight," said John. "I haven't seen him for a while."

"I'm thirsty," said Renee. "Let's get some beer." She wrapped her arm around Frank and guided him to the kitchen with her hand in his back jeans pocket.

John thought about following them to tell Frank he wanted to leave. But he did not want to overhear Alan and Sheila at it in the bathroom, and he doubted Frank would go since he had just hooked up with a girl. John strained his eyes to find Steve and Derek in the crowd, but before he spotted them, Doreen appeared.

Doreen worked in the cafeteria and lived on the floor below John and Frank. Everyday she tried to flirt with Frank when he came through the lunch line, and everyday he scowled at her.

"Hi, John," she said.

"Hi," he muttered. He did not wish to be rude, but he could not be friendly to her. He would rather be a wallflower than be seen talking to a weird girl.

"Having fun?" she asked.

He nodded.

"You come with Frank?"

"Yeah."

"I came with Lori. That's my roommate."

"I know," he said. He heard the slur in her voice. She was toasted, which made him less willing to talk to her. He wondered whether his own voice were slurred.

"John, you've been working out," she said, touching his bicep, visible through his short sleeve shirt. "Ooh, make it hard for me."

Not knowing what possessed him, John flexed his arm.

"Mmm, I'd like to feel those strong arms around me at night," she said, running her tongue along her lips.

John felt frightened yet flattered. He could not get away from her without pushing her; she was planted in front of him. He wondered what would be her next move.

"Hey, John, you seen Steve?"

It was Derek. He stepped up beside John, but Doreen refused to budge to make way for the newcomer.

"No," said John, his eyes pleading with his friend for help.

Derek, seeing the look, said, "Doreen, get lost. John's too good for you."

"What would you know?" she said.

"I'm not afraid to hit girls, especially not ugly ones," Derek replied.

She looked at Derek, then at John. John felt he should apologize, but he did not. She turned and stormed off. At times, John was glad to have rude friends.

"Man, stay away from her. She's nothing but trouble," said Derek. "I drank too much. I've got to sit down."

John followed Derek over to a couch in the corner. They sat down and tapped their feet to the booming stereo. John had a headache. He thought about Doreen touching his bicep. He had liked it. He wished he had let her touch more. Then he saw her across the room, her hand up some fat, bald guy's shirt, stroking his hairy chest. John felt he would puke, and not because of the liquor. He looked over and saw Derek had fallen asleep. He did not know how long he sat there. He was half-asleep himself and his stomach was gurgling. Finally, he got up and stumbled through the kitchen to the bathroom; thankfully Alan and Sheila had vacated it.

When he came out, he found Frank kissing Renee goodbye while her roommate watched. When Frank saw John from the corner of his eye, he said goodnight to Renee; then she and her roommate disappeared out the back door.

"You ready to go?" asked Frank.

"Yeah," said John, relieved. He looked at the kitchen clock. It was just past one.

"I guess the party broke up early," said Frank.

They walked back to the living room. John caught a glimpse of Alan walking up the stairs, his arm around Sheila. John pretended not to see his cousin, but Alan hollered, "Hey John! You guys have a good night. Come over anytime."

"Okay," said John.

"Thanks for everything, Alan," said Frank, wishing to ingratiate himself with his host.

"No problem, man." He let out an excited giggle as Sheila grabbed him where John wished he had not seen. Then Alan chased her upstairs. John and Frank went out the front door.

"Man, Alan gives great parties," said Frank, grabbing John's shoulder for support as he stumbled down the front steps. "You're a real bonehead not to tell me he's your cousin. He's the one who buys for all the undergrads."

Before John could reply, Frank stepped off the sidewalk and bent over to puke in the front yard. John wanted to tell Frank how stupid he was, but he did not want Frank angry at him; he knew most people only spoke to him because he was friends with Frank. He tried not to listen to Frank vomiting. He figured he was just tired and would be less cranky in the morning.

He tried to clear his head by inhaling the crisp night air. It was early October, the autumn colors just past their prime; the smell of decaying leaves filled his nostrils; he noticed the familiar smell for the first time that autumn; it reminded him of his walks with Dickens down the Blueberry Trail. Soon the snow would come. After just a month at college, John felt homesick. He decided to go home tomorrow, to take Dickens for a walk, maybe watch a movie with his mom and stay for supper. He had not spent a day at home since he moved into the dorm. He needed a day at home, away from all this strange college world, so different from how he had been raised.

"Don't worry; I'll drive," said John when Frank lifted his head from the ground. Frank tossed his arm around John and said, "Take me home, man."

John led Frank to the car, opened the passenger door so Frank could crawl in, then walked around the car and got into the driver's side.

"Man, I ain't never been this drunk," Frank said. "I mean I drank a few times after my high school football games, but never like this. Never seen so many good looking girls either. That Renee. I've thought she was hot since the first day I seen her. Been meaning to ask for her phone number, only I was too nervous, until she started rubbing up against me tonight; then I knew she liked me. Man, I want to bang her. Well, at least I got her phone number. John, you don't even know. Right when we left there, when you were in the bathroom, man, she let me French kiss her, and put my hands up her sweater. Course she had her bra on, but I could still feel how sweet her tits are – biggest ones I've ever seen. I mean like watermelons, man. She's could totally be a total porn star."

"Uh huh."

John was glad to get back to the dorm, although Frank had to stop before they went inside so he could puke all over the grass.

"Come on, Frank," John whispered, "before our R.A. catches us."

"Yeah, he's a hardass," said Frank, wiping drool on his shirt sleeve.

John warned him to be quiet, but Frank tripped on his way up the stairs, letting out a loud laugh. John shooshed him, grabbed his shoulders, and guided him to their door. Thankfully, they lived right by the stairwell. In a few seconds, he had the door unlocked, and they were safely inside with no R.A. in sight.

Frank meandered his way into the shower. John sat on the bed, his head against the wall, trying to stay awake until Frank finished in the bathroom. Then Frank came out, too drunk to have remembered to put his underwear on. He collapsed naked on his bed and started snoring. John got up and pulled the bedspread out from beneath him, then covered him with it. Shaking his head in disgust, he showered, then crawled into his own bed.

Once in bed, however, he did not feel sleepy. Actually, he felt quite good. The beer and tequila had given him quite a buzz. He recalled Doreen feeling his bicep. Then he remembered Frank and Alan's comments about girls; even with Frank, he had never before talked about a girl's breasts. He felt he should disapprove of such remarks, but now he replayed the words over and over in his mind. He tried to remember whether Renee's chest had really been as big as Frank claimed. He remembered Frank and Renee rubbing against each other as they danced. He wondered whether he would ever rub against a girl like that. But not in public, that was for sure; he would not want a girl who would do that in public. But he knew it would sure feel good to do it. He used to think such behavior was sinful, but everyone at the party had been doing it. Now he felt it was just natural, normal. He fell asleep, wishing –

A few nights later, John turned down going to the Hyper with Frank so he could study for a physical geography test. Frank went, and Frank returned, but John still did not understand Einstein's theory of relativity nor have the faintest idea how it related to physical geography.

"Man, that's the best workout I've had in weeks," said Frank, stripping out of his sweaty clothes. "Guess what? I broke three hundred pounds today. Most I ever lifted." He flexed his biceps and admired his mammoth chest in the mirror. John was too frustrated with Einstein to reply. He wished he could be as careless about school as Frank – but John knew better; he would have to use his brains to get ahead; Frank had muscles and a certain amount of charm, despite his crudeness, that would get him the respect he needed to climb the corporate ladder; at least, Frank believed that was the case, and John had seen too many jocks treated with favoritism to argue.

Frank got into the shower, leaving the bathroom door open. John went back to Einstein, but his stomach was growling. It was eight o'clock, and he craved pizza. He thought maybe he could talk Frank into going to Pizza Hut – just for an hour's break. Then he could come back and study until bedtime.

As Frank turned off the shower, John heard a knock on the door. He was about to answer it when Frank hollered, "It's open!" John looked up to see Doreen standing in the doorway.

"Hi, John. I was going to ask you if – oh, hi, Frank."

She had caught Frank out of the corner of her eye. He was standing in the bathroom, wearing only a towel as he put on his deodorant.

"Hello," John heard Frank say. He heard embarrassment in his roommate's tone, but Frank did not tell her to get lost as Steve or Derek would have done. Instead, John watched Doreen step into the bathroom. Then she was out of his range of vision, but he could imagine. He heard a few muffled words, a couple bumps against the sink counter, then some rumbling and the clanging of a belt and shoes against the tiled bathroom floor. In a couple minutes, definite grunting was audible. John listened, unable to move.

Suddenly, he saw Renee standing in the hallway door. She smiled and started to say, "Hello, John," and step into the room; then she heard the grunting and looked into the bathroom.

"Oh. Oh!" Renee screeched. She stepped away, then turned back to shout, "You pig!" and ran down the hall.

Frank rushed out of the bathroom, a towel clutched in front of his crotch.

"Renee! No!" he shouted. "Come back! It's not like that! It's not what you think!"

But she was gone, and he could not run down the hall with his bare ass.

He came back and looked into the bathroom. Doreen was still not visible to John, but he heard her say, "It's okay, Frank. You don't need her. You were real good. I can do for you the – "

"Get your clothes on and get the Hell out of here," said Frank. He went to his dresser to grab his underwear.

Frank's eyes flared so that John dared not speak. Frank put on his underwear, then sat down on his bed to put on his socks. John could hear Doreen sobbing. Frank jumped up and went back into the bathroom.

"I'm sorry I yelled," he said to keep her quiet. "But you surprised me before I knew what was happening. You don't touch a guy like that. It's not fair."

John heard muffled cries, then some whispering. Finally, Doreen emerged, Frank's hand on her shoulder, gently propelling her toward the door.

"I'm sorry," he said, pecking her on the cheek in a brotherly manner.

She stepped into the hallway. Frank shut the door. John stuck his nose in his book, too embarrassed to look at his roommate.

Frank reached into the closet for his pants. After he put them on, he pulled a shirt over his large chest.

"Hey, John, I'm hungry. You wanna go out for pizza?"

"I was going to ask you the same thing," said John, trying to sound natural. "How about Pizza Hut?"

John cleared his throat, embarrassed by his trembling voice. "Okay."

They found their wallets. Frank grabbed his car keys. They said nothing on the way to the restaurant. They found a booth and ordered a pizza. After the waitress took their order, Frank said, "I don't know what came over me. I know I shouldn't have done it."

John wanted to say, "No, you shouldn't have," but he was still too shocked to discuss the situation.

"I guess I just wasn't thinking," Frank thought out loud. "My hormones took over because I've been wanting to get laid for so long. Once she touched me I couldn't stop. She was rubbing my chest and then she put her hand under the towel. I told her I didn't have a condom, but she said it was okay 'cause she's been on the pill since she was fourteen, so I guess it was safe enough. I'm sorry about Renee and all. It was awful quick, but I guess that's normal the first time. I was burning so bad I couldn't have stood it another minute. I don't know why I never did it before. I had other opportunities, but geez, it was awesome."

John lowered his head, embarrassed and not wanting to hear more. He was glad when the pizza came so he could avoid talking by eating.

"Maybe it was wrong, John, but it made me feel like such a man. I mean, I've always known I was attractive to women – I know I have the physique to turn them on, but now I'm certain the girls want me. I can't blame Doreen; I mean I did look good – I always look all pumped up after a workout, and especially when I get out of the shower. But I won't get involved with Doreen anymore. I'm sure I can get lots better girls, especially with biceps like these."

Frank set to admiring his arms. John knew Doreen was a loose woman, but now he did not think Frank any better. John thought of his grandparents; they had been engaged for years, but he doubted they had ever given into temptation before their wedding day. That was real love, meaningful love. John did not understand how people could just fool around. Maybe he was too old-fashioned, too serious, but he did not know how in this day of rampant AIDS, anyone could do what Frank and Doreen had done, and even if there were no fear of disease, such rash behavior only created emotional chaos and pain.

Once back at the dorm, John buried himself in physical geography while Frank went to play video games with Derek and Steve. When Frank told the other guys about his escapade, they joked that he was a stud; he took the compliment seriously. In the next couple weeks, he picked up several girls, and a couple times, the girls spent the night in his room. John started spending his evenings at the library, and if Frank had a girl over, he often spent the night sleeping on his suitemates' floor. Derek told him, "Frank's become a slut himself," and Steve told John to complain to the R.A. for being forced out of his room. Both were disgusted with Frank, partly from envy. After a few weeks, John tried to tell Frank how he felt, but Frank said, "Don't be such a tight ass. If you got laid, you'd be a lot less crabby."

Ellen would no longer leave her mother alone at night. She and her cousins took turns staying with her. Beth's health was fine, but Ellen feared her mother's knees might give out, and if she fell and broke a hip, she might suffer for hours before she was found. Beth was too stubborn to use a cane or her lifeline button.

During Christmas break, John stayed with his grandmother several nights to give her other caretakers a break. These evenings with his grandmother were spent sitting together in the living room. Grandma read the newspaper and watched the Nashville Network. She said she had always wanted to see the Grand Ole Opry, but now she was too old to make the trip. John read *A Tale of Two Cities,* and out of politeness, he occasionally commented on something on TV or asked whether she needed anything. Neither really knew what to talk to the other about – gone were the days when Grandma could captivate John's interest by reading *I Can Lick Thirty Tigers Today.*

When a commercial came on that featured kittens, Beth said, "I remember once when I was a girl I got to hold six kittens in my lap."

John perked up his ears. "Whose kittens were they?"

"The neighbors next door."

"How old were you?"

"Oh," she said, looking troubled, "I don't know, maybe eight."

"Who were your neighbors?"

"Oh, I don't remember their names. Isn't that funny. Well, it was so long ago. They had a little boy a bit older than me. They lived there a long time too because they were my cousin Thelma's neighbors when she bought my parents' house."

John tried to think of other things he might ask Grandma about her childhood, but he had found since his grandpa died, that when he asked Grandma questions, she would say she did not remember.

By nine o'clock, Beth was sound asleep in her chair. John got up to shower, then returned to the living room in his pajamas. Grandma mumbled in embarrassment, "Oh, I guess I nodded off. I don't know why I'm so tired tonight."

"It's the holidays; they're always tiring," he excused her.

Ten minutes later, oblivious to Dolly Parton being on *The Ralph Emory Show,* Grandma had fallen back asleep. At eleven o'clock, she woke up and said she would go to bed. John quickly went to the bathroom while Grandma set out her pills for the next morning. Then he went to his mother's old room, but he did not sleep. He lay in bed, listening to make sure Grandma made it safely into the bathroom, then down the hall to her room. He did not close his eyes until he heard her snoring.

In the morning, they listened to "Telephone Time" on WJPD, the Country Giant. For breakfast, they had fried eggs and Trenary Toast, the only toast Grandma would eat, although it was so hard she had to dunk it in her coffee. She insisted on washing the breakfast dishes, no matter how tiring it was for her. Then she disappeared into her bedroom to get dressed, a two hour task. Despite her age, John could not imagine why it took her so long. She never came back out until lunchtime. He liked to think she was in there writing – that's what he would have done – but Grandma was no writer. Neither did she clean the bedroom, other than to run a dustcloth over the furniture. He wondered whether she just sat on the edge of the bed and remembered the past, even though she claimed she could not remember much anymore – perhaps she just rested, having lived so many years, that she was no longer concerned about time or needed to think.

While Grandma was in her bedroom, John planned to work on his novel. At least he intended to write. He sat at the dining room table, pen in hand, and stared around the room. The morning sun poured across the lace tablecloth. The old furnace came on and spread a dusty, cozy smell through the house.

Christmas tree tinsel sparkled in the sunlight. Christmas had been good, but since Grandpa's death, it was bittersweet. John stared at the artificial tree and recalled his mother telling him how when she was a girl, her father would bring home a real tree, then cut off branches and drill holes in the trunk to insert the cut branches so the tree would look full for Grandma. Grandpa would have done anything to please Grandma. John looked at the ornaments, old pink, green, and blue glass balls with sparkling glitter, pieces from the Depression years that his grandparents had bought to celebrate their first Christmas together as man and wife. Other ornaments were more elaborate, given by friends and family members – ornaments with little winter scenes inside or with Norman Rockwell paintings and "Christmas 1962" or "Christmas 1977" written on them. A few ornaments had photographs of grandchildren, John and Chad, or Uncle Jim's children when they were little, all these ornaments nearly antiques already. The tree's bubble lights were so old they had come back in fashion. And on a side branch, half hidden by garland, hung a green glass pickle – a traditional German symbol of friendship, a sign of how the past surrounds us even when we forget it; it was evidence that John's Great-Great-Grandfather Fritz Bergmann had come to America so many years before, and how his son, Karl Bergmann, had gone to Germany eighty years ago in search of his father's past; Karl had returned and presented the pickle to his sister, Beth's mother, John's great-grandmother. Now no one living remembered where the whimsical ornament had come from, but it was granted a bough of the Christmas tree every year.

Not even his parents' house, not his very own room, had the same feeling of comfort John felt in this house his grandfather had built. The living room's furniture consisted of a green tweedish looking couch so old the cushions no longer fit it properly, an upholstered recliner ripped beneath the footrest, half its buttons on the back long since fallen off, and Grandma's burgundy rocking chair with a green throw over it. There were cream colored footstools, one punctured by Bandit's paws and repaired with masking tape, a couple formica tables made by Grandpa, a floor television topped with black and white graduation photos of John's mother and Uncle Jim, two lamps that did not match, and on the wall, a wooden moon with steps for little porcelain angels to stand upon. The brown carpet did not match the furniture. The ceiling had, in 1960s style, been spackled, swirled, and sprinkled with white, blue, and pink sparkles; as a boy, John had imagined the ceiling looked like billowy clouds with stars peeking through. Grandpa and Grandma's living room was devoid of faults because he had always been welcomed there. It represented a simple life to him, a place of safety even his grandparents had perhaps not felt there. It was so different from the world he now found himself living in.

John started to think he hated college. The day before classes started again, his mother offered to drop him off in time for him to have supper with Frank. John did not refuse; he felt uncomfortable telling his mother just how lonely he was, and how Frank's behavior troubled him.

When he reached his room, he found Frank was not back yet. He stuck the key in the lock, turned the handle, and switched on the lights. After setting down his suitcase, he walked through the bathroom and into Steve and Derek's room, but they were also not there. It was five o'clock, so if Frank did not show up soon, John would have to eat supper alone. He decided to put away his clothes and wait half an hour for his roommate to show up. As he started stuffing his underwear in a dresser drawer, he noticed a little box sitting on his bed.

He walked over and picked up the package. It was wrapped in Christmas paper. The label read, "To my best friend John."

He knew the gift was from Frank. No one else would have left him a present. He had not gotten Frank anything.

He ripped off the paper. Inside the box was a Swatch, the coolest wrist-watch a person could own. He had always wanted one. This Swatch was suave, with a blue face, red stripes, and white swatch guard. Conservative, yet classy colors. John put it on his wrist and became mesmerized by the little red second hand circling around the face. There were no numbers to tell the time – only a place for the date at the three o'clock spot. What had possessed Frank to buy such a smart thing for him? Again he looked at the tag.

"To my best friend John."

He never would have suspected Frank was sentimental. Then he saw headlights flash through the window. He looked outside and was surprised to realize he hoped it was Frank. He saw the car stop in the parking lot. Someone got out and walked toward the dorm. It was a girl. He sat down on his bed, feeling anxious. He heard footsteps in the hall and jumped up again. He wished Frank would come; he was hungry. He finished putting away his clothes, but stopped to listen at every little creak or the sound of a door opening. He felt anxious. He sat down to read, but his eyes wandered from the page. He heard another footstep in the hall. His heart pounded. When the steps faded away, he knew they were not Frank's. He went to the bathroom and quickly washed his hands, then was back staring out the window, waiting for Frank. He looked at his watch. It was six o'clock. It was such a gorgeous watch. How could Frank have given him something so cool? Was it true, what Frank had written?

He sat back down on the bed in frustration. He tried to read, but whenever he turned a page, he realized he had absorbed nothing from the previous one.

He heard the doorknob turn. He wanted to jump up, knowing it had to be Frank, but he kept his eyes glued to the page.

"Hey," he heard Frank say.

"Hello," said John, looking up.

"Did you eat?" Frank asked, setting down his suitcase. "I'm starving."

"No, I didn't," said John.

Frank smiled as he noticed John's wrist.

"I see you got your present."

"Yeah, thanks."

"Do you like it?"

"Sure. It's really cool."

"Good."

"I'm sorry I didn't get you anything," said John. "Can I buy you supper?"

"Okay, but you don't have to."

"No, I want to. Where do you want to go?"

"I doubt the cafeteria's open," said Frank.

"How about somewhere nice, like the Villa," said John. "Let's start the semester off right."

"Okay."

Frank broke into a goofy grin.

John jumped up from the bed and put on his coat. In a minute, they were walking down the hallway. Frank draped his arm over John's shoulder. "I'm glad to be back. My family nearly drove me nuts over Christmas, and I haven't worked out in two weeks. I'm too tired tonight, but maybe tomorrow we can start going to the Hyper again."

"Sure," said John.

John would rather write than weightlift, and he still had issues with Frank's loose behavior with women, but overall, Frank was a good guy. And John would rather have a buddy than read a book.

For the first time since his grandfather's death, John felt the good days had returned.

1989-1990

John hesitated before getting out of the car. He wished he could just hand the giant envelope to the postman, but instead, he would have to have it weighed, then affix enough postage to the return envelope in case the publisher rejected his manuscript. He tried not to think about that possibility, but he still had to pay the postage both ways.

He got out of the car, clutching his completed novel under his arm. He hoped he would not see anyone he knew. He had decided not to mail the package at the university bookstore from fear he would meet one of his professors who would be aghast to learn he dared think himself worthy of publication. He crossed Washington Street, gazing up at the tall Post Office and Federal Building. He remembered seeing a photograph of his grandfather peering out of one of those upper windows. John's novel had started out from an idea based on his grandfather's life; he missed his grandpa so much he had wanted to immortalize his memory, but the story had gotten away from him, creating a character only loosely based on Henry Whitman; nevertheless, John knew it was the best piece he had ever written. He thought it might bring luck that he was mailing his novel at the post office his grandfather had helped to build.

Inside, three people waited in line before him. John stared at the painting of Father Marquette standing up in a canoe while Indians paddled it; everyone in Upper Michigan knows you cannot stand in a canoe, and the Indians looked crabby, as if irritated that Father Marquette was not helping to paddle. But since John had set the novel in the city named for this Jesuit priest, he thought seeing the picture might bring him good luck.

When it was his turn, John slid his package over the counter to the postman.

"Hi. I need to have this weighed and then buy stamps for return postage."

"Okay," said the postman, placing the envelope on the scale. "What is it?"

"Um, it's a manuscript." He was too shy to call it a novel.

"That's a big one," replied the man, who had seen his share of amateur writers in the twenty years he had stood behind the post office counter. "It's going to be $5.60 both ways. $11.20 total."

"All right," said John, opening his wallet to fish out a ten and two one dollar bills. He could not believe it was so expensive. He had expected to pay no more than six or seven dollars – he only made about fifty dollars a week working at the cafeteria – but it would be worth it if his book were published.

The postman handed John the stamps. He licked them and stuck them on the envelopes while the postman counted out his change. John took one last look at the nearly five hundred double-spaced pages. He silently said a little prayer over them, then sealed the outside envelope and handed it to the postman.

He walked quickly out of the post office to where he had parked. Once inside his car, he felt safe and able to breath again. He looked at his swatch. Quarter to ten. He better hurry if he were going to be on time for his British literature class.

After his class that day, John had an hour to spend at the library doing research for his paper on James Joyce's *A Portrait of the Artist as a Young Man* before meeting Frank for lunch downstairs at Bookbinders. Throughout Olson Library, snuck in between bookshelves, were arrangements of rectangular shaped tables, each table with four chairs around it. John knew these study sections best by the colors of the metal bookshelves that surrounded them. His favorite section was across the aisle from the volumes of Joyce criticism, in a dark area of the library where the fluorescent lights were not too bright and the bookshelves had metal book holders the same shade of shamrock green as Ireland, where John and Joyce's ancestors had lived. Here John usually sat to study.

He was relieved today to find his study area empty of other, less dedicated scholars. He pulled out a chair, set his bookbag on the table, dug out his notecards, then went to the Joyce shelf, returning a few minutes later with half a dozen books he had not yet consulted. He would not settle for the ten minimum sources required. A research paper was not a research paper if he had not looked at every book for every scrap and tidbit that might be remotely useful to his paper's argument. Soon he was skimming books for relevant information, and scribbling out one notecard after another.

In the midst of this literary ecstasy, he was distracted by the sound of a coat unzipping, then a bookbag being plunked down on the table opposite. Raising his eyes, he saw a female had come to interrupt his solitude.

She caught his glance and stared back. His eyes returned to his book, but he sensed her approaching him.

"John?"

He looked up, not recognizing her.

"Yes."

"It's Holly."

Momentary confusion. A struggling study of her face. Then his face transformed into a smile.

"Holly! I haven't seen you in years."

"I know," she said.

"Are you going to school here?"

"Yes. I just transferred this semester from U of M."

"Sit down," he said. She had already pulled out a chair. "How have you been?"

"Good," she said.

He had not seen her in so long he did not know what more to say. They had spent hundreds of their childhood hours together, yet she was a stranger now. He could not ask whether she wanted to go build a fort in the woods.

"Why'd you transfer up here?" he finally asked.

"My dad still lives here. I never have liked it downstate. I wanted to get far away from my mom and stepfather. They live in Grosse Pointe, and I hate it there. My stepfather thinks he's a big shot, and my mom's become just like him. I like it here a lot better."

"I remember your address was Grosse Pointe last time you wrote," said John.

"I can't believe you remember that since I haven't sent you a letter in years. I'm afraid I wasn't a very good correspondent."

"That's okay," said John. He did not tell her how hurt he had been when she quit writing.

She asked after his parents and Chad.

"I should go visit them," she said. "I really miss that old neighborhood. Are there still lots of woods like where we built forts and played Poseidon Adventure. Do you remember that?"

"Yes," he said. "All the woods are still there. I take Dickens for walks in them whenever I go home to visit."

"Oh, Dickens," said Holly. "I miss him too."

"What are you going to school for?" he asked.

"Business."

"Oh, my best friend is in marketing," said John.

"Maybe he's in one of my classes," she said. "What's his name?"

"Frank Jarvi."

"Oh, sure, I know Frank. I know who he is anyway."

John looked at his swatch, remembering he had to meet Frank for lunch. "Do you have to go to class?" she asked.

"No, I'm meeting Frank for lunch at Bookbinders. Do you want to join us?"

"Sure," she said. "Then we can do some more catching up."

John stuffed his notecards into his bag. Holly grabbed her bookbag from the other table. They walked out of the library together.

"What are you going to school for?" she asked.

"English."

"I should have known. You always were a bookworm," she said.

They went down to the main floor of the library, then down another floor to Bookbinders coffee shop at the end of the academic mall. When they entered, they found Frank had already found them a table.

"Hey, John. What's up?" said Frank.

"This is Holly," said John. "We grew up next door to each other. She's been living downstate, but she just moved back up here to go to school."

"Hi, I'm Frank Jarvi," he said, taking Holly's delicate hand in his giant one. "I think I've seen you around campus."

"You're in my marketing class," she replied.

"Oh yeah, sure. Now I'll know someone to get notes from when I skip."

"Holly," John said. "I'll watch your purse and bookbag if you want to go up to the counter and order."

"What's good here?" she asked.

"Frank usually gets a salad and yogurt."

"That's all you eat? A big guy like you?" she said with surprise.

"Have to keep my abs rock hard," he said, smacking his stomach with his fist. "I'll have a power shake this afternoon."

"What do you usually get, John?"

"Nachos and a chocolate milkshake."

"That's his lunch everyday," laughed Frank. "I'm starving. I'll go up with you and order John's food too."

John held the table while Holly and Frank stood in line. Maggie was the manager of Bookbinders, and the students who worked there loved her. Today, she was in a grand mood fussing and joking at them. John listened to the banter. When Frank got to the register, Maggie told him he needed to eat more – maybe he and John should switch meals for once. Holly smiled, glad to be in a friendly environment. She had been lonely at U of M, but now, she hoped John would be her friend again.

Frank and Holly returned to the table. In a couple minutes, Maggie shouted, "Nachos and a chocolate shake" and John went up to gather his lunch.

Frank asked Holly about Grosse Pointe and U of M and why she had left.

"I'd rather be downstate," he told her. "I imagine I'll be moving down there when I graduate – all the good jobs are down there. There's nothing in the U.P. for anyone with half a brain."

"It's beautiful up here," Holly said. "And people are more friendly. I missed it."

"Did you miss all the snow? I'm sick of the snow."

"Yes, I even missed the snow. We hardly get any down there."

"I couldn't live where there wasn't snow," said John. "Remember, Holly, how we used to build snowforts and snowmen, and pretend we were Eskimos."

"Yes, remember the snowman we pretended was an Eskimo goddess because of some story we read in school?"

"Yes, we were rather pagan children," John laughed. "I remember we also used to build Egyptian temple sand castles."

"But we played stories out of the Bible too," she reminded him.

Frank inserted a word here or there, but most of the hour's conversation was John and Holly reminiscing until John looked at his swatch and said, "I better get to class."

"Will I see you again?" Holly asked as John put on his coat.

"Sure, why don't you come to lunch again tomorrow?"

"Okay. I'll meet you here."

"Frank, are you coming?" asked John. Frank had a class at the same time as John so they usually walked to Jamrich Hall together.

"No, we're having a test today, and I didn't study for it. I'll call the prof later to say I was sick so I can take it next week."

"Frank," John said, but left it at that. One of the conditions of being Frank's friend was not to gripe at him for his faults. John left his friends at Bookbinders while he went to his world religions class, but the only religion he thought about for the next hour was the worship of the pagan Eskimo snow goddess.

Soon John and Holly made it a point to get together at least a couple times a week besides lunch everyday with Frank. One fall afternoon, they had just returned to campus from a walk around Presque Isle in time for Holly to go to her four o'clock class. John went back to his dorm room to wait until Frank got out of class so they could go to the Hyper. On his bed, John saw Frank had left his mail, including a large envelope from the publisher to whom he had submitted his novel. His heart pounding, John ripped open the package to find his manuscript returned with a rejection letter.

> Dear Mr. Vandelaare:
> Thank you for submitting your manuscript to us. I am sorry that we must decline your offer to have us publish your novel. Because of the number of manuscripts we receive, we are not able to make extensive comments. However, we do not feel that you write effective dialogue, an important concern, you will agree, in marketing a work of fiction.
> Respectfully yours,
> Kristen Novak
> Editor

John reread the letter in disbelief. He had thought of a dozen reasons why no one would want to publish his book, but not because he could not write effective dialogue. He was angry. The editor did not know what she was talking about. He picked up the returned manuscript and read a page of dialogue. He felt unsure. He started to read it out loud, listening to the diction. It was awful. The language was stilted. No one talked that way. Why, the sentences were complete and grammatically perfect. How could he have been so stupid? He would have to rewrite the whole thing. He felt like tearing out his hair at the thought. Maybe he was wrong. Maybe he should just send it out again, but it had cost eleven dollars to mail it. Three hours wages. He would not spend more money mailing it out until he had rewritten it. Or maybe he should just throw it out and try to write something else, but it had taken him two years to write this book. He had not expected to become famous overnight, but he had thought he had written a decent novel. Mary Shelley had written *Frankenstein* at age eighteen; its writing was atrociously bad, but it had been published and long admired for its content.

He did not know what to do. He lay down on the bed, not even caring when his legs crinkled the pages of his novel. He lay there for nearly an hour pitying himself and wondering whether he should quit writing. Then he got up off the bed so Frank would not think him pathetic. He wanted to tell Frank about the rejection, but he did not want Frank to think him a loser; Frank was impressed by how much time John labored at his writing, although he had never asked to read a word of it. John stuffed the manuscript and letter under his bed, turned on his computer and tried to look as if he had been busy working on his James Joyce paper. James Joyce did not write realistic dialogue. John had yet to meet anyone at college who spoke like the students in *A Portrait of the Artist as a Young Man*.

When Frank came home, he and John changed into their gym clothes and went to the Hyper. Frank was too focused on pumping up his biceps to notice John's depressed mood, and John was not ready to reveal the defeat of his literary dreams. As they left the Hyper, Frank said, "By the way, John, I saw Holly this morning."

"Oh," said John. "She didn't mention seeing you when I walked around Presque Isle with her this afternoon."

"That's because I told her I would tell you."

"Tell me what?" asked John.

"I asked her out. We have a date Friday night."

"Oh," said John. They walked a few yards in silence.

"You don't mind, do you?" asked Frank.

"I – I didn't know you liked Holly that way."

"Well, I didn't either, but when we all went to the movie last Sunday, she put her hand on my knee."

"She did?"

"Yeah. It was kind of weird because you were sitting next to me so I didn't know what to do. She left it there a long time too. I thought maybe you would notice, but I guess not. I've always thought she was hot, but I didn't think I'd ever be with her. But then the more I thought about it, the more I wanted to ask her out. I always thought she was interested in you, but she says you're just friends."

John's heart jumped. Anger rose in him. He wanted to accuse Frank of going behind his back. Why had Frank not asked him whether he were interested in Holly? But John was more hurt that Holly had said they were just friends – even if it were true. He had hoped they might someday be more.

"You don't mind, do you?" asked Frank. "I mean, I figured if you were interested in her, you would have asked her out by now. We've been hanging out together for weeks."

"No, I don't mind." John tried to smile. "I'd be happy if my two best friends were a couple."

"Thanks, man," said Frank, carelessly draping his arm around John's shoulder.

Frank did not notice John flinch. John had thought it too early in their renewed friendship to ask Holly out, but secretly, he had already imagined marrying her. Now he had lost his chance. What was he thinking? Apparently, he had never had a chance; she had never put her hand on his knee.

"Where will you go on your date?" asked John.

"I don't know," said Frank. "I thought maybe you could suggest a nice restaurant since you know more places around here than I do."

John suggested several restaurants until Frank settled on the Garden Room because its view overlooking Lake Superior would make dinner romantic. Then after supper, Frank and Holly would go to a movie; Frank decided on a chick flick so it would be more romantic for her. John imagined the movie would provide a prime opportunity for more knee-stroking.

"Frank?" John said.

"What?"

"I – I wonder if – "

"What?"

John was afraid to ask. Their friendship was strong because they overlooked each other's faults. John was grateful that Frank ignored all his deficiencies, his physical inferiority and social ineptitude. When the two friends had encountered problems, it was because Frank was thoughtless rather than from any direct attempt to antagonize John. But John told himself that if Frank fooled around with Holly, then abandoned her as he had other girls, they would no longer be friends. Several times over the phone John had made excuses to crying girls for why Frank would not return their calls. Since Frank was his friend, John had kept his mouth shut on these occasions, but with Holly it would be different. He would not let Frank hurt her.

"Frank, you're serious about Holly, aren't you? I mean – "

"I'm crazy about her," said Frank. "She's about the nicest girl I ever met. I want to impress her all I can. I was thinking I would wear a suit on our date."

"That might be a bit much," said John, "but maybe you could wear a tie."

"Okay. Can I borrow one of yours?"

"Sure," said John, begrudging loaning a tie to the guy stealing his girl. Should he warn Frank that if he hurt Holly, their friendship would be over? Should he warn Holly what Frank was really like? But he suspected she already knew. He and Holly had gone to the movies a couple times so Frank could be alone with a girl in the dorm room. Holly was such a nice girl that John did not know what she could see in Frank. Was she as dumb as all those other girls who were brainwashed by a guy's muscles?

That evening, John was relieved when his mother called to ask whether he could stay with Grandma on Friday night; he did not want to be in their room if Frank brought Holly back there after their date.

Saturday morning, John returned to his dorm room. Frank was not home because he had gone out running. When John went into the bathroom, he spotted a condom in the wastebasket.

"He didn't even try to hide it," he muttered to himself.

He sat down at his desk, thinking he would start rewriting his novel. He did not want to think about Frank and Holly. In ten minutes, Frank returned.

"Hey," Frank said.

"Hey," John replied, his eyes glued to his computer.

"Aren't you going to ask me how it went?"

"What?"

"My date with Holly."

"Oh yeah, how did it go?"

Frank told him all about dinner, the movie, the sweet things he had said to Holly that had totally worked, how good she kissed.

"What's wrong?" he asked when he saw John's face fall.

"Nothing," said John.

"You're upset about me and Holly, aren't you? I knew you would be."

"No," said John.

"What is it then?"

"Well, my novel," said John, unable to think of another excuse. "I sent it to a publisher and it was rejected."

"Oh," said Frank. "You didn't even tell me you had sent it out."

"No, I wanted it to be a surprise when it was accepted, and I didn't want anyone to know if it were rejected."

"Buddy," said Frank, putting his hand on John's shoulder, "you know you can tell me anything."

"I know, but I got the rejection letter the day you told me about Holly, and you seemed so happy I didn't want to depress you."

"You could have told me anyway," said Frank. "Did you tell your folks?"

"No," said John. "You know I'm shy talking about my writing."

"Well, cheer up. That publisher doesn't know everything. Just send it out again. I know my best friend can write circles around everyone else."

Frank punched John in the arm so that he could not help but smile. He could not stay mad at his friend. Frank did not go out with Holly to hurt him, and he would not hurt Frank. He was glad he had told Frank about his book being rejected, although he had barely thought about it since he had found out about Frank and Holly. He was okay with everything now. He told himself he did not want to be involved with Holly anyway; she would just suck up his writing time.

Frank asked John to go for a ride with him and Holly that afternoon to the Copper Country to look at the fall colors, and they might stop by Frank's parents' house so he could introduce Holly to his family. John had never known Frank to bring a girl home to his parents. He felt disillusioned about Holly since she had slept with Frank on their first date, yet if they were going to be in a serious relationship, he would be happy for them. Still, John told Frank he could not go because he had too much homework to do.

"Suit yourself," said Frank.

After his roommate left, John went into the bathroom and threw toilet paper over the condom so he would not have to look at it. Then he sat down at his desk. He did not have any homework to do. He would work on his novel; what he wanted most was to be a novelist, and he would not let anything interfere with that dream.

1990-1991

John, Frank, and Holly became a bit of a trio. Both Holly and Frank said John was their best friend. After a few months of his friends dating, John adapted and began to spend time with them as a couple. Frank frequently spent the night at Holly's apartment, which made things easier for John, who enjoyed having a dorm room to himself so he could write in the evenings. He also joined Sigma Tau Delta, the English Honor Society; he befriended the other members and spent time with them discussing the latest art films, laughing over the oddities of their English professors, and going to plays at the college's Forest Roberts Theatre.

One night, Frank fixed John up with Holly's roommate. John had only met Mandy a couple times, but he thought her pretty, and Holly said Mandy was a psychology major and really smart. John thought she would be interesting; maybe her knowledge of psychology would help him come up with ideas for interesting characters in his novels. He had gone out with so few girls that he anxiously anticipated the date. Then the day before John would see Mandy, Frank came home from Holly's house to say the date was off. Disappointed, John asked why until Frank admitted that Mandy had said, "John isn't the kind of guy you can have fun with."

"What does that mean?" John asked. "I'm fun. You and Holly think I'm fun. My other friends think I'm fun."

"John," said Frank, "you know you're my best friend and all; you're smart and loyal and kind, but you're not exactly fun."

"Why not?" John asked.

"Your idea of fun is watching *Masterpiece Theatre*. Girls want more excitement than that."

"Then maybe she just isn't the girl for me," said John, "but there are girls who like to read. I can't believe a psychology major would think – "

"John, what she means is you're not the kind of guy who'll fool around with a girl."

"Oh."

John did not know what to say. Mandy was right – he was not that kind of guy. He did not see the point in fooling around – it was not worth all the risks for a few minutes of pleasure. He would only go out with a girl who wanted a commitment.

"John," said Frank, "I'm only trying to help you here, but you know, you'd find more girls if you made some effort to be attractive."

"What do you mean by that?" John asked.

"Well, for one thing you pig out on chocolate ice cream."

"I'm not fat," said John.

"No, but what's the point of going to the Hyper if you're just going to eat junk food. Girls like guys who are cut like me, with tight asses and veins popping out of their ripped arms, not guys who are soft in the stomach and have no chest."

"I'm not soft," John said. He could not pinch an inch on his waistline, even if his abdominal muscles were not defined.

"Girls want hunks, John. You'll never be one if you don't try harder."

John had always been self-conscious about his body. He was hurt that Frank would now pick on him about it.

"Maybe I don't want a girl," he said. "I don't even like Mandy. I only said yes to get you and Holly off my back."

"And you could do something with your hair," Frank said. "Why do you always part it on the side like that? It's practically a comb-over."

John was speechless. His best friend had never attacked him before.

"No girl wants a guy with hair like that," said Frank. "And it's really hard for me to say this, but sometimes I'm embarrassed even to be seen with you."

"Shut the hell up!" John said. He was furious. He had always kept his mouth shut about Frank's faults.

"Well, it's true. You've got a comb-over and a cowlick sticking up, and – "

"As if being seen with you isn't an embarrassment to me," John said.

"What does that mean?" Frank had been sitting on his bed, but now he stood up and walked over to where John was sitting in front of his computer. John felt intimidated, but he did not care if Frank hit him. He was too mad.

"Half the school thinks you're a male slut," said John. "I'm almost afraid to sit on our toilet seat from fear you'll give me some venereal disease."

"You're an asshole," said Frank, turning toward the door.

John did not reply. He would not lower himself to using Frank's vulgar language.

Frank turned around. "I suppose you'll tell Holly I'm a slut, but I haven't been with another girl in the last year since I started dating her. You have a lot of nerve to say that to me when you know I've tried my damnedest to change. Your whole problem is that you're just jealous and sexually frustrated."

John felt ashamed. He was jealous of Frank – at least for his popularity. He wanted to apologize before they said more words they would regret, but Frank had already gone out and slammed the door behind him.

They made up the next day. It was exam week, and neither wanted to leave for Christmas vacation sore at the other. Besides, they had bought each other presents so it was senseless to waste them. A few weeks later, when the winter semester began, the fight was forgotten, but Frank did not try to fix John up with any more women.

That year, Northern Michigan University's hockey team was phenomenal. NMU had long been one of the premier hockey schools in the nation. It was a rare game when the Lakeview Arena was not packed with hundreds of screaming fans. Frank had befriended a couple hockey players at the weight room that year, and one of them often gave him free tickets, meaning John, Holly, and Frank came home many nights with sore lungs from cheering the home team. As the NMU Wildcats won game after game, the university community burst with exuberance. By March, the Wildcats were going to the championship finals. The team hoped to score big.

Frank also hoped to score.

"John," he said one afternoon, "you weren't planning to go to Minnesota for the championship game were you?"

"No. I'd like to, but I really can't afford it right now. Why? Do you want to go?"

"I thought I'd take Holly. It would be a little romantic getaway for us."

"Oh," said John. "That's fine. I have a lot of work to do this weekend anyway."

Thinking the conversation was over, John went to brush his teeth, but a minute later, Frank came into the bathroom.

"John, I want to tell you something, but you have to keep it secret."

John spit out a mouthful of toothpaste. "Of course. What is it?"

"I'm going to ask Holly to marry me."

John was stunned. Frank and Holly were not yet twenty-one. But they did care about each other, and Frank had not been with any other girls since he started dating Holly.

"Are you sure?" John asked.

"Yeah, that's why I want to go to St. Paul with her. I thought we'd get a hotel room together, and I would ask her then."

"Oh," said John.

"What do you think?" Frank looked like a frightened rabbit.

"Are you sure about it?" John asked.

"Yeah. Every minute I'm not with her I'm half-crazy thinking about her. I could barely stand being away from her when I went home for spring break. I came back two days early just to be near her again. I love her like mad. I never felt that way about anyone before. But do you think I'm ready for marriage?"

"Well," said John, knowing well his role as best friend, "any girl would be lucky to have you. I can't imagine her saying 'No'. But you probably shouldn't get married right away; at least, not until you finish school. But ask her first. Don't look so scared. Ask her, and then when she says yes, you'll be a lot happier."

"I will then," said Frank, relieved that John did not think him foolish. "You won't tell anyone until I ask her?"

"No," John promised.

After they were both in their beds and the lights turned out, the friends talked about how John would be best man at the wedding, and what kind of house Frank and Holly would have, and what they would name their kids, and how John would be uncle to the kids, and where they would live once they graduated, and all the good things in life to come for the happy couple.

Sunday was the big hockey game. John spent the afternoon working on his novel, although he kept wondering whether Frank would ask Holly before or after the game. John and Frank had discussed over and over again whether Frank should ask Holly at dinner, in their motel room, in the special jacuzzi in the motel room, at half-time, or when the NMU Wildcats won, if they won. But Frank had left undecided. John waited all day for the phone to ring. When evening came, he turned on the TV to watch the usual FOX shows, *In Living Color* and *Married With Children*; he felt lonely not having his friends there to laugh with him over the antics of Jim Carrey and Al Bundy. Then, as he got ready for bed, he heard shouting in the hall.

The second he heard chants and cheers, he knew the Wildcats had scored victory. He joined the crowd to learn the details. After a thrilling triple-overtime game, the Wildcats had defeated Boston University by a score of 8-7. Northern's hockey team was NCAA national champion. The school went crazy. Guys in their pajamas and underwear were dancing in the hallway, oblivious to any embarrassment caused by the girls' downstairs who came up to drink and party with them. Not until one o'clock did John hear the telephone ring; he ran back into his room to grab it.

"Did you hear the big news? We won the national championship."

John could barely hear, but he knew Frank's voice.

"Yeah, I know. Can you hear all the excitement here?"

"Yeah. It's awesome, isn't it?"

"Yeah. How did you make out?" John asked.

"I said YES!" Holly screamed into the phone.

"Congratulations!" John shouted back.

"We're driving home tonight," said Frank. "We'll see you first thing in the morning. We better go now."

"All right," John said. "Congratulations. Drive safely."

After hanging up, he jumped up and down with glee, then went back into the hall to find his suitemates and tell them the news.

The next Friday night, the engaged couple and their future best man celebrated with dinner at Entre Amigos. John, glowing with happiness for his friends, informed Frank and Holly that they were celebrating their engagement where once the Marquette Opera House stood, where his grandfather had proposed to his grandmother. Frank and Holly did not care where they were – they were happy just staring into each other's eyes; John contented himself by indulging in Entre Amigos' incredible Mexican lasagna smothered in sour cream.

They were in a riotously joyous mood, cracking jokes, planning the wedding, playfully tossing nacho chips at each other, enjoying the stuffed feeling of eating too much, getting tipsy off coca-cola – they were all a few months shy of being old enough for margaritas; that hardly mattered – they were drunk on happiness.

"My mother," Frank said, "wants us to get married in our church back home."

"Married in Pelkie?" said Holly. "I'm not getting married in that little town."

"Well, my mother doesn't want us to get married in Marquette. She says it's too far for my family to travel."

"But all our friends are here," said Holly, "and except for my mom and step-dad, so is my family."

"You'd have more options for the wedding reception in Marquette," said John.

"I told my mother that," said Frank, "but she said I was becoming a snob like all the other people in Marquette who think they're better than the rest of the U.P."

"We don't think we're better," said John. "It's just that we are the cultural metropolis of the Upper Peninsula."

"Whatever!" laughed Frank.

John laughed too, but as he did, he spotted a familiar face in the back of the restaurant. A minute later, Robert O'Neill was walking toward him; John stood up to greet his grandpa's old friend.

"What are you doing?" Frank asked John before seeing the old man he imagined was one of John's many relatives.

"Hello, sir, how are you?" said John.

"Just fine," said Robert, walking slowly but steadily for his advanced age. "I haven't seen you in some time. I used to bump into your mother every now and then, but it's been awhile. This is my daughter, Helen. Helen, this is John Vandelaare. You may remember his grandfather, Henry Whitman, used to do some carpentry work for us; his Uncle Jim is friends with your brother."

"It's nice to meet you," said Helen O'Neill, shaking John's hand, although she had been away from Marquette so long she did not remember the Whitmans at all.

"Helen is home visiting."

"I'm trying to convince Father to move to Florida with me," said Helen. "I worry about him living in that big empty house by himself."

"Oh," said John, suddenly remembering the news his mother had given him a few weeks before. "I was sorry to hear that Mrs. O'Neill passed away."

"Thank you. So was I," said Robert. "I'm not leaving my house, though; I've lived there fifty-seven years, and I can't leave Marquette when all my friends are here. My best friend, Tom Hampton, lost his wife last year, so I can't leave him here alone."

"Tom has children to look after him, Father. You don't; that's why you should come to Florida with me," said Helen.

"Don't argue with me in public," said Robert. "John, introduce me to your friends here."

"This is Frank, my college roommate, and this is Holly," said John.

"It looks like you're having a celebration – I bet you're excited about NMU winning the hockey game. Wasn't that spectacular? And just think, now that they're the national champions, they'll have the world's largest dome to play in – I never imagined anything like that would be in Marquette. I guess it should be done in time for next hockey season."

"I don't think they'll play hockey in it," said Frank, "just football."

"I wish they'd settle on a name," said Robert. "I'm with the majority in thinking they should call it the Yooper Dome. It was a clever person who turned the initials U.P. into Yooper to describe us. It beats being called Trolls like those below the Mackinac Bridge. But I imagine the university will spoil everyone's fun by going with one of the more dignified suggestions like the Great Lakes Dome or the Superior Dome."

"I imagine so," said Holly.

"Well, John, will you come visit me sometime? It's been a while."

John's face lit up as it had years ago when he had first visited Mr. O'Neill.

"Yes, sir, I'd like that."

"You're still writing, aren't you?"

"Ye-es," said John, always shy about discussing his novels.

"Good, keep it up. Well, I'll see you sometime then. It was nice to meet all of you," said Robert, shaking John's hand and smiling at Frank and Holly.

"Goodbye," said Helen.

"Who's that?" Frank asked once the O'Neills had gone out the door.

"Robert O'Neill," said John.

"Is he your uncle or something?" asked Holly.

"No," said John. "My grandpa knew him. He's a famous writer."

"Never heard of him," said Frank.

John named off some well known O'Neill novels.

"I never heard of him either," Holly said. "Frank, either you agree that we get married in Marquette, or I'll have my bridesmaids wear fuschia."

"What am I getting myself into?" Frank grinned.

John was busy as the semester came to its close and final exams loomed before him. He had every intention of going to visit Mr. O'Neill, especially since he was sorry Mrs. O'Neill had passed away; he remembered that pleasant after-noon several years ago of drinking tea and eating cheesecake in that beautiful Victorian library; he remembered how full of life Mrs. O'Neill had been, even when well into her eighties; Mr. O'Neill must be terribly lonely to have lost such a lively source of happiness. But John's good intentions were forgotten when greater concerns arose.

One day, John came back from the library to find Frank sitting on his bed, his face buried in his hands. When John entered the room, Frank lifted his head, revealing a terrified look no man Frank's size should have reason to exhibit.

At first, John was afraid someone had died; he knew all Frank's grandpar-ents were gone, so he suspected it must be Frank's mother or father. Then John thought it might be his own grandmother, and Frank was trying to find the words to tell him. But Frank just stared at him. John set down his bookbag, then asked, "What's wrong?"

Frank searched for words. "I have to tell you something."

"What is it?"

"Please don't yell at me," Frank said. John thought it ludicrous Frank would fear his temper.

"I won't. Just tell me what it is," said John, sitting down on his own bed, terrified of what could have crushed his friend into this crouching, frightened shell.

"Remember when I went home for spring break?" Frank asked.

"Yeah."

"Well, something happened that I didn't tell you about."

"What?"

"I met this girl at a bar. A girl I knew from high school. Her name's Dawn. I – we – I drank too much, and we – I was just – "

He could not say the words, but John understood.

"You slept with her?"

Frank's eyes confirmed his guilt.

"I thought you promised you'd be faithful to Holly."

"Don't get mad at me, John. I can't bear it," said Frank, tears welling in his eyes. "That's the only time I've ever been unfaithful to her. Please, you're my best friend. I need your help."

"What can I do about it?" John felt more exasperated than willing to help.

"I got Dawn pregnant."

"Oh," said John. "Shit."

Even Frank was surprised to hear such a word from John's mouth.

"I know you're ashamed of me," said Frank. "I'm sorry to disappoint you. I – "

"It's all right," said John, angry, but not enough to increase his friend's agony. "I'm sorry. I just wish it hadn't happened."

"I don't know what I was thinking," said Frank. "It meant nothing to me. I didn't even enjoy it with her – that was when I knew Holly is the only girl for me. But I never thought my one mistake could be so awful that the girl would get pregnant."

John did not know what to say. He wished he could undo the past for Frank, but it was impossible. Now they had to worry about the future. Would this girl expect Frank to marry her? Poor Holly would be heartbroken, no matter what happened.

"When are you going to tell Holly?" John asked.

"I don't know. If Dawn has an abortion, maybe I won't have to."

"Is she planning to have an abortion?" asked John, stunned by the added complexity. He was against abortion, but he did not want to see four lives ruined – Holly and Frank's, and this Dawn girl's, plus that of the baby who might end up without a parent, or with two parents who did not love each other but married for its sake.

"She doesn't know what she wants. She thinks she wants to keep the baby, but I'm hoping to talk her out of it."

"What if she does keep it? Will you marry her?"

"No, I can't. She's – no, for one thing she's too ugly. I must have been really drunk to do anything with her that night."

Then John blew up. "You mean the best reason you can come up with for not marrying her is that she's ugly? You mess up your life and hers and Holly's, and you won't try to make it right because the girl is ugly?"

"I don't mean it like that," Frank said. "Please, John. Don't get mad at me."

"I don't know what to think," said John. "I'm sorry for you, sorry that you've been so stupid. I'm sorry if I'm mad, but this is a shock for me too. I don't like to see my best friend ruin his life."

"I don't want to ruin it; I want to fix it, but I don't know how."

"First, I think you need to tell Holly," said John.

"I can't yet. I need to figure out what to do about the baby first. I can't deal with losing the woman I love right now. I need to figure out what Dawn wants and then figure out how that will effect Holly and me."

John did not know what to say. He could not believe what was happening.

"John, please don't tell Holly. I'll tell her when I'm ready. The baby isn't due until December. I've got lots of time to tell her."

"You don't have lots of time. She's already planning the wedding. You have to tell her soon."

"I will. I just – I need to think all this through."

"All right," said John. "I won't say anything to anyone." He would not tell Holly. She was his friend, but his first loyalty was to Frank. A numbness set in as he tried to imagine how Frank's one drunken escapade could so mess up all their lives; he was angry to think how he had found so much joy in Frank and Holly's happiness, and now, his joy was over. He told himself he should live his own life, rather than live vicariously through his friends' relationships, but by doing so, at least he did not hurt himself as Frank and Holly had done. He still hoped for the best for them, but he did not feel there was much hope.

The next few days, John avoided Holly. One evening she called and asked why he had not come over the night before with Frank to watch TV. He made the excuse that he had to study for exams, although he had taken his last exam that day. He was looking forward to the end of the semester. Holly's roommate, Mandy, was graduating, so Frank was going to move in with Holly for their senior year, a decision Frank had made before he learned he would be a father. John decided to move home his senior year to save money. At first, he had been disappointed not to be Frank's roommate anymore, but now he felt relieved he would not have to spend so much time around the happy couple who had a volcano about to erupt beneath them.

The day before he moved out of his dorm, John was alone, packing, when the phone rang. Since Frank was gone to class, and Holly knew Frank's schedule perfectly, John could not imagine who except a telemarketer would call him in the middle of the day.

"John?"

It was his mother.

"John, listen. Grandma's in the hospital."

There was silence as the words sunk in.

"What's wrong with her?" Why, he asked himself, did bad things always come in groups?

"She wasn't feeling well last night when I stayed with her, but when I checked on her before leaving for work this morning, she said she was fine.

Then Aunt Eleanor came over to have breakfast with her and found she was still in bed and had vomited all over. Your Grandma didn't respond to her, so she cleaned up the mess and took Grandma's temperature. When she saw Grandma had a fever, she called an ambulance. I'm at the hospital now, waiting for the doctor's diagnosis. They think she has the stomach flu."

"Is she going to be all right?" John asked.

"I hope so, but it's scary right now. Could you come over and sit with me? You're done with your classes, right?"

"Yeah, I'll walk right over. I'll be there in fifteen minutes."

His mother gave him directions for where to meet her at the hospital. Then he was out the door and trekking uphill from down campus. He walked quickly, afraid his grandmother was so sick she might pass away before he saw her one last time. He walked past Olson Library, the Hedgcock Field House, then around the curbing road past the Cohodas Building and the Don H. Bottum University Center before crossing the parking lot to reach College Avenue. Before him was the former St. Luke's Hospital where he had been born. Since then, it had merged with St. Mary's Hospital to form Marquette General Hospital, now the largest hospital for hundreds of miles in any direction. While yet a boy, John had seen built a towering skyscraper on the west of the hospital's property. Now, to the astonishment of even Marquette's proudest residents, another towering structure was being built on the opposite side of College Avenue. The future Neldberg building, named for the hospital's current administrator, would contain the first and only escalator in Upper Michigan, and perhaps most amazing of all, it would be connected by a skywalk to the hospital buildings across the street. John was thankful his mother had said she would meet him in the hospital lobby; otherwise, he would have been lost amid the maze of medical buildings where two thousand people were employed.

"Is it serious?" he asked the moment he saw his mother.

"They're giving Grandma an IV because she's so dehydrated. I'm not surprised since she barely ate or drank anything yesterday, and she had diarrhea. The IV will help her, but it's scary considering her age."

"I know," said John. He wished he could squeeze his mother's hand, but much as they loved each other, they were not a touching family. John thought it odd how Frank could affectionately fling his arm around just about anyone, then be crass the next moment to his closest friends, yet the Vandelaares and Whitmans, closer to each other than most families, rarely expressed physical affection.

John and Ellen waited in a lounge until they could see his grandmother.

After a minute, Ellen said, "Poor Aunt Eleanor, having found Grandma like that. She was nearly hysterical when she called me. She's got enough problems right now without having to worry about Grandma."

"Why, what's wrong with her?" asked John. Since he lived in the dorms, he often felt left out of the family gossip.

"She's worried about Uncle Bill's son, Alan – she's always been fond of that boy – he's gotten himself into a mess by getting his girlfriend pregnant."

"Who's his girlfriend?" asked John.

"I don't know her name. Apparently, he just found out the girl was pregnant yesterday."

John wondered whether the girl were Sheila, whom he had met at Alan's party his freshman year.

"Apparently, Aunt Eleanor was so upset she got into an argument with Uncle Bill and told him he had set a bad example for his sons by the way he's always run around with women. She told me she wished she had said something to him years ago, but it's too late now. She's always been fond of Alan, although I never thought Alan all that promising."

"I always liked Alan; he was always friendly to me," said John, remembering childhood moments of kindness from his older cousin.

"I don't understand the young people these days," said Ellen.

John had kept Frank's secret, but now he felt the need to unburden himself, and his mother would not tell anyone.

"I feel sorry for Frank," said Ellen when John had finished the story, "but he has been stupid. You're right that he should tell Holly. He shouldn't let her make any wedding plans until he has, but don't get caught in the middle of it, or you could lose both your friends."

"Lately," said John, "I'm not so sure I care. I think they're both rather stupid. Holly knows from all the gossip around campus how wild Frank used to be, and I don't think Frank will ever grow out of it. I wouldn't be surprised if he's been sleeping around on her all the while, and just never told me because he knew I'd disapprove. He had no reason to tell me until he got a girl in trouble and needed advice."

"He sounds like a selfish young man," said Ellen. "Since he's your friend, I understand why you want to be there for him, but maybe you should find some other friends."

John had thought the same, hard as it was to realize he had outgrown his friendships. Maybe when the fall semester began, Frank, Holly, and he would all be friends again, but he was looking forward to having a break from them over summer vacation.

"Ellen, your mother's in her room now," said a nurse at the front desk. "You can go see her if you like."

"Thank you," said Ellen. John and his mother took the elevator up to his Grandma's room, dreading what the doctor might tell them.

Excerpts from John Vandelaare's Journal:

Wednesday, May 1, 1991

This morning at 8:30, my Grandma Whitman passed away. Mom was the only one at the hospital with her when she died.

Grandma first got sick last Wednesday; she had some pains in her stomach and diarrhea. Then on Thursday morning, Aunt Eleanor found she had vomited all over her bed. Her temperature was 103 so Aunt Eleanor called the ambulance to bring her to the hospital. It was down to 99.8 on Friday, but then on Sunday her kidneys started to fail and she could not go to the bathroom.

From Monday morning until Grandma died, Mom never left her side, even sleeping in a chair next to her hospital bed for two nights. I spent most of Monday afternoon with Mom and Grandma at the hospital, and I went up there again in the evening with Chad. On Monday afternoon, Grandma knew I was there even if she did not know exactly who I was. I held her hand and she looked into my eyes, but she could say little since she had her oxygen mask on. She looked as if she were scared, but by evening she did not seem to know any of us were there. Mom thinks Grandma was seeing things we couldn't see; she hoped maybe Grandma saw Grandpa coming for her. Yesterday, Aunt Eleanor, Uncle Bill, Lucy and Maud spent several hours at the hospital with Mom, me, and Chad, taking turns going into her room to sit with her, and sitting in the waiting room the rest of the time. Mom called Uncle Jim in California on Monday night and told him he better come home, but he couldn't get a flight until this morning.

Mom said when Grandma died this morning, she watched Grandma's breathing getting slower and slower until her last breath looked like her soul were leaving her body. The breath just passed down from her face and cheeks until they shrunk inward and her shoulders lowered. Mom sat there alone with her a few minutes, then called for the nurse.

Mom said she told Dad when she married him that she would never move away because she wanted to take care of her parents when they needed her, and now she is thankful that she did.

Sunday, May 5, 1991

I've been too busy with Grandma's funeral and family visiting to write lately, but I want to record what has happened the last few days.

Uncle Jim and Aunt Lisa arrived in Marquette's airport just three hours after Grandma died. Uncle Jim was upset that he wasn't there when his mother passed away, but Mom was afraid that if Grandma saw Uncle Jim, she would have been scared and realized she was dying.

Mom, Chad, and I went with Aunt Lisa and Uncle Jim to the funeral home to make the arrangements. The casket we picked out was a beautiful ivory color with a copper tint on the top. Pink flowers were painted on the side and embroidered on the inside material. The cloth was a pink so pale it was almost white, and it matched the brand new pink and white dress Mom had bought for Grandma on her last birthday, but which she had never gotten the chance to wear. Grandma also wore her white pearl necklace. Mom insisted Grandma be buried with her wedding and engagement rings on her fingers because she had worn those rings everyday for fifty-six years until this last year when her fingers had shrunk so the rings wouldn't fit anymore, and then she had carried those rings with her everywhere in her purse, just as if she were still married to Grandpa.

The funeral was Saturday morning at St. Michael's. I was the lector, and also a pallbearer along with Chad and Uncle Bill's sons, William and Jason.

Losing Grandma has been really hard for me, but I think it's been hardest on Mom and then Chad. Mom took care of Grandma nonstop these past four years so now she doesn't quite know what to do with herself. I went to college the year after Grandpa died, so Chad spent more time with Grandma, always helping her find the right page in the missalette at church and always letting her hang onto his arm when they went anywhere since she was always too stubborn to use her cane. I guess Chad was always a little closer to

Grandma, while I was closer to Grandpa. For me, almost the hardest thing about losing her is that it brings back memories of how hard Grandpa's passing was. If it hurt me so much to lose him, I can't imagine how Grandma felt about his death, although she never mentioned it. Mom was always afraid if she or Grandma mentioned it, they would break down in tears. I'm glad Grandma is with Grandpa now. I don't think they ever should have been apart.

Frank and Holly went to the funeral. John sat with them at the luncheon. They had just moved into their apartment together, and they told John he was welcome to stop by anytime. He promised to visit, but he said right now, he wanted to spend more time with his family. He decided to use his grandmother's death as an excuse to distance himself from his friends.

Uncle Jim and Aunt Lisa returned to California a few days after the funeral. They planned to return next summer when Grandma's house was sold and the estate settled; in the meantime, Ellen would clean out her parents' house and prepare to sell it. John and Chad promised to help their mother sort through their grandparents' belongings. No one wanted to sell the house, but it was smaller than the Vandelaares' home, and since John was in college, he could not afford to buy it. The house would have to be sold and the money split between Ellen and Uncle Jim.

A year was a short time to clean out an entire house. John had never realized how much a family can acquire by living in one house for half a century. Many things in it no one wanted such as Grandpa's old saw, sanders and tools, worn out old furniture, and clothes long out of date. The workshop was filled with cardboard boxes, wood and nails, screws, putty, sandpaper, mounds of sawdust and dirt by the dustpanful. The attic was a cobwebbed sacristy for loved but broken toys from Ellen's childhood, tin pails for berry-picking that had come filled with peanut butter during Eisenhower's presidency, encyclopedias too old to include the Korean War, magazines with covers discussing the 1968 presidential election. Grandma's hutch cabinet was packed with china she received for her wedding, most of it now cracked, its painted flowers rubbed off, but John carefully wrapped it and decided to keep the dozen pieces that were still whole. Ellen discovered the silver that had been her Grandma McCarey's, which her mother had once shown to her forty years before. Saddest of all was an old cigar box filled with photographs, faded black and white pictures of ladies in long dresses, men with turn of the century mustaches, people sitting in carriages. Forgotten faces. Ellen and John searched for family resemblances. They guessed who might be Grandma's parents or brothers, but they did not know for sure. Aunt Eleanor came over to identify multitudes of deceased Whitmans and Dalrymples, but the camera's attempt to preserve the McCareys and Bergmanns had failed because names had not been written on the backs of photographs.

"Grandma sure didn't like to throw anything away," said John one day when he and Ellen were cleaning out his grandparents' bedroom. He was folding up old flannel shirts to send to St. Vincent de Paul's.

"Look at this!" said Ellen, reverently unfolding a handkerchief she had found stuffed away in the dresser's bottom drawer. "Look what's embroidered on it, 'Paris 1918'." John stepped over to peer at the antique words stitched on satin cloth. "Grandma must have gotten it from one of her brothers," said Ellen. "She told me her brothers fought in World War I."

"Really?" said John. "Grandma never told me that."

"No, she wasn't one to talk about the past. She had three brothers, but I only knew my Uncle Michael, the one who became a priest. I don't think he would have been old enough to go to the war, so it must have been the other two brothers who went. It's sweet she kept this handkerchief all these years. She must have been just a little girl when her brother brought it home for her. I wish I could remember her brothers' names. I think one actually died in the war."

An hour later, John found a box in the closet which contained an old Catholic prayerbook. Stuffed inside were several obituaries.

"Mom, look at these."

"Oh, yes," said Ellen, sitting down on the bed as John handed an obituary to her. "This was her cousin, Thelma Bergmann. Oh, and look, here's my Grandma Whitman's obituary."

"Mom, look at this one," said John, stunned by the headline. "This must be the brother who brought Grandma the handkerchief. He died in a mining accident."

"Really? Read me what it says."

"It's from *The Mining Journal* in 1926," said John.

JEREMY MCCAREY

McCarey Among Dead In Barnes-Hecker Mining Disaster

Jeremy McCarey, Marquette native, was among the victims who died in the Barnes-Hecker tragedy on November 3. He was working on one of the lower levels of the mine and was unable to escape to safety.

Mr. McCarey, age 35, was the son of Patrick and Katherine (Bergmann) McCarey of Marquette. McCarey had lived in Marquette all his life until he went to serve his country in the Great War in Europe. He had been employed at the Barnes-Hecker mine for the past six years. He is survived by a widow and one child.

His remains have not been recovered. A funeral service will be held for him at St. Peter's Cathedral on Monday.

"How horrible," said Ellen. "I wonder what happened to his wife and child. That child would be my cousin, but I never met it – I don't even know whether it was a boy or girl. They must have moved away."

"Grandma never told you she had a brother who died in the mine?"

"No, I would have remembered if she did. I suppose it was too painful for her to mention, just as she never mentioned Grandpa after he died."

"Grandpa was always telling stories about the past," said John. "I wish Grandma had. It seems as if we know a lot more about the Whitmans than we do about the McCareys."

John looked through the rest of the obituaries, one for his Great-Grandpa Whitman, one for Uncle Roy, but there were no more for the McCareys.

"I'm disappointed," John said.

"Why?" asked Ellen.

"I just hoped we'd find more."

"Well, you know your grandparents weren't rich. They hoarded a little, but like most people, they just tried to get by from one week to the next."

"No, I don't mean money," said John. "It's just, Grandma used to spend so much time in her room every morning; I used to imagine she was in here writing in a diary or something."

"Well, there are those letters we found that Grandpa wrote to Grandma the year he built that house in Florida."

"I know, but I can imagine what they say before I even read them because Grandpa was more open," said John. "Grandpa must have thrown away the ones Grandma wrote to him, and I really wish they had survived so I could know more about what Grandma was like when she was younger."

"Just be thankful you knew your grandparents," said Ellen. "Not everyone is so lucky."

🍁　🍁　🍁

John was not satisfied. He wished his grandparents had lived longer, so he could have asked them more questions about their lives. Grandpa had at least been talkative; John was determined to write down every story Grandpa had told him from being paid a quarter as a kid to scrub the kitchen floor so he could treat him and Uncle Roy to a movie, to how Grandpa had proposed to Grandma at the Opera House, even though her cousin had to tag along as chaperone. He wished Grandma had told him how she felt on her wedding day, unable to be married in a Catholic church. He wondered how she had felt about moving to California. John asked his mom why they had moved to California, but she could not even remember. Aunt Eleanor thought it was because of Grandpa's poor health, but no one was sure.

John wondered why he had spent so much time writing historical fiction on events he knew nothing about. Even the novel he had intended to write about his grandfather he had tried to make sensational and adventure-filled so it would be more interesting. He suspected he could have made it more interesting by basing it solely on the truth. He should be writing about his own life and experiences; only now did he realize he did not know much about his own background. He was John Vandelaare, but he had been shaped by his environment and his family. Now he began to wonder about things such as why he was a Catholic; he knew Grandma had been Catholic, but he vaguely remembered her saying her father had not gone to church, so did his Catholicism then come from Great-Grandma McCarey? Who exactly had Great-Grandma McCarey been? All he knew about her was that her maiden name had been Bergmann. Wasn't that a German name? But were Germans Catholics or Protestants? Maybe it depended on where in Germany they came from. Why had his German or his Irish ancestors come to America? What had it been like to leave their own countries, and why had they settled in Upper Michigan of all places? Had they already known someone here, or did they come for money or work? Had they stayed because they fell in love here, or were they already married when they came? What would knowing such things mean to him? Would he understand himself any better or be any happier for knowing the hundreds of decisions his ancestors had made that resulted in his birth and life in Marquette?

Something must be gained from knowing such things. John did not know where to begin, but he brought home from his grandparents' house the obituaries, photographs, and torn newspaper clippings and began to record family names, dates, and birthplaces. From Grandma's cousin Thelma's obituary, he learned her parents' names – her father, Karl Bergmann, would have been Great-Grandma McCarey's brother. He wracked his memory for hints his grandparents had given him. He remembered at Uncle Roy's funeral, Grandpa had pointed out the graves of his own grandparents. John did not remember what the stones looked like, but he knew the approximate area where they were. One Saturday afternoon, he talked Chad into going with him to Park Cemetery.

"What were Grandpa's grandparents' names?" Chad asked as they got out of the car.

"Whitman I imagine," said John.

"Are you sure those are the grandparents he meant?"

"I don't know," said John. "His other grandparents were named Dalrymple."

They found Uncle Roy's stone beside the grave of their Great-Grandpa and Great-Grandma Whitman. Then they walked downhill in the direction Grandpa had pointed, carefully looking at the name on each stone.

After ten minutes, Chad said, "Here's a Whitman. Jacob Whitman and wife Agnes. Maybe they're great-grandpa's parents. Jacob was born in 1843 and died in 1897 and Agnes was born in 1851 and died in 1884."

"Yes, those were Great-Grandpa Whitman's parents' names according to his obituary," said John. "They died so young."

John scribbled down the names and dates. Then they wandered about, looking at other stones, searching for familiar names.

"Hey," said Chad. "Remember in Grandma's stuff we found that picture of Uncle Roy and Great-Grandma standing next to a gravestone. There were some trees near it. Maybe those are Great-Grandma's parents' graves."

"Were the trees big in the picture?" asked John, who could not remember.

"No," said Chad, "they were little, but it was a black and white picture, so the trees are probably grown now."

Twenty minutes later, they found the stone beside the trees. There lay Charles and Christina Dalrymple, and beside them was a smaller stone for Arthur Dalrymple. All three stones had birth and death dates on them, and below Arthur's name was written, "who was born in Pictou, Pictou, Nova Scotia".

"Great-Grandma had a brother named Charles," Chad reminded John. "Remember he was married to that Aunt Harriet everyone says was really mean."

"But this Charles is too old to be Great-Grandma's brother. It must be her father."

"Then Arthur must have been her grandfather."

John thought for a minute. "That would make Arthur our great-great-great-grandfather."

John wrote down their names and dates. He doubted many people knew the names of their great-great-great grandfathers. He felt he had made a successful start.

A few evenings later, John tried to draw a chart showing all his ancestors and their descendants, as far as he knew. The family lines soon grew out of control until he had to tape several pieces of paper together; then the Vandelaares' neighbor Jane stopped by.

"You know," she said, when she saw John's project, "if you go down to the Mormon Church in Harvey, they have a Family History Center there for genealogy. I have a friend who goes down there; she says they have records from all over the world on their computers. They might be able to help you."

John had never dreamt Marquette would have a place devoted to genealogy. When he went to the church, he was overwhelmed by the books, microfilm readers, and computers. He was soon spending his free evenings reading through microfilm rolls of Marquette County's censuses, birth, death, marriage, and property records, and he searched on the computer for distant relatives who had submitted information on his ancestors. He found Jacob and Agnes Whitman's marriage record, which gave him their parents' names, and then he found in the censuses the places those people had come from. The Whitmans had come from New York. Agnes's parents had been the Hennings, and they had come from Massachusetts. And then he did searches on the computer and he found out that Cordelia Whitman's maiden name had been Brookfield. Some distant relative in Utah had submitted information on the Brookfields, and traced the family back in New England to the seventeenth century. John wanted to cry and at the same time, jump up and down. He printed off the ancestral lines and came home to display his treasure.

"This is my ten-greats grandfather," John said, pointing at the chart.

"I can't even begin to wrap my mind around all that," said Ellen when he showed her the charts. "How are we related to the Brookfields again?"

John's genealogical interest soon made his family and friends think him fanatical, even a little nuts. In a couple more months, he learned he was descended from King Edward III of England. He told his friends the number of his ancestors who had signed the Magna Carta; his friends said they had never heard of the Magna Carta. He was fascinated by the overwhelming concept of all these ancestors; he could claim descent from the Emperor Charlemagne thirty different ways, and the Emperor Charlemagne's ancestry could be traced back to the first century A.D., nearly two thousand years ago. And had his great-grandma, Margaret Dalrymple Whitman, been alive, she would have been pleased to find finally proven that she was indeed a descendant of the

Stewarts, even if from a distant branch related to the Scottish royal family without any claim to the throne.

John found it almost impossible to keep track of all these people and their descendants; he finally resolved he would only keep track of descendants of ancestors who had lived in North America, but even that undertaking would take years if not decades to complete. He had to buy a computer program to keep the records straight – six enormous three ring binders were not sufficient, not when he had some nine thousand relatives to document.

He could have easily gotten lost in the magnitude of the numbers of people he found, but he also tried to learn what he could of each individual. Thousands of them would remain simply names, the rest of their identities lost to history. But when he did find information, he marveled over each ancestor's fascinating story; the Irish potato farmer thrilled him no less than the Puritan colonial governor. Eventually, he found he could claim descent from someone who had lived in every country in Europe. He had been raised to believe America was the great melting pot, but now he realized the world was a melting pot; no such thing as race existed, so how foolishly ignorant was racism. The Scots and English might hate each other, but here he was descended from a sister of Robert the Bruce as well as from the English King Edward I, Hammer of the Scots. He could claim descent from William the Conqueror and the Conquered King Harold. One ancestor was a Byzantine Emperor whose daughter married a Spanish Lord, whose son married a Hungarian Princess, whose grandson married a Countess in France, whose granddaughter married an English baron, whose grandson migrated to the seventeenth century Colony of Connecticut. No legitimate reason existed for anyone to hate anyone of a different race because not too many centuries back in history, they were both descended from the same blood. Nor did John consider himself special because he could claim descent from a king or a saint; he knew each one of his ancestors living in the year 1500 had tens of thousands of descendants living today; everyone alive could claim such lineages.

Unspeakable greatness existed in the shared ancestral past of the human race. Each ancestor had triumphed over incredible odds to continue humanity; if just one of his ancestors had not lived, John knew he would not have existed. Every individual ancestor was significant, no matter whether that person's story had been recorded or forgotten. John felt the tribulations of his own life were minor compared to his forebears' struggles, and in knowing their stories, he felt great courage to face life's trials. After all, he had the blood and perseverance of tens of thousands of magnificent human beings running through his veins.

1992

The first weekend of January, Tom Vandelaare was convinced the three feet of snow on his roof, and the several more feet still to come before winter ended, were certain to bring the ceiling crashing down, burying his family under a blanket of snow and ice. After days of hemming, hawing, and hoping for a warm day to melt the snow, he resigned himself to shoveling off the roof.

"John, you want to come up and help your dad?" Tom asked at breakfast.

"No."

"Come on, be a nice boy and help Dad."

"I'd probably fall off the roof," John said.

"No, you won't. Not if you're careful."

"I can't, Dad. I don't think I'm coordinated enough to keep my balance."

"Chad, will you help me?"

"No," said Chad. "You always yell when I help you. Besides, I have to go to work."

Chad worked at the NMU cafeteria. John had a job as a tutor at the campus Writing Center, but he could not use work as an excuse today.

"It wouldn't hurt you boys to help your father," said Tom.

"Tom," said Ellen, "they don't need to go up there. I wouldn't risk breaking my neck up there either. If you don't think you can clean the roof off on your own, we'll hire somebody."

"The neighbor's son goes up on the roof to help his dad. I've even seen him up there shoveling by himself," said Tom as he put on his boots. No one replied until he had gone out and slammed the door.

"Maybe I should help him," said John.

"Just ignore him," Ellen replied. "If you don't think you can keep your balance, you shouldn't go up there. I don't need two of you falling off."

"Well, it's a big job," said John, "and Dad'll wear himself out doing it alone."

"You'll just fall off because you're so uncoordinated," said Chad, putting on his coat and kissing his mother goodbye.

"Don't worry about it," Ellen said. "Your father's a fanatic about cleaning snow. He wouldn't even clean it today if he had someone to go ice fishing with."

John helped his mother clear the breakfast table. When she started the dishes, he went in his room. He tried to work on his novel since it was the last day of Christmas vacation and tomorrow he would be busy with school. He had wanted to write all during vacation, but instead he had spent his time doing genealogy and watching movies. He sat down at his desk, turned on the computer and waited for it to boot up. He found himself staring out the window as shovelfuls of snow were thrown off the roof. He could hear his father stamping his feet so no one would forget he was up there working. If Tom had to clean off the roof, no one else would be able to concentrate on anything until he was done.

"Negative attention, that's all he wants," John thought. He opened the document that contained his novel, rewrote a paragraph, then found himself staring out the window again.

"Darn it," he thought. "Why do I always have to feel guilty?"

"Where are you going?" Ellen asked when he passed through the kitchen in his winter jacket.

"To help Dad."

"Oh, John, just ignore your father. He doesn't need your help."

"It'll take hours to shovel off all that snow. It won't hurt me to help him for an hour."

"Well, just be careful," said Ellen.

"Dad, I'm coming up!" John shouted once he was outside, shovel in hand.

"Okay, I'll hold the ladder for you," Tom shouted down.

John had expected at least a "Thank you" for his help, but he should have known better. Now wishing he had stayed inside, he climbed up the ladder, careful not to let his feet slide off the slippery rungs. Soon he lifted one foot onto the roof.

"Be careful," his dad warned.

For a minute, John imagined himself falling backward, plummeting into a five foot snowbank, but once his feet were planted on the roof and he stepped away from the edge, he felt secure.

"Start shoveling there," said Tom. "Try to throw the snow as far as you can so it doesn't land on the bushes beside the house."

John only partly listened. He gaped at all the snow. He wondered how long this job would take; he imagined it would be time consuming if the roof were slippery. He wished there were a way to bring the snowblower up here.

"Don't worry about getting close to the edge," Tom said. "I'll do that since I'm more steady on my feet up here."

"All right," said John, stepping only where snow on the shingles gave him traction. He had expected to have trouble balancing himself, but other than shoveling on a slope, he did not feel as endangered as he had expected. The work was tiring, but he did not mind. He stopped every few minutes to catch his breath and to watch his father work like a machine. Tom liked to complain about work, but he was only happy when he was occupied.

John threw the snow onto the already imposing banks. Soon his back hurt from his crooked stance and the repetitive movement of shoveling. The snow was coming down lightly, but it was a warm winter day, nearly twenty-five degrees. The constant movement kept John warm, and he enjoyed the cool air; he had nearly forgotten how fresh air tasted after two months of being cooped up in the stale house.

Father and son stopped a moment to watch an air force jet fly overhead.

"They can make planes fly and send men to the moon," said Tom, "but they won't heat our highways in winter or find ways to make the snow melt off our roofs. The government sure has its priorities messed up."

John ignored his father's complaints. He wondered where the plane was going and what it felt like to fly one. He decided it was worthwhile to help his dad, if only to see the snow covered trees stretching in all directions and the chimneys peeking out of snowcovered roofs. He could even see Marquette Mountain's ski hill and the edge of town where the trees ended. Up here, he realized how small Marquette was – only a little clearing in a giant northern forest; it had grown from a village of a hundred people to over twenty-thousand, but when compared to the size of the forests, it had grown little. All the snow burying the houses reminded John how insignificant people were beside the power of Nature. All people could do was to build shelter for protection, to claim a piece of land for a little while, maybe a few generations, a piece of land that would remain long after its owners were gone. Yet John was descended from the rugged pioneers of Upper Michigan, and here he wanted to stay. John had not traveled much – he wanted to see the land of English literature, and Ireland, India and the pyramids of Egypt, and the Netherlands where his father's father had come from, but wherever life might lead him, he knew he would always come home to his snowy little town on Lake Superior.

He began to shovel again so his father would not yell that he was being lazy. But John had only thrown a few more shovelfuls off the roof before a familiar car pulled into the yard.

"Hello, Frank!" he yelled when his friend got out of the car.

Frank looked up. "What are you doing up there?"

"What does it look like?" shouted Tom. "We gotta get this roof cleaned off before it caves in!"

Frank looked at them as if they were crazy.

"Why didn't you call before you came out?" John asked.

"If we get a couple more big storms," Tom said, "I don't know what we'll do. Don't know where we're gonna put all this damn snow."

"I need to talk to you," Frank said.

"Okay," said John. "I'll be down in a minute. Go inside and stay warm."

"I s'pose I can finish up," Tom told John. "Thanks for your help. There's not much left to do anyway."

John felt the shoveling had not been that bad. His father had said "Thank you" after all and could not now complain that John had not helped.

John went down the ladder, then brushed the snow from his coat and shook out his hat. In the garage, he took off his boots and pounded them together to knock off the snow before bringing them inside.

"Frank said you were coming in so I made some hot chocolate," said his mom at the door. "Is your dad coming in too?"

"Not for a little while yet."

"John, you wanna go for a ride?" asked Frank, sitting at the table and sipping hot chocolate. His face said something was wrong.

"Sure, just let me put on some dry clothes. My pants are all wet."

As he changed his clothes in his bedroom, John could hear his mother asking Frank about school. He wondered what was wrong. He had not talked to Frank in a month. In fact, he had only spoken to Frank three or four times since last summer. He had told Frank he wanted to spend more time with his family since his grandmother had died, and he knew Frank had Holly now, but Frank must have suspected he wanted a break from their friendship. Still, John knew he would be there for his friend when he had a problem.

"Would you boys like me to fix sandwiches for you?" asked Ellen when John returned to the kitchen and sat down to drink his hot chocolate. "It's almost lunch time."

"No, I thought maybe I'd take John out for lunch," said Frank. "I haven't seen much of him lately."

"Sorry, I've been busy," said John.

"Is Holly joining you?" Ellen asked.

"No," said Frank. "She's working actually."

"Well, you boys have a nice time. I imagine I'll just bake some cookies this afternoon, and do up the laundry. Then maybe I'll call Aunt Eleanor later."

John swallowed down his hot chocolate and stood up. He could see Frank was miserable and not up to listening to his mother's daily household itinerary.

"I'll see you later, Mom," he said, kissing her cheek. Then he threw on his jacket and shoes and followed Frank to the car.

Tom came inside a minute later.

"That Frank sure is lazy," he said. "You would think he'd offer to help."

"Why should he?" said Ellen. "It's not his roof."

"Well, it would be nice if he gave me a hand."

"You don't need a hand," said Ellen. "Why didn't you brush that snow off before you came in? And take off those boots. You're going to track up my kitchen floor, and I just mopped it yesterday."

"So what's up?" Frank asked as he backed the car out of the driveway.

"Nothing," said John. "What's wrong? You look upset about something."

Frank did not reply until he turned the car onto the highway.

"Holly found out."

It took John a minute to realize what Frank meant.

"Oh," he said. "Well, it's about time. You should have told her months ago."

"I tried, but I couldn't," said Frank. "She found out because my brother came to visit yesterday and let it slip that Dawn had had the baby."

"Oh, when was it born?"

"The week before Christmas."

"Did you see it yet?"

"No, I don't want to go over there."

"Cripe, Frank. Why not? You're a father now."

"I don't care about that," said Frank. "I just want to be with Holly."

"I take it Holly's angry?"

"She says there's no way in hell she's going to marry me, not after I've lied to her for nine months."

"I don't blame her," said John.

He wanted to tell Frank how childish he had been not to tell Holly sooner, but he restrained himself when he saw a tear running down his friend's cheek.

"Don't cry," he said, for the first time feeling sorry for Frank.

"I can't help it. You don't know what it's like. I never felt about any girl the way I do about Holly. If I lose her, I think I'll kill myself."

"Don't talk crazy," said John.

"I mean it," said Frank. "I can't stand the thought of being separated from her."

"You can't kill yourself. You have a baby to support."

"Will you talk to her, John? Will you reason with her?"

"What am I supposed to say?" he asked, willing to help his friend, but doubting anything he said would change Holly's mind.

"Tell her I love her, that I know I made a mistake, and I promise I'll never do it again."

"Why don't you tell her that?"

"I tried, but she won't listen to me."

"Man, you've got yourself into a mess," said John. "I don't know what's wrong with you. You never could control yourself around women. I tried to warn you."

"Don't be mad at me, John. I would have told her sooner, only I love her so much I didn't want to hurt her."

"If you loved her that much, you wouldn't have gotten Dawn pregnant."

"I wish you'd been there that night, John. You would have stopped me."

"You would have done the same thing some other night."

Frank said nothing. He knew John was right.

"So, did Holly throw you out?"

"No, she went to stay with a friend of hers. I've called there about twenty times, but she won't speak to me."

"What if she won't ever speak to you? Then what will you do? And don't tell me you'll kill yourself."

"Leave."

"What do you mean?"

"Move away. I can't stay where I have a bad reputation."

"Where would you go?"

"Downstate or maybe Chicago or Minneapolis. I'll graduate, then go somewhere to find a job. Would you come with me?"

"No, I'm going to get my M.A. at Northern next year."

"You could do that anywhere. You know we won't find decent jobs around here. Come with me, John. You're the only true friend I have."

John was tempted. He remembered being on the roof and seeing the airplane. He wanted to see more of the world. He could go to school wherever Frank got a job. He could always come back to the U.P. after he finished his M.A.

"But what about the baby?" he asked. "Don't you want to be near it?"

"I can send child-support. I don't want to be around Dawn. She's a total bitch. I don't think she even wanted the baby; she just refused to get an abortion or put the baby up for adoption to spite me."

"I doubt that," said John.

"She wanted me to marry her, but that would only mess me up more. She's no catch compared to Holly. And the baby – she doesn't need a screw-up father around."

"She? You mean it's a girl?"

"Yeah," laughed Frank. "Delta Dawn Jarvi. Can you believe that? Dawn must really hate me to name our kid that."

John felt sorry for Frank, but he could not understand Frank's lack of paternal interest. He feared if he said anything more, he would only make Frank angry.

"Let's go eat something," he said. "I'll buy."

They stopped at Togo's to get subs, then drove over to Frank's place. Frank did not want to eat in a restaurant because he admitted he was afraid he might start crying in public, and he did not want to miss Holly if she came home, even if only to pick up her things. While they ate, Frank talked John into calling her.

As he dialed the phone, John looked out the window at the gently falling snow and thought how his pleasant afternoon had been destroyed.

Holly's friend answered. She was screening Holly's calls, but since it was not Frank, she passed the phone to Holly. John tried to explain how Frank was feeling, but Holly immediately cut him off.

"John, if you're calling for that jerk, you can just forget it. You never should have introduced me to him in the first place, and I can't believe you've pretended to be my friend all this time when you knew he was cheating on me."

"Holly, he told me he was going to tell you, so I trusted he would. He – "

"Then I guess that's two of us whose trust he's broken. I can't believe I wasted two years of my life with that jerk."

"Holly, he's heartbroken. He's sitting here crying. If you could see – "

"Don't you think I've been crying? Don't call me again if you're going to take his side."

The line went dead.

Frank did not need to be told what she had said. The two friends sat on the couch and watched TV, Frank interjecting his worries every few minutes. When it started to get dark, John asked Frank to drive him home.

"Will you be all right by yourself?" John asked when he was dropped off.

"Yeah."

"You're not going to try anything stupid, are you?"

"No."

"Meet me for lunch tomorrow at Bookbinders."

"All right," said Frank.

Holly did not change her mind. A week later, she came over with her friend to collect her things. Frank tried to talk to her, but her friend only shouted insults at him until he broke down crying and went to lock himself in his room. Once Holly was gone, Frank called John and told him what had happened. John had never seen Frank so upset; he was sickened by it. Even Frank did not deserve to be hurt so badly.

A few weeks later, Frank sought John out at the library to tell him, "I got a job in Milwaukee. I'm leaving the first week of May. Will you come with me?"

"No, I can't," said John. "This is home."

"There's nothing here for you," said Frank. "You can go to school there. You need to get out of this small town. Even if you get an M.A., there won't be any jobs here in your field. You'll end up moving anyway, so you might as well move now."

"Maybe I'll come to Milwaukee when I finish my M.A., but I'm not ready to leave my family yet."

"I don't know why you want to stay in this sucky town. People here don't give you a chance once they form an opinion of you. They stick you in a box, and you can never get out. You'll be happier somewhere else."

"I have to get to class," said John, packing up his bookbag.

"Fine, leave. I should have known better than to think I could depend on you. Best friend? Ha! You're like all the others. I hope you rot to death in this town."

John knew if he replied they would end up in a shouting match in the library. He was sorry his friend was hurting, but Frank had made his own troubles. He wondered now whether they had ever really been best friends; they had never had anything in common. If they parted ways now, it would probably be for the best.

At graduation that spring, John watched Holly walk across the stage, but they did not speak. He heard through a mutual friend that she had gotten a job in Minneapolis. The day after graduation, Frank moved to Milwaukee. He was no letter writer, and too broke when he first moved to call long distance. John sent him a few letters, but after he got no response from a Christmas card, he accepted that the friendship was over.

1993

Ellen had had a fine Saturday until now. She had finished all her housework, baked her cookies, and had time that afternoon to watch her favorite movie, *Guess Who's Coming to Dinner*. But when the Vandelaares arrived at St. Michael's, Ellen experienced a heartwrenching blow. She had read in the *Mining Journal* that J.D. Pierce School was to be torn down, but in her busy life, she had given it little thought. Now, before her eyes, she saw the demolition of her alma mater had begun; most of the walls were already a pile of rubble. She felt a sudden headache as if someone had cut into her skull to wrench out her memories.

She said nothing as she followed her family into church; she dipped her finger in the holy water font, made the sign of the cross, knelt to pray, then rose to join in the opening hymn. But she did not hear a word of the service. She recalled the faces of all the children she had known who had once walked through the halls and sat in the classrooms of J.D. Pierce forty years before. Now all those children were grown, and so were their children – they were spread across the country, most no longer living in Marquette. Whatever they had accomplished, they had first dreamt of achieving while sitting in a classroom of their grade school. Most of those adults did not even know their old school was gone, or if they knew, it did not matter to them. Ellen was surprised by how much she cared. Until now, she had not considered what a significant role the school had played in her life – in childhood, it had been her second home.

Last year she had sold her parents' house. She had lost her mom and dad, then her childhood home, and now her school. Her past was being forgotten – now only Uncle Bill, Aunt Eleanor, and her cousins remembered when she was a little girl, and none of them would be around that many more years.

As she knelt for the Eucharistic prayers, Ellen looked up at the rose window hanging above the altar; it had been hung in St. Michael's last year when the church celebrated its fiftieth anniversary. Preserved from when St. John the Baptist had been torn down, the window was another memorial to an unappreciated past.

She felt homesick for her childhood the rest of that evening, so homesick she decided to call her brother.

"They knocked down Pierce school," she told him. "And Longyear Hall will probably be torn down too. Some people are trying to raise money to save it, but it doesn't look hopeful."

Jim replied, "Well, I guess it's time the old school was torn down. Here in L.A., we don't keep old buildings long. It's more cost effective to build a new one than to renovate an old building."

Ellen asked Jim how his kids were. She did not want to talk about her school anymore, not if her brother were unsympathetic to her feelings. How could she and her brother be so different? She wondered what odd gene she had inherited that kept her in her hometown, clinging to her family and her past while her brother had left Marquette without once looking back.

When she got off the phone, she tried to read the newspaper. John came into the kitchen after a minute to pour himself a glass of coke.

"Mom," he said, distracting her attention from the editorials.

"What?" she asked, peering at him through her new bifocals.

"I'm going to write a letter to the newspaper about Longyear Hall. I think it's awful they're going to tear it down."

Ellen paused, then said, "So do I."

"I think it's bad enough," said John, "that St. John's was torn down to build a parking lot, and there's only going to be a parking lot where J.D. Pierce was. But I don't see how they can tear down the oldest building on campus."

"Neither do I," said Ellen.

John went to his room to write his letter; he did not suspect how he had cheered his mother by letting her know another family member shared her feelings.

Extract from the *Mining Journal*'s editorials:

> To the Editor:
> As an NMU graduate and seventh generation Marquettian, I believe the decision to demolish Longyear Hall is nothing short of a major tragedy, both to NMU and Marquette.

Anyone who has read the recent articles in the *Mining Journal* cannot help but be appalled. NMU repeatedly states it cannot afford the $2.9 million to save its oldest structure. At the same time, it is planning to spend $38 million to heat the campus sidewalks, build a parking ramp, renovate the University Center, and repair the leaking Superior Dome. If $38 million can be spent in this way, why cannot $2.9 million be found for the university's most historical building?

Longyear Hall is a significant historical monument for Northern Michigan University, reflecting the pioneer spirit that founded Marquette. The Longyear family is a legend in the Marquette area. John M. Longyear's contributions to the Marquette area include being elected mayor in 1890, donating the land for the Peter White Public Library, helping found the Marquette County Historical Society and its John M. Longyear Research Library, founding the Huron Mountain Club, and battling to get a normal school, today's Northern Michigan University, located in Marquette.

Do those who question the historical value of Longyear Hall even know about the Longyear family? Several of the board members who have decided the building should be demolished are not even Marquette natives. What right do they have to take what belongs to us? Those of us whose ancestors came and built this city out of the wilderness are appalled by the situation. Just because people do not share our heritage does not mean they have the right to take it from us

Marquette, when will you stop letting this happen? Why didn't you learn your lesson when beautiful Kaye Hall was destroyed? Do we really want another historical building torn down after we watched St. John the Baptist's Church replaced with a parking lot? What will be next? Will St. Peter's Cathedral be toppled to the ground? Will the Peter White Library's pristine limestone walls come to feel the wrecking ball?.

In 1999, not only will NMU celebrate its 100th anniversary, but Marquette will celebrate its 150th birthday. What will we have to celebrate if there is nothing left to remind us of our past?

John Vandelaare, Proud Marquette Native

The past was disappearing. John's letter, and countless others in the same vein, made no difference. Longyear Hall was demolished. Ironically, Northern Michigan University soon after announced preparations for its one hundredth anniversary by locating historical places on campus.

John had enjoyed his years at NMU, but once he finished school, he decided he would move away to get a Ph.D. in creative writing. Frank had been right; once he finished his M.A., Marquette would hold nothing for him.

During his last year at Northern, John delved more deeply into his genealogy in an attempt to preserve his heritage for his own knowledge. He would return from long hours spent at the Peter White Public Library, the Latter Day Saints' Family History Center, or the J.M. Longyear Research Library, with new revelations for his family.

"Mom, you know how I've been trying to find Gerald and Clara's marriage record?" he said one evening.

"Whose?" asked Chad.

"Gerald and Clara Henning. Our ancestors. I've been looking for their marriage record."

"I know you've mentioned them a lot," said Ellen, "but I still can't remember how we're related to them."

"They were your Grandpa Whitman's grandparents. Their daughter Agnes married Jacob Whitman."

"Okay," said Ellen, pretending she now had them straight in her head. "So did you find what you were looking for?"

"Yes, they were married in Boston. And the marriage record listed Clara's maiden name as Wilson. So then I found her parents' marriage record, and her mother's maiden name was Lyte!"

"So?" asked Ellen, wondering why her son sounded so excited.

"Don't you know who the Lytes were?"

"No," said Chad, "but I'm sure you're going to tell us."

"The Lytes were one of the most important families in colonial New England. Three of them were colonial governors, including two of our direct ancestors, and the other is our ancestral uncle. The uncle was a governor in Connecticut, while the two direct ancestors were colonial governors of the Massachusetts Bay Colony."

"That's interesting," said Ellen.

"It's not that interesting," said Chad. "It's not as if anyone ever heard of them before. Let us know when you find out we're related to someone who really matters like a president."

"Well, I found out something else interesting. You know how Grandma Vandelaare's maiden name was Varin."

"Yeah," said Tom, looking up from scratching a lottery ticket.

"Well, Mom's great-great-great grandfather, Lucius Brookfield, was married to a Suzanne Varin, and her son by her other husband, Jean Varin, is dad's ancestor. They were living in Marquette in the 1860s when Mom's family was also here."

"Wait a minute," said Ellen, "are you telling me I'm related to your father?"

"Gross," said Chad.

"No, you're not related, but Dad's ancestor and yours were married for a short time. Suzanne's husband was killed in the Civil War, and Lucius's wife died about the same time, so Lucius and Suzanne got married. Lucius was an old man then, and Suzanne only in her thirties. He died soon after, and then Suzanne married again and moved to Wisconsin. Dad is descended from Suzanne by her first husband Jean. They had a son, Gervase, who was actually born in Marquette. Gervase is Dad's great-grandfather."

"That's funny," said Ellen. "Tom, could you move so I can set the table?"

"Yeah, I'm done," said Tom, brushing the shavings of his lottery ticket onto the floor. "Just another loser. I don't know why I waste my money on these tickets."

"I don't know either," said Chad. "Mom, will you press my blue shirt after supper?"

"Sure," said Ellen. "John, do you want to watch a movie with us later?"

John saw his family was unimpressed by his genealogical discoveries. He did not want to watch a movie with them. He wanted to type his latest findings into his computer so his information would be documented properly while he still understood the notes he had made. But he reminded himself it was almost Christmas, and soon he would be moving away from home. The ancestors could wait until tomorrow; he should enjoy what time he had with his family before he left home.

1994

Excerpts from John Vandelaare's Journal:

April 7, 1994

Today I was accepted into a Ph.D. program. I wrote to the university and told them I accepted the teaching assistantship and would be there this fall. It's strange to think I'll be moving. Everyone has been congratulating me and telling me they know it must be hard to get into a Ph.D. program, but they are sure I'll be an excellent candidate because I love literature and writing so much. My whole life seems to have led up to this moment when I can finally devote myself to my writing in hopes that my dissertation will become a published novel or short story collection. It will be hard to live so far from home, but I feel a calling to do this and prove once and for all that I can be a writer. Maybe someday I'll return to Marquette, but right now, if I don't go, I feel I will regret it the rest of my life. This chance will bring me new opportunities and chances to meet people. Writing and literature are really only a means to better understanding the human condition, and knowledge is what I wish for more than anything.

May 3, 1994

I graduated with my M.A. a few days ago. It was a nice ceremony in the Superior Dome. The English Department had a special party for all the graduates; I received many congratulations and best wishes in pursuing my Ph.D. Although it was a happy day, I kept thinking of Frank; he had been my best friend through my undergraduate years, but now he is not here to see me get my M.A. I also thought about Grandpa and Grandma and how proud they would be to know I've done so well for myself so far in life. Looking back, the six years I've spent at Northern have been the happiest of my life, taking away much of the pain I felt after Grandpa died. Now they are over, and it is hard to imagine what the future will be, but as Tennyson wrote:

> The old order changeth, yielding place to new,
> And God fulfills himself in many ways,
> Lest one good custom should corrupt the world.
> Comfort thyself.

So I am off to a new life in a few months. I will go, like Stephen Dedalus, "to forge in the smithy of my soul the uncreated conscience of my race". I will miss Marquette, but I can always come back to visit.

August 18, 1994

Next week I'll be moving away. I've been working on my family tree some more, trying to do what I can before I move since it'll be harder to access the local Marquette records downstate. I could try the internet – I guess there are getting to be lots of genealogy websites, but I haven't gotten online yet at home and haven't had the time to search at the library.

This afternoon I happened to drive past Holy Cross Cemetery so I decided to stop and say goodbye to Grandpa and Grandma, who are buried there. Then I went to the Westwood Mall and realized that just a few years ago, I would have gone to the Marquette Mall, but that mall is now nearly empty. Marquette has changed a lot since I was a kid. At the mall, I did not even see one person I knew. When I was little, I remember going places with Grandpa, and it seemed it would take an hour to go in and out of a store because Grandpa constantly met people he knew. Now a Walmart is going to be built, and one building after another seems to be appearing along US 41; soon Marquette and Negaunee will have merged together. It's easier to think about moving away when I realize Marquette will soon no longer be the city I knew. There's even talk of closing K.I. Sawyer Air Force Base now that the Cold War is over. If that happens, it will really hurt the local economy, so I'm probably better off to leave. I'll always love Marquette, but Frank was right – there really is nothing here for me anymore.

September 10, 1994

I've lived downstate for a couple weeks now. It's been a difficult experience. My parents came down to help me move in; I drove down the '89 Chevy I bought while they came down in my dad's truck. I'm glad we didn't all ride in the same vehicle because I cried from Munising to Seney. My eyes got so blurry I don't know how I managed to stay on the road. But I've been fine since then, other than a little scared. I'm enjoying my classes and already learning new things about literature. It is strange to live where I don't know anyone, but I hope to meet people, and more importantly, to learn to write better. I must stay positive; the strangeness of it all will wear off eventually; right now it seems like a game, as if I were a child playing house in someone else's apartment. I'll write more in my journal when I feel more settled. I'm going to work on my novel the rest of this evening.

After two long months downstate, John made his first weekend trip home. He barely slept before leaving early Friday morning. He was on the road before daylight because he wanted to beat the morning rush hour traffic. On future trips, he would find the drive long and tedious, but today, despite pouring rain, and his getting lost for twenty minutes from a wrong turn, the nearly eight hour drive flew by because every mile brought him closer to home.

When John crossed the Mackinac Bridge and saw the sign welcoming him to the Upper Peninsula, his spirits rose. From that moment on, everywhere were familiar sights from his childhood's summer vacations to Mackinac Island or Sunday drives to Newberry and Munising. The best part of the drive was the last stretch along Lake Superior, down a hill and around a curve until, across the bay, he saw Marquette.

Whenever in the past he had come home from a vacation or a night excursion, he had come around those same curves, and driving through Harvey, he had seen Marquette's lights spreading out across the water, through the openings in the old ore dock, like a festive beacon, welcoming all to its warm harbor. Today, the pouring rain in the afternoon did not cast a welcoming glow upon Marquette, but John's heart glowed within him. St. Peter's red cathedral roof, the first distinguishable building, was enough to make him happy.

Although he did not have to go through Marquette to reach home, he could not resist driving through his favorite town. He drove slowly through Harvey to relish the sight of the old Harvey House, the Marquette Prison's gates, the Garden Room Restaurant. Then he went up a hill and came down it to find himself in the Queen City of the North. He drove through the town he had not seen in two months, and felt as if he had been away half a lifetime. He drove to Washington Street to look at the old downtown, the Old Savings Bank, the First National Bank, the Delft Theatre, the Post Office his grandfather had helped to build. He went up Third Street's hill and turned onto Ridge Street, past the Peter White Library and then past all the grand old historical homes. He turned onto Lakeshore Boulevard, and drove along the beach to Presque Isle. He circled the island, even spotting some deer, now freed from their zoo cages, but so at home on the island that they roamed it freely to the delight of Marquette's residents. Then he drove back through town along Fourth Street, fondly gazing at each familiar house, surprised to see one repainted a different color. Down the hill he went as St. Peter's Cathedral loomed up before him. He turned onto Fisher, then Champion – he knew the names of all the streets, so unlike downstate – then Genesee and Division Streets, and finally, he started down County Road 553 to his parents' house.

When John reached home, the garage door was closed, signifying no one was home. He felt disappointed not to be greeted immediately upon his return when he had anticipated his visit for so long. He carefully opened the back door, knowing Dickens usually lay against it because it was near the heater. But Dickens was not by the back door. John stepped inside, set his suitcase down, and took off his shoes. Still no Dickens greeted him. He walked through the kitchen and dining room. Everything looked familiar, yet out of proportion as if he had not quite remembered things properly, or perhaps because the exhausting drive had made him a little dizzy. Then he saw Dickens, lying on the carpet, taking a sunbath in a beam of light that stretched across the living room. John bent over to pet him and say hello.

Dickens awoke at the familiar but long unheard voice. For two months he had not understood where his best friend had gone. When Grandpa and Grandma had gone away, they had never come back; he had loved them, but they were not John. He had feared John would not come back, and that meant no more walks with John, no more treats from him, no more of his singing while John played the piano, no more laying against John's feet at the end of his bed. Since John had gone away, Dickens had not felt like doing much of anything. He thought he must be dreaming now, but John's hand on his back felt so real, and he could smell John, and hear John's voice. John was not gone forever as he had thought. He was overwhelmed with happiness. He jumped up, pawing the air, scratching John's legs until John sat down beside him and let him jump into his lap. He licked John's face full of kisses.

"It's okay, Dickens; it's okay. Calm down. Calm down." Finally Dickens lay down to have his belly rubbed until John's arm grew sore. John told Dickens how happy he was to be home. He promised they would go for a long walk, but before they could carry out this plan, the back door opened.

"Hello!" Ellen and Chad called. John shouted back "Hello!" He heard them set down grocery bags on the kitchen counter. Then they came into the living room.

"Welcome home!" said Ellen, laughing at the sight of Dickens getting his belly rubbed. "He sure is happy to see you."

"He jumped all over me," said John. "I've never seen him so excited."

"Well, he missed you," said Ellen, unable to say how much she had herself missed him. "How long have you been home?"

"Just ten minutes."

"Did you have a good trip?" Chad asked.

"Yeah, it rained most of the way, but I didn't have any trouble."

"Good," said Ellen. "Give me a hug."

John got up from the floor and hugged his mother, although that only caused Dickens to jump up, sit on his haunches and paw the air for more attention.

"It's okay, Dickens," John said, patting him on the head. "I'll be home for two whole days. I'll have plenty of time to pet you."

"Your dad should be home any minute, so we might as well eat. I got hamburgers from McDonalds because you said on the phone you had plans to go out with Derek tonight. I figured you wouldn't want to wait for me to make supper."

"All right," said John. "I'll call Derek real quick to see what time he wants me to come over. I think we're going to the late movie anyway, and then maybe out to the Shamrock."

"That's fine," said Ellen, taking off her coat. "Just don't tire yourself out. You had a long drive, and you'll have to make it again on Sunday."

John called Derek – his only friend from college still left in Marquette. In the meantime, Tom came home. In a few minutes, they were all eating at the table, even Dickens, who sat impatiently at John's feet, waiting for bites from the hamburger the family always specially ordered and chopped up for him.

Ellen was so intent on telling John everything that had happened while he was gone that he could barely say anything about his own experiences at school. But he did not really mind. He did not want to think about school this weekend. He kept looking at the clock, conscious of how quickly this weekend was already passing away; he wanted to enjoy every minute he could. He insisted on washing the dishes, although his mother wanted him to rest until he went out. They did the dishes together while Tom went into the living room to wait for the lottery numbers to come on TV. Then, the family sat together and watched a rerun of *Roseanne*.

At eight o'clock, John went to get his coat so he could go out.

"Mom!" he heard Chad shout. "Dickens is throwing up!"

John ran into the kitchen. Dickens was gagging, spitting up saliva. Then his back legs collapsed and he lay down.

"Is he okay?" John asked as Ellen knelt down to wipe up the mess.

He began to pet Dickens, who lay there panting.

"It's all right," said Ellen. "Seeing you probably just overexcited him. He's not young anymore."

"Maybe we shouldn't have given him that hamburger," said John.

"He'll be fine," said Ellen. "Go out with your friends and don't worry. He'll be okay if he just rests a little."

John was reluctant to leave, but tonight was his only chance to see Derek, who had a date tomorrow night. John wanted to hear all about Derek's life and what he planned to do when he finished school – Derek was taking the seven years to finish a four year degree plan. John forgot about Dickens once he and Derek were at the movie and then at the Shamrock Bar. He enjoyed talking to Derek, but he felt odd at the Shamrock, suddenly realizing how much younger than him were most of the students; it was a college hangout, while he was now a Ph.D. student. He felt like an outsider now, but he dismissed the feeling as simply being tired from his long drive. When he crawled into bed that night, he fell asleep to recurring dreams of the seemingly neverending freeway that had brought him home.

Early in the morning, Ellen heard a whimpering sound in the kitchen. She imagined Dickens was just dreaming, but when the noise continued, she crawled out of bed and went to the kitchen, hoping he was not sick again.

When she turned on the light, she saw Dickens had vomited all over the rug by the back door. Now he was sitting up, trembling and looking frightened. She grabbed some paper towel to wipe up the mess before he decided to walk through it. She talked soothingly to him. He raised his head, although he was too old and blind now to see her. Then he opened his mouth as if to be sick again. Instead, a convulsion shook his body and he fell over shaking. Ellen was too shocked to know what to do. Then the shaking ended. He lay still.

Dickens was gone. Ellen tried not to cry. She looked at the clock. It was just six in the morning. She grabbed more paper towel and wiped up the rest of the mess. Then she quietly went into the bathroom to get dressed and take the curlers out of her hair. Fifteen minutes later, she woke up Tom. When she told him, he said he would dig a hole in the backyard and build a box to put Dickens in. Then he got dressed and went outside. Ellen was thankful for a husband this morning.

She went back into the kitchen but did not know what to do with herself. She had planned to bake cookies that afternoon, but she felt so fidgety she decided to do it now and get it over with. Cookies might cheer up the boys. She did not know what to do with Dickens. She just could not bring herself to cover him with a blanket while he lay there. She wanted to pretend, as she saw him out of the corner of her eye, that he was just sleeping as always, usually with his snout in one of the boys' shoes, finding comfort in the scent of his loved ones.

When she heard the boys stirring, Ellen went to tell them about Dickens before they saw him. Both came and looked at their dog's still form, then quietly sat down at the kitchen table. They were still in their pajamas, feeling unmotivated to do anything in the early morning quiet.

"It had to be expected," said John. "He was fourteen years old and blind."

"It's better that he went this way than our having to put him to sleep," said Chad. "That's what I was afraid of."

Tom came in from digging the hole. Then they all sat down to breakfast. After they ate, the boys helped Tom build a wooden box. Chad placed his tattered childhood quilt, made by Aunt Eleanor, into the box so Dickens would be comfortable. By noon, Dickens was buried. He rested beneath a tree in the backyard where he had often lain in the grass on a warm summer's day while John sat beside him, reading a book and petting him.

The Vandelaares' neighbor, Jane, came over that afternoon. When told what had happened, she said, "Maybe Dickens was just waiting to see John one last time before he died."

John knew Jane's words were intended to console. He also knew he was not to blame, but after looking forward to this visit for two months, the weekend had become bittersweet. He wished he had never moved away, but the nagging voice in his head kept reminding him the U.P. held nothing for him. Now that Dickens was gone, John felt another tie to home was broken. If he were ever to have a decent job, to make anything of himself, he would have to finish his Ph.D. and find a teaching job at a university somewhere.

John Vandelaare lived downstate for four years, only visiting home at Christmas or for a few weeks in the summer. At the end of that time, he expected he would earn a Ph.D., and then everything he had wanted and worked for, whatever everything was, would finally happen.

1998

"There he is," said Aunt Eleanor, greeting John when he opened the door. "Here, Bill," she said, shoving the cake at her brother, "Hold this. I have to hug Dr. Vandelaare."

John gently wrapped his arms around his fragile but active old aunt.

"Aunt Eleanor, I'm still just John," he replied.

"Congratulations, John," said Uncle Bill, shaking his great-nephew's hand once his sister had taken back the cake.

"Thank you. Come on in."

The week before, John had graduated with his Ph.D., then packed up his belongings and moved back home. He had searched the country for a position teaching creative writing, but the market for English professors was oversaturated. The two hundred applications he had sent out had been responded to with letters saying, "While your credentials are impressive, please understand, we had seven hundred applicants for this position." He had not even gotten a single interview. He had achieved his goal of earning a Ph.D., but without any employment prospects, he did not know what else to do except return home while he continued looking for a job. He felt depressed, but his mother insisted on throwing him a graduation party, and knowing how proud she was of him, he did not have the heart to disappoint her.

Aunt Eleanor and Uncle Bill were followed by Lucy and Maud, bringing bags full of graduation presents for him. His father's hunting buddy, Mr. Richmond, greeted him with a pat on the back and said, "There's the professor!" Their neighbor Jane kept saying, "We're all so proud of you."

Family friends flooded through the door, handing John graduation cards. Hardly in a festive mood, he felt overwhelmed by the attention. Ellen scurried about, pouring glasses of pop and making sure everyone had coffee. Tom kept getting in her way, fussing about the food, asking why she had made so much potato salad, telling her he did not know why she got a vegetable tray when no one would eat the broccoli or cauliflower on it. Chad helped his mother while John greeted each guest.

Once they all finally sat down to eat, John got the questions he dreaded.

"John, are you going to keep teaching?" asked Jane.

He bought time to think of an answer by finishing chewing on some celery, but there was only one answer he could give.

"I don't know. It depends on whether I can find a job."

"With all the teaching you did while earning your degree, that should be no problem for you," said Mr. Richmond. "I bet all the colleges will want to hire you."

"He says he can't find a job," said Tom.

"Well, but you just graduated; you've barely started looking," said Jane.

"I've been looking for the last year," said John, "ever since I started my dissertation. I've already gotten rejection letters for two hundred teaching positions."

"Two hundred!" said Bill. "Why, I never applied for more than three or four jobs in my life."

"Well, with the economy being so bad, Uncle Bill," said Lucy, "it's harder for young people to find a job than when you were young."

"They liked you at NMU. Why won't they hire you there?" asked Aunt Eleanor.

"They don't have an opening for a creative writing professor."

"But you were one of their top students," said Jane.

"That doesn't matter if there aren't any job openings," said John.

"Well, don't be too disappointed," said Maud, seeing John's glum face. "You'll do just fine for yourself. It'll just take time."

"People fall into jobs. It's often strange how things work out," said Jane.

"Maybe you could just find a part-time job in the U.P. and keep writing in the meantime," said Lucy.

"Everyone will think he's too overqualified to work around here," said Chad, personally knowledgeable of the Upper Peninsula's sluggish job market. "Most of the jobs are low-paying, so no one will think someone with a Ph.D. will stick around here."

"You've worked so hard," said Jane, "that it won't hurt you to have a little break until you find work. Rather than worry about the future, you should be proud of everything you've already accomplished at your young age."

The conversation changed. Bill and Tom talked about fishing. Jane and Maud discussed their gardens. Mr. Richmond told Lucy about his last trip to Walmart to get his oil changed. Ellen finished eating, then took orders for cake. John retreated from the company by offering to help her. After the cake, John opened his graduation cards. Lively chatter followed for an hour before everyone said their goodbyes.

Once the guests were gone, John helped his mother clean up. Then she went to wash her hair, and he went in the living room to watch TV just to be sociable with his family. But Chad soon decided to go home to his apartment, and Tom fell asleep on the couch. John could not concentrate on *Dr. Quinn, Medicine Woman*. He was replaying the party in his mind.

He told himself it had not been that bad. That he had no job prospects was now common knowledge among his friends and family. While everyone was proud of him, he felt let down. They all knew he had earned a Ph.D., but no one had asked what he had learned during all those years of school. They only thought of his degree as a way to get a good job, which he knew was unlikely. None of them were interested in discussing teaching, writing, or literature with him. He did not know what to say to these people, not even those of his own flesh and blood; they did not care about *Lyrical Ballads*, revenge tragedies, deconstructionism, or the devastating effects of Darwinism upon Victorian literature. He had often heard academia referred to as the "ivory tower". Now he realized that outside of the ivory tower, no one cared it existed. Even the people he was closest to were so involved in the details of their own lives that they were not interested in the problems or crises of his own. And now that he had no teaching position, he wondered what use was a Ph.D.? Granted, he had enjoyed gaining so much knowledge, but it was knowledge with only limited purpose. He could have just read on his own and worked during the last four years. He began to wonder whether he had gone to school out of sheer vanity to become Dr. Vandelaare.

During his graduate school years, he had also found himself questioning the usefulness of creative writing classes. The undergraduates to whom he had tried to teach writing had rarely listened to his advice. The professors who tried to teach him to write were more interested in distorting his work into what they considered as properly innovative literary forms than letting him search for his own unique means of expression.

He left the living room and went to find the copy of his dissertation. Picking it up, he began to read one of the short stories in the collection; he found what he had always suspected: it was not very good. He had plugged along at writing these stories to earn his professors' praise and to meet the dissertation requirements of the doctoral program; the stories were approved because they were the model of current postmodern trends, exemplifying the cleverness of style that had replaced emphasis on character and insight. After four years of studying writing and literature, John had produced mere mediocrity. He had intended to send these stories to magazines, or even publishers. But he knew even if they sold, they would not bring him any significant amount of money, so why should he attach his name in print forever to such inferior work? Everything suddenly seemed pointless.

His first week home, John had resisted unpacking his belongings from downstate. Now he realized his chance of finding a teaching job for the fall semester was so slim he might as well make himself comfortable in his old bedroom; he never felt comfortable until his books were arranged alphabetically and categorized as British, American, French, or World literature, history, religion, and psychology. He had acquired so many books that what had filled his apartment downstate could not now fit into his bedroom; he delegated boxes of books to the basement. He spent an entire morning sorting and arranging his library. Then at noon, he cooked a frozen pizza, poured a glass of coke, and because it was a warm spring day, sat on the porch while he ate.

During his graduate school years, a book had always been propped beside his plate as he ate his solitary meals; he had rarely dared give himself a break from the work demanded to earn his degree. Today, after sorting so many books, he felt no desire to open and read one. He slowly ate his pizza while looking across the backyard and telling himself he was home. Coming into bloom was the lilac bush that had been transplanted from Grandma's house. The bird feeder had a flock of junkos around it. Chipmunks were scurrying about the lawn, chasing each other, collecting seeds that had fallen from the feeder. At the end of the yard was a little cluster of trees under whose shade Dickens had been buried. Chad had planted a garden over the grave.

"It's been a long time since I just sat here and enjoyed nature," John thought. He felt as he often had when after hours of reading, he had lifted his head from a book to refocus his eyes. Four years of stress and hard work had ended; he felt he deserved the right to breathe again, but he only felt more stressed now than he had during those years in the doctoral program. He turned his head toward the woods where he had spent his childhood climbing trees; for a moment, he relived how he and Holly had picked ferns to make roofs for their forts. Happier, more innocent times. He had spent so many recent years trying to progress toward a goal that had led to naught, he had forgotten the simple pleasures along the way.

He doubted he would ever find a teaching job – he had wasted four years to earn a Ph.D. He would have to start over now. He would begin by looking for a job in Marquette. He would be cautious before he made any giant decisions about his future.

If nothing else, the rigors of the Ph.D. program had taught him not to be fainthearted; he had watched many doctoral candidates leave the program, but he had persevered, and he would persevere again. If he could earn a Ph.D., he could accomplish just about anything. He now realized he had limited himself by thinking that if he wanted to write, teaching was the only way to support that desire. He started to feel excitement about the numerous paths that might lay before him. He finished eating and washed his dishes. Then he booted up his computer to compose a new resume.

John applied for every full-time job and many part-time jobs listed in the *Mining Journal*. He went to Manpower and signed up for temporary office work. After three weeks, he got an interview for a secretarial position at eight dollars an hour. He had barely stepped into the office when he knew he would not get the job. The man who interviewed him suggested that if John were hired, he would only stay until he could get a teaching position at NMU. John explained NMU had no job openings, and since he would not teach this coming year, he would have little chance of getting a teaching position at any school in the future. Nevertheless, the man said, "We want to hire someone we believe will stay long-term." John wondered how any employer could expect someone to stay long-term for a measly eight dollars an hour; no one could support himself on that, much less support a family. The man said he would let John know. Two days later, John found a rejection letter in the mailbox.

Why was he kidding himself? He would never find work in Marquette. But he did not want to move where he knew no one; he had already spent four sad years alone, hardly making a friend downstate while he overworked himself to earn his Ph.D. He wished he had not lost touch with Frank or Holly – they probably had great jobs in big cities now – had he stayed in touch with them, he might have moved to one of those cities, and they would have helped him get settled. He had also lost touch with his suitemate Steve. He still emailed Derek once in a while. Derek lived in Flint – the few times John had visited Derek, he had felt he could never live there. Still, Derek was making good money now, despite the seven years he spent going to college. But John could not look to Derek for aid; Derek had a fiancee and was too busy for a friend he barely spoke to once every couple months. John knew he would have to leave Marquette, but he could not yet resolve himself to that decision.

A couple weeks later, he found a temporary job. Everyone in the office was friendly, and they were impressed by his typing and proofreading skills and his pleasant personality; most of the workers were Marquette natives; one girl had even gone to high school with him. John listened to his coworkers talk about their teachers from high school, the ministers or priests at their churches, their friends, relatives, and dentists. Someone was bound to say, "Sure I know Donna," or "Barry's my cousin." John knew many of the people mentioned, and he found that his coworkers were friends to friends of his old friends. For the first time since he had come home, he started to feel he belonged here. In Marquette, people knew each other's stories, and they cared about each other. One day, two of his coworkers mentioned their husbands putting new kitchen cabinets in their homes. John's boss said, "You know, thirty years ago, I had my cabinets built by Henry Whitman, and they're still holding up." John could not resist saying, "Henry Whitman was my grandfather." "Really," said his boss. "Well, he did excellent work."

The temporary job ended after a month, but it made John feel Marquette's sense of community. The next day he got two rejection letters from colleges in Alabama and New Mexico. "I don't care," he thought, throwing the letters in the garbage. "I don't want to live in Alabama or New Mexico."

He kept looking for a job in Marquette, but one Friday, he took a break by going to Jean Kay's Pasties to buy a pasty, the favorite food of Upper Michigan, brought to the Marquette mining range over a century before by the Cornish as a practical food to eat in the mines below. With a pasty and a coke, John drove to Presque Isle, parked his car, and sat at a picnic bench. Watching the seagulls fly over the breakwall, he wondered whether their lives were as carefree as they seemed.

He tried to relax as he ate, but he could not help wondering how the sun could shine when he was so miserable. A nagging feeling told him he should go home and look in the newspaper at the daily job listings. Yet when he threw his trash into a garbage can, his wandering spirit overpowered him.

John had never visited Presque Isle without finding the solace he craved from Nature. Today he felt love stirring in his heart for this special place as he walked down the trail past Kawbawgam's grave to the magnificent cliff overlook; he remembered his grandfather telling him how his father and grandfather had come here to fish with the last Chief of the Chippewa. As a child, John had come here with his father and brother to pick dandelion leaves to feed the deer when the Shiras Zoo existed. He recalled one of his birthday parties held here, and how he and Chad had walked these same trails with Uncle Roy, not long before that great lover of the forest had passed away. He remembered a happy night with Frank and Holly when the three of them had walked to the island at night and stood on the breakwall to watch the black waves in the moonlight.

John left the wooded path and returned to the road, marveling at the stately pines, and the full foliage of the maples and oaks that leaned over the road; he could hear squirrels scurrying along the tree branches. A car passed him, but he soon saw it up ahead, stopped on the road, the driver watching a deer in the wood. John realized he had taken the deer's presence at Presque Isle for granted; that they willingly remained here, nearly tame, reflected the good hearts of the local people. He felt how fortunate he was to have grown up in this land where he could be so close to Nature and become so familiar with the seasons' natural rhythms which most of the human race had forgotten. Downstate, he had taught many students who, reared in metropolitan areas, had been unable to identify with the poems of Wordsworth and Frost which John read as if they described his childhood; his students had been ignorant of Nature save for the sky, and even then, the stars had been blocked from their view by the flashing of neon lights. Not one of those city children had ever swung from a birch tree or known the tingling sensation of a fawn eating a carrot from his hand.

He walked off the main road and down the dirt path to the cove. For a warm summer day, the spot was strangely lonely. Yielding to a childish impulse, he walked up to the pebble filled beach between the black rocks and shoreline cliffs. He removed his shoes and socks, rolled up his pant legs, and waded into the water. For centuries, the lake had pushed pebbles up from its floor into the cove; the little rocks were Nature's tokens to the children of Marquette, who collected the neverending supply of brilliant red, white, yellow, brown, green, black, and blue stones. John leaned over to dip his arm in the lake; the cool water was refreshing as he pulled up one rock after another to look at their marvelous colors, then return them to the lake, thankful to have admired them, and wanting others to have the same pleasure. A gentle wind rustled the trees; the breeze stirred miniature waves that plunked up against the rocks on the shore. He looked straight out into the lake until he could not tell where it merged with the sky. He had admired the beauty of the cove's rocks but ignored the magnificent vista. He felt his entire life could be described as focusing on little rocks without seeing the grander view. He had limited himself to his writing and teaching until his writing had become lifeless, and his life dull. He had squelched all but the strict voices of academia, perhaps worthy voices, but not all knowing. The lake, rocks, trees, the wind – all had their voices, voices which never ceased to whisper patiently until he would listen.

"I think," he said aloud – so stunned by this sudden knowing, "that I'm going to stay in Upper Michigan. I've been so worried about getting a job, making money, and trying to prove I'm intelligent that I forgot to be happy. Until now, I don't think I've realized how unhappy I was downstate. This is my home. Here I will stay."

As John stepped into the house, freshly returned from Presque Isle, the telephone rang.

"Hello."

"Is John Vandelaare there, please?"

"This is he," said John. He hoped it was someone offering him a job, but he suspected it was a telemarketer.

"Hello. This is Brian Johnson. I'm the Chair of the English Department at the University of Texas. I'm calling regarding the application you sent us a couple months ago for an instructor position."

"Yes," said John. His stomach tightened. Was this a job interview? Would there be a campus visit? He could not even remember applying at the University of Texas – he had applied to so many schools. He had applied for tenure track positions, and then only for instructor positions out of desperation. This job must have been one of those he had applied for in April, three months ago now.

"We'd like to consider you for the position. We just got funding for six instructors, and we need to fill them as soon as possible. If you're still interested, I'd like to tell you a little about the position, and then ask you a few questions if you don't mind."

"Yes, I'm still interested," said John. He tried not to sound nervous, although his mind raced into near shock at an actual interview after so many attempts.

"It's a one year position," said Dr. Johnson. "It requires teaching four sections of composition per semester. The pay is $24,000 a year. Depending on funding, the position may be renewed up to four years." Dr. Johnson went on to describe the university, its location, the student population, and departmental goals. John scarcely listened as he tried to believe he was being offered a job. The salary was horribly low; he and his fellow graduate students had often joked about getting jobs paying only $30,000 after they had spent ten years going to college. Would it be worth moving to Texas for only one year for such a small sum of money? He had never been to Texas, but he imagined it was dry, flat land, and he hated hot weather. He was used to water and vibrant green forests. His heart cried "NO!" but his brain counseled, "If you take it, it might lead to a tenure track position, and at least you'll be teaching."

Dr. Johnson asked him about his theories of composition, how he would teach various rhetorical essays, and what had been his coursework in the Ph.D. program. John gave the best answers he could considering the lack of warning he had received to prepare for an interview. He felt overwhelmed by the thought of teaching four sections of composition; that would be one hundred students, all taking a class they did not want, a class viewed as the least interesting course at the university. He would have about six hundred essays to grade each semester.

"Well, I want to get these positions filled as quickly as possible," said Dr. Johnson, "so I see no reason to hold off. I'm happy to offer you the position. I can get the contract drawn up and mailed to you today if you think you want to come."

"I – well," John hesitated.

"Do you need time to think about it?"

John wanted to say he needed time to think about it, but he knew that would only be delaying the inevitable. He was afraid if he took time to think about it, he might break his resolve. He had a flashback to an hour ago when he had stood in the cove at Presque Isle; now he was sweating from anxiety and longing to wade again into those cool waters. From the depth of his soul, a strong, sure voice said, "Thank you, sir, but I'm not interested." He did not give a reason. He felt instantly relieved.

"Have you had another offer?" asked Dr. Johnson.

"No, I just don't think Texas is the right place for me."

"You realize how bad the job market is right now? This late in the summer, chances are you won't receive another offer, and if you don't teach this year, no one is likely to hire you next year."

John was well aware of what his refusal meant; he would not be badgered.

"I think I would rather stay in Michigan near my family, even if it means no longer being in academia."

"All right," said Dr. Johnson, sounding annoyed and unsympathetic to John's emotional dilemma. "There are plenty of others who want to teach."

"I'm sorry," said John, in disbelief at the chance he was giving up. "I do appreciate your offer."

"You're welcome. Goodbye."

John heard the phone click, then the dial tone. It was too late to change it now. He hung up the phone. Had he been wrong? If he had had more time – if he had known the call was coming, then he would have had more time to think about it. But he had gone to graduate school to learn to write better – even if he were unsure whether that had happened – he had not gone to teach freshman composition to students uninterested in writing. With hundreds of student papers to grade, where would he find time to write? He told himself he did not care about the money or some impressive career. He would plug along in Marquette – he would rather work at a low paying secretarial job in his home-town than swelter in the Texas heat, without trees, without Lake Superior, without his family. If he could only find a job here, he would be content, but he did not even have that promise.

His mother was the first to come home that night. John debated how to tell her what had happened. She read the anxiety on his face.

"What's wrong?"

"I got a job offer today – for a teaching job."

"Oh," she said. She sat down at the kitchen table. "Where is it?"

"The University of Texas."

"That's so far away," she said, staring out the patio window, not wanting to believe this disruptive change could occur when her son had just come home.

"Is it a good job?"

"No," he said. "I – I turned it down."

She looked at him in astonishment.

"Why?"

"I would have to teach four sections of composition which would be way too much work for what they were paying, and I couldn't stand the heat in Texas anyway."

"But it might have led to something better. Are you sure about this?"

"Yes, it was only for one year, not a tenure track position. It might have been renewed, but after a couple years, I would have had to move to another school. There are so few tenure track positions now that if I kept teaching, I would probably end up moving from one instructor position to another for years. I don't want to do that."

"Are you okay with your decision?"

"Yes, I want to stay in Marquette, and I don't think I'll change my mind. I'll keep looking for a job here. Something will turn up."

He did not really believe anything would turn up. He feared he had made a huge mistake.

"Well," said Ellen, starting to put away the groceries. "You know I'm happy to have you here."

"I know."

"I'm sure it was hard for you to be away for so long," Ellen said. "You're a lot braver than me. After living in California when I was a little girl, I never really wanted to leave Marquette again. I don't know how you stood being downstate by yourself all the years you did. It's sad that these days the economy forces people to move away from home."

"You don't care that I won't be a professor? That I might end up being a secretary or a ditchdigger or something."

"If ditchdigging makes you happy, then I'll be proud my son learned how to be happy. That's more important. Just be patient. Everything will work out."

John found it hard to be patient. By the time supper was over, his stomach was upset, and by bedtime, his heart was pounding. For hours that night, he lay on his bed in the dark, wondering whether he had made a mistake. He wished God would explain to him why, just after he had resolved to stay in Marquette, he had been tempted with an offer to move away. He kept asking himself whether he had made all wrong decisions: to get a Ph.D. that made him overqualified and unemployable, to turn down a teaching job that would have been like bondage, to return to Marquette rather than move to a large city where he would have more opportunities. Was he wasting his time and talents remaining in this small town? What was wrong with him that he needed to be near his family when thousands of other young men and women moved away from home without ever looking back? What strength did they possess that he lacked?

Or were they the weak ones who followed the call of money and prestige at the cost of sacrificing their families and personal happiness? And where had that brave, deep voice come from? That voice he had scarcely recognized as his own when it had welled up in his chest and said "No" to moving to Texas. He would not be a coward. He told himself he had more courage than the others who had left here out of fear over the economic struggles of life in Upper Michigan.

"God, I know you have a reason for all this," he said, "and if I'm patient and true to myself, everything will work out."

"John, what are you going to do today?" Ellen asked the following Saturday morning as she made him pancakes for breakfast.

"Read the want ads I guess."

"Don't sound so depressed. Something will turn up."

"I know. I just wish I had a job so I could quit wondering whether I made the wrong decision. All this stress has given me writer's block."

He had started to wonder whether continuing to write was even worthwhile, but he could not yet bring himself to say so.

"I was wondering whether you'd do me a favor," said Ellen. "There are all those photographs from your grandparents' house that we never did put into albums. Maybe you could help me get a start on those today."

"Where are they?" He was glad for anything to keep him occupied.

Half an hour later, they had pulled out some sparsely filled photograph albums and two large boxes filled with pictures.

"What are these?" asked John, digging out an old cigar box.

"Those are the letters your grandpa wrote home while he was building that house in Florida."

"I forgot these even existed," said John. When he had started working on the family tree, he had felt he knew enough about his grandparents so he had ignored the letters while searching for information from earlier generations.

"You can read them if you want to," said Ellen.

"Maybe later."

All afternoon, John helped his mother put together the photograph albums. They found a picture of a church group from the turn of the century. "I remember my mother showed me this picture when I was a girl. She pointed out her mother and father in it to me," said Ellen, "but now I don't remember which ones they were. Isn't that sad?" They kept the picture anyway and inserted it into the album. There was a picture of Grandpa as a little boy. There were pictures of Great-Great-Grandpa and Grandma Dalrymple with Aunt Eleanor and Uncle Roy as children sitting on their knees. A picture of Grandma in a wild hat from the 1920s. Pictures of Ellen as a little girl playing with her cousins, pictures of Uncle Jim as a little boy, pictures of the rodeo Grandpa and Grandma had attended in California. "I know Roy Rogers and Dale Evans were there," said Ellen, "but all I really remember was how miserably hot it was that day even though it was the middle of winter. I hated California. All the while there, all I wanted to do was come home." John thought he must be a lot like his mother in that respect. Here was a picture of his mother making her First Communion, of Christmas trees with the family standing before them in their outlandish 1960s clothes. Pictures of huge family dinner parties taken in the 1950s. "There's Uncle Charles and Aunt Harriet, and that's their son, Joseph, and his sons the twins, and there's Uncle Bill and his first wife, and there's my mother's cousin, Thelma, and my grandmother," said Ellen. "And here's a picture of you as a baby." John ignored his baby picture and looked again at the pictures of the family get-togethers. That was how he remembered his grandparents, part of a large loving family now severely diminished. He still thought of his grandparents everyday. He wondered what they would say about his getting a Ph.D., and about his turning down a teaching job. Would they understand? They had come home from California to be near the family. Although they had lived in a different era, when few went to college, John wished they were here now to give him advice.

"We better get ready for church," said Ellen, setting down the pictures.

At Mass, John prayed for guidance. Then they went to Main Street Pizza to pick up supper and bring it home. While they ate, Ellen said, "I'm too tired to work on those photograph albums anymore tonight. I'm just going to sit and watch *Lawrence Welk*."

John had seen every rerun of *Lawrence Welk*; even if it had been Grandma's favorite show, he had no desire to watch it again.

"Then maybe I'll go read Grandpa's letters," he said.

He disappeared into his bedroom with the letters. The stack consisted of fifty-four envelopes, and according to the postmarks, they had been written over the course of three months while Grandpa was in Florida. Grandpa had worked everyday, yet he had still found time almost every evening to write to his wife.

John carefully opened the first envelope and pulled out a letter written on small lined paper, with blue ink that had soaked through the page, making illegible blots where Grandpa had written on both sides. Written almost daily, the letters were often repetitive in content, but Grandma would doubtless have been disappointed if she had not found one of her husband's letters in the mailbox. Back in those days, few people made long distance phone calls, so the letters had been the only means of communication between a couple who after more than twenty years of marriage had endured their first separation. John wished Grandma's letters had also survived, but that Grandpa had discarded them did not reflect any lack of affection on his part as apparent in so many passages that made John smile.

> March 20, 1957
> Dear Honey,
>   I hope you like the beautiful slip I'm sending you. You aren't allowed to wear it until I get home to see you in it. It sure is made of beautiful cloth, isn't it? I hope you like the apron and the dress too. I thought you'd like the flowers on the dress. I want you to have beautiful things to show your friends because I couldn't think of a better way to keep you happy and show you how much I love you. But you can't show anyone but me the slip. HAHA.
>   Well darling, there's only 4 more weeks before I'll be coming home. I've saved up quite a bit of money. After I get home and we get things paid off, I want us to take a nice vacation for just the two of us, and boy, are we sure going to enjoy ourselves. I thought maybe we could go to Escanaba for two days and stay overnight. Then we could take it easy shopping and not hurry. We can buy you a new summer coat while we're there. You know you need one. You and I have never really been out by ourselves like that on a trip, and it would be a good rest for you away from home, no dishes or cooking for two days, wouldn't it, darling? Tell me in your next letter whether you want to. Then you can look forward to it and you won't miss me so much.
>   Love you, Henry

"My gosh, Grandpa, your letters sure are corny," said John, shaking his head. He could not imagine anyone outside of the family would find the letters interesting, not when they were full of stuff like buying aprons, but they were Grandma's personal letters, and she had appreciated Grandpa's simple, thoughtful gifts more than if they had been diamonds or furs. John could not help smiling at the thought of an overnight shopping trip to Escanaba. Most people went to Green Bay or Appleton these days, but Grandpa had seen the excursion as a vacation for Grandma. And buying Grandma a slip – well, it was nice to know that even though Grandma had been overweight and middle-aged, Grandpa had thought her beautiful.

If some passages were corny, others were quite moving.

> April 1, 1957
> Dear Honey,
>
> Only two more weeks. Then we'll stop by Ada's to visit for a couple days before heading home. I hope the time goes by quickly. I sure am awful lonesome without you. You and me were ever pals weren't we, wifey dear? I know you must miss me holding your hand in the evenings. I sure do miss you. We have never been apart a night until now since we were married except that time of the big fire in '38 remember, and I hope we never have to be apart again. I know that I will never do this again. There isn't any amount of money that is worth being away from you for a day.

John knew from his mother that Grandma had not wanted to leave Marquette again after the trip to California, and Grandpa had never left Grandma for another day after he came home from Florida. Just being together, in their hometown, had been enough for them. "I must be a lot like my grandparents," he thought.

He felt confirmed once again in his decision to stay in Marquette. He would be plagued by daily doubts for months to come, but he began to feel if he wanted to stay, he should not care what kind of ambitious career others might think he should pursue. He must seek his own joy because as his grandpa had said, no amount of money mattered by comparison. His grandparents had left Marquette, only to return because they were homesick, and his mother had refused to leave, resulting in his father leaving the air force. And even Uncle Jim's decision to leave Marquette, his family and all that was familiar, must have taken tremendous courage. He felt all his family before him, whether they had stayed or gone, had showed great courage, and now like the six generations before him, John had to make his decision.

The following week, John found a month long temporary job. Alone in the basement of a downtown office building, he spent eight hours a day entering data into a computer. The task was mind-numbingly miserable, and he constantly watched the clock, so bored he would count the minutes until he could leave even when hours of work remained. Still, he found the job better than being unemployed.

He might have taken greater advantage of the times he did not work if he did not suffer from writer's block. Ever since he had decided the short stories from his dissertation were not worth publishing, he had felt drained of good ideas. Writer's block was like constipation; his inability to write made him more irritable than being unemployed. He found it almost unbearable to know he had earned a Ph.D. yet he had no job and was forced to live with his parents. Sometimes he almost wished he had taken the teaching job in Texas, no matter how horrible it would have been.

His miserable temporary job ended on a stormy Friday afternoon. At five o'clock that day, he raced from the office building through the pouring rain to where his car was parked on the top floor of the downtown ramp. By the time he unlocked the car door, he was thoroughly drenched. The heat in his car no longer worked, and he had no money to have it fixed. He had hoped to buy a new car before winter, but he had also thought he would have a teaching job before winter. By the time he reached home, he was wet, cold, and bitter toward the world and everyone around him. His parents sensed his moodiness and said little to him at supper. He did the dishes for his mother, then went to his room and tried to read, but he was too tired to concentrate. He lay on his bed and flipped through the TV channels with the remote control. Exhausted mentally and physically, he fell asleep despite the television and the thunderstorm outside.

The next morning, John saw the storm had done so much damage that he found it hard to believe he had slept through it. The grass was littered with broken tree branches, the roof of the bird feeder had blown ten feet across the yard, and the lawn chairs had toppled over.

For breakfast his mother made blueberry pancakes. She wanted to bake a blueberry pie, but she did not have enough berries.

"John, do you want to pick some berries with me after breakfast?" she asked.

He agreed, although he was in no mood to do anything. He and his mother crossed the yard and entered the neighboring woods where John had played as a child. He had on his shorts because it was such a hot day, but once outside, he found it comfortingly cool to walk through the woods with the wet ferns brushing against his bare legs. He and his mother only walked a few feet before they came across a giant oak – grandfather to half a dozen young saplings nearby – fallen across the Blueberry Trail.

"The storm must have knocked it over," said Ellen. "It looks as if it were struck by lightning since the top is split in two."

"No, it started splitting years ago," said John. "When I was a kid, I used to climb it near to the top where it was just starting to divide."

"Hmm," said Ellen. "Well, let's walk down farther. There might be some berries in that patch up ahead."

"Mom, remind me later to come out here with my camera."

"Why?"

"I want to take a picture of the tree."

"Why?" she repeated while scanning the nearby bushes for hidden blueberries.

"It was my favorite climbing tree when I was a kid. Don't you remember?"

"No. I didn't pay much attention to which trees you boys climbed; I just worried about you falling out of them."

"I must have climbed that tree every summer day when I was a kid," said John. "Chad and I named it Frederick. Don't you remember that?"

"No. Why Frederick?" asked Ellen, walking on ahead while John still hovered over his fallen friend.

"It just looked like a Frederick. I guess we thought it sounded kind of elegant."

"Here's a good-sized patch," said Ellen, bending over a blueberry bush. John began to pick berries a few feet away from her. He remembered how as a child he used to count each berry he put in his bucket, only to lose count after two or three hundred. He remembered how he used to swing his bucket upside down so fast the blueberries would not fall out, only later to stumble on a root and drop them all. Then his memories went back to the tree.

"I wish it hadn't fallen over," he thought. "I know that just because I moved back home doesn't mean everything will stay the way I remember, and I have to accept that, but it's hard to lose an old friend."

He had known so many changes already – St. John's torn down, Longyear Hall demolished, the Marquette Mall with its beautiful fountain now nearly empty, the fountain long gone. He could not see how any of these changes were for the better, but he would have to be content with loving what remained.

"Even if Frederick is gone," thought John, "the rest of the forest is still here, and it's better that Frederick die of old age in a storm than he be chopped down when someone finally buys and clears this lot."

"There are so many berries in this patch," said Ellen, standing up to relieve her backstrain, "that I should have my bucket filled in no time. Maybe we can pick enough to make two pies. Then I can send one home with your brother when he comes over."

When John and his mother finished berrypicking, John returned outside with his camera to take a picture of Frederick.

"No matter how things change," he told himself, "I'll always remember Frederick once stood here, and over there was Bernard, the Poseidon Adventure Tree, which fell the year before I moved downstate. Because of my memory, I can always be back in the past again – like when I drive along County Road 553, and I come around the curve into Marquette, still expecting to see the old Brookridge Estate standing there, momentarily forgetting it's been torn down. As long as I remember, the past is still part of the present for me, and I'll always be able to live in Old Marquette. As I get older, I imagine I'll live even more in the past, but maybe that's what it means to get older."

He no longer felt sad, but simply felt that he had grown up; part of growing up was having memories.

The family had blueberry pie for supper; that evening, so many blueberries were left that John helped his mother clean them. Tom drifted into the living room to watch TV and wait for the lotto numbers. It was a beautiful evening; the patio door was open and a warm breeze blew in. It was August, and the summer was almost over so John and his mother decided to sit on the porch and enjoy the evening as they cleaned the berries. John patiently picked through his bucket, sorting mushy from firm berries, and removing the occasional leaf or little spider who had haphazardly fallen into his berry bucket. Sitting on the porch where he had spent so many happy hours of childhood playing and reading books, he felt clothed in the golden illusion that summer will last forever, with its luscious green trees and warm breezes, morning glory flowers, and buckets brimming over with blueberries. These summer evenings were bridges across the years that calmed the soul until nightfall's gray replaced the striking pink rays of sunset.

"Isn't this nice," said John.

"Yeah right," said Ellen, wiping soggy blueberry juice from her fingers onto a paper towel.

"No, I mean it, Mom. There's something so pleasant about the simplicity of picking and cleaning blueberries. Sort of like a "back to Nature" thing, only here we never have to go back because we're constantly surrounded by Nature."

"I guess so. Summer wouldn't be the same without blueberry pie, although I do get sick of cleaning the berries."

"Things like blueberries make me feel I made the right decision to stay here," said John.

Ellen did not reply. She wanted her son to stay, but she also wanted him to be happy, and while a man should not be defined by his work, John had always worked hard even at his play; she doubted he would find anything in Marquette that was creative or challenging enough for him. In time, she imagined he would leave again. Until then, she would say nothing to influence his decisions; it was best to let him work things out on his own.

John continued to work temporary jobs for a week or two at a time, then find himself again unemployed. His few interviews ended in rejection because his Ph.D. made him overqualified, and employers did not believe he would stay in a low paying job. He knew he would have stayed at any job if he were just offered benefits. He could not understand why all the hard work he had done, which should prove him a good employee, should instead make him unemployable. Deep down, he feared he would give into fear and move to Chicago or Detroit.

One evening as he helped his mother wash the dishes, she said, "I met Mr. O'Neill in the IGA today."

"Oh yeah," said John. "How is he? He must be in his nineties now. Wasn't he Grandpa's age?"

"I think so," said Ellen. "He has a cane now, and he had a healthcare worker with him, but he seemed to be getting along okay. He said he quit driving last year."

"He must be awful lonely since his wife died and his children don't live around here."

"I imagine so," said Ellen. "He asked how you were."

John was afraid to hear what his mother had told Mr. O'Neill. He wanted to avoid everyone now, especially people he knew at the university, and people who had encouraged him to get a Ph.D. He imagined everyone must think him a failure for choosing to be near his family rather than follow his career.

"He wanted me to congratulate you on getting your Ph.D.," said Ellen, "and he asked whether you would stop by sometime to visit him."

"I always liked Mr. O'Neill," said John, "but I don't want to visit him; he won't understand my situation. I don't understand it myself."

"He always asks about you when I see him. It wouldn't hurt you to stop by his house. You have plenty of free time, and maybe he'll know someone who might give you a job."

John dreaded such a visit. How could a successful writer like Mr. O'Neill understand the failure he felt?

"I don't know," he said.

"He would probably enjoy talking to you about books and writing. I'm sure he's lonely."

John did not call Mr. O'Neill, but two days later while John was reading the want ads, Mr. O'Neill called him, and John, too polite to refuse a personal invitation, agreed to come over for lunch the next day; worse, he agreed to bring Mr. O'Neill a copy of his dissertation. He dreaded the meeting, but the following day at noon, he promptly appeared at the O'Neill house.

When he rang the bell, the door was opened by a young woman.

"You must be John," she said. "Come on in."

He stepped into the hallway and let her take his coat. She introduced herself as Tina, a college student who helped Mr. O'Neill with the housekeeping. Then John heard Mr. O'Neill call out, "Hello". The distinguished author appeared a second later in the dining room doorway. Robert O'Neill clutched his cane to support his hunched back and weakening legs. What hair he had left clung to the sides of his face, leaving him bald on top. But John could see behind Mr. O'Neill's spectacles two witty, intelligent eyes, vibrantly interested in the life around them.

"So good to see you again, John," he said, offering his hand. "How are you?"

"Fine," John lied. "Thank you for inviting me to lunch."

"Thanks for coming. Most young people don't want to be bothered with an old geezer like me, but you and Tina here seem to be the exceptions."

Tina smiled, then went to fetch the tea and sandwiches she had prepared.

John followed Mr. O'Neill's tottering steps into the dining room. He helped Mr. O'Neill into a chair, then sat down and looked about him at the old pictures, wallpaper, and fine mahogany table, none of which he had forgotten from his visit years before.

Mr. O'Neill asked after John's parents, and then John inquired after Mr. O'Neill's children, both of whom were pursuing successful careers. "I wish though," said Mr. O'Neill, "that they would both retire and move back here."

Tina brought in lunch. John had been holding onto the copy of his dissertation all this time, but now he set it on the table so he could eat. Mr. O'Neill instantly asked to see it. John pushed it across the table, then waited to eat while Mr. O'Neill looked at the table of contents.

"Can I get you anything else?" asked Tina.

"No, thank you. I know you have to get to class," said Mr. O'Neill.

"All right, I'll be going then. It was nice to meet you," she said to John, then disappeared into the hallway. A minute later, they heard the front door open and close.

"We better eat before the soup's cold," said Mr. O'Neill, setting down John's manuscript. "I'll be eager to read this. I feel you have some real talent from the couple short stories you've published. Your stories are more real than some of that self-conscious dribble they call writing these days – all that stylistic pseudo-intellectual nonsense that fills the literary magazines. The task of a writer is first and foremost to create real characters in real situations with whom readers can identify. I don't care how clever a writer is if he can't tell a good story."

"Thank you," said John, smiling as he silently named to himself some of the postmodern novelists he imagined Mr. O'Neill was denouncing. Yet Mr. O'Neill was praising stories John had written before he entered the Ph.D. program and distorted his literary talents.

"The story of yours I liked the best," Mr. O'Neill said, "was the one you set in the Upper Peninsula. Your descriptions of the area were vividly accurate, just as if you were looking at a photograph as you described them. I remember I read it in summer, but you set it during winter. The story made me feel cold even though the heat was scorching that day. Not every writer has that power."

"That one was easy to write because I knew the experiences in it so well," said John.

"Not that the other story wasn't good," said Mr. O'Neill, "but I thought that winter story was amazing."

John had thought his other published story better because he had labored over it more. By comparison, the story set in the U.P. had been easy to write.

"Write what you know," said Mr. O'Neill. "It's old advice and everyone gives it, but it's the best advice there is."

"I agree," said John, realizing he had usually failed to take that advice.

"I don't write fiction anymore," said Mr. O'Neill. "I'm too old to keep track of the characters. I still keep a journal – not that there's much for me to write in it nowadays. But if I were young and could start over again, I would write more about the U.P. So many of its stories are still waiting to be told. This area has played one of the most important roles in U.S. history. Most of the wars, from the Civil War on, would not have been won if not for the Upper Peninsula's iron ore, and then there's the copper, and the lumber, the shipping on the Great Lakes, and the incredible beauty. I wish I had written more about all of it, but maybe being a Southerner by birth, I wasn't meant to do it."

"Yes, there are great stories here," John agreed, unsure what more to say.

"But what are you writing now?" asked Mr. O'Neill, between spoonfuls of soup.

"Nothing really. Looking for a job is taking up all my energy."

John waited for Mr. O'Neill's face to change expression as the successful author realized he was talking to a failure, a man who did not live up to his potential.

Instead, Mr. O'Neill said, "Well, a good paying job will come. But your real job is to write. That's the talent God gave you that you must not waste."

"I just don't feel very inspired right now. I seem to have writer's block."

"Inspiration isn't everything. Writing is nine-tenths perspiration. Everyone thinks writers sit around waiting for ideas. No one should lack for ideas – subjects are all around you to write about. The U.P. is so rich with folklore and history – you'll never be able to write everything to be said about it. Your mother tells me you moved back here because you missed the U.P. so you must appreciate all of its story potential."

"I did miss it," said John, "especially the lake, and the autumn colors, and the snow. Downstate, there are barely seasons by comparison."

"Exactly." Mr. O'Neill's eyes twinkled. "And now that you're back, you must have memories that are reawakening. I remember your grandpa was quite a storyteller. You should write down his stories – all your family memories – that could be your start, and then you'll have no excuse for writer's block."

John was stunned. He had spent years letting academia dictate how he should write. Now he realized all the material he had ever needed had been here in his hometown.

"But," he said, "would anyone outside Upper Michigan be interested in reading it?"

"Why read Joyce when you've never been to Ireland, or Dickens when you've never been to England, or Faulkner if you've never been to the South?" Mr. O'Neill said. "The human story is everywhere, and here we have fine tales of courage, of men and women struggling against the wilderness, making a living from the earth, falling in love with the land. Most writers should be so lucky to have such fantastic material."

"I never thought of it that way," said John. "I've never been to England, but I love British literature."

"People move around so much in this crazy modern world," said Mr. O'Neill, "that no one knows who he is anymore. But you grew up here, and your family has been here a long time. You have an identity shaped by this land,

and you can use your sense of belonging here to help illuminate other people's lives."

"I have done a lot of research on my family tree," said John.

"I bet there are fascinating stories in your family's past for you to tell."

John silently finished his lunch, ideas flooding his thoughts, ideas that had always been there, but it had taken Mr. O'Neill to draw them out.

"Let's go into the library to have our tea," said Mr. O'Neill. "At my age, I like to be comfortable after I eat."

John found himself once more sitting in that pleasant room of William Morris wallpaper, gilded books, Boston ferns, and nineteenth century knick-knacks. He remembered his previous visit with his grandfather, when Mr. and Mrs. O'Neill had sat in their chairs, a glowing old couple. Now Mr. O'Neill looked so frail, his loneliness reflected in his talkativeness.

The author rambled about the meaning of his writing. "It's all that's kept me going at times. I was devastated when my first wife died, but writing helped me carry on. Even if I had never been published, I would have still written. If only one person someday reads your words and appreciates them, it will have been worthwhile. We can never know what an influence we are upon others. Think of our ancestors who first came to Marquette – they never could have foreseen what this city would look like today, or what we, their descendants, would be like, but they did not live in vain. We're better off because those pioneers had the courage to come here."

Mr. O'Neill began to talk of the famous people he had met, the painter George Dewbey, famous writers, including his favorite, Willa Cather, politicians including President Eisenhower, President Nixon, several Michigan governors, and he spoke of his travels all over North America and Europe. "But I always came back here," he said. "Marquette is home. Most days I've divided up between my writing and being with my family, and that has been more than enough."

At four o'clock, just as the grandfather clock chimed in the hall, another college girl came to make Mr. O'Neill his supper. She would later be relieved by a young man who would stay overnight to make sure Mr. O'Neill was safe.

"I have three girls and one young man who take care of me. I sometimes confuse the girls' names," Mr. O'Neill said, "but they're all good to me, and they can use the extra money. I like to encourage the young, and they're good enough to put up with my idiosyncrasies."

John thanked Mr. O'Neill for a pleasant afternoon. He knew Mr. O'Neill had the best intentions toward him, but John still doubted he could ever write anything remarkable. Yet he also felt he had obsessed about the wrong things since he had returned home. He would find a paying job eventually, but his vocation was to write. Even if he never wrote anything significant, he had wanted to be a writer since childhood, and if he did not follow that dream at all costs, he would forever regret it.

A few days later, John had another temporary work assignment downtown. Although he had not written anything since he had visited Mr. O'Neill, the author's words simmered in the back of his mind. During his lunch break, he popped into Snowbound Books, thinking he might like a British novel, something by Galsworthy or Waugh, but when he entered the store, the local history section caught his eye. He skimmed the shelf, noting he had read most of the books there, but he had never before seen *Ojibwa Narratives*, a compilation of tales told by Chief Kawbawgam, recently printed and edited by Marquette native, Professor Arthur Bourgeois. John had been unaware such stories existed. He felt interested in them because he knew his Great-Grandpa Whitman had known Chief Kawbawgam.

John bought the book as well as a Galsworthy novel, then returned to work. He began the Galsworthy novel that evening and finished it by the end of the week. Then he turned to *Ojibwa Narratives*. He read it in small pieces for several days, smiling at the humorous stories. Then one night, as he was about to turn off the light and go to bed, he came across the following tale.

> In the spring, Kitchi Nonan took a walk to another lake, and there he saw several swans. Wanting to catch them but not knowing how in the world to do it, he finally dove under the water and swam around till he found where the swans were; then tied all their feet together with a line and gave it a jerk. Away went the swans through the air, with Kitchi Nonan hanging on to the line. After being carried for miles, he lost his hold and fell. As luck would have it, he landed right in the top of a hollow pine just as a bear was coming out. Nonan tumbled on the bear and surprised it so it scrambled out of the tree and ran away.

"Oh my gosh!" said John, sitting up with a jolt. "That's grandpa's story – the one he told at my birthday party years ago at Presque Isle. It's almost exactly the same, except he told it about his father. Actually, he said his father had told it to him, but I bet his father heard it from Chief Kawbawgam, then adapted it to be about himself."

John could hardly hold in his excitement. He went into the living room where his parents were dozing in front of the television.

"Mom," he said, waking her to kiss her goodnight. "I'm going to bed, but I want to tell you something."

"What?" she yawned.

He told her about the story. "Grandpa must have heard it from his dad and his dad must have heard it from Chief Kawbawgam. It's as if our family helped continue an oral tradition we borrowed from the Ojibwa."

"Uh huh," said Ellen, falling back asleep.

John was disappointed by her lack of enthusiasm. He went to bed, but lay awake, fascinated by his discovery. His grandfather and great-grandfather had adapted the story for their own purposes; they had plagiarized, but also improved it, reflecting what good storytellers they were. If his grandfather had embellished the story, then John saw no reason why he could not embellish his grandfather's stories. "Maybe Mr. O'Neill was right. There is material here for me to write about."

The next day his temporary work assignment ended. Rather than job search, he turned on his computer and from a drawer dug out the wrinkled, yellowing manuscript of his first novel, the one intended to be about his grandfather, but which had drifted into a completely different story. He had received numerous rejection letters for it while he was an undergraduate.

"It's not that bad," he said, as he skimmed it over. "It's wordy and the dialogue is pretty stilted, but the idea was good. I can rewrite it, saving the good parts and reworking them into something better."

He began immediately to cross out extraneous paragraphs, writing notes on how to rearrange scenes, build tension, and develop the characters. He would have to retype the entire novel. He had handwritten it, then typed it up on a computer that long since had died; the saved version was on unusable floppy disks. Retyping the salvageable parts would further allow him to rethink and improve the work. The original story had some passing references to the historical period the novel was placed in, with mention of streetcars, ice wagons, the golden age of radio, but now John felt a major factor of the story should be the influence of the Upper Peninsula and its environment upon the novel's characters.

As autumn approached, he became aware again of the Upper Peninsula's special environment. That year, the autumn colors appeared more brilliant than he had remembered them in past years. In the mornings, the smell of rotting leaves gripped his nostrils with a comforting feeling he had not known since childhood's countless autumn walks with Dickens. The sunlight sparkling on orange and yellow foliage reawoke a sensitivity to light and color he had long forgotten. Soon, the snow would come with its blinding reflections, its cold, its white wonderland possibilities. One evening, he heard the harmonious honking of the Canadian geese on their southern flight. He looked up into the cold northern sky as darkness spread across it. Quickly he tried to count the V of geese – twenty-six, twenty-seven – he was not quite sure how many, but they were a miracle.

His senses had reawakened to the voices of birds and the wind, the beauty of leaves and the lake, the smell of snow and an approaching rain shower, the taste of blueberries, the bitter cold biting at his cheeks and fingertips. The singular elements of this land began to mold his imagination, to heighten his senses and his aesthetic appreciation. He had been isolated from Nature's powerful influence while downstate. If he moved away again, he would not have this oneness with his environment that was so essential to his writing; he refused to let himself again forget these little details that made life so splendid. This land had shaped seven generations of his family, until it had seeped into his being, claiming him as its native son.

He began to make lists of his sensual memories – the feel of deer munching dandelion leaves from his hand at the Shiras Zoo, the smell of his Grandpa's cheek when he kissed it, the ivory soap smell of Grandma's bathroom, the glow of light streaming over Grandma's lace tablecloth, the comforting dusty warmth of his grandparents' old furnace turning itself on, of going sledding and then coming home with frozen fingers he had to thaw in hot water, his mother always baking until the house smelled perpetually of chocolate chip cookies, the texture of Aunt Eleanor's crumby date bars, the festive wrapping paper on presents brought to him by Lucy and Maud. Memories came flooding back, one leading to another, and with them came back stories, memories of childhood, tales Grandpa had told him of his own grandparents and of his mother's childhood, of Aunt Eleanor's divorce, Grandpa and Grandma's religious differences that had postponed their marriage, a hundred little family dramas. He quit worrying about writing – that would come. For now, he was cataloging memories. He began reading historical articles whenever they appeared in the *Mining Journal, Marquette Monthly*, and *Marquette Magazine*. He cut out articles and filed them, realizing the potential source of fiction in

Marquette's history, in the environment, the buildings, lake, trees, all of this land that had helped to form him.

A few days before Thanksgiving, he called Mr. O'Neill.

"I've begun to write again," he said proudly. He asked whether he might come to lunch to discuss the novel he wanted to set in the Upper Peninsula. They set a date for the following week, by which time, John intended to have drafted a few chapters to show his prestigious mentor.

"Splendid," said Mr. O'Neill. "I can't wait to see it."

"Hello. How was your day?" asked Ellen when John came home from another temporary job a few days before Christmas.

"Awful," he said. "All day I folded newsletters and stuffed envelopes. I can't believe I went to school all those years to end up doing something a child can do."

"I have something to tell you," said Ellen.

John took off his shoes and coat while Ellen waited.

"What is it?" he asked, feeling tired and crabby.

"Mr. O'Neill died. It's in the paper today."

For a moment, John did not move. Then he asked, "How?"

"The paper said he died at home in his sleep."

"At least he went peacefully," said John.

"We'll have to go to the funeral," Ellen said.

"Of course."

John was stunned. Mr. O'Neill was the only one outside his family who had understood him since his return to Marquette, even though they had only spoken a couple times. Mr. O'Neill had made him feel hopeful again. Now, when he was working so hard on a new novel, and had eighty pages he wanted to get approval upon, Mr. O'Neill was gone. John felt it was the last blow he could take. He spent that evening staring at his computer screen, wondering what Mr. O'Neill would have said had he read the draft of John's new novel. "What's the point of even trying anymore?" he asked the universe. He might as well just move away, find a decent job, and settle for an ordinary life. The U.P. held nothing for him. He could not write anything worthwhile. No one would ever want to read about Marquette. After he turned off the light and crawled into bed, John buried his face in his pillow and begged God for one ounce of hope before he broke completely under the despair consuming him.

The next morning, John was surprised to receive a phone call from Mr. O'Neill's lawyer. John planned to attend the funeral, but he could not believe it when his presence was requested at the reading of the Will following the funeral.

"He probably just left me a book or something," he told his mother.

At the funeral, John and Ellen spoke to Mr. O'Neill's children, Bernie and Helen, but no one mentioned the reading of the Will to John, and he did not feel it his place to mention it. At the funeral luncheon, John and Ellen sat across the table from Tina, whom John had met when he went to have lunch with Mr. O'Neill. When Tina learned Ellen was a nurse, she told her she was going to nursing school. The two women struck up a lively conversation, while John sat awkwardly, wondering whether anyone would object to his being at the reading of Mr. O'Neill's Will. He tried to imagine what Mr. O'Neill might have left him – maybe an autographed copy of Willa Cather's *O Pioneers*, or one of the beautiful pre-Raphaelite paintings in the library; at the same time, he felt guilty to think he would receive anything. He felt he would have benefited more from Mr. O'Neill's advice.

After the funeral luncheon, he said goodbye to his mother, then drove alone to the Ridge Street house, and nervously knocked on the door.

Helen O'Neill greeted him. Then a man in a suit came forward and introduced himself as Mr. Hampton, Mr. O'Neill's lawyer and a cousin of some sort. "All right, everyone. Let's get started," the man called. "Please come into the dining room." John hesitantly followed the others. He looked at the men in the room and tried to figure out which one was Bernie, his Uncle Jim's old friend. He surmised the young men and women must be Mr. O'Neill's grandchildren or his great-nephews and nieces. Tina was also there and a couple other college students John imagined had helped care for Mr. O'Neill. John hoped his bequest was something small; he did not want to anger all these people.

The lawyer began to read the will, specifying sums of money to be left to Mr. O'Neill's children and grandchildren, monetary gifts to servants, a scholarship bequest to Northern Michigan University and to his church. John began to think the lawyer had forgotten him. He wished to be anywhere but sitting in this room. Then he heard his name read.

> Finally, to my friend, John Vandelaare, I leave in trust my house at
> – East Ridge Street, with the stipulation that he take up residency
> there, and he open the house as a historical home with the assistance
> of the Marquette County Historical Society. Along with the house, I

bequeath to him a trust fund to be used for his living expenses and
the needed repairs and upkeep of the house. To this trust, I bequeath
the publication rights and royalties of my autobiography, which will
be found among my papers. The royalties from this work are to be
used for the support of the house. My attorney is instructed to
present John Vandelaare with a personal letter in which I explain my
reasons for making him this bequest.

John was beside himself with disbelief. He had never expected a true
legacy. He did not fully understand. He remained in shock as the lawyer laid
down the will and handed John an envelope containing Mr. O'Neill's letter.
John stared at everyone. Everyone stared at him. He did not know what to say.

"Go ahead and read the letter," Helen O'Neill told him.

He nervously slit it open with his finger and read silently.

November 30, 1998
Dear John,

No doubt you were surprised to be asked to the reading of my
will and even more surprised to learn you are my primary heir.
Granted, I have left money of more value to my children and grandchildren. But none of them want to live in Marquette. If I let them sell
the house, it will probably end up being divided into apartments like
so many other historical homes in Marquette. Marquette has seen
enough of its grand old buildings destroyed, but after Dandelion
Cottage was saved, I decided I wanted to preserve my own home. I
know you share my love of local history, and you will appreciate this
house all the more when you understand my reasons for leaving it to
you. Of course, I am seeking to encourage your writing by giving you
this house to provide a source of income. Although I am not now the
famous writer I once was, I imagine there are still students of American literature who will be interested to visit here when I am gone.
You, and your wife and children should you marry, may live in the
rooms upstairs, and you may use the main rooms downstairs for
historical tours. The house will provide you with an income, but
more importantly, it is part of your heritage.

I know your interest in Marquette's history is intertwined with
your own family background. I have told you I wished I had written
more about this area. With that intention, I did some research into
local history. Imagine my surprise when I stumbled upon property
records at the Marquette County Courthouse that this house, which
I had always assumed was built by my Great-Uncle and Great-Aunt

Smith, was bought by my great-uncle from Gerald Henning. I am sure you are aware of your descent from the Hennings, perhaps even that they lived on Ridge Street, but since neither you or your grandfather ever mentioned it, I am guessing you did not know this house had originally belonged to your ancestors. They only lived here a short time, from when the house was built in 1868 until they sold it in 1876. You are probably aware that Gerald and Sophia Hennings' daughter, Madeleine, drowned in Lake Superior, and as a result, the family left Marquette and moved back East. Since then, Marquette seems to have forgotten Gerald Henning's significance as one of the first promoters of the city's industry. Gerald had another daughter, Agnes, who married Jacob Whitman. In my research, I learned that Jacob and Agnes were the grandparents of your own grandfather, Henry Whitman. That makes you, John, directly descended from the original owners of the house. Consequently, I wish to return this house to its original family, and to the person who most shares my literary and historical concerns.

I know you will care for this beautiful home better than anyone else. I also know you will continue to work on your writing, which has so much promise. I only regret I will not live to see your talents come to full fruition. This bequest is not a gift, but an investment in a brilliant writer's future. My children understand and are in concurrence with my decision. My lawyer will explain to you the details of the trust fund. My family and the Marquette County Historical Society will give you full cooperation in making the house a living museum. You have worked hard toward your goals. I hope this is the first of many deserved rewards.

My Best Wishes,
Robert O'Neill

John looked up from the letter to see several faces smiling at him.

"Father wanted it this way," said Helen O'Neill.

"I don't feel I deserve it," he replied.

"Father felt you had real talent," said Helen. "My brother and I are happy to know the house will be preserved, and now you will be able to remain in Marquette as you want and still be a writer. Father thought you would be better able to capture the magic of this place in your writing than anyone else, and from the pieces of your writing he let us read, we agree with him."

"I don't know what to say," said John. " 'Thank you' is so insufficient."

"It's all right," said Bernie. "Helen and I have lives elsewhere, but we couldn't bear to sell this old house. This is how we want it."

"Why don't you come back tomorrow morning when you're better used to the idea," said Helen. "Dad left detailed plans we'll go over with you in the next few days before we return to our own lives. People from the historical society will want to meet with you as well. And of course, you'll want to explore the house to decide what will be your personal living space and how the tours will be conducted."

John remained speechless. This house was his for his lifetime, and then in trust for his heirs, or if there were none, it would be placed in the hands of the historical society to manage, while the trust would always exist to preserve it. He was forbidden to sell it, not that he would ever want to. He felt as if this bequest were something from a movie, yet it somehow seemed natural that he would live here, in the home of his ancestors and his literary predecessor.

John met with Mr. O'Neill's lawyer and the historical museum's representative. By that time, the O'Neills had removed the personal items they wanted. Most of the furniture, especially pieces that had belonged to the O'Neills and Smiths and even a few pieces that had belonged to the Hennings, remained in the house. Robert had requested that certain items, including his books, desk, manuscripts, and paintings would remain so the house would closely resemble how it had looked during his life.

The lawyer and the museum director sat down with John to explain how the house would operate as a museum with the threefold purpose of preserving Marquette's history, a significant piece of Victorian architecture, and the home of one of America's great writers.

A few days before Christmas, John moved into his new home. He was still overwhelmed by his good fortune and how swiftly his worries had vanished. He could not remember being so carefree since childhood. The work required to prepare the house to open as a museum would be a labor of love. With some basic work, the house could open for tours by summer. Until then, winter would be spent cleaning, sorting through objects in the attic, and moving John's own belongings into the suite of upstairs rooms for his personal use. He spent his days with plasterers, painters, and stonemasons, but he devoted his evenings to his writing. When he finally took up his pen again, it was with an enthusiastic loyalty to Mr. O'Neill and their shared dream.

A happier Christmas had not existed for the family in many years. At first, John had feared people would be jealous of him, but instead, everyone was exuberant about visiting the grand old house. When John learned that Mr. O'Neill's Great-Aunt Carolina Smith had once hosted annual Christmas Eve parties in the house, and that Robert and Eliza O'Neill had continued this tradition for many years, he decided he did not have time to be ready for Christmas Eve, but he would have a New Year's party to show off the house to his family and friends. After months of embarrassment over his lack of job prospects, he no longer felt like a failure but wanted to share his happiness with everyone. Even Great-Aunt Ada and her daughter, Judy, came home to visit for the holidays that year, primarily to see John's house.

Everyone at the party marveled at the fine old mansion, the lace curtains that had hung nearly a century, the Pre-Raphaelite paintings that had been in vogue when the house was built, the William Morris wallpaper, the exquisite chandelier in the front parlor, the fine woodwork of the staircase.

"It's as if I've stepped back into my childhood," said Aunt Eleanor, who recalled elderly people eighty years before whose homes had been similarly furnished.

"Your grandfather would have been proud," said Uncle Bill. "He was the best carpenter in this town, and he did a lot to preserve this house. He'd be happy to know you're continuing his work."

"I'm glad everything has worked out for you," said Aunt Ada. "I thought you were right to move back to Marquette. I'd have done the same if I didn't have my children and grandchildren down South. You've proven that if you follow your heart and work hard, eventually you'll be rewarded."

For the first time that night, John slept in the house. After the last of his guests departed, he climbed upstairs to his bedroom. The curtains were still open, and the darkness was pierced by moonlight streaming across the bed. Rather than turn on the light and shut the curtains, he looked out at Lake Superior. He could see ice floes nestling on the water's surface. He knew the moon controlled the rhythm of the tides. Tonight he felt the moon held a strange control over him. He remembered the picture from his childhood book of Bible stories: the boyish Prophet Samuel, bathed in moonlight, who sat up in bed and said, "Speak Lord, your servant is listening." John had listened to his heart, and now God had rewarded him. He felt overwhelmed. Perhaps the moon did make you mad, but he felt he had returned from exile to the promised land – a land not of milk and honey, but fresh water, pristine snow, and rich minerals. The land of his ancestors, the land where holy men – Father Marquette, Bishop Baraga, his own great-uncle Monsignor McCarey had walked, blessing the land beneath their feet. As a child, he had been told that people who left this land were haunted by its lake and forests until they were drawn back. He had been drawn back, but only now did he understand why. He thought of all those who had lived here before him – the Brookfields and Hennings, the Whitmans and Dalrymples, the Bergmanns and McCareys, the Varins and Vandelaares, even the Smiths and O'Neills, each family making this land its home. He was the seventh generation of his family to live in Marquette. He was meant to be here, and to write of this place.

1999

Winter passed, the first true winter John had known since he had left Marquette. While downstate, John had been homesick for magnificent northern winters. Now with every fresh snowfall, a boyish enthusiasm rekindled within him. During these winter months, he rose early each morning, made a pot of coffee, opened the curtains to the darkness and wrote until lunchtime as he watched the day slowly dawn. He chopped apart his first novel, rejecting and rewriting sentences and paragraphs until the work showed little trace of its original content. Then in the afternoons, he sorted the papers of the Smiths and O'Neills, discarding or preserving as necessary, or he hung replica period piece wallpaper, or painted a closet, or met with people who could help restore the O'Neill House. But the best days were those of the snowstorms, when he would take a break just to stare out the window or to cozy up in a quilt and read while listening to the thundering, roaring wind. One afternoon, he went outside to build a snowman so large it nearly rivaled the statue of Father Marquette overlooking the Lower Harbor. And when the sun came out, John reveled in the shadows of tree branches stretching across the snow.

But by late March, winter seemed as if it would never end. Spring was not taken for granted here. Storm followed storm. Snowbanks piled themselves into small mountains. When it seemed impossible to lift a shovel any higher to throw snow on top of a bank already six feet tall, and a cavernous driveway looked ready to crash inward, only then, and sometimes not even until one more storm hit, would spring hint of its coming.

First, a warm day would arrive – forty degrees – amazingly warm after so many frigid months. You flung open your window, for the ice around it had melted so you could finally open it again. Fresh air poured in, freeing the house of winter's staleness and germs. Your heart now pounded in anticipation of spring; no matter what you were doing, you stopped to listen to the melody of melting snow, of water dripping off your roof. Then a week or so later, you might see a flattened blade of grass, a little patch, perhaps two inches of bare ground; the patch slowly grew, the snow receding until the patch became a plot, and then other little patches would appear, first around the tree trunks. Hourly you would peer out the window to check the progress of those patches, estimating how long before they would connect to one another to create a foot or two of grass.

Then another storm would come. Two feet of snow burying the grass, but in a few days, that snow had melted. Two or three more snowfalls might still cover the grass, but likewise, they would melt. Even if it snowed now, you knew the time had come. Winter was defeated. The Snow Queen's terrible reign had begun its decline. It was spring. Crocuses reared their heads through melting slush, daffodils appeared where grass was turning green. Color thickened in the tree branches; then buds appeared. Soon lilacs would be in bloom.

John beheld all this glorious metamorphosis of Nature. He had felt content with restoring the house and writing his novel, but now with the coming of spring, he felt a new restlessness in him. He was thankful he could remain in Marquette, yet he yearned for something more. He wrote all the more furiously when this strange mood came upon him, but no matter how many pages he wrote, he felt something was yet missing.

In early June, the scent of lilacs wafted through the open library window. John sat at his desk, pen in hand, but he stared at the bookshelves filled with thousands of volumes. He had always dreamed of owning such a library; a room of wall to wall books. He still could not believe this beautiful house was his home. He felt nearly overwhelmed by his life, by the swift, great responsibility thrust upon him; he wished more people could be so lucky since most Upper Peninsula natives found themselves forced into exile by the area's economic conditions. He knew he would never cease in gratitude for the fortune that was his.

The telephone broke his happy musings. When the genius burned and his fingers flew over the keyboard, scarcely fast enough to capture his thoughts, John would leave the answering machine on. But today, since he was only daydreaming, he picked up the phone.

"Hello."

"Is John Vandelaare there, please?"

"This is he."

Imagining it was a telemarketer, he prepared to hang up the minute the female voice mentioned she was with a credit card or long distance phone company.

"Hi, this is Wendy Dawson. I'm researching my family tree, and I think we may be related. I'm doing some research this morning at the Marquette Historical Society, and the librarian here told me you're researching the Brookfield and Henning families. Are you related to them?"

"Yes, I'm descended from them," John replied.

"Oh, good. I'm related to them as well, but I don't have a lot of information. I'm only in Marquette for a few days, but would you be interested in meeting to share notes?"

"Sure," said John.

"Great. Is there a time that's best for you?"

"I'm pretty open. You can come over now if you want."

"Oh, that would be wonderful."

John gave her his address and directions to the house. He was always pleased to talk to anyone who might add a nugget of information to the family history. After he hung up the phone, he went to watch for her from the front window since she had called from the historical society, only a few blocks away. He was curious to know how she was related to the Hennings and Brookfields. His best guess was she was descended from his great-grandfather's sister, Mary, but Mary had been a Whitman, and Wendy had not mentioned the Whitmans.

Ten minutes later, a car pulled up in front of the house and a young woman emerged. John opened the front door as she came up the walk.

"Hello," he said.

"Hello. I'm Wendy Dawson, the one who thinks we might be cousins."

John shook her hand, then showed her into the dining room. She had a bundle of notebooks and papers with her, which she set on the table, and then they both sat down.

"You have a beautiful home," she said.

"Thanks," said John. "I should have mentioned on the phone that this house belonged to the Hennings – Gerald and his wife, Sophia Brookfield."

"Really?" she glowed. "I can't believe that. I'm actually in their house. Have you always lived here? Has the house always been in the family?"

"No, I sort of inherited it," John said. "It's a long story I'd be happy to tell you, but first, let's figure out how we're related. I'm descended from Gerald and Clara Henning's daughter Agnes. She married Jacob Whitman, son of Nathaniel Whitman and Cordelia Brookfield. Jacob and Agnes were my great-great-grandparents."

"I'm descended," said Wendy, "from Gerald by his second wife, Sophia."

"Sophia was Cordelia Brookfield's sister," said John. "That would make us relatives twice over – only," he paused, trying to bring up the family tree in his mind. "But how can that be? Gerald and Sophia didn't have any children who lived."

"Oh yes," said Wendy. "I'm descended from their daughter, Madeleine."

John was shocked. "Madeleine? But you can't be. She drowned in Lake Superior when she was only sixteen. Agnes was Gerald's only child who married. Sophia had a son named Caleb by her first husband, but he also died without children."

"Oh no, I'm definitely descended from Madeleine," said Wendy. "I know the family thought she drowned, but remember, her body was never found."

"I don't understand." John was baffled.

"Madeleine didn't drown. She managed to make it to shore. Then when she realized people would think she was dead, she decided to run away. See, she was in love with a man her mother didn't approve of, so she eloped with him."

John laughed. "That sounds like a soap opera. How do you know this?"

"Madeleine was still alive when my mother was a little girl. My mother was her great-granddaughter. Madeleine also kept a diary which I've read."

"I don't believe it!" said John, although more surprised than doubtful. He had always relished the family scandals he had uncovered over the years, but this story surpassed them all. "How could Madeleine have let her parents think she was dead? They were so heartbroken they could not bear to live in Marquette after she drowned."

"I'm not saying what she did was right," said Wendy. "She was young and stubborn. Later, she regretted it, but she could never bring herself to contacting her parents to tell them the truth."

"I don't know what to say," said John. He looked about him at the walls, imagining the sadness that had enveloped the house when Madeleine had been believed drowned and her body never found.

"Here, I have a copy of the diary with me," said Wendy, digging through her bag. "You can read it. It's not very long because Madeleine only wrote sporadically, but it covers thirty-eight years. The original's in the Montana Historical Society's collection."

She passed to John a three ring binder labeled "The Diary of Madeleine Henning Carew 1876-1914". He opened the binder to the first page and eagerly read the word-processed page transcribed from Madeleine's own handwriting.

November 4, 1876

Four months ago today I nearly drowned in Lake Superior. I look back now on that day, July 4th, as the date of my independence. I have been happier these past four months than any time previously. I know I have caused my parents great pain by my pretense to be dead, but I cannot regret it because it was the only way I could be with Lazarus. Perhaps someday I will reveal the truth to them, and I hope then they will forgive me. It is not, however, for myself that I am beginning this diary, but rather because I am expecting a child. If anything should ever happen to me, or to Lazarus, this diary will prove my child's identity as the grandchild of Gerald and Sophia Henning of Marquette, Michigan. My handwriting here will verify the authenticity of this document.

I was born in Marquette, Michigan in 1860 to wealthy parents. My childhood was happy until I was fifteen and met Lazarus Carew. We immediately fell in love, but my mother did not approve because Lazarus was only a laborer and a poor immigrant without family in her eyes. My mother could not see the great nobility of his character which was so visible to me. After my mother quarreled with me over Lazarus, a quarrel in which she forbade me ever to see him again, I was heartbroken. That evening, the 4th of July, 1876, I went on a picnic with some friends. We took a boat out on Lake Superior, but it grew dark and the boat ran up onto a rock. The sudden jolt knocked me overboard, and the waves pulled me underwater while pushing the boat away so my friends could not rescue me. I called for help while being tossed up and down in the waves, struggling to breathe. It was the most terrifying experience of my life. I tried to swim to the distant shore, but before I could get very far, the waves overwhelmed me, and I lost consciousness.

I awoke to find myself on the beach while it was still dark out. I do not know how long I lay there, but it must have been a good while because morning broke an hour or so later. At first, I was dazed and could not recollect how I got there. Then I slowly realized everyone must think me dead. I wanted to go back to town, but I could not see where to walk in the darkness. After a little while, I saw a lantern, and then I dimly spotted a figure who turned out to be my Lazarus. He had come searching for me. We were overjoyed to see each other. He told me a search party had been formed to look for me. Then I recalled the argument with my mother. I knew I would not get to be with him once I returned to Marquette. It occurred to me that if my mother thought I was dead, Lazarus and I could elope without anyone following us. He did not want to deceive my parents, but I convinced him it was the only way we could be together. He agreed to return to Marquette and collect what we needed while I hid in the woods and waited for him. Then when he returned, we walked to Negaunee, where we took a train to the West.

We came to Montana because Lazarus has an uncle here who came over from Cornwall. Here we were married on July 21st. Lazarus bought me a brand new dress for the wedding, the finest I have ever owned because it is my wedding dress, even if it does not have all the fancy frills my mother would have insisted upon. Lazarus has now gotten a job working in the mine with his uncle. Last week, we got our own place, a small cottage just down the road from his uncle. On the side, I have been earning money by sewing, which my older sister Agnes taught me to do so well. I miss her and my father. I even miss my mother now that my anger has subsided, but I do not regret my actions. Maybe after the baby is born, I will write to tell my parents the truth. I am sorry to cause them pain, but I do not see how I had any other choice.

When John finished the first entry, he wished to read on, but he felt it would be rude to do so in front of his guest.

"I still can't believe it," he said, passing the binder back to Wendy. "It's unbelievable."

"Yes, it's a fascinating story."

"So what happened next?"

"Oh, they had a wonderful life together," said Wendy. "Lazarus was young and strong and extremely smart. He soon left the mines and got a job with a local railroad, then worked his way up to be vice president of the company. They were so rich by the time they were middle-aged that they built a large mansion near the Yellowstone River. Believe it or not, they built it out of Lake Superior sandstone which they had shipped from Marquette to Montana. Now that I've seen this house, I imagine Madeleine must have wanted it that way because it would remind her of her childhood home. They ended up having one son and four daughters. The third daughter was my great-grandmother, Sophia Carew. That's basically it – Madeleine didn't write very faithfully in her diary – sometimes there are gaps of a year or two, and most of the rest is about parties or what she did daily, none of it overly exciting, but I think she was an interesting woman nevertheless. My mother remembers her as being quite a lady even in her old age. She died when my mother was a little girl."

"And she never contacted her parents again?" said John.

"No. She doesn't mention her parents very often in the diary. I imagine that as the years went by, she found it harder to contact them and adjusted to the consequences of her secret. The only other major mention of her parents was when she learned her mother had died. Let me see whether I can find that passage."

Wendy paged through the binder until she stopped to read aloud the following passage:

April 3, 1908
    Today I found out that both my father and mother are dead. It makes me wonder again how wrong I was to pretend to have drowned. My father has been dead these fourteen years. Fourteen years! How hard it is to believe. My mother just died a few days ago. I found out in a newspaper column that mentioned her death. The headline was "New York Society Hostess Dies in Utah at Age 88". I happened to read it, never imagining the subject would be my own mother. The article mentioned she had been predeceased by my half-brother, Caleb, my father, and myself. From what I can gather from the article, my parents moved to New York after my disappearance, and my father grew extremely rich and my mother became a leader in society just as she had always wanted. After my father died, my mother moved to Utah to be near my cousins Esau and Edna Brookfield.
    How amazing to think all these years my parents and I have lived completely separate and unknown existences from each other! I always imagined they were growing old in their house in Marquette. How sad that with all that money, they ended up with no children to leave it to; the paper says my cousins were my mother's heirs so I wonder whether that means my half-sister Agnes is also dead. What became of Agnes's children that they inherited nothing? After all, the money was my father's so it should have gone to his descendants, not my mother's relatives. I almost want to write to my cousins in Utah, but I know I never will. It is all too late now, but I feel I would give anything just to see my parents one more time and to tell them I love them and ask them to forgive me for the pain I must have caused them. I do not regret marrying Lazarus – he's been wonderful to me – but I was young and headstrong then. Had I been older and wiser, perhaps I could have found a way to compromise with my mother. I hope my parents are at peace now.

"How sad," said John.
"Yes, it is sad," said Wendy.

"And so surprising," John repeated. "Here I've spent years researching the family tree, but it never occurred to me that Madeleine might not have drowned. There's even a stone in Park Cemetery for her, although I knew her body was never found."

"Would you be willing to show me the cemetery?" asked Wendy. "I'd like to see the ancestors' graves."

"Sure, I'd be happy to," said John. "Gerald and his first wife, Clara, and Sophia and her first husband, and her son Caleb, and her parents are all buried there."

"Tell me more about the family. I don't really know anything about the ancestors before Madeleine except for her parents' names. I only started working on the family tree this year."

"I don't know where to start," said John. "I've spent the last seven years doing research. I've traced thousands of ancestors, some branches going back to before the Middle Ages."

"Really?" said Wendy. "I can't even imagine that."

"I'll show it all to you if you have time," said John.

Then they both heard Wendy's stomach growl. She laughed and said, "I worked so intensely this morning at the historical society that I skipped lunch and came right over here."

John looked at the clock. It was almost five.

"Why don't we go somewhere for supper?" he said. "Then I can tell you more about the family, and after we eat, we can come back here and I'll show you the documents and the family tree I've constructed."

"Are you sure? I don't want to keep you from anything."

"Sure, I'm sure," said John. "I'm not much of a cook so I'd probably just be ordering a pizza or something anyway."

"Okay," said Wendy. "You pick the restaurant since I'm not from around here."

Fifteen minutes later, John and Wendy found a booth at the Portside Inn.

"They're famous here for their breadsticks, or rather the special cheese spread for the breadsticks," said John. "You have to try them."

"All right," Wendy said, glad not to eat alone in an unfamiliar town.

After they ordered, Wendy stared awkwardly at John until he lowered his eyes to the table, looking at the funny placemat with a drawing of the U.P. in which you had to search for the hidden moose and waterfalls.

"I'm not surprised we're related," said Wendy. "You look a lot like one of my cousins."

"Really?" said John. "We're not that closely related that you would think there'd be a resemblance?"

Both silently spent a couple minutes figuring out their exact relation.

"We're fourth cousins," Wendy concluded.

"Fourth half-cousins," said John, "since our great-great grandmothers, Agnes and Madeleine, were half-sisters."

"That's somewhat close," said Wendy.

"I wonder," John mused, "if your cousin and I look like a mutual Henning or a Brookfield ancestor."

"I don't know," said Wendy. "Do you have photographs of any ancestors?"

"I have a photograph of Gerald, but it was taken when he was about sixty. There's a tintype of Lucius and Rebecca Brookfield, but they must be in their sixties as well in the picture."

"Well, I guess you'll have to wait thirty or forty years before you can compare your looks to Gerald and Lucius's pictures."

"I can wait," said John.

"So," Wendy asked, "how did you come to live in Gerald and Sophia's house?"

John started at the beginning with the house's history. He detailed how when the Hennings left Marquette, they had sold the house to the Smiths. Then when Carolina Smith died, she gave the house to her grandson Mark Hampton and his wife Eliza. When Mark Hampton died in World War I, Eliza inherited the house, then married her first husband's second cousin, Robert O'Neill, who upon his death, had left the house to John.

"I love Robert O'Neill's books," said Wendy. "I had no idea he was from Marquette."

"Really? You've read Robert O'Neill?" said John. "Most people seem to have forgotten him now."

"I had to read one of his books in college and since then I've read several more. I'm sure there'll be lots of people who want to visit his house. But I'm still confused why he chose you to inherit the house, even though you are descended from the original owners."

John explained how Robert O'Neill had wanted to preserve the house as a significant part of Marquette's history, and equally, that he had wanted to encourage John to write about the area.

"I'd love to read your novel," said Wendy. "I used to think I wanted to be a writer, but I soon learned I had no talent for it, so I became a high school

English and history teacher. But if I weren't a teacher, running a historical museum would definitely interest me. When will the house open for tours?"

"During the Fourth of July week," said John. "This year is Marquette's hundred and fiftieth birthday so we're building a float for the parade to advertise the grand opening."

"What perfect timing," said Wendy. "I don't suppose after supper, you would give me an early tour of the house."

"Sure, I'd love to," said John.

She asked more questions about Marquette's history and why the Hennings and Brookfields had come to the area. John explained about the discovery of iron ore, and the area's mining, shipping, and logging industries. He detailed his own descent from the Hennings and Brookfields through the Whitmans, and he stunned her by revealing how they were both descended from kings and queens, saints and soldiers, the greatest people of medieval European history, not to mention all the peasants whose lives had failed to be recorded.

When they finished eating, both ordered dessert to prolong the conversation.

"I wonder," said Wendy, "whether it's a coincidence we're so similar, or whether it's really because of some gene we inherited from a mutual ancestor."

"It's probably an eccentric gene from the Brookfield side," laughed John. "I think the Brookfields were all a little eccentric, especially Lucius, who was willing to come to this outpost in his old age, or Uncle Darius, who vanished out West for many years. Madeleine probably took after Uncle Darius in being willing to leave her family."

"But why does that make us eccentric?" asked Wendy.

"I think anyone who is insane about genealogy must be eccentric, especially when we're so young. Ever notice that most genealogists are over fifty?"

"That's true," said Wendy.

They finished dessert and drove back to the O'Neill House. John gave Wendy the grand tour, indicating which aspects of the house represented the ownership of the Hennings, Smiths, or O'Neills.

"The Hennings took pretty much everything with them, so really just the structure itself recalls their time here, except the conservatory built off the library – that was added on by Carolina Smith. All the nineteenth century furniture was hers. Mr. O'Neill told me he and his wife were a little too scared of his great-aunt, even after her death, to make many changes to the house. The modern furniture, if you can still call the 1950s and 60s modern, was the O'Neills'. I actually think they mixed it in nicely with the older pieces."

Wendy loved every inch of the house. She continually stopped to admire the woodwork, the wallpaper patterns, and the three families' photographs that John had hung about the house.

"But, John, where are your family pictures now that you own the house?"

"I don't really want my picture up. The visitors will see me when I give guided tours. That's enough."

"Well, once you marry and have a family, you should have your pictures up. Actually, what you really need are two large genealogy charts so visitors can see how you are descended from the original owners, as well as charts detailing the Smiths and O'Neills' family tree."

"That's a good idea," John replied.

Upstairs, they walked through the various bedrooms.

"I bet this room was Madeleine's," said Wendy.

"I don't know," said John.

"It must be – in her diary she mentions it looked out on Lake Superior. Except for the large master bedroom her parents probably had, this is the only bedroom facing the lake."

"That's true."

"You should name the rooms. This would be Madeleine's room."

Saving the best for last, John ended Wendy's tour with the library.

"Oh!" Wendy squealed. "This room is definitely the house's showpiece."

They sat down in the library while John showed her the family photographs he had of the Brookfields, Hennings, and Whitmans. Only one photograph existed of Madeleine, taken with her parents, sister Agnes, and brother Caleb when she was only six. Wendy dug through her papers until she found two more photographs, one of Madeleine with her husband Lazarus and their five children, the second of Madeleine at age eighty. Wendy promised to make copies of both pictures for John.

"It's just so sad," he said. "It's almost as if you're being here finally reunites the family. Just think, Gerald and Sophia never even saw their grandchildren. I want to hang that picture of Madeleine and her children next to the picture of Gerald and Sophia, so the grandparents and grandchildren can be together on the wall, even if they were not together in life."

When ten o'clock arrived, Wendy admitted she was exhausted and prepared to return to her motel.

"How long are you staying in town?" asked John.

"Just two more days," said Wendy. "I didn't expect to find so much information."

"I've barely started to show you everything," said John. "If you come back tomorrow, we can go somewhere to make photocopies, and I could give you a tour of the town. I could show you where the old Brookfield farmhouse is. Of course, it's got modern aluminum siding so it doesn't look at all like it did when Lucius built it. And you have to see the cemetery, and Presque Isle and Sugarloaf Mountain, and the Methodist Church that the Brookfields helped to found."

"I would like that," said Wendy. "I think I would understand the family better if I knew what the town was like where they lived."

John promised to meet her at her motel the next morning so they could have breakfast together.

He walked her to her car, then watched her drive down the street. It was a warm summer night; a slight breeze sent lilac perfume through the air. His spine tingled, not because he was cold, but because he had spent years researching the family tree, yet Wendy was the first relative to share his interest. He went inside and got ready for bed, then sat down, intending to read and watch the eleven o'clock news; instead, he found himself planning tomorrow's itinerary for how he would show his favorite city to someone who would share his enthusiasm. Even after he went to bed, he remained fascinated to think Madeleine Henning had not drowned; he felt the house itself must have had some of its sadness lifted by the visit of Madeleine's descendant.

John met Wendy the next morning in the lobby of the Holiday Inn. Then he drove her to the Bavarian Inn for breakfast, telling her how in the 1980s, it had been the most popular breakfast restaurant in town, and he had frequented it on Sundays with his grandparents. While they ate, she asked him more questions about Marquette's history. After breakfast, he drove her to Negaunee to visit the Michigan Iron Industry Museum so she could better understand what had attracted the Hennings and Brookfields to Marquette. After the museum, they returned to Marquette, and John drove her past the Brookfield farmhouse. Lucius Brookfield would not have recognized his home with its aluminum siding, an added two car garage, electric lines running into the roof, and a satellite dish. Once on Marquette's extreme outskirts, the Brookfield farmhouse was on the East side of McClelland Avenue, which now divided the old city from the commercial and mall strip district. Once seated amid acres of farmland, the house was now one of twenty on a city block.

"I can't imagine what the house looked like during the Civil War," said Wendy.

"If the barn hadn't been torn down, it would look more like a farmhouse."

"Well, it's still neat to know our ancestors lived here," Wendy said.

They drove onto the bypass heading toward the lake. Wendy spotted St. Peter's giant towers and asked what church it was.

"I'd like to visit it if we could," she said.

"Sure," said John. "It's very impressive inside; actually, it's been called the world's most beautiful sandstone building."

"And then can we see the Methodist church the Brookfields belonged to?"

"All right," said John. "I should have pointed it out to you last night since it's just down the street from my house."

"I never saw anything like this in Montana," said Wendy when they reached the cathedral.

John took her through the side door that leads downstairs to Bishop Baraga's crypt. He explained that since the 1970s, the cause for the canonization of Bishop Baraga as a saint of the Roman Catholic Church had been underway; John told Wendy how the Marquette Diocese's founding bishop had spent decades dedicated to the conversion of the local Chippewa and the spiritual welfare of the miners, sailors, and entrepreneurs who flooded the area when iron ore was discovered.

"It sounds as if he deserves to be made a saint," said Wendy.

"When he died," John said, "nearly everyone in Marquette attended the funeral. Despite a blizzard that day, the cathedral was so packed that people stood out in the street to pay their respects."

"I wonder whether Gerald and Sophia were there," Wendy said, as John led her upstairs to the graceful little Chapel of the Blessed Sacrament and then into the much larger, magnificently Romanesque Church with its marble pillars, an exquisite mosaic of Christ and the apostles, and stained glass storied windows.

"This church is so much nicer than the Catholic church I go to," said Wendy. "We have one of those ugly modern ones, without a pane of stained glass or a single statue. It's really a crime even to call it a church."

"I know," said John. "That reminds me of the one I went to downstate – it looked more like a nuclear bomb shelter than a church. Are you Catholic then, even though Madeleine would have been a Methodist?"

"Yes, my grandmother was Catholic, so my grandpa converted for her," Wendy said. John told her about his own grandparents' religious difficulties in getting married. "There's the courthouse where my grandparents finally tied the knot," he pointed across the street as they emerged from the cathedral's front doors.

They walked a couple blocks down Fourth Street to the old Harlow house.

"Amos Harlow was Marquette's founder," John said. "He's the one who convinced Gerald Henning to come here. I always imagine Sophia must have made social calls here to Mrs. Harlow."

Once back in the car, they drove to Park Cemetery. As John parked the car, his cousin exclaimed over the beautiful pond filled with water lilies.

"It's a beautiful cemetery," John said. "It was designed, as its name indicates, to be both a park and a cemetery. In the Victorian period, people used to have family picnics here."

Wendy laughed. "I guess the Victorians wanted Grandpa and Grandma to be at the family picnic, even if they were below the earth."

John led her along the path to where his great-grandparents and Uncle Roy lay buried. "My grandparents aren't here since Grandma was Catholic," he said, "so they're buried in Holy Cross Cemetery on the other side of town. My grandma's whole family is there – her parents and grandparents."

They walked down a little hill to where Jacob and Agnes Whitman rested peacefully, the grave marked by a flag commemorating Jacob's Civil War service. Nearby was a stone with the names of Nathaniel Whitman and Cordelia Brookfield on it, but no death date was given for Cordelia, because as John explained, Cordelia had moved to Utah to live with her daughter and son-in-law after her husband died, and in Utah, she had been buried. John and Wendy next went to the oldest portion of the cemetery, John pointing out the graves of the Dalrymples on his way, although they were not Wendy's relatives. They visited Lucius and Rebecca Brookfield's stone. Then they stopped beside the stone for "Madeleine Henning, Beloved Daughter, 1860-1876."

"Maybe we should have it removed now," said John.

"No," said Wendy. "It's presence only makes her story more interesting. I wonder what they buried there?"

"I don't know," said John, "maybe a doll or some clothing?" John then pointed out the stones of Caleb Rockford and his father George. "Caleb was Madeleine's half-brother by her mother. He also drowned in the lake, or at least, he was found dead in the lake. Apparently, he fell in while trying to help people rescue their belongings and place them on the dock during the great fire of 1868 that burned down most of Marquette."

"How sad," said Wendy, "that Sophia should lose both her children by drowning. From what Madeleine writes, Sophia was not the most pleasant woman, but even so, no mother deserves that pain."

They made one last stop at the grave of Gerald Henning and his first wife, Clara, a woman who was no more than a name to John and Wendy, her bravery in Marquette's infancy long forgotten.

John and Wendy walked back to the car in a roundabout way, allowing John to point out the mausoleum of the Peter White family and to explain the role of that great pioneer in Marquette's history. "We'll have to visit Presque Isle before you go," he said. "It's Peter White's greatest legacy to Marquette."

"John, you're so knowledgeable about the area's history," said Wendy once they were back in the car. "I bet you'll have plenty of students visit the O'Neill house, and even if they're not interested in it, the girls will be thrilled to have such a handsome tour guide."

John was embarrassed. He had never thought himself handsome.

"I hope I'll be a good tour guide," he said. "I want visitors to be interested in the O'Neill House."

"You will," said Wendy. "You have such a personal connection to this place that you're able to appreciate it and make it interesting. Even though I have a history degree, I don't think I ever really appreciated history's impact until I started researching my family tree; now I appreciate it even more since you've shown me how I'm connected to people who lived hundreds and even a thousand years ago. I envy you being able to live in your hometown and feel so connected to the past. I've never known what that was like because my dad was always moving us around the West wherever his job took him. I would have liked just to stay in one place and come to know it well as you have."

"It wasn't that easy," said John. "I could have moved about to different teaching jobs, but the only offer I got was in a place I didn't want to be. If I had found a teaching job somewhere else, I know I would have been so homesick I would have come back here eventually. It's unexplainable the sense of belonging I have when I visit the cemetery and see all the members of my family who were here before me, or when I walk past the Post Office my grandpa helped to build, or I drive past the prison and remember my great-grandfather worked there. And now I live in the house my great-great-great grandparents built. I guess I can never escape the past."

"Knowing about the ancestors," said Wendy, "makes me feel I'm not alone in the world but part of a chain that spreads back through countless generations, and maybe someday I'll be linked to future generations as well. I would almost like to move here so when I have children, they can share this heritage."

"You'd have a hard time finding a job here," said John, "but otherwise, it's a great place to live, with all the beautiful scenery, fresh air, and hardly any crime."

"You've managed to make a life here," said Wendy. "Maybe I could be as lucky."

"Well," said John. "Few people have the good fortune Mr. O'Neill entrusted to me in the form of the house and an income so I can write."

"If your writing is as interesting as your conversation, I'm sure you'll be a successful novelist," Wendy smiled. John noted she was always smiling. He felt exhilarated as he drove her back to his house. Rather than go inside, they walked along Ridge Street, admiring all the grand old homes that were neighbors to the O'Neill House. They stopped to peek inside the Methodist Church that Rebecca Brookfield had helped to found and where Esau Brookfield and Edna Whitman had been married. Then they went on to visit the library and look at the historical books.

For supper, they went to the Villa Capri. Then they returned to the O'Neill House to watch the newly released video *On Iron Bay* produced locally to celebrate Marquette's sesquicentennial. When the film was over, they sat on the back porch, in the dark, looking up at the moon as it spread gleams along the lake. They talked about literature. Wendy loved to read Dickens and Trollope, Willa Cather and Emerson and many another author John admired. It was midnight before he drove her back to her motel with the promise to pick her up in the morning for another full day.

The next morning was spent making photocopies. John copied Madeleine's entire diary for his records, along with birth and death records and censuses and photographs that Wendy had brought with her. Wendy received copies of Lucius Brookfield's letters that John had discovered at the Marquette County Historical Society without any idea how they had arrived there. Copies were also made for Wendy of the Henning, Brookfield, and Whitman photographs.

Then John took Wendy on a walking tour around Presque Isle. Luckily, an ore boat was in the harbor, so they walked out on the breakwall to watch the boat load its cargo from the pocket dock. Next they left the hot sun behind to sit in the cool gazebo and admire the sparkling lake for a few minutes before beginning their trek around the island. John told stories about the island, such as how Jacob Whitman had fished there with Chief Kawbawgam. They paused at the lookout sites to admire the towering cliffs, then trudged through the thick forests of birch, pine, and oak. They came across a deer in the path, staring at them as awestruck by people as they were of it. "I've never been so close to a deer before," Wendy whispered as the creature turned its head to trot into the forest. Wendy thought the Black Rocks remarkable. They stopped to admire the new Presque Isle Pavilion, receiving its finishing touches, a gift from the people of Marquette to celebrate their city's sesquicentennial. Finally, they stopped to get Jilbert's Mackinac Island Fudge ice cream, without peer throughout the nation.

As they walked back to the car, John told Wendy about the filming of *Anatomy of a Murder* in Marquette. Wendy revealed herself to be a huge fan of the film's star, Jimmy Stewart. John then insisted on taking her to Big Bay to show her the site of the real murder as well as where the movie was filmed. The leaves were stunningly green as they drove along the twisting curves of the Big Bay Road. After looking about the Thunder Bay Inn and its gift shop, they settled down to supper in the restaurant where Wendy felt it only proper to order the Jimmy Stewart sandwich.

After supper, they both felt a little sleepy. John offered to take her back to the motel so she could rest before her early morning flight, but she adamantly refused. "Actually," she said, "I wouldn't mind going for another walk."

"I'll make you regret saying that," John smiled. "I'll take you for a climb up Sugarloaf Mountain."

Wendy thought he was kidding about climbing a mountain, especially since when they began, the trail only slightly inclined. They walked at a leisurely pace, pausing to admire bleeding hearts, mayflowers, and luscious ferns bordering the path. John spent several minutes scanning the forest before finding lady's slippers. "I'm afraid they're illegal to pick," he said, "but they're definitely my favorite flower."

"I never saw one before," said Wendy. "They'd make a lovely wedding bouquet – they're so very delicate."

Then came the stairs, one flight after another, over giant rocks and between towering pines. Robins sang as the evening sun lit the treetops. John knew the climb was strenuous and Wendy was growing tired, but she was clearly enjoying herself too much to complain. After many, many steps, they were finally high enough to glimpse Lake Superior, and then, reinvigorated, they climbed the last two flights of stairs until they reached the rocky mountain peak.

Before them rose the obelisk to Bart King's memory; John proudly mentioned that his grandfather had helped build it, nearly eighty years before.

Wendy was overwhelmed by the scenic view, and as always, John was awestruck by the cloudlike appearance of the cold, pristine lake encircling little green islands.

"It's so beautiful here I feel as if I never want to leave," said Wendy.

"I know," said John. "It makes me wonder how I ever left Marquette."

"I'm surprised we're the only ones up here," said Wendy. "I would think lots of teenagers come up here so they would have privacy to make out."

"I'm sure quite a few do," laughed John. "Actually, my father proposed to my mother up here."

As dusk approached, Marquette's city lights flickered on, then cast a solid glowing beam across the lake. Neither John nor Wendy needed to express their awe. Both instinctively knew the other appreciated the sight.

After a couple minutes, John said, "We should probably go before it's too dark to find our way back down."

"Just one more minute," Wendy said. "I want to memorize how beautiful everything is."

And then, John felt a strange tingling run through him. He told himself the breeze was making it chilly, but if it were just a breeze, then why did he want to lean over to kiss Wendy? If he did kiss her, how would she react? Clearly they were friends, good friends even if they had only known each other a few days, and tomorrow she would be gone, and he did not want to end their happy time with awkwardness between them. Maybe he should ask permission to kiss her, but then she might just think him foolish.

"I guess we better head back," said Wendy, turning toward the stairs. "It's getting pretty dark."

"All right," said John. He stupidly followed her, wondering why he had felt so foolish a moment before, wondering why he was such a coward.

At the bottom of the first flight of stairs, Wendy missed the last step and tumbled onto the rock below. John was instantly beside her as she insisted she was fine. He gave her his hand to help her up. Once she was standing, although she could only brush off her pants with one hand, she did not pull her hand from his.

"You don't mind, do you?" she asked.

"No," he said. "We don't want to get lost."

"You go first," she said. "You know this place better, and if we meet a bear, you'll have to protect me."

"I'll try," he laughed. His eyes peered into the darkness while his feet felt for the trail. They talked little during the walk back which took twice as long because of the dark. John told himself they were quiet because they were concentrating on finding their way back, but he found it hard to concentrate with Wendy's hand in his.

Finally, they were at the car, and then John drove Wendy back to the Holiday Inn. She had an early flight the next morning, but they promised to call and email each other so they could continue to exchange information. She gave him an awkward hug before climbing out of the car. He waited until she had walked into the motel; then he drove home, trying to remember all the things he would have to catch up on since the O'Neill House would be opening in a few more weeks. He felt more confident now about the grand opening since Wendy had been so impressed by the house. He wished she could be there for the celebration.

The telephone rang as John fixed breakfast the next morning.

"Where have you been?" asked his mother. "I must have called you a half-dozen times yesterday."

"Why didn't you leave a message on the answering machine?" John asked.

"I hate talking to those things. You know that. So where were you?"

He explained that a distant cousin had been in town, a descendant of the Hennings.

"Oh," said Ellen. "Listen. I talked Lucy and Maud into helping make flowers for the float. I told them we would start working on it Wednesday, and your brother said he'd come over after work to help."

"That's fine," said John. "I'm going shopping today to buy material for it."

"Okay, I'll see you then."

Chad, being the true artist in the family, had actually given John the idea for the float, but John knew the technicalities of its construction were up to him. They would build a large wooden stand resembling the O'Neill House. Beside it would be pictures of Robert O'Neill and Father Marquette. John's father would drive the truck pulling the float. Ellen was too shy to be in the parade, but Lucy and Maud had agreed to walk with John alongside the float, handing out flyers to announce the opening of the Robert O'Neill Historical Home.

John tried to keep himself busy with work all day, but he kept finding himself pausing, lingering over memories of Wendy as she sat beside him, pouring over the family history; she had been the first relative, though only a fourth or fifth cousin, he had met who shared his interest in genealogy. He wished again she could have stayed for the house's grand opening.

He drove around a lot that day to Kmart, Walmart, and Shopko. Driving along US 41, he noticed a car like the one Wendy had rented, and that tingling feeling went through him again until he peered inside and realized it was not her, but an old man. In Walmart, he looked twice at a woman in the shoe department who, from the corner of his eye, had hair resembling Wendy's, but when she turned toward him, he clearly saw the woman was nowhere near as lovely. He considered calling Wendy that night to make sure she had reached home safely, but he feared she would think it odd when they had not known each other that long. He thought he would email her instead, but then he decided tomorrow would be better. He did not want her to think him obsessive. He asked himself why he was obsessing.

Marquette's combined Sesquicentennial and Independence Day parade was scheduled for Saturday, July 3rd. That morning, the city residents woke to the sounds of rumbling thunder. By nine o'clock, the rain was pouring down and people worried the parade would be postponed. John and his family had worked hard on their float, and they had printed thousands of fliers announcing the grand opening of the Robert O'Neill Historical Home following the parade; now they worried that if the parade were canceled, they would also have to cancel the open house. Four of the house's downstairs rooms were to be opened for the reception, and the dining room table would be filled with punch and hors d'oeuvres. No one wanted to serve leftover food on a later day. John was so anxious he just wanted to get the entire thing over with. He had felt listless for days, and his enthusiasm for the house's grand opening was quickly waning. He was suddenly feeling very lonely, especially at night when he lay alone in a giant bed in a giant, empty house.

The rain continued all morning. Hours of listening to the radio without hearing any announcements about the parade suggested it would be held in the rain; John was sure the drizzle would destroy his float before it was halfway down the parade route. He looked out the window overlooking the Lower Harbor's Mattson Park where the residents had celebrated the sesquicentennial by decorating hundreds of log poles to represent different Marquette families and businesses. The family poles were complete with family trees, photographs, and histories. John had convinced his father to help him carve a pole; then he and his mother had drawn the family tree and attached pictures. Perhaps the pole, the flyers he had posted around town, and the advertisement he had placed in the *Mining Journal*'s special "Marquette at 150" issue would still attract people to the O'Neill House's grand opening, even if the parade were canceled.

Then, shortly after twelve, TV6 ran a message across the screen saying the parade would be delayed until three o'clock. Shortly after, the parade organizers called to inform John where to meet to be ready for the parade. The weather should clear up by then, and John was determined that whatever gloom existed in the air or in his heart, even if the rain meant he would catch pneumonia, he would proudly help celebrate his hometown's birthday.

The parade began on West Washington Street, near Shopko, and headed East to downtown. John met his father, Lucy, and Maud at the departure point. Ellen and Chad, Aunt Eleanor, and Uncle Bill, set up their lawnchairs on the sidewalk in front of Harlow Park to watch the festivities. Just before three o'clock, the sun came out and the rain let up. Mother Nature was being gracious to Marquette on its birthday.

It was the longest and finest parade in Marquette's history. Blocks and blocks of floats rolled down Washington Street; hundreds of people participated while thousands of spectators lined the streets. Historical cars drove the city's elected officials down Washington Street. Monumental size floats depicted Marquette's favorite buildings, including St. Peter's Cathedral and the Peter White Public Library. Old Jerry, Marquette's 1920s fire engine, proudly rolled along followed by modern fire trucks and ambulances. Children demonstrated what they had learned in dance classes, or they rode bicycles covered in streamers. Native Americans turned out to remind people they had been there before the city. Emphasis was given to the discovery of iron ore that had brought the city into existence. People bought commemorative buttons, and the old-timers, Aunt Eleanor and Uncle Bill among them, reminisced about the centennial celebrations of half a century before.

As the O'Neill House's float started down the street, John, Lucy, and Maud began to hand out flyers to the spectators. After a few minutes, John heard people cheering, and in a few more seconds, he realized his float was being applauded by a crowd enthusiastic that one of its city's most beautiful homes, and one of that city's favorite sons, Robert O'Neill, should be honored. John continued down the parade route, beaming to know all his advertising had made people excited about the preservation of a historical and literary home.

Slowly the float passed McDonalds and Burger King, then Kentucky Fried Chicken, the bakery, the Holiday Cleaners and the auto sales buildings. As it descended a little hill, into view came Harlow Park, the old City Hall, the Old Savings Bank's clock tower, and in the far distance, Lake Superior. John felt an upsurge of love for his city; happily, he shook hands and handed out flyers. As he walked past Harlow Park, he waved at his family on the sidewalk. Then, just as the float crossed the intersection at Washington and Seventh Streets, Ellen asked Chad, "What is your brother doing?"

Chad's mouth dropped as he watched John run across the street, practically shouting. A young woman broke from the crowd. In a second, John had thrown his arms around her, nearly lifting her from the ground.

"What are you doing here?" he asked. "Why are you crying?"

"I don't know," Wendy laughed as she wiped the tears away. "I was afraid you wouldn't be so happy to see me."

"I – I've missed you," said John, "but why are you here?"

"I knew this was your big day. I didn't want to miss it. I – I – "

"Wendy," John broke in, "I know this isn't the place, but I can't help myself. I'm in love with you."

"I love you too," she cried.

"Kiss her!" shouted a teenager in the crowd. John rarely acted on impulse, but he needed no prompting now. He wrapped his arms around her again, and this time, he was so excited, he did tilt her up off the ground as she rose to meet his lips.

"I told you I thought I could be happy in Marquette," said Wendy, "as long as it's all right with you."

"Will you marry me?" John asked. "I know we've only just met, but I never met anyone like you before. I can't explain it, but it just feels right."

"It's too soon to ask me, John."

In his truck, Tom honked his horn, warning John that the parade was moving on.

"You better get going," Wendy told him.

He did not know what to do. He started to turn back toward the parade.

"John!" Wendy shouted. He turned back toward her. "Yes!" she said. "The answer's yes." Somehow she knew it was the right answer.

She had barely said the words before his lips were again pressed to hers.

"Go! I'll come to the house after the parade," she said, laughing as the crowd cheered them. She pushed him toward the float. He looked back at her as he jogged down the street. She disappeared into the crowd, but not before an old lady, sitting beside her wrinkled, husband, told Wendy, "You're lucky. I wish I'd found a good-looking guy like that when I was young."

John remembered nothing more about the parade. For the rest of the walk, his heart was racing as he anticipated seeing Wendy at the house. At the parade route's end, his father and cousins asked who the girl was, but he only told them he would explain later. When he reached the O'Neill House, John half-expected Wendy would already be there, but he only found his mother, Chad, and Aunt Eleanor setting up for the reception.

"Who was that girl?" asked Ellen, as he stood in the front hall, waiting for his first visitors.

"Her name's Wendy Dawson. She's the girl I told you came to visit Marquette a few weeks ago."

"Why were you kissing her?" Chad asked. "Do you know what a spectacle you – "

"Someone's coming up the walk," John cut off his brother. He did not want to explain he was in love while a crowd of strangers traipsed through the house.

"Welcome to the O'Neill Home," John greeted everyone. "There are four open rooms for you to view and a guide in each room to answer questions. We have refreshments in the dining room."

"I guess he's not going to tell us why he was kissing her," said Chad to his mother as the guests walked by.

"Shh," Ellen said. "He can tell us later."

A half dozen more people came up the sidewalk. Soon the house was flooded with visitors, most of whom John did not know, but each one wanted to shake his hand to congratulate him on the beautiful float and the historical home's grand opening. They asked him questions about how he was related to the house's original owners, as yesterday's *Mining Journal* article had mentioned.

"I think he made a fool of himself," John could hear Chad saying to his mother in the front parlor. "People must think he lost his mind. Why didn't he ever tell us about this girl?"

John was about to explain, when the front door opened again. On the doorstep, behind three little old ladies, stood Wendy. John politely greeted the ladies and ushered them into the dining room while Wendy patiently smiled at him. When the hall was empty of all but the two lovers, John said, "I was starting to worry you weren't coming."

"No need to worry about that," she said, slipping her hand into his. More guests arrived. This time, Wendy greeted them herself, encouraging them not to miss the beautiful fireplace or the gilt-covered books in the library. John realized what a perfect hostess she would be. Once the guests had been ushered into the dining room, he could not resist taking her in his arms.

"I love you," he said. "Come meet my family."

Gently, he led the future mistress of his home into the front parlor.

COMING SOON!

Tyler R. Tichelaar has written three more novels set in Marquette. Each novel stands on its own, yet readers of the Marquette Trilogy will recognize many familiar characters. More than spin-offs of the trilogy, these novels provide fresh perspectives on old characters and complex psychological portraits of new ones.

✦

BLACK NO MORE

Black No More is the story of Lysander Blackmore, the sinister banker in *The Queen City*. Focusing on minor characters from Mr. Tichelaar's Marquette Trilogy, the novel is really a collection of short stories, each told in first person by a different character. The variety of characters' voices provides multiple perspectives on the novel's events. *Black No More* depicts the influence one person has, even in death, upon others, and it explores the prisons of grief, loneliness, and fear self-created when people doubt their own worthiness.

✦

THE ONLY THING THAT LASTS

The story of Robert O'Neill, the famous novelist introduced in the Marquette Trilogy. As a young boy during World War I, Robert is forced to leave his South Carolina home to live in Marquette with his grandmother and aunt. He finds there a cold climate, but many warmhearted friends. An old-fashioned story that follows Robert's growth from childhood to successful writer and husband, the novel is written as Robert O'Neill's autobiography, his final gift to Marquette by memorializing the town of his youth.

✦

SPIRIT OF THE NORTH

Perhaps Tyler R. Tichelaar's finest novel. Readers of the Marquette Trilogy will find out more about the past of *Iron Pioneers* lumberjack Ben and the truth behind the ghost story of Annabella Stonegate told by Will Whitman in *The Queen City*. The novel's heroines, Barbara and Adele Traugott, travel to Marquette in 1873 to live with their uncle, only to find he is deceased. Penniless, they are forced to survive a terrible winter in their uncle's remote wilderness cabin. Through their difficulties they find love, heartache, and ultimately, the miracle of their own being.

Be sure to read all of the Marquette Trilogy:
IRON PIONEERS
THE QUEEN CITY
SUPERIOR HERITAGE

For more information on book release dates, ordering, and author events, visit: www.MarquetteFiction.com